PRAISE FOR PAULLINA SIMONS

Eleven Hours

"Keeps poking its way back into your head long after you've finished it."
—*Chicago Tribune*

"*Eleven Hours* reminded me of Steven Spielberg's *Duel*—a story with minimalist style and a powerful scare."
—Martin Cruz Smith

"*Eleven Hours* is a harrowing, hair raising story that will keep you turning the pages late into the night."
—Janet Evanovich

"Simons does a wonderful job pulling you into the story . . . it's a ticking time bomb!"
—Adrianne Lee
Author of *Little Girl Lost* and *Night Terror*

Red Leaves

"A haunting page-turner."
—*Los Angeles Times*

"Suspenseful. Creates a mystery from the ordinary, protected lives of Ivy League kids, slowly peeling away their deceptions to reveal denial, cowardice, and chilling indifference. Engrossing."
—*Publishers Weekly*

"Simons's characterizations are excellent, and she quickly draws the reader deeply into the nuances of the story. Highly recommended."
—*Library Journal*

"A wonderful mystery-suspense story with marvelous twists and turns that keep you guessing—and turning pages—right to the very end."
—*Detroit Free Press*

Tully

"Reads fast, like a sudden surge of wind over the plains, and the book's momentum builds to tornado force."
—*USA Today*

"What a lovely and resonant evocation of that first great bond between women—it's deeply moving."

—Anne Rivers Siddons

"An impressive and enviable first novel . . . Powerful and telling . . . There is a reader involvement that almost becomes a compulsion."

—*Richmond Times-Dispatch*

"Complex, diverse, multi-faceted . . . Lush in emotion and rich in detail."

—*The Denver Post*

"Beautifully written . . . Hard to put down . . . Highly recommended."

—*Library Journal*

"An extraordinary and massive novel . . . Simons piques your curiosity with delicate finesse at every turn . . . Impressive . . . Remarkable . . . Truly exciting . . . One hopes we will see other books by Paullina Simons."

—*Bookpage*

"You'll never look at life the same way again . . . experiences of pain, despair and betrayal are offset by moments of dazzling joy, love and, above all, friendship. Read and weep—literally."

—*Company*

The Bronze Horseman

"Extraordinary . . . right up there with *The Thorn Birds* and *Gone with the Wind*."

—Teresa Medeiros
Author of *After Midnight*

"A love story both tender and fierce."

—*Publishers Weekly*

"Readers will come to care about these characters and their plight and will take away a definite sense of what the siege of Leningrad actually meant on a personal level."

—*Booklist*

"This has everything a romance glutton could wish for: a bold, talented and dashing hero, a heart-stopping love affair."

—*Daily Mail* [UK]

"Tatiana and her Alexander are powerful, complex and compelling characters easily capable of demanding and sustaining a readers' attention. This is a real three-hanky weepy."

—*Historical Novels Review*

TATIANA
AND
ALEXANDER

By Paullina Simons

TATIANA
AND
ALEXANDER

PAULLINA
SIMONS

MADISON
PARK PRESS™

NEW YORK

Published by Madison Park Press™, 15 E. 26th Street, New York, NY 10010

Book design by Christos Peterson

ISBN: 1-58288-191-X

Printed in the United States of America

Once again for my grandfather and grandmother,
ninety-eight and ninety-four, who still plant cucumbers
and grow flowers and live happily ever after,
and
for our good friend Anatoly Studenkov,
still as ever left behind in Russia, who does not.

CONTENTS

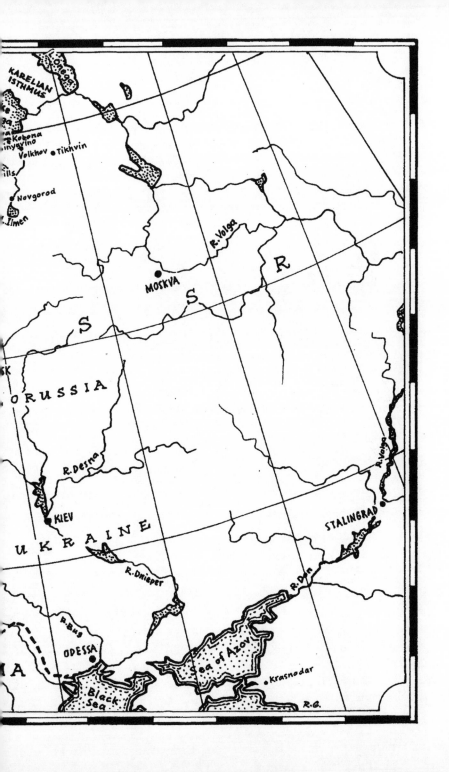

And in the moonlight's pallid glamour
Rides high upon the charging brute
Head held high 'mid echoing clamour
The Bronze Horseman in pursuit.

And all through that long night no matter
What road the frantic wretch might take
There would pound with ponderous clatter
The Bronze Horseman in his wake.

—Aleksandr Pushkin

TATIANA
AND
ALEXANDER

PROLOGUE

ALEXANDER BARRINGTON STOOD IN front of the mirror and adjusted his red Cub Scout tie. Rather, he was *attempting* to adjust his Cub Scout tie, because he couldn't take his eyes off his face, a face uncharacteristically glum. His mouth was turned down. His hands were fidgeting with the gray-and-white tie, unable to do a good job, today of all days.

Stepping away from the mirror, he looked around the small room and sighed. It wasn't much, a wood floor, drab brown-branch wallpaper, a bed, a nightstand.

It didn't matter about the room. It wasn't his room. It was a rented room, a furnished rented room and all the furniture belonged to the landlady downstairs. His real room was not in Boston but back in Barrington, and he had really liked his old room and hadn't felt the same way about any other room he had lived in since. And he had lived in six different rooms since two years ago when his father sold their house and took Alexander out of Barrington.

Now they were leaving this room, too. It didn't matter.

Rather, that's *not* what mattered.

Alexander looked in the mirror again. He came up flush to the mirror, stuck his face against the glass and breathed out deeply. "Alexander," he whispered. "What now?"

His best friend Teddy thought it was the most exciting thing in the world, Alexander's leaving the country.

Alexander couldn't have disagreed more.

Through his partly open door, he heard his mother and father arguing. He ignored them. They tended to argue through stress. Presently the door opened and his father, Harold Barrington, came in.

"Son, are you ready? The car is waiting for us downstairs. And your friends are downstairs, too, waiting to say goodbye. Teddy asked me if I would take him instead of you." Harold smiled. "I told him I just might. What do you think, Alexander? You want to trade places with Teddy? Live with his crazy mother and crazier father?"

"Yes, because my own parents are so sane," said Alexander. Harold was thin and of medium height. His one distinguishing feature was a resolutely set chin on a broad, square-jawed face. At the age of forty-eight his light-brown, graying hair was still thick upon his head, and his eyes were intense and blue. Alexander liked it when his father was in a good mood because then the eyes lost some of their seriousness.

Pushing Harold out of the way, his mother, Jane Barrington, strolled in, wearing her best silk dress and white pillbox hat, and said, "Harry, leave the boy alone. You can see he's trying to get ready. The car will wait. And so will Teddy and Belinda." She smoothed out her thick, long dark hair arranged under the hat. Jane's voice still carried traces of the lilting rounded Italian accent that she had not been able to lose since coming to America at seventeen. She lowered her voice. "I never liked that Belinda, you know."

"I know, Mom," said Alexander. "That's why we're leaving the country, isn't it?" He watched them in the mirror. He looked most like his mother. In personality he hoped he was more like his father. He didn't know. His mother amused him, his father confounded him. "I'm ready, Dad," he said.

Harold came over and put his arm on Alexander's shoulder. "And you thought Cub Scouts was an adventure."

Cub Scouts was plenty for me. "Dad?" he asked, looking not at his father but at his own reflection. "If it doesn't work out . . . we can come back, right? We can come back to—" He stopped. He didn't want his father to hear his voice crack. Taking a steadying breath, he finished, "To *America*?"

When Harold didn't reply, Jane came up to Alexander, who now stood between his parents, his mother in small heels three inches taller than his father, who was a good foot and a half taller than Alexander. "Tell the boy the truth, Harold. He deserves to know. Tell him. He is old enough."

Harold said, "No, Alexander. We are not coming back. We are going to make the Soviet Union our permanent home. There is no place for us in America."

Alexander wanted to say that there had been a place for *him*. Alexander had a place in America. Teddy and Belinda had been his friends since they were all three. Barrington was a tiny, white-shingled, black-shuttered town with three steepled churches and a short main street that ran four blocks from one end of town to the other. In the woods near Barrington, Alexander had had a happy childhood. But he knew his father didn't want to hear it, so he said nothing.

"Alexander, your mother and I, we are absolutely sure this is the right thing for our family. For the first time in our lives, we are finally able to do what we believe in. We are no longer paying lip service to the communist ideals. It's easy to propound change while living in absolute comfort, isn't it? Well, now we are going to live what we believe. You know it's what I fought for my whole adult life. You've seen me. And your mother, too."

Alexander nodded. He *had* seen them. His father and mother arrested for their principles. Visiting his father in jail. Being unwelcome around Barrington. Being laughed at in school. Constantly getting into fights for his father's principles. He had seen his mother stand by his father's side, picketing and protesting with him. The three of them had gone to Washington D.C. together to parade communist pride in front of the White House. They were arrested there, too. Alexander had spent a night in a juvenile detention center when he was seven. But on the plus side, he was the only boy in Barrington who had been to the White House.

He had thought all that was sacrifice enough. And then he had thought that breaking with their family and giving up the house that had been the Barrington homestead for eight generations was sacrifice enough. He thought that living in small rented rooms in busy and dusty Boston while disseminating the socialist word was sacrifice enough.

Apparently not.

Frankly, Alexander was surprised by the move to the Soviet Union, and not happily surprised. But his father believed. His father thought the Soviet Union was the place where they would finally belong, where Alexander would not be laughed at, where they would be welcomed and admired instead of shunned and ridiculed. The place where they could build their life up from "meaningless" and make it "meaningful." Power was to the toiling man in the new Russia, and soon the toiling man would be king. His father's belief was enough for Alexander.

His mother pressed her painted red mouth on Alexander's forehead, leaving a bright greasy pucker, which she then rubbed off—not well. "You know, don't you, darling, that your father wants you to learn the right way, to grow up the right way?"

A little petulantly, Alexander said, "This is really not about *me*, Mom—"

"No." Harold's voice was adamant. His hand never left Alexander's shoulder. "This is *all* about you, Alexander. You're only eleven now, but soon you will become a man. And since you have only one life, you can be only one man. I'm going to the Soviet Union to make you into the man you need to be. *You*, son, are my only legacy to this world."

"There are plenty of men in America, too, Dad," Alexander pointed out. "Herbert Hoover. Woodrow Wilson. Calvin Coolidge."

"Yes, but not good men. America can produce greedy and selfish men, prideful and vengeful men. That's not the man I want you to be."

"Alexander," said his mother. "We want you to have advantages of character that people in America just don't have."

"That's right," said Harold. "America makes men soft."

Alexander stepped back from his parents, never taking his eyes off his solemn reflection. That's what he had been looking at before they came in. Himself. He was looking at his face and wondering, *when I grow up, what kind of a man am I going to be?* Saluting his father, he said, "Don't worry, Dad. I'll make you proud. I'll be ungreedy and unselfish, unprideful and unvengeful. I'll be as hard a man as they come. Let's go. I'm ready."

"I don't want you to be a hard man, Alexander. I want you to be a good man." Harold paused. "A better man than me."

As they were walking out, Alexander turned around and caught himself in the mirror one last time. I don't want to forget this boy, he thought, in case I ever need to come back to him.

Stockholm, May 1943

I am on a stake, thought eighteen-year-old Tatiana, waking up one cold summer morning. I cannot live like this anymore. She got up from the bed, washed, brushed her hair, collected her books and her few clothes, and then left the hotel room as clean as if she had not been in it for over two months. The white curtains blowing a breeze into the room were unrelenting.

Inside herself was unrelenting.

Over the desk there was an oval mirror. Before Tatiana tied up her hair she stared at her face. What stared back at her was a face she no longer recognized. Gone was the round baby shape; a gaunt oval remained over her drawn cheekbones and her high forehead and her squared jaw and her clenched lips. If she had dimples still, they did not show; it had been a long time since her mouth bared teeth or dimples. The scar on her cheek from the piece of the broken windshield had healed and was fading into a thin pink line. The freckles were fading too, but it was the eyes Tatiana recognized least of all. Her once twinkling green eyes set deep into the pale features looked as if they were the only ghastly crystal barriers between strangers and her soul. She couldn't lift them to anyone. She could not lift them to herself. One look into the green sea, and it was clear what raged on behind the frail façade.

Tatiana brushed her shoulder blade-length platinum hair. She didn't hate her hair anymore.

How could she, for Alexander had loved it so much.

She would not think of it. She wanted to cut it all off, shear herself like a lamb before the slaughter, she wanted to cut her hair and take the whites out of her eyes and the teeth out of her mouth and tear the arteries out of her throat.

Tying the hair up in a bun on top of her head, Tatiana put a kerchief over it, to attract as little attention as possible, though in Sweden— a country full of blonde girls—it was easy to become lost in the crowd.

Certainly she had become that.

Tatiana knew it was time to go. But she could find nothing inside to propel her forward. She had the baby inside her, but it was as easy to have a baby in Sweden as it was in America. Easier. She could stay. She wouldn't have to make her way across an unfamiliar country, get a passage on a freighter headed for Britain and then travel across the ocean to the United States in the middle of a world war. The Germans were blowing up the northern waters on a daily basis, their torpedoes detonating the Allied submarines and the blockade ships into high flame balls encircled by black smoke, incongruous against the serene seas of Bothnia and the Baltic, of the Arctic and the Atlantic. Staying safe in Stockholm required nothing more of her than what she had been doing.

What *had* she been doing?

She'd been seeing Alexander everywhere.

Everywhere she walked, everywhere she sat, she would turn her head to the right, and there he would be, tall in his officer's uniform, rifle slung on his shoulder, looking at her and smiling. She would reach out and touch thin air, touch the white pillow on which she saw his face. She would turn to him and break the bread for him and sit on the bench and watch him making his slow sure way to her, crossing the street for her. She would walk after Swedish men during the day, men whose backs were broad, whose stride was long, she would stare impolitely into the faces of strangers because it was Alexander's face she saw etched there. And then she would blink, blink again and he would be gone. And she would be gone, too. She would lower her gaze, and walk on.

She raised her eyes to the mirror. Behind her Alexander stood. He brushed the hair away from her neck and bent to her. She couldn't smell him, nor feel his lips on her. Just her eyes saw him, almost felt his black hair on her neck.

Tatiana closed her eyes.

She went and had breakfast at Spivak café, her usual two helpings of bacon, two cups of black coffee, three poached eggs. She pretended to read the English paper she had bought at the kiosk across the street; *pretended* because the words were gases inside her head, her mind could not catch them. She read better in the afternoon when she was calmer. Leaving the café, she walked to the industrial pier, where she sat on the bench and watched the Swedish dockhand load up his barges full of finished paper to be taken over to Helsinki. She watched the longshoreman steadily. She knew that in a few minutes, he would go off to talk to his friends fifty meters down the pier. He would have a smoke and a small cup of coffee. He would be gone from the barge thirteen minutes. He would leave the covered barge unattended, the plank connected to the cabin of the shipping vessel.

Thirteen minutes later he would come back and continue loading the paper from the truck, wheeling it down the plank on his hand trolley. In sixty-two minutes the captain of the barge would appear; the longshoreman would salute him and untie the ropes. And the captain would take his barge across the thawed Baltic Sea to Helsinki.

This was the seventy-fifth morning Tatiana had watched him.

Helsinki was only four hours from Vyborg. And Tatiana knew from the English newspapers she bought daily that Vyborg—for the first time since 1918—was back in Soviet hands. The Red Army had taken Russia's Karelian territories back from the Finns. A barge across the sea to Helsinki, a truck across the forests to Vyborg, and she too would be back in Soviet hands.

"Sometimes I wish you were less bloody-minded," Alexander says. He had managed to receive a three-day furlough. They're in Leningrad—the last time they're in Leningrad together, their last everything.

"Isn't that the pot calling the kettle black?"

He grunts. *"Yes. I wish the kettle were less black."* He snorts in frustration. *"There are women,"* he says, *"I know there are, who listen to their men. I've seen them. Other men have them—"*

She tickles him. He does not seem amused. "All right. Tell me what to do," she says, lowering her voice two notches. "I will do exactly as you say."

"Leave Leningrad and go back to Lazarevo instantly," Alexander tells her. "Go where you will be safe."

Rolling her eyes, she says, "Come on. I know you can play this game."

"I know I can," Alexander says, sitting on her parents' old sofa. "I just don't want to. You don't listen to me about the important things . . ."

"Those aren't the important things," Tatiana says, kneeling in front of him and taking hold of his hands. "If the NKVD come for me, I will know you are gone and I will be happy to stand against the wall." She squeezes his hands. "I will go to the wall as your wife and never regret a second I spent with you. So let me have this here with you. Let me smell you once more, taste you once more, kiss you once more," she says. "Now play my game with me, sorrowful as it is to lie down together in wintry Leningrad. Play the miracle with me—to lie down with you at all. Tell me what to do and I will do it."

Alexander pulls on her hand. "Come here." He opens his arms. "Sit on top of me."

She obeys.

"Now take your hands and place them on my face."

She obeys.

"Put your lips on my eyes."

She obeys.

"Kiss my forehead."

She obeys.

"Kiss my lips."

She obeys. And obeys.

"Tania . . ."

"Shh."

"Can't you see I'm breaking?"

"Ah," she says. "You're still in one piece then."

She sat and watched the dockhand when it was sunny and she sat and watched him when it rained. Or when it was foggy, which is what it was nearly every morning at eight o'clock.

This morning was none of the above. This morning was cold. The pier smelled of fresh water and of fish. The seagulls screeched overhead, a man's voice shouted.

Where is my brother to help me, my sister, my mother? Pasha, help me, hide in the woods where I know I can find you. Dasha, look what's happened. Do you even see? Mama, Mama. I want my mother. Where is my family to ask things of me, to weigh on me, to intrude on me, to never let me be silent or alone, where are they to help me through this? Deda, what do I do? I don't know what to do.

This morning the dockhand did not go over to see his friend at the next pier for a smoke and a coffee. Instead, he walked across the road and sat next to her on the bench.

This surprised her. But she said nothing, she just wrapped her white nurse's coat tighter around herself, and fixed the kerchief covering her hair.

In Swedish he said to her, "My name is Sven. What's your name?"

After a longish pause, she replied. "Tatiana. I don't speak Swedish."

In English he said to her, "Do you want a cigarette?"

"No," she replied, also in English. She thought of telling him she spoke little English. She was sure he didn't speak Russian.

He asked her if he could get her a coffee, or something warm to throw over her shoulders. No and no. She did not look at him.

Sven was silent a moment. "You want to get on my barge, don't you?" he asked. "Come. I will take you." He took her by her arm. Tatiana didn't move. "I can see you have left something behind," he said, pulling on her gently. "Go and retrieve it." Tatiana did not move.

"Take my cigarette, take my coffee, or get on my barge. I won't even turn away. You don't have to sneak past me. I would have let you on the first time you came. All you had to do was ask. You want to go to Helsinki? Fine. I know you're not Finnish." Sven paused. "But you are very pregnant. Two months ago it would have been easier for you. But you need to go back or go forward. How long do you plan to sit here and watch my back?"

Tatiana stared into the Baltic Sea. "If I knew, would I be sitting here?"

"Don't sit here anymore. Come," said the longshoreman.

She shook her head.

"Where is your husband? Where is the father of your baby?"

"Dead in the Soviet Union," Tatiana breathed out.

"Ah, you're from the Soviet Union." He nodded. "You've escaped somehow? Well, you're here, so stay. Stay in Sweden. Go to the consulate, get yourself refugee protection. We have hundreds of people getting through from Denmark. Go to the consulate."

Tatiana shook her head.

"You're going to have that baby soon," Sven said. "Go back, or move forward."

Tatiana's hands went around her belly. Her eyes glazed over.

The dockhand patted her gently and stood up. "What will it be? You want to go back to the Soviet Union? Why?"

Tatiana did not reply. How to tell him her soul had been left there?

"If you go back, what happens to you?"

"I die most likely," she barely whispered.

"If you go forward, what happens to you?"

"I live most likely."

He clapped his hands. "What kind of a choice is that? You must go forward."

"Yes," said Tatiana, "but how do I live like this? Look at me. You think, if I could, I wouldn't?"

"So you're here in the Stockholm purgatory, watching me move my paper day in and day out, watching me smoke, watching me. What are you going to do? Sit with your baby on the bench? Is that what you want?"

Tatiana was silent.

The first time she laid eyes on him she was sitting on a bench, eating ice cream.

"Go forward."

"I don't have it in me."

He nodded. "You have it. It's just covered up. For you it's winter." He smiled. "Don't worry. Summer's here. The ice will melt."

Tatiana struggled up from the bench. Walking away, she said in Russian, "It's not the ice anymore, my seagoing philosopher. It's the pyre."

BOOK ONE
The Second America

. . . Hold your head up all the more
This tide
And every tide
Because he was the son you bore
And gave to that wind blowing and that tide

Rudyard Kipling

CHAPTER ONE

In Morozovo Hospital, March 13, 1943

IN THE DARK EVENING, in a small fishing village that had been turned into Red Army headquarters for the Neva operation of the Leningrad front, a wounded man lay in a military hospital waiting for death.

For a long time he lay with his arms crossed, not moving until the lights went out and the critical ward grew tired and quiet.

Soon they would be coming for him.

He was a young man just twenty-three, ravaged by war. Months of lying wounded in bed threw a pallor on his face. He was unshaven, and his black hair was cropped close to his scalp. His eyes, the color of toffee, were blanks as he stared into the far distance. Alexander Belov looked grim but he was not a cruel man, and he looked resigned but he was not a cold man.

Months earlier on the ice during the Battle of Leningrad, Alexander had run out for his lieutenant Anatoly Marazov, who lay on the river Neva with a bullet in his throat. Alexander ran out to the hopeless Anatoly, and so did a doctor with no sense—an International Red Cross doctor from Boston named Matthew Sayers, who fell through the ice, and whom Alexander had to pull out and drag across the river to the armored truck for cover. The Germans were trying to blow up the truck from the air, and in their attempts they blew up Alexander instead.

It was Tatiana who had pulled him back from the four horsemen who came for him, counting his good and bad works on their black-gloved fingers. Tatiana, whom he had told, *"Leave Leningrad and go back to Lazarevo instantly."* Lazarevo, deep at the foot of the Ural Mountains, a small fishing village buried in the pine woods, nestled on the shores of the Kama River, Lazarevo, where for an instant in time she could have been safe.

But she was like the doctor: she had no sense. No, she said to him. She was not going. And she said *no* to the four horsemen, shaking her fist at them. It's too early for you to claim him. And then defiantly: I won't let you take him. I will do everything in my power to keep you from taking him.

And she did. With her own blood, she had kept them from Alexander. She poured her blood inside him, she drained her arteries and filled his veins, and he was saved.

Alexander may have owed Tatiana his life but Dr. Sayers owed Alexander his, and he was going to take Alexander and Tatiana to Helsinki, from where they would make their way to the United States. With Tatiana's help they concocted a plan, and for months Alexander lay in the hospital while his back healed and carved figures and cradles and spears out of wood and imagined driving through America with her, their hurt all vanished, just the two of them, singing to the radio.

He had lived on the fleeting wings of hope. It was such a translucent hope. He knew it even as he drowned in it. It was the hope of a man surrounded by the enemy, who, as he makes his last run to safety, his back turned, prays he will have a chance to dive into a pit of life before the enemy reloads, before they send the heavy artillery out. He hears their guns, he hears their shouts behind him, but still he runs, hoping for a reprieve from the whistle of the shell. Dive into hope, or die in despair. *Dive into the River Kama.*

Alexander's fate was sealed. He wondered how long ago it had been sealed, but he did not want an answer to that question.

Since he left his small room in Boston back in December 1930, that's how long.

Alexander could not leave Russia. But one small thread of hope still dangled in front of him. One small flicker of the waning candle.

To get Tatiana out of the Soviet Union, Alexander Belov grit his teeth and closed his eyes. He clenched his fists and backed away from her; he pushed her away, he let her go.

There was only one thing left for him to do in his old life, and that was to stand up and salute the doctor who could save his wife. For now there was nothing to do but wait.

Deciding he did not wish to be taken out of bed in his hospital clothes, Alexander asked the night shift nurse to bring him his Class A major's uniform and his officer dress cap. He shaved with his knife and a bit of water by the side of his bed, dressed and then sat in the chair, arms folded. When they came for him, as he knew they would, he wanted to go with as much dignity as the lackeys for the NKVD would allow. He heard loud snoring from the man in the bed next to him, hidden from view by the isolation tent.

Tonight—what was Alexander's reality? What was it that determined Alexander's consciousness? And more important, what would happen to him in an hour or two when everything Alexander had ever been would come into question? When the secret police chairman General Mekhlis would lift his beady, lard-encrusted eyes and say to him, "Tell us who you are, Major," what would be Alexander's answer?

Was he Tatiana's husband?

Yes.

"Don't cry, honey."

"Don't come, yet. Please. Don't. Not yet."

"Tania, I have to go." He told Colonel Stepanov he was going to be back for Sunday night roll call and he could not be late.

"Please. Not yet."

"Tania, I'll get another weekend leave—" He is panting. *"After the Battle of Leningrad. I'll come back here. But now . . ."*

"Don't, Shura, please don't."

"You're holding me so tight. Release your legs."

"No. Stop moving. Please. Just . . ."

"It's nearly six, babe. I have to go."

"Shura, darling, please . . . don't go."

"Don't come, don't go. What can I do?"

"Stay right here. Inside me. Forever inside me. Not yet, not yet."

"Shh, Tania, shh."

And five minutes later, he is bolting out the door. "I've got to run, no, don't walk me to the barracks. I don't want you walking by yourself at night. You still have the pistol I gave you? Stay here. Don't watch me walk down the corridor. Just—come here." He envelops her in his coat, hugging her into himself, kissing her hair, her lips. *"Be a good girl, Tania,"* he says. *"And don't say goodbye."*

She salutes him. *"I'll see you, the captain of my heart,"* says Tatiana, her tears having fallen down her face from Friday till Sunday.

Was he a soldier in the Red Army?

Yes.

Was he the man who had entrusted his life to Dimitri Chernenko, a worthless demon disguised as a friend?

Yes, again.

But once, Alexander had been an American, a Barrington. He spoke like an American. He laughed like an American. He played summer games like an American, and swam like one and took his life for granted like one. He had friends he thought he was going to have for life, and once there were forests of Massachusetts that Alexander called home, and a child's bag where he hid his small treasures—the shells and the eroded glass bits he had found on Nantucket Sound, the wrapper from one of the cotton candies, bits of twine and string, a photograph of his friend Teddy.

Once there was a time he had a mother, her tanned, made-up, large-eyed familiar face laughing into his memory.

And when the moon was blue and the sky black and the stars beaming down their light on him, for a stitch in eternity Alexander had found what he thought was going to elude him all of his Soviet life.

Once.

Alexander Barrington was coming to an end. Well, he wasn't going to go quietly.

He put on his three military valor medals and his medal of the *Order of the Red Star* for driving a tank across the barely frozen lake, he put on his cap, sat in the chair by his bed and waited.

Alexander knew how the NKVD came for people like him. They needed to cause as little commotion as possible. They came in the middle of the night, or they came in a crowded train station while you were on your way to a Crimean resort. They came in a fish market, they came through a neighbor who wanted you to come into his room for just a sec. They asked to sit next to you in the canteen where you were having your *pelmeni*. They hemmed and hawed their way through a store and asked you to join them in the special order department. They sat next to you on a bench in the park. They were always polite and quiet and smartly dressed. The car that would pull up to the curb to take you to the Big House and the concealed pistols they carried were nowhere in sight. One woman, who had been arrested in the middle of a crowd, started to scream loudly and climbed a lamppost and continued carrying on so that even the normally indifferent passers-by stopped and stared; she made the NKVD work impossible. They had to leave her alone, and she, instead of disappearing somewhere to the middle of the country, went home to sleep, and they came for her in the night.

For Alexander they had previously come one afternoon after school. He was with a friend, and two men came up to him and told him he had forgotten about his meeting with his history teacher, could he possibly step back in for a moment and speak to him? He knew right away, he smelled their lies on them. Not budging, he grabbed his friend's arm and shook his head. His friend left—precipitously—knowing when he wasn't wanted. Alexander remained alone with the two men, reviewing his options. When he saw the black car slowly pull up to the curb, he knew his options were narrowing. He wondered if they would shoot him in the back in broad daylight while there were other people around. He decided they wouldn't and took off. They gave chase, but they were in their thirties, not seventeen. Alexander lost them in a few minutes, side-stepped into an alley, hid and made his way to a market near St. Nicholas church. After buying a bit of bread, he was afraid to go home. He thought they would go there next to look for him. Alexander spent the night outdoors.

The next morning he went to school, thinking he would be safe in the classroom. The principal himself brought a note to Alexander, saying he was needed in the office.

As soon as he left the room, he was grabbed and quietly taken outside and placed inside the car already waiting at the curb.

In the Big House he was beaten and then transferred to the Kresty prison where he awaited the resolution of his fate. He had few illusions.

But however they came for him tonight, Alexander knew they would not want to make a ruckus in the middle of a military hospital critical ward. The charade, the pretense they were using—of taking him across to Volkhov to be promoted to lieutenant colonel—would serve the *apparatchiks* well until they got him alone. Alexander's goal was to make sure he did not get to Volkhov, where the facilities for his "trial" and execution were well set up. Here in Morozovo, among the inexperienced and bumbling, he had a much better chance of living.

He knew that Article 58 of the Soviet Criminal Code of 1928 didn't even specify him as a political prisoner. If he was accused of crimes against the state, then he was a criminal, and would be sentenced accordingly. The code, in fourteen sections, defined his offences only in the most general terms. He didn't need to be an American, he didn't need to be a refugee from Soviet justice, he didn't need to be a foreign provocateur. He didn't need to be a spy or a flag waver. He didn't even need to commit a crime. Intention was just as criminal and equally punishable. Intention to betray was as severely looked upon as betrayal itself. The Soviet government prided itself on this clear sign of superiority to the Western constitutions, which senselessly waited for the criminal act before meting out punishment.

All actual or intended action aimed at weakening either the Soviet state or the Soviet military strength was punishable by death. And not just action. Inaction, too, was counter-revolutionary.

And as for Tatiana . . . Alexander knew that one way or another, the Soviet Union would have shortened her life. Long ago Alexander had planned to run to America—leaving her behind, the wife of a Red Army deserter. Or Alexander was going to die at the front—leaving her widowed and alone in the Soviet Union. Or his *friend* Dimitri was going to point out Alexander to the NKVD, Stalin's secret police, as indeed he had done—leaving her as Alexander Barrington's sole survivor, the Russian wife of an American "spy" and a class enemy of the people. These were the choking choices of Alexander and the unlucky girl who became his wife.

When Mekhlis asks me who I am, am I going to salute him and say, I am Alexander Barrington and not look back?

Could he do that? Not look back?

He didn't think he could do that.

Arriving in Moscow, 1930

Eleven-year-old Alexander felt nauseated. "What is that smell, Mom?" he asked, as the three of them entered a small, cold room. It was dark, and he couldn't see well. When his father turned on the light, it wasn't much better. The bulb was dim and yellow. Alexander breathed through his mouth and asked his mother again. His mother did not reply. She took off her prim hat and her coat, and then when she realized it was too cold in the room, she put her coat back on and lit a cigarette.

Alexander's father walked around with a manly gait, touching the old dresser, the wooden table, the dusty window coverings, and said, "This is not bad. This will be great. Alexander, you have your own room, and your mother and I will stay here. Come, I'll show you your room."

Alexander followed him. "But the smell, Dad . . ."

"Don't worry." Harold smiled. "You know your mother will clean. Besides, it's nothing. Just . . . many people living close together." He squeezed Alexander's hand. "It's the smell of communism, son."

It had been late at night when they were finally brought to their residential hotel. They had arrived in Moscow at dawn that morning after a sixteen-hour train ride from Prague. Before Prague they had traveled twenty hours by train from Paris, where they had spent two days waiting either for papers or permission or a train, Alexander wasn't sure. He liked Paris, though. The adults were fretting, and he ignored them as much as possible. He was busy reading his favorite book, *The Adventures of Tom Sawyer*. Whenever he wanted to tune out the adults, he

opened Tom Sawyer and felt better. Then of course, his mother afterward would try to explain what had just gone on between her and his
father, and Alexander wished he had a way to tell her to follow Dad's
lead and not say anything.

He didn't need her explanations.

Except now. Now he needed an explanation. "Dad, the smell of
communism? What the hell *is* that?"

"Alexander!" his father exclaimed. "What did your mother teach
you? Don't talk like that. Where do you even pick up that stuff? Your
mother and I don't use that kind of language."

Alexander didn't like to disagree with his father, but he wanted to
remind him that every time he and his mother argued they used that
kind of language—and worse. His father was always under the impression that just because the fighting didn't concern Alexander, Alexander
couldn't hear it. As if his parents weren't in the next room, or right next
door, or even right in front of him. In Barrington, Alexander had never
heard anything. His parents' bedroom was at the opposite end of the
hallway upstairs, there were rooms and doors in between, and he had
never heard a thing. It was as it should be.

"Dad," he tried again. "Please. What is that smell?"

Uncomfortable, his father replied, "That's just the toilets, Alexander."

Looking around his bedroom, Alexander asked where they were.

"Outside in the hall." Harold smiled. "Look on the bright side—
you won't have to go far in the middle of the night."

Alexander put down his backpack and took off his coat. He didn't
care how cold he was. He wasn't sleeping in his coat. "Dad," he said,
breathing through his mouth, wanting to retch. "Don't you know I
never get up in the middle of the night? I'm a deep sleeper."

There was a small cot with a thin wool blanket. After Harold left
the room, Alexander went to the open window. It was December, well
below freezing. Looking down onto the street from the second floor,
Alexander noticed five people lying on the ground in one of the doorways. He left the window open. The fresh cold air would clear out the
room.

Going out into the hall, he was going to use the toilet but couldn't.
He went outside instead. Coming back, he undressed and climbed into
bed. The day had been long and he was asleep in seconds, but not before
he wondered if capitalism had a smell also.

CHAPTER TWO

Arriving at Ellis Island, 1943

TATIANA STUMBLED OUT OF bed and walked to the window. It was morning, and the nurse was going to bring the baby soon for a feed. She pushed the white curtains away. Opening the latch, she tried to lift the window, but it was stuck, the white paint having sealed the frame to the wall. She tugged on it. It popped open and she pulled it up, leaning her head outside. It was a warm morning that smelled like salt water.

Salt water. She breathed in deeply, and then she smiled. She liked that smell. It was unlike the smells that were familiar to her.

The seagulls cutting the air with their screeching were familiar.

The view was not familiar.

New York harbor in the foggy dawn was a misty glass-like expanse of greenish sea, and off in the distance she saw tall buildings, and to the right, through the pervading fog, a statue lifted its right arm in a flame salute.

With fascinated eyes, Tatiana sat by the window and stared at the buildings across the water. They were so tall! And so beautiful, and there were so many of them crowding the skyline, spires, flattops jutting out, proclaiming the mortal man to the immortal skies. The winding birds, the calmness of the water, the vastness of the buildings, and the glass harbor itself emptying out into the Atlantic.

Then the fog lifted and the sun came up into her eyes, and she had to turn away. The harbor became less glassy as ferries and tugboats, all manner of lighters and freighters, and even some yachts, started criss-crossing the bay, sounding their whistles and horns in such cacophonous delight that Tatiana thought about closing the window. She didn't.

Tatiana had always wanted to see an ocean. She had seen the Black Sea and the Baltic Sea and she had seen many lakes—one Lake Ladoga too many—but never an ocean, and the Atlantic was an ocean on which Alexander once sailed when he was a little boy, watching fireworks on the Fourth of July. Wasn't it Fourth of July soon? Maybe Tatiana could see some fireworks. She would have to ask Brenda, her nurse, who was a bit of a cow, and conveyed all her information rather gruffly, the bottom part of her face—and all of her heart—covered by a mouthpiece to protect against Tatiana.

"Yes," Brenda said. "There will be fireworks. Fourth of July is in two days. They're not going to be like in the days before the war, but there will be some. But don't you go worrying about fireworks. You've been in America less than a week and you're asking about fireworks? You've got a child to protect against an infectious disease. Have you been outside for a walk today? You know the doctor told you you've got to take walks in the fresh air, and keep your mouth covered in case you cough on your baby, and not lift him because that will tire you out— have you been outside? And what about breakfast?" Brenda always talked too fast, Tatiana thought, almost deliberately so that Tatiana wouldn't understand.

Even Brenda couldn't ruin breakfast—eggs and ham and tomatoes and milky coffee (dehydrated milk or no). Tatiana ate and drank sitting on her bed. She had to admit that the sheets, the softness of the mattress and the pillows, and the thick woolen blanket were comforts like bread—crucial.

"Can I have my son now? I need to feed him." Her breasts were full.

Brenda slammed the window shut. "Don't open the window anymore," she said. "Your child will catch cold."

"Summer air will make him catch cold?"

"Yes, *moist*, wet summer air will."

"But you just said me to go outside for walk—"

"Outside air is outside air, inside air is inside air," Brenda said.

"He has not caught my TB," Tatiana said, coughing loudly for effect. "Bring me my baby, please."

After Brenda brought the baby and Tatiana fed him, she went to open the window again and then perched herself up on the window sill, cradling the infant in her arms. "Look, Anthony," whispered Tatiana in her native Russian. "Do you see? Do you see the water? It is pretty, right? And across the harbor there is a big city with people and streets, and parks. Anthony, as soon as I am better, we will take one of those loud ferry boats and walk on the streets of New York. Would you like that?" Stroking her infant son's face, Tatiana stared across the water.

"Your father would," she whispered.

CHAPTER THREE

Morozovo, 1943

MATTHEW SAYERS APPEARED BY Alexander's bed at around one in the morning and stated the obvious. "You're still here." He paused. "Maybe they won't take you."

Dr. Sayers was an American and an eternal optimist.

Alexander shook his head. "Did you put my *Hero of the Soviet Union* medal in her backpack?" was all he said.

The doctor nodded.

"Hidden, as I told you?"

"As hidden as I could."

Now it was Alexander's turn to nod.

Sayers brought from his pocket a syringe, a vial, and a small medicine bottle. "You'll need this."

"I need tobacco more. Have you got any of that?"

Sayers took out a box full of cigarettes. "Already rolled."

"They'll do."

Sayers showed Alexander a small vial of colorless liquid. "I'm giving you ten grains of morphine solution. Don't take it all at once."

"Why would I take it at all? I've been off it for weeks."

"You might need it, who knows? Take a quarter of a grain. Half a grain at most. Ten grains is enough to kill two grown men. Have you ever seen this administered?"

"Yes," said Alexander, Tania springing up in his mind, syringe in her hands.

"Good. Since you can't start an IV, in the stomach is best. Here are some sulfa drugs, to make sure infection does not recur. A small container of carbolic acid; use it to sterilize your wound if all the other drugs are gone. And a roll of bandages. You'll need to change the dressing daily."

"Thank you, Doctor."

They fell silent.

"Do you have your grenades?"

Alexander nodded. "One in my bag, one in my boot."

"Weapon?"

He patted his holster.

"They'll take it from you."

"They'll have to. I'm not surrendering it."

Dr. Sayers shook Alexander's hand.

"You remember what I told you?" Alexander asked. "Whatever happens to me, you'll take this"—he took off his officer cap, handing it to the doctor—"and you will write me a death certificate and you will tell her that you saw me dead on the lake and then pushed me into an ice hole, and that's why there is no body. Clear?"

Sayers nodded. "I'll do what I have to," he said. "I don't want to do it."

"I know."

They were grim.

"Major . . . what if I do find you dead on the ice?"

"You will write me a death certificate and you will bury me in Lake Ladoga. Make a sign of the cross on me before you push me in." He shuddered slightly. "Don't forget to give her my cap."

"That guy, Dimitri Chernenko, is always around my truck," Sayers said.

"Yes. He won't let you leave without him. Guaranteed. You must take him."

"I don't want to take him."

"You want to save her, don't you? If he doesn't come, she has no chance. So stop thinking about the things you can't change. Just watch out for him. Trust him with nothing."

"What do I do with him in Helsinki?"

Here Alexander allowed himself a small smile. "I'm not the one to be advising you on that one. Just—don't do anything to endanger you or Tania."

"Of course not."

Alexander spoke. "You must be very careful, nonchalant, casual, brave. Leave with her as soon as you can. You've already told Stepanov you're headed back?" Colonel Mikhail Stepanov was Alexander's commander.

"I told him I'm headed back to Finland. He asked me to bring . . . your wife back to Leningrad. He said it would be easier for her if she left Morozovo."

Alexander nodded. "I already spoke to him. I asked him to let her leave with you. You'll be taking her with his approval. Good. It'll be easier for you to leave the base."

"Stepanov told me it's policy for soldiers to get transported to the Volkhov side for promotions. Was that duplicity? I can't understand anymore what's truth and what's a lie."

"Welcome to my world."

"Does he know what's happening with you?"

"He is the one who told me what's about to happen to me. They have to take me across the lake. They don't have a stockade here," Alexander explained. "But he will tell my wife what I have told her—I'm getting promoted. When the truck blows up, it will be even easier for the NKVD to go along with the official story—they don't like to explain arrests of their commanding officers. It's so much easier to say I've died."

"But they do have a stockade here in Morozovo." Sayers lowered his voice. "I didn't know it was the stockade. I was asked to go check on two soldiers who were dying of dysentery. They were in a tiny room in the basement of the abandoned school. It was a bomb shelter, divided into tiny cells. I thought they had been quarantined." Sayers glanced at Alexander. "I couldn't even help them. I don't know why they didn't just let them die, they asked for me so late."

"They asked for you just in time. This way they died under doctor's care. An International Red Cross doctor's care. It's so legitimate."

Breathing hard, Dr. Sayers asked, "Are you afraid?"

"For her," said Alexander, glancing at the doctor. "You?"

"Ridiculously."

Alexander nodded and leaned back against the chair. "Just tell me one thing, Doctor. Is my wound healed enough for me to go and fight?"

"No."

"Is it going to open again?"

"No, but it might get infected. Don't forget to take the sulfa drugs."

"I won't."

Before Dr. Sayers walked away, he said quietly to Alexander, "Don't worry about Tania. She'll be all right. She'll be with me. I won't let her out of my sight until New York. And she'll be all right then."

Faintly nodding, Alexander said, "She'll be as good as she can be. Offer her some chocolate."

"You think that'll do it?"

"Offer it to her," Alexander repeated. "She won't want it the first five times you ask. But she will take it the sixth."

Before Dr. Sayers disappeared through the doors of the ward, he turned around. The two men stared at each other for a short moment, and then Alexander saluted him.

Living in Moscow, 1930

When they were first met at the train station, even before heading to their hotel they were escorted to a restaurant where they ate and drank all evening. Alexander delighted in the fact that his father was right—life seemed to be turning out just fine. The food was passable and there was plenty of it. The bread was not fresh, however, and, oddly, neither was the chicken. The butter was kept at room temperature, so was the water, but the black tea was sweet and hot, and his father even let Alexander have a sip of vodka as they all raised their crystal shot glasses, their boisterous voices yelling, *"Na zdorovye!"* or "Cheers!" His mother said, "Harold! Don't give the child vodka, are you out of your mind?" She herself was not a drinker, and so she barely pressed the glass to her lips. Alexander drank his vodka out of curiosity, hated it instantly, his throat burning for what seemed like hours. His mother teased him. When it stopped burning, he fell asleep at the table.

Then came the hotel.

Then came the toilets.

The hotel was fetid and dark. Dark wallpaper, dark floors, floors that in places—including Alexander's room—were not exactly at right angles with the walls. Alexander always thought they needed to be, but what did he know? Maybe the feats of Soviet revolutionary engineering and building construction had not made their mark on America yet. The way his father talked about the Soviet hope, Alexander would not have been surprised to learn that the wheel had not been invented before the Glorious October Revolution of 1917.

The bedspreads on their beds were dark, the upholstery on their couches was dark, the curtains were dark brown, in the kitchen the wood-burning stove was black, and the three cabinets were dark wood. In the adjacent rooms down the dark, badly lit hall lived three brothers from Georgia by the Black Sea, all curly dark-haired, dark-skinned and dark-eyed. They immediately embraced Alexander as one of their own, even though his skin was fair and his hair was straight. They called him Sasha, their little Georgian boy, and made him eat liquid yogurt called *kefir*, which Alexander did not just hate but loathe.

There were many Russian foods that—much to his misfortune—he discovered he loathed. Anything bathed in onions and vinegar he could not share the same table with.

Most of the Russian food placed before them by the other well-meaning compatriots of the hotel was bathed in onions and vinegar.

Except for the Russian-speaking Georgian brothers, the rest of the people on their floor did not speak much Russian at all. There were thirty other people living on the second floor of Hotel Derzhava, which meant "fortress" in Russian; thirty other people who came to the Soviet Union largely for the same reasons the Barringtons did. There was a communist family from Italy, who had been thrown out of Rome in the late twenties, and the Soviet Union took them in as their own. Harold and Alexander thought that was an honorable deed.

There was a family from Belgium, and two from England. The British families Alexander liked most because they spoke something resembling the English he knew. But Harold didn't like Alexander continuing to speak English, nor did he like the British families very much, nor the Italians, nor really anyone on that floor. Every chance he got, Harold tried to dissuade Alexander from associating with the Tarantella sisters, or with Simon Lowell, the chap from Liverpool, England. Harold Barrington wanted his son to make friends with Soviet girls and boys. He wanted Alexander to be immersed in the Moscow culture and to learn Russian, and Alexander, wanting to please his father, did.

Harold had no problem finding employment in Moscow. During his life in America he, who didn't *have* to work, had dabbled in everything, and though he could do few things expertly, he did many things well, and what he didn't know he learned quickly. In Moscow the authorities placed him in a printing plant for *Pravda*, the Soviet newspaper, for ten hours a day cranking the mimeograph machine. He came home every night with his fingers ink-stained so dark blue they looked black. He could not wash the ink off.

He could have also been a roofer, but there wasn't much new construction in Moscow—"not yet," Harold would say, "but *very very* soon." He could have been a road builder, but there wasn't much road building or repairing in Moscow—"not yet, but *very very* soon."

Alexander's mother followed his father's cues; she endured everything—except the shabbiness of the facilities. Alexander teased her ("Dad, do you approve of Mom's scrubbing out the smell of the proletariat? Mom, Dad doesn't approve, stop cleaning."), but Jane would nonetheless spend an hour scrubbing the communal bathtub before she could get in it. She would clean the toilet every day after work—before she made dinner. Alexander and his father waited for their food.

"Alexander, I hope you wash your hands every time you leave that bathroom—"

"Mom, I'm not a child," said Alexander. "I know to wash my hands." He would take a long sniff. "Oh, l'eau de communism. So pungent, so strong, so—"

"Stop it. And in school, too. Wash your hands everywhere."

"Yes, Mom."

Shrugging, she said, "You know, no matter how bad things smell around here they're not as bad as down the hall. Have you smelled Marta's room?"

"How could you not? The new Soviet order is especially strong in there."

"Do you know why it's so bad? She and her two sons live in there. Oh, the filth, the stench."

"I didn't know she had two sons."

"Oh, yes. They came from Leningrad to visit her last month and stayed for good."

Alexander grinned. "Are you saying they're stinking up the place?"

"Not them," Jane replied with a repugnant sneer. "The whores they bring with them from the Leningrad rail station. Every other night they have a new harlot in there with them. And they do stink up the place."

"Mom, you're so judgmental. Not everyone is able to buy Chanel perfume as they pass through Paris. Maybe you should offer the whores some—for *French* cleansing." Alexander was pleased at his own joke.

"I'm going to tell your father on you."

Father, who was right there, said, "Maybe if you stop talking to our eleven-year-old son about whores, all would be well."

"Alexander, darling, Merry Christmas Eve." Having changed the subject, Jane smiled wistfully. "Dad doesn't like us to remember the meaningless rituals—"

"It's not that I don't like to," interjected Harold. "I just want them placed in their proper perspective—past and gone and unnecessary."

"And I agree with him completely," Jane calmly continued, "but it does get you in the chest once in a while, doesn't it?"

"Particularly today," said Alexander.

"Yes. Well, that's all right. We had a nice dinner. You'll get a present on New Year's like all the other Soviet boys." She paused. "Not from Father Christmas, from us." Another pause. "You don't believe in Santa Claus anymore, do you, son?"

"No, Mom," Alexander said slowly, not looking at his mother.

"Since when?"

"Since just now," he replied, standing up and gathering the plates off the table.

Jane Barrington found work lending books at a university library but after a few months was transferred to the reference section, then to the maps, then to serving lunch in the university cafeteria. Every night, after cleaning the toilets, she cooked a Russian dinner for her family, once in a while lamenting the lack of mozzarella cheese, the absence of olive oil to make good spaghetti sauce, or of fresh basil, but Harold and Alexander didn't care. They ate the cabbage and the sausage and the potatoes and the mushrooms, and black bread rubbed with salt, and Harold requested that Jane learn how to make a thick beef borscht in the tradition of good Russian women.

⌘

Alexander was asleep when his mother's shouting woke him. He reluctantly got out of his bed and came into the hall. His mother in her white nightgown was yelling obscenities at one of Marta's sons, who was skulking down the hall not turning around. In her hands, Jane held a pot.

"What's going on?" said Alexander. Harold had not gotten up.

"There I was, going to the bathroom, and I thought, let me go get a drink of water. It's the middle of the night, mind you, what could be the problem with that? And what did I find in the kitchen but that hound, that filthy animal, with his disgusting paw in my borscht, digging out the meat and eating it! My meat! My borscht! Right out of the pot! Filth!" she called down the hall. "Filth and slime! No respect for people's property!"

Alexander stood and listened to his mother, who kept on for a few more minutes and then, with angry relish, threw the entire pot of recently cooked soup into the sink. "To think that I would eat anything after that animal's hands were in it," she said.

Alexander went back to bed.

The next morning Jane was still talking about it. And the next afternoon, when Alexander came home from school. And the next dinner—which was not delicious borscht but something meatless and stewed that he did not like. Alexander realized he preferred meat to no meat. Meat filled him up like few other things did. His growing body confounded him, but he needed to feed it. Chicken, beef, pork. Fish if there was some. He didn't care much for an all vegetable dinner.

Harold said to Jane, "Calm down. You're really getting yourself worked up."

"How could I not? Let me ask you, do you think that scum washed his hands after he pawed the whore from the train station that was with fifty other filthy scum just like him?"

"You threw the soup out. Why such a fuss?" said Harold.

Alexander tried to keep a serious face. He and his father exchanged a look. When his father didn't speak, Alexander cleared his throat and said, "Mom, um, may I point out that this is not very socialist of you. Marta's son has every right to your soup. Just as you have every right to his whore. Not that you would want her, of course. But you would be entitled to her. As you are to his butter. Would you like some of his butter? I'll go and get some for you."

Harold and Jane stared at Alexander cheerlessly.

"Alexander, have you lost your mind? Why would I want anything that belongs to that man?"

"That's my point, Mom. Nothing belongs to him. It's yours. And nothing belongs to you, either. It's his. He had every right to rummage in your borscht. That's what you've been teaching me. That's what the Moscow school teaches me. We are all better for it. That's why we live like this. To prosper in each other's prosperity. To rejoice and reap benefit from each other's accomplishment. Personally, I don't know why you made so little borscht. Do you know that Nastia down the hall hasn't had meat in her borscht since last year?" Brightly Alexander looked at his parents.

His mother said, "What in the name of the Lord has gotten into you?"

Alexander finished his cabbagy, oniony dinner and said to his father, "Hey, when's the next Party meeting? I can't wait to go."

"You know what? I think no more meetings for you, son," said Jane.

"Just the opposite," said Harold, ruffling Alexander's hair. "I think he needs more of them."

Alexander smiled.

They had arrived in Moscow in the winter, and after three months they realized that to get the goods they needed, the white or rye flour, or electric bulbs, they had to go to the private sellers, to the speculators who loitered around railroad stations selling fruit and ham out of their fur-lined coat pockets. There were few of them and their prices were exorbitant. Harold objected to it all, eating the small rationed black bread portions, and borscht without meat, and potatoes without butter but with plenty of linseed oil—previously thought to be good only for making paint and linoleum and for oiling wood. "We have no money to give away to private traders," he would say. "We can live one winter without fruit. Next winter there will be fruit. Besides, we don't have any extra money. Where is this money to buy from speculators coming from?" Jane would not reply, Alexander would shrug because he did not know, but in the dark after Harold was asleep, Jane would creep into his room and whisper to him to go the next day and buy himself oranges so the scurvy wouldn't get him, and ham so dystrophy wouldn't get him, or some rare and dubiously fresh milk. "Hear me, Alexander? I'm putting American dollars in your school bag, in the inner pocket, all right?"

"All right, Mom. Where is this American money coming from?"

"Never mind that, son. I brought a little extra, just in case." She would creep to him and in the dark her mouth would find his forehead. "Things are not expected to be good overnight. Do you know what's going on in our America? The Depression. Poverty, unemployment, things are difficult all over; these are difficult times. But we are living according to our principles. We are building a new state not on exploitation but on camaraderie and mutual benefit."

"With a few extra American dollars?" Alexander would whisper.

"With a few extra American dollars," Jane would agree, gathering his head into her arms. "Don't tell your father, though. Your father would get very upset. He'd feel as if I'd betrayed him. So don't tell him."

"I won't."

The following winter, Alexander was twelve and there was still no fresh fruit in Moscow. It was still bitterly cold, and the only difference between the winter of 1931 and the winter of 1930 was that the speculators near the railroads had vanished. They had all been given ten years in Siberia for counter-revolutionary anti-proletarian activity.

CHAPTER FOUR

Living on Ellis Island, 1943

TATIANA TRIED TO READ to improve her English while she got better. In the small but well-stocked Ellis library, she found many books in English donated by nurses, by doctors, by other benefactors. The library even had some books in Russian: Mayakovsky, Gorky, Tolstoy. Tatiana read in her room, but reading in English could not keep her attention and when her attention wandered, images of rivers and ice and blood mixed with images of bombing, planes, mortars, and ice holes, and knitting, and sewing, and motionless mothers on sofas with their body bags in their hands and famished frozen sisters on piles of dead bodies and brothers who vanished on exploding trains and fathers who burned down to ashes and grandfathers with infected lungs and grandmothers dying of grief. White camouflage, pools of blood, wet matted black hair, an officer's cap strewn to the side, lying on the ice, images all so visceral she would have to stagger down the hall and throw up in the shared bathroom and afterwards force herself into learning better and better English that sufficiently commanded her attention so that her mind did not wander and go where the heart could not help but wander, meander into the emptiness in the middle of her chest, a black void that felt so much like fear that when she closed her eyes, her whole body choked on it.

She would lift a sleeping Anthony out of his bassinet and lay him on her chest for comfort, for closeness. But no matter how good Anthony smelled, and how silky his black hair felt against her lips, she could not keep her mind from wandering. If anything . . .

But she liked to smell him. She liked to undress him if it was sufficiently warm, and feel his chubby pink soft body. She liked to smell his hair and his neck and his milky baby breath. She liked to turn him over and touch his back and his legs and his long feet, and smell the back of his neck. Contentedly he slept and did not wake up, not even with all the prodding and caressing.

"Does this child ever wake up?" asked Dr. Edward Ludlow on one of his rounds.

In slow English Tatiana replied, "Think him as lion. He sleeps twenty hours in day and wakes up in night to hunt."

Edward smiled. "You must be getting better. You're making a joke."

She smiled wanly. Dr. Ludlow was a thin, graceful man of fluid motion. He did not raise his voice, he did not jerk his hands. He was soothing in his eyes, in his speech, in his movements. He had a good bedside manner, a must for a fine doctor. He was in his mid-thirties, Tatiana guessed, and carried himself so upright that she suspected he might have been a military man once. She felt that she could trust him. He had serious eyes.

Dr. Ludlow had delivered Anthony when she had arrived in the Port of New York and gone into labor, a month early. He now came every day to check on her, even though Brenda said that normally he worked at Ellis only a couple of days a week.

Glancing at his watch, Edward said, "It's almost lunchtime. Why don't we take a walk if you're up to it, and eat in the cafeteria? Put on your robe and we'll go."

"No, no." She didn't like to leave her room. "What about TB?"

He waved her off. "Put on your face mask and walk down the hall."

Reluctantly she went. They had lunch at one of the narrow rectangular tables lining the large open room with high windows.

"It's not great," Edward said, looking at his meal. "I get a little beef. Here, have some of mine." He cut half of his chipped beef with gravy and put it on her plate.

"Thank you, but look at all food I have," said Tatiana. "I have white bread. I have margarine. I have potatoes and rice and corn. There is so much food."

In the dark room she sits and in front of her is a plate and on the plate lies a black hunk of bread the size of a deck of cards. The bread has sawdust in it, and cardboard. She takes a knife and a fork, and cuts it slowly into four pieces. She eats one, chews it deliberately, pushes it with difficulty through her dry throat, eats another and another and finally the last one. She lingers especially on the last one. She knows after this piece is gone there will be no more food until tomorrow morning. She wishes she could be strong enough to save half of the bread until dinner, but she isn't, she can't. When she looks up from her plate, her sister, Dasha, is staring at her. Her plate is long empty.

"I wish Alexander was coming back," says Dasha. "He might have food for us."

I wish Alexander was coming back, thinks Tatiana.

She shuddered; her potato fell to the floor. She bent and picked it up, dusted it off, and ate it without saying a word.

Edward stared at her, his fork full of beef suspended between the plate and his mouth.

"There is sugar and tea and coffee and condensed milk," Tatiana tremulously continued. "There is apples and oranges."

"There's hardly any chicken, there's practically no beef, there's only very little milk and there's no butter," Edward said. "The wounded need all the butter we have and we don't have any, you know they'd get better faster if they had some but they don't."

"Maybe they do not want to get better faster. Maybe they like it here," Tatiana said, and found Edward studying her again. She thought of something. "Edward, you say you have milk?"

"Not much, but yes, regular milk, not condensed."

"Bring me some milk and a large vat, and long wooden spoon. Maybe ten liters of milk, twenty. The more the better. Tomorrow we will have butter."

Edward said, "What does milk have to do with butter?"

Now it was Tatiana's turn to study Edward, who smiled and said, "I'm a doctor, not a farmer. Eat, eat. You need it. And you're right. Despite everything, there is still plenty."

CHAPTER FIVE

Morozovo, 1943

THEY CAME FOR HIM a few hours into the night. Alexander, sleeping in the chair, was roughly shaken awake by four men in suits, motioning him to stand.

Slowly he stood.

"You're going to Volkhov to get promoted. Hurry. There is no time to waste. We've got to get across the lake before it gets light. The Germans bomb Ladoga constantly." The sallow man who was speaking in hushed tones was obviously in charge. The other three never opened their mouths.

Alexander picked up his rucksack.

"Leave that here," said the man.

"Well, I'm a soldier. I always take my ruck with me if it's all the same to you."

"Have you got your sidearm?"

"Of course."

"Let's have that."

Alexander took a step toward them. He was a head taller than the tallest. They looked like thugs in their drab gray winter coats. On top of the coats they had small blue stripes, the symbol of the NKVD—the People's Commissariat of Internal Affairs—the way the Red Cross was a symbol of international empathy. "Let me understand what you're asking me," he said quietly but not *that* quietly.

"So it's easier for you," the first man stammered. "You're wounded, no? It must be hard for you to carry all your gear—"

"This isn't all my gear. These are just my few personal things. Let's go," Alexander said loudly, moving out from the side of the bed, pushing them out of his way. "Now, comrades. We're wasting time." It was not an even fight. He was an officer, a major. He couldn't see their rank in their shoulder bars or demeanor. They had no authority until they were out of the building and took his away from him. This police liked to do its work in private, in the dark. They did not like to be overheard by barely sleeping nurses, by barely sleeping soldiers. This police liked it to seem as if everything was just as it should be. A wounded man was being taken in the middle of the night across the lake to get a promotion. What was so out of the ordinary about that? But they had to leave his gun with him to continue with the pretense. As if they could have taken it away.

As they were walking out, Alexander noticed that the two beds next to him were empty. The soldier with the breathing difficulties and another had gone. He shook his head. "Are they going to get promoted, too?" he asked dryly.

"No questions, just go," said one of the men. "Quickly."

Alexander had slight trouble walking quickly.

As he made his way through the corridor, he wondered where Tatiana was sleeping. Was it behind one of those doors? Was she there now, somewhere? Still so close. He took a deep breath, almost as if he were smelling for her.

The armored truck was waiting outside behind the building. It was parked next to Dr. Sayers's Red Cross jeep. Alexander recognized the white and red emblem in the dark. As they got closer to their truck, a silhouette hobbled out from the shadows. It was Dimitri. He was hunched over his casted arm, and his face was a black pulp with a swollen protuberance instead of a nose—earlier courtesy of Alexander.

He stood for a moment and said nothing. Then, "Going somewhere, Major Belov?" His hissing voice placed special emphasis on Belov. It sounded like *Belofffff*.

"Don't come close to me, Dimitri," Alexander said.

Dimitri, as if heeding the advice, took a step back, then opened his mouth and laughed silently. "You can't hurt me anymore, Alexander."

"Nor you me."

"Oh, believe me," said Dimitri in a smooth sweet-sour voice, "I can still hurt you." And right before Alexander was pushed into the NKVD truck by the militia men, Dimitri threw his head back as if in studied delirium and wagged a shaking finger at Alexander, baring the yellow teeth under his bloodied nose and narrowing his slit eyes.

Alexander turned his head, squared his shoulders, and without even looking in Dimitri's direction as he jumped into the truck, said very loudly and clearly and with as much satisfaction as he could get his voice to muster, "Oh, fuck you."

"Get in the truck and shut up," barked one of the NKVD men to Alexander, and to Dimitri: "Go back to your ward, it's past curfew. What are you doing skulking around here?"

In the back of the truck, Alexander saw his two shivering ward mates. He hadn't expected two other people, two Red Army *soldiers*, to be in the truck with him. He had thought it would be just him and the NKVD men. No one to risk or sacrifice except them and himself. Now what?

One of the NKVD men grabbed his ruck. Alexander yanked it away. The man did not let go. "It looks as if it's hard for you to carry it," he said, struggling. "I'll take it and give it back to you on the other side."

Shaking his head, Alexander said, "No, I'll keep it." He wrenched it from the man.

"Belov—"

"Sergeant!" said Alexander loudly. "You're talking to an officer. Major Belov to you. Leave my belongings alone. Now, let's start driving. We've got a long way ahead of us." Smiling to himself, he turned away, dismissing the man. His back didn't hurt as badly as he had imagined: he was able to walk, jump up, talk, bend, sit down on the floor of the truck. But his weakness upset him.

The truck's idling motor revved up and they began driving away— from the hospital, from Morozovo, from Tatiana. Alexander took a deep breath and turned to the two men sitting in front of him.

"Who the fuck are you?" he said. The words were gruff but the tone was resigned. He looked them over briefly. It was dark, he could barely make out their features. They were huddled against the wall of the truck, the smaller one wore glasses, the larger one sat, body wrapped in his coat, head wrapped in a bandage, and only his eyes, nose, and mouth showed. His eyes were bright and alert, discernible even in the dark, even at night. Bright perhaps wasn't quite the right word. Mischievous. You couldn't say the same about the smaller man's eyes. They were lackluster.

"Who are you?" Alexander repeated.

"Lieutenant Nikolai Ouspensky. This is Corporal Boris Maikov. We were wounded in Operation Spark, on January fifteenth, over on the Volkhov side—we were housed in a field tent until we—"

"Stop," Alexander said, putting his hand out. Before he continued with them he wanted to shake their hands. He wanted to feel what they were made of. Ouspensky was all right—his handshake was steady and friendly and unafraid. His hand was strong. Not frail Maikov's.

Alexander sat back against the truck and felt for the grenade in his boots. Damn it. He could hear Ouspensky's rattling breathing. Ouspensky was the one Tania had moved next to Alexander and put a tent around, the one with only one lung, the one who could not hear or speak. Yet here he was sitting, breathing on his own, hearing, speaking.

"Listen, both of you," said Alexander. "Summon your strength. You're going to need it."

"For getting a medal?" Maikov said suspiciously.

"You're going to be getting a posthumous medal if you don't get hold of yourself and stop shaking," said Alexander.

"How do you know I'm shaking?"

"I can hear your boots knocking together," Alexander replied. "Quiet, soldier."

Maikov turned to Ouspensky. "I told you, Lieutenant, this didn't seem right, to be woken in the middle of the night—"

"And I told you to shut up," said Alexander.

There was a bit of dull blue light coming in from the narrow window in the front of the truck.

"Lieutenant," Alexander said to Ouspensky, "can you stand up? I need you to stand up and block the view from the window."

"Last time I heard that, my quartermate was getting some blow," said Ouspensky with a smile.

"Well, rest assured, no one is getting blow here," Alexander said. "Stand up."

Ouspensky obeyed. "Tell us the truth. *Are* we getting promoted?"

"How should I know?" Once Nikolai blocked the small window, Alexander took off his boot and pulled out one of the grenades. It was dark enough that neither Maikov nor Ouspensky saw what he was doing.

He crawled to the back of the truck and sat with his back against the doors. There were only two NKVD men in the front cabin. They were young, they had no experience, and no one wanted to cross the lake: the danger of German fire was ever-present and unwelcome. The driver's lack of experience broadcast itself in his inability to drive the truck faster than twenty kilometers an hour. Alexander knew that if the Germans were monitoring Soviet army activity from their positions in Sinyavino, the truck's leisurely speed would not escape their reconnaissance agents. He could walk across the ice faster.

"Major, are *you* getting promoted?" asked Ouspensky.

"That's what they told me, and they let me keep my gun. Until I hear otherwise, I'm optimistic."

"They didn't let you keep your gun. I saw. I heard. They just didn't have the strength to take it from you."

"I'm a critically injured man," Alexander said, taking out a cigarette. "They could have taken it from me if they wanted to." He lit up.

"Have you got another one?" said Ouspensky. "I haven't smoked in three months." He looked Alexander over. "Nor seen anyone but my nurses." He paused. "I've heard your voice, though."

"You don't want to smoke," Alexander said. "From what I understand, you have no lungs."

"I have one lung, and my nurse has been keeping me artificially sick so I don't get sent back to the front. That's what she did for me."

"Did she?" asked Alexander, trying not to close his eyes at the image of Nikolai's nurse—the small, clear-eyed bright sunny morning of a girl, the crisp Lazarevo morning of a sweet blonde girl.

"She brought in ice and made me breathe the cold fumes to get my lungs rattling and working. I wish she would have done a little more for me."

Alexander handed him a cigarette. He wanted Nikolai to stop talking. He did not think Ouspensky would be particularly pleased to discover that Tatiana had saved him only long enough to be now sent into Mekhlis's clutches.

Taking out his Tokarev pistol, Alexander got up, pointed at the back door and fired, blowing out the padlock. Maikov squealed. The truck slowed down. There was obviously some confusion in the driver's cabin as to the source of the noise. Now down on the floor, Ouspensky was no longer blocking the window. Alexander had seconds before the truck stopped. Flinging the doors open, he pulled the pin out of the grenade, pulled himself above the roof of the creeping vehicle and threw the grenade forward. It landed a few meters in front of the truck's path; seconds later there was a shattering explosion. He had just enough time to hear Maikov bleat, "What is that—" when he was thrown from the truck onto the ice. The pain he felt in the unhealed wound in his back was so jolting he thought his scars were tearing apart a millimeter at a time.

The truck jerked and began to rumble to a sliding stop. It skidded, teetered and fell sideways onto the ice, crunching to a halt at the ice hole made by Alexander's grenade. The hole was smaller than the truck, but the truck was heavier than the broken ice. The ice cracked and the hole became wider.

Alexander got up and ran limping to the back doors, motioning for the two men to crawl to him. "What was that?" Maikov cried. He had bumped his head and his nose was bleeding.

"Jump out of the truck!" Alexander yelled.

Ouspensky and Maikov did as he commanded—just in time, as the front end of the truck slowly sank beneath the surface of the Ladoga. The drivers must have been knocked unconscious by the impact against the glass and ice. They were making no attempts to get out.

"Major, what the hell—"

"Shut up. The Germans will begin shooting at the truck in three or four minutes." Alexander had no intention of actually dying on the ice. Before he saw Ouspensky and Maikov, he had had a small hope he might be alone, and would, after blowing up the truck with the NKVD men in it, make his way back to the Morozovo shores and into the woods. All of his hopes seemed to have this one common denominator nowadays: short-fucking-lived.

"You want to stay here and observe the efficient German army in action, or you want to come with me?"

"What about the drivers?" asked Ouspensky.

"What about them? They are NKVD men. Where do you think those drivers were taking you at dawn?"

Maikov tried to stand up. Before he could say another word, Alexander pulled him down onto the ice.

They weren't far from the shore, maybe two kilometers. It was predawn. The cabin of the truck was submerged and cracking a larger hole in the ice, large enough soon for the whole truck to fit through.

"Pardon me, Major," Ouspensky said, "but you're talking out of your ass. I've never done anything wrong in my entire military career. They haven't come for me."

"No," Alexander said. "They've come for me."

"Who the fuck are *you*?"

The truck was disappearing into the water.

Ouspensky stared at the ice, at the shivering, dumbfounded and bleeding Maikov, at Alexander, and laughed. "Major, perhaps you could tell us your plans for what the three of us are going to do alone on the open ice once the truck sinks?"

"Don't worry," said Alexander with a heavy sigh. "I guarantee you, we won't be alone for long." He nodded in the direction of the distant

Morozovo shore and took out his two pistols. The headlights of a light
army vehicle were getting closer. The jeep stopped fifty meters from
them, and out of it jumped five men with five machine guns all pointing
at Alexander. "Stand up! Stand up on the ice!"

Ouspensky and Maikov stood instantly, hands in the air, but
Alexander didn't like to take orders from inferior officers. He would not
stand up and with good reason. He heard the whistling sound of a shell
and put his hands over his head.

When he looked, two of the NKVD men were lying face down,
while the other three were crawling to Alexander, rifles aimed at him,
hissing, *stay down, stay down.* Maybe the Germans will kill them before
I have a chance to, Alexander thought. He tried to make out the shore.
Where was Sayers? The NKVD jeep was stationary, providing a convenient practice target for the Germans. When the NKVD men got
very close, Alexander suggested to them that maybe they should get
back inside their vehicle and return to Morozovo with all deliberate
speed.

"No!" one of them yelled. "We have to get you across to Volkhov!"

Another shell whistled by, this one falling twenty meters from the
jeep—the only transport they had to get either to Volkhov or back to
Morozovo. Once the Germans hit their jeep, the cluster of men would
last several unprotected seconds on the open lake against German artillery.

On his stomach, Alexander stared at the NKVD men on their
stomachs. "You want to drive to Volkhov under German fire? Let's go."

The men looked at the armored truck that had carried Alexander. It
had nearly gone below the surface of the water. Alexander watched
with amusement as self-preservation battled it out with orders.

"Let's go back," said one of the NKVD. "We will return to Morozovo and await further instructions. We can always get him to Volkhov
tomorrow."

"I think that's wise," said Alexander.

Ouspensky was watching Alexander with amazement. Alexander
ignored him. "Come on, all of you. On three. Run to your jeep before
it's blown up." Aside from wanting to keep alive, Alexander wanted to
remain dry. His life wasn't worth much to him wet. He knew that
whether he was in Volkhov or Morozovo he would get dry clothes when
donkeys flew. The wet clothes would remain on his body until after
they'd given him pneumonia and killed him, and still they'd be wet on
his corpse in the March damp.

All six men crawled to the jeep. The three NKVD troops ordered the men to get into the back. Both Ouspensky and Maikov glanced at Alexander with considerable anxiety.

"Just get in."

Two of the NKVD men got into the back with them. Ouspensky and Maikov breathed out in relief.

Alexander took out a cigarette and passed one to Nikolai and to white-faced Maikov who refused.

"Why did you do that?" whispered Ouspensky to Alexander.

"I'll tell you," said Alexander. "I did it because I just didn't feel like getting promoted."

Back on shore, the jeep proceeded to headquarters, passing a medical truck heading for the river. Alexander spotted Dr. Sayers in the passenger seat. Alexander managed a smile as he smoked, though he noticed the tips of his fingers trembling. It was going as well as could be expected. The scene on the lake genuinely looked like the aftermath of a German onslaught. Dead men on the ice, one truck down. Sayers would write out the death certificate, sign it, and it would be as if Alexander had never existed. The NKVD would be grateful—they preferred making their arrested parties invisible anyway—and by the time Stepanov learned of what had really happened, and that Alexander was still alive, Tatiana and Sayers would be long gone. Stepanov would not have to lie to Tatiana. Lacking any actual information, he himself would believe that Alexander, with Ouspensky and Maikov, had perished on the lake.

He ran a hand over his capless head and closed his eyes, quickly opening them again. The bleak Russian landscape was better than what was behind his closed lids.

Everybody won. The NKVD would not have to answer questions from the International Red Cross, the Red Army would pretend to mourn a number of downed and drowned men, while Mekhlis still had his paws on Alexander. Had they wanted to kill him, they would have killed him instantly. Those were not their orders. He knew why. The cat wanted to play with the mouse before he ripped the mouse to pieces.

It was eight in the morning by the time they got back to Morozovo, and since the base was coming to life and since they had to be hidden until they could be safely transported to *unsafety*, Alexander, Ouspensky and Maikov were thrown into the stockade in the basement of the old school. The stockade was a concrete cell just over a meter wide and less than two meters long. The militia ordered the three soldiers to lie flat on the floor and not move.

The cell was too short for Alexander; there was not enough room to lie down on the floor. As soon as the guards left, the three men crouched on the ground, drawing their knees up to their chests. Alexander's wound was throbbing. Sitting on the cold cement wasn't helping.

Ouspensky kept on at him. Alexander said, "What do you want? Stop asking. This way when you're questioned you won't have to lie."

"Why would we be questioned?"

"You've been arrested. Isn't that clear?"

Maikov was looking into his hands. "Oh, no," he said. "I've got a wife, a mother, two small children. What's going to happen?"

"You?" said Nikolai. "Who are you? I've got a wife and two sons. Two *small* sons. I think my mother is still alive, too."

Maikov didn't reply, but both he and Ouspensky turned to stare at Alexander. Maikov lowered his gaze. Ouspensky didn't.

"All right," said Ouspensky. "What did you do?"

"Lieutenant!" Alexander pulled rank whenever and wherever necessary. "I've heard enough from you."

Ouspensky remained undaunted. "You don't look like a religious zealot."

Alexander was silent.

"Or a Jew. Or a skank." Ouspensky looked him over. "Are you a *kulak*? A member of the Political Red Cross? A closet philosopher? A socialist? A historian? Are you an agricultural spoiler? An industrial wrecker? An anti-Soviet agitator?"

"I'm a Tatar drayman," said Alexander.

"You will get ten years for that. Where is your dray? My wife would find it very useful for hauling onions from nearby fields. Are you telling me we were arrested because we had the fucking bad luck to be bedded next to you?"

Maikov emitted a whimper that bordered on a wail. "But we know nothing! We did nothing!"

"Oh?" said Alexander. "Tell that to the group of musicians and a small audience that used to gather in the early thirties for an evening of piano without clearing it first with the housing council. To help defray the costs of the wine, they would collect a few kopecks from each person. When they were *all* arrested for anti-Soviet agitation, the money they had collected was deemed to have gone to prop up the nearly extinct bourgeoisie. The musicians and the audience all got from three to ten years." Alexander paused. "Well, not all. Only those who confessed to their crimes. Those who refused to confess were shot."

Ouspensky and Maikov stared at him. "And you know this how?"

Alexander shrugged. "Because I, being fourteen, escaped through the window before they had a chance to catch me."

They heard someone coming and fell quiet. Alexander stood up, and as the door was opened, Alexander said to Maikov, "Corporal, imagine your old life is gone. Imagine they've taken from you all they can and there is nothing left—"

"Come, Belov, let's go!" shouted a stout man with a single-shot Nagant rifle.

"It's the only way you will make it," Alexander said, stepping out of the cell and hearing the door slam closed behind him.

⚬⚬⚬

He sat in a small room in the abandoned school, in a school chair, in front of a table that was in front of a blackboard. He thought at any minute the schoolmaster was going to come in with a textbook and proceed with the lesson on the evils of imperialism.

Instead two men came in. There were now four people in the room, Alexander in the chair, a guard at the back of the class and two men behind the teacher's table. One man was bald and very thin with a long, thoughtful nose. He introduced himself kindly as Riduard Morozov. "Not the Morozov of this town?" asked Alexander.

Morozov smiled thinly. "No."

The other man was extremely heavy, extremely bald and had a round bulbous nose with broken capillaries. He looked like a heavy drinker. He introduced himself—somewhat less kindly—as Mitterand, which Alexander found almost humorous since Mitterand was the leader of the tiny French "Resistance movement in Nazi-occupied France.

Morozov began. "Do you know why you're here, Major Belov?" he asked, smiling warmly, speaking in polite, friendly tones. They were having a conversation. In a moment Mitterand was going to offer Alexander some tea, maybe a shot of vodka to calm him. Alexander thought of it as a joke, but oddly, the bottle of vodka actually did materialize from behind a desk, along with three shot glasses. Morozov poured.

"Yes," Alexander said brightly. "I was told yesterday I'm getting promoted. I'm going to be lieutenant colonel. And no, thank you," he said to the drink being offered to him.

"Are you refusing our hospitality, Comrade Belov?"

"I am Major Belov," Alexander said, standing up and raising his voice to the man in front of him. "Do you have a rank?" He waited. The man said nothing. "I didn't think so. You're not wearing a uniform. If you had a uniform to wear, you would be wearing it. Now, I will not have your drink. I will not sit down until you tell me what you want with me. I will be glad to cooperate in whatever way I can, comrades," he added, "but don't sit there and insult me by pretending we're the best of friends. What's going on?"

"You're under arrest."

"Ah. So no promotion then? It only took you since four this morning. Ten hours. You have not told me what you want with me. I don't know if you know yourselves. Why don't you go and find someone who can actually tell me? In the meantime, take me back to my cell and stop wasting my time."

"Major!" That was Morozov. The voice was less kind. The vodka, however, had been drunk by both men. Alexander smiled. If he kept them in the classroom drinking, they'd be leading him to the Soviet-Finnish border themselves, talking to him in soft English. They called him major. Alexander understood the psychology of rank extremely well. In the army there was only one rule—you never spoke rudely to your superiors. The pecking order was precisely established. "Major," Morozov repeated. "Stay right here."

Alexander returned to his chair.

Mitterand spoke to the young guard by the door; Alexander didn't hear the individual words. He understood the essence. This was not only out of Morozov's hands, this was out of his league. A bigger fish was needed to deal with Alexander. And soon the fish would be coming. But first they were going to try to break him.

"Put your hands behind your back, Major," said Morozov.

Alexander threw his cigarette on the floor, twisted his foot over it, and stood up.

They relieved him of his sidearm and his knife and pillaged through his rucksack. Having found bandages and pens and her white dress—nothing worth removing—they decided to take Alexander's medals off his chest, and they also tipped his shoulder bars and they told him he was not a major anymore and had no right to his title. They still hadn't told him the charges against him, nor had they asked him any questions.

He asked for his ruck. They laughed. Almost helplessly, he glanced at it once, in their hands, knowing Tatiana's dress was there. Just one more thing to be trampled on, to be left behind.

Alexander was taken to a solitary concrete cell with no window, no Ouspensky, no Maikov. He had no bench, he had no bed, and he had no blanket. He was alone, and his only sources of oxygen came from the guards opening the door, or from opening the sliding steel reinforced window on the door, or from the peephole they peered at him through, or from the small hole in the ceiling that was probably used for poison gas.

They left him his watch, and because they didn't search his person they did not find the drugs in his boots. He had a feeling the drugs were not safe. But where to put them? Slipping off the boots, he took the syringe, the morphine vial and the small sulfa pills and stuffed them in the pocket of his BVDs. They would have to search more thoroughly than they usually did to find them there.

Bending reminded him of his sharply throbbing back, which, as the day wore on, felt as if it were swelling and expanding. He debated giving himself a morphine shot, then decided against it. He didn't want to numb himself to what was about to come. He did chew one of the sulfa tablets, bitter and acidic, without crushing it, without asking for water. He just put it into his mouth and chewed it, shuddering with the swallow. Alexander sat quietly on the floor, realizing they couldn't see him because it was so dark in the cell, and closed his eyes. Or maybe they had remained open; it was hard to tell. It didn't matter in the end. He sat and waited. Had the day gone? Had it been one day? He wanted a smoke. He remained motionless. Had Sayers and Tatiana left? Had Tania allowed herself to be convinced, to be goaded, to be comforted? Had she taken her things and got into Sayers's truck? Had they fled Morozovo? What Alexander wouldn't give for a word. He was very afraid that Dr. Sayers would break down, not convince her, and she would still be here. He tried to feel for her up close, sensing nothing but the cold. If she were still in Morozovo, he knew that once they started interrogating him for real and once they knew of her, he would be finished. He couldn't breathe thinking of her still so close. He needed to stall the NKVD for a little while longer until he knew for sure she was out. The sooner she left, the sooner he could give himself over to the state.

She seemed very close. He could almost reach for his ruck and feel for her dress, and see her, white dress with red roses, hair long and flowing, teeth gleaming. She *was* very close. He didn't have to touch the dress. He didn't need comfort. She needed comfort. *She* needed him so much, how was she going to get through this without him?

How was she going to get through losing him without him?

Alexander needed to think about something else.

Soon he didn't have to.

"Idiot!" he heard from the outside. "How do you plan to observe the prisoner if he has no light? He could have killed himself in there for all you know. Stupid moron!"

The door opened and a man walked in with a kerosene lamp. "You need to be illuminated at all times," said the man. It was Mitterand.

"When is someone going to tell me what's going on around here?" said Alexander.

"You are not to question us!" Mitterand shouted. "You are not a major anymore. You are nothing. You will sit and wait until we are ready for you."

That seemed to be the sole purpose of Mitterand's visit—to yell at Alexander. After Mitterand left, the guard brought Alexander some water and three-quarters of a kilo of bread. Alexander ate the bread, drank the water, and then felt around the floor for a drain hole. He did not want to be illuminated. He also did not want to compete for oxygen with a kerosene lamp. Opening the bottom of the lamp, he poured the kerosene down the drain, leaving just a little left at the bottom that burned out in ten minutes. The guard opened the door and shouted, "Why is the lamp out?"

"Ran out of kerosene," Alexander said pleasantly. "Have you got more?"

The guard did not have more.

"That's too bad," Alexander said.

He slept in the darkness, in a sitting position, in the corner, with his head leaning against the wall. When he woke up it was still pitch black. He didn't know for sure he had woken up. He dreamed he had opened his eyes, and it was black. He dreamed of Tatiana, and when he woke up, he thought of Tatiana. Dreams and reality were mingled. Alexander didn't know where the nightmare ended and real life began. He dreamed he closed his eyes and slept.

He felt disconnected from himself, from Morozovo—from the hospital, from his life—and he felt strangely comforted in his detachment. He was cold. That attached him back to his cramped and uncomfortable body. He preferred it the other way. The wound in his back was merciless. He grit his teeth and blinked away the darkness.

Harold and Jane Barrington, 1933

Hitler had become the Chancellor of Germany. President Von Hindenburg had "stepped down." Alexander felt an inexplicable stirring in the air of something ominous he could not quite put his finger on. He had long stopped hoping for more food, for new shoes, for a warmer winter coat. But in the summer he didn't need a coat. The Barringtons were spending July at their dacha in Krasnaya Polyana and that was good. They rented two rooms from a Lithuanian widow and her drunken son.

One afternoon, after a picnic of hard-boiled eggs and tomatoes and a little bologna, and vodka for his mother ("Mom, since when do you drink vodka?"), Alexander was lying in the hammock reading when he heard someone behind him in the woods. When he languidly turned his head, he saw his mother and father. They were near the clearing by the lake, throwing pebbles into the water, chatting softly. Alexander was not used to his parents talking quietly, so strident had their relationship become with their conflicting needs and anxieties. Normally he would have looked back into his book. But this quiet chatter, this convivial closeness—he didn't know what to make of it. Harold took the pebbles out of Jane's hands and brought her to stand close to him. One of his hands was around her waist. He was holding her other hand. And then he kissed her and they began to dance. They waltzed slowly in the clearing, and Alexander heard his father singing—*singing*!

As they continued to waltz, their bodies spinning in a conjugal embrace, and as Alexander watched his mother and father in a moment they had never had before in front of him and would never have again, he was filled with a happiness and longing he could neither define nor express.

They drew away from one another, looked at him, and smiled.

Uncertainly he smiled back, embarrassed but unable to look away.

They came over to his hammock. His father's arm was still around his mother.

"It's our anniversary today, Alexander."

"Your father is singing the anniversary song to me," said Jane. "We danced to that song the day we were wed thirty-one years ago. I was nineteen." She smiled at Harold.

"Are you going to stay in the hammock, son? Read for a while?"

"I'm not going anywhere."

"Good," said Harold, taking Jane by the hand and heading with her toward the house.

Alexander looked into his book, but after an hour of turning the pages, he could not see or remember a single word of what he had just read.

⸻

Winter came too soon. And during the winter on Thursday evenings after dinner Harold would take Alexander by the hand and walk with him in the cold to Arbat—the Moscow street vendors' mall of musicians and writers and poets and troubadours and old ladies selling *chachkas* from the days of the Tsar. Near Arbat, in a small, smoke-filled two-room apartment, a group of foreigners and Soviet men, all devout communists, would meet for two hours from eight to ten to drink, smoke and discuss how to make communism work better in the Soviet Union, how to make the classless society arrive faster at their doorstep, a society in which there was no need for the state, for police, for an army because all grounds for conflict had been removed.

"Marx said the only conflict is economic conflict between classes. Once it's gone, the need for police would be gone. Citizens, what are we waiting for? Is it taking longer than we anticipated?" That was Harold.

Even Alexander chipped in, remembering something he had read: "'While the state exists, there can be no freedom. When there will be freedom, there will be no state.'" Harold smiled approvingly at his son quoting Lenin.

At the meetings Alexander made friends with sixty-seven-year-old Slavan, a withered, gray man who seemed to have wrinkles even on his scalp, but his eyes were small blue alert stars, and his mouth was always fixed in a sardonic smile. He said little, but Alexander liked the look of his ironic expression and the bit of warmth that came from him whenever he looked Alexander's way.

After two years of meetings, Harold and fifteen others were called into the Party regional headquarters or Obkom—Oblastnyi Kommitet—and asked if the focus of their future meetings could perhaps be something other than how to make communism work better in Russia since that implied it wasn't working quite so well. After hearing about it from his father, Alexander asked how the Party knew what a group of fifteen drunk men talked about once a week on Thursdays in a city of five million people. Harold said, himself quoting Lenin, "'It is true that liberty is precious. So precious that it must be rationed.' They obviously have ways of finding out what we talk about. Perhaps it's that Slavan. I'd stop talking to him if I were you."

"It's not him, Dad."

After that the group still met on Thursdays, but now they read aloud from Lenin's *What Is To Be Done?* or from Rosa Luxembourg's pamphlets, or from Marx's *Communist Manifesto*.

Harold often brought up the approval of American communist supporters to show that Soviet communism was slowly being embraced internationally and that it was all just a matter of time. "Look what Isadora Duncan said about Lenin before she died," Harold would say and quote: "'Others loved themselves, money, theories, power. Lenin loved his fellow men ... Lenin was God, as Christ was God, because God is love, and Christ and Lenin were all love.'"

Alexander smiled approvingly at his father.

During one full night, many hours of it, fifteen men, except for a silent and smiling Slavan, tried to explain to a fourteen-year-old Alexander the meaning of "value subtraction." How an item—say shoes—could cost less after it was made than the sum total value of its labor and material parts. "What don't you understand?" yelled a frustrated communist who was an engineer by day.

"The part of how you make money selling shoes."

"Who said anything about making money? Haven't you read the *Communist Manifesto*?"

"*Yes.*"

"Don't you remember what Marx said? The difference between what the factory pays the worker to make the shoes and what the shoes actually cost is capitalist theft and exploitation of the proletariat. That's what communism is trying to eradicate. Have you not been paying attention?"

"I have, but value subtraction is not just eliminating profit," Alexander said. "Value subtraction means it's actually costing more to make the shoes than the shoes can be sold for. Who is going to pay the difference?"

"The state."

"Where is the state going to find the money?"

"The state will temporarily pay the workers less to make the shoes."

Alexander was quiet. "So in a period of flagrant worldwide

inflation, the Soviet Union is going to pay the workers *less?* How much less?"

"Less, that's all."

"And how are *we* going to buy the shoes?"

"Temporarily we're not. We'll have to wear last year's shoes. Until the state gets on its feet." The engineer smiled.

"Good one," Alexander said calmly. "The state got on its feet enough to cover the cost of Lenin's Rolls Royce, didn't it?"

"What does Lenin's Rolls Royce have to do with what we're talking about?" screamed the engineer. Slavan laughed. "The Soviet Union will be fine," the engineer continued. "It is in its infancy stages. It will borrow money from abroad if it has to."

"With all due respect, citizen, no country in the world will lend money to the Soviet Union again," said Alexander. "It repudiated all of its foreign debt in 1917 after the Bolshevik Revolution. They will not see any foreign money for a long time to come. The world banks are closed to the Soviet Union."

"We have to be patient. Changes will not happen overnight. And you need to have a more positive attitude. Harold, what have you been teaching your son?"

Harold didn't reply, but on the way home he said, "What's gotten into you, Alexander?"

"Nothing." Alexander wanted to take his father's hand, like always, but suddenly thought he was too old. He walked alongside him, and then took it anyway. "For some reason, the economics are not working. This revolutionary state is built foremost on economics, and the state has figured out everything except how to pay the labor force. The workers feel less and less like proletariat than like the state-owned factories and machines. We've been here over three years. We just finished the first of the Five-Year Plans. And we have so little food, and nothing in the stores, and—" He wanted to say, *and people keep disappearing,* but he kept his mouth shut.

"Well, what do you think is going on in America?" Harold asked. "Thirty per cent unemployment, Alexander. You think it's better there? The whole world is suffering. Look at Germany: such extraordinary inflation. Now this man Adolf Hitler is promising the Germans the end of all their troubles. Maybe he will succeed. The Germans certainly hope so. Well, Comrades Lenin and Stalin promised the same thing to the Soviet Union. What did Stalin call Russia? The second America, right? We have to believe, and we have to follow, and soon it will be better. You'll see."

"I know, Dad. You may be right. Still, I know that the state has to pay its people somehow. How much less can they pay you? We already can't afford meat and milk, not that there is any, even if we could. And will they pay you less until—what? They'll realize they need more money, not less, to run the government, and your labor is their largest variable cost. What are they going to do? Reduce your salary every year until—until what?"

"What are you afraid of?" Harold said, squeezing Alexander's reluctant hand. "When you get big, you will have meaningful work. You still want to be an architect? You will. You will have a career."

"I'm afraid," said Alexander, extricating himself from his father, "that it's just a matter of time before I am, before we *all* become nothing more than fixed capital."

CHAPTER SIX

Edward and Vikki, 1943

TATIANA WAS SITTING BY the window, holding her two-week-old baby with one hand and a book with the other. Her eyes were closed, and then she heard a breath, and instantly opened her eyes.

Edward Ludlow was standing a few feet away from her with an expression of curiosity and concern. She could understand. She had been very silent since her baby was born. She did not think that was so unusual. Many people who came here, leaving their life behind, must have been silent, as if the enormity of what was behind and what was ahead was just dawning on them in their small white rooms as they stared at the robes of Lady Liberty. "I was worried about you dropping the baby," he said. "I didn't mean to startle you . . ."

She showed him how tightly she was holding Anthony. "Don't worry."

"What are you reading?"

She looked at her book. "I'm not reading, just . . . sitting." It was *The Bronze Horseman and Other Poems* by Aleksandr Pushkin.

"Are you all right? It's the middle of the afternoon. I didn't mean to wake you."

She rubbed her eyes. The baby was still sleeping. "This child not sleep at night, only day."

"Much like his mother."

"Mother on his schedule." She smiled. "Everything all right?"

"Yes, yes," said Dr. Ludlow hurriedly. "I wanted to let you know that an INS worker is here to talk to you."

"What he want?"

"What does he want? He wants to give you a chance to stay in the United States."

"I thought because my son . . . because he was born on American ground . . ."

"American soil," Dr. Ludlow corrected her gently. "The Attorney General needs to look at your case personally." He paused. "We don't have many stowaways coming to the United States during war, you have to understand. Especially from the Soviet Union. It's unusual."

Tatiana said, "Does he feel is safe to come here? Did you say him I have TB?"

"I told him. He'll be wearing a mask. How are you feeling, by the way? Any blood in the cough?"

"None. And fever is gone. I feel better."

"You've been going out a bit?"

"Yes, salty air is good."

"Yes." He stared at her solemnly. She stared solemnly back. "The salt air is good." He cleared his throat and continued. "The nurses are all amazed your boy hasn't caught TB."

"Explain to them, Edward," said Tatiana, "that if ten thousand people come to see me every day for whole year and I had TB every day for whole year, only ten to sixteen people contract disease from me." She paused. "It's not so contagious as people think. So send in INS man if he thinks he strong enough. But tell him odds. And tell him I don't speak so good English."

Smiling, Edward said her English was just fine and asked if she wanted him to stay.

"No. No, thank you."

The INS man, Tom, talked to her for fifteen minutes to see if she spoke rudimentary English. Tatiana spoke rudimentary English. He asked about her skills. She told him she was a nurse, and that she could also sew and cook.

"Well, there is certainly a shortage of nurses during the war," he said.

"Yes, much of it here at Ellis," said Tatiana. She thought of Brenda being in the wrong profession.

"We don't get many cases like you."

She made no reply.

"You want to stay in the United States?"

"Of course."

"You think you could get a job, to help in the war effort?"

"Of course."

"Not be a public charge? That's very important to us in time of war. You understand? The attorney general comes under scrutiny every time he lets a person like you slip through his fingers. The country is in turmoil. We must make sure you stay productive, and that you have allegiance to this country, not your old country."

"Don't worry about that," she said. "As soon as my TB goes and they let me work, I will get job. I will be nurse, or seamstress, or cook. I will be all three, if need to. I will do what I have to after I am good again."

As if suddenly remembering she had TB, Tom stood up and went to the door, tightening the mask around his mouth. "Where will you live?" he said in a muffled voice.

"I want to stay here."

"After you get better, you'll have to get an apartment."

"Yes. Do not worry."

He nodded, writing something down in his book. "And the name you want to go by? I saw on the documents you brought with you that you got out of the Soviet Union as a Red Cross nurse named Jane Barrington."

"Yes."

"How fake are those documents?"

"I do not understand what you mean."

Tom fell silent. "Who is Jane Barrington?"

Now Tatiana was silent. "My husband's mother," she said at last.

Tom sighed. "Barrington? Not very Russian."

"My husband was American." She lowered her gaze.

Tom opened the door. "Is that the name you want to use to get your permanent residency card?"

"Yes."

"No Russian name for you?"

She thought about it.

Tom came closer to her. "Sometimes refugees who come here like to cling to a little bit of their past. Maybe they leave just the first name the same. Change the last name. Think about it."

"Not me," she replied. "Change all. I don't want to—how you put it? Cling to anything."

He wrote something down in his book. "Jane Barrington it is, then."

When he left, Tatiana opened her *Bronze Horseman* book as she sat once more by the window, looking out onto the New York harbor and the Statue of Liberty. She touched the picture of Alexander she had kept in there; without looking at it she touched his face and his uniformed body, and she whispered small short words in Russian to comfort *herself* this time, not Alexander, not his child, but herself. Shura,

Shura, Shura, whispered Jane Barrington, once known as Tatiana
Metanova.

༺ꞏꞏꞏꞏꞏꞏꞏꞏ༻

Tatiana's days consisted of feeding Anthony and changing Anthony and
washing Anthony's few nightgowns and cloth diapers in the bathroom
sink and going on short, fragrant walks outside the hospital and sitting
on benches with Anthony wrapped in blankets in her arms. Brenda
brought her breakfast to her room. Tatiana ate lunch and dinner in her
room. Unless Anthony was sleeping, Tatiana had him in her arms. She
looked at only two things: the New York harbor and her son. But whatever comfort she received from holding her baby was dissipated from
being alone day in and day out. Brenda and Dr. Ludlow called it convalescing. Tatiana called it solitary confinement.

One morning at the end of July, tired of herself, of sitting in her
room, Tatiana decided to take a walk down the corridor while Anthony
was sleeping.

She heard groans from the corridor and followed the groans into a
ward filled with wounded men. Brenda was on duty—the only one on
duty—looking less than pleased with her lot and showing the wounded
men exactly how she felt. Grumbling, curt, displeasingly surly, she was
washing out a wound on a soldier's leg despite repeated and loud pleas
from the soldier to either do it more gently or to shoot him.

Tatiana walked over and asked Brenda if she needed help, to which
Brenda replied that she certainly didn't need a sick girl making her prisoners sicker, and could Tatiana immediately go back to her room. Not
moving, Tatiana stood, stared at Brenda, stared at the raw hole in the
soldier's thigh, at the soldier's eyes, and said, "Let me bandage leg, let
me help you. Look, I have mask over my nose and mouth. You got four
men screaming for you on other side of hospital. One just lose a tooth in
his morning coffee. One have raging fever. One is oozing blood through
his ear."

Brenda let go of the bucket and the soldier's leg and left, though Tatiana could see that for a moment Brenda had struggled with what actually gave her more displeasure: taking care of the soldiers or letting
Tatiana have her way.

Tatiana finished washing out the wound; the soldier never peeped,
looking soothed and asleep; either asleep or dead, Tatiana concluded as
she bandaged his leg, still without motion from him, and moved on.

She disinfected an arm wound and a head wound, started an IV, and administered morphine, wishing for a bit of morphine for herself to dull her inner aching, at the same time thinking how lucky the German submarine men were to have had the luck to be brought to American shores for imprisonment and convalescence.

Suddenly Brenda appeared and, as if surprised that Tatiana was still in the ward, asked her to immediately go back to her room before she infected all her patients with TB, sounding almost as if she cared what happened to the patients.

As Tatiana was heading back, out in the corridor by the water fountain, she saw a tall, slim girl in a nurse's uniform standing and crying. Long-haired and long-legged, she was quite beautiful; if you didn't look at her mascara-streaked, tear-streaked, swollen eyes and cheeks. Tatiana needed a drink of water, and so with great discomfort she proceeded past the girl, stopping just half a foot away from her to get to the fountain. The girl sobbed loudly. Tatiana put her hand on the girl's elbow and said, "Are you all right?"

"I'm fine," the girl sobbed.

"Oh."

The girl continued to cry. She held a slightly moist cigarette in her hands. "If you only knew how freakishly miserable I am at the moment."

"Can I do anything?"

The girl looked out of her wet hands at Tatiana. "Who are you?"

"You can call me Tania."

"Aren't you the TB stowaway?"

"I am better now," Tatiana said quietly.

"You're not Tania. I processed your documents myself. Tom gave them to me. You're Jane Barrington. Oh, what do I care? My life is in shambles and we're talking about your name. I wish I had your problems."

Trying quickly to find the words to say something comforting in English, Tatiana said, "It could be worse."

"That's where you're so wrong, missy. It's as bad as can be. Nothing worse can happen. Nothing."

Tatiana noticed the wedding band on the girl's finger, and her sympathy flowed. "I am sorry." She paused. "Is it about your husband?"

Without looking away from her hands, the girl nodded.

"It is terrible thing," said Tatiana. "I know. This war . . ."

The girl nodded. "It's the pits."

"Your husband . . . he is not coming back?"

"*Isn't* coming back?" the girl exclaimed. "That's the whole point! He is very much coming back. Very much so. Next week."

Tatiana took a puzzled step away.

"Where are you going? You look like you're ready to fall down. It's not your fault he is coming back. Don't look so upset. I guess worse things have happened to girls at war, I just don't know of any. You want to go grab a coffee? Want a cigarette?"

Tatiana paused. "I have coffee with you."

They sat down in the long dining room at one of the rectangular tables. Tatiana sat across from the girl who introduced herself as Viktoria Sabatella ("But call me Vikki."), shook Tatiana's hand vigorously and said, "You here with your parents? I haven't seen any immigrants come this way in months. The boats are not bringing them in. So few—what? You're sick?"

"I am better now," said Tatiana. "I am here with myself." She paused. "With my son."

"Get out!" Viktoria slammed her coffee cup on the table. "You don't have a son."

"He almost month old."

"How old are you?"

"Nineteen."

"God, they start early where you're from. Where are you from?"

"Soviet Union."

"Wow. How'd you get this baby anyway? You have a husband?"

Tatiana opened her mouth, but Vikki went on as if the question had not been asked. Before she drew her next breath, she told Tatiana that she herself had never known her father ("Dead, or gone, all the same") and barely knew her mother ("Had me too young") who was in San Francisco, living with two men ("Not in the same apartment") and pretending to be either sick ("Yes, mentally") or dying ("From all that *passion*"). Vikki had been raised by her maternal grandparents ("They love Mumsy but they don't approve of her") and was living with them still ("Less fun than you might think"). She had originally wanted to be a journalist, then a manicurist ("In both professions you work with your hands; I thought it was a natural progression") and finally decided ("Was forced to, more like it,") to go into nursing when the European war looked like it would suck the United States into it. Tatiana was listening quietly and attentively when Vikki suddenly looked at her and said, "Got a husband?"

"Once."

"Yeah?" Vikki sighed. "Once. Would that I had a husband once—"

At that moment their conversation was interrupted by a painfully angular, very tall, immaculately dressed woman in a white brim hat, walking briskly through the dining hall, swinging her white purse and yelling, "Vikki! I'm talking to you! Vikki! Have you seen him?"

Vikki sighed and rolled her eyes at Tatiana. "No, Mrs. Ludlow. I haven't seen him today. I think he is still cross-town at NYU. He is here on Tuesday and Thursday afternoons."

"Afternoons? He's not at NYU! And how do you know his schedule so well?"

"I've worked with him for two years."

"Well, I've been married to him for eight and I still don't know where the hell he is." She came up to the table and towered over the two girls. She eyed Tatiana suspiciously. "Who are *you*?"

Tatiana pulled up her cloth mask from her neck to her mouth. Vikki stepped in. "She is from the Soviet Union. She barely speaks English."

"Well, she should learn, shouldn't she, if she expects to earn her keep in this country. We're at war, we have no business supporting wards." And swinging her purse, nearly hitting Tatiana on the head, the woman swept from the dining room.

"Who she?" asked Tatiana.

Vikki waved her hand. "Never mind her. The less you know about her, the better. That's Dr. Ludlow's crazy wife. She storms in here once a week looking for her husband."

"Why she keep losing him?"

Vikki laughed. "The question I think should be why does Dr. Ludlow let himself be lost so often."

"All right, why?"

Vikki waved Tatiana off. Tatiana understood. Vikki did not want to be talking about Dr. Ludlow. With a small smile, Tatiana appraised Vikki. Now that she had stopped crying, Tatiana could see that Vikki was a striking girl, a proper girl who was pretty and knew it and did everything to make sure everyone knew it. Her hair was shiny and long and swept over her face and shoulders, her eyes were outlined in black eyeliner and runny mascara, and her full lips had traces of bright red lipstick. Her white uniform was tight on her long-limbed figure and came just a touch too high above the knee. Tatiana wondered how the wounded men responded to so much . . . Vikki.

"Vikki, why you cry? You not love your husband?"

"Oh, I love him, all right. I love him." She sighed. "I just wish I could love him from five thousand miles away." Lowering her voice, she continued. "This is really not a good time for him to come back."

"For husband to come back to his wife?" When was not a good time for that?

"I wasn't expecting him." She started to cry again, into her coffee. Tatiana moved the cup away slightly so Vikki could finish the coffee later if she wanted to.

"When were you . . . ?" What was the word? Expecting?

"At Christmas!"

"Oh. Why he coming home so soon?"

"Can you believe it? He was shot down over the Pacific."

Tatiana stared.

"Oh, he's fine," Viktoria said dismissively. "It's a scrape. A little superficial shoulder wound. He flew the plane ninety miles after he was shot. How bad could it be?"

Tatiana stood from the table. "I think I go feed my son."

"Yes, but Chris is going to be miserable."

"Who is Chris?"

"Dr. Pandolfi. You haven't met him? He comes here with Dr. Ludlow."

Chris Pandolfi. That's right. "Oh, I met him." Dr. Pandolfi was the doctor who had come aboard the ship she was on and decided he was *not* going to help to deliver her baby on U.S. . . . soil. He wanted to send her back to the Soviet Union, broken amniotic waters, TB and all. It was Edward Ludlow who had said no and made Dr. Pandolfi help get Tatiana to the hospital on Ellis Island. Tatiana patted Vikki on the shoulder. She wasn't sure Chris Pandolfi was such a great catch. "You be fine, Viktoria. Maybe stay away from Dr. Pandolfi. Your husband is coming home. You are *so* lucky."

Viktoria got up and followed Tatiana down the hall to her room. "Call me Vikki," she said. "Can I call you Jane?"

"Who?"

"Isn't your name Jane?"

"You call me Tania."

"Why would I call you Tania when your name is Jane?"

"Tania my name. Jane just on documents." She saw Vikki's uninterested and confused face. "Call me what you like."

"When are you getting out?"

"Getting out?"

"Out of Ellis."

Tatiana thought about it. "I do not think I am getting out," she said. "I have nowhere to go."

Vikki followed Tatiana into her room and glanced at her son sleeping in his bassinet. "He's kind of little," she said absent-mindedly, touching Tatiana's blonde hair. "His father was dark-haired?"

"Yes."

"So what's it like being a mother?"

"It's—"

"Well, when you're all better, I want you to come home with me. Meet Grammy and Grampa. They love little babies. They keep wanting me to have one." Vikki shook her head. "God help me." She glanced again at Anthony. "He's sort of cute. Too bad his father has never seen him."

"Yes."

The boy was so helpless. He couldn't move, or turn his head, or hold his head. He was so difficult to dress—his floppy arms and head defying Tatiana's awkward mothering skills—that some days she kept him naked just in a cloth diaper, swaddled underneath the blankets. She had no clothes for him except for the few nightgowns Edward had brought for her. It was summer and warm and he didn't need much, thank goodness, for the head would not fit in the nightgown hole, the arms refused to go into the long sleeves. Bathing him was even harder, if that were possible. His bellybutton had not healed completely, so she washed his body with a cloth, and that was not too bad, but washing his hair was outside her expertise. He couldn't do anything, he could not help her in any way, he could not lift his arms or stay still when she needed him still or be propped up. His head bobbed backward, his body slipped out of her grasp, his legs dangled precariously above a sink. She lived in fear that she would drop him, that he would slither out of her arms and onto the black-and-white tile floor. Her feelings about his absolute dependence on her fluctuated from intense anxiety over his future to an almost suffocating tenderness. Somehow, and maybe that was how nature intended it, his need for her made her stronger.

And she needed to be made stronger. Too often when he was asleep and safe, Tatiana herself felt that her own bobbing head, her own dangling arms and legs, her fragile body would slip on the sill and plummet down to the concrete ground below.

And so to draw sustenance from him, she would uncover him, unwrap him and touch him. She would lift him from his bed and place him on her chest, where he would sleep, head on her heart. He was long, his limbs were long, and as she caressed him, she imagined looking at another boy through the eyes of his mother, a baby boy, long like Anthony, dark like him, soft like him, touched by his mother, bathed, nursed, caressed by his new mother who had waited her whole life to have this one boy.

CHAPTER SEVEN

The Interrogation, 1943

HE HEARD VOICES OUTSIDE, and the door opened.

"Alexander Belov?"

Alexander was going to say yes but for some reason thought of the Romanovs shot in a small basement room in the middle of the night. Was it the middle of the night? The same night? The next night? He decided to say nothing.

"Come. Now."

He followed the guard to a small room upstairs, this one not a classroom. It was an old storage area, maybe a nurses' station.

He was told to sit in the chair. Then he was told to stand up. Then to sit back down again. It was still dark outside. He couldn't figure out what the time was. When he asked, he was met with a "Shut up!" He decided not to ask again. After a few moments, two men entered the room. One of them was the fat Mitterand, one of them was a man he did not know.

The man shined a bright light into Alexander's face. He closed his eyes.

"Open your eyes, Major!"

Fat Mitterand said softly, "Vladimir, now now. We can do this another way."

He liked that they were calling him major. So they still couldn't get a colonel to interrogate him. As he had suspected, they didn't have anyone to deal with him here in Morozovo. What they needed to do was get him to Volkhov where things would be different for him, but they didn't want to risk any more of their men for a drive across the river. They had already failed once. Eventually he would go in a barge, but the ice would have to melt first. He could spend another month in the Morozovo cell. Could he take another minute in it?

Mitterand said, "Major Belov, I am here to inform you that you are under arrest for high treason. We have irrefutable documents accusing you of espionage and treason to your mother country. What say you to these charges?"

"They're baseless and unfounded," said Alexander. "Anything else?"

"You are accused of being a foreign spy!"

"Not true."

"We are told you have been living under a false identity," said Mitterand.

"Not true, the identity is my own," said Alexander.

"In front of us we have a few words we would like you to sign, to the effect that we have informed you of your rights under the Criminal Code of 1928, Article 58."

"I am not signing a single thing," said Alexander.

"The man next to you in the hospital told us that he thought he heard you speaking English to the Red Cross doctor who came to visit you every day. Is that true?"

"It is not."

"Why did the doctor come to visit you?"

"I don't know if you are aware of why soldiers go to the critical ward of a hospital, but I was wounded in action. Maybe you should talk to my superiors. Major Orlov—"

"Orlov is dead!" snapped Mitterand.

"I'm sorry to hear that," said Alexander, momentarily flinching. Orlov was a good commanding officer. He was no Mikhail Stepanov, but then who was?

"Major, you stand accused of joining the army under an assumed name. You stand accused of being an American named Alexander Barrington. You stand accused of escaping while en route to a corrective camp in Vladivostok after having been convicted of anti-Soviet agitation and espionage."

"All bald-faced lies," said Alexander. "Where is my accuser? I'd like to meet him." What night was it? Was it at least the next night? Had Tania and Sayers gotten out? He knew that if they had, they would have taken Dimitri with them, and then it would be very difficult for the NKVD to maintain that there was an accuser when the accuser himself disappeared like one of Stalin's Politburo cabinet ministers. "I want to get to the bottom of this as much as you do," said Alexander with a helpful smile. "Probably more so. Where is he?"

"You are not to ask questions of us!" Mitterand yelled. "*We* will ask the questions." Trouble was, they had no more questions. Rather, they had the same question over and over again: "Are you an American named Alexander Barrington?"

"No," would reply the American named Alexander Barrington. "I don't know what you're talking about." Alexander could not tell how long this continued. They shined a flashlight into his face; he closed his eyes. They ordered him to stand up, which Alexander took as an opportunity to stretch his legs. He stood gleefully for what seemed like an hour, and regretted being told to sit back down. He didn't know it was precisely an hour but to keep himself occupied during the repetitive questioning, he started counting the seconds it took for each round to be completed from "Are you an American named Alexander Barrington?" to "No. I don't know what you're talking about."

It took seven seconds. Twelve if he drew out his response, if he tapped his feet together, if he rolled his eyes, or if he sighed heavily. Once he started to yawn and could not stop for thirty seconds. That made the time go faster.

They asked the question 147 times. Mitterand had to take a drink six times to continue. Finally he passed the reins to Vladimir, who needed less to drink and fared much better, even asking Alexander if *he* wanted a drink. Alexander politely declined, grateful for the diversion. He knew he must never accept anything they offered him. That was their invitation into his graces.

Still not diverting enough. One hundred and forty-seven times later Vladimir said, with naked frustration in his voice and on his face, "Guard, take him back to his cell." And then he added, "We will make you confess, Major. We know the accusations against you are true and we will do all it takes to make you confess."

Usually, when the Party *apparatchiks* interrogated prisoners with the intention of convicting them as soon as possible and sending them to a forced labor camp, everyone knew the charade being played. The interrogators knew the charges were bogus, and the stunned and dazed prisoners knew the charges were bogus, but in the end, the alternatives presented to them were too stark for them to continue to deny the obvious fallacies. Tell us, you-who-have-lived-next-door-to-an-anti-proletarian-revolutionary, that you are in collusion with him, or it will be twenty-five years in Magadan for you. If you confess you will get only ten. That was the choice and the prisoners confessed—to save themselves, or to save their families, or because they were beaten, degraded, broken-down, paralyzed from thought by the barrage of lies. But Alexander wondered if this was the first time since these sham interrogations began decades ago that the prisoner was accused of the actual truth—that he indeed was Alexander Barrington—and the interrogators for the first time were armed with truth, and truth stood in front of them, truth that Alexander had to deny, truth that Alexander had to bury under a barrage of lies if he were to live. He thought about pointing this out to Mitterand and Vladimir but he didn't think they would either understand or appreciate the grim irony.

After he was taken back to his cell, two guards came in and, with their two rifles pointed at him, ordered Alexander to undress. "So we can launder your uniform," they said. He undressed down to his BVDs. They asked him to remove his watch and boots and socks. Alexander was unhappy about the socks, for the floor in his cell was numbingly cold. "You need my boots?"

"We will polish them."

Alexander was grateful for the foresight that had made him move Dr. Sayers' drugs from his boots to his BVDs.

Reluctantly he handed over the boots, which they snatched from him and left without a word.

After the door had closed and he was left alone, Alexander picked up the kerosene lamp and held it close to his body to warm himself up. He didn't care about losing oxygen any longer.

The guard saw and yelled not to touch the lamp. Alexander did not put the lamp down. The guard came in and took the lamp out, leaving Alexander cold and in darkness again.

His back wound, though having been bandaged thoroughly by Tatiana, was throbbing. The dressing was wrapped around his stomach. He wished he could wrap his whole body in the white bandage.

He needed as little of his body touching the cold as possible. Alexander stood in the middle of his cell, so that only his feet were on the icy floor. He stood and imagined warmth.

His hands were behind his head, they were behind his back, they were in front of his chest.

He imagined . . .

Tania standing in front of him, her head on his bare chest, listening for his heart, and then lifting her gaze at him and smiling. She was standing tiptoed on his feet holding on to his arms, as she reached up with her neck extended and lifted her head to him.

Warmth.

There was no morning and no night. There was no brightness and no light. He had nothing to measure time with. The images of her were constant, he could not measure how long he had been thinking of her. He tried counting and found himself swaying from exhaustion. He needed to sleep.

Sleep or cold? Sleep or cold?

Sleep.

He huddled in the corner and shook uncontrollably, trying to stave off misery. Was it the following day, the following night?

The following day from what? The following night from what?

They're going to starve me to death. They're going to thirst me to death. Then they will beat me to death. But first my feet will freeze and then my legs and then my insides, they will all turn to ice. And my blood, too, and my heart, and I will forget.

Tamara and Her Stories, 1935

There was an old babushka named Tamara who had lived for twenty years on their floor. Her door was always open and sometimes after school Alexander would stop in and talk to her. He noticed that old people loved the company of young people. It gave them an opportunity to impart their life experience to the young. Tamara, sitting in her uncomfortable wooden chair near the window one afternoon, was telling Alexander that her husband was arrested for religious reasons in 1928 and given ten years—

"Wait, Tamara, Mikhailovna, ten years where?"

"Forced labor camp, of course. Siberia. Where else?"

"They convicted him and sent him there to work?"

"To prison . . ."

"To work for *free*?"

"Oh, Alexander, you're interrupting, and I need to tell you something."

He fell quiet.

"The prostitutes near Arbat were arrested in 1930 and not only were they back on the street months later but had also been reunited with their families in the old cities they used to frequent. But my husband, and the band of religious men, will not be allowed to return, certainly not to Moscow."

"Only three more years," Alexander said slowly. "Three more years of forced labor."

Tamara shook her head and lowered her voice. "I received a telegram from the Kolyma authorities in 1932—*without right of correspondence*, it said. You know what that means, don't you?"

Alexander didn't want even to hazard a guess.

"It means he is no longer alive to correspond with," said Tamara, her voice shaking and her head lowering.

She told him how, from the church down the block, three priests were arrested and given seven years for not putting away the tools of capitalism, which in their case was the organized and personal and unrepentant belief in Jesus Christ.

"Also forced labor camp?"

"Oh, Alexander!"

He stopped. She continued. "But the funny thing is—have you noticed the hotel down the street that had the harlots right outside a few months ago?"

"Hmm." Alexander noticed.

"Well, have you noticed how they all disappeared?"

"Hmm." Alexander noticed that too.

"They were taken away. For disturbing the peace, for disrupting the public good—"

"And for not putting away the tools of capitalism," Alexander said dryly, and Tamara laughed and touched his head.

"That's right, my boy. That's right. And do you know how long they had been given in that forced labor camp that you care so much about? Three years. So just remember—Jesus Christ, seven, prostitutes, three."

"All right," said Jane, coming into the room, taking her son by the hand and leading him out. Before she left, she turned around and said in an accusatory tone to Tamara, but addressed to Alexander, "Can we *not* be learning about prostitutes from toothless old women?"

"Who would you like me to learn about prostitutes from, Mom?" he asked.

৩৩৩৩

"Son, your mother wanted me to talk to you about something." Harold cleared his throat. Alexander crimped his lips together and sat quietly. His father looked so uncomfortable that Alexander had to sit on his hands to keep himself from laughing. His mother was pretending to clean something in another part of the room. Harold glared in Jane's direction.

"Dad?" said Alexander in his deepest voice. His voice had broken a few months ago, and he really liked the way his new self sounded. Very grown-up. He also had shot up, growing more than eight inches in the course of the last six months, but he couldn't seem to put any flesh on his bones. There just wasn't enough of . . . anything. "Dad, do you want to go for a walk and talk about it?"

"No!" said Jane. "I can't hear a thing. Talk here."

Nodding, Alexander said, "All right, Dad, talk here." He scrunched up his face and tried to look serious. It wouldn't have mattered if he were sitting cross-eyed and sticking his tongue out. Harold was not looking at Alexander.

"Son," said Harold. "You're getting to be at that age where you're, well, I'm sure, you're—and also you're—you're a fine boy, and good-looking, I want to help, and soon, or maybe already—and I'm sure that you're—"

Jane tutted in the background. Harold fell quiet.

Alexander sat for a few seconds, then got up, slapped his father on the back and said, "Thanks, Dad. That *was* helpful."

He went into his room, and Harold didn't follow him. Alexander heard his parents bickering next door, and in a minute there was a knock. It was his mother. "Can I talk to you?"

Alexander trying to keep a composed face, said, "Mom, really, I think Dad said all there was to say, I don't know if there's anything to add—"

She sat down on his bed while he sat in the chair near the window. He was going to be sixteen in May. He liked summer. Maybe they would get a room at a *dacha* in Krasnaya Polyana again like they did last year.

"Alexander, what your father didn't mention—"

"*Was* there something Dad didn't mention?"

"Son . . ."

"Please—go ahead."

"I'm not going to give you a lesson in girls—"

"Thank goodness for that."

"Listen to me, the only thing I want you to do is remember this—" She paused.

He waited.

"Martha told me one of her derelict sons has had his horn removed!" she whispered. "*Removed*, Alexander, and do you know why?"

"I'm not sure I want to."

"Because he got *frenchified*! Do you know what that is?"

"I think—"

"And her other son's got *French pigs* all over his body. It's the most revolting thing!"

"Yes, it—"

"The *French curse*! The *French crown*! Syphilis! Lenin died from it eating up his brain," she whispered. "No one talks about it, but it's true all the same. Is that what you want for yourself?"

"Hmm . . ." said Alexander. "No?"

"Well, it's all over the place. Your father and I knew a man who lost his whole nose because of it."

"Personally, I'd rather lose the nose than—"

"Alexander!"

"Sorry."

"This is very serious, son. I have done all I can to raise you a good, clean boy, but look where we are living, and soon you'll be out on your own."

"How soon you think?"

"What do you think is going to happen when you don't know where the harlot you're with has been?" Jane asked resolutely. "Son, when you grow up, I don't want you to be a saint or a eunuch. I just want you to be careful. I want you to protect what's yours at all times. You must be clean, you must be vigilant, and you must also remember that without protection, you will get a girl up the stick, and then what? You're going to marry someone you don't love because you weren't careful?"

Alexander stared at his mother. "Up the *stick*?" he said.

"She'll tell you it's yours and you'll never know for sure, all you'll know is that you're married, and your horn is falling off!"

"Mother," said Alexander. "Really, you must stop."

"Do you understand what I'm telling you?"

"How can I not?"

"Your father was supposed to explain to you."

"He did. I think he did very well."

Jane got up. "Will you just once stop with your joking around?"

"Yes, Mom. Thanks for coming in. I'm glad we had this chat."

"Do you have any questions?"

"Absolutely none."

The Changing of the Hotel's Name, 1935

One frostbitten late January Thursday, Alexander asked his father as they headed out to their Party meeting, "Dad, why is our hotel's name changing again? It's the third time in six months."

"Surely not the *third* time."

"Yes, Dad." They walked side by side down the street. They weren't touching. "When we first moved in, it was the Derzhava. Then the Kamenev Hotel. Then the Zinoviev Hotel. Now it's the Kirov Hotel. Why? And who is this Kirov chap?"

"He was the Leningrad Party Chief," said Harold.

At their meeting, the old man Slavan laughed raucously after he heard Alexander's question repeated. He beckoned Alexander to him, patted him on the head and said, "Don't worry, son, now that's it's Kirov, Kirov it will stay."

"All right, enough now," Harold said, trying to pull his son away. But Alexander wanted to hear. He pulled away from his father.

"Why, Slavan Ivanovich?"

Slavan said, "Because Kirov is dead." He nodded. "Assassinated in Leningrad last month. Now there's a manhunt on."

"Oh, they didn't catch his killer?"

"They caught him, all right." The old man smirked. "But what about all the others?"

"What others?" Alexander lowered his voice.

"All the conspirators," said the old man. "They have to die, too."

"It was a conspiracy?"

"Well, of course. Otherwise how can we have a manhunt?"

Harold called sharply for Alexander, and later on, when they were walking home, he said, "Son, why are you so friendly with Slavan? What kinds of things has that man been telling you?"

"He is a fascinating man," Alexander said. "Did you know he's been to Akatui? For five years." Akatui was the Tsarist Siberian hard labor prison. "He said they gave him a white shirt, and in the summer he worked only eight hours and in the winter six, and his shirt never got dirty, and he got a kilo of white bread a day, plus meat. He said they were the best years of his life."

"Unenviable," grumbled Harold. "Listen, I don't want you talking to him so much. Sit by us."

"Hmm," said Alexander. "You all smoke too much. It burns my eyes."

"I'll blow my smoke the other way. But Slavan is a troublemaker. Stay away from him, do you hear?" He paused. "He is not going to last long."

"Last long where?"

Two weeks later, Slavan disappeared from the meetings.

Alexander missed the nice old man and his stories.

✎

"Dad, people keep disappearing from our floor. That lady Tamara is gone."

"Never liked her," put in Jane, sipping her vodka. "I think she is sick in the hospital. She was old, Alexander."

"Mom, two young men in suits are living in her room. Are they going to share that room with Tamara when she returns from the hospital?"

"I know nothing about that," said Jane firmly, and just as firmly poured herself another drink.

"The Italians have left. Mom, did you know the Italians have left?"

"Who?" said Harold loudly. "Who is disappearing? The Frascas have not disappeared. They are on vacation."

"Dad, it's winter. Vacation where?"

"The Crimea. In some resort near Krasnodar. Dzhugba, I think. They're coming back in two months."

"Oh? What about the van Dorens? Where have they gone? Also the Crimea? Someone new is living in their room, too. A Russian family. I thought this was a floor only for foreigners?"

"They moved to a different building in Moscow," said Harold, picking at his food. "The Obkom is just trying to integrate the foreigners into Soviet society."

Alexander put down his fork. "Did you say moved? Moved where? Because Nikita is sleeping in our bathroom."

"Who is Nikita?"

"Dad, you haven't noticed that there is a man in the bathtub?"

"What man?"

"Nikita."

"Oh. How long has he been there?"

Alexander exchanged a blank look with his mother. "Three months."

"He's been in the bathtub for three months? Why?"

"Because there is not a single room for him to rent in all of Moscow. He came here from Novosibirsk."

"Never seen him," Harold said in a voice that implied that since he had never seen Nikita, Nikita must not exist. "What does he do when I want to have a bath?"

Jane said, "Oh, he leaves for a half-hour. I give him a shot of vodka. He goes for a walk."

"Mom," said Alexander, eating cheerfully, "his wife is coming to join him in March. He begged me to talk to everybody on the floor to ask if we could have our baths earlier in the evening, to let them have a bit of—"

"All right, you two, you're having me on," said Harold.

Alexander and his mother exchanged a look, and then Alexander said, "Dad, go check it out. And when you come back, you tell me where the van Dorens could have moved to in Moscow."

When Harold came back, he shrugged and said, "That man is a hobo. He is no good."

"That man," said Alexander, looking at his mother's vodka glass, "is the head engineer for the Baltic fleet."

⌀ౠ৩

A month later, in February 1935, Alexander came home from school and heard his mother and father fighting—again. He heard his name shouted out once, twice.

His mother was upset *for* Alexander. But he was fine. He spoke Russian fluently. He sang and drank beer and played hockey on the ice in Gorky Park with his friends. He was all right. Why was she upset? He wanted to go in and tell her he was fine, but he never liked to interrupt his parents' fights.

Suddenly he heard something being thrown, and then someone being hit. He ran into his parents' room and saw his mother on the floor, her cheek red, his father bending over her. Alexander ran to his father and shoved him in the back. "What are you doing, Dad?" he yelled. He kneeled down next to his mother.

She half sat up and glared at Harold. "Fine thing you're showing your son," she said. "You brought him to the Soviet Union for this, to show him how to treat a woman? His wife, perhaps?"

"Shut up," said Harold, clenching his fists.

"Dad!" Alexander jumped to his feet. "Stop!"

"Your father has abandoned us, Alexander."

"I'm not abandoning you!"

Squaring off, Alexander pushed his father in the chest.

Harold shoved Alexander and then hit him open-handed across the face. Jane gasped. Alexander swayed but did not fall. Harold went to strike him again, but this time Alexander moved away. Jane grabbed Harold's legs, yanked, and sent him down on his back. "Don't you dare touch him!" she yelled.

Harold was on the floor, Jane, too; only Alexander was standing. They couldn't look at one another; everyone was panting. Alexander wiped his bleeding lip.

"Harold," Jane said, still on her knees. "Look at us! We're being destroyed by this fucking country." She was crying. "Let's go home, let's start over."

"Are you crazy?" hissed Harold, looking from Alexander to Jane. "Do you even know what you're saying?"

"I do."

"Have you forgotten that we gave up our U.S. citizenship? Have you forgotten that at the moment you and I are citizens of no country; that we're waiting for our Soviet citizenship to come through? You think America is going to want us back? Why, they practically kicked us out. And how do you think the Soviet authorities are going to feel once they find out we're turning our backs on them, too?"

"I don't care what the Soviet authorities think."

"God, you are so naïve!"

"Is that what I am? What does that make *you*? Did you know it was going to be like this and brought us here anyway? Brought your son here?"

He stared at her with disappointment. "We didn't come for the good life. The good life we could have had in America."

"You're right. And we had it. We'll make do with what we have here, but Harold, Alexander is not meant to be here. At least send *him* back home."

"What?" Harold could not find his voice to say it above a whisper.

"Yes." She was helped off the floor by Alexander as she stood in front of Harold. "He is fifteen. Send him back home!"

"Mom!" said Alexander.

"Don't let him die in this country—can't you see? Alexander sees it. I see it. Why can't you?"

"Alexander doesn't see it. Do you, son?"

Alexander was silent. He did not want to side against his father.

"You see?" Jane exclaimed triumphantly. "Please, Harold. Soon it will be too late."

"You're talking rubbish. Too late for what?"

"Too late for Alexander," Jane said brokenly, pale with despair. "For him, forget your pride for just one second. Before he has to register for the Red Army when he turns sixteen in May, before tragedy befalls us all, while he is still a U.S. citizen, send him back. He has not relinquished his rights to the United States of America. I will stay with you, I will live out my life with you—but—"

"No!" Harold exclaimed in an aghast voice. "Things didn't turn out the way I had hoped, look, I'm sor—"

"Don't be sorry for me, you bastard. Don't be sorry for me—I lay down in this bed with you. I knew what I was doing. Be sorry for your son. What do you think will happen to him?"

Jane turned away from Harold.

Alexander turned away from his parents. He went to the window and looked outside. It was February and night.

Behind him, he heard his mother and father.

"Janie, come on, it'll be all right. You'll see. Alexander will be better off here eventually. Communism is the future of the world, you know this as well as I do. The wider the chasm between the rich and the poor in the world, the more essential communism is going to become. America is a lost cause. Who else is going to care about the common man, who else will protect his rights but the communist? We're just living through the toughest part. But I have no doubt—communism is the future."

"God!" Jane exclaimed. "When will you ever stop?"

"Can't stop now," he said. "We're going to see this through to the end."

"That's right," Jane said. "Marx himself wrote that capitalism produces above all its own gravediggers. Do you think that perhaps he wasn't talking about capitalism?"

"Absolutely," agreed Harold, while Alexander looked the other way. "The communists hate to conceal their views and aims. They openly declare that their ends can be attained only by the forcible overthrow of all existing conditions. The fall of capitalism is inevitable. The fall of selfishness, greed, individuality, personal attainment."

"The fall of prosperity, comfort, humane living conditions, privacy, liberty," said Jane, spitting the words out, as Alexander doggedly stared out the window. "The second America, Harold. The second fucking America."

Without turning back, Alexander saw his father's angry face and his mother's despairing one, and he saw the gray room with the falling plaster, and the broken lock held together by tape, and he smelled the washroom from ten meters away, and he was silent.

Before the Soviet Union, the only world that had made sense to him was America, where his father could get up on the pulpit and preach the overthrow of the U.S. government, and the police that protected that government would come and remove his father from the pulpit and put him into a Boston cell to sleep off his insurrectionist zeal, and then in the next day or two they would let him out so he could recommence with renewed fervor preaching to the curious the lamentable deficiencies of 1920s America. And according to Harold there were plenty, though he himself admitted to Alexander that he could not for the life of him understand the immigrants who poured into New York and Boston, who lived in deplorable conditions working for pennies and put generations of Americans to shame because they lived in deplorable conditions and worked for pennies with such joy—a joy that was diminished only by the inability to bring more of their family members to the United States to live in deplorable conditions and work for pennies.

Harold Barrington could preach revolution in America and that made perfect sense to Alexander, because he read John Stuart Mill's *On Liberty* and John Stuart Mill told him that liberty didn't mean doing what you damn well pleased, it meant saying what you damn well pleased. His father was upholding Mill in the greatest tradition of American democracy; what was so wrong with that?

What didn't make sense to him when he had arrived in Moscow was Moscow. As the years passed, Moscow made only less and less sense to him; the privation, the senselessness, the discomfort encroached upon his youthful spirit. He had stopped holding his father's hand on the way to Thursday meetings; what he keenly felt absent from his own hand, however, was an orange in the winter.

Hailing Russia as the "second America," Comrade Stalin proclaimed that in a few years the Soviet Union would have as many railroads, as many paved roads, as many single family houses, as the United States. He said that America had not industrialized as fast as the USSR was industrializing because capitalism made progress chaotic, whereas socialism spearheaded progress on all fronts. The U.S. was suffering thirty-five per cent unemployment, unlike the Soviet Union which had near full employment. The Soviets were all working—proof of their superiority—while the Americans were succumbing to the welfare state because there were no jobs. That was clear, nothing confusing about that. Then why was the sense of malaise so pervasive?

But Alexander's feelings of confusion and malaise were peripheral. What wasn't peripheral was youth. And he was young, even in Moscow.

He turned back to his mother, handing her a napkin to wipe her face while wiping his own with his sleeve. Before walking out and leaving them to their misery, Alexander said to his father, "Don't listen to her. I will not go to America alone. My future is here, for better or worse." He came a little closer. "But don't hit my mother again." Alexander was already several inches taller than Harold. "If you hit her again, you'll have to deal with me."

༄

A week later Harold was removed from his job as a printer because as the new laws would have it, foreigners were no longer allowed to operate printing machinery, no matter how proficient they were and how loyal to the Soviet state. Apparently there was too much opportunity for sabotage, for printing false papers, false affidavits, false documents, false news information, and for disseminating lies to subvert the Soviet cause. Many foreigners had been caught doing just that and then distributing their malicious propaganda to hard-working Soviet citizens. So no more printing for Harold.

He was redeployed to a tool-making factory, melting metal into screw-drivers and ratchets.

That job lasted a few weeks. Apparently it also wasn't safe. Foreigners had been caught making knives and weapons for themselves instead of tools for the Soviet state.

He was then employed as a shoemaker, which amused Alexander ("Dad, what do you know about making shoes?").

That job lasted only a few days. "What? Shoe-making isn't safe either?" Alexander asked.

Apparently it wasn't. Foreigners had been known to make galoshes and mountain boots for good Soviet citizens to escape through marshes and through mountains.

༄

A somber Harold came home one April evening in 1935 and instead of cooking (it was Harold who cooked dinner for his family now), sat down heavily at the table and said that a Party Obkom man had come to see him at the school where he was working as a floor sweeper and asked him to find a new place to live. "They want us to find our own rooms. Be a little more independent." He shrugged. "It's only right. We've had it relatively easy the last four years. We need to give something back to the state." He paused and lit a cigarette.

Alexander saw his father glance at him furtively. He coughed and said, "Well, Nikita has disappeared. Maybe we can take his bathtub."

There was no room for the Barringtons in all of Moscow. After a month of looking, Harold came home from work and said, "Listen, the Obkom man came to see me again. We can't stay here. We have to move."

"By when?" Jane exclaimed.

"Two days from now. They want us out."

"But we have nowhere to go!"

Harold sighed. "They offered me a transfer to Leningrad. There is more work—an industrial plant, a carpentry plant, an electricity plant."

"What, no electricity plants in Moscow, Dad?"

Harold ignored Alexander. "We'll go there. There'll be more rooms available. You'll see. Janie, you'll get a job at the Leningrad public library."

"Leningrad?" Alexander exclaimed. "Dad, I'm not leaving Moscow. I got friends here, school. Please."

"Alexander, you'll start a new school. Make new friends. We have no choice."

"Yes," Alexander said loudly. "But once we had a choice, didn't we?"

"Alexander! You will not raise your voice to me," Harold said. "Do you hear?"

"Loud and clear!" shouted Alexander. "I'm not going. Do *you* hear?"

Harold jumped up. Jane jumped up. Alexander jumped up.

Jane said, "No, stop it, stop it, you two!"

"You will not speak to me this way," Harold said. "We are moving, and I don't want to talk another minute about it."

He turned to his wife and said, "Oh, and one more thing." Sheepishly, he coughed. "They want us to change our name. To something more Russian."

Alexander scoffed. "Why now? Why after all these years?"

"Because!" Harold shouted, losing control. "They want us to show our allegiance! You're going to be sixteen next month. You're going to register for the Red Army. You need a Russian name. The fewer ques-

tions, the better. We need to be Russians now. It will be easier for us."
He lowered his gaze.

"God, Dad," Alexander exclaimed. "Will this ever stop? We can't even keep our name anymore? It's not enough to kick us out of our home, to move us to another city? We need to lose our name, too? What else have we got?"

"We are doing the right thing. Our name is an American name. We should have changed it long ago."

"That's right," said Alexander. "The Frascas didn't. The van Dorens didn't. And look what happened to them. They're on vacation. Extended vacation, right, Dad?"

Harold raised his hand to Alexander, who pushed him away. "Don't touch me," he said coldly.

Harold tried again. Alexander pushed him away again, but this time he didn't let go of his father's hands. He did not want his mother to see him lose his temper, his poor mother, who stood shaking and crying, clasping her hands at her two men, pleading, "Darlings, Harold, Alexander, I beg you, stop it, stop it."

"Tell him to stop it!" Harold said. "You've raised him like this. No respect for anybody."

His mother came over to Alexander and grabbed hold of his arms. "Please, son," she said. "Calm down. It'll be all right."

"You think so, Mom? We're moving cities, we're changing our name just like this hotel. You call that all right?"

"Yes," she said. "We still have each other. We still have our lives."

"How the definition of being all right changes," said Alexander, extricating himself from his mother and taking his coat.

"Alexander, don't walk out that door," said Harold. "I forbid you to walk out that door."

Alexander turned to his father, looked him in the eye, and said, "Go ahead and stop me."

He left and did not come back home for two days. And then they packed up and left the Kirov Hotel.

His mother was drunk and unable to help carry the suitcases to the train.

When did Alexander first begin to feel, to know, to sense that something was desperately wrong with his mother? That was the point: something wasn't desperately wrong with her all at once. At first she had been slightly not herself, and it wasn't for Alexander to say what was the matter with his adult parent. His father could have seen, but his father had no eyes. Alexander knew his father was the kind of man who simply could not keep the personal and the global in his head at the same time. But whether Harold was aware and plainly ignored it, or whether he was actually oblivious, didn't matter, and it didn't change the simple fact that Jane Barrington gradually, without fanfare, without much to-do, much introduction and much warning permanently ceased to be the person she once was and became the person she wasn't.

CHAPTER EIGHT

Ellis Island, 1943

EDWARD CAME IN TO check on Tatiana in the middle of August. She'd been in America seven weeks. She was sitting in her usual place by the window, with a naked and diapered Anthony on her lap, tickling him between his toes. She had been feeling much better, her breathing was deep, she was almost not coughing. She had not seen blood in her cough for a month. The New York air was doing her good.

Edward took the stethoscope from her chest. "Listen, you are doing much better. I think I'm going to have to discharge you."

Tatiana said nothing.

"Do you have anywhere to go?" Edward paused. "You will need to get a job."

"Edward," said Tatiana, "I like it here."

"Well, I know. But you're all better."

"I was thinking, maybe I work here? You need more nurse."

"You want to work at Ellis?"

"Very much."

Edward talked to the chief surgeon at the Public Health Department, who came in to talk to Tatiana, informing her that she would have to be put on something called a three-month probation to see if she could keep up with the work, if she had the necessary skills. He told her that she would not be employed by Ellis Island but by the PHD and as such would sometimes have to pull duty at the New York University hospital downtown if they had a shortage of nurses there. Tatiana agreed, but asked if she could live at Ellis, "maybe work as night nurse?" The surgeon was not keen. "Why would you want to? You could get yourself an apartment right across the bay. Our citizens don't live here."

Tatiana explained as best she could that she hoped some of the detained refugees at Ellis could look after her son while he was still small, and though she wanted to work, she had no one to leave him with and to make matters easier for everyone she could stay in her current convalescent room.

"But it's so small!"

"One room just right for me."

Tatiana asked Vikki to buy her a uniform and shoes. "You know you only get two pairs of shoes?" said Vikki. "War rationing. You want one of them to be nurse's shoes?"

"I want my only pair to be nurse's shoes," said Tatiana. "What I need more shoes for?"

"What if you wanted to go dancing?" asked Vikki.

"Go where?"

"Dancing! You know, do a little lindy hop, a little jitterbug? What if you wanted to look nice? Your husband isn't coming back, is he?"

"No," said Tatiana, "my husband isn't coming back."

"Well, you definitely need nice new shoes if you're going to be a widow."

Tatiana shook her head. "I need nurse's shoes and white uniform, and I need to stay at Ellis, and I not need nothing else."

Vikki shook her head, her eyes flickering. "It's *anything* else. When can you come have dinner with us? How about this Sunday? Dr. Ludlow says you're being discharged."

Vikki bought Tatiana a uniform that was slightly big, and shoes that were the right size, and after Edward discharged her, she continued to do what she had been doing in her white hospital gown and gray hospital robe—look after the foreign soldiers who were shipped to New York, treated, and then sent elsewhere on the continent to do POW labor duty. Many of them were German soldiers, some were Italian, some Ethiopian, one or two French. There were no Soviet soldiers.

⁕

"Oh, Tania, what am I going to do?" Vikki was in her room, sitting on the bed, while Tatiana lay in bed, breastfeeding Anthony. "Are you on a break?"

"Yes, a lunch break." Tatiana smiled, but the irony went past Vikki's unlistening ears.

"Who takes care of your boy while you do rounds?"

"I take him with me. I put him on empty bed while I take care of soldiers." Brenda palpitated every time she saw it, but Tatiana didn't like to leave him sleeping alone in the room, so she didn't care how much

Brenda palpitated. If only there had been more immigrants, someone could take care of her baby while she worked. But there were very few people coming through Ellis. Twelve in the month of July, eight in the month of August. And they all had their own children, their own problems.

"Tania! Can we talk about *my* situation? You know, don't you, that my husband is home with me now."

"I know. Wait little while," Tatiana said. "Maybe war will take him again."

"That's the problem! They don't want him. He can't operate heavy machinery. He's been honorably discharged. He wants us to have a baby. Can you even imagine?"

Tatiana was quiet. "Vikki, why you get married?"

"It was war! What do you mean, *why* did I get married? Why did *you* get married? He was going off to war, he asked me to marry him, I said yes. I thought, what's the harm? It's war. What's the worst that can happen?"

"This," said Tatiana.

"I didn't think he'd be coming back so soon! I thought he'd be back for Christmas, once, twice. Maybe he'd be killed. Then I could say I had been married to a war hero."

"Is he not war hero now?"

"It doesn't count—he's alive!"

"Oh."

"Before he came back I had been going dancing every weekend, but now I can't do anything. God!" she exclaimed. "Being married is a real drag."

"Do you love him?"

"Sure." Vikki shrugged. "But I love Chris, too. And two weeks ago, I met a radiologist who was nice . . . but it's all over for that now."

"You right," Tatiana said. "Marriage very inconvenient." She paused. "Why do you not get, what is it called?"

"A divorce?"

"Yes."

"What are you, crazy? What kind of country do you come from? What kind of customs do you have there?"

"In my country," said Tatiana, "we faithful to our husbands."

"He wasn't here! Surely I can't be expected to be faithful to him when he is thousands of miles away, and getting up to no good in the Far East? As far as divorce . . . I'm too young to get divorced."

"But not too young to be widow?" Tatiana flinched when she said it.

"No! There is an honor that comes with being a widow. I can't be a divorcée. What am I, Wallis Simpson?"

"Who?"

❧

"Tania, you're doing well. Brenda tells me, albeit grudgingly"—Edward smiled—"that you are very good with the patients." Edward and Tatiana were walking between the patient beds. Tatiana was carrying an awake and alert Anthony.

"Thank you, Edward."

"Are you afraid your boy is going to get sick from being around sick people?"

"They not sick," Tatiana replied. "Right, Anthony? They wounded. I bring my boy, and he makes them happy. Some of them have wives and sons back home. They touch him and they happy."

Edward smiled. "He is a very fine boy." Edward stroked Anthony's dark head. Anthony paid Edward back by grinning toothlessly. "You take him outside?"

"All time."

"Good. Babies need fresh air. And you, too." He cleared his throat. "You know, on Sundays the doctors from NYU and PHD play softball in Sheep Meadow, in Central Park, and the nurses come to cheer us on. Would you like to come this Sunday with Anthony?"

Tatiana was too flustered to answer. They were on the stairs when they heard the clomping of high heels. "Edward?" a voice screeched from the ground floor. "Is that you?"

"Yes, sweetheart, it's me." Edward's voice was calm.

"Well, thank goodness I found you. I've been looking everywhere for you."

"I'm right here, sweetheart."

Mrs. Ludlow walked up the stairs, panting, and the three of them stopped on the landing. Tatiana held her baby closer. Disapprovingly, Edward's wife eyed Tatiana and said, "A new nurse, Edward?"

"Nurse Barrington? Have you met Marion?"

"Yes," said Tatiana.

"No, we never met," declared Marion. "I never forget a face."

"Mrs. Ludlow," said Tatiana. "We meet every Tuesday in dining room. You ask me where Edward, and I say I don't know."

"We have never met," repeated Mrs. Ludlow, with extra firmness to her voice.

Tatiana said nothing. Edward said nothing.

"Edward, can I talk to you in private? And you," she added, glaring at Tatiana, "are too young to be carrying a child. You're not carrying him correctly. You're not holding his head. Where is the baby's mother?"

"Marion, she *is* the baby's mother," said Edward.

Mrs. Ludlow was critically silent for a moment, then tutted and before anyone could say anything, she tutted again with emphasis, muttered the word "immigrants" and dragged Edward away.

⚬〜⚬

Vikki stormed into the hospital ward, grabbed Tatiana by the arm and pulled her out into the corridor. "He asked *me* for a divorce!" Vikki whispered in an indignant and offended hiss. "Can you believe it?"

"Um—"

"I said I wasn't giving him a divorce, it wasn't proper, and he said he would sue me for a divorce and win because I—I don't even know what he said—broke some covenant. Oh, I said to him, like you weren't with Far Eastern whores while you were away from me, and you know what he said?"

"Um—"

"He said *yes*! But it's different for soldiers, he said. Do you even believe it?" Vikki shook, Vikki shrugged, Vikki warded off the insulted glint in her eyes. Her mascara did not run, and her lips never lost their shine. "Fine, I said, just fine, you're the one who is going to be sorry, and he said he was already sorry. Ugh." She shuddered and brightened. "Hey, come for dinner on Sunday. Grammy is making Sunday lasagna."

But Tatiana didn't.

Come for dinner, Tania. Come to New York, Tania. Come play softball in Sheep Meadow with us, Tania. Come on the ferry ride with us, Tania, come for a car ride to Bear Mountain with us, Tania. Come, Tania, come back to us, the living.

CHAPTER NINE

With Stepanov, 1943

WHEN ALEXANDER OPENED HIS eyes—did he open them?—it was still black, still cold. He was shaking, his arms around himself. There is no shame in dying in war, in dying young, in dying in a cold cell, in saving your body from humiliation.

Once, when he was convalescing, Tatiana asked without looking at him as she was dressing his wound, did you see the light? And he replied, no, he had not seen.

It was only a partial truth.

Because he had heard . . .

The gallop of the red horse.

But here all the colors had run dry.

෴

As if in a stupor, Alexander dimly heard the sliding of the metal bolt, the turning of the key. His commander, Colonel Mikhail Stepanov, came into his cell with a flashlight. Alexander was hunched in the corner.

"Ah," said Stepanov. "So it's true. You *are* alive."

Alexander wanted to shake Stepanov's hand, but he was too cold and his back was too sore. He did not move and said nothing.

Stepanov crouched by him. "What in the world happened to that truck? And I saw the Red Cross doctor's death certificate for you myself. I told your wife you were dead. Your pregnant wife thinks you're *dead*!"

"Everything is as it should be," replied Alexander. "It's good to see you, sir. Try not to inhale. There is not enough oxygen here for both of us."

"Alexander," said Stepanov. "You didn't want to tell her what was happening to you?"

Alexander shook his head.

"But why the truck explosion, the death certificate?"

"I wanted her to think there was no hope for me."

"Why?"

Alexander didn't answer.

"Anywhere you go—I will go with you," Tatiana says. *"But if you are staying, then I'm staying, too. I'm not leaving my baby's father in the Soviet Union."* She bends over an overwhelmed Alexander. *"What did you say to me in Leningrad? What kind of a life can I build, you said, knowing I have left you to die—or to rot—in the Soviet Union? I'm quoting you back to you. Those were your words."* She smiles. *"And on this one point, I will have to agree with you."* She lowers her voice. *"If I left you, no matter which road I took, with ponderous clatter indeed, the Bronze Horseman would pursue me all through that long night into my own maddening dust."*

He couldn't tell that to his commander. He didn't know if Tatiana had left the Soviet Union.

"You want a smoke?"

"Yes," replied Alexander. "But can't here. Not enough oxygen for a smoke."

Stepanov pulled Alexander up to his feet. "Stand for a few minutes," Stepanov said. "Stretch your legs." He looked at Alexander's bent-sideways head. "This cell is too small for you. They didn't expect that."

"Oh, they did. That's why they put me here."

Stepanov stood with his back to the door, while Alexander stood across from him.

"What day is it, sir?" asked Alexander. "How long have I been here? Four, five days?"

"The morning of the sixteenth of March," said Stepanov. "The morning of your third day."

Third day! Alexander thought with shock.

Third day! Alexander thought with excitement. That would probably mean that Tania . . .

He didn't continue with his thoughts. Very quietly, almost inaudibly, Stepanov leaned forward and Alexander thought he said, "Keep talking loudly, so they can hear, but listen to me so that I can laugh with you when you come back in the clover field, and I will show you how to eat clover."

Alexander looked at Stepanov's face, more drawn than ever, his eyes gray, his mouth turned down with sympathy and anxiety. "Sir?"

"I didn't say anything, Major."

Shaking off the hallucination in his head, of a meadow, of sun, of clover, Alexander repeated in a low voice, "Sir?"

"Everything's gone to shit, Major," whispered Stepanov. "They're already looking for your wife, but . . . she seems to have disappeared. I convinced her to go back to Leningrad with Dr. Sayers, just as you asked me. I made it easy for her to leave."

Alexander said nothing, digging his nails into the palms of his hands.

"But now she's gone. You know who else disappeared? Dr. Sayers. He had informed me he was going back to Leningrad with your wife."

Alexander dug his nails harder into his palms to keep himself from looking at Stepanov and from speaking.

"He was on his way to Helsinki, but he was supposed to have gone to Leningrad first!" Stepanov exclaimed. "To drop her off, to pick up his own Red Cross nurse he had left in Grechesky hospital. Listen to me, are you listening? They never reached Leningrad. Two days ago his Red Cross truck was found burned, pillaged and turned over on the Finnish-Soviet border at Lisiy Nos. There was an incident with the Finnish troops and four of our men were shot and killed. No sign of Sayers, or of Nurse Metanova."

Alexander said nothing. He wanted to pick up his heart from the floor. But it was dark, and he couldn't find it. He heard it roll away from him, he heard it beating, bleeding, pulsing in the corner.

Stepanov lowered his voice another notch. "And Finnish troops shot and killed, too."

Silence from Alexander.

"And that's not all."

"No?" Alexander thought he said.

"No sign of Dr. Sayers. But . . ." Stepanov paused. "Your good friend, Dimitri Chernenko, was found shot dead in the snow."

That was small comfort to Alexander.

But it was *some* comfort.

"Major, why was Chernenko at the border?"

Alexander did not answer. Where was Tatiana? All he wanted to do was ask that question. Without a truck how could they have gotten anywhere? Without a truck what were they doing—walking on foot through the marshes of Karelia?

"Major, your wife is missing. Sayers is gone, Chernenko is dead—" Stepanov hesitated. "And not just dead. But shot dead in a *Finn's uni-*

form. He was wearing a Finnish pilot's uniform and carrying Finnish ID papers instead of his domestic passport!"

Alexander said nothing. He had nothing to hide except the information that would cost Stepanov his life.

"Alexander!" Stepanov exclaimed in a hissing whisper. "Don't shut me out. I'm trying to help."

"Sir," Alexander said, attempting to mute his fear. "I'm asking you please not to help me anymore." He wished he had a picture of her. He wanted to touch her white dress with red roses one more time. Wanted to see her young and with him, standing newly married on the steps of the Molotov church.

The fear, the stabbing panic he felt prohibited Alexander from thinking of Tania past. That's what he would have to learn to do: forbid himself from looking at her even in his memory.

With trembling hands he made a sign of the cross on himself. "I was all right," he finally managed to say, "until you came here and told me my wife was missing." He began to shiver uncontrollably.

Stepanov came closer to Alexander. He took off his own coat and gave it to him. "Here, put this around your shoulders."

Immediately he heard a voice from the outside yell, "It's time!"

In a whisper, Stepanov said, "Tell me the truth, did you tell your wife to leave with Sayers for Helsinki? Was that your plan all along?"

Alexander said nothing. He didn't want Stepanov to know—one life, two, three, was enough. The individual was a million people divided by one million; Stepanov did not deserve to die because of Alexander.

"Why are you being so stubborn? Stop it! Having gotten nowhere, they're bringing in a new man to question you. Apparently the toughest interrogator they have. He has never failed to get a signed confession. They've kept you here nearly naked in a cold cell, and soon they'll come up with something else to break you; they'll beat you, they'll put your feet in cold water, they'll shine a light in your face until you go mad, the interrogator will deliberately tell you things you will want to kill him for, and you need to be strong for all that. Otherwise you have no chance."

Alexander said faintly, "Do you think she is safe?"

"No, I don't think she is safe! Who is safe around here, Alexander?" Stepanov whispered. "You? Me? Certainly not her. They're looking everywhere for her. In Leningrad, in Molotov, in Lazarevo. If she is in Helsinki, they'll find out, you know that, don't you? They'll bring her back. They were calling the Red Cross hospital in Helsinki this morning."

"It's time!" someone yelled again.

"How many times in my life will I have to hear those words?" Alexander said. "I heard them for my mother, I heard them for my father, I heard them for my wife, and now I hear them for me."

Stepanov took his coat. "The things they accuse you of—"

"Don't ask me, sir."

"Deny them, Alexander."

As Stepanov turned to go, Alexander said, "Sir . . ." He was so weak he almost couldn't get the words out. He didn't care how cold the wall was, he could not stand on his own anymore. He pressed his body against the icy concrete and then sank down to the floor. "Did you see her?"

He lifted his gaze to Stepanov, who nodded.

"How was she?"

"Don't ask, Alexander."

"Was she—"

"Don't ask."

"Tell me."

"Do you remember when you brought my son back to me?" Stepanov asked, trying to keep his voice from breaking. "Because of you I had comfort. I was able to see him before he died, I was able to bury him."

"All right, no more," said Alexander.

"Who was going to give that comfort to your wife?"

Alexander put his face into his hands.

Stepanov left.

Alexander sat motionlessly on the floor. He didn't need morphine, he didn't need drugs, he didn't need phenobarbital. He needed a bullet in his fucking chest.

☙

The door opened. Alexander had not been given any bread or water, or any clothes. He had no idea how long he had been left undressed in the cold cell.

A man came in who apparently did not want to stand. Behind him a guard brought in a chair and the tall, bald, unpleasant-faced man sat down and in a pleasant-sounding nasal voice said, "Do you know what I'm holding in my hands, Major?"

Alexander shook his head. There was a kerosene lamp between them.

"I'm holding all your clothes, Major. All your clothes and a wool blanket. And look, I've got a nice piece of pork for you, on the bone. It's still warm. Some potatoes too, with sour cream and butter. A shot of vodka. And a nice long smoke. You can leave this damn cold place, have some food, get dressed. How would you like that?"

"I would like that," Alexander said impassively. His voice wasn't going to tremble for a stranger.

The man smiled. "I thought you would. I came all the way from Leningrad to talk to you. Do you think we could talk for a bit?"

"I don't see why not," Alexander replied. "I don't have much else to do."

The man laughed. "No, that's right. Not much at all." His non-laughing eyes studied Alexander intently.

"What do you want to talk about?"

"You, mostly, Major Belov. A couple of other things."

"That's fine."

"Would you like your clothes?"

"I'm sure," Alexander said, "that to a smart man like yourself, the answer is obvious."

"I have another cell for you to go to. It's warmer, bigger and has a window. Much warmer. It must be twenty-five degrees Celsius in there right now, not like this one, it's probably no more than five Celsius in here." The man smiled again. "Or would you like me to translate that into Fahrenheit for you, Major?"

Fahrenheit? Alexander narrowed his eyes. "That won't be necessary."

"Did I mention tobacco?"

"You mentioned it."

"All these things, Major—comfort things. Would you like any of them?"

"Didn't I answer that question?"

"You answered that question. I have one more for you."

"Yes?"

"Are you Alexander Barrington, the son of Harold Barrington, a man who came here in December of 1930, with a beautiful wife and a good-looking eleven-year-old son?"

Alexander didn't blink as he stood in front of the sitting interrogator. "What is your name?" he asked. "Usually you people introduce yourselves."

"Us people?" The man smiled. "I tell you what. You answer me and I will answer you."

"What's your question?"

"Are you Alexander Barrington?"

"No. What is your name?"

The man shook his head.

"What?" said Alexander. "You asked me to answer your question. I did. Now you answer mine."

"Leonid Slonko," said the interrogator. "Does that make any difference to you?"

Alexander studied him very carefully. He had heard the name Slonko before. "Did you say you came from Leningrad to talk to me?"

"Yes."

"You work in Leningrad?"

"Yes."

"A long time, Comrade Slonko? They tell me you're very good at your job. A long time in your line of work?"

"Twenty-three years."

Alexander whistled appreciatively. "Where in Leningrad?"

"Where what?"

"Where do you work? Kresty? Or the House of Detention on Millionnaya?"

"What do you know about the House of Detention, Major?"

"I know it was built during Alexander II's reign in 1864. Is that where you work?"

"Occasionally I interview prisoners there, yes."

Nodding, Alexander went on. "Nice city, Leningrad. I'm still not used to it, though."

"No? Well, why would you be?"

"That's right, why would I? I prefer Krasnodar. It's warmer." Alexander smiled. "And your title, comrade?"

"I'm chief of operations," Slonko replied.

"Not a military man, then? I didn't think so."

Slonko bolted up, holding Alexander's clothes in his hands. "It just occurred to me, Major," he said, "that we are finished here."

"I agree," said Alexander. "Thanks for coming by."

Slonko departed in such an angry rush that he left the lamp and the chair. It was some time before the guard came in and took them.

Darkness again.

So debilitating. But nothing so diminishing as fear.

This time he didn't wait long.

The door opened and two guards came in and ordered him to come with them. Alexander said, "I'm not dressed."

"You won't need clothes where you're going."

The guards were young and eager—the worst kind. He walked between them, slightly ahead of them, barefoot up the stone stairs, and down the corridor of the school, out the back way to the woods, barefoot in the March slush. Were they going to ask him to dig a hole? He felt the rifles at his back. Alexander's feet were numb, and his body was going numb, but his chest wasn't numb, his heart wasn't numb, and if only his heart could stop hurting, he would be able to take it much better.

He remembered the ten-year-old Cub Scout, the American boy, the Soviet boy. The bare trees were ghostly but for a moment he was happy to smell the cold air and to see the gray sky. It's going to be all right, he thought. If Tania is in Helsinki and remembers what I told her, then she would have convinced Sayers to leave as soon as possible. Perhaps they've gone already. Perhaps they're already in Stockholm. And then nothing else matters.

"Turn around," one of the guards said.

"Do I stop walking first?" Alexander said. His teeth chattered.

"Stop walking," said the flustered guard, "and turn around."

He stopped walking. He turned around.

"Alexander Belov," said the shorter guard in the most pompous voice he could muster, "you have been found guilty of treason and espionage against our Motherland during the time of war against our country. The punishment for military treason is death, to be carried out immediately."

Alexander stood still. He put his feet together and his hands at his side. Unblinkingly he looked at the guards. They blinked.

"Well, now what?" he asked.

"The punishment for treason is death," the short guard repeated. He came over to Alexander, proffering a black blindfold. "Here," he said. Alexander noticed the young man's hands were shaking.

"How old are you, Corporal?" he asked quietly.

"Twenty-three," replied the guard.

"Funny—me too," said Alexander. "Just think, three days ago I was a *major* in the Red Army. Three days ago I had a *Hero of the Soviet Union* medal pinned to my chest. Amazing, isn't it?"

The guard's hands continued to shake as he lifted the blindfold to

Alexander's face. Alexander backed away and shook his head. "Forget it. And I'm not turning around, either."

"I'm just following orders, Major," said the young guard, and Alexander suddenly recognized him as one of the corporals who had been in the emplacement with him three months ago at the storming of the Neva to break the Leningrad blockade. He was the corporal Alexander had left on the anti-aircraft gun as he ran out to help Anatoly Marazov.

"Corporal . . . Ivanov?" Alexander said. "Well, well. I hope you do a better job shooting me than you did blowing up those fucking Luftwaffe planes that nearly killed us."

The corporal wouldn't even look at Alexander. "You're going to have to look at me when you aim, Corporal," Alexander said, standing tall and straight. "Otherwise you will miss."

Ivanov went to stand by the other guard. "Please turn away, Major," he said.

"No," Alexander said, his hands at his sides, and his eyes on the two men with rifles. "Here I am. What are you afraid of? As you can see I'm nearly naked and I'm unarmed."

He pulled himself up taller. The two guards were paralyzed. "Comrades," said Alexander. "I will not be the one to issue you an order to lift your rifles. You're going to have to do that on your own."

The other corporal said, "All right, lift your rifle, Ivanov."

They lifted their rifles. Alexander looked into the barrel of one of the guns. He blinked. *O God, please look after Tania all alone in the world.*

"On three," said the corporal, as the two men cocked their rifles.

"One—"

"Two—"

Alexander looked into their faces. They were both so afraid. He looked into his own heart. He was cold, and he felt that he had unfinished business on this earth, business that couldn't wait an eternity. Instead of seeing the trembling corporals, Alexander saw his eleven-year-old face in the mirror of his room in Boston the day he was leaving America. What kind of man have I become? he thought. Have I become the man my father wanted me to be? His mouth tightened. He didn't know. But he knew that he had become the man he himself wanted to be. That would have to be good enough at a time like this, he thought, squaring his shoulders. He was ready for "three."

But "three" did not come.

"Wait!" He heard a voice shout from the side. The guards put down their rifles. Slonko, dressed in a warm coat, felt hat and leather gloves, walked briskly to Alexander. "Stand down, Corporals." Slonko threw a coat he was carrying onto Alexander's back. "Major Belov, you're a lucky man. General Mekhlis himself has issued a pardon on your behalf." He put his hand on Alexander. Why did that make Alexander shudder?

"Come. Let's go back. You need to get dressed. You'll freeze in this weather."

Alexander studied Slonko coldly. He had once read about Fyodor Dostoyevsky's similar experience with Alexander II's guards who were ready to execute him. Dostoyevsky was spared at the last minute with a show of mercy from the emperor and exiled instead. That experience of looking death in the face and then being shown mercy transformed Dostoyevsky. Alexander, on the other hand, did not have time to look so deep into his soul as to be changed even for five minutes. He thought it wasn't mercy they were showing him but a ruse. He was calm before, and he remained calm now except for an occasional shiver from his skin to his bones. Also, unlike Dostoyevsky, he had stared death in the face too often in the last six years to have been daunted by it now.

Alexander followed Slonko back to the school building with the two corporals bringing up the rear. In a small, warm room he found his clothes and his boots and food on a table. Alexander got dressed, his body shaking. He put his feet into his socks, which had been— surprisingly—laundered, and rubbed his feet for a long time to get the blood flowing again. He saw some black spots on his toes and momentarily worried about frostbite, infection, amputation; but only momentarily because the wound in his back was on fire. Corporal Ivanov came and offered him a glass of vodka to warm his insides. Alexander drank the vodka and asked for some hot tea.

Having slowly eaten his food in the warm room and drunk his tea, Alexander felt full and sleepy. Not just sleepy, close to unconsciousness. The black spots on his feet became fainter and grayer. He closed his eyes for a moment and when he opened them again, Slonko sat in front of him. "Your life has been saved by General Mekhlis himself," Slonko said. "He wanted to show we are not unreasonable and that we believe in mercy."

Alexander made no move even to nod. It required all he had to stay awake.

"How do you feel, Major Belov?" asked Slonko, getting out a bottle of vodka and two glasses. "Come, we're both reasonable men. Let's have a drink. We have no differences."

Alexander acknowledged Slonko by shaking his head. "I ate, and I had my tea," he said. "I feel as good as I possibly can." He couldn't keep himself upright.

"I want to talk to you for a few minutes."

"You seem to want a lie from me, and I cannot give it to you. No matter how cold you make me." He pretended to blink. Really he was just closing his eyes.

"Major, we spared your life."

With great effort, Alexander opened them again. "Yes, but why? Did you spare it because you believed in my innocence?"

Slonko shrugged. "Look, it's so simple." He pushed a piece of paper in front of Alexander. "All you need to do is sign this document in front of you that says you understand your life has been spared. You will be sent to exile in Siberia, and you will live out your days in peace and away from the war. Would you like that?"

"I don't know," said Alexander. "But I'm not signing anything."

"You have to sign, Major. You are our prisoner. You have to do as you're told."

"I have nothing to add to what I already told you."

"Don't add, just sign."

"I'm not putting my name on anything."

"And exactly what would your name be?" Slonko said suddenly. "Do you even know?"

"Very well," said Alexander, his head bobbing forward.

"I can't believe you're making me drink by myself, Major. I find it almost rude."

"Maybe you shouldn't drink, Comrade Slonko. It's so easy to fall into the abyss."

Slonko lifted his eyes from the vodka and stared at Alexander for what seemed to be minutes. Finally he said slowly, "You know, a long time ago, I knew a woman, a very beautiful woman who used to drink."

No reply was required of Alexander, so he made none.

"Yes. She was something. She was very brave and suffered terribly not to have a drink in prison. When we picked her up for questioning, she was drunk. It took her several days to get sober. When she became sober, we talked for a long time. I offered her a drink, and she took it, and I offered her a piece of paper to sign and she signed it gratefully. She wanted only one thing from me—do you know what it was?"

Alexander managed to shake his head. *That's* where he heard the name Slonko!

"To spare her son. That was the only thing she asked. To spare her only son—Alexander Barrington."

"That was good of her," said Alexander. He clenched his hands together to still them. He willed his body to remain still. He wanted to be like the chair, like the desk, like the blackboard. He didn't want to be like the glass rattling in the March wind. Any minute now the glass was going to pop out of the frame. *Like the stained glass in a church in Lazarevo.*

"Let me ask you, Major," Slonko said amiably, downing his drink and tapping the empty glass on the wooden table. "If you yourself were going to ask for one thing before *you* were put to death, what would it be?"

"To have a cigarette," Alexander replied.

"Not for mercy?"

"No."

"Do you know your father also begged me to show you mercy?"

Alexander paled.

Slonko said in English, *"Your mother begged me to fuck her but I refused."* He paused, and then smiled. *"At first."*

Alexander ground his teeth together. Nothing else on him moved. In Russian he said, "Are you speaking to *me*, comrade? Because I speak only Russian. They tried to get me to learn French in school, but I'm afraid I wasn't very good at languages." After that he said nothing. His mouth was dry.

"I'm going to ask you again," said Slonko. "I'm going to ask you patiently and politely. Are you Alexander Barrington, son of Jane and Harold Barrington?"

"I will answer you patiently and politely," said Alexander patiently and politely. "Though I have been asked this a hundred and fifty times already. I am not."

"But Major, why would the person who told us this lie? Where would he get this information from? He couldn't have made it up. He knew details about your life no one could have had any idea about."

"Where is this person?" Alexander said. "I'd like to see him, I'd like to ask him if he is sure it's me he is talking about. I for one am certain he made a mistake."

"No, he is sure you're Alexander Barrington."

Alexander raised his voice. "If he is so sure, let him identify me. He is an upstanding comrade, this man you talk about? He is a proper Soviet citizen? He is not a traitor, he has not spat on his country? He served it proudly as I have? He's been decorated, he never shied away from battle, no matter how one-sided, no matter how hard-won? This man you speak of, he is an example to us all, correct? Let me meet the paragon of new Soviet consciousness. Let him look at me, point his finger and say, "This is Alexander Barrington." Alexander smiled. "And then we will see."

Now it was Slonko's turn to pale. "I came from Leningrad to talk to you like a reasonable man," he hissed, losing some of that effacing false humility, baring his teeth, narrowing his eyes.

"And I am certainly glad to talk to you," Alexander said, feeling his own dark eyes darken. "As always I am happy to talk to an earnest Soviet operator, who seeks the truth, who will stop at nothing to find it. And I want to help you. Bring my accuser here. Let's clear up this matter once and for all." Alexander stood up and took one half-menacing step in the direction of the desk. "But once we get this cleared up, I want my besmirched name back."

"Which name would that be, Major?"

"My rightful name. Alexander Belov."

"Do you know that you look like your mother?" Slonko said suddenly.

"My mother has long died. Of typhus. In Krasnodar. Surely your moles told you that?"

"I'm talking about your real mother. The woman who would suck off any guard to get a shot of vodka."

Alexander did not flinch. "Interesting. But I don't think my mother, who was a farmer's wife, had ever seen a guard."

Slonko spat and left.

A guard came to stand over Alexander. It was not Corporal Ivanov. All Alexander wanted to do was close his eyes and fall asleep. But every time he closed his eyes, the guard rammed the butt of the rifle under his chin with a call to wake up. Alexander had to learn to sleep with his eyes open.

The bleak sun set and the room became dark. The corporal turned on the bright light, and shined it into Alexander's face. He became rougher with the rifle. The third time he tried to slam the barrel into Alexander's throat, Alexander grabbed the barrel, twisted it out of the guard's hands and turned it on him. Standing over him, he said, "All you have to do is ask me not to fall asleep. No stronger measures are required. Can you do that?"

"Give me my rifle back."

"Answer me."

"Yes, I can do that."

He gave the guard the weapon back. The guard took it, and struck Alexander in the forehead with the butt of the rifle. He flinched, saw black for a moment but made no sound. The guard left the classroom and returned shortly with his replacement, Corporal Ivanov, who said, "Go ahead, Major. Close your eyes. When they come I will yell. You will open your eyes then, yes?"

"Instantly," Alexander said in a grateful voice, closing his eyes in the most uncomfortable of chairs, which had a short back and no arms. He hoped he wouldn't fall over.

"That's what they do, you know," he heard Ivanov say. "They keep you from sleeping day and night, they don't feed you, they keep you naked, wet, cold, in darkness at day and in light at night until you break down and say white is black and black is white and sign their fucking paper."

"Black is white," Alexander said without opening his eyes.

"Corporal Boris Maikov signed their fucking paper," said Ivanov. "He was shot yesterday."

"What about the other one? Ouspensky?"

"He's back in the infirmary. They realized he had only one lung. They're waiting for him to die. Why waste a bullet on him?"

Alexander was too exhausted to speak. Ivanov lowered his voice another notch, and said, "Major, I heard Slonko arguing with Mitterand a few hours ago. He said to Mitterand, 'Don't worry. I will break him or he will die.'"

Alexander made no reply.

He heard Ivanov's whispering. "Don't let them break you, Major."

Alexander didn't answer. He was sleeping.

Leningrad, 1935

In Leningrad, the Barringtons found two small rooms next to each other in a communal apartment in a ramshackle nineteenth-century building. Alexander found a new school, unpacked his few books, his clothes, and continued being fifteen. Harold found work as a carpenter in a table-making factory. Jane stayed home and drank. Alexander stayed away from the two rooms they called home. He spent much of his time walking around Leningrad, which he liked better than Moscow. The pastel stucco buildings, the white nights, the river Neva; he found Leningrad historic and romantic with its gardens and palaces and wide boulevards and small rivers and canals criss-crossing the never-sleeping city.

At sixteen, as he was obliged to, Alexander registered for the Red Army as Alexander Barrington. That was his rebellion. He was not changing his name.

In their communal apartment they tried to keep to themselves—having so little for each other and nothing for other people—but a married couple on the second floor of their building, Svetlana and Vladimir Visselsky, made friendly approaches. They lived in one room with Vladimir's mother, and at first were quite taken with the Barringtons and lightly envious of the two rooms they had for themselves. Vladimir was a road engineer, Svetlana worked at a local library and kept telling Jane there was a job for her there, too. Jane got a job there, but was unable to get up in the mornings to go to work.

Alexander liked Svetlana. In her late thirties, she was well-dressed, attractive, witty. Alexander liked the way she talked to him, almost as if he were an adult. He was restless during the summer of 1935. Emotionally and financially broke, his parents did not rent a *dacha*. The summer in the city without a way to make new friends did not appeal much to Alexander, who did nothing but walk around Leningrad by day and read by night. He got a library card where Svetlana worked, and often found himself sitting and talking to her. And, very occasionally, reading. Frequently she walked home with him.

His mother brightened a bit under Svetlana's casual attention but soon went back to drinking in the afternoons.

Alexander spent more and more of his days at the library. When she walked home with him, Svetlana would offer him a cigarette, which he stopped refusing, or some vodka, which he continued to refuse. The vodka he could take or leave. The cigarettes he thought he could take or leave too, but he had gradually begun to look forward to their bitter taste in his mouth. The vodka altered him in ways he did not like, but the cigarettes provided a calming crutch to his adolescent frenzy.

One afternoon they had come home earlier than usual to find his mother in a stupor in her bedroom. They went to his room to sit down for a second, before Svetlana had to go back downstairs. She offered Alexander another cigarette, and as she did so, she moved closer to him on the couch. He studied her for a moment, wondering if he was misreading her intentions, and then she took the cigarette out of her mouth and put it into his, kissing him lightly on the cheek. "Don't worry," she said. "I won't bite."

So he was not misreading her intentions.

He was sixteen and he was ready.

Her lips moved to his mouth. "Are you afraid?" she said.

"I'm not," he said, throwing the cigarette and the lighter on the floor. "But you should be."

They spent two hours together on the couch, and afterward Svetlana moved from the room and down the hall with the shaken walk of someone who had come into the battle thinking it was going to be an easy conquest and was now stumbling away having lost all her weapons.

Stumbling away past *Harold*, who was coming home from work, and who passed Svetlana in the hall with a nod and a "You don't want to stay for dinner?"

"There is no dinner," Svetlana replied weakly. "Your wife is still asleep."

Alexander closed his own door and smiled.

Harold cooked dinner for himself and Alexander, who spent the rest of the evening holed up in his room pretending to read, but really just waiting for tomorrow.

Tomorrow couldn't come fast enough.

Another afternoon of Svetlana, and another, and another.

For a month in the summer she and Alexander met in the late afternoons.

He enjoyed Svetlana. She never failed to tell him exactly what he needed to do to bring her pleasure, and he never failed to do exactly as he was told. Everything he learned about patience and perseverance, he learned from her. Combined with his own natural tendency to stay until the job was done, the result was that Svetlana left work earlier and earlier. He was flattered. His summer flew by.

On the weekends when Svetlana came over with her husband to visit the Barringtons, and she and Alexander barely acknowledged their intimacy, he found the sexual tension to be almost an end in itself.

Then Svetlana began to question the evenings he spent out.

Trouble was, now that Alexander had seen what was on the other side of the wall, all he wanted was to be on the other side of the wall, but not just with Svetlana.

He would have gladly continued with her and made time with girls his own age, but one Sunday evening as the five of them were sitting down to a dinner of potatoes and a little herring, Vladimir, Svetlana's husband said to no one in particular, "My Svetochka, I think, needs to get a second job. The library has apparently reduced her hours to part-time."

"But then when would she come and visit my wife?" said Harold, spooning another helping of potatoes onto his plate. They were all crowded in Alexander's parents' room around the small table.

"You come and visit me?" asked Jane of Svetlana. No one at the table responded for a moment. Then Jane nodded. "Of course you do. Every day. I see you in the afternoon."

"You girls must have a great time around here," said Vladimir. "She always comes home full of such good spirits. If I didn't know better, I'd say she was having a raucous affair." He laughed in the tone of a man who thought the very *idea* of his wife's having an affair was so absurd as to be almost delicious.

Svetlana herself threw her head back and laughed. Even Harold chuckled. Only Jane and Alexander sat stonily. For the rest of the dinner Jane said nothing to anyone but got drunker and drunker. Soon she was passed out on the couch while the rest of them cleaned up. The next day, when Alexander came home, he found his mother waiting for him in his room, somber and sober.

"I sent her away," she said to him as he came in and threw down his bag of library books and jacket on the floor and stood in front of his mother with his arms folded.

"Okay," he said.

"What are you doing, Alexander?" she asked quietly. He could tell she had been crying.

"I don't know, Mom. What are *you* doing?"

"Alexander . . ."

"What are you concerned about?"

"That I'm not looking after my son," she replied.

"You're concerned about that?"

"I don't want it to be too late," she said in a small, remorseful voice. "It's my fault, I know. Lately I haven't been much of . . ." She broke off. "But whatever is happening in our family, she can't come here anymore, not if she wants to keep this from her husband."

"Like you're keeping what you do in the afternoons from yours?"

"Like he cares," retorted Jane.

"Like Vladimir cares," retorted Alexander.

"Stop it!" she yelled. "What's the point of this? To wake me up?"

"Mom, I know you will find this hard to believe, but it has nothing to do with you."

"Alexander," Jane said bitterly, "indeed I find that very hard to believe. You, the most beautiful boy in all of Russia, you're telling me you could not have found a young school girl to parry with instead of a woman nearly my age who just happens to be my friend?"

"Who says I haven't? And would a school girl have gotten you sober?"

"Oh, I see, so this does have something to do with me after all!" She didn't get up off the couch while Alexander, with his arms crossed, stood in front of her. "Is this what you want to do with your life? Become a toy for bored older women?"

Alexander felt his temper rising. He grit his teeth. His mother was too upsetting for him.

"Answer me!" she said loudly. "Is this what you want?"

"What?" he said, just as loudly. "Does it seem to you as if I've got so many more attractive options? Which part do you find so repellent?"

Jane jumped up. "Don't go forgetting yourself," she said. "I am still your mother."

"Then act like my mother!" he yelled.

"I've looked after you!"

"And look where it's gotten all of us—all of us Barringtons making a life for ourselves in Leningrad while you spend half of Dad's wages on vodka, and still that's not enough. You've sold your jewelry, you've sold your books, your silks and your linens for vodka. What's left, Mom? What else have you got left to sell?"

For the first time in her life, Jane raised her hand and slapped Alexander. He deserved it and knew it, but couldn't keep himself from saying it.

"Mom, you want to offer me a solution, offer me a solution. You want to tell me what to do—after months of not speaking to me—forget it. I will not listen. You're going to have to do better." He paused. "Stop drinking."

"I'm sober now."

"Then let's talk again tomorrow."

But tomorrow she was drunk.

School started. Alexander busied himself with getting to know a girl named Nadia. One afternoon, Svetlana met him at the school doors. He was laughing with Nadia. Excusing himself, Alexander walked down the block with Svetlana.

"Alexander, I want to talk to you." They walked to a small park and sat under the autumn trees. "Your mother knows, doesn't she?"

"Yes." He cleared his throat. "Listen . . . we needed to stop anyway."

"Stop?" She said the word as if it had never actually occurred to her. He looked at her with surprise.

"Not stop!" she exclaimed. "Whatever in the world for?"

"Svetlana . . ."

"Alexander, can't you see?" she said, trembling and taking hold of his arm. "This is just a test for us."

He pulled his arm away. "It's a test I'm meant to fail. I don't know what you could possibly be thinking. I'm in school. I'm sixteen. You're a married thirty-nine-year-old woman. How long did you imagine this would go on?"

"When we first started," she said hoarsely, "I imagined nothing."

"All right."

"But now . . ."

His gaze dropped. "Oh, Sveta . . ."

She got up off the bench. The throaty cry she emitted hurt Alexander's lungs—as if he had breathed inside himself her miserable addiction to him. "Of course. I'm ridiculous." She struggled with her breath. "You're right. Of course." She tried to smile. "Maybe one last time?" she whispered. "For old times' sake? To say goodbye properly?"

Alexander bowed his head by way of replying.

She stumbled a step back from him, composed herself and said as steadily as she could, "Alexander, remember this as you go through your life—you have amazing gifts. Don't squander them. Don't give them out meaninglessly, don't abuse them, don't take them for granted. You are the weapon you carry with you till the day you die."

They did not see each other again. Alexander got himself a card at a different library. Vladimir and Svetlana stopped coming over. At first Harold was curious why they no longer visited and then he forgot about them. Alexander knew his father's inner life was too unsettled to worry about why he no longer saw people he didn't like very much to begin with.

Fall turned into winter. 1935 turned into 1936. He and his father celebrated New Year's by themselves. They went to a local beer bar, where his father bought him a glass of vodka and tried to talk to him. The conversation was brief and strained. Harold Barrington—in his own sober, defiant way—was oblivious to his son and his wife. The world his father lived in Alexander did not know, stopped understanding, didn't want to understand even if he could have. He knew that his father would have liked Alexander to side with him, to understand him, to believe in him, the way he did when he was younger. But Alexander did not know how to do that anymore. The days of idealism had gone. Only life was left.

Giving Up One Room, 1936

Could it get less tolerable?

Shortly.

An undergrown man from Upravdom—the housing committee—arrived at their doorstep one dark January Saturday morning, accompanied by two people with suitcases, and waved about a piece of paper, informing the Barringtons that they were going to have to give up one of their rooms to another family. Harold didn't have the strength to argue. Jane was too drunk to object. It was Alexander who raised his voice but only briefly. There was no point. There was no one to go to, to correct this.

"You can't tell me this is unjust," the smirking Upravdom member said to Alexander. "You have two nice rooms for the three of you. There are two of them, and they have no rooms at all. She is pregnant. Where is your socialist spirit, comrade soon-to-be Comsomol?" The Comsomols were young members of the Communist Party of the Soviet Union.

Alexander and Harold moved the cot and his small dresser and his few personal belongings and his bookshelf. Alexander put his cot next to the window, and the dresser and bookshelf between himself and his parents as an angry barrier. When his father wanted to know if he was upset, Alexander barked, "It's been my dream to share a room with you at sixteen. I know you don't want any privacy either." They talked in English, which was more natural and more colloquial, and provided an opportunity to say the word *privacy*, a word that did not exist in Russian.

The next morning when Jane woke up she wanted to know what Alexander was doing in their room. It was a Sunday.

"I'm here for good," said Alexander, and went out. He took a train to Peterhof and walked the grounds by himself, sullen and confused.

The feeling he had had all his young life—that he was brought on this earth for something special—had not left Alexander, not quite; what it did was dissipate inside him, became translucent in his blood vessels. It no longer pulsed through his body. He was no longer filled with a sense of purpose. He was filled with a sense of despair.

I could have lived through it all if only I continued to have the feeling that at the end of childhood, at the end of adolescence, there was something else in this life that would be mine, that I could make with my bare hands, and once I had made it, I could say, I did this to my life. I made my life so.

Hope.

It was gone from Alexander on this sunny crisp Sunday, and the feeling of purpose had vanished, was vanquished in his veins.

The End, 1936

Harold stopped bringing vodka into the house.

"Dad, you don't think Mom will be able to get vodka any other way?"

"With what? She has no money."

Alexander didn't mention the thousands of American dollars his mother had been hoarding since the day they came to the Soviet Union.

"Stop talking about me as if I'm not here!" Jane shouted.

They looked at her with surprise. Afterward Jane started stealing money from Harold's pockets and going to buy the vodka herself. Harold started keeping his money out of the house. Jane was then caught in someone else's apartment, going through their things, already drunk on some French perfume she had found.

Alexander began to be afraid that the next natural step for his mother would be to drink her way through the money she had brought with them from America. It wouldn't end until all the money was gone. First the Soviet rubles she had saved from her job in Moscow, then the American dollars. It would take his mother a year to buy vodka with all her dollars on the black market, but buy it she would, gone the money would be, and then what?

Without that money, Alexander was finished.

Alexander had to get his mother sober for long enough to let him hide the money in a place that was not home. He knew that if she found out he had taken it without her knowledge or permission her hysteria would not cease until Harold knew of her treachery. Once Harold knew his wife had mistrusted him from the moment they left the United States, mistrusted him even in her love and her respect, mistrusted him and his motives and his ideals and all the dreams he thought she shared with him from the very start, once he knew that, Alexander felt his father would not recover. And he didn't want to be responsible for his father's future, all he wanted was the money to help him be responsible for his own. That's what his sober mother wanted, too. He knew that. Sober, she would let him hide the money. The trick was to get her sober.

Over the course of one difficult and contemptible weekend Alexander tried to dry out his mother. She, in her convulsing rage, flooded him with such obscenities and vitriol that finally even Harold said, "Oh, for God's sake, give her a drink and tell her to shut up."

But Alexander didn't give her a drink. He sat by her, and he read aloud from Dickens, in English, and he read Pushkin to her, in Russian, and he read her the funniest of Zoshchenko's anecdotes, and he fed her some soup and he fed her some bread, and gave her coffee, and put cold wet towels on her head, but still she wouldn't stop ranting. Harold, in a quiet moment, asked Alexander, "What did she mean about you and Svetlana, what was she talking about?"

"Dad, haven't you learned by now, you have to shut her off? You can't listen to a word she is saying."

"No, no, of course not," muttered Harold thoughtfully, walking away from Alexander, though not far, because there wasn't anywhere in the narrow room to go.

On Monday, after his father left for work, Alexander cut school and spent all day convincing his morosely, miserably sober mother that her money needed to be put in a safe place. Alexander tried to explain to her, first patiently and quietly, then impatiently and shouting, that if something, God forbid, were to happen to them, and they were arrested—

"You're talking nonsense, Alexander. Why would they arrest us? We're their people. We're not living well, but then we shouldn't be living any better than the rest of the Russians. We came here to share their fate."

"We're doing that gallantly," said Alexander. "Mom, wise up. What do you think happened to the other foreigners that lived with us in Moscow?" He paused. His mother considered. "Even if I'm wrong, I'm saying it's not going to hurt us to be a little prudent and hide the money. Now how much money is left?"

After thinking for a few moments, Jane said she did not know. She let Alexander count it. There was ten thousand dollars and four thousand rubles.

"How many dollars did you bring with you from America?" he asked.

"I don't know. Maybe seventeen thousand. Maybe twenty."

"Oh, Mom."

"What? Some of that money went to buy you oranges and milk in Moscow, or did you forget already?"

"I didn't forget," Alexander replied in a weary voice. How much for the oranges and milk, he wanted to know. Fifty dollars? A hundred?

Jane, smoking and watching Alexander, narrowed her eyes at him. "If I let you hide the money, will you let me have a drink, as a thank you?"

"Yes. Just one."

"Of course. One small one is all I want. I feel much better when I'm sober, you know. But just one small drink to get me through the heebie-jeebies would help me stay sober, you know that, don't you?"

Alexander wanted to ask his mother just how naïve she thought he was. He said nothing.

"All right," said Jane. "Let's get it over with. Where are you planning to hide it?"

Alexander suggested gluing the money into the back binding of a book, producing one of his mother's good, thick-covered hardbacks to show exactly what he meant.

"If your father finds out, he will never forgive you."

"He can add it to the list of things he won't forgive me for. Go on, Mom. I have to get to school. After the book is ready, I'm putting it in the library."

Jane stared at the book Alexander was proposing. It was her ancient copy of Pushkin's *The Bronze Horseman and Other Poems*. "Why don't we glue it inside the Bible we brought from home?"

"Because finding a Pushkin book in the Pushkin section of the Leningrad library is not going to alert anyone. But finding a Bible in English anywhere in the Russian library just might." He smiled. "Don't you think?"

Jane almost smiled back. "Alexander, I'm sorry I haven't been well."

He lowered his head.

"I don't want to talk to your father about this anymore because he no longer has any patience for me, but I'm having trouble with our life."

"We know," Alexander said. "We've noticed."

She put her arms around him. He patted her on the back. "Shh," he said. "It's all right."

"This money, Alexander," she said, looking up at him, "you think it will help you somehow?"

"I don't know. Having it is better than not having it."

He took the book with him, and after school went to the Leningrad public library and in the back, in the three-aisle-wide Pushkin section, found a place on a bottom shelf for his book. He put it between two scholarly-looking tomes that had not been checked out since 1927. He thought it was a good bet no one would check out his book, either. But still, it didn't feel completely safe. He wished there were a better hiding place for it.

When Alexander came home later that evening, his mother was drunk again, showing none of the remorseful affection he had seen in her eyes earlier in the day. He ate dinner quietly with his father, while listening to the radio.

"School good?"

"Yes. It's fine, Dad."

"You have good friends?"

"Sure."

"Any good friends who are girls?" His father was trying to make conversation.

"Some friends who are girls, yes."

His father cleared his throat. "Nice Russian girls?"

Smiling, Alexander asked, "Compared with what?"

Harold smiled. "Do the nice Russian girls," he asked carefully, "like my boy?"

Alexander shrugged. "They like me all right."

Harold said, "I remember you and Teddy hung out with that girl, what was her name again?"

"Belinda."

"Yes! Belinda. She was nice."

"Dad." Alexander laughed. "We were *eight*. Yes, she was nice for an eight-year-old."

"Oh, but what a crush on you she had!"

"And what a crush on her Teddy had."

"That about sums up all the relationships on God's earth."

They went out for a drink. "I miss our home in Barrington a little," Harold admitted to Alexander. "But it's only because I have not lived a different way long enough. Long enough to change my consciousness and make me into the person I'm supposed to be."

"You have lived this way long enough. That's *why* you miss Barrington."

"No. You know what I think, son? I think it's not working so well here, because it's Russia. I think communism would work much better in America." He smiled beseechingly at Alexander. "Don't you agree?"

"Oh, Dad, for God's sake."

Harold didn't want to talk about it anymore. "Never mind. I'm going over to Leo's for a little while. You want to come?"

The choice was, either go back home to the room with his unconscious mother or sit in a smoked-out room with his father's communist cronies regurgitating obscure parts of *Das Kapital* and talking about bringing the war back home.

Alexander wanted to be with his father but alone. He went home to his mother. He wanted to be alone with somebody.

☙

The next morning, as Harold and Alexander were getting ready for their day, Jane, still inebriated from the night before, held on to Alexander's hand for a moment and said, "Stay behind, son, I have to talk to you."

After Harold left, Jane said in a hurried voice, "Collect your things. Where is that book? You have to run and get it."

"What for?"

"You and I are going to Moscow."

"Moscow?"

"Yes. We'll get there by nightfall. Tomorrow first thing in the morning I'll take you to the consulate." They'll keep you there until they contact the State Department in Washington. And then they'll send you home."

"What?"

"Alexander, yes. I'll take care of your father."

"You can't take care of yourself."

"Don't worry about me," said Jane. "My fate is sealed. But yours is wide open. Concern yourself only with you. Your father goes to his meetings. He thinks by playing with the grown-ups he won't be punished. But they have his number. They have mine. But you, Alexander, you have no number. I have to get you out."

"I'm not going without you or Dad."

"Of course you are. Your father and I will never be allowed to return. But you will do very well back home. I know it's hard in America these days, there aren't many jobs, but you'll be free, you'll have your life, so come and stop arguing. I'm your mother. I know what I'm doing."

"Mom, you're taking me to Moscow to surrender me to the Americans?"

"Yes. Your Aunt Esther will look after you until you graduate secondary school. The State Department will arrange for her to meet your ship in Boston. You're still only sixteen, Alexander, the consulate won't turn you away."

Alexander had been very close to his father's sister once. She adored him, but she had an ugly fight with Harold over Alexander's dubious future in the Soviet Union, and they had not spoken or written since.

"Mom, two things," he said. When I turned sixteen, I registered for the Red Army. Remember? Mandatory conscription. I became a Soviet citizen when I joined. I have a passport to prove that."

"The consulate doesn't have to know that."

"It's their business to know it. But the second thing is . . ." Alexander broke off. "I can't go without saying goodbye to my father."

"Write him a letter."

The train ride was long. He had twelve hours to sit and think. How his mother managed those hours without a drink, he didn't know. Her hands were shaking badly by the time they arrived at the Leningrad Station in Moscow. It was night; they were tired and hungry. They had no place to sleep. They had no food. It was a fairly mild late April, and they slept on a bench in Gorky Park. Alexander had strong bittersweet memories of himself and his friends playing ice hockey in Gorky Park.

"I need a drink, Alexander," Jane whispered. "I need a drink to take an edge off my life. Stay here, I'll be right back."

"Mother," said Alexander, putting his steady hand on her to keep her from getting up. "If you leave, I will go straight to the station and take the next train back to Leningrad."

Deeply sighing, Jane moved closer to Alexander and motioned to her lap. "Lie down, son. Get some sleep. We have a long day tomorrow."

Alexander put his head on his mother's shoulder and eventually slept.

The next morning they had to wait an hour at the consulate gate until someone came to see them—only to tell them they could not come in. Jane gave her name and a letter explaining about her son. They waited restlessly for another two hours until the sentry called them over and said the consul was unable to help them. Jane pleaded to be let in for just five minutes. The sentry shook his head and said there was nothing he could do. Alexander had to restrain his mother. Eventually he led her away and returned by himself to speak to the guard. The man apologized. "I'm sorry," he said in English. "They did look into it, if you want to know. But the file on your mother and father has been sent back to the State Department in Washington." The man paused. "Yours, too. Since you're Soviet citizens, you're not under our jurisdiction anymore. There is nothing they can do."

"What about political asylum?"

"On what grounds? Besides, you know how many Soviets come this way asking for asylum? Dozens every day. On Mondays, near a hundred. We're here by invitation from the Soviet government. We want to maintain our ties to the Soviet community. If we started accepting their people, how long do you think they'd allow us to stay here? You'd be the last one. Just last week, we relented and let a widowed Russian father with two small children pass. The father had relatives in the United States and said he would find work. He had a useful skill, he was an electrician. But there was a diplomatic scandal. We had to give him back." The sentry paused. "You're not an electrician, are you?"

"No," replied Alexander. "But I am an American citizen."

The sentry shook his head. "You know you can't serve two masters in the military."

Alexander knew. He tried again. "I have relatives in America. I will live with them. And I can work. I'll drive a cab. I will sell produce on the street corner. I will farm. I will cut down trees. Whatever I can do, I will do."

The sentry lowered his voice. "It's not you. It's your father and mother. They're just too high profile for the consulate to get involved. Made too much of a fuss when they came here. Wanted everyone to know them. Well, now everyone knows them. Your parents should have thought twice about relinquishing their U.S. citizenship. What was the hurry? They should have been sure first."

"My father was sure," said Alexander.

The trip back from Moscow was only as long as the trip *to* Moscow; why did it seem decades longer? His mother was mute. The countryside was flat bleak fields; there was still no food.

Jane cleared her throat. "I desperately wanted to have a baby. It took me ten years and four miscarriages to have you. The year you were born the worldwide flu epidemic tore through Boston, killing thousands of people, including my sister, your father's parents and brother, and many of our close friends. Everybody we knew lost someone. I went to the doctor for a check-up because I was feeling under the weather and was terrified it might be the dreaded flu. He told me I was pregnant. I said, how can it be, we'll fall sick, we've given up our family inheritance, we are broke, where are we going to live, how will we stay healthy, and the doctor looked at me and said, "The baby brings his own food."

She took Alexander's hand. He let her.

"You, son—you brought your own food. Harold and I both felt it. When you were born, Alexander—when you were born, it was late at night, and you came so suddenly, I didn't even have time to go to the hospital. The doctor came, delivered you in our bed, and said that you seemed in a great hurry to get on with living. You were the biggest baby he had ever seen, and I still remember, after we told him we were naming you Anthony Alexander after your great grandfather, he lifted you, all purple and black-haired, and exclaimed, "Alexander the great!" Because you were so big, you see." She paused. "You were such a beautiful boy," she whispered.

Alexander took his hand away and turned to the window.

"Our hopes for you were extraordinary. I wish you could imagine the kinds of things we dreamed for you as we strolled down the Boston Pier with you in the carriage and all the old ladies stopping to gaze at the baby with hair so black and eyes so shining."

The flat fields were rushing by.

"Ask your father—ask him—when next you can, if his dreams for you ever included *this* for his only son."

"I just didn't bring enough food, did I, Mom?" said Alexander, with hair so black and eyes so shining.

CHAPTER TEN

The Ghosts of Ellis Island, 1943

THERE WAS SOMETHING UNDENIABLY comforting about living and working at Ellis. Tatiana's world was so small, so insular, and so full that there was little left of her to imagine a different life, to move forward in her imagination to New York, to the real America, or backward in her memory, to Leningrad, to the real Alexander. So long as she stayed at Ellis with her infant son, lived with him in a small stone room with the large white window, slept in her single bed on her white linen, wore her one set of white clothes and sensible shoes, so long as she lived in that room with Anthony and her black backpack, she didn't have to imagine an impossible life in America without Alexander.

Desperately trying to get away from that black backpack, she frequently longed for the noise of her family, for the chaos and the arguing, for the music of loud vodka drinkers, for the smell of incessant cigarette smokers. She wished for her impossible brother, for her sister, for her bedraggled mother, her gruff father and for her grandmother and grandfather—revered by her. She ached for them the way she used to ache for bread during the blockade. She wished for them to walk loudly down the Ellis halls with her as they did now every day, silent ghosts by her side, helpless before his screaming ghost also by her side.

During the day she carried her boy and bandaged and fed the wounded, leaving her own festering wounds until night-time when she licked them and nursed them, and remembered *the pines and the fish and the river and the axe and the woods and the fire and the blueberries and the smell of cigarette smoke and the loud laughter coming from one male throat.*

It was impossible to walk the stripped bare corridors of Ellis Island Three without hearing the millions of footsteps that had walked there on the black-and-white checkered floor before Tatiana. When she ventured across the short bridge to the Great Hall on Ellis Island One, the sense grew. Because unlike Ellis Three, where present life was continuing, Ellis One was deserted. All that remained in the gothic building, on the stairs, the corridors, the gray dusty rooms was the spirit of the past—of those who came before, since 1894, those who came by shiploads, seven times a day, who docked across the water at Castle Garden or who came off the planks here, right into Immigration Hall, and then trudged upstairs into the Great Registry Room clutching their bags and children, adjusting their head coverings, having left behind everything in the Old World: mothers and fathers, husbands, brothers and sisters, having either promised to send for them or having promised nothing. Five thousand a day, eighty thousand a month, eight million one year, twenty million from 1892 to 1924, without visas, without papers, without money, but with the clothes they wore and whatever useful skills they had—as carpenters, seamstresses, cooks, metalworkers, bricklayers, salesmen.

Mama would have done well here, sewing. And Papa would have fixed their water pipes, and Pasha would have fished. And Dasha would have looked after Alexander's boy while I worked. Ironic and sad as that would have been, she would have done it.

They came with their children, for no one left the children behind—it was for the children they had come, wanting to give them the halls of America, the streets, the seasons, the New York of America. New York, right across the water, so close yet impossibly far for those who had to be cleared through immigration and medical examinations before they could step on the shores of Manhattan Island. Many had been sick like Tatiana, and worse. The combination of contagious illness, no language skills, and no work skills occasionally made the doctors and the INS officers turn the immigrants away—not a lot, handfuls a day. Older parents and their grown children could be split up. Husbands and wives could be split up.

Like I was split up. Like I am split up.

The threat of failure, the fear of return, the longing to be admitted was so strong that it remained in the walls and the floors, permeating the stone between the cracked glass windows, and all the yearning hope echoed off the walls of Ellis and into Tatiana as she walked the herringbone tile corridors with Anthony in her arms.

After the clampdown in 1924, Ellis Island stopped being the nucleus for nearly all immigration into the United States. Nonetheless, ships with immigrants arrived each day, then each week, then each month. Processing at Ellis dwindled from millions a year to thousands, to hundreds. Most people came to Port of New York with visas already in hand. Without visas, the immigrants could now be legally turned away and often were, and so fewer and fewer people risked making a life-changing, life-threatening journey only to be turned back at the port of call. But still, 748 people smuggled themselves in between crates of tomatoes in the year before the war, without papers, without money.

They were not turned away.

Just as talk was beginning to swell about closing down the largely unneeded Ellis Island, World War II broke out, and suddenly in 1939, 1940, 1941, Ellis became useful as a hospital for refugees and stowaways. Once America entered the war, it would bring the wounded and captured Germans and Italians from the Atlantic and detain them at Ellis.

That's when Tatiana arrived.

And she felt needed. No one wanted to work at Ellis, not even Vikki, who instinctively felt that her natural and prodigious flirting skills were utterly wasted on the foreign wounded men who would be going back to their home country or to work on U.S. farms as field-hands. Vikki grudgingly pulled her duty at Ellis but she much preferred the NYU hospital, where the wounded, if they did not die first, had a hope of pleasing Vikki—the medium-term gal—in the medium-term.

Quietly the German wounded continued to be brought to Ellis Island, and continued to convalesce. The Italian men, too, who talked even as they were dying, talked in a language Tatiana did not understand; yet they spoke with a cadence, with a fervor and a fury that she did understand. They had hearty laughs and throaty cries and clutching fingers with which they would grab onto her as they were carried off the boats, as they stared into her face and muttered hopes for life, chances for survival, words of thanks. And sometimes before they died, if holding her hands wasn't enough, and if they had nothing contagious or infectious, she brought them her boy and placed him on their chests, so that their war-beaten hands could go around his small sleeping form and they would be comforted, and their hearts would beat at peace.

She wished she could have brought Alexander his sleeping son.

Something about Ellis Island's contained, confined nature soothed *her*. She could stay in her whitewashed, clean-linen room with Anthony, and she could eat three meals at the cafeteria, saving her meat rations and her butter rations. She could nurse her son, pleased by the heft of him, by the size of him, by the health and shine of him.

Edward and Vikki, one late summer afternoon, sat her down in the cafeteria, put a cup of coffee in front of her and tried to convince her to move to New York. They told her New York was booming during war, there were night clubs, there were parties, there were clothes and shoes to buy and perhaps she could rent a small apartment with a kitchen and perhaps she could have her own room, and Anthony could have another, and perhaps perhaps perhaps.

Thousands of miles away there was war. Thousands of miles away there was the River Kama, the Ural Mountains which had watched it all, seen it all, known it all. And the galaxies. They knew. They bent their midnight rays to shine through Tatiana's window at Ellis Island, and they whispered to her, keep going. Let *us* weep. You live.

The echoes spoke to Tatiana, the corridors felt familiar, the white sheets, the salty smell, the back of the robes of Lady Liberty, the night air, the twinkling lights across the bay of a city of dreams. Tatiana already lived on an island of dreams, and what she needed, New York could not give her.

The fire has gone out. The clearing is dark, but on the cold blanket they remain. Alexander sits with his legs open and Tania sits between them, her back to his chest. His arms swaddle her. They are both looking up at the sky. They are mute.

"Tania," Alexander whispers, kissing her head, "do you see the stars?"

"Of course."

"You want to make love right here? We'll throw the blanket off and make love and let them see us—so they will never forget."

"Shura . . ." Her voice is soft and sad. "They've seen us. They know. Look, can you see that constellation up to the right? You see how the cluster stars at the bottom form a smile? They're smiling at us." She pauses. "I've seen them many times, looking beyond your head."

"Yes," Alexander says, wrapping his arms and the blanket tighter around her. "I think that constellation is in the galaxy of Perseus, the Greek hero—"

"I know who Perseus is." She nods. "When I was a little girl, I lived inside the Greek myths." She presses against him. "I like that Perseus is smiling at us while you make love to me."

"Did you know that the stars in Perseus that are yellow might be close to imploding, but the stars that are blue, the biggest, the brightest—"

"And they are called novas."

"Yes, they shine, gain in brilliance, explode, then fade. Look how many blue stars there are around the smile, Tatia."

"I see."

"Do you hear the stellar winds?"

"I hear rustling."

"*Do you hear the stellar winds, carrying from the heavens a whisper, straight from antiquity . . . into eternity . . .*"

"*What are they whispering?*"

"*Tatiana . . . Tatiana . . . Ta . . . tiana . . .*"

"*Please stop.*"

"*Will you remember that? Anywhere you are, if you can look up and find Perseus in the sky, find that smile, and hear the galactic wind whisper your name, you'll know it's me, calling for you . . . calling you back to Lazarevo.*"

Tatiana wipes her face on Alexander's arm and says, "*You won't have to call me back, soldier. I'm not ever leaving here.*"

CHAPTER ELEVEN

Baseball in Central Park, 1943

JULY HAD GONE BY, and August, too, and September. Seven months since she left the Soviet Union. Tatiana stayed at Ellis, not venturing once across the harbor, until finally Edward and Vikki had had enough of her, and they took her and Anthony—nearly by force—in the ferry one Saturday afternoon to see New York. Against Tatiana's objections ("Vikki, I don't have carriage to put Anthony.") Vikki bought a carriage for four dollars at a second-hand shop. "It's not for you. It's for the baby. You can't refuse a present for your baby."

Tatiana didn't refuse. She often wished her boy could have a few more clothes, a few more toys. A carriage perhaps for the walks around Ellis. In the same shop Tatiana bought Anthony two rattles and a teddy bear, though he preferred the paper bags they came in.

"Edward, what's your wife going to say when she finds out you're out with not one but two of your nurses, gallivanting around gay New York?" asked Vikki with a grin.

"She will scratch out the eyes of the wench who told her."

"My mouth is shut. What about you, Tania?"

"I'm not speak English," said Tatiana, and they laughed.

"I can't believe this girl has never once been to New York. Tania, how do you keep from going to the Immigration Department? Don't you need to speak to them every few weeks so they can see how you're doing?"

Looking at Edward gratefully, Tatiana said, "Justice Department come to me."

"But three months! Didn't you want to go to New York and see for yourself what all the fuss is about?"

"I busy working."

"Busy nursing," punned Vikki, and laughed at herself. "He is a nice boy. He is not going to fit into the carriage soon. I think he is extra big for his age. All that milk." She glanced at Tatiana's abundant chest and coughed loudly.

"I do not know," said Tatiana, looking at Anthony with swelling pride. "I do not know boys his age."

"Trust me, he is gigantic. When are you going to come for dinner? How about tomorrow? I don't want to hear it from Grammy about my divorce anymore. It's official, you know. I'm divorced. And my grandmother every Sunday dinner says to me that no man shall ever want me again, a tainted divorced woman." Vikki rolled her eyes.

"Vikki, but why do you have to prove her so wrong?" said Edward. Tatiana stifled a laugh.

"I have eyes but for one man. Chris Pandolfi."

Tatiana snorted. Edward smiled. "Our Tania doesn't much like Chris, do you, Tania?"

"Why?" asked Vikki.

"Because he calls me Nurse Buttercup. I think he make fun of me. What is this buttercup?"

Shaking his head and smiling, Edward placed his arm on Tatiana's back and said, "Happy yellow flower," but Vikki was already talking about how Chris was going to take her to Cape Cod for Thanksgiving weekend, and how she had found the most exquisite chiffon dress to go dancing in next Saturday.

The market in front of Battery Park was teeming with people.

Tatiana, Vikki, and Edward pushed a sleeping Anthony past the market, through Church Street and then turned down Wall Street and crossed downtown to go to South Street, through the Fulton Fish Market and then up to Chinatown and Little Italy. Edward and Vikki were exhausted. Tatiana walked on, mesmerized by the tall buildings, by the swarming crowds, everyone shouting, cheerful, hot, by the street vendors selling candlesticks, candles, old books, apples, by the musicians on street corners, playing harmonica and accordion. She walked as if her feet did not belong to her and did not touch the hard pavement. She was amazed at the potatoes and peas and cabbages spilling out of bushels onto the sidewalks, by the peaches and apples and grapes, by the horse-drawn carriages selling cottons and linens, by the cabs and cars, thousands of them, millions of them, by the double-decker buses, by the constant clang of the el on Third Avenue, on Second Avenue, amazed, open-mouthed by it all.

They stopped at a coffee house on Mulberry Street, and Vikki and Edward sank into the sidewalk chairs. Tatiana remained standing, her hand on the carriage. She was looking at the bride and groom descending the church steps into the courtyard across the street. There were many people around them. They looked happy.

"You know she's a tiny girl and looks deceptively as if she will fall down any second, but look at her, Edward. She's not even out of breath," said Vikki.

"I, however, have lost several pounds. I have not walked this much since my days in the army," said Edward.

Ah, so Edward *was* a military man. "Edward, you walk this much through hospital beds every day," Tatiana said, not turning away from the couple at the church. "But your New York, it is something."

"How does it compare to the Soviet Union?" asked Vikki.

"Favorably," Tatiana replied.

"Someday, you'll have to tell me about it," said Vikki. "Oh, look, peaches! Let's go buy some."

"New York is always like this?" said Tatiana, trying not to sound wide-eyed.

"Oh, no. It's only like this because of the war. Usually it's very lively."

Two Sundays later, Tatiana went with Anthony and Vikki to Central Park to watch Edward play softball against the health officials at PHD, including Chris Pandolfi. Edward's wife did not come. He said she was resting.

Tatiana smiled at the passers-by and at the fruit stand sellers. The birds were joyous overhead and life bustled forward in freshwater color spurts, and she bowed her head and held her son with one hand and the peaches in the other, and said, yes, these are ripe and smell sweet. She was contemplating taking a ride with Vikki and Edward up to Bear Mountain one Sunday, when Edward had a few gallons of rationed gasoline and his wife was home resting and the leaves were changing. But this Sunday Tatiana was in Central Park, in New York, in the United States of America, holding Anthony while the sun was bright and Edward played softball, and Vikki jumped up and down at every hit and every catch, and Tatiana was not dreaming.

But where *is* Anthony's mom? What's happened to her? Tatiana wanted that girl back, the girl before June 22, 1941, the girl who sat on the bench in her French-made, Polish-bought white dress with red roses and ate ice cream on the day war started for Russia. The girl who swam with her brother, Pasha, who read away her summer days, the girl with everything in front of her. With the Red Army first lieutenant in his

Sunday best Class As standing across the sunlit street in front of her. She could have not bought the ice cream, she could have gotten on the earlier bus and hurtled across town in a different direction toward a different life. Except she had to have bought the ice cream. That was who she was. And because of that ice cream now she was here.

Now, wartime New York with its bustling fervor and Vikki with her brightest laugh and Anthony with his fiercest cry, and Edward with his gentle good humor were all trying to bring that girl back. Everything that had been in front of Tatiana was behind her now. The very worst and the very best, too. She lifted her freckled face at a loud and jumping Vikki on the baseline and smiled and went to the drink stand to buy some Coca Cola for her friends. Tatiana's long blonde hair was in a long braid, as always. She was wearing a simple blue sundress that was too big for her, too long and too wide.

Edward caught up with her and asked if he could carry Anthony for a bit. Tatiana nodded. She bent her head low so she wouldn't see Edward carrying Alexander's boy, so the ancient ruins would stay in Rome where they belonged, far away from an afternoon in Sheep Meadow with Vikki and Edward.

He bought the Cokes, water and some strawberries, and the three of them slowly walked back to her blanket on the grass. Tatiana didn't speak.

"Tania," said Edward. "Look at how he's smiling." He laughed. "The infant smile, nothing quite like it, is there?"

"Hmm," said Tatiana, not looking. She knew Anthony's toothless ear-to-ear smile. She'd seen it in action in the infirmary at Ellis. The German and Italian soldiers worshipped Anthony.

"I bought something nice for you and him. You think it's too early for him to eat strawberries?"

"I do, yes."

"But look—aren't they nice? I bought too many. Have some. Maybe you can cook them up or something."

"I can," Tatiana said quietly, taking a long drink of water. "I can make jam, I can make jelly, I can preserve them whole in sugar, I can make pie out of them, and crumble, I can cook them and freeze them for winter. I am queen of preserving fruit."

"*Tania—how many ways are there of cooking blueberries?*"

"*You'd be surprised.*"

"*I'm already surprised. What are you making me now?*"

"*Blueberry jam.*"

"I like the skim off them."

"Come here and have some."

She brings the spoon to his mouth and lets him taste. He licks his lips.
"I love that."

"Hmm." She sees the look in his eyes. "Shura, no. I have to finish this. It
needs to be stirred constantly. This is for the old women for the winter."

"Tania . . ."

"Shura . . ."

His arms go around her. "Did I mention that I'm sick to death of
blueberries?"

"You're impossible."

CHAPTER TWELVE

Conversations with Slonko, 1943

"MAJOR!"

Instantly, Alexander opened his eyes. He was still in the interrogation classroom, still in the wooden chair, still guarded by Ivanov. In walked Slonko with grim strides.

"Well, Major, it looks like you're going to have to stop playing games."

"That'll be fine," said Alexander. "I'm not in a playing mood."

"Major!"

"Why is everyone shouting?" Alexander rubbed his head. His skull was cracking.

"Major, do you know a woman by the name of Tatiana Metanova?"

It was harder for Alexander to stay composed. He kept still through willpower. If I can live through this, he thought, I can live through anything. If I can live through this, I *will* live through anything. He wasn't sure whether to lie, whether to tell the truth. Slonko was obviously planning something.

"Yes," said Alexander.

"And who would she be?"

"She was one of the nurses at Morozovo hospital."

"*Was?*"

"Well, I'm not there anymore, am I?" Alexander said mildly.

"Turns out she is not there either."

That was not a question. Alexander said nothing.

"She is more than just a nurse, though, isn't she, Major?" said Slonko, producing Alexander's domestic passport out of his pocket. "Why, right in here, it says that she is your wife."

"Yes," Alexander said. His whole life in one line. He steadied himself. He knew Slonko was not done by a long shot. He needed to be ready.

"Ah. And where is she at the moment?"

"I would have to be omniscient to know that," Alexander said.

"She is with us," said Slonko, bending forward. "We have her in our custody." He laughed with satisfaction. "What do you think of that, Major?"

"What do I think of that?" said Alexander, not taking his gaze away from Slonko. He folded his arms around his chest and waited. "Could I have a smoke?" he asked, and was brought one. He lit it with steady hands. Before anyone spoke again, Alexander decided Slonko was bluffing. He decided to *believe* Slonko was bluffing. Just yesterday, was it, Stepanov had told Alexander that Tatiana was missing and no one could find her. Stepanov said Mekhlis's men were all in a panic. Yet there was nothing about that from Slonko in their previous two conversations. Nothing at all, as if the matter were unknown to him. Suddenly now, he had pulled Tatiana out of his hat with the proud air of a peacock. He was bluffing. Had they caught her, Alexander would have been asked about her sooner. Slonko would have certainly brought up that they were looking for her and could not find her. But there had been not a word from him about Dimitri, not a word about Sayers, and not a word about Tatiana.

Still, he was alone, and Slonko was with three guards. There was bright light shining directly into Alexander's face, there was the feeling of weakness all over his body, of no sleep, of mental exhaustion, of an aching wound in his back, and there was his weighted-down heart. He said nothing, but the effort cost him considerable resources. How many resources did he have left? In 1936 when he was arrested he had all his resources and he had not been wounded. Why couldn't he have met Slonko then? Alexander grit his teeth and waited for the rest.

"Your wife is being questioned at this very moment—"

"By someone other than you?" said Alexander. "I'm surprised, comrade, that you would entrust someone else with such an important job. You must have many qualified men working for you."

"Major, do you remember what happened three years ago in 1940?"

"Yes, I fought in the war with Finland. I was wounded and received a medal of valor and was promoted to second lieutenant."

"I'm not talking about that."

"Ah."

"In 1940, the Soviet government established rules for women who failed to renounce their husbands for crimes committed under Article 58 of the Penal Code. Failure to renounce your spouse was a crime punishable by ten years in a hard labor camp. Do you know anything about that?"

"Not much, comrade, thankfully. I was not married in 1940."

"I'm going to level with you, Major Belov, because I'm tired of

playing games. Your wife, Dr. Sayers, and a man named Dimitri Chernenko tried to escape—"

"Wait," said Alexander. "Surely Dr. Sayers was not escaping?
Wasn't he with the Red Cross? They're free to cross international borders, no?"

"Yes," snapped Slonko. "But your wife and her companion were not.
There was a border incident in which Private Chernenko was shot."

"Was he your witness?" Alexander smiled. "I hope he wasn't your
only witness."

"Your wife and Dr. Sayers made it to Helsinki."

Alexander remained smiling.

"But the doctor was gravely wounded. Do you know how we know
that, Major? Because we called the hospital in Helsinki. We were told
that the doctor died two days ago."

The smile was frozen on Alexander's face.

"We were also told by the very helpful Red Cross doctor that Sayers
had come in with a wounded Red Cross nurse. She fits the description
of Tatiana Metanova. Small, blonde, apparently pregnant? A gash on
her face? That would be her?"

Alexander made no motion.

"I thought so. We had asked him to keep hold of her until our men
got there. We met up with her in the Helsinki hospital and brought her
back early this morning. Do you have any questions?"

"Yes," said Alexander, struggling with himself to stand. He decided
to remain sitting. He steeled his face and he steeled his arms and he
steeled his entire body. But it was no use. His legs were shaking. Yet in a
steely voice he said, "What do you want from me?"

"The truth."

Time—what a funny thing it was. In Lazarevo, it had blinked
through them; blink and gone. What was it doing now, standing still, as
he tried to breathe through the seconds, as he tried to keep calm. For a
moment as he looked down onto the dirty wood floor, he thought, to
save her, I will tell him the truth. I will sign his fucking paper. From me,
there actually *is* truth. I *am* who he says. But then he thought, what
about Corporal Maikov? His truth was that he had known nothing; certainly he had not known me. What truth could he have given them before they shot him? To Slonko, lies are truth and truth is a lie. The
answers we give, the answers we keep hidden, he knows it's all a sham,
yet his life's achievement is measured by the success of how many lies he
can get out of us. He doesn't think I'm anymore Alexander Barrington

than Stepanov is, than Maikov was. What he wants is for me to lie so he can declare his mission a success. What he wants is the seventeen-year-old boy he never got to question. The nerve—the audacity!—of a convicted agitator to escape and not die. That's what he's responding to. What he wants is for me to sign a piece of paper that will tell him it's all right to kill me, now, seven years later, whether or not I'm Alexander Barrington. He wants absolution for killing me. With my confession I would give it to him.

Slonko was twisting the truth, trying to make Alexander weak. Tatiana had disappeared, that was true. They were looking for her—also true. Maybe they did call the Helsinki Red Cross. Maybe they did find out that Sayers had died. Poor Sayers. Maybe they did find out there was a nurse with him and without knowing her name, just from the description alone, they deduced it was Alexander's wife. It had only been a few days. Could they really have gotten one of their operatives to Helsinki that quickly? They had trouble retrieving supply trucks from Leningrad barely seventy kilometers away. Helsinki was five hundred kilometers from here. Could they really have not just intercepted her, but brought her back, too?

Would Tania have stuck around Helsinki? True, Alexander had told her they couldn't stay in that city, but in her abandoned distress, would she have remembered?

Alexander lifted his gaze back to Slonko, who was staring at him with the expression of a man who is rubbing his hands together before he digs into the feast in front of him. With the expression of a man who is about to witness the goring of the matador.

Coldly Alexander said, "Is there some truth you haven't gotten from me, comrade?"

"Maybe, Major Belov, you don't care for your own life, but surely you will talk to us when the life of your pregnant spouse is at stake?"

"I will repeat my question to you, comrade," said Alexander, "in case you didn't hear me the first time. Is there something you want I haven't given you?"

"Yes, you haven't given me the truth!" exclaimed Slonko, slapping Alexander very hard across the face.

"No!" Alexander's teeth were grit. "What I haven't given you is the satisfaction of knowing you were right. You think you've finally caught the man you've been chasing. I'm telling you, you are wrong. You will not take your impotence out on me. I need to be brought in front of a military tribunal. I am not one of your small-time Party prisoners you can bully into submission. I am a decorated officer in the Red Army. Have you ever served your country in a war, comrade?" Alexander stood up. He was a head taller than Slonko. "I didn't think so. I want to be brought up in front of General Mekhlis. We will resolve this matter immediately. You want to get at the truth, Slonko? Let's get to it. The war still needs *me*. While you," Alexander said, "have to run back to your Leningrad jail."

Slonko cursed. He ordered the two guards to restrain Alexander, which they did with difficulty.

"You've got nothing on me," Alexander said loudly. "My accuser is dead, otherwise you would have brought him to me. The authority over me lies with my commanding officer, Colonel Stepanov, and with General Mekhlis who has ordered my arrest. They will tell you that I received an *Order of the Red Star* in front of five Red Army generals prior to Operation Spark. I was wounded in the storming of the river, and for my effort in the war I received the *Hero of the Soviet Union* medal."

Slonko could barely get the words out. "Where is this medal, Major?"

"My wife took it for safekeeping. Surely, if you have her in your custody, you'll be able to take a look at the medal." Alexander smiled. "It will be the only time you'll get a chance to look at one."

"*I* am the interrogating officer!" Slonko yelled, red in the face and his bald head, striking Alexander again.

"Ah fuck!" Alexander yelled back. "You are not an officer! *I* am an officer. You have no power over me."

"That's where you're wrong, Major," said Slonko. "I do have power over you, and do you know why?"

When Alexander didn't answer, Slonko leaned closer. "Because very soon I am going to have power over your wife."

"Really?" Alexander said, ripping his arms away from his guards, jumping up, kicking away the chair behind him. "Do you have power even over your own? I doubt you'll have power over mine."

Slonko did not back away as he replied, "Oh, be sure I will and I intend to tell you all about it."

"Please do," Alexander said, stepping away from the fallen chair. "Then I will instantly know you're lying."

Slonko snarled into his face.

"Comrade," said Alexander, "I am not the man you're looking for."

"You are that man, Major. Everything you say and do only convinces me further of it."

ᏟᎲᎲᎲᎲᎧ

Back in his small cold cell, Alexander thanked God for his clothes.

They had left the kerosene lamp in his cell and the eye of the guard never left the porthole.

Alexander could not *believe* that what was happening to him came down not to ideology, not to communism, not to treason, or even to espionage, but to the pride of one small man.

Dimitri and Slonko were cut from the same cloth. Dimitri, petty-minded and small-hearted, was first cousin to Slonko who actually had some clout to back up his malice. Dimitri had nothing and his helplessness infuriated him all the more. Now he was dead. Not soon enough.

Alexander was sitting in the corner when he heard the lock turn. He sighed. They just weren't going to leave him alone, were they?

Slonko walked in, leaving the door open behind him. The guard remained just outside. Slonko stood a good twenty centimeters below the ceiling of the cell. He ordered Alexander to stand. Alexander reluctantly stood, bent at the knees, his own head five or six centimeters above the ceiling of the cage. Because of that, his slightly forward-leaning form looked ready to spring, though his head was bent in a way that may have seemed to Slonko like subservience.

"Well, well. Your wife Tatiana is quite an interesting woman," said Slonko. "I just finished with her." He rubbed his hands together. "Quite interesting indeed."

Alexander glanced at the open door. Where was the guard? He reached into the inside pocket of his BVDs and Slonko yelled, "What are you doing?" But he wasn't armed. He did not pull out a weapon.

"I'm getting my penicillin shot," Alexander said. "I was wounded." He smiled. "I need to take my medicine. I'm not the man I used to be in January, comrade."

"That's good to know," Slonko replied. "Are you the man you used to be in 1936?"

"Yes, I am still that man," said Alexander.

"While you're fixing yourself up, let me tell you what your wife told us about you—"

"Before you continue," interrupted Alexander, opening the vial of morphine and not even looking at Slonko, "I have read that there are some countries in the world where it is against the law to force a wife to give information about her husband. Amazing, isn't it?" He dipped the needle into the vial and then slowly drew the morphine solution up into the hollow barrel.

"Oh, we didn't force her," Slonko smiled. "She gave it up quite willingly." He smiled again. "And it's not the only thing—"

"Comrade!" Alexander yelled, taking a small step forward. "I am warning you. Do *not* continue." He was a half-meter away from Slonko. He could put his hands on Slonko's shoulders in a fraternal gesture if such a gesture were called for at this time. It wasn't.

"No?"

"No," said Alexander. "Trust me with this, Comrade Slonko. You are inciting the wrong man."

"Oh, why is that?" Slonko asked warmly. "Because you *won't* be incited?"

"Quite the opposite," replied Alexander. "Because I will be."

Slonko fell quiet.

Alexander fell quiet.

"Well, aren't you going to shoot yourself full of penicillin, Major?"

"When you leave, yes."

"I'm not leaving."

Alexander shook his head without stepping back to the wall. "Stick to the business at hand. Have you gotten me a tribunal in front of a military command? I'm sure you will be welcome to sit in on the proceedings, to hear an innocent man acquit himself in your country."

"In *your* country, Major," Slonko corrected Alexander.

"In my country," agreed Alexander, not moving any part of his body. The cell was barely two meters long, a meter wide. He waited. He knew that Slonko did not have a tribunal set up. He had not been given the authority for anything—for a tribunal, for an execution, for a thorough investigation. He wanted a confession out of Alexander while no one else gave a damn. For all Alexander knew, since the star witness was lying dead in the snow, Mekhlis himself could have already said to Slonko, free Belov. We can't afford to lose good men, we have no information on his espionage except from a dead deserter, and Stalin did not issue an order for Belov's death, which is the only order I will listen to. At the same time, Slonko was not giving up. Why?

Slonko could not touch him. Alexander would pass a man like Slonko on the street and not acknowledge him. That's how far the proletariat had come. A man like Slonko, a Party pig all his life, had no power over a man like Alexander, his prey for seven years.

That was so right in Alexander's world, yet obviously so wrong in Slonko's.

Alexander waited. After a few moments, he said, "Why don't you leave, comrade, and come back when you've got something more. Bring me before the generals. Or bring me my release order."

"Major, you will never be free again," said Slonko. "I have recommended that you will never be free."

"When I die I will be."

"I will not allow your death. Your mother has died. Your father has died. I want you to live the life they planned for you, the life they brought you here for. They both thought so much of you, Alexander Barrington. They both told me so. Do you think you have fulfilled their dreams?"

"I don't know about *them*, but I have fulfilled my own mother and father's dreams, yes. They were simple farmers. I have gone far in the Red Army. They would be proud of me."

"What about your wife's hopes, Major? Do you think you have fulfilled your wife's?"

"Comrade, I have already told you—do not speak to me about my wife."

"No? She was quite willing to talk about you. When she wasn't—ahem—otherwise—"

"Comrade!" Alexander stepped toward Slonko. "That will be the *last* time," he said. "There will be no more."

"I will not leave."

"You will leave. You are dismissed. Come back when you've got something."

"Oh, I'm not leaving, Major," said Slonko. "The more you want me to, the more I want to stay."

"I don't doubt it. You *will* leave, though." Not a flicker moved through Alexander, who stood as if he were a statue. He was barely breathing.

"Major! I'm not the one arrested. I'm not the one whose wife has been arrested. I'm not the American."

"As to the last, I'm not either."

"You are, you are, Major. Your own wife told me so when she finished sucking my cock."

Alexander's hand slammed into Slonko's throat. Slonko didn't even have time to breathe in his surprise. His head snapped back against the concrete wall, eyes bulging, mouth open. With his free hand, Alexander plunged a syringe filled with ten grains of morphine through Slonko's sternum, straight into the right chamber of his heart. He pressed his palm against the thumb plate and snapped Slonko's jaws shut. Slonko could not emit a single sound even if he wanted to.

In English, Alexander said, "I'm surprised at you. Didn't you know who you were dealing with?" Gritting his teeth, he squeezed Slonko's neck, and saw the eyes first cloud, then glaze over. He whispered, "This is for my mother . . . and my father . . . and for Tatiana."

Convulsing, Slonko was sinking to the ground. Alexander held him up with one hand on his throat, as Slonko's neck muscles stretched and relaxed, as his pupils dilated, and when Slonko stopped blinking, Alexander let go of his neck. The chief investigator dropped to the floor like a heap of stones. Alexander pulled out the empty syringe from Slonko's chest, threw it down the drainpipe, came up to the door and yelled, "Guard! Guard! Something is wrong with Comrade Slonko!"

The guard ran in, looked around the room, looked at Slonko limp on the floor and said in a confused voice, "What happened?"

"I don't know," Alexander said calmly. "I'm not a doctor. But maybe you should get one. The comrade may have had a heart attack."

The guard didn't know whether to run, to stay, to leave Alexander, to take him along. He didn't know whether to lock the door or to leave it open. The confusion was so apparent on his frightened and pale face that Alexander, smiling kindly, said, "Leave him here, and take me with you. Don't bother locking the cell. He is not going anywhere."

The guard took Alexander and they both ran up the stairs, through the school, outside, and to the commandant's building. "I don't even know who I should speak to," the guard said helplessly.

"Let's go and talk to Colonel Stepanov. He'll know what to do."

To say that Stepanov was surprised to see Alexander would have been an understatement. The guard by this time was in such a panic he was not able to speak. He mumbled something about Slonko and no noise and just doing his job, just standing right by the door, hearing nothing. Stepanov asked him several times to calm down, but the guard was unable to follow simple orders. Finally, Stepanov had to offer the boy a drink of vodka, and turned to Alexander with a perplexed face.

"Sir," said Alexander, "Comrade Slonko collapsed while he was in my cell. The guard was obviously away for a few moments"—Alexander paused—"perhaps attending to some private business. He is afraid it will seem that he was derelict in his duty. Yet, I know firsthand he is a diligent and dedicated guard. There was nothing he could have done for the comrade."

"Oh, my God, Alexander," said Stepanov, getting up and quickly getting dressed. "Are you telling me Slonko is dead?"

"Sir, I don't know. I'm not a doctor. I would recommend finding one, though. Probably soon."

They procured a medic who came to the cell, shuddered once, and without even listening for Slonko's pulse pronounced the man dead. The cell had a filthy stench it had not had before. Everyone held their breath as they filed out.

"Oh, Alexander," said Stepanov.

"Yes, sir," said Alexander, "I seem to have bad fucking luck."

No one had any idea what to do with Slonko. He had come to Alexander's cell at two in the morning. Everyone else was soundly asleep. There was nowhere to put Alexander, who offered to sleep in Stepanov's anteroom with the guard by his side. Stepanov agreed. "Thank you, sir," said Alexander, lying down on the floor and putting his head down. Stepanov glanced at the trembling guard in the corner, and then back at Alexander. "What the hell is going on, Major?" he whispered, crouching by him.

"You tell me, Colonel," said Alexander. "What did Slonko want with me? He kept telling me they've brought Tatiana back from Helsinki, that she's confessed. What was he talking about?"

"They're beside themselves," Stepanov said. "They tried to find her, but she is nowhere. People don't just disappear in the Soviet Union—"

"Actually, sir—"

"Not without a trace."

"Actually, sir—"

"Alexander, stop being impossible."

"Yes, sir."

"I'm telling you that once the Grechesky hospital told the NKGB—"

"The what?"

"Oh, they haven't informed you? NKVD is gone. Now it's the NKGB. The People's Kommitet on Government Security. Same agency, different name. First name change since 1934." Stepanov shrugged. "Anyway. Once the NKGB was informed that Sayers and Metanova had not made it to the Leningrad hospital, they got very suspicious. They have a turned-over truck, they have four dead Soviet troops and a handful of Finnish ones, no first aid kit in the truck, and in fact, the Red Cross symbol had been torn out of the cabin's canvas. No one can explain it. There is no trace of either the doctor or his nurse. Yet six border stations along the way say they checked through a doctor and his nurse returning to Helsinki with a wounded Finnish pilot in a prisoner exchange. They cannot remember the nurse's name, but they swear it was American. Well, we have the wounded Finnish pilot. He is neither Finnish, nor a pilot, and wounded is a euphemism for what he is. He is your friend Dimitri and he is ripped full of holes. That's the situation on the ground. He's dead, and the doctor and the nurse have vanished into thin air. So Mitterand called the Helsinki Red Cross hospital and found a doctor who doesn't speak any Russian. It took the bumbling idiots"— Stepanov was barely whispering at this point—"it took them a whole day to find someone to talk to the doctor in English." Stepanov smiled. "I was going to suggest you."

Alexander stayed impassive.

"Anyway, they finally got someone from Volkhov to speak to the doctor in English. From what I can understand, Matthew Sayers has died."

"So that much was true." Alexander sighed. "They all have such a way of mixing their lies with just enough truth that you go mad trying to uncover what's real and what isn't."

"Yes, Sayers died in Helsinki. Blood poisoning from his wounds. As for the nurse with him, the doctor said that she had gone and he hadn't seen her for two days. He assumed she was no longer in Finland."

Alexander stared at Stepanov with sadness and relief. For a sick moment he actually felt regret that they hadn't brought Tatiana back; he thought maybe he could lay his eyes on her one last time. But finally something real bobbed to the surface. "Thank you, sir," Alexander whispered.

Stepanov patted Alexander on the back. "Sleep now. You need your strength. Are you hungry? I have some smoked sausage and some bread."

"Leave it for me, but right now I sleep."

Stepanov disappeared into his quarters and Alexander, the heaviness from his soul having lifted like morning fog, thought before he fell asleep that indeed Tania had listened to his every word and did not remain in Helsinki. She must have gone on to Stockholm. Perhaps she was in Stockholm now. He also thought that Sayers must have done right by her to the end, because had he broken and told Tatiana the truth about Alexander's "death," then Tatiana would have already been back in the Soviet Union right in the clutches of the man who—Oh, Tatiana, my—

But that was all he had.

At least fucking Dimitri was dead.

Fitfully, he slept.

The Bridge over the Volga, 1936

Alexander was asked who he was at seventeen, at the Kresty prison after he was arrested. They were indifferent about it then—they knew. They asked, they went away—for days at a time—they came back, and then they said, "Are you Alexander Barrington?"

"I am, yes," said Alexander, because then he did not have another answer and he thought the truth would protect him.

And then they read him his sentence. There was no courtroom for Alexander in those days, no tribunal presided over by generals. There was an empty windowless concrete cell with bars for doors and a toilet bucket on the concrete floor and no privacy, and there was a naked bulb up high. They made him stand as they read to him from a piece of paper in sonorous voices. There were two men, and as if Alexander didn't understand the first one, the second one took the paper and read it to him again.

Alexander heard his name, loud and clear, "Alexander Barrington," and he heard the sentence, louder and clearer: "Ten years in forced labor camp in Vladivostok for anti-Soviet agitation in Moscow in 1935 and for efforts to undermine Soviet authority and the Soviet state by calling into scurrilous and spurious question the economics lessons of the Father and Teacher." He heard ten years; he thought he had *mis*heard. It was a good thing they read it to him again. He almost said, where is my father, he will solve this, he will tell me what to do.

But he didn't say that. He knew that whatever befell him, befell his mother and father as it had befallen the seventy-eight people who had once lived at the hotel with them in Moscow, the piano group Alexander sometimes went to, the group of communists he and his father belonged to, his friend Slavan, the old Tamara.

They asked him if he understood the charges against him; did he understand the punishment meted out to him?

He didn't understand. He nodded anyway.

He was busy trying to envision the life he was meant to live. The life his father had wanted him to live. He wanted to ask his father if spending his youth fulfilling two of Stalin's Five Year Plans for the industrialization of Soviet Russia—part of the fixed capital that Alexander understood so well because he knew precisely what was not working in the socialist state—was what Harold had wanted for Alexander. But his father wasn't around to ask.

Was Alexander's destiny to mine for gold in the tundra of Siberia because the utopian state couldn't afford to pay him?

"Do you have any questions?"

"Where is my mother?" asked Alexander. "I want to say goodbye to her."

The guards laughed. "Your mother? How the fuck should we know where your mother is? You're leaving tomorrow morning. See if you can find her by then."

Laughing, they left. Standing, Alexander remained.

And the next day he was put on a train to Vladivostok. The scarred, knotted man next to him said, "We're lucky they're taking us to Vladivostok. I just came back from Perm-35. Now *that* is hell on earth."

"Oh, where is that?"

"Near the city of Molotov. Have you heard of it? Near the Ural Mountains on the Kama River. It's not as far as Vladivostok, but it's much worse. No one who goes there survives."

"You survived."

"Because I served only two years, and they let me out. I exceeded my production quota for five quarters in a row. They were pleased with my capitalist productivity. They thought the proletariat in me had worked hard enough for the common man."

Once Alexander placed Vladivostok on a map of the Soviet Union, he knew that, though he had no money and no home, he had to escape if he were to have any chance of living. The city was in the bowels of the world, and if there was a Hades on earth, then to him Vladivostok seemed it. To travel by cattle train through the Ural Mountains, through the west Siberian plain, through the central Siberian plateau, past all of Mongolia, and around all of China to rot in an industrial cement city on a thin strip of land on the shores of the Sea of Japan. Alexander was sure there was no return from the catacomb that was Vladivostok.

For a thousand kilometers Alexander looked out of the small porthole in the train, or out of the doors the guards sometimes left open to give the prisoners some air. He saw his chance when they were coming up to cross the River Volga. I will jump, he thought. The Volga was far down below, the wobbly rail bridge high over a precipice, maybe thirty meters high, a hundred feet by American standards. Alexander didn't know much about the Volga; was it rocky? Was it deep? Was it fast? But he saw it was wide, and he knew it emptied a thousand kilometers south in Astrakhan into the Caspian Sea. He didn't know if he would get another—better—chance. But he knew that if he managed to survive the Volga, he could make his way into one of the southern republics, Georgia, maybe, or Armenia, and then cross the border into Turkey. He wished he had his mother's American dollars. After they returned from the failed trip to Moscow he had put the book back in the library and then was arrested so quickly he never had a chance to retrieve it. But even without the money, he knew escape or death were his only choices.

He looked down and his stomach twisted. Could he survive? It struck him that he didn't want to die. He remembered William Miller in Barrington. Nice, blond, popular William Miller. Had been taking swimming lessons since he was five weeks old. He could jump and somersault and hold his breath under water, he could outswim and outjump any other kid in Barrington, including Alexander, who certainly didn't shy away from trying. And then one summer afternoon when they were eight, they were playing Tarzan in the Olympic-sized pool at William's house, jumping cannonball into the deep end, into what was supposed to be twelve feet of water. William jumped from a diving board *two* feet high into twelve feet of water. But what William didn't consider was large-boned Ben down the street, who, at the moment of William's ill-timed upside-down cannonball, was treading water too close to the diving board. William saw Ben just a millisecond too late and lurched to the left to avoid Ben's substantial form. William's head hit the concrete wall of the pool, snapped and popped, and from then on William Miller was wheeled around by a twenty-four-hour-a-day nurse and was fed through a tube in his stomach. Strange? Could it be any more strange than a seventeen-year-old boy, nearly six foot three and 180 pounds, throwing himself down one hundred feet into what might be eight feet of water with boulders for a bottom? Alexander couldn't recite the immutable laws of physics on that one, but something was telling him they were not in his favor. There was no time to panic and no time to think. He knew he could be jumping to his death. He knew it. His stomach knew it. His exploding heart knew it. But this death would at least be quick. He crossed himself. In Vladivostok he would be dying for the rest of his life.

He mouthed, *help me God*, and jumped from the train with only the prison clothes he was wearing.

A hundred feet was a long way to fall, though it took but a few seconds; the train was nearly on the other side of the river by the time he reached the water. He had jumped feet first and hoped the Volga was deep enough to withstand his fall. It was. It was also cold and very fast. The river current grabbed him and carried him half a kilometer, fighting the whole way for a gulp of air, and by the time he turned his head to the bridge, the train was just a speck in the distance. It didn't look as if it had stopped. He wasn't sure if anyone even noticed, except for the convict next to him, who had been smirking from Leningrad to the Volga, and muttering, "A strapping young lad, just wait till Vladivostok, wait to see what'll become of ya."

He didn't want to risk getting out of the water until he could no longer see the bridge. He swam with the current, maybe five kilometers, and finally became tired and crawled out. It was summer and drying off was quick. Alexander dug some potatoes out of the ground, ate them raw, took off his clothes, made himself a bed out of leaves, and a lean-to canopy out of twigs (thank God for Cub Scouts) and then slept. When he woke up, his clothes were damp and his legs sore. He didn't know how to make himself new clothes, so he built a fire, dried the clothes and turned them inside out, so the prison gray wouldn't be as clearly visible. He smeared green leaves all over himself to further disguise the color, some mud, some strawberry pulp, and when the clothes were unrecognizable as having been issued by the NKVD, he set out again, staying close to the river.

Alexander traveled downstream on the Volga on barges and fishing boats, offering his fishing services until one fisherman asked him for his domestic passport. After that, Alexander veered away, walking deeper inland, hoping to find his way to the mountains between Georgia and Turkey. He stayed away from fisherman and from farmers—he knew sooner or later someone from whom he could not get away would ask for his domestic passport. His had been taken from him, and he had been issued a prison workbook; certainly he could not have shown that. He burned it.

Traveling without accepting help had the great disadvantage of slowness. Walking would only get him thirty or less kilometers a day. Alexander had to risk hitching rides in horse carriages to get south a little faster.

It was the fifteen-year-old girl working in the fields through which he was passing who stopped him. Long enough to ask for a drink, to ask for some bread, to ask if there was any work he could do to make some spare cash. She brought him home by the hand to her open-hearted parents. She of the large warm calloused farmer's hand, she of the thick long light-brown hair, the round face, the round flesh, the perspiration around the neck and the arms, and a glistening chest on which a small gold cross lay, nearly horizontally, so healthy and young was she.

Alexander didn't get as far as Georgia. He ended up staying in Belyi Gor, a village near Krasnodar by the Black Sea, still in the republic of Russia where—because he had noticed Larissa and it was August and harvesting season—he offered his fieldhand services to the farmer's family, the Belovs. Yefim and Maritza Belov had four sons, Grisha, Valery, Sasha, Anton, and a daughter.

The Belovs had no room for him in their small farmhouse, but he stayed gladly in the barn, slept on hay, worked from sunup to sundown and at night thought about Larissa. She smiled at him with her parted mouth, pretending to be constantly out of breath. Alexander knew it was a ruse, but it worked, for he had been starved and needed feeding. His body had been too tense for too long, on the run and on guard. Larissa was the promise of relief.

But Alexander stayed away. Her brothers were not the trifling types. Working in the fields digging potatoes, carrots, onions, threshing wheat for the collective farm or *kolkhoz* without the help of animals had made them like oxen, and living around their adolescent, tumescent, eager sister had made them more than a little wary of migrant workers like Alexander, who took off their shirts and worked in their trousers, getting slicker and more tanned by each sun-drenched day. Alexander was seventeen, but he looked like a man and ate like a man, and worked like a man. In all ways, he had the appetites of a man and the heart of one. Larissa saw it. The brothers saw it. He stayed away. He offered to make hay bales. He offered to chop winter wood for the family. He offered to build them a new—bigger—table, hoping he would remember from the childhood days with his father what it was like to use the saw, a plane, hammer and nails. He offered all this, hoping his work would keep him out of the fields and in the barn.

Of course the more Alexander remained aloof, the more Larissa pushed forward, becoming as brazen as a fifteen-year-old girl could get living in a small farmhouse with her parents and four brothers.

It was late August in scorching Krasnodar by the Black Sea. And one afternoon when he was in the barn tying up the hay into neat stacks, he saw the light stream on the ground and when he turned around, the light stream was gone, blacked out by Larissa who stood in front of him.

In his hands he held a pitchfork, a ball of twine, and a knife. She asked him in a low voice what he was doing. Making hay bales, he was going to reply, but realized she knew and he didn't have to say a word. Under different circumstances, he would have not stopped himself. He could barely stop himself now. But the girl was trouble; he felt it.

"Larissa, this is going to end in no good," he said.

"I don't know what you mean," she said, sauntering closer. She was barefoot and was wearing what was barely a dress. "It's godlessly hot out there. I came in for a little shade in the middle of the day. You don't mind, do you?"

He turned his back to her, bending to the hay. "Your brothers will kill me."

"Why would they do that? You're working so hard. They'll applaud you." She came closer. He could smell the summer sweat on her body. She inhaled. She could smell his.

"Stop."

She took another step toward him and stopped. His back was still to her but with his peripheral vision he saw her jump on top of a wooden stable gate. "I'll just sit here and watch you," he heard her say.

He watched *her* for a moment, and then went back to his work. His body was nearly giving out. In one moment, he thought, in one moment, I could have such sweet relief, and it would take but a moment. No harm done. She was close enough to him that he could smell her farm fresh body, her washed hair, her breath. He closed his eyes momentarily.

"Alexander," she said huskily. "Look. I want to show you something."

Aching, reluctant, desperate, he looked. She slowly pulled up her skirt and slightly opened her legs. Her hips were just below Alexander's eye level. His gaze stopped between her bare thighs. A groan escaped him.

"Come here, Alexander."

He came. Pushing her hands away, he stood between her legs, and pulled down her dress to expose her body. Panting, perspiring, ravenous, he raised his head to her lips and then feverishly bent to her breasts, while his fingers caressed her, the softness, the warmth . . . she was moaning as she clutched the bar—and then laughter sounded right outside the barn, and Larissa tried to push Alexander away. He wasn't moving from her.

Larissa shoved him hard, jumping down from the beam, and the light was on the grass, and Grisha, her oldest brother, came in and said, "Larisska, there you are, I've been looking all over for you. Get out of here. Stop trying to corrupt our Alexander. Can't you see he's got real work to do? Go to Mama. She wants to know why you haven't gotten the cows from the pasture yet. The *kolkhoznik* will be here for the milk soon."

"I'm going," said Larissa, walking past Alexander. Grisha left first, and before Larissa disappeared she turned around and with a delicious smile on her face whispered, "Alexander, next time we won't be interrupted and my mouth will be *all* over you, I promise. And afterward I will call you Shura, instead of Sasha like my brother. Just you wait."

Alexander could think about nothing else for the rest of the day, or the evening, or certainly the night alone in his barn. But the next day something happened that stopped him from self-immolation. It was Larissa's pale face in the morning. When he approached her, she put her hands up and without looking at him said, "I'm not feeling well."

"I don't mind," he said. "I'll make you feel better."

She pushed him weakly away and, without glancing at him, said, "Stay away, Alexander. Do yourself a favor. Stay away from me."

Perplexed he went to do his work. He didn't see her for the rest of the day, but in the evening during dinner, Larissa's now extremely pale face was accompanied by fever. The fever was higher the following evening and was miserably followed by a red raised rash on her face a day later.

Oh no, the grown-ups said in a panic. She is *sick*.

And then came Alexander's fever and his rash, but by the time he was sick, no one said *oh no* in a panic. Because the horseman of the apocalypse sat atop a pale horse that they all knew was typhus, the incurable, contagious, deadly pestilence. The headache that preceded the onset of the disease was so severe, so throbbing, so eye-poppingly wretched that by the time the 105°F fever and the scabby, scratchy, inflamed rash came, Alexander welcomed the distracting delirium that accompanied it. The brothers were feverish and Larissa was hemorrhaging, and then the parents were delirious, and Larissa was dead. One minute pressed against Alexander's burning hands, the next dead and unburied as they were all too weak to dig a hole for her, and so she lay in the *izba*, and they all panted feebly and waited for the horseman to come for them. And it did.

In the end, only Larissa's father, Yefim, and Alexander remained. They had not been outside in many days, weeks maybe? They held on to each other and drank water, and prayed, and Alexander started praying in English, mixing it with Russian, pleading for peace, for his mother and father, pleading for their lives, praying for America, for health, for his life, for his mother, for Teddy, Belinda, Boston, Barrington, for the woods, for death finally because he couldn't take it anymore, and then he saw Yefim's tormented eyes watching him, felt Yefim's hand on him, heard Yefim's bleeding mouth whispering to him, "Son, don't die, don't die here like this. Go back to your father and mother. Find your way back home. Where is your home, son?"

Yefim died. Alexander did not. After spending six weeks in quarantine, he got better. The Soviet authorities, to prevent the outbreak of disease in the fall heat over the Caucasus region, burned the village of Belyi Gor and all the bodies and huts and barns and fields contained therein. Alexander, who remained alive but had no identity, got himself a new identity as Yefim's third son Alexander Belov. When the Soviet council workers came with masks on their faces and clipboards to their chests and in muffled voices asked, "Your name?" Alexander without hesitation said, "Alexander Belov." They checked against the birth records for Belyi Gor, against the available records for the Belov family and issued Alexander a new domestic passport that allowed him to travel in the Soviet Union without getting stopped and arrested for lack of documents. Alexander was put on a train and with written permission from the regional *Soviet* made his way back to Leningrad and went to live with Mira Belov, Yefim's sister. Mira was taken aback to see him. Fortunately for Alexander, she had not seen the family and the real Alexander Belov in twelve years and though she pointed out with surprise Alexander's black hair and dark eyes, the leanness and the height ("Sasha, I can't get over it. You were so short and blond and chubby when you were five!"), she couldn't remember well enough to become suspicious. Alexander stayed, sleeping on a cot in the hall, a cot that was half a meter too short for him. He ate dinner with Mira and her husband and her husband's parents and tried to be in their apartment as little as possible. He had a plan. He needed to finish school and then he would join the army.

Alexander didn't have time to remember, to think, to ache. He had only one mission—to see his parents again—and he had only one goal and one imperative—one way or another to leave the Soviet Union.

A New Best Friend, 1937

In the last six months of secondary school, Alexander met Dimitri Chernenko. Dimitri, nondescript and diminutive, kept sidling up to Alexander and asking questions, his curiosity pervasive, invasive and sometimes irritating. Dimitri was like the puppy Alexander never had. He seemed lonely and in need of friendship—and harmless. He was a scrawny kid with shaggy hair and eyes that constantly darted from one face to the next, never staying for more than a few seconds on anyone or anything. Yet the way he looked up to Alexander, literally looked up to him, the way his mouth opened in fawning awe when Alexander spoke, amused Alexander. Dimitri was easy to tease; he laughed at himself for always coming last in a race, for always missing the goal at football, for falling out of trees.

Once or twice, however, Alexander saw Dimitri bullying the younger boys in the school yard, and the second time when Dimitri tried to get Alexander to join in on the taunting of a petrified kid, Alexander pulled Dimitri aside and said, "What are you doing?" And Dimitri apologized and didn't do it again. Alexander attributed this lack of propriety to never being the popular one and overlooked it, just as he overlooked his off-color remarks about girls ("Doesn't she have a hot ass? Hey, you, hotass!"). Alexander would patiently point out the errors in tact and judgment and Dimitri was a willing student, reforming himself to the best of his abilities, though nothing Alexander could teach would make Dimitri kick the ball into the goal or finish first in a race, or listen to a girl talk about her hair without a bored sneer around his mouth. But in other ways, Dimitri became better behaved. And he laughed at all of Alexander's jokes, and that went a long way in friendship.

Dimitri was very interested in Alexander's tinge of an accent, but Alexander brushed off the questions. He didn't trust Dimitri, which said less about Dimitri than it said about Alexander who didn't trust anybody. Other than talking to Dimitri about his American past, Alexander and Dimitri managed to cover many other topics: communist politics (in hushed, mocking terms), girls (Dimitri had less experience than Alexander, i.e. none), and parents.

And that's when one afternoon while walking home, Dimitri let slip that his father was a guard at one of the city prisons, and not just any prison, but (in a glorious stage whisper) in *the House of Detention*, the most feared and hated of the Leningrad prisons. He said it, Alexander knew, because his father's position of power made Dimitri seem more powerful in Alexander's eyes. But it was at that moment that Alexander looked differently at Dimitri.

Suddenly he saw an opening in the porthole of destiny, a possibility of discovering what happened to his family, and that opportunity was enough for Alexander to swallow his hard-earned mistrust and confide in Dimitri. Alexander told Dimitri the truth about his past and asked for Dimitri's help in locating Harold and Jane Barrington. Dimitri, his eyes shining, said he would be glad to help Alexander, who in his gratefulness gave Dimitri a hug and said, "Dima, if you help me, God help me, I swear, I'll be your friend for life. I'll do anything for you."

Patting Alexander on the back, Dimitri replied that no thanks were necessary, he would help Alexander gladly because they were best friends, weren't they?

Alexander agreed that they were.

A few days later, Dimitri brought him the news about his mother. She had been "imprisoned without a right of correspondence."

Alexander remembered the old babushka Tamara and her husband. He knew what that meant. He remained composed in front of Dimitri, but that night he cried for his mother.

With Dimitri's father's help, they managed to get into the House of Detention for five minutes under the auspices of visiting Dimitri's father and doing a school report on the progress of the Soviet state against agitators and foreign traitors to the socialist cause.

Alexander saw his father for a few minutes one incongruously sunny and warm June afternoon. He had hoped for ten; maybe one or two alone. He got one or two, with Dimitri, Dimitri's father, and another guard. No privacy for Harold and Alexander Barrington.

Alexander had gone over what he wanted to say to his father until the few words were cut into his memory that neither anxiety nor fear could obliterate.

Dad! he wanted to say. Once when I was barely seven, you, me and Mom went to Revere Beach, remember? I swam until my teeth chattered, and you and I dug a large sand hole and built a sand bar and waited for the rising tide to wash the ocean in. We got so burned those hours on the beach, and then we went on the awesome Cyclone—three times—and ate cotton candy and ice cream until my stomach hurt and you smelled of sand and salt water and the sun, and you held my hand and said I too smelled like the sea. It was the happiest day of my life, and you gave that day to me, and when I close my eyes that's what I will remember. Don't worry about me. I will be all right. Don't worry about anything.

But he wasn't alone with his father for a moment to say those words to him, in any language. Alexander became afraid that Harold's emotion would alert the guard. Fortunately the apathetic sentry wasn't looking for subterfuge.

His father was the only one who spoke, in English, with a little lead-in help from Alexander. "Could the prisoner say something to us in English?" Alexander had asked the guard, who grunted and said, "All right. But make it short. I don't have time to waste."

"I'll say something short in English," said Harold. His voice barely strong enough to get the words out, he grasped Alexander by the hands and whispered, holding him tight, his eyes spilling over, "Would that I had died for thee, O Absalom, my son, my son!"

Saying nothing, Alexander stepped away and blinked back his father. At the end of those few short minutes in a bare concrete cell, Alexander's cost for keeping himself in control was a chipped tooth and a bit of his immortal soul. *I love you*, he mouthed silently, and then the door closed.

⌒⚭⚬

After that, Dimitri never left Alexander's side, which was all right with Alexander: he needed a friend.

It didn't take long for Dimitri to start formulating plans to get him and Alexander out of the Soviet Union. Since much of what Dimitri was saying echoed what Alexander already had been thinking and planning, Alexander saw no reason to stop him. And he saw no reason not to get Dimitri out with him. Two could fight better than one, could cover each other, could watch each other's back. That's what Alexander imagined. That Dimitri would be like a battle buddy. That Dimitri would watch his back.

But Alexander was patient, and Dimitri was not. Alexander knew the right time had to come, and would. They talked about taking trains down to Turkey, they talked about making their way to Siberia in the winter and walking across the Bering Strait ice. They talked about Finland and finally settled on it. It was the nearest and most accessible.

Alexander went every week to check on his *Bronze Horseman* book. What if someone checked it out? What if someone kept it? He couldn't help but feel that his money was not safe.

Having graduated secondary school, Alexander and Dimitri decided to enroll in the three-month program at the Officer Candidate School of the Red Army. The OCS was Dimitri's idea. He thought it would be a good way to impress girls. Alexander thought it would be an entry way into Finland if the Soviet Union and Finland went to war, which seemed likely: Russia did not like having a foreign country, a historical enemy, only twenty kilometers from Leningrad, arguably Russia's greatest city.

OCS was nothing like Alexander had imagined. The brutality of the instructors, the grueling schedule of the training, the constant humiliation by the sergeants in charge were all meant to break your spirit before war could. The humiliation was harder to bear than the running, the sweating in the cold, the rain. But worse than everything was being awoken after taps and told to stand for hours while some fucking cadet got taken to task for forgetting to shine his boots.

Alexander learned about imperfection in OCS, and about leadership, and about respect. He learned about keeping his mouth shut and about keeping his locker spotless and about being on time and about saying *yes, sir* when he wanted to say *fuck you*. He also learned that he was stronger and faster and quicker than other trainees, that he was neater, that he was more calm under pressure, and that he was less afraid.

He also learned that words spoken to him that were meant to rattle him actually did.

After experiencing the grunt duality of officer school—they wanted to make a man out of you by breaking your spirit until you had none left—Alexander was grateful only that he wasn't an enlisted man: they must have had it even harder.

And then Dimitri flunked OCS.

"Can you believe it? What bastards they all are, after putting me through such hell, to not let me graduate! What kind of stupid bullshit is that? I've got a good mind to write the commander a letter—who is the commander of OCS, Alexander? Do you see this letter? They're telling me I unloaded and loaded my weapon too slowly, and that I crawled on my belly like a fucking snake too slowly, and that in battle tests I didn't keep quiet enough, or exhibit enough leadership quality to be considered for an officer rank. Look at this: they're inviting me to join the enlisted ranks. Well, if I can't load my weapon fast enough for them as an officer, what good am I going to be as a fucking grunt?"

"Perhaps the standards are different for officers and regular soldiers."

"Sure they are! But they should be tougher for the frontoviks! After all, those are the guys who are first at the battle line. So they're flunking me out of a program that would have kept me in the rear where I would do the least damage, but instead offering me a position where I'm going to be thrown into the fucking war zone? No, thanks." Dimitri looked up at Alexander. "Did you get your letter?"

He had gotten it, of course, and was informed of his impending graduation as a second lieutenant, but he didn't think Dimitri was in any mood to hear that. To lie was impractical. Alexander told Dimitri the truth.

"Alexander, this is just idiotic. Our plans are completely fucked. What good are we to each other, with you an officer and me a private?" Dimitri hit himself on the head for emphasis. "I've got it! Great idea. Only one thing left to do—do you see it?"

"I don't see it."

"You've got to reject your second lieutenantship. Tell them you're honored and grateful, but you've reconsidered. They'll enlist you as a private in a few days, and then we'll be together in one unit and able to run together when the opportunity arises." He was gleefully smiling. "And for a moment I thought all was lost and our plans were as good as dead."

"Hold on, hold on." Alexander looked at Dimitri askance. "Dima, you want me to *what?*"

"Decline your officership."

"Why would I do that?"

"So we can execute our plans."

"Our plans haven't changed. If I'm second lieutenant, then I'm commanding a unit that has a sergeant who's in charge of your squad. We'll go to Finland together no matter what."

"Yes, but what good is it if we're not in the same unit? Those were our plans, Alexander."

"Our plans were to become officers together. We didn't say anything about becoming privates."

"All right, but our plans changed. We have to be flexible."

"Yes. But if we're both privates, we've got no power whatsoever."

"Who said anything about power? Who wants power?" Dimitri narrowed his eyes. "You?"

"I don't want power," Alexander said. "I want to be in a position to help us. You've got to admit, one of us being an officer gives us more options, more opportunity to get to where we need to be. I mean, if it were reversed and I flunked and you became an officer, I'd definitely want you to stay an officer. You could do so much for us."

"Yes," Dimitri said slowly, "but I didn't become an officer, did I?"

"Just dumb luck, Dima," Alexander said. "I'd think no more about it."

"I'm hardly going to be able to help thinking about it," said Dimitri, "since I'm about to become everybody's shitting pot."

Alexander said nothing. Dimitri spoke again. "I think it would be better if you and I were in the same squad."

"There is no guarantee of being in the same squad," Alexander said. "They'll send you to Karelia and me to the Crimea . . ." Alexander broke off. It was ridiculous. There was no way he was declining his officership. But by the look in Dimitri's eyes, by the hunched manner of Dimitri's shoulders, by the unpersuaded sneer of Dimitri's mouth, Alexander heard the first tear in the fabric of his and Dimitri's friendship. Shoddy Soviet workmanship, Alexander decided, and worked harder to convince Dimitri that this was going to work out. "Dima, think how much better your life will be in the army if I'm in the commissioned ranks, helping you out every step of the way. Better food. Better cigarettes. Better vodka. Better assignments. Better girls."

Dimitri looked skeptical.

"I'm your ally and your friend, and I'll be in a position to help you."

Dimitri still looked skeptical.

And rightly so, for, despite Alexander's proffered hand, life was only marginally easier for Dimitri. But there was no denying it—it was *considerably* easier for Alexander. He was quartered better, he was fed better, he was allowed more privileges and liberties, he was paid better, he received better weapons, he was privy to sensitive military information, and a better class of woman threw herself at him at the officers' club. The benefit to Dimitri was that Alexander *was* his commanding officer at the Leningrad garrison—with two sergeants and a corporal in between. But it was a dubious benefit the first time Alexander shouted at Dimitri for not maintaining order during a forward march and saw Dimitri coil up. Alexander knew he was either going to continue to shout orders at everyone including Dimitri, which was clearly not acceptable to Dimitri, or not shout orders at anyone, which was clearly not acceptable to the Red Army.

Alexander transferred Dimitri into another unit, placing him under the command of one of his quartermates, Lieutenant Sergei Komkov—permanently damaging his relationship with Komkov.

"Belov, you ought to be drawn and quartered," the short, nearly bald Komkov said to him one evening at cards. "What were you thinking asking me to take Chernenko? He is the biggest pussy I've ever seen! He is a worthless excuse for a soldier. My little sister is braver. He can't do anything right but hates to be told what to do. Can we court martial him for cowardice?"

Alexander laughed. "Come on, he's a good guy. You'll see he'll be good in battle."

"Belov, cut the shit. Today I was nearly going to shoot him for desertion when he dropped his rifle during a march and then had to step three paces out of formation to pick it up. I actually cocked my weapon at him, for which I was sorry. Then, to make it up to him, I put him in charge of cleaning the officers' latrine."

"Stop it, Komkov. He'll be all right."

"Do you know that one of our rifles was accidentally fired and Chernenko dropped to the ground in the courtyard and covered his head? Didn't protect his assigned buddy, I might add. I don't know why you defend him all the time as you do. He'll be the death of us in battle."

Here Come the Girls, 1939

When they first started going to clubs, he got together with a girl named Luba and she started coming around more often, and Alexander started being less interested in meeting new girls, but then he found Dimitri talking to her, and then Dimitri expressed an interest in her and Alexander nodded and stepped away. Luba was hurt, while Dimitri played with her for a while and dropped her.

That happened twice, three times more. Alexander didn't mind; he could always find himself another girl. He tried leaving Dimitri at the Sadko bar and going to the officers' club instead, but Dimitri disapproved. So Alexander continued to go to Sadko with Dimitri and to pretend that he wasn't that interested in any specific girl. And that was true. He quite liked all women.

Oksana only liked to be on top and did not want to be touched.

Olga liked to be touched. *Only* touched.

Milla talked too much about communism and economics.

Agafia talked too much period.

Isabel came once, returned for more, and on the third try, asked if he wanted to be married.

Dina said she liked him more than any other man she'd ever been with, and then he found her with Anatoly Marazov the next weekend.

Maya wanted it any which way, and he gave it to her any which way, and then again, and again, and afterward she said all he cared about was himself.

Megan talked all the while she was using her mouth on him.

Nina talked all the while he was using his mouth on her.

Nadia wanted to play cards, not before, not after, but instead of.

Kyra said she would do it only if her best friend Lena could join in.

Zoe was brazen all around and was done in fifteen minutes.

Masha was brazen all around and was done in two hours.

Marisa was the girl who liked to be talked to, and Marta was the girl who didn't.

Sofia was the girl who liked most everything as long as she had to do nothing herself.

Sonia was the almost funny girl until suddenly, after one Saturday night too many, she became the girl with a broken heart, and suddenly she wasn't funny and she wasn't broken-hearted. She was just livid.

Valentina wanted to know if he ever killed another human being.

Zhenya wanted to know if he wanted to have a baby.

And then Alexander started forgetting their names.

That happened when he started to keep himself from release longer and longer. He kept coming back to them, looking into their eyes, their mouths, trying to get them completely naked, wanting a connection, wanting something else, but wanting and forgetting and continuing. A few a night, Friday night, Saturday night, Sunday night, and sentry evenings, and Sunday afternoons—not many during daylight, much to his dissatisfaction, for he so liked to look at them in their fervor.

Alexander started to withdraw from them, still liking them, still needing them, still wanting them, but with a resigned face, an unsmiling face, with a detached manner and a growing indifference to their pleasure, and suddenly and inexplicably their attachment to him grew!

There seemed to be more and more of the girls who liked his company, who wanted to walk with him along Nevsky Prospekt and hold his arm, who squeezed him gratefully at the end, and whispered thank you, who would come back the following weekend when he would already be on his next girl, on his next three. More and more of them seemed to want something from him—what, he did not know and, more to the point, could not give.

"I want more, Alexander," she said to him. "I want more."

And he smiled and said, "*Believe* me, I gave you all I got."

"No," she said. "I want more."

As they were walking back, he said in a resigned voice, "I'm sorry, but—what you want, it's just not possible. This is about as much as I'm capable of."

Still every girl he looked at, every girl he said hello to, every girl he touched, he thought, *is she the one?* I've had nearly all of them, has *the* one come and gone? *Come*—and gone, and I did not know?

But every once in a while, before dreams, before the black of night took him, for a moment, for a second, under the stars, on trains, and barges, and in other people's carriages, Alexander saw the barn and smelled Larissa, and heard her pleasure breath, and felt regret for something lost he was afraid would never come again.

CHAPTER THIRTEEN

Dinner at the Sabatellas', 1943

FINALLY, ON A SUNDAY in late October, Tatiana agreed to come for dinner at Vikki's. The Sabatellas lived in Little Italy, at the corner of Mulberry and Grand.

As they walked through the door, Tatiana heard a bellow and a screech and then an alto voice hollered, "Gelso-MEE-nah!" A dark-haired, tanned woman of large size and short stature came out from the kitchen. "You said you were going to be here three hours ago."

"I'm sorry, Grammy. Tania wasn't done with—I don't even know what she does in that hospital. Tania, meet my grandmother, Isabella, oh, and this is Tania's little boy, Anthony."

Tatiana was hugged but Anthony was scooped up by the floury hands, and taken, all three and a half months of him, into the kitchen, where he was splayed out on the counter, on his back, and Tatiana thought if she didn't instantly come to her son's rescue, Isabella might just make a zeppole out of him.

"*Gelsomina?*" Tatiana inquired quietly of Vikki as they stood in the kitchen and drank wine.

"Don't ask. It means jasmine. It has something to do with my dead mother."

"Your mother is not dead!" Isabella shouted without rancor, caressing the baby. "She is in California."

"She's in California," Vikki explained. "That means purgatory in Italian."

"Stop it. You know how ill she is."

"Your mother is ill?" Tatiana whispered.

"Yes," Vikki whispered back, "*mentally* ill."

"Stop it, you impossible child," Isabella boomed, beaming at Anthony.

"I told them under no circumstances to ask you about the baby's father," Vikki loudly whispered. "Is that good?"

"That's good, Vikki," Tatiana quietly whispered back.

Tatiana liked the apartment, which was large and lived-in, with oversized windows and tall bookshelves and big furniture, but she was slightly unsettled by the decorating colors: the entire apartment from the carpeted floors to the walls to the crown molding to the velvet curtains was the color of the red wine she was drinking.

In the burgundy and dark-wood parlor room, she met Travis, Isabella's thin, small and less-boisterous-than-his-wife husband.

"When I met my Travis," Isabella said over dinner, holding Anthony with one hand and serving lasagna to Tatiana with the other, "Vikki, pass the bread to Tania, and the salad, and don't just sit there, pour her some wine for the sake of Mary and Jesus, where was I? When I met Travis—"

"You already said that, woman," said Travis, glancing at Tatiana and scratching his bald head as if in apology.

"*Prego*, don't interrupt. When I met you, you were on your way to marry my Aunt Sophia."

"Don't tell *me*! *I* know. Tell *her*!"

A little more bread was going to keep her mouth nice and occupied. She could eat and they could talk and a good time would be had by all.

"My mother's younger sister," elaborated Isabella. "Travis and I met in a small town in Italy. Near Florence. You know where Florence is?"

"Yes," Tatiana said. "My husband's mother was from Italy."

"I was sent by my mother to meet Travis at the train station. Because he never could have found his way. We lived deep in the valley between the mountains. I was sent to meet him and bring him to my Aunt Sophia who was waiting."

Vikki said, "Grammy, with your help, he *never* found his way."

"Be quiet, child. It was ten kilometers—about six miles—back to my house. By the time we had walked two kilometers I knew I could not live a day without him. We had stopped at a local tavern for some wine. I never drank. I was too young, just sixteen, but Travis offered me some of his. We drank from the same chalice . . ." She had stopped serving, smiled and turned to Travis who was eating lasagna and pretending not to pay any attention.

"We didn't know what to do," continued Isabella. "My aunt was twenty-seven, and so was Travis. They were going to be married, there was no way out. We sat in that tavern in the hills near Florence and we didn't know what to do. So you know what we did?" Isabella poked Travis, who dropped his fork and groused. "We didn't come home. We just said, let's go to Rome, we'll write to the family from there. Instead of Rome, we took a train to Naples, and then a boat from Naples to El-lis Island. We came here in 1902. With nothing but each other."

Tatiana had stopped eating and was watching Isabella and Travis. "Did your aunt forgive you?"

"Nobody forgave me," said Isabella.

"Her mother doesn't write to her to this day," said Travis, his mouth full.

"Well, she's dead, Travis, she can hardly write to me now."

"Alexander, how long have you loved my sister?" asks a starved and dying Dasha.

"Never. I never loved her," replies Alexander. "I love you. You know what we have."

"You said when you get furlough in the summer you would come to Lazarevo and we would get married," says Dasha, coughing.

"Yes. I will come to Lazarevo on furlough, and we will get married," says Alexander to Tatiana's sister, Dasha.

Tatiana deeply lowered her head, kneading and pinching her stiffened fingers.

"We had two daughters in America," continued Isabella. "Travis wanted a son, but God decided otherwise." She sighed. "We tried for a boy. I had three miscarriages." Isabella looked longingly at Anthony, so longingly in fact that Tatiana wanted to get hold of her son again, as if desire somehow equaled possession.

"In 1923, our oldest daughter Annabella had Gelsomina—"

"And called me *Viktoria*," pointed out Vikki.

"What does she know?" Isabella said dismissively. "What kind of an Italian name is Viktoria? Gelsomina, now that's a beautiful Italian name, fitting for a beautiful girl like you. Our youngest, Francesca, lives in Darien, Connecticut. She comes once a month. She's married to a nice man, no children yet."

"Grammy, Aunt Francesca is thirty-seven. No one has children at thirty-seven," declared Vikki.

"We were meant to have a son," said Isabella mournfully.

"No, we weren't," said Travis. "If we were meant to have a son, we would have had a son. Now give the boy back to his rightful mother and eat, woman."

"Tania, who takes care of him while you work?" asked Isabella, with regret handing Anthony to Tatiana, who took him gratefully.

"I take him with me, or he sleeps, or refugee or soldier looks after him."

"Well, that's not very good," Isabella said. "If you want, I can take care of him for you."

"Thank you," Tatiana said. "But I don't think . . ."

"I could come to Ellis and pick him up for you. And then I could bring him back for you."

"Isabella!" exclaimed Travis.

Tatiana smiled at Isabella. "I think about your question, all right?" she said. "And you two are very lucky you have each other. That is wonderful story."

"You're lucky to have your boy," said Isabella.

"Yes," said Tatiana.

"Where is your family?"

Tatiana said nothing at first. "The Germans blockaded Leningrad two years ago," she said. "There was no food." She fell silent.

It is June 23, 1940—Tatiana and Pasha's birthday. They're turning sixteen and the Metanovs are celebrating at their dacha in Luga. They have borrowed a table and put it out in the brambled yard because there's no room in the porch for seventeen people—the seven Metanovs, Papa's sister, husband and niece, Tatiana's Babushka Maya and the six Iglenkos. Papa brought black caviar from Leningrad and smoked sturgeon. He brought herring with potatoes and onions and Mama made hot borscht and five different types of Russian salad. Cousin Marina made a mushroom pie, Dasha made an apple pie, Tatiana's paternal grandmother made her cream puffs, Babushka Maya painted her a picture, and Papa even brought some chocolate from the city because he knows how much Tatiana loves chocolate. Tatiana wears her white dress with red roses. It is the only nice dress she owns. Papa brought it from Poland two years earlier. It is her favorite dress.

Everyone drinks vodka, everyone but Tatiana. They drink until they can't hold the glass in their hands. They tell endless political Russian anecdotes and they eat to bursting. Papa plays the guitar and sings hearty Russian folk songs and everyone else joins in even though they can't remember the words; even though they can't carry a tune.

> "If you only knew
> Oh how dear to me,
> Are these Moscow nights . . ."

"When you turn eighteen, Tania," says Papa, "I will rent out a banquet hall in the Astoria Hotel for you and Pasha, and we're going to have ourselves a real proper feast, not this."

"You didn't have a party like that for me, Papa," Dasha says, who turned eighteen five years earlier.

"Times were very tough in 1935," says Papa. "We had so little, but things are better now and they'll be better still in two years. I'll raise a glass to you too at the Astoria, Dasha, all right?"

Tania wants to turn eighteen tomorrow so she can have another day like this day. The night air is warm and smells of faded lilacs and blooming cherry blossoms, the crickets are deafening and even the mosquitoes are at bay. Her brother and sister fall on top of her on the grass and they tickle her until she yells, screeches, squeals, stop it, stop it, stop it, my dress my dress, while the adults raise another shaky glass and Papa picks up the guitar again and Tatiana hears his deep inebriated voice carry through the brambles and the nettles and the white cherry trees, scratching out exiled Alexander Vertinsky's lament for Leningrad . . .

> "Uncertain talk by chance brought
> Sweet and needless words
> Summer Garden, Fontanka, and Neva
> Why did you fly here oh words so fleeting?
> Here the noise is made by foreign cities
> And foreign waters lap against the shores here."

CHAPTER FOURTEEN

In the Volkhov Prison, 1943

SLONKO WAS DEAD, BUT nothing was resolved about Alexander's fate. He was transferred to Volkhov and had to deal with a more malicious class of idiot. He found himself in a different state of mind after he learned that Tatiana had escaped the clutches of the Soviet Union. His relief was mingled with an unrelenting melancholy. Now that he knew she was irrevocably gone, he didn't know who to rail at first, the person who interrogated him or the guard who pointed a rifle at him. But he hated himself most of all.

She was gone—that was *his* doing.

Volkhov, like Leningrad and unlike Morozovo, actually had two prisons—one for criminals, one for *politicals*. The distinction was fine, and Alexander was being housed in the prison for criminals. They seemed to have better cells. He remembered his few days in Kresty after his arrest in 1936 before he was put on a train to Vladivostok. The cells had been small and odorous. In this prison in Volkhov the cells were bigger, had two bunks, a sink, a toilet. The cell had a steel door with a barred window, which was opened briefly to pass through his tray of food.

There was bread and oatmeal and occasionally meat of unknown origin. There was water, tea once in a while, and Alexander received vouchers which he could trade for tobacco or vodka.

Alexander kept his vouchers, of which he got two or three every day, and did not use them. Vodka he had no use for. Tobacco was a different story. He thirsted for tobacco. His mouth, his throat craved the burn, the smoke; his lungs craved the nicotine. But he forbade himself tobacco. His desire for nicotine slightly dulled his thirst for Tatiana; slightly numbed the aching emptiness in his body left by her absence. It had been about five months since his back was ripped open in the Battle of Leningrad; only twitching nerve endings remained around the raised, ridged scar that had managed to heal at last.

Alexander saved his tobacco vouchers and paced. He kept his uniform, he kept his boots. His sulfa drugs were long gone. The morphine had gone to Slonko. His rucksack was gone. He hadn't seen Stepanov since the night of Slonko's death, so he couldn't ask what had happened to his ruck, which, though filled with many stupid and replaceable things, had one thing in it that was neither—Tania's wedding dress. As if he could bear to look at it anyway. He could hardly bear to think of it.

Six paces from one wall to the other, ten paces from the front door to the back window. All day, while the sun was up, Alexander ran the length of the cell, and when he could not think anymore he would count the steps. One afternoon he paced 4,572 steps. Another he paced 6,207. Between early breakfast and early lunch and late dinner, Alexander walked between his prison walls, walking out Tatiana, living out the darkness. He had no foresight and no hindsight. He could barely tell what was right in front of him. Alexander didn't know what was ahead of him in the coming years and maybe if he had known, he would have chosen death in those gray pacing days, but because he didn't know, he chose life.

෴

Finally he got his military tribunal. After a month of pacing in his cell and collecting ninety tobacco vouchers, he went before three generals, two colonels and one Stepanov. He stood before them in his uniform, wearing his visor cap—his better-looking officer's cap having been given over to his wife.

"Alexander Belov, we are here to decide what to do with you," said General Mekhlis, a thin, tense man who looked like a weathered crow.

"I'm ready," said Alexander. It was about time. A month in one cell. Why couldn't the Lazarevo month with Tatiana have passed as slowly?

"Charges have been brought against you."

"I'm aware of the charges, sir."

"Charges that you are a foreigner, an American, disguised as a Red Army officer with the purpose of sabotage and subversion during the worst crisis our great country has ever faced. We are faced with our extinction at the hands of the Germans. You understand why we cannot allow foreign spies to infiltrate our ranks?"

"I understand. I have a defense."

"Let's hear it."

"All the things you just mentioned are baseless lies. They were presented to you to besmirch my character. My record in the Red Army since 1937 speaks for itself. I have been nothing but a loyal soldier, I have obeyed my superior officers, I have not shied away from any conflict. I served my country proudly against Finland and against Germany. In the Great Patriotic War, I have participated in four attempts to break the blockade on Leningrad. I was wounded twice, the second time nearly mortally. The man who accused me of foreign provocation is dead, shot by our own troops while trying to escape the Soviet Union. I will remind you that man was a *private* in the Red Army. He was a rear supply man for the border troops. His attempted escape constitutes nothing less than desertion and treason. Are you taking the word of a *known* deserter from the Red Army against the word of one of your decorated officers?"

"Don't tell me what to think, Major Belov," snapped Mekhlis.

"I wouldn't presume to, sir. I was posing a question." Alexander waited. The men behind the table conferred with each other briefly while Alexander stared out of the window. There was open air outside those windows. He breathed in. He had not been outside in so long.

"Major Belov, are you in fact Alexander Barrington, son of Jane and Harold Barrington who were executed for treason in 1936 and 1937?"

Alexander blinked; that was his only reaction. "No, sir," he said.

"Are you the Alexander Barrington who jumped off a train headed for corrective camps in 1936 and was presumed dead?"

"No, sir."

"Have you ever heard of Alexander Barrington?"

"Only through these charges."

"Are you aware that your wife, Tatiana Metanova, has disappeared and is presumed to have escaped with Private Chernenko and Dr. Sayers?"

"No. I am aware that Dr. Sayers was not escaping and that Private Chernenko was shot dead. I am aware that my wife is missing. Comrade Slonko, however, told me before he died"—Alexander coughed once loudly for emphasis—"that she was in NKVD—NKGB, I mean— custody. He told me she had signed a confession implicating me as the man Comrade Slonko had been looking for since 1936."

The generals exchanged a surprised look.

"Your wife is not in our custody," Mekhlis said slowly. "And Comrade Slonko is no longer here to defend himself. Chernenko is not here to defend himself."

"Of course."

"Major Belov, how do you explain the actions of your wife? Does it seem at all peculiar to you that she would leave you here while escaping—"

"Wait, if I may, General. My wife was not escaping. She had come to

Morozovo with Dr. Sayers at his request and with the permission of the Grechesky hospital administrator. She was under his supervision."

"I think that even under his supervision, your wife was not allowed to leave the Soviet Union," said Mekhlis.

"I'm not entirely convinced she has. I have been hearing much conflicting information."

"Has she been in touch with you?"

"No, sir."

"That doesn't trouble you?"

Blink. "No, sir."

"Your pregnant wife has disappeared, has not contacted you and that doesn't trouble you?"

"No, sir."

"The patrol units who checked the accompanying nurse's identification all adamantly deny that she had Soviet papers. While they cannot remember her name, they're sure her documents were with the American Red Cross. This does not bode well for you or your wife."

Alexander wanted to point out that it boded better for his wife, but kept silent. "My wife is not on trial here, is she?" he asked.

"She would be if she were here."

"But she is not on trial here," Alexander repeated. "You asked me if I was Alexander Barrington, the American, and I told you I was not. I don't know what my wife's whereabouts have to do with the accusations against me."

"Where is your wife?"

"I do not know."

"How long have you been married?"

"A year this June."

"I hope, Major, you keep track of the men under your command better than you have kept track of your wife."

Blink.

The generals studied Alexander. Stepanov's eyes never left him.

Mekhlis said, "Major, let me ask you something. Why would anyone accuse you of being an American if it weren't true? The facts that Private Chernenko provided us with were too detailed to be made up."

"I'm not saying he made them up. I'm saying that he is confusing me with another man."

"Who?"

"I don't know."

"But why would he point the finger at *you*, Major?"

"I don't know, sir. Dimitri Chernenko and I have had a difficult relationship over the years. Sometimes I thought he was jealous of me, angry at me for succeeding so far beyond him in the Red Army. Perhaps
he wanted to hurt me, to sabotage my progress. He also may have had
unrequited feelings for my wife. I'm fairly certain of it. Our friendship
had cooled considerably in the years before his death."

"Major, you are exasperating the high command of the 67th Army."

"I'm sorry for that. But all I have is my record and my good name. I
don't want both dishonored by a dead coward."

"Major, what do you think will happen to you if you tell us the
truth? If you are Alexander Barrington we will confer with the proper
authorities in the United States. We may be able to arrange a transfer for
you back to America."

Alexander laughed softly. "Sir, with all due respect, I'm here on
charges of treason and sabotage. The only transfer that will be arranged
for me will be to another world."

"You're wrong, Major. We are reasonable men."

"Surely, if all it took was for me to say I am from America, or England, or France in order to be transferred back to the country of my
choice, what would stop any of us?"

"Mother Russia, that's what!" exclaimed Mekhlis. "Your allegiance
to your country."

"It is that allegiance, sir, that is stopping me from telling you I am
an American."

Mekhlis took off his pince-nez and looked Alexander over. "Come
closer to the table, Major Belov. Let me take a good look at you."

Alexander stepped forward until he was at the edge of the tall desk.
He didn't need to straighten up. He was already straightened. Unwa-
veringly he stared into Mekhlis's face. Mekhlis stared silently back and
finally said, "Major, I will ask you one more time, but before you hastily
reply as you have been doing, I am going to give you thirty minutes to
think about your answer. You will be taken outside, and then brought
back here and asked one last time. These are the questions I am putting
before you. Are you Alexander Barrington, son of Jane and Harold Barrington of the United States? Were you arrested for crimes against the
Motherland in 1936 and did you escape while en route to your final
destination in Vladivostok? Did you, under the false name of Alexander Belov, infiltrate the officer ranks of the Red Army in 1937 after
graduating from secondary school? Did you attempt to desert the Red
Army and escape through Karelia during the war with Finland in 1940,

only to be stopped by Dimitri Chernenko? Have you been a double agent during your seven years in the Red Army? No, no, don't answer. You have thirty minutes."

Alexander was led out of the room and outside, outside! He sat on the bench while two guards stood either side of him, while the breezy warm May wind blew around him. He realized he would soon be turning twenty-four. He sat while the sun shone and the sky was blue and the air smelled of distant lilacs and blooming jasmine and lake water.

Then Came the War, 1939

As part of the Leningrad garrison, quartered at the Pavlov barracks—formerly the barracks that belonged to the Tsar's Imperial Guards—Alexander was responsible for patrolling the streets, for sentry duty over the Neva, and for the fortifications of the Finland–Russia border. Vladimir Lenin had whored half of Russia in March 1918—Karelia, Ukraine, Poland, Bessarabia, Latvia, Lithuania, Estonia—to ensure survival of the fledgling communist state. The Karelian Isthmus had been given up to Finland.

After Hitler and Stalin divided Poland in September 1939, Stalin received assurances from Hitler that a "campaign" against Finland to reclaim the disputed land would not be seen as a sign of aggression against Germany. In November 1939, Stalin attacked Finland to get the Karelian Isthmus back. No matter how much the command insisted on it, Alexander refused to call the war with Finland a campaign with Finland. A campaign was two grown men driving around the country shaking hands with the electorate and then going to the polls. Any time you tried to take territory with tanks and rifles and mortars and the lives of men it ceased being a campaign and became a war.

Alexander's first battle was fought in the swamps of the vast Karelian forest. Unfortunately, Komkov had been completely right about Dimitri. In battle, Dimitri turned out to be a fainthearted, yellow-bellied, miserable, craven coward, words Komkov shouted straight into Dimitri's cowering face before tying him to a tree to prevent him from deserting. Komkov would have shot him but Alexander stayed his hand, regretting it every minute since.

Even without Dimitri's help, the Soviets managed eventually to overpower the unconquerable Finns. When it was over, Alexander counted the Finnish bodies. There had only been twenty Finns in the woods. Now all twenty were dead, which was good, but to kill them they had sacrificed 155 Red Army soldiers. Twenty-four came back to Lisiy Nos with Alexander. Twenty-four plus Dimitri. Komkov did not come back.

In 1940, the Finns sent more troops into southern Karelia and took back the trees and the thirty meters the Soviets had won, and another twenty kilometers besides, and the lives of thousands more Soviet men. Alexander found himself in charge of three platoons of strangers and his orders were to push the Finns from the Karelian Isthmus, back to Vyborg. Vyborg needed to be in Soviet hands, according to the Red Army—and according to Alexander, since penetrating the border there would leave him only a few hundred kilometers from Helsinki, Finland. Him and Dimitri. Despite everything, he would honour his promise to Dimitri. Alexander felt their opportunity for escape was close.

During the last days of the so-called *campaign*, in March 1940, Alexander served under Major Mikhail Stepanov, a stoic commanding officer with impenetrable eyes. Alexander was given a mortar and thirty men, including the commander's young son, Yuri, to clear the area in the swamps near Vyborg. Thirty rifles and three light mortars just did not do the job against a well entrenched Finnish army. Alexander's platoon was unable to penetrate enemy lines, and neither could the five other platoons that stretched inland from the Gulf of Finland.

When Alexander finally returned to the rear at Lisiy Nos with only four of his thirty men, Major Stepanov asked about his son. Alexander told him that he didn't know what had happened to Yuri. He knew that Yuri's battle buddy had been killed. Alexander volunteered to go back into the swamps by himself to bring back Yuri Stepanov. The major instantly agreed and ordered Alexander to take one more man with him into the forest.

Alexander took Dimitri. He also took his ten thousand dollars, and they set off with nothing but his money and their rifles and grenades into the marshy lands near the gulf without any intention of coming back to the Soviet Union.

They found Yuri Stepanov.

"God, he's alive, Dima," said Alexander, turning Stepanov over. The soldier could barely breathe. Alexander pushed Stepanov's tongue down with his fingers to help the boy breathe better. "He's alive," he repeated, looking up at Dimitri.

"Yeah. Barely." Dimitri glanced around. "Come on, let's go. We don't have much time. We need to get going. It's perfect right now. Quiet."

Alexander cut open Stepanov's uniform to see where he was hit. He saw blood over the young man's torso. The blood was viscous and brown. Alexander couldn't tell how much blood Stepanov had lost. Judging by the pallid look of him, quite a bit.

Mumbling, Yuri Stepanov opened his eyes and his hand reached up to touch Alexander. He tried to say something but couldn't.

"Alexander!" Dimitri exclaimed. "Let's go."

"Dimitri!" Alexander exclaimed, not even looking up. "Stop your shouting and let me think for a minute. Just for one minute, all right."

He continued to crouch in the marsh by Stepanov's side, listening to the boy's labored breathing, looking at the boy's gray face. Thirty meters away was the unprotected Finnish border. Thirty meters away were the low-lying bushes near the gulf coast. Thirty meters away was a country other than the Soviet Union. And in that country was the sea that would take Alexander to Stockholm, and in Stockholm was a building where Alexander would go to beg for his freedom. And afterward . . . Alexander could see the whitewashed shingles, the whitewashed clapboard of the Barrington houses in between the cinnabar sugar maples. He could smell Barrington. He breathed deeply in, his lungs hurting. He would save himself, he would save Dimitri who helped him see his father, he would breathe the air of home once more.

He had expected to fight, he expected to freeze, to fire his weapons and to suffer, to swim, to sleep knee deep in mud, to die if he had to, to kill men who stood in his way. He did not expect this—a wounded son and a waiting father.

Alexander took another breath. It was not Barrington anymore. All he smelled was the organic, slightly stale old blood, the metal of the weapons, the burnt sulfur odor of gunpowder. And all he heard was Yuri Stepanov's lungs laboring through each breath.

Alexander would be leaving a young man to die. He would be leaving a father's son to die. He would be buying his freedom with this boy's death. Alexander crossed himself. This is God's test, he thought. To show me what I'm made of.

Alexander grabbed Stepanov by his arms and legs and lifted him off the ground. "Dima, I have to bring him back."

Dimitri paled. "What?"

"You heard me."

"Are you out of your fucking mind? You can't go back. We are not going back."

"I am."

A silent scream came from Dimitri in the quiet woods. Drip, drip, trickle, crackle, birds gone, crickets gone, drip, crackle and Dimitri's mute fury. "What are you talking about?" he hissed. "We didn't come back for him. He was a ruse. We came here to continue forward."

"I know we did," said Alexander. "But I can't."

"This is war, Alexander! What? You're suddenly going to care about each of the thousands of men you let die under your command?"

"I didn't let them die," Alexander said.

"We're going forward." Dimitri grit his teeth.

"Fine," said Alexander. "If you're going, then let me give you half of my money. You will get yourself to Stockholm one way or another, and from there you will know what to do. You will get yourself to America."

"What are you talking about? What do you mean, *me*? You mean us."

"No, Dimitri, I told you. I'm going back with Yuri. But no reason for you to go back."

"I'm not going without you!" Dimitri nearly shrieked through the woods, his voice pitched high.

"All right," said Alexander. "Let's go back while he is still alive."

Dimitri didn't move. "If you tell me you're returning to Lisiy Nos, then bringing Stepanov back will be the last thing you will do as a Soviet soldier."

With Stepanov flung over his shoulders, Alexander came up very close to Dimitri and said, through his own grit teeth, "Dimitri, are you threatening me?"

"Yes," Dimitri said.

Alexander backed away a step and looked at Dimitri with grim resignation. "Well, I'll tell you what," he said slowly, "you go ahead and do what you like. Go ahead and inform on me. Then it's even more important that the last thing I do is save another man's life."

"Oh, fucking hell!"

"We're going to have another chance! Look at what we found in these woods. We'll be able to come back here again. This is our first chance, not our last. We'll come back here and we'll escape. If you're threatening me with the NKVD, then you will never yourself get out of the Soviet Union. You'll rot here. I'll be dead, but you'll be here for the rest of your life." Alexander paused. "Mark my words, Europe is going to war with Hitler. We'll have another chance, but not if I'm dead. So what will it be? If you want to run, you'll keep your mouth shut long enough for me to get us out." Alexander paused. "Don't be an ass. Let's bring the boy back to his father."

"No!" said Dimitri.

"Then do what you fucking like." Alexander was done speaking. Without waiting for Dimitri to catch up, he turned around and started walking. He heard Dimitri's sullen footsteps in the distance behind him. Dimitri was a coward, and as a coward perhaps he could shoot another man in the back, but not when the man had promised to someday carry him on it.

They returned to base after hours of slogging in the dismal swamp. It was nearly dark, but the first thing Alexander saw by the line of the pines was Mikhail Stepanov, standing with one of the NKVD border guards, looking for them through the trees. His legs shaking, Stepanov walked towards Alexander and was barely strong enough to ask, "Is he alive?"

"Yes," said Alexander. "But he needs a doctor."

Mikhail Stepanov took his son from Alexander and carried him to the field tent where he laid him on an empty cot and sat by him quietly, as they got a transfusion into Yuri, and some morphine too, and even some sulfa drugs. Together Stepanov and Alexander washed Yuri's body, and the doctor stitched up the three bullet wounds. Yuri had been too long in the woods with metal in his body. The wounds were infected.

Alexander went to get something to eat and to have a smoke, and then came back and sat by Stepanov's side. Yuri had come to a bit, and was faintly talking to his father. "Papochka," he said, "I'm going to be all right?"

"Yes, son," said Stepanov, holding Yuri's hand.

"I was lucky. It could have been so much worse." Yuri glanced at Alexander. "Right, Lieutenant?"

"Right, Private," said Alexander.

"Mama will be proud of me," said Yuri. "Am I going to fight again?"

He saw Major Stepanov's stricken face. Alexander said nothing for a moment. "Where *is* his mother?" he asked at last.

"Dead since 1930," replied Stepanov.

"Papa?"

"Yes?"

"Are *you* proud of me?"

"Very proud, son."

They sat by Yuri like this, the two warriors, listening to Yuri's labored breathing, watching his slowly blinking eyes.

And then the breathing was no longer labored, and the eyes were no longer blinking, and Major Stepanov hung his head and cried, and Alexander, unable to take it, walked out of the medic's tent.

He was leaning against a supply truck, smoking, when Stepanov walked outside.

"I'm sorry, sir," said Alexander.

Stepanov extended his hand to Alexander. "You're a fine soldier, Lieutenant Belov," he said, in a tight voice. "I have been in the Red Army since 1921, and I will tell you right now—you're a fine soldier. Your refusal to retreat, to leave your dead behind, where does it all come from? Don't say you're sorry. Because of you, I said goodbye to my only child. Because of you he will be buried. He will have rest. And I will, too." Stepanov did not let go of Alexander's hand.

"It was nothing, sir," said Alexander, lowering his head.

The Winter War ended days later on 13 March, 1940.

The Soviets never did regain Vyborg.

In Front of Mekhlis, 1943

The question before him was who he was. His time was up. He knew. Standing up, he remembered verse of Kipling's "If," almost as if his own father were speaking to him.

> *If you can make one heap of all your winnings,*
> *and risk it on one turn of pitch and toss,*
> *and lose, and start again, at your beginnings,*
> *and never breathe a word about your loss.*

They called for him, and when he was led back before the tribunal, he was almost cheerful.

"Well, Major, have you thought about it?"

"Yes, sir."

"What is your answer?"

"My answer is that I am Alexander Belov, from Krasnodar, a major in the Red Army."

"Are you the American expatriate Alexander Barrington?"

"No, sir."

And then they were all quiet. Outside was a fresh May day. Alexander wanted to be outside again. The faces on him were somber, unblinking. He became somber and unblinking himself. One of the generals was tapping a pencil against the wooden desk. Stepanov's eyes were discreetly on Alexander and when their glances locked, Stepanov nodded lightly.

Finally General Mekhlis spoke. "I was afraid that would be your answer, Major. Had you said yes, we would be talking to the U.S. State Department. Now the question before me is what do I do with you? I have been given complete authority over the disposition of your fate. My colleagues and I have conferred while you were outside. The decision before us is a difficult one. Even if you are telling the truth, the accusations against you rest on your shoulders along with all your bars and follow you in the Red Army wherever you go. The swirl of rumor, of suspicion, of innuendo, it doesn't end. It won't end. And if makes your job as an officer so much harder, and our job of defending you against other false accusations, against men afraid to fight under your command, so much harder."

"I'm used to challenges, sir."

"Yes, but we don't need them." Mekhlis raised his hand. "And don't interrupt, Major. If you're lying, however, all the same things apply, except now we as a government and a protector of our people have made a terrible mistake and will be made to look foolish and humiliated when the truth is eventually revealed. And you know one thing about truth— it always comes out in the end. Do you see how, whether you are lying or telling the truth, you are tainted property to us?"

"If I may, General," interjected Stepanov. "We are fighting a frantic war in which we are losing men faster than we can conscript them, we are losing weapons faster than we can make them, and we're losing ranking officers faster than we can replace them. Major Belov is an exemplary soldier. Surely we can find something for him to do in the name of the Red Army?" When Stepanov encountered no argument, he continued. "He can be sent to Sverdlovsk to make tanks and cannons. He can be sent to Vladivostok to mine iron ore, he can be sent to Kolyma, or to Perm-35. In any of those places he can remain a productive member of Soviet society."

Mekhlis scoffed. "We have plenty of other men to mine iron ore. And why should we waste a Red Army major on making a cannon?"

Alexander imperceptibly shook his head with amusement. Well done, Colonel Stepanov, he thought. A moment from now you will be having them beg for me to remain in the army, whereas a moment ago they were ready to shoot me themselves.

Stepanov continued on Alexander's behalf. "He is not a major any longer. He has been stripped of his rank upon his arrest. I see no problem with sending him to Kolyma."

"Then why are we still calling him Major?" Mekhlis puffed.

"Because he remains what he is even if the bars have been removed from his shoulders. He has been a commanding officer for seven years. He commanded men during the Winter War, he has fought to keep the Germans on the other side of the Neva, he has manned the Road of Life, and he fought alongside his men in four Neva campaigns last summer trying to break the blockade."

"We have been made aware numerous times of his record, Colonel Stepanov," Mekhlis said, painfully rubbing his forehead. "Now we need to decide how to dispose of him."

"I suggest sending him to Sverdlovsk," said Stepanov.

"We cannot do that."

"Then reinstate him."

"We cannot do that either."

Mekhlis was silent for a while, thinking. After a heavy sigh, he said, "Major Belov, near Volkhov in the valley between Lake Ladoga and the Sinyavino Heights there is a railroad that is getting bombed by the Germans from their hilltop positions several times a day. Are you familiar with it?"

"Yes, sir. My wife helped build that railroad after we broke the blockade."

"Please don't bring up your wife, Major, it's a sore subject. In any case, that railroad is vital for getting food and fuel to the city of Leningrad. I've decided to sentence you to a penal unit in charge of rebuilding the railroad along a ten-kilometer stretch between Sinyavino and Lake Ladoga. Do you know what a penal battalion is?"

Alexander was silent. He knew. The army was filled with thousands of men sent to storm bridges without cover, to cross rivers without cover, to build railroads under fire, to go first into battle without artillery support, without tanks or rifles for each man. In penal battalions, the men were given alternating rifles. When the man next to you fell, you picked up his rifle, unless it was you who fell. Penal battalions were Soviet walls of men sent before Hitler's firing squads.

Mekhlis was silent. "Anything to add, Major? Oh, and you are formally relieved of your rank."

"That's fine. I'm being asked to be part of a battalion, not to command the men, correct?"

"Incorrect. You are being ordered to command the men."

"In that case, I have to keep my rank."

"You cannot keep your rank."

"Sir, with all due respect, I cannot command a squirrel, much less hardened and fearless men in a penal battalion constantly under threat of death without authority bestowed on me by the Red Army. If you want me to be in charge, you have to give me the tools required to command men. Otherwise I will be no good to the Red Army, no good to the war effort and no good to you. The men will not obey a single order from me, the railroad will remain unbuilt, and supply people and soldiers will perish. You cannot ask me to remain in the army—"

"I'm not asking you, I'm ordering you."

"Sir, put me in a penal battalion, certainly, but do not ask me to be in charge. I will be an NCO, a sergeant, a corporal, whatever you decide is fine with me. But if you actually want to use me to the army's advantage, I must keep my bars." Alexander was unflinching when he said, "Certainly you as a *general* understand that better than anyone. Have you forgotten General Meretskov? He sat in the dungeons of Moscow waiting for his execution. The powers-that-be decided he should command the Volkhov front instead. So he was promoted to general and given an army instead of just a division. How do you think he would have fared commanding his army as the peasant he actually was? How many men do you think he would have been able to send to their deaths if he had been a non-commissioned corporal instead of a commissioned general? Do you want to get the Germans out of Sinyavino Heights? I will get them out for you. But I must keep my rank."

Mekhlis was staring at Alexander with frank, resigned understanding. "You have worn me out, Major Belov. You will be sent to Sinyavino in one hour. The guard will escort you back to your cell to collect your things. I will demote you and allow you to keep the rank of captain, but that is all. Where are your medals?"

Alexander wanted to smile but didn't. "Taken from me before the interrogation. I'm missing the *Hero of the Soviet Union* medal."

"That's unfortunate," Mekhlis said.

"Yes, sir, it is. I also need new BDUs, new weapons, and new supplies. I need a knife, and a tent—I need new gear, sir. My old gear has disappeared."

"Have to keep better track of your equipment, Major Belov."

Alexander saluted him. "I'll keep that in mind. And it's Captain Belov, sir."

CHAPTER FIFTEEN

Running into Ouspensky, 1943

ALEXANDER WAS ESCORTED TO the rear of the current front, where he resupplied himself, dressed appropriately and rode in a truck to the barracks that housed a penal battalion of hundreds of used-up men, men who were either criminals or political survivors. They were on the wet ground resting, smoking, playing cards. Three of them were engaged in a fight which Alexander broke up. One of the men in the struggle was Nikolai Ouspensky.

"Oh, no, not you," said Ouspensky.

"What the hell are you doing here, soldier?" Alexander said, shaking his hand. "You have only one lung."

"What are *you* doing here? I was sure you were dead," Ouspensky said cheerfully. "I thought they shot you. Certainly after the interrogation I got on your behalf I thought nothing would be left of *you.*"

Alexander offered Nikolai a cigarette and led him away. "What's your rank here? Are you a corporal?"

"I'm still a lieutenant," Ouspensky said indignantly and then quieter, "demoted from first to second lieutenant."

"Good. I am your commanding officer. Choose twenty men and take them to lay the tracks for the train to get through. Do me a favor and don't fight with your charges anymore. It diminishes your authority."

"Thanks for the tip."

"Go pick your men. Who was your superior officer before me?"

"You're joking. No one. We had three captains die in the last two weeks. Then they started sending the majors to the railroad. Two of them died. We've got no one left. The idiots have not yet figured out that if the Germans have such a good view of the railroad they're constantly blowing up, they have just as good a view of the vertical men who are fixing it. Just this morning we lost five men before we laid a single millimeter of track."

"Let's see how we do under the cover of night."

It turned out not much better. Twenty men went with Ouspensky, and thirteen came back, including Ouspensky. Out of the thirteen, three were injured critically, two were superficially wounded, and one man was blind.

The blind man escaped in the night, was stopped at the Lake Ladoga shore and shot on the spot by the NKGB.

The army base between Sinyavino Heights and Lake Ladoga was set up on a flat, boggy stretch of land with canvas tents and some wooden structures erected for the colonels and the brigadier generals. Two battalions were quartered here, comprising six companies, eighteen platoons, and fifty-four squads, 432 men in all. Because of a lack of commanding officers, Alexander had a battalion all to himself, 216 men he could send to their deaths.

Stepanov was not here. Alexander didn't get to see Stepanov again after the tribunal hearing. He must have gone back to the Leningrad garrison, his only home for many years. Alexander hoped so.

Meeting Dasha Metanova, 1941

Alexander was at Sadko, standing near the bar as usual. He preferred going to the officers' club; he found it awkward socializing with non-coms. The gulf between them was too large now.

On this June Saturday night, Alexander was standing talking to Dimitri when two girls came and stood near them. He glanced at them briefly. The second time he looked, he found one of them staring at him with frank interest. He smiled politely. Dimitri turned his head, looked them both over, raised his eyes at Alexander, and stepped around so the two men could face the two women.

"Could we buy you girls a beer?" Dimitri asked.

"Sure," said the taller, darker one. She was the one who had been staring at Alexander. Dimitri was making friendly conversation with the shorter, less attractive one. It was hard to talk in the bar. Alexander asked if the dark girl wanted to go for a walk. She smiled. "Sure."

They went outside into the warm barely dusky night. It was just after midnight, and still quite light out. The girl sang a bit, then took his hand and laughed into his face. "So am I going to have to guess," she asked, "or will you tell me your name?"

"Alexander," he said, and did not ask for hers because he had trouble remembering names.

"Aren't you going to ask me my name?"

He smiled. "You sure you want me to know?"

She looked at him with surprise. "Do I want you to know what my name is? Is that what you soldiers have regressed to? You don't even ask the girl's name anymore?"

"Hey, listen," said Alexander, patting her. "I don't know what the other soldiers regressed to. I just know that I tend to forget names."

"Well, maybe after tonight, you will never forget my name." She smiled suggestively.

Slightly shaking his head, Alexander wanted to tell her that she would have to do something pretty extraordinary for him not to forget her name, but he said nothing except, "All right. What's your name?"

"Daria," she said. "But everyone calls me Dasha."

"All right, Daria-Dasha. Do you have a place you want to take me to? Is anyone at home?"

"Is anyone at home? Where are you living? Of course. I'm never alone for a second. I've got everybody at home. Mama, Papa, Babushka, Dedushka, my brother. And my sister sleeps in the same bed as me." She raised her eyebrows and laughed. "I think even an officer would have trouble having two sisters at the same time?"

"It depends," Alexander said, putting his arm around her. "What does your sister look like?"

"About twelve," Dasha replied. "Is there anywhere *you* can take me?"

Alexander took her to his barracks. It was his turn tonight.

Dasha asked if she should undress. "I don't want anyone to walk in on us."

"Well, this is the army barracks," said Alexander, "not the European Hotel. Undress, Dasha, but at your own peril."

"Are you going to undress?"

"They've all seen *me*," Alexander pointed out.

Dasha undressed, and so did Alexander.

He enjoyed her as much as many other girls. Her body was a typical Russian fleshy body—large hips, large breasts—the kind that drove men like his quartermate Grinkov crazy. What Alexander liked about Dasha, though, was a slightly familiar quality, a friendly, easy-going manner that came from knowing someone a while. Also, her response to him was somewhat above the mill. She actually said, "Oh, my . . . Alexander, *where* do you come from?"

They had an hour together until Grinkov came back with a girl and wouldn't take no-it's-not-your-day for an answer.

After they dressed, Alexander walked Dasha to the sentry gate. "So, tell me," she asked, "are you going to remember my name next week when I come by?"

"Sure . . . Dasha, right?" He smiled.

Next week she came by with her friend again; unfortunately Dimitri had already gone with someone else, and Dasha didn't want to leave her friend in the lurch. The three of them ended up walking down Nevsky Prospekt together. Then—finally—her friend caught a bus back home, and Alexander took Dasha back to the barracks, where it wasn't his turn and his quarters were already full.

"You've got two choices," Alexander said. "You can either go home, or come inside and ignore the other soldiers."

Dasha looked at him. He couldn't quite tell what was in her eyes. "Well," she said, "why not? My mother and father have to ignore us kids as we pretend to sleep. Are they sleeping?"

"Not even close," said Alexander.

"Oh. That's a bit too strange for me."

Alexander nodded. "Do you want me to walk you home?"

"No, it's all right." She came up close to him. "I had a really good time last week."

Alexander paused. "Me too," he said. "Let's go to the Admiralty Gardens."

The third Saturday night he met her, they found a quiet place under the embankment of the Moika Canal, where the boats quayed. It was secluded enough and Dasha didn't make any noise, and Alexander had certainly trained himself not to utter a sound. There was nowhere for Dasha to lie down, but Alexander could sit.

"Alex—do you mind if I call you Alex?" she asked.

"No," he said.

"Alex, tell me something about yourself." Dasha smiled at him. "You're very interesting."

They had finally finished, and he was hoping to get back. He wanted to sleep. His Sunday morning began at seven regardless of how late the girls kept him up. "Why don't you tell me something about *your*self?"

"What do you want to know?"

"Many soldiers before me?"

"Not many." Dasha smiled. "Alexander, you don't want to be having *that* conversation. Because then I'll have a question for you."

"All right."

"Many women before me?"

He smiled. "Not many."

She laughed.

He laughed, too.

"I tell you what, Alex. Since I met you three weeks ago, I haven't been able to stop thinking about you."

"Really?"

"Really. And I haven't been with any men since then." She paused. "Can you say the same?"

"Absolutely. I haven't been with any men since then either."

She punched him lightly. "Stop. You have time for more?"

"No." He didn't want to tell her he didn't have another condom. "Come and see me next week. I'll have time then."

"Come on," she said teasingly, her hands on him. "I promise it'll be quick."

"No, Dasha. Next week."

After Dasha left and Alexander returned to the barracks, he found a girl in the corridor that he had been with back in May, a girl who was friendly and drunk and attractive and who would not stop or would not leave until he unbuttoned his trousers. Alexander unbuttoned his trousers.

And the week was long, and during the week, Alexander had sentry duty which included a couple of girls Dimitri had set up for them. When Saturday night came, Alexander went to Sadko, having only a cursory interest in getting together with a girl, as in, it's Saturday night, so he might as well. He ran into one he hadn't seen for a while, and after having a couple of drinks and buying her a couple of drinks, he went to the back alley of Sadko and had her against the wall, and when she said, "Aren't you going to throw your cigarette out?" he was surprised it was still in his mouth. He sent the girl home and returned to Sadko.

He felt arms go around his head and a voice say, "Guess who."

It was Dasha. He smiled. She had come alone this time.

He thought he was finished for tonight. But Dasha's evening was just beginning, so Alexander felt obliged to buy her a few beers and talk to her. They smoked, joked a bit, and then she pulled him out of the bar. "Dasha, it's getting late," he said. "I've got to be up tomorrow at seven."

"I know," she said, rubbing his arm. "You're always in a hurry. Always rushing off somewhere. What's the hurry, Alex?"

Sighing, he looked at her with wearied amusement. "What are you proposing?"

"I don't know." She smiled. "Same as last week?"

He tried to remember. For some reason last week had flown out of his head. He could see that if he didn't remember it would upset Dasha, and so he tried. But between last week and this week there had been . . . he tried to focus his mind. There had been much talk of imminent war.

"Don't you remember? Down by the parapets on Moika?"

Now he recalled. He had taken her down by the canal. "You want to go there again?"

"More than anything."

"Let's go."

Afterward, it was nearly one. "Alexander," she said, sitting on top of him, panting, "I must say, you're quite a strenuous lover . . . and I don't say that lightly."

"Thank you."

"Are you having a good time?"

"Of course."

"You don't talk much, do you?"

"What do you want to talk about?"

She laughed. "Do you feel we're saying it all?"

"We're saying all I need to."

"You want to meet next week?"

"Sure."

"Do you have a free day? Maybe you can come to my place for dinner? I don't live too far from here. On Fifth Soviet. You can meet the family."

"I don't have many free days."

"What about Monday or Tuesday?"

"This Monday or Tuesday?"

"Yes."

"I'll see. No, wait, I've got to—listen, maybe in a week or so."

"We can't keep meeting like this."

"No?"

"Well, we could." She grinned. "But maybe we could go somewhere?"

"Where would you like to go?"

"I don't know. Somewhere nicer. Maybe to Tsarskoye Selo, or Peterhof?"

"Maybe," he said noncommittally, lifting her off, getting up, stretching. "It's getting late, Dash. I have to get back."

He returned to base where he sat for a few minutes with Sergeant Ivan Petrenko, the sentry, sharing some vodka and a cigarette before he went back to his quarters.

"You think the rumors are true, Lieutenant? You think we're going to war with Hitler?"

"I think it's unavoidable, Sergeant, yes."

"But how is it possible? It's like England going to war with France. Germany and the Soviet Union have been allies for nearly two years. We signed a pact."

"And divided Poland just like old friends." Alexander smiled. "Petrenko, do you trust Hitler?"

"I don't know. I don't think he'll be stupid enough to invade us."

"Let's hope you're right," said Alexander, stubbing out his cigarette. "Good night."

All he wanted was to go to sleep; why was that so much to ask? But both Marazov *and* Grinkov were with women on their beds, covered with sheets up to their hair. Alexander averted his glance as he climbed atop his bunk, put a pillow over his head, and closed his eyes.

"Alexander," he heard a strident female voice say. "You *bastard*."

Sighing heavily, he pulled the pillow off and opened his eyes. The girl who had just been with Grinkov was standing in front of his bunk. Behind him, Alexander heard Grinkov chuckling.

"What did I do?" he asked tiredly. He recognized her slightly bloated, greatly drunken face.

"Don't you remember? You told me last week to come and meet you here tonight. I waited for three hours for you at the damn gate! Finally, I gave up and went to Sadko and what do I see but you making time with some girl who is not *me*."

Alexander did not want to get up, but he felt that at any second he was going to be slapped, and he didn't want to be slapped while he was lying down. "I'm really sorry," he said, rising and sitting with his legs dangling off the bunk. He vaguely remembered her. "I didn't mean to upset you."

"No?" she said, very loudly. Grinkov was laughing into his pillow. Marazov and his girl were going at it and couldn't be less interested. Neither could Alexander.

He couldn't remember her name. He wanted to tell her to get out, but he didn't want to make her feel worse in front of listening ears. He jumped off the bed, and as soon as he did, she made a fist and went to strike him in the face. Grabbing her wrist, he pushed her away, and shook his head. "I am *not* in the mood for this."

"You're all the same, aren't you?" she said. "You are all just woman haters and whoremongers, you don't give a shit about any of us."

"We're not woman haters," Alexander said with surprise. "*I'm* not. But—" God, *what* was her name! "If we're whoremongers, what does that make *you?*"

She gasped.

"Oh, listen . . ." he said. "I'm tired. What do you want from me?"

"A little respect, Alexander. That's all. Just a little consideration."

Alexander rubbed his eyes. This was ludicrous. "Look, I'm sorry—"

She broke in with, "You can't even remember my name, can you?" Her hand went up again. Alexander almost didn't stop her that time.

But he did stop her. He hated to be hit by anyone. All the hair on his body stood on end.

"God, I feel sorry for the girl who is going to fall in love with you, you bastard. Because you're going to shred her to pieces, you heartless swine!"

As she walked down the corridor to the stairs, Alexander called after her, "I remember—you're Elena."

"Fuck you," said Elena, disappearing down the hall.

Well, if that's not a soldier's farewell, I don't know what is, Alexander thought, going back to his quarters. He wanted to smoke and smoke again inside these prison walls, and he wanted a quiet room where he could remain composed and alone, and where he could nurse his wounded pride and think of how far he had come away from Krasnodar and from young Larissa, who had given him some of her sweetness right before she died, and from Comrade Svetlana Visselskaya, his mother's friend, who had said to him, Alexander, your gifts are so abundant, don't squander them. Well, Alexander thought, any minute now, one of the girls he had carelessly discarded was going to come by the barracks with a gun and blow his brains out and on his tombstone the epitaph would read, "Here lies Alexander, who couldn't remember the name of any girl he had fucked."

With a touch of self-hatred, he tried to look for sleep. It was three in the morning, June 22, 1941.

CHAPTER SIXTEEN

The Railroad at Sinyavino Heights, 1943

ALEXANDER CALLED OUSPENSKY INTO his tent. "Lieutenant, what's wrong with Sergeant Verenkov?"

"I don't know what you mean, sir."

"Well, just this morning, he brought me not only his coffee ration, but some of his gruel, too, though thankfully not all of it."

"Yes, Captain."

"Lieutenant, why is Verenkov bringing me his gruel? Why is Sergeant Telikov offering me his French letters? Why would I require condoms from my sergeant? What's going on here?"

"You're our commanding officer, sir."

"I did not command gruel. Nor French letters."

"He wants to be nice."

"Why?"

"I don't know, sir."

"I'm going to get the truth out of you, Lieutenant."

⚬⚬⚬

The rear of the base was a kilometer from Lake Ladoga and every morning Alexander walked to the lake to wash. In the early, still, tepid summer, the lake smelled like what it had turned into—a burial ground for thousands of Soviet men.

One morning he was returning from the lake as he passed the mess tent, and through the canvas he heard Ouspensky's voice. Normally he would have just kept going, but he heard his own name mentioned in a conspiratorial tone. Alexander slowed down.

Ouspensky was talking to Sergeant Verenkov, a young political convict who had previously never been in the army, and Sergeant Telikov, who had been in the army for ten years and was a career sergeant. Ouspensky was saying, "Sergeants, you stay away from our commander. Do not talk to him directly. Don't look him in the eye. You have something to ask him, ask me. And pass it down to all your men. I'm here as your buffer."

Alexander smiled.

"Do we need a buffer?" That was Telikov. He was a careful man.

"Oh," said Ouspensky, "believe me. You need a buffer. Captain Belov acts like a reasonable man. He acts like a rational man, he acts like a patient man. But he will kill you with his bare hands if you're not careful."

Verenkov was skeptical. "Fuck off, you are full of shit."

Ouspensky continued undaunted, but in a lower voice. "Do you know he ripped the arm off a supply runner named Dimitri Chernenko, ripped the arm right off its hinges! Left him with nothing but a bloodied stump. And that's not even the worst of it. The severed arm didn't kill him. But one punch in the face nearly killed him. One punch, Verenkov. Just think about that."

Alexander laughed soundlessly. If only that had been true.

"And when Chernenko still would not die, our commander ordered his execution on the border with Finland, while he was still laid up in the hospital in Morozovo."

"You're fucking with us."

"I'm telling you, he is not afraid of anything. Not of runners, not of the Germans, not of death, not even of the NKGB. Now listen carefully and don't repeat this to anyone . . ." Ouspensky's voice was down to a whisper. "When he was in a cell back in Morozovo, an interrogator came to see him—"

"Why was he arrested?"

"For being a double agent."

"Fuck off!"

"It's true."

"A double agent for who?"

"I think the Japanese. It's not important. Listen. An interrogator came to see him. Our commander was not armed, he had no weapons on him, but do you know what happened?"

"He killed the interrogator?"

"Sure as shit he killed the interrogator!"

"How?"

"No one knows."

"He punched him?"

"There wasn't a mark on him."

"He choked him?"

"Not a mark on him, I tell you."

"How, then? Poison?"

"Nothing!" Ouspensky said with excitement. "That's the whole point! No one knows. But just remember—our commander is a man who can kill another in a tiny cell with nothing. Just by the sheer force of his will. So stay the fuck away from him. Because he eats runts like you for lunch."

"Lieutenant!" Alexander walked into the tent.

Ouspensky, Verenkov, and Telikov jumped up. "Yes, sir."

"Lieutenant, stop terrorizing our sergeants. I don't like you telling lies about me. For the record, I am not a double agent for the Japanese. Is that clear?"

A pause. In shaky voices, "Yes, sir."

"Now go back to your duties. All of you."

"Yes, sir."

They did not look at him as they hastily filed out. Alexander could barely keep the smile off his face.

⌀⟋⟋⟍⟍⌀

After a few weeks, Alexander began to see a pattern: He would send two squads, three, a platoon, two platoons, fifty men to the railroad, and they would not come back. For those who did come back there were no bandages, no antibiotics, no blood, no morphine. The Germans were protected by the Sinyavino hills and the trees, but they had an unfettered view of the broken railroad. Still provisions had to get to Leningrad one way or another, the railroad had to be rebuilt one way or another, and Alexander had no choice but to send his men to the railroad.

Though the stretch that kept getting knocked out of order was always the same five kilometers, Alexander could not put his men on the railroad at any time of day, at any one-hundred-meter stretch of the broken rails without an instant barrage from the hills. It was June and the weather was mild. Every afternoon Alexander carried the casualties off the railroad tracks and onto the field behind the poplars where they were lowered into mass graves that were not even covered over by dirt. The graves had been dug by mines a few weeks before and the holes were not yet filled up with dead men. The entire area smelled of dug dirt, and fresh water, and fresh death.

June 22, 1943 came and went. Two years since the start of war. Two years since the start of everything.

Orbeli and His Art, 1941

Alexander was woken up at four in the morning, after sleeping for barely an hour. His small consolation was that everyone else was also woken up, and told to go outside into the courtyard.

It was June 22, summer solstice, the longest day of the year, 1941. Sunday morning. Outside was pink dawn and light. Colonel Mikhail Stepanov addressed his garrison troops.

"About an hour ago, Hitler wiped out our Crimean naval fleet stationed in the Black Sea. Our planes, our ships and our men have been destroyed. His men are now on Soviet ground. He has also invaded our border from the Ukraine north through Prussia. Defense Minister Comrade Molotov is going to make an announcement at noon. It's war."

There was a rumble among the barely awake troops. Alexander stood silent. He wasn't surprised; there had been talk of war for a long time among the Red Army officers, and there had been rumors about Hitler's border fortifications since winter, but Alexander's first thought about war was, "War! That will give me another chance for escape."

Alexander kept himself awake with coffee and cigarettes as he listened for four hours to defense plans. He was then assigned to patrolling Leningrad until six in the evening, at which time he had to be back at the barracks for sentry duty. He left the garrison gladly at eleven in the morning.

He strolled breezily through the Haymarket and down Nevsky Prospekt, where he broke up a fight between a woman and a much bigger man. The woman was hitting the man with her bag, screaming at him. It took Alexander a few minutes to figure out that the woman was upset with the man for trying to cut in line. "Doesn't he know that war has started? What does the comrade think we're all doing here? He is not getting in front of me. I don't care if the whole Red Army comes down here."

Raising his eyebrows to the man, Alexander said, "You heard her. You're not getting in front of her."

Down by the Grand Elisey food store, he broke up a mêlée that included eight women who were all clawing at each other over a sausage that belonged to one woman, fell out of her bag and was quickly picked up by another. While this was going on, a third woman walked off with someone's flour. Alexander played King Solomon only briefly. He felt this was not his strength, arguing about sausage with eight irate women.

He walked away, straight into another fight over who was getting on the bus first.

Alexander decided to get away from Nevsky. It was worse than being in a war. In a war, at least you could take out your gun and shoot the enemy. He walked down to St. Isaac's, to the statue of the Bronze Horseman where things were more peaceful. He stood for a few minutes, smoking, looking at the statue. It had been several weeks since he had checked on his book in the Leningrad library. Now that war had started, he thought it would be wise to get the book out and keep it with him; it would probably be safer. The libraries and the museums no doubt would be shipping their precious volumes out of Leningrad—just in case. As he smoked, Alexander tried to remember bits of the "Bronze Horseman" poem he liked: *And in the moonlight's pallid glamor, rides high upon his charging brute, hand outstretched in echoing clamor, the Bronze Horseman in pursuit.* Smiling at himself for remembering words he had not read in many years, lighting another cigarette, Alexander proceeded down the embankment, past the Admiralty Gardens, past the Palace Bridge, past the Hermitage Museum, where he walked past a tall man in a suit, hunched over the parapet, looking into the river. The man took out a cigarette and nodded to Alexander without smiling. Alexander nodded back and slowed down. The man said, "Have you got a light?"

Alexander stopped and took out his lighter. "Left my matches inside," the man said quickly. "Thank you." He extended his hand. "Josif Abgarovitch Orbeli," he said, flicking the ashes out of his long, graying, unkempt beard.

"Lieutenant Alexander Belov." They shook hands.

"Ah," said Orbeli, looking into the river. "Lieutenant, is it true? War has started?"

"It's true, citizen. Where did you hear?"

Without turning around, Orbeli pointed to the Hermitage. "At work; I'm the curator. So tell me honestly, what do you think? Will the Germans get to Leningrad?"

"Why not?" said Alexander. "They got to Czechoslovakia, Austria, France, Belgium, Holland, Denmark, Norway, Poland. Europe is in Hitler's hands. Where else is Hitler going to go? He can't go to England. He's afraid of water. He had to come here. This was his plan all along. And he will come to Leningrad." With the Finns' help, he wanted to add, but didn't. The curator looked too upset.

"Oh, *Bozhe moi*," Orbeli said. "Oh, *koshmar*. What's going to happen? What's going to happen to my Hermitage? They'll bomb it like they bombed London. There will be nothing left of our city, nothing left of our spires, our churches, our national monuments. There will be nothing left of our art," he said in a breaking voice.

"St. Paul's is still standing," said Alexander, by way of comfort. "Westminster Abbey. Big Ben. London Bridge. The Germans couldn't touch the British national monuments. Forty thousand Londoners are dead, though."

"Yes, yes." Orbeli waved him off impatiently. "People always die at war. But what about my art?"

Alexander stepped slightly away. "Well, we can't evacuate St. Isaac's Cathedral, or the Bronze Horseman statue. But we will evacuate our people. And we can evacuate your art."

"Where can we possibly ship it?" Orbeli exclaimed in a high voice. "Who will look after it? Where will it be safe?"

"The art will have to take care of itself," said Alexander. "Ship it anywhere, it doesn't matter. It will be safer than in Leningrad."

"My Tamerlane? Renoir? Rembrandt? Fabergé? My precious, priceless treasures. All of it, without me?"

Alexander tipped his cap lightly. "All of it will be safer somewhere else. And someday the war will be over. Good day, citizen."

"Nothing good about this day," Orbeli muttered, and turned to walk across the road to his museum.

Alexander, amused, continued down the Neva embankment, past the Winter Palace, past Moika Canal. It was a Sunday afternoon in Leningrad, and here on the embankment everything was quiet, unlike the harried rabble that crowded on Nevsky where the lines in all the stores were out the door, people shoving and screaming obscenities at each other. There was no one here and Alexander liked it better. He passed the Summer Garden, strolling down to Smolny monastery with a rifle on his shoulder.

At the corner of Ulitsa Saltykov-Schedrin Alexander paused briefly. A few blocks to the right of the river, Tauride Park stretched pleasantly down the street and he quite liked walking past it in the summer. But Smolny and its grounds straight ahead might have some problems, some crowds in need of control. Which way to go? To go straight to Smolny and then circle around the Tauride Park or to walk along the park road and then circle around to the monastery?

He lit a cigarette and stood for a few seconds, looking at his watch. He had a bit of time. What was the rush, anyway? Any crowd problems would still be there in a half-hour just as well as in fifteen minutes. He was only one man; he couldn't be everywhere at once. Alexander turned right and walked down Ulitsa Saltykov-Schedrin.

The street was deserted, and the trees were rustling in the summer wind. He was thinking about Barrington. He remembered the woods by Barrington. He and Teddy used to lie down in the woods and listen to the trees swaying above them. He liked the sound.

He heard another sound. A soft sound, of someone singing.

It was very faint. Alexander looked down the street and saw no one.

Alexander looked across the street and saw a girl on a bench.

The first thing he noticed was a mass of light, long blonde hair covering the girl's face and the second thing he noticed was her white dress with red roses. Covered by a leafy canopy of forest-green trees, she sat on a bench like a white flurry, her golden hair, her white dress, her blood-red roses. She was eating ice cream and softly singing to herself in between the licks of the cone. Alexander recognized the tune. She was singing "We'll Meet Again in Lvov, My Love and I"—a current popular song. She somehow managed to sing, to lick her ice cream, to bounce her bare leg, her foot gussied up with a red sandal, and to pull the hair back from her face. All at once. She was oblivious not just to Alexander standing across the street dumbly staring at her, but also to the war, to the world, to all the things that guided Leningraders on this Sunday. In the moment she was in, she had herself and her lustrous hair and her magnificent dress and her ice cream and her soft voice. She was in a world Alexander had never seen, swimming on the moon in a sea of tranquility. He could not move from the spot on the pavement.

And he still could not move from that spot on the pavement, from seeing her for the first time. That's where he was to this day, knowing that had he walked straight ahead instead of making a right, he would be living a different life. Had he walked by her even at the moment of seeing her. He could have been provident, he did not have to cross the street. He could have gaped at her and gone on, couldn't he?

But on that sunlit Sunday, Alexander knew nothing, thought nothing, imagined nothing. He forgot Dimitri and war and the Soviet Union and escape plans, and even America, and crossed the street for Tatiana Metanova.

Later he watched her hands gesticulating as she spoke. Her fingers were slender and well formed. Her nails were meticulous. He asked her why she kept them so spotless and she replied that she had once known a girl with dirty fingernails. The girl had been much trouble. She had never forgotten it.

"Do you think she was trouble because of the dirty fingernails?"

"I'm almost sure of it."

Alexander wanted her spotless hands on him.

He was afraid she was too young for his man's gaze, much less for his man's hands.

"Where do you live, Tania?"

"On a street called Fifth Soviet. Do you know where that is?"

He patrolled that area. "It's near Grechesky Prospect. There's a church nearby."

"Yes, it's right across the street," she said.

"Though I think church is a strong word for that building. It's a document storage facility."

She laughed. "Yes," she said, bubbling. "It's a *Soviet* church."

The simple time with her on Sunday was so markedly brief.

All his time with her was markedly brief, encircled by war wagons, by his mother and father, by his false name, by Dimitri's perceived power over his humanity, by Dasha, oh that Dasha! Surrounded by Slonko and Nikolai Ouspensky, assailed by the Soviet Union from all sides. He had to learn how to live, not remember, not hear the never-ending echoes that those one hundred minutes alone with her kept thundering into him. One bus ride with her, when he had her all to himself, sitting on the seat next to her, walking across one Field of Mars by her side, one glimpse into what might have been, one flare of an inflamed heart and the consequence? Eternity in Soviet Russia.

Where could they have gone to hide? Where could they have disappeared?

Sunday came and went.

The Field of Mars, June, death, life, white nights, Dasha, Dimitri, they all came . . .

And went.

But there Alexander still was, standing on that street, on that curb, in the sun, looking at her under the elms, looking at provenance across from him, provenance in a white dress with red roses, licking her ice cream with red lips, singing. His and only his for one hundred minutes, blink of an eye and gone. It all was, it was, but now it had passed and the blizzard cloaked it, leaving emptiness and light. Passed forever, and he was here forever, still on the street forming and reforming his screaming heart.

Losing Pasha, 1941

Her twin brother Pasha had disappeared. It all seemed innocent enough at first, going to a boy's summer camp—but then the Luftwaffe flew over the boy's camp, and the Red Army sent in the boys to stand in front of the Panzer tanks, and Pasha vanished. She refused to accept it and went to find him in Luga with Hitler across the river, because she was crazy, and he went to bring her back because he was crazy for her.

Another tainted moment of having her this time *almost* to himself. When they lay in his tent, there was no other place they wanted to be, and they both knew it. Despite Hitler's forces a hundred meters away, despite Tania's broken ribs, her broken leg and her broken spirit, despite losing Pasha.

He felt her short sobs. "Shura, we have to find him."

"Oh, Tania."

"We have to. I can't go back home without finding him. I can't fail like this. Please. You don't know my family. You don't know me."

"I know Tania. They—and you—will have to learn to live with what you still have."

"Don't say that. I can't live without him."

Alexander could barely get his words out. "I'm sorry, Tania."

"I can't, you don't know. He is my brother, don't you understand? And what if he is somewhere waiting for me and I don't come? Who else should go and rescue you if not your family? Who else? Oh, Alexander, what if he is wondering why it's taking me so long to come and find him, and I don't come? Why don't I come?"

"Why would he be waiting?"

"Because he knows what I am. I won't leave him."

Alexander fell quiet. Lucky Pasha having someone like Tatiana on his side. "Tania, there's no trace of him. Two million German men stand between you and Pasha. You can't walk, nor bend. You're broken, and he is lost. Leave him be. Let him go with God."

And the next morning alone in the woods under the falling bombs, covering her with his body to shield her from harm, he couldn't take it anymore, couldn't stop himself. Alexander kissed Tatiana. They could have died there in the woods; he almost wanted to when he recalled dimly what lay ahead of them—desperation, deceit, Dasha, Dimitri, Hitler, Stalin, war all around them.

Pasha was never found. Weeks later they got word that he had died on a burning train. The father didn't recover, drinking down, burning down his grief until there was nothing left of him either. Pasha had been his only son. Alexander had one more grateful thought for easing his own father's heart in prison. He was also his father's only son. Could he even remember what it was like to have a father, a mother, bending over him at night, kissing him, crying?

He couldn't.

More and more Tatiana seemed to him to be a chance not taken, a moment gone. He could not stop what he felt for her, yet she seemed for another life, for another time, for another man.

She wanted more from Alexander. Didn't they all.

Except he didn't have more. He didn't have anything.

CHAPTER SEVENTEEN

Christmas in New York, 1943

TATIANA AND ANTHONY WERE invited to spend Christmas Eve with Vikki and her grandparents.

When she arrived she found Edward there.

"Why did you invite him?" she whispered to Vikki in the kitchen.

"He celebrates Christmas, too, Tania."

Tatiana sat next to Edward on the couch, sipping something called eggnog and holding on her lap six-month-old Anthony, who wanted some eggnog too. Edward told Tatiana that four days earlier he had been kicked out of his home. His wife apparently had had enough of him working such crazy hours and spending so little time with her.

"Let me understand," said Tatiana. "You weren't spending time with her so she throw you out?"

"That's correct."

Tatiana asked slowly, "But won't this mean you be spending even less time with her?"

Edward laughed. "I don't think she liked me very much, Tania," he said.

"That's unfortunate in wife," she commented.

Vikki, who had brought them some biscuits covered with honey, had a self-satisfied look about herself, a look that later prompted Tatiana to quietly call Vikki a trouble maker.

There was soothing caroling Christmas music on, there was the smell of ginger, of apple pie, of spaghetti sauce filled with garlic, the burgundy colors in the apartment became somehow appropriate, and Vikki was wearing a brown velvet dress that went well with her brown velvet hair and her brown velvet eyes. Isabella and Travis fed everybody as though there were no war. The conversation was as light as the wine.

Later, she sat in the quiet bedroom and nursed her son while the happy noises full of Christmas graces filled the apartment. Inside the room was quiet and warm and dark. She closed her eyes and rocked.

There was no comfort for a young woman named Tatiana this Christmas Eve, not at the candlelight mass, not at the celebration dinner, not during prayer, not in sleep, not with Vikki, not in Ellis. As she nursed her boy, Tatiana's salty tears fell on his face that she didn't bother to wipe, and in her tears and in her milk and in her heart only one word struck the clock of her soul on the stroke of every minute: *Alexander.*

Ellis at Christmas was a grim place. Why was that so soothing to her? Because the wounded needed her. Because someone besides her son needed her. She fed the soldiers lying in their white beds, and she whispered to them to think of their brothers in arms, who had neither bed nor solace. "Well, Nurse Tania, that's because they don't have you looking after them," said a wounded German pilot named Paul Schmidt in accented English. He had been flying over the North Channel, bombing the tankers bringing food and arms into the North Sea. He had been brought down into the water. En route to the U.S. he had both his legs amputated and was now convalescing long enough to be sent back home. He told Tatiana that he didn't really want to be sent home. "If I still had my legs, the Americans would send me to work for their war effort, wouldn't they? Like they do the rest of our boys?"

"They just might send you anyway. You could sit and milk cows."

"What I'd like," he said with a smile, "is to have a nice American girl marry me and keep me from going back."

Tatiana smiled back. "You might ask one of other nurses," she said. "I not American."

"I don't care," he said, the interest in his eyes not waning.

"You think your wife back home would like that? You marrying?"

"We wouldn't have to tell her." He grinned.

She told him a little about herself. Tatiana found it remarkably easy to tell the German and Italian soldiers about her life before America, compared with how remarkably difficult she found it to talk to Vikki or Edward. She could not let her friends know where she lived every day of her life, among the snows of Leningrad and the waters of Lazarevo. Yet these men, homeless and dying strangers, understood her well, knew her well.

"I'm glad I'm not on the Eastern Front anymore," said Paul Schmidt.

I'm not, Tatiana wanted to say. Because when I was on the Eastern Front, my life meant something. "You weren't wounded on the Eastern Front," she said finally. Bending her head, she continued to feed him, looking down into the metal spoon touching the white enamel plate. She concentrated on the chicken broth smell, concentrated on the feel of white crisp starched linen under her arms, on the wool of his blanket, on the slight chill of the ward. She tried to detach herself from visions of the Eastern Front. *Feeding her husband . . . bringing the spoon to his lips . . . sleeping in the chair next to him . . . walking away from his bed, and turning around—*

No. NO.

"You have no idea what the Soviets are doing to us," he repeated.

"I have some idea, Paul," Tatiana said. "I was nurse in Leningrad last year. Not long before that, I saw what you German boys did to our Soviet men."

He shook his head while swallowing the broth, so vehemently that some of the liquid escaped his mouth and ran down his chin. Tatiana wiped it and brought another spoonful to his mouth.

"The Soviets are going to win this war," he said, lowering his voice. "And do you know why?"

"Why?"

"Because they don't value the lives of their men."

And then they were both quiet.

"Does Hitler value your life?" asked Tatiana.

"More than Stalin would. Hitler tries to heal us so he can send us back to the front, but Stalin doesn't even bother. He lets his men die and then sends thirteen- and fourteen-year-olds to the front. And then they die."

"Soon," Tatiana said, "there will be no one left to send."

"The war will be Stalin's before that happens."

Tatiana was called away to tend to the other wounded, but returned to Paul with some Christmas cookies, giving him what remained on her tray and pouring him tea with milk.

"You're wrong, by the way, about me," he told her. "I was wounded in Russia. Over the Ukraine. I was flying bombing missions and was knocked down. When I fell, I nearly lost my stomach." He stopped, remembering. "Literally, lost my stomach."

"I understand," said Tatiana.

"After I healed, they transferred me to the North Channel—less dangerous. Ironic, isn't it? My captain thought I'd lost my edge. But do

you know, when I fell over the Ukraine, I fell into the hands of the Soviet partisans, who didn't kill me. They took pity on me, I don't know,
maybe because it was Christmas of last year."

"I don't think they took pity on you because it was Christmas," Tatiana said gently. "The Soviets don't celebrate Christmas."

He glanced at her. "Is that why you're here? The holidays don't
mean much to you?"

She shook her head. She wanted to cross herself to give herself
strength, but didn't. She wanted to cry, but didn't. She wanted to be
strong, to be impenetrable, to be like a rock, to be like Alexander. But she
couldn't be. "I'm here," she said, "because it makes wounded here happy
that they not alone so far from home." Her voice faltered. "I'm here, because I hope that if I do something nice for you, if I bring you just a bit of
comfort, then maybe, somewhere else, someplace else, someone might
bring comfort to . . ." A small tear fell from her eye.

Paul stared at her with surprise. "You think that's how it works?"

"I do not know how it works," Tatiana said.

"Is he on the Eastern Front?"

"I don't know where he is," she said. She couldn't lend voice to the
death certificate in the black backpack in her room.

"Well, you better pray he's not on the Eastern Front. He won't last a
week there."

"No?" Her face must have shown the paling of her already weak-
ened spirit, because Paul patted her hand and said, "Ah, hell, don't
worry about it, Nurse Tania. Wherever he is, here or in the hereafter,
you know what he is hoping for?"

"What?" she whispered.

"That *you're* safe," Paul replied.

⟨⟩

Christmas in New York.

Christmas in New York in wartime. The year before, Tatiana had
spent New Year's Eve in Grechesky hospital with Dr. Matthew Sayers,
surrounded by Soviet nurses. They had drunk some vodka and passed
the glass to a few patients who had been awake enough and strong
enough to raise their glasses. Tatiana had thought only about going to
the front to meet up with Alexander. They were leaving in five days.
Alexander didn't know it yet, but one way or another she was going to

get herself and her husband out of the Soviet Union. Leningrad had no lights. Leningrad was covered in broken ruins. German shells flew from Pulkovo on New Year's Eve, German planes bombed the city on New Year's Day. Four days later, Tatiana had left Leningrad in Dr. Sayers' Red Cross truck and thought to herself, will I see Leningrad again?

And now it looked as if she never would.

Instead she was seeing New York at Christmas. She saw Little Italy, covered with green and red flickering lights, and she saw 57th Street, decked out with white lights, and she saw the Empire State Building, with its red and green spire, and she saw the Christmas tree at Rockefeller Center. The lights in the tall buildings were on for an hour because it was Christmas, and then were dimmed out for war.

She walked in the cold and the snow, pushing Anthony in the carriage, and all around her was noise and bustling people with shopping bags. Tatiana had no bags. Tatiana wasn't buying presents. She was walking through a snowy, excited New York at war, thinking that Alexander had lived ten Decembers like this, in Boston. Ten Decembers of Christmas carols, and packages under arms, and bells constantly ringing, and trees covered with lights, and a big sign on top of one coffee shop saying "JESUS IS THE REASON."

He had lived with it all, and his mother and father gave him gifts and Santa came to him on Christmas. So Tatiana went into a toy store and bought Anthony a train set from Santa. He was too little for a train set, but he would grow into it.

At Bergdoff's on 58th and Fifth Avenue, Tatiana saw some beautiful Christmas blankets in the window display, and because she was cold and because she was thinking of Alexander, she walked into Bergdoff and inquired about them. The blankets were one hundred per cent cashmere and one hundred outrageous dollars each. The lady told her that and turned away, as if the conversation were over. Then, remembering, she turned back to Tatiana, took the blanket out of her hands and turned away again.

"I'll take it," Tatiana said, getting out her money. "I will take three. What colors do you have?"

That night at Ellis, mother and son slept together in her single bed under two cashmere blankets. The third she was saving for Anthony's father.

New York at Christmas time. There was ham, and there was cheese, and there was milk and chocolates and a couple of ounces of steak for everyone, and there was the lively spirit of women trying to get the last of the toys for their boys. And there were men who came home from the war for Christmas.

Not Vikki's man, because she divorced him.

And not Tatiana's man, because she had lost him.

But other men.

The trees all glowed with white lights, and even at Ellis, the nurses decorated a tree for the German and Italian soldiers, except that no one wanted to work Christmas Day, not for double pay, not for triple pay, not for a week's vacation. Tatiana worked for triple pay and a week's vacation.

New York at Christmas.

As she walked down Mulberry Street in Little Italy on the way to Vikki's apartment, pushing Anthony in the carriage, Tatiana sang under her breath, "A Long Long Trail," a song she had heard on the hospital radio.

> *"There's a long long trail unwinding*
> *Into the land of my dreams,*
> *Where the nightingales are singing*
> *And a white moon beams.*
> *There is a long long night of waiting*
> *Until my dreams all come true,*
> *Till the day when I'll be going*
> *Down that long long trail with you."*

CHAPTER EIGHTEEN

Alexander and the Germans, 1943

THE SOVIET MEN WERE still dying at Sinyavino, and the Germans remained in the hills.

Alexander would send more and they would get killed. Lieutenant-colonel Muraviev, in charge of both the penal and the non-penal battalions, had no interest in hearing from Alexander. "It's a penal battalion," he said. "Do you know the meaning of that, Captain?"

"I do. But let me ask you, I haven't taken math since secondary school, but at the rate of thirty men a day, how long will I keep my two hundred men?"

"I know the answer to that one," Muraviev exclaimed. "Six!"

"Yes. Not even one week. The Germans still have three thousand troops in the hills, while we have virtually none."

"Don't worry. We will get you more men to send to the railroad. We always do."

"Is that the goal? To let the Germans use our men for target practice?"

Muraviev narrowed his eyes. "I've been told about you. You're a troublemaker. You're forgetting, you're in charge of a *penal* battalion. The safety of your men is not my concern. Just fix the railroad and shut up."

Alexander left without saluting Muraviev. Clearly he needed to take matters into his own hands. He didn't wish for another man like Stepanov to guide him. He wished for three men a tenth of Stepanov to let him do as he knew best. Well, why would Alexander's men mean anything to Muraviev? They were all convicted criminals. Their crimes included having had mothers who had been in musical groups that corresponded with people in France, even though the musical groups had been long defunct and even though the mothers had been long dead. Some of them had been found in churches, before late last year when Stalin had admitted, according to Pravda, that he himself believed in a "kind of God." Some of them unwittingly shook hands with people who were about to be arrested. Some of them had rooms next to people who had been arrested. Ouspensky said, "I was one of those people. I had the bad luck to be bedded next to you, Captain." Alexander smiled. They were walking to the armaments tent. He had asked Ouspensky to come with him. Alexander was going to requisition a 160-millimeter mortar.

The previous dawn, Alexander had climbed up behind the bushes on the slopes that led to the railroad and watched his men become fodder for the German bombs. With a pair of field binoculars he observed where the three German bombs came from. They were a good two kilometers away. He needed the 160-millimeter mortar. Nothing else would reach.

Of course the commissar's office didn't want to give it to him. The desk sergeant said the penal battalion was not entitled to one, and the order to requisition one had to come from Alexander's commanding officer, who was Muraviev and who with a flat snicker refused.

"I've lost a hundred and ninety-two men in seven days. Do we have enough convicts to repair this road?"

"Orders are orders, Belov! The mortar is going to be needed by the company storming Sinyavino Heights next week."

"Your men intend to carry a three-ton weapon *up* a mountain, Colonel?"

Muraviev ordered Alexander out of his tent.

Alexander had had enough. He called one of his sergeants, Melkov. In the evening, Melkov, who tolerated vodka best in the battalion, got the armament guard good and drunk, so drunk in fact that the guard—when he fell asleep in his chair—did not hear Alexander and Ouspensky open the creaky door of the wooden weapons facility and wheel the mortar out. They had to wheel it a kilometer in the dark. Meanwhile Melkov, taking his assignment very seriously, sat by the armaments guard and every fifteen minutes poured more vodka down his throat.

Right before five a.m., seven of Alexander's men used themselves as bait on the railroad.

Through his binoculars, Alexander watched the origination point of the first bomb from the hills arch its whistling way into the tracks. His men ran, escaping unharmed. It took both Alexander and Ouspensky to load the detonation explosive chemical rocket bomb into the breech. "Now just remember, Nikolai," said Alexander as he pointed the cannon to the hills. "We only have two bombs. Two chances to blow up the Fritzes. We need to return this damn thing in twenty minutes before the changing of the guard at six."

"You don't think req will notice the two biggest bombs gone?"

Alexander watched the blue morning hill through the binoculars. "After we blast the fucking Germans, I really don't care if anyone notices the missing bombs. I bet they won't notice. Who do you think keeps an inventory of this stuff? The drunk guard? Melkov is taking care of him. He is also taking thirty sub-machine guns for our men."

Ouspensky laughed.

"Don't laugh," said Alexander. "You'll disturb the delicate balance of the charge. Ready?" He lit the fuse.

The fuse burned for two seconds, there was recoil straight down into the ground, which rumbled as though it were an earthquake fault line, and the first bomb whistled out of the barrel, in an arc through the air. It flew a kilometer and a half; Alexander watched it fall into the trees and burst. By the time it reached its target, the second bomb was already on its way. Alexander didn't even look to see where the second one landed. He had already begun to dismantle the mortar. Leaving Ouspensky in charge of the remaining men, he wheeled the heavy artillery back to the requisition house and managed to attach the lock and throw the keys back to the unconscious guard at two minutes to six. "Well done," he said to Melkov as they hurriedly walked back to their tents for morning inspection.

"Thank you, sir," said Melkov. "It was my pleasure."

"I can see that," Alexander said, smiling. "Don't let me catch you drinking so much again. Or you're going straight to the brig."

The requisition guard remained unconscious for another four hours and was summarily taken off guard duty for gross dereliction. "It's a good thing for you, Corporal, that nothing was missing!" Muraviev hollered.

The guard's punishment consisted of serving a week under Alexander's railroad repair command. Alexander said, "You're lucky the Germans have been quiet the past two days, otherwise you'd be going to your death, Corporal."

While the Germans were regrouping, Alexander's men fixed the railroad tracks unharmed, and five trains with food and medical supplies made it through to Leningrad.

After that the Germans resumed shelling the Soviet soldiers, but not for long because Muraviev *gave* Alexander the mortar. Having exposed the German position and after a few more mortar attacks on the

Sinyavino area, a battalion of the 67th Army stormed the hills, leaving Alexander's men down below on artillery support.

The battalion did not return, but the Germans stopped shooting at the railroad for good.

⚬᠁᠊᠊᠊᠊ᠣ

In the fall of 1943, the 67th Army ordered Alexander's penal battalion—shrunk to two minimal companies, 144 men in total—across the river Neva south to Pulkovo, to the last holdout of the German blockade ring around Leningrad. This time, Alexander received some artillery—heavy machine guns, mortars, anti-tank bombs, and a case of grenades. Each of his men had a light machine gun and plenty of ammunition. At Pulkovo, for twelve days in September 1943, Alexander's 7th battalion, with two others and a motorized company, bombarded the Germans. They even had some airpower helping them, two Shtukareviches. It was all to no avail.

The leaves fell off the trees. Sergeant Melkov was killed. It got cold, another winter came, the fourteenth winter since the Barringtons came to the Soviet Union. Alexander continued to push his way up the hill day after bloodied bitter day. He received new men—200 of them. The eastern side of the hill was liberated from the Germans in December 1943.

Up on a Pulkovo hill, Alexander could look north and see in the distance the few twinkling lights of Leningrad. And in the near distance during a clear winter day, he could see the smokestacks of the Kirov factory, which continued to produce arms for the city. If he looked through his binoculars, he would be able to see the Kirov wall, in front of which he could see himself standing day after day, week after week with his cap in his hands, waiting for Tatiana to run out of the factory doors.

He didn't need to stand on the Pulkovo crest to see it.

⚬᠁᠊᠊᠊᠊ᠣ

New Year's Eve, 1943, Alexander spent in front of a fire near his officer's tent with his three first lieutenants, three second lieutenants, and three sergeants. He drank vodka with Ouspensky by his side. Everyone seemed optimistic about 1944. The Germans were on the way out of Russia. After the summer of 1943, after Sinyavino, after the Battle of

Kursk, after the liberation of Kiev in November and Crimea just a few weeks ago, Alexander knew that 1944 was going to be the last year the Germans would be on Soviet soil. His mission was to proceed westward with his penal battalion, to push the Germans back into Germany—at all costs, at whatever the cost.

That was Alexander's New Year resolution—to make his way west. His only hope lay there.

He allowed himself another drink. Someone, already drunk, told a bad Stalin joke. Someone cried for his wife. Alexander was almost certain it wasn't him. On the outside he tried to be fashioned of concrete. Ouspensky clinked a glass of vodka with him and finished off the bottle.

"Why can't we get furlough like other soldiers?" Ouspensky complained, drunk, sentimental, disheveled. "Why can't we go home for a day on New Year's?"

"I don't know if you've noticed, Lieutenant, but we're fighting a war. Tomorrow we sleep away the hangover and on Tuesday we're in battle again. The German blockade around Leningrad will be lifted completely this month. The Nazis will leave our city and it will be because of your efforts."

"I don't care about the fucking Nazis. I want to see my wife," said Ouspensky. "You've got nowhere to go—that's why you want to push the Germans out of Russia."

"I've got somewhere to go," said Alexander slowly.

Studying him carefully, Ouspensky asked, "You have a family?"

"Not around here, no."

For some reason this made Ouspensky only more glum.

"Look on the bright side, Nikolai," said Alexander. "We're not among the enemy, right?"

Ouspensky said nothing.

Alexander continued. "We drank a whole bottle of vodka in a few hours. We had ham, some smoked herring, some pickles, and even some fresh black bread. We told jokes, we laughed, we smoked. Think how much worse it could be." Alexander wasn't going to let his mind go down the corridors of its own torture chambers.

"I don't know about you, Captain, but I've got a wife and two small boys I haven't seen in ten months. Last time I saw them was right before I got shot. My wife thinks I'm dead. I can tell my letters aren't getting to her. She is not replying to them." Ouspensky paused and wavered like a sapling.

Alexander said nothing. I have a wife and a child I've never seen. What's happened to her, to the baby? Have they made it anywhere? Are they safe? How can I live not knowing if she's all right?

I can't.

I can't live not knowing if she is all right.

Thou shall not be afraid for the terror by night . . . nor for the arrow that flieth by day . . .

Ouspensky drank straight from a newly opened bottle. "Ah," he said, waving his hand. "Hell with it. Life is so fucking hard."

Alexander took the vodka bottle from Ouspensky and drank from it himself. "Compared to what?" he asked, taking a smoke, inhaling the acrid fumes into his constricted throat.

"Tania, let's get drunk."

"Why, what for?"

"Let's smoke, get drunk, celebrate your birthday, our wedding, and be really rowdy." He raises his eyebrows.

"You're a goose. My birthday was a week ago." She smiles. "We celebrated already. You married me. Remember?"

He grabs her off the pine needle ground.

She throws her arms around him. "All right, all right, I'll drink a little vodka with you."

"Not a little. An unconscionable amount. We'll raise our cups . . ." He pours for the two of them near the fire in the clearing. She is kneeling on the blanket, expectantly. He kneels in front of her. "And we'll drink to our wonderful life."

Tatiana raises her cup. "All right, Shura. Let's drink to our wonderful life."

CHAPTER NINETEEN

New York, June 1944

THE ROOM IS STARK white. The curtains, white, barely move. The window is closed. There is no wind. There is no draft. There is no pink and lucid air.

I sit on the floor of my stark white room. The beige door closed. The silver lock latched. There is rust on the hinges that creak as they swing.

Open and shut.

In front of me I hold my black bag, and in this bag, he lives. His beige cap, his black-and-white photo with his white teeth and caramel eyes.

On the gray-tile floor I sit, but outside, not an hour away, lies Bear Mountain. And the trees on the mountain are sepia and cinnabar, colored with copper and sunset. Like his copper eyes and sunset lips. In Sheep Meadow I can play baseball with my cream wooden bat. Like he played when he was a boy . . .

Scout.

I can make a noose knot like he taught me.

I can climb a green tree.

I can swing under the silver moon in the sinking water under the plum sky.

Through my window just beyond the red, white and blue of the American flag, beyond the Golden Door and the Coral Gothic of Ellis gleams the lazurite bay that leads to the living sea, to the wailing ocean.

My colors run from moon to sun, from rust to sky. The oceans divide us as we fail, as we fall into the whiteout of my once and future life. The whiteout of sky and fog and mist and ice. The ice is cracked and bleeding. You're underneath it. And I am, too.

I sit on the gray-tile floor, touching the black canvas, the metal rim of the gun, the yellowing papers of your savior book, your green crisp dollar bills.

I touch the picture of you and me newly married exploding on red wings, flying to each other on the cyclamen wings of Promethean fire.

Outside, the siren wails, the ball cracks against the bat, the baby cries, the gray ice bleeds. I remain on the floor with the black canvas bag of our surprise hope at my feet. Forever on the floor, black with the colors of my grief.

⟨෧෨⟩

"Tania, what's the matter?" It was Vikki, standing at the open door of Tatiana's room. Anthony was on the floor playing with his toys. Tatiana was on the floor with her head on the tiles.

"Nothing."

"Are you working today?"

"I'm up, I'm up."

In a startled voice, Vikki said, "What's the matter with you?"

"Not much," Tatiana said. She knew she must have been a sight. Her eyes felt swollen shut. She could barely see.

"It's eight! Have you been crying? The day hasn't begun yet!"

"Let me get dressed. I have to make my rounds."

"Do you want to talk?"

"Not at all. I'm fine. It's my birthday today. I'm twenty."

"That's why you're like this? Happy birthday! Why didn't you say so? What's so awful about your birthday?"

"I can't believe we're getting married on my birthday!" she says.

"This way, you'll never forget me."

"Who could ever forget you, Alexander?" she asks, groping gently for him.

Standing in the stained-glass light, her hair, her heart flying in the air.

Tatiana didn't celebrate. She worked all day and played with her nearly one-year-old boy in the evening. At night, with the curtains open, the windows open, the briny air wafting through the room, Tatiana kneeled by the side of her bed, grasping the wedding rings hanging at her chest. She'd been in the United States nearly a year. On the night of her twentieth birthday, Tatiana sat on the floor of her room at Ellis after nursing Anthony and took everything out of her black backpack—for the first time since she left the Soviet Union. One by one, she took out the loaded German-issue pistol, the *Bronze Horseman* book, the Russian-English phrasebook, the photo of him, the wedding photos of them, his officer cap, and everything out of the pockets.

That's when she found the *Hero of the Soviet Union* medal that had once belonged to Alexander.

She stared at it with incomprehension for what seemed half the night, and then she went out into the hall and looked at it under the light, to see if maybe she had made a mistake.

The sun went up, came down. It was warm. The water shimmered. And she still stared at the medal. She was dumbstruck. Was it a mistake?

As clearly as she saw the sailboats in the bay, Tatiana saw the medal hanging on the back of Alexander's chair the last evening she saw him with Dr. Sayers by her side. Alexander had said, "I'm going to come back tomorrow afternoon a decorated lieutenant colonel," and Tatiana had beamed and glanced at the medal hanging on the back of the chair by his hospital bed.

How did this medal end up in her backpack? She could not have taken it—it was not hers to take.

What does it mean? she whispered to herself, but was no closer to understanding; in fact was further away. The more she tried to think clearly, the more she came up against the concrete blocks her mind had put up.

But Dr. Sayers had brought her the backpack when she was on the floor in his office after she'd learned about Alexander's truck blowing up and sinking in Lake Ladoga. Sayers brought the backpack for her before they got into his Red Cross jeep and drove to Finland.

And on that floor she still remained—in the morning and at night, between patients and shopping, between lunch and dinner, between Vikki and Edward, between Ellis and Anthony. She hopped on the ferry and remained on the floor, and on that floor was her backpack and in it was Alexander's *Hero of the Soviet Union* medal.

Did Alexander give the medal to her? Could she have forgotten that?

When Dr. Sayers told her about Alexander, he gave her Alexander's officer cap. Did the doctor give her the cap *and* the medal?

She did not think so.

Did Colonel Stepanov?

Not him either.

She got up off the floor, and draped the medal over her neck next to the rope that held their wedding rings.

A day passed and then another and then another.

A German soldier saw the medal and in broken English said, "Where you get that? That's very powerful medal. Only given to most honor soldiers. Where you get that?"

Every time Tatiana nursed her boy, every time he lay in her arms and she watched him, she could not help thinking, *if Alexander was wearing that medal when he died, it would still be on his neck*. Because Tatiana knew that when you went to get promoted, you went draped in your honor. You carried your flag with you.

The doctor might have given me his cap, but he wouldn't have taken a medal off Alexander's neck. And even if he did, the doctor would have *handed* the medal to me. Wouldn't he? *Here, Tania, here is your husband's cap, and here is his medal, too. Keep it all.*

No, this medal was hidden from her; it was placed in the smallest compartment in the bag, inside a secret pocket. There was nothing else in that pocket, and she never would have found it had she not taken everything out and felt through the canvas.

Why would Dr. Sayers have hidden the medal?

Why not give it to her with the cap?

Because he was afraid it would raise too many questions.

Would she have become too suspicious? But suspicious of what?

Tatiana was groping blindly for the false note. She couldn't figure it out. She slept, worked, nursed, and in the middle of one late June night, she opened her eyes and gasped.

She knew what it was.

Perhaps she would have flared up at the medal had she been given it, thought about it too much, wondered about it. Become too suspicious of one thing or another.

But Dr. Sayers wouldn't have known that.

Only one person would have known that.

Alexander wanted her to have his highest medal of honor, but knew she couldn't see it right away, that it would raise too many questions for her. So he told Dr. Sayers to hide it. On the ice, in the hospital, some-where, he asked Dr. Sayers to hide it.

Which meant there had been a deception and Dr. Sayers was in on it.

Was Alexander's death in the plan, too?

Was Dimitri's?

"Tatiasha—remember Orbeli."

That was the last thing he had said to her. Remember Orbeli. Was he asking her if she remembered, as in "Remember Orbeli?"

Or was he telling her to remember? "Remember Orbeli."

Tatiana did not sleep for the rest of the night.

Byelorussia, June 1944

Alexander called Nikolai Ouspensky into his tent. They had set up camp in western Lithuania for two days of rest and further instructions. "Lieutenant, what's wrong with Sergeant Verenkov?"

"I don't know what you mean, Captain."

"Well, just this morning, he cheerfully informed me that the tank had been fixed."

Ouspensky beamed. "It has been, Captain."

"This surprises me, Lieutenant."

"Why, sir?"

"Well, for one," Alexander said patiently, "I didn't know the tank needed fixing."

"Badly, sir. The diesel pistons were misfiring. They needed to be aligned."

Nodding, Alexander said, "That's very good, Lieutenant, but it does bring me to my second point of surprise."

"And that is, sir?"

"We don't *have* a fucking tank!"

Ouspensky smiled. "Oh, yes, we do, sir. We do. Come with me."

Outside near the woods, Alexander saw a green light battle tank with the Red Star and the emblem "For Stalin!" emblazoned on the side. Like the ones Tania used to make at Kirov. Only this one was smaller. A T-34. Alexander walked around the tank. It was battle-weary but generally in good condition. The treads were intact. He liked the number on the tank: 623. The turret was large. The cannon was larger. "A 100-millimeter!" said Ouspensky.

Alexander glanced at him. "What the fuck are you so proud of? You built this yourself?"

"No. I stole it myself."

Alexander could not help laughing. "Where from?"

"Fished it out of the pond over there."

"Was it completely covered with water? Is all the ammo soggy?"

"No, no, just the wheels and the tread were in the water. It had stalled; they couldn't get it started."

"How did *you* get it started?"

"I didn't. I had thirty men help me push it out. That's when Verenkov fixed it. Now it works like a music box."

"Where did it come from?"

"Who the fuck cares? From the battalion before us?"

"There is no battalion before us. You haven't figured out yet that we're the first in the line of fire?"

"Well, maybe they were retreating from the woods. I don't know. I saw a corpse floating in the pond. Maybe it was the gunner."

"Not a very good one," commented Alexander.

"Isn't it fantastic?"

"Yes, it's great. They're going to take it away from us. Does it have much ammo?"

"It's loaded. I think that's why it sank. It's supposed to store only three thousand 7.62-millimeter rounds, and it's got six thousand!"

"Any 100-millimeter?"

"Yes." Ouspensky grinned. "Thirty. Five hundred of the 11.63-millimeter rounds—for the mortars. It's got fifteen rockets, and look, a fixed heavy-machine-gun. We're set, Captain."

"It'll all be taken away from us."

"They'll have to get past you first." Ouspensky saluted him. "You'll be our tank commander."

"It's always a pleasure when a lieutenant assigns duties to the captain, you bastard," said Alexander.

With Ouspensky as his driver, and Telikov as his gunner, and Verenkov as his loader, he was able to protect his men with the tank in skirmishes from spring to summer 1944 for three hundred kilometers from Byelorussia to eastern Poland. The fighting in Byelorussia was the worst. The Germans did not want to leave. Alexander did not blame them. With his helmet on, he plowed through the Byelorussian countryside, not stopping at ponds, or woods, or loss of men, or villages, or women, or even sleep. The tread wearing out on his tank, Alexander forged ahead, keeping only one thought in front—Germany.

Field after field, forest after forest, marsh, mud, mines, rains. They would set up their tents and catch fish in rivers, cook it in steel bowls over fires, eat two to a bowl—Ouspensky always ate with Alexander—and then restless sleep, and then onward again into German bullets and German arms. There were three Soviet armies pushing the Germans out of Russia, Army Group Ukraine, the most southern, Army Group Center and Army Group North, of which Alexander was part, under General Rokossovsky. The Soviets were not content to merely push the Germans out of Russia. There was going to be retribution on German soil for the evil inflicted on Russia the past two and a half years and for that, millions of men had to plow through Lithuania, Latvia, Byelorussia, and Poland. Stalin wanted to be in Berlin by fall. Alexander did not think that was possible but even so, it was not because of a lack of effort on his part. Onward field after mined field, and the men lay afterward dead and unburied in the fields that once grew potatoes. The remaining men took their rifles and went on. There were a dozen engineers in Alexander's battalion who could find and de-prime mines. They kept getting killed, and Alexander kept getting new engineers. Finally he trained everyone in his battalion how to find a mine and how to pull out the fuse. After crossing the un-primed field, they would come to a wood, and in the wood the Germans awaited them. Five penal battalions would push their way through the wood first, through the rivers first, through the marsh first, to clear the way for the regular divisions. And then more woods, more fields.

It was good that it wasn't winter, but it was still cold and wet at night. The rivers weren't frozen, and the men could clean themselves, thus avoiding typhus—just barely. Alexander knew: typhus meant death by firing squad—the army could not afford an epidemic. The penal battalions were the first to be killed, but also the first to be replenished: there seemed to be no shortage of political convicts sent to die for Mother Russia. To boost sagging morale, Stalin decided to put honor and dignity back into the Red Army by introducing new uniforms— new after a fashion. Following Stalin's directive in 1943, even the officers in penal battalions wore the uniforms of the old Tsar's *Imperial Army,* with red emblazoned shoulder boards, gray felt fabric and gilded epaulets. It made dying in the mud so much more dignified and stepping on mines a matter of great honor. Even Ouspensky seemed to breathe easier with his one lung while wearing the uniform he would have died protecting the emperor in.

The men had no hair anywhere on their bodies. Under Alexander's directive, they shaved themselves daily to prevent the spread of lice. After heavy fighting, they would spend a day in the river shaving.

Alexander was often unable to tell his men apart from one another. Some were slightly taller than average, some were slightly smaller, some had birthmarks, others were clean, some were dark-skinned, most were white and sunburned. Only a few were freckled. Some had green eyes, some brown, and one Corporal Yermenko had one green eye, one brown.

In civil life, hair defined men. Head hair, body hair, but now the men were defined by war and their scars. The scars were the most distinguishing features. Scars from battle, from knife wounds, from bullets, from compound fractures, from shell grazings, from gunpowder burns. On the arms, maybe on the upper shoulders, perhaps on the lower legs. There were not too many living with scars on their chests, abdomens, or scalps.

Alexander knew his Lieutenant Ouspensky by the wheezing noise he made when he breathed, and by the scar over his right lung, and he knew his Sergeant Telikov by his white, wiry, long body, and Sergeant Verenkov by his squat body that must have been once nearly completely covered with black hair and was now nearly completely covered with black stubble.

Alexander preferred them to have fewer distinguishing features. It made losing the men easier. One loss, one replacement with another shaved, bald, smooth, scarred man.

Alexander's battalion started up in northern Russia and moved down to Lithuania and Latvia. By the time they got to Byelorussia, he had been ordered to switch fronts and go from Rokossovsky's Army Group North, to Zhukov's Army Group Center. In flat and largely woodless Byelorussia there was a rousting of the Germans such as Alexander had never seen; to do it the Red Army lost over 125,000 men and twenty-five divisions in Byelorussia alone, while Alexander's battalion pushed forward and south, forward and south, finally connecting with Konev's northern divisions of southernmost Army Group Ukraine.

After June 1944, when news came that the American and British forces landed in Normandy, Alexander's battalion covered a hundred kilometers in ten days, knocking out four German companies of 500 men each. The Soviet trucks rallied behind with supplies and food, and more men to replace the losses. Alexander was unstoppable. Like Comrade Stalin, he needed to get into Germany. Stalin may have wanted retribution, but Alexander felt his deliverance lay there.

The Black Horseman of the Apocalypse, 1941

Fed up and frustrated, Alexander volunteered himself to fight the Finns in Karelia to get as far away from the Metanovs as possible.

He asked Dimitri to come with him, mentioning valor, medals, promotions, but thinking shootings, stabbings, casualties.

True to form, Dimitri refused to go to Karelia to fight, and then was promptly sent to the slaughterhouse of Tikhvin where he was outmanned and outarmed by the Germans.

Alexander was sent with a thousand troops to push the Finns back from the supply line to Leningrad. Weeks went by of savage fighting, of gaining territory meter by hard won bloody meter. Finally, after a day of gunfire that left three hundred Red Army soldiers dead, Alexander, surveying the damage in the near dark, found himself one icy late September evening alone in a field with dead Soviet men around him and with dead Finnish men in front of him. All quiet on the Karelian front and the NKVD were half a kilometer back in the bushes, away from the front line. The fires from the shells still burning, branches broken from trees crackling, snow black from the blood of man, smell acrid of singed human flesh, a few isolated groans, and Alexander alone.

All was quiet, except the roaring in Alexander's chest. He looked back; there was no movement behind him. The machine gun was in his hands. He took a step, then another, then another. He had his Shpagin, his rifle, his pistol, his uniform. He was now walking amid the dead Finns close to the woods. In one and a half minutes he could be wearing a Finnish uniform, stripped from the body of a dead officer and holding a Finnish machine gun.

Dark. Quiet. He glanced back again. The NKVD weren't coming any closer.

Mere months with her. Months. In the vast landscape of his life, the weeks, the stolen moments, the Luga night, the hospital minutes, the moment on the bus, the white dress, the green eyes, all of it just a burst of color on the periphery, a red splash in the corner of the canvas of his life. He took another step. He could not help her. Not her, not Dasha, not Dimitri. Leningrad was going to swallow them all and Alexander would be damned if he stayed and watched. Another step. Dead on the icy blown-apart streets of a starved Leningrad.

No one moving on the flat terrain, no trucks, no roads, no men, just trenches, and downed bodies, and Alexander, another step in the right direction and another. And another. He was deep amid the Finns now. Bend down, find a tall body, take its uniform, pick up his machine gun, drop yours, drop the life you hate, one more step and go. Go, Alexander. You cannot save her. Go.

For many minutes he stood on Finnish soil amid the fallen enemy.

The life he hated had in it one thing he could not leave behind.

He turned around and slowly walked back to his platoon, his only light the flares of flashlights and the failing fires . . . glancing back once at the forest that was Finland.

If only he could have found a way out of Russia that cold dark September night in Finland, he would not be so heavy-hearted now. Empty-hearted, yes, but not fear-hearted, leaden-hearted like now.

෴

Stalin gave up Leningrad to Hitler, fighting for his life in Moscow. Hitler in turn said he wouldn't waste a bullet on Leningrad preferring instead to starve it out, and in a matter of months the city became lined with unburied corpses. The bodies lying in the white streets covered in white sheets were pristine. The barely living called them "dolls."

The less Tatiana and her family had—as their supplies of flour and oatmeal evaporated—the more their faces crowded around Alexander, longingly asking him if he had more for them, more food, more rations, more, more, the more Tatiana withdrew and stood near the door, away from him, the more feeling he began to have for her. In the middle of war, in the middle of raging fighting, of unburied dead, of being cold and wet, in famine, Alexander's feelings for Tatiana grew as if they were a well-watered, well-nourished plant.

What Leningrad gave them, 250 grams of cardboard bread, what Alexander stole for them, soy beans and linseed oil, was not enough, but the sawdust and cottonseed black cake he was eating was enough for his heart.

She had to be evacuated. One way or another she simply had to be.

November died into December. The white and bombed out streets of Leningrad remained littered with corpses no one could either move or bury. All the movers and buriers were dead. The electricity wasn't working. Neither was water. There was no kerosene to fire up the kilns to bake the bread, which was just as well because there was no flour.

"Alexander, tell me, how long have you loved my sister?" asked the dying Dasha.

"Tell me, how long have you loved my sister?"

"How long—have you—loved my sister?"

Alexander should have replied, Dasha, if you had seen me standing mute, hearing the day fly, the May fly, an ephemera on a Sunday street singing, "Someday We'll Meet in Lvov, My Love and I," you would have your answer.

CHAPTER TWENTY

Lazarevo, 1942

LAZAREVO—EVEN THE NAME itself was reminiscent of myth, of legend, of revelation. Lazarus, the brother of Mary and Martha, raised from four days dead by Jesus. A miracle given by God to reaffirm man's faith that so angered His enemies they started plotting to kill both the mortal and the divine.

Lazarevo—a small fishing village on the needle banks of the mighty Kama, the river that for ten million years flowed a thousand miles south into the world's largest sea.

Alexander went to Lazarevo on faith.

He had heard nothing from her. Nothing for six months. All he had to say was, I do not believe she could have survived because I have seen with my own eyes thousands stronger than her, healthier than her that had not survived. They got sick, and she was sick. They had no food, they were starved and she was starved. They had no defences and she had none. They were alone, and she was also. She was small and she was weak and she didn't make it.

That would have required nothing of Alexander. He could have said, it must be so. All he had to do was nothing. How easy!

But Alexander learned by now: there was no easy step in his life, no easy day, no easy choice, no easy way.

He had his one life. In June 1942 he went to Lazarevo holding it in his hands.

By the shores of the Kama, he found her gorgeous and restored, and not just restored to her original shining brilliance but enlarged and clarified. Light reflected off her, no matter which way she turned.

They ran down to the almighty river. She never even looked back.

She would never know what it meant to him, an unremitting sinner, after all the unsacred things he had seen and done, to have her innocence. He held her to him. He had dreamed of it too long, touching her. Dreamed of seeing her naked too long, beautiful, bare, ready for him.

He was afraid to hurt her. He had never been with an untouched girl before; he wasn't sure if he was supposed to do something first.

In the end, he did nothing first, but she baptized him with her body. There was no Alexander anymore; the man he knew had died and was reborn inside a perfect heart, given to him straight from God, to him and for him.

He had lived the last five years of his life being with women whose names he could not remember, whose faces he could not recall, women to whom he meant nothing but a well spent moment on a Saturday night. The connections he had made with those women were transient links, gone as soon as the moment was gone. Nothing lasted in the Red Army. Nothing lasted in the Soviet Union. Nothing lasted inside Alexander.

He had lived the last five years of his life amid young men who could die instantly as he was covering them, as he was saving them, as he was carrying them back to base. His connections to them were real but impermanent. He knew better than anyone the fragility of life during Soviet war.

Yet Tatiana had lived through the hunger, made her blind way through the snow on the Volga, made her way inside his tent to show Alexander that in his life there was one permanence. In Alexander's life there was one thread that could not be broken by death, by distance, by time, by war. Could not be broken. As long as I am in the world, she said with her breath and her body, as long as *I* am, you are permanent, soldier.

And he believed.

And before God they were married.

გადად

Alexander was sitting on a blanket, his back against the tree, and she was on top of him, straddling him, kissing him so deeply he couldn't get his breath. "Tania . . ." he whispered. ". . . Hang on . . ."

It was their third morning as husband and wife. They got up, washed, drank and were now deeply ensconced under the birch.

"Shura, darling, I can't believe you're my husband. My *husband*."

"Mmm."

"Shura, my husband for *life*."

"Mmm." His hands were caressing her thighs.

"Do you know what that means? You've sworn to make love only to me for life."

"I'll *take* that job."

"Do you know I read that in some African cultures I get to have your liver as a sign of your love for me." She giggled.

"You can take my liver, Tatia, but I won't be much good to you afterward. Maybe you should make love to me first."

"Shura, wait."

"No. Take your dress off. Take it all off."

She obliged.

"Now sit on top of me."

"But you're completely dressed!"

"Just sit on top of me." He gazed at her hungrily. Tatiana had a beautiful body. And Alexander had seen them all. Lithe, smooth, crème, from her clavicles to her carpals, Tatiana was formed to fit Alexander's desire. Everything he liked in a woman's body, his tiny maiden wife unsparingly had. She had a small waist and rounded hips, she had soft thighs and lush breasts. She had the gift of silk and velvet from her golden hair to the soles of her feet and all within her. Alexander's breath was short. He opened his arms.

Tatiana straddled him. "Like this?"

"This is good," he said, his hands over her, groaning at the feel of her. Tatiana lifted herself up to let him kiss her warm breasts. His hands grasped her hips. He closed his eyes. "Tania, do you know that in Ethiopia a woman, to make herself more attractive to her new husband, makes a series of cuts on her torso and then rubs ash into them to raise them into scars?"

Sitting back down on him, Tatiana stared at him. "You would find this attractive?"

"Not particularly." Alexander smiled. "It's the *sacrifice* that appeals to me."

"I'll show you, sacrifice. I think it's in the same Ethiopia," she said, "that the women get shaved from the neck down."

"Mmm."

"Does *that* appeal to you?"

He was pressing her body into himself and licking her lips. "Let's just say it doesn't not appeal to me."

"Shura!"

"What? You know in some African cultures the women are not allowed to speak to their husbands unless they're spoken to first?"

"Yes, and in others, they can flirt with both the husband and his cousin and both men can share the marriage bed if the woman so desires. How does *that* strike you?" She went on without letting him respond. "And in some, I keep myself completely covered in a, in a—what is that thing called . . ."

"A black box," Alexander said, smiling.

"No, the real name."

"A burka."

"Yes! A burka. I keep myself covered with a burka from head to toe my entire life, but at the beginning of the marriage you have to lift the burka off my face and I have to reach up and help you, and the one whose hand is on top gets to be the boss in the marriage." She laughed infectiously. "Which one of those appeals to you, husband?"

He couldn't speak for a moment as she continued to kiss him to end all wars. "Well, first of all," he said hoarsely, "my father's sister had no children, so the cousin thing is out. And yes, I would like for you to wear a black box so no one else can lay their eyes on you. And to address your third point, I find it hard to imagine a tadpole like you being the boss of anything."

"Imagine away, soldier," Tatiana said bravely. Her fire lips consumed him.

It was time for him to get undressed. But he couldn't move. Her knees were against his ribs, her arms were holding his head, and her lips were ravishing his mouth.

Alexander groaned. "In Barrington, do you know what we did? It wasn't Africa, but we cut our palms and pressed our blood together to say we were going to be friends for life."

"If you *want* we can press our palms together, but in Russia, when we want to reaffirm marriage, we just have a baby." She bit his neck.

"I tell you what," said Alexander. "Let me up, and we'll see what we can do to reaffirm our marriage." Not only did she not move off him, but she held him tighter. "Tania . . ." he said. Nothing from her except her lips. He was feeling weaker by degrees.

"A minute ago, I was a tadpole," she whispered. "Now suddenly you can't move me off you."

He didn't just move her off him. Holding her with one hand, he jumped up off the ground into a standing position while continuing to hold her. "You, my dear," Alexander said, "are lighter than all of my gear and my weapons and the mortar that I carry." With his free hand he unzipped his trousers.

"Where is that mortar that you carry," Tatiana said huskily, her lips at his neck.

❦

Time, time, time.

❦

They were walking back to the cabin. Alexander's blueberry bucket was half full. Tania's was flowing over. "I don't know how you're going to survive in the wilderness," she said.

"By not picking blueberries, that's for sure." He took her hand. "Want me to carry that?"

"I'm fine."

"Say something in English."

"*I'm hungry*," she complied in English.

"Something else." He smiled.

She tutted.

"Something else," he repeated, squeezing her hand emphatically.

In English, she asked, "Do you ever went to *doghouse*?"

Alexander didn't understand. "A doghouse—"

He understood. "Tania . . ." He laughed. "It's the *cathouse*."

"Oh." She blushed. Alexander pulled her to him.

"Careful with the blueberries," she said in English. "Don't spill my full backet."

"Okay." Alexander shook his head. "And it's *bucket*." Balling up her hand into a fist, he brought it to his lips.

At the cabin, Tania immediately perched down to pick through the blueberries while Alexander went for a swim. Drying off, Alexander stood in front of Tatiana, buckets between her parted legs. She looked up at him expectantly. He extended his hand.

❦

After they had finished making sweet slow afternoon love, and she was cradled in his arms, he said, "Yes, I've been to a cathouse. A long time ago."

She shuddered briefly, not looking at him. "Often?"

"No, not often."

"Didn't you ever—all those skanks have been with so many men. Do they even wash in between?"

Alexander smiled at her innocence, at her blinding blondeness. "Not all women can be untrampled snow like you," he said. He paused, slightly shuddering himself. "I'll never go again, all right?"

She looked at him, puzzled. "Why would you?" she asked, her expression full of love, full of faith. "You're married now. To me."

"I know who I'm married to." He thought a moment. "Besides," he added slowly, "I was very careful. I always wore a safety sheath."

"A what?"

Oh, dear God. "A false scabbard," he said. She was heartbreaking. "Over the sword."

Tatiana was thoughtful. "When you say *always* . . ."

"Always."

"Not *always*, right?"

"Always, Tania. How can you not believe me? A second ago you didn't even know what—"

"Shura."

"What?"

"Not always," she said firmly, propping herself up on her arm. "You don't wear one with me."

Alexander smiled. "Why would I?" He took her in his arms. "Why should I?" he whispered.

"Wait, wait!" She disentangled herself. "Are you telling me that you were never uncovered . . ."

"That's what I'm saying."

"*Never?*"

"Never."

"I don't believe you."

Alexander laughed. "The truth is not dependent on your belief, Tania."

"All those women, all those good-time girls, all those garrison hacks, not a single one?"

"Particularly not them."

"But Shura, you—" She paused. "You must have needed quite a lot of them." She smiled. "Scabbards, not girls."

He smiled back.

"What did you do when you ran out?"

"I stayed away until I got some more."

Tatiana was very quiet. "What about Dasha?"

"What about her?"

"With her, too?"

"Tania, with everyone."

"Shura . . ." Tatiana jumped on him, hugging him to kill the alive. She was shaking him. When she lifted her face from his neck, tears were in her eyes. "You're such a beast. How could you have not told me this for five whole days? And after I told you all about me in the first five minutes."

He grinned, his hands running up and down her bare back. "You never asked."

She shook him again. He stroked her arms, her neck, her lips. Caressing her, he watched her face, her closed eyes, her slightly parted mouth. "Say something in English."

"No," she said. "But now I am going to go and make you blueberry jam."

"Great," Alexander muttered, watching her hop down. "Can't wait. Much better than a *bit of fresh*."

Tatiana turned to him and smiled. "Shura," she said in halting English, "show me your *marriage bait*."

Alexander laughed. "Tania, come here. Please. Forget the blueberries."

"What did I say now?" she said, coming back, kneeling in front of him and smiling.

"It's not *marriage bait*, it's the *wedding tackle*. And here it is." He smiled. "But stop using your English as a source of comedy on our marriage rack. Touch me."

Fondling him and grinning, she said in English, "All right, you well drawn soldier."

"Tania . . . oh, no." His stomach was beginning to hurt. "Stop, I said. You're killing me."

"Come, give me *a slice of tail*."

"Tania!"

"What?" she said, her eyes twinkling.

"I don't give *you* a slice of tail!"

"Well, all right then." She lay down next to him.

"You're playing with me? Stop. I'll be no good to you in a minute."

"Then who has the *sugarstick*?"

He grabbed her, pulling her to him. "That would be me."

"Well, give me some."

"All right, then." She *was* teasing him.

"*Come, come, come.*" She smiled. "How is my English tongue?"

"Perfect," Alexander said. "And it's the English *language*. But you've reduced a formerly whole man to his frazzled parts."

"What will make you whole again?" asked Tania. "A little trip to the cathouse?"

"A little trip to your cathouse, maybe," said Alexander, his lips devouring her laughing face.

⁂

Stop, stop, stop.

⁂

He was teaching her how to fire a pistol. She was a reluctant—"and poor"—student. "Attention! You are completely not paying attention."

"I am."

He nudged her with his hand. "You would make a terrible soldier. You don't listen, you don't obey. They'd throw you out of boot camp. Let's try it again. Where's the safety?"

She showed him.

"Where's the magazine catch?"

She showed him.

"Where's the hammer? Where do the bullets go? Do you remember how to put a new magazine in?"

She popped the magazine catch, pulled the old clip out, snapped the new clip in place, cocked the hammer and with both hands aimed the pistol at a tree. From behind her he reached over and took the gun away. "If you fire it, we'll lose dinner for a week. All the fish will leave."

"I see." She jumped up and down. "So how did I do?"

"You get good marks for memory but you completely fail on attitude."

Saluting him, she stood to attention. "Yes, sir. What's the punishment for poor attitude?" She grinned and then burst out laughing and ran away.

⁂

Tania is across from him on the wood floor in front of the fire in their cabin. It has rained all morning and afternoon, it is nearing dinner time, which she is supposed to be preparing, but Alexander isn't letting her go—until he wins one, just *one* idiotic game of dominoes. She asks him, "You have one-ones," almost like it's not a question. And he says yes! because one-ones start the game and give you an advantage. But he has said that before. They've been playing since one. They must have played 40 times. Maybe 50. He's had one-ones and two-twos, he's had, in a seeming impossibility, all seven double tiles at once. He's had every combination of tiles imaginable. He has not won. Alexander *cannot* believe it. "Wouldn't the law of averages swing my way just *once?*" he demands of Tatiana who smiles sweetly across the floor.

"Husband, I think your luck is changing."

"You think?"

"I'm almost positive."

She is wearing a knee-length skirt and a blue cardigan over a yellow shirt. Her hair is swept up on top of her head, falling into her face. She looks warm and small. Alexander feels the aching in the pit of his stomach. Not even bothering to study her tiles, she is merrily humming, sitting with her legs drawn up. If he weren't so intent on winning, he would ask her to pull up her skirt a little to let him peek.

"But I just want to say, Shura," says Tatiana philosophically, "that you can't win everything."

"Watch me."

"Do I complain when you always beat me across the river?" she asks. "When you catch the perch with your bare hands and I can't? When you unfairly beat me at arm wrestling just because you're bigger? And what about poker? Do I complain when you always beat me at strip poker?" She grins, and Alexander wants to fall on top of her that instant.

"Actually, yes, you do complain," he says, his voice deepening an octave. "And I don't want to win everything. I want to win one lousy game out of fifty, is that too much to ask?"

Her eyes twinkling, she gets all demure. "Would you like me to *let* you win, darling?"

"That's it," he exclaims. She laughs. "I'm winning this game, Tania, I don't care what kind of black magic you weave over my tiles."

Alexander comes close. Very close. He has one tile left when she lays down her last and claps joyously, falling back on the floor. Her hitched-up skirt lifts, exposing the flushed backs of her bare thighs, her sheer underwear. He watches her a moment and then falls on top of her.

"Shura, dinner!" She is laughing, feral, trying to get away, and does, and bolts out the door into the clearing and he chases her down to the river in the gloomy dusk, in the miserable rain. He catches her as she is about to dive in, clothes on, into the Kama.

"Oh, no, you don't," he says, lifting her into his arms. "Not this time."

Squealing, she struggles against him, cheerfully and symbolically. He carries her wet inside the house, kicks the door shut behind him and, setting her down, pulls all the blankets and pillows down on the floor in front of the fire.

"Shura, dinner!" she repeats mock-plaintively.

"No, Tania, *me*."

It is very warm in the cabin.

Undressing her, he lays her naked on the blanket and, undressing himself, lies down next to her.

"One of two things is going to happen after I'm done with you," he says in his most soothing erotic voice. Tatiana can't take it; she moans.

"That's right, one of two," he says, caressing her trembling body. "I am going to make love to you until you either beg me to stop, or promise me that you will *never* and I mean, never, play dominoes with me again."

She closes her eyes as her hands reach for him, grasp for him. "I'll tell you right now," she whispers. "I will not be begging you to stop."

"We'll just see about that," says Alexander.

꧁꧂

Stop time, stop time, stop time.

꧁꧂

One less day. In the late evening, Tatiana climbed into his lap. "No, no, don't stop reading," she purred, snuggling up to him. "I'm cold." She curled into his chest. Enfolding her in his arms, Alexander resumed reading, but only every tenth word was getting through because she was nestled against him, and her silky hair was rubbing against his neck, his throat, his jawbone. Alexander listened to her breath. It was rhythmic. He put the book down and peeked at her. Her eyes were closed.

An aching tenderness filled him. He sat, not moving, inhaling her sleeping soapy feminine smell. She fit into him like a cat under his chin, on his collarbone, her legs tucked in over him, she was warming him as he warmed her. He wanted to squeeze her closer to him but didn't want to do anything to wake her up. Unlike him, she was a light sleeper, and he knew when she got up, she would get off his lap.

Minutes, crystalline, wet, chilly, breathless minutes, and the time tick tock, tick tock, it moved, without a watch, without a clock, without the chime of the hour, the bell of the church, but with every sunrise, every sunset, with the waning cycle of the moon it steamrolled ahead without a backward glance.

How many days left? He didn't want to think about it. When they got married they had twenty-six days in front of them and they said, oh, we've been married three days, five days, ten days. But now Tatiana had stopped talking about it, and Alexander was thinking, how many days *left?*

Dear Tania. I am so happy, yet I've never been more miserable in my whole life. Can you possibly understand? You with your wings of joy, can you understand what you carry on your shoulders, and how heavy I am? No, you are made of gossamer, nothing can weigh you down, not even me. You float, while I founder—in my fear, in my folly, in my fierce weakness.

A short quake went through her, and she opened her eyes. "Oh," she murmured. "Did I fall asleep?"

"Shh," he said. "Don't get up."

"How long have I been on you?"

"Not long enough. Stay here," he said quietly. "Stay. I'll sit up and you bend your head and sleep on me. I'll hold you all night."

"And tomorrow you won't be able to walk, your back will be so bad," she replied. She tickled his neck. They sat. "Well? Are we just going to sit here, or do you plan to do your husbandly duty?"

"We're just going to sit here."

Her fingers caressed his neck, her lips kissed his throat, her hips nested into his lap. "What's the matter?" she asked, nuzzling him. "Come on. Let me make you happy."

"I *am* happy."

"Happier. Lie down," she whispered.

When they roughhoused, Tatiana was as assertive as a cougar, but during lovemaking, Alexander couldn't get her to be anything but intemperately tender with him. "Harder," he would tell her. "Touch me harder, Tatia. Don't be so gentle with me."

"Shura . . ." The fire flickered its harvest moonlight around the cabin. She stroked his face with her gentle fingers, her tongue ran in smooth circles around his lips, her fingers sloped down to his neck and throat and caressed his chest, lightly circled his upper arms where she rested before continuing. "I love your arms," she whispered. "I keep imagining you holding me with them."

"You don't have to imagine," Alexander whispered back. "I'll hold you with them right now."

"You lie still." She continued to caress his chest and his stomach; her fingers were silky and fragile, like small nightingales with webbed feet.

"Tatia," he whispered. "I'm dying."

"No," she said, moving lower. "Not yet."

"Yes, yet," he replied. "Come on, don't make a grown man beg."

Adoring and worshipful, groaning from pleasure, she was bent over him, breathing over him, murmuring. "God, Shura, you are—I love you, I can't take it."

She couldn't take it? His eyes shut, he clasped her head between his hands.

⚬⚮⚬

A few days. A few nights. Later, later. Tomorrow. The next day, the next evening, another breakfast, a waning quarter-moon night.

She sat on the blanket every night before the fire he built outside in the clearing, and called him to her. And he would come, like a lamb to the slaughter, and lie down and put his head into the lion's lap and she would sit over him and stroke his face, and murmur. Every night she murmured to him, soothing him with her lilting stories or her questions, or her jokes, and sometimes she sang to him. Lately all she sang to him was "Moscow Nights":

> "The river flows and flows
> All made from moonsilver
> A song is faintly heard and then subsides
> During these quiet nights."

"Shura, are you hungry?"

"No." They were sitting side by side. He wasn't looking at her.

"You sure? We haven't eaten since six, and it's—"

"I said no."

Silence. "Are you thirsty? Want another cup of tea?"

"No, thank you," he said a little gentler.

"What about a little vodka?" She nudged him. "I'll drink with you."

"No, Tania. I don't want anything."

"Can I get you a cigarette?"

"Tania!" he exclaimed. "I'm fine. Believe me, if there is something I want, I'll let you know, all right?"

He felt her body tense. She took her hands away. He put them back. "I want you to continue to touch me, I don't want to move, or have you move. I'm fine, right here." He didn't look at her.

"Come here, darling," she said. "Come. Put your head on me."

The lion spoke. The lamb obeyed.

His head was in her lap and she was lightly tickling his neck and murmuring.

"Tania, can you just stop?" he whispered. "Can you just quit for a second? Please. I can't take you."

She cradled him, bending over him, kissing his hair. He felt her breasts soft against his head. "Shura . . . Shura . . ." she purred in her sing-song voice. "Husband man, lovely man, big man, soldier man, beautiful man, Tania's man . . . Shura, beloved man, adored man, worshipped man, alive man, Shura . . ."

Alexander couldn't speak.

"Shura, listen. Look at me, and listen. Are you listening?"

"Yes," he said, opening his eyes and looking up.

Her eyes were twinkling. She cleared her throat. "In the year 2000, three crocodiles lie on a river bank. One says, 'We were green once.' The other one says, 'Yes, and we could swim.' The third one says indignantly, 'Enough of this. Stop wasting your time. Let's fly around and gather some honey!'"

Laughing, Alexander put his hands to his face. The crocodiles might not have known what they were, but he knew very well what he was.

"Shura, stop, come on now. Don't laugh yet. My mission is to make you laugh until you cry." Tatiana peeled his hands away from his face and said, "A husband says to his wife—"

"Please, no more."

"A husband says to his wife, 'Dear, did you hear the rumor that the postman has had all the women in the village except one?' And his wife exclaims, 'Oh, I bet it's that stuck-up Mira in hut number thirty!'"

Alexander laughed. "Okay, here is mine: 'A pest is a man you'd rather make love to than explain why you'd rather not.'"

Tatiana hugged him and said, "And here's mine: 'Honey, what do you prefer—my beautiful body or my beautiful face?' "

"Your sense of humor," returned Alexander, holding her to him until she couldn't breathe. Nine days left, he wanted to say, but didn't. Couldn't.

⊙⊙

She was struggling with a large basket of wet clothes near the water while he sat on the bench smoking. He had been hacking away at the forest all morning, swinging the axe at the branches as if it were some kind of absolution from his sins. He spent three hours making kindling bundles for her, because he knew it would get cold at night after he had left. But he was upset with her—again. She had been gone all morning, helping the old women clean their house, or plant, or fuck knows what else.

Alexander watched her resentfully as she struggled with their wet sheets. Tatiana couldn't lift the heavy basket to bring it to the line. He watched her and smoked. Finally she turned around, saw him sitting on the bench and looked surprised and then disheartened.

"Shura," she called to him reproachfully, motioning him to her. "What are you doing? Come and help me."

He didn't move.

"Shura!"

Alexander got up and walked over. Without looking at her, he swung the basket up with one hand and carried it to the line, where he dropped it on the ground and went back to the bench. As he turned to sit down, Tatiana was standing in front of him.

"What?" she said. "What *now*?"

"Don't give me the 'what now,' all right?"

"What?" she said. "What did I do too much of, or not enough of?"

He opened his mouth, but her hand went over it as she brought her face to his and said quietly, "Stop it. Stop yourself before you say something you will have to apologize for in ten seconds." She held her hand over his mouth and then kissed his forehead. Patting him lightly on the cheek, she went to hang the laundry, leaving him dumbfounded and stung by conscience.

Alexander went inside and made her tea. Walking over, he handed her the cup and said guiltily, "Here, you drink, let me do this."

She sat down on a tree stump while he fiddled with the clothes pins.

When he was done, he went to her, watched her for a moment, and then slowly descended to his knees. Tatiana parted her legs to let him closer.

"Tania . . ." he said in a stilted voice.

She stopped him. "Shh. You don't have to apologize for anything. Be whatever you want, Shura, just *be*."

"Why do you do that?" he asked. "Why can't you just tell me to stop being an idiot? Why can't you raise your voice, tell me to shut the hell up?"

"Is that what you want, Alexander?" she said. "You want me to fight with you? We have a handful of days left and you want me to fight with you?"

He hugged her. "Not a handful. Eight. Now tell me what can I do for you? What do you want me to do? You want me to carry something for you? Can I chop wood? Make another fire? Chase you through the woods? Can I carry you?"

He heard her say something in a broken, muted whisper that didn't sound like happiness or even love. It sounded like a gasp torn from a lifetime of grief.

Alexander couldn't respond, couldn't look at her. He pretended he hadn't heard, patted her back, kissed her neck.

Her voice a little happier and thickening, Tatiana answered. "You can do anything you want to me. As you know—I like it all."

Alexander knew Tatiana loved to be carried by him. She loved to be lifted in his arms, or slung over his back, or carried like a backpack. He knew she was remembering Luga every time he picked her up . . . Luga, when all of Lazarevo was still ahead of them.

When Leningrad was still ahead of them. When Dasha was alive. When she had a family. Could Alexander love her enough for all of them who once sat around her, drinking their tea, smoking, teasing her, neglecting her, loving her? Could he give her enough?

Yes, he could. For the next few days.

And then what?

Alexander brought her inside and laid her on their bed. The stove was still warm from morning.

"I know what you like . . ." Alexander whispered. Lifting her dress, he exposed her hips and opened her legs. He loved looking at her as he alternately caressed her and put his mouth on her.

He heard her moaning for him. He stopped touching her for a moment and listened. "Shura . . . Shura . . . come up, please, come up."

He knew what she wanted. And he wanted to give it to her. "What do you want, Tatia?"

"Come on, Shura," she whispered. "Come on . . ."

Alexander went back to touching her. "Look at you," he whispered, lowering his face to her.

He had to stop. He could tell she was moments away. "Not yet, Tania. Who is my good girl . . ." he whispered. "Who is my beautiful good girl . . ."

In frustration, she tried to move away. He held her in place, while his careful tender fingers stroked her.

Tatiana was nearly crying from tension. Alexander wanted to put his mouth on her again—but he waited.

She clutched at him, moaning for him to climb to her. He resisted.

Finally she breathed out the words he longed to hear.

Groaning from the excitement of hearing her say it, Alexander whispered, "All right, Tatiasha." He barely had time to enter her, before he was flooded with her relief. Eight days left, Alexander's body cried, his tingling throat cried.

Alexander was going sick out of his mind. He was on a suicide mission—he wanted Tatiana to stop loving him before he left. He wanted her to be glad he was leaving.

What he wanted was to *make* her glad he was leaving, not for her to be glad out of her own accord. He wanted to be the one to facilitate this change in her.

Her vulnerability ate at him so much he couldn't look her in the face.

What was happening to him? It was so hateful.

⚬〜〜⚬

"Come on, lift me up," Tatiana said another night. "Lift me, take me standing like I know you love, take me however you want, but please don't be upset with me, Shura."

He turned from her.

"Honey," she whispered. "Husband . . . Alexander . . ."

He couldn't look at her.

Tatiana stood in front of him, topless, nipples erect, her loving face, her wet lips. They forgot the tea, forgot his cigarettes, forgot his anger, forgot it all, all they did, pleading, moaning through the crescent night, was forget it all.

As always. There was nothing else when they were in their cabin.

Just Tania and Shura, and they adored each other, and their hearts were breaking, as they implored the God who made them, let us have this for another wordless moment, let us have *us* for a moment longer. Alexander took her against the wall and kneeling on the hard floor and on the high counter he had made, and on their bed, he took her gently and roughly and slowly and quickly, but in the end his heart was still breaking.

There was a desperation to their lovemaking—a brutal relinquishing of happiness that was as gradual and inevitable as the low tide. Whereas before Tania and Shura were starving for each other and made love to wake the gods to proclaim the eternal *We* to life, now they made love to stave off death, to stem the flood of destruction that awaited them upon his leaving—itself as inevitable as sunset.

Their feverish arrhythmic, broken, violent coupling was a cry to the gods, to any gods who would listen. Pleasure was mixed with a propellant ache; the greater the pleasure, the emptier the heart was after.

Five days left.

The following rainy night on the floor by the fire, he once again stopped himself from release. Alexander thought if he stopped himself, maybe he could stop time.

How long can he keep himself? How long can he watch her, how much longer can he hear her voice, smell her breath when she moaned and when she whispered, like now, what was she saying . . . I can't even hear her, I want to finish, but no, I can't . . . "What, Tania?"

"Alexander, please don't leave me."

"Babe, don't worry," he said. "There is life after grieving. Look at us. *We* felt again." He kissed her. "You will want to love again, and you will." Alexander wanted to add, *thank God*, but he didn't mean it. My heart on a fucking stake, twisting in the fire.

"Wait, stop, honey, stop, Shura, I can't breathe, I can't breathe—"

But Alexander wouldn't stop. Until he was finally done. It took her long minutes to get her breath back, while he lay on the floor and smoked. The ash fell on the hardwood. It fell on his chest. He didn't even brush it off. Tatiana brushed it off.

When she was calmer, Tatiana whispered, "Sometimes when you

hold me like that, when you constrict me the way you do, when you suffocate me, when I feel your hands on my throat, over my face, when my
lungs are crushed by you and your body is on me, I can't help thinking
you almost wish I *would* stop breathing."

"That's crazy."

"Is it?"

"Absolutely."

"You hold me, Shura, as if you don't want me to live past this." Tatiana paused. "Past us."

"Crazy."

Four days left.

◦꧂◦

"I don't want you to touch me anymore." These words were spoken by
Tatiana as Alexander was holding her against the wall. "I'm serious,"
she said. "I don't want you to make love to me. I want you to stop. I don't
want to need you anymore. I don't want to love you anymore."

"All right," he whispered, not letting her go, not moving away from
the wall.

"What are we going to do? What am *I* going to do? You'll be dead,
but what am I going to do the rest of my life in Lazarevo?"

"I'll be back, Tatia," Alexander said.

"You'll be dead. And I'll be alone in Soviet Russia."

"I won't be dead."

"There is no place for us here," she said.

He disagreed. "The Ural Mountains were three hundred million
years in the making. We found a place among the round hills. This is
our place."

"Please don't." Her body shook. "They were once larger, these
mountains. They are nearly flattened out by erosion, by time. But they're
still standing."

"Yes. And we with them," whispered Alexander, squeezing her to
him. "But this is just the beginning of your life, Tatiana. You'll see. After three hundred million years you'll still be standing, too."

They weren't looking at each other.

"Yes," she whispered. "But not with you."

◦꧂◦

Alexander was leaving tomorrow. Today he couldn't look at her, couldn't touch her, couldn't talk to her. He didn't know how he was going to go on. He didn't know how she was going to go on.

He knew he would have to. He knew she would have to.

But how?

Where did they teach you how to live after you'd lost it all?

Who taught you how to go on after you had lost everything?

Tatiana.

Tatiana taught me how to go on after she had lost everything.

Alexander got up early, went for his swim, but afterward didn't come inside like always. Instead he sat on the bench outside and smoked, smoked with closed eyes, so he wouldn't see Lazarevo.

Just behind his closed eyes were the birches and the pines and the cones on the ground and the gray-green mountains beyond the rushing river. He smelled the remnants of the fire, he wanted tea, he wanted another cigarette. He wanted his life to be over.

He was getting *that* wish, wasn't he?

"Tania, I'm telling you, don't cry. That was our deal, do you hear me? I can't take it."

"Am I crying?" she said.

"I'm serious," Alexander said. "I can't do this. I need you—"

"You know what?" she said to him. "All the things you need me to be, I can't be right now. I'll be what I can." She was crying.

His throat burning, Alexander lay next to her. Side by side they steeled themselves in their bed, and she cradled his head to her breasts, and she whispered and whispered and whispered and by the time she was done, his hair was damp from her tears. But she wasn't done. She was never done. Her capacity to heal him, to harvest her love in him was endless.

"There was once a time," she said, "when you placed your hand on my chest, and I thought my whole life was in front of me. In front of the Hermitage. In front of that broken man and his crates of art. Do you remember?"

"How could I forget?" Alexander said. "I never forget that man."

Tatiana turned her face to him. They kissed. She cradled against him, tiny against him, she lay buried in his chest, and Alexander knew she was listening to his heart. She did that all that time; it was comforting and disquieting.

She was as resolute as ever, as fully loving, as completely giving, intensely tender, unbearably moving, as always affecting him utterly. But there was something else. She was holding him so desperately, crying over him, almost as if she were mourning him already, almost as if she were already grieving. She made love to him without letting go of his head, choking him against her and crying, as if she were not just saying goodbye, but saying goodbye to him for good.

As if she were leaving herself with him because he needed her more. She was saying goodbye not only to him but to herself. There you go, Alexander, Tatiana was saying, take me and go. Have it all. There will be nothing left, but I will grow something new for myself. The Tania you love will remain with you. Take her. And he did, until there was nothing left.

Her warm wet space engulfed him. He was not returning to the womb, he was giving himself back to eternity. He was closing his eyes and surrendering to the universe that loved them and believed in their youth. To the stars and the mystery moon and the River Kama rushing onward to its thousand-kilometer trek, for ten million years feeding into the Caspian Sea. Long after Tania and Shura will have returned to the earth, the river, the pines, the mountains, the imploding stars would still be here, constant and changeless over Lazarevo. They were eternal, and Alexander's Tatiana, too . . . she was eternal, moaning softly against his neck, warm breath, warm breasts and lips and legs around him, surrounding him, all things to him.

Limpid morning became desert evening. He wished he could help her, but he knew what they were losing, better than she who was still an innocent. But he knew everything.

Alexander knew what was ahead.

It was tomorrow.

He was leaving.

It was tomorrow.

He had left.

It was tomorrow.

And he was without her.

CHAPTER TWENTY-ONE

Sam Gulotta, Washington DC, July 1944

TATIANA COULDN'T LEAVE ALEXANDER'S medal alone. Couldn't leave Orbeli alone. She took an unprecedented day off, took Anthony with her, went to Pennsylvania Station, bought a train ticket and traveled to Washington DC where she found the United States Department of Justice on Pennsylvania Avenue. After four hours of shuffling from the Executive Office for Immigration Review to the Office of Immigration and Naturalization, to the National Central Bureau or Interpol Office, she finally found a clerk who told her she was in the wrong building and the wrong department entirely and needed to go to the Department of State on C Street. She and Anthony went to a small coffee shop where they had soup and, with their ration cards, warm bacon sandwiches. It remained a small marvel to her that delicious meat products were readily available in a country at war.

At the Department of State, Tatiana slogged from the Bureau of European Affairs to the Bureau of Population, Refugees and Migration and finally found the Office of Consular Affairs where she, with her tired legs and tired baby, would not move from the receptionist's desk until she was put in touch with someone who knew something about expatriate emigration *out* of the United States.

That is how she met Sam Gulotta.

Sam was an athletic-looking man in his thirties with curly brown hair. Tatiana thought he looked less like an under secretary for consular affairs than a physical education teacher, and she wasn't far wrong—he told her that he coached his son's Junior League baseball team in the afternoons and summer camps. Fingers tapping, Sam leaned over the scuffed wooden counter messy with scattered papers and said, "Now what's this all about?"

Tatiana took a deep breath, held the cranky Anthony to her chest and said, "Here?"

"As opposed to where? Over dinner? Yes, here." He smiled when he said it. He wasn't gruff, but it was five o'clock on a government Thursday.

"Mr. Gulotta, when I was in Soviet Union, I met and married a man who come to Moscow as young boy. I think he was still American citizen."

"Really?" Gulotta said. "What are you doing in the States? And what is your name now?"

"My name is Jane Barrington," said Tatiana, taking out her residence card and showing it to him. "I have permanent residence in United States. Soon to be citizen. But my husband . . . how to explain?" She took a breath and told him, beginning with Alexander and ending with the Red Cross death certificate and Dr. Sayers smuggling her out of the Soviet Union.

Gulotta listened silently and then said, "You are telling me too much, Jane Barrington."

"I know. I need your help. I want to find out what happen to my husband," she replied in a faint voice.

"You know what happened to him. You have the death certificate."

How to explain the *Hero of the Soviet Union* medal? Gulotta would not have understood. Who could? How to explain Orbeli?

"Maybe he not dead?"

"Mrs. Barrington, you have much more information on that than I have."

How to explain to an American the penal battalions? She tried.

"Mrs. Barrington, excuse me for interrupting," Gulotta interrupted. "What penal battalions? What ranking officers? You have the death certificate. Your husband, whoever he was, wasn't arrested. He drowned. He is out of *my* jurisdiction."

"Mr. Gulotta, I think maybe he not drowned. I think maybe certificate was fake and he was arrested and maybe he in one of those penal battalions now."

"Why would you think that?"

That, she could not adequately explain. She couldn't even try. "Due to unforeheard circumstances—"

"Unforeheard?" Gulotta could not help a small smile.

"I . . ."

"Do you mean unforeseen?"

"Yes." Tatiana blushed. "My English—I still learning—"

"You're doing very well. Please continue."

In the corner over the wide counter under the fluorescent lights, a middle-aged, overweight woman squinted grimly at Tatiana with delighted disapproval. "Mr. Gulotta," said Tatiana. "Are you right person for me to talk to? Maybe there someone else?"

"I don't know if I'm the right person." He squinted at her himself over the counter. "Since I don't know why you're here. I could be the wrong person. But my boss has already left for the day. Tell me what you need."

"I want you to find out what happened to my husband."

"Is that all?" he said with irony.

"Yes," she said without irony.

"Let me see what I can do. Would next week be soon enough for you?"

Now she understood. "Mr. Gulotta—"

He clasped his hands. "Listen to me. I don't think I'm the right person after all. I don't think there is a right person in this entire department—heck, in this entire government who can help you. Tell me again your husband's name."

"Alexander Barrington."

"Never heard of him."

"Were you working for State Department in 1930? That's when he and his family emigrated."

"No, I was still at university then. But that's not the point."

"I told you—"

"Oh, yes, unforeheard circumstances."

Tatiana turned around and was about to walk away when she felt his hand on her arm. He had stepped out from the counter and was now on her side. "Don't go yet. It's quitting time. Why didn't you come to me earlier in the day?"

"Mr. Gulotta, I took five A.M. train to come from New York. I have only these two days off, Thursday and Friday. I spent until now walking between State and Justice Department buildings. You first person talking to me. I was going to White House next."

"I think our President is busy. Something about an invasion of Normandy. I hear there's a war on."

"Yes," said Tatiana. "I was nurse in that war. I am still nurse in that war. Can Soviets help you? They our allies now. All you want is little information." She squeezed her hands in a palsy around the handle bars of the baby carriage.

Sam Gulotta stared at her.

Tatiana might have given up, but Sam had good eyes. Listening, seeing, feeling eyes.

"Look up his file," she continued. "You must have file on people who emigrate to Soviet Union? How many people can there be? Look up his file. Maybe something there. You'll see—he was just small boy when he left America."

Sam made a small disbelieving sound, somewhere between a chortle and a groan. "All right, say I look up his file, and learn that yes, indeed, he was a small boy when he left the United States. So what? You already know that."

"Maybe there will be something else. Soviet Union and United States communicate, yes? Maybe you find out what happened to him. For certain."

"How much more certain than a death certificate can I get?" Gulotta muttered, and then louder said, "all right, say I find out, by some miracle, that your husband is still alive. Then what?"

"You let me worry about then what," said Tatiana.

Sam sighed. "Come back tomorrow morning. Come back at ten. I will try to locate his file. What year did you say his family left?"

"Nineteen thirty, December," Tatiana said, smiling at last.

She stayed with Anthony in a small hotel on C Street near the State Department. It pleased her to get a room in a hotel. No trepidation, no refusal, no demand for papers. She wanted a room, she produced three dollars, she got a nice room with a bathroom. That simple. No one looked at her twice even after they heard the Russian accent.

The next morning she came back to Consular Affairs before nine and sat on the bench for an hour with her son on her lap, playing with his fingers, looking at a picture book. Gulotta came out at nine forty-five and motioned for her to follow him to his office. "Sit, Mrs. Barrington," he said. In front of him lay a dossier ten inches thick. For a few moments, maybe a minute, he didn't say anything. His hands were on the file and his eyes were on it too. Then he sighed heavily. "What relation did you say you are to Alexander Barrington?"

"His wife," Tatiana said in a small voice.

"Jane Barrington?"

"Yes."

"Jane Barrington was the name of Alexander's mother."

"I know. That's why I took it. I'm not Alexander's mother," Tatiana said, glancing at him suspiciously as he studied her suspiciously. "I took her name to get out of Soviet Union." She tried to figure out what he was worried about. "What you worried about? That I'm communist?"

"What is your real name?"

"Tatiana."

"Tatiana what? What was your Soviet name?"

"Tatiana Metanova."

Sam Gulotta stared at her for what seemed to her to be solemn hours. His hands, clenched around the dossier, never unclenched, not even when he said, "May I call you Tatiana?"

"Of course."

"Did you say you got out of the Soviet Union as a Red Cross nurse?"

"Yes."

"Well, well," Gulotta said. "You were very lucky."

"Yes." She looked down into her hands.

"No more Red Cross in the Soviet Union. Verboten. Forbidden. A few months ago the U.S. State Department asked to have the Red Cross to help at the Soviet hospitals and the Soviet POW camps, and Foreign Minister Molotov himself refused. Quite amazing for you to have left." He looked at her with renewed surprise. She wanted to look down again.

"Tatiana, let me tell you about Alexander Barrington and his parents. He left the United States with his parents in 1930. Harold and Jane Barrington sought voluntary asylum in the Soviet Union despite repeated requests from us not to do so. We could not guarantee their safety. Despite his seditionary activities on our soil, Harold Barrington was still an American citizen and we had an obligation to him and his family. Do you know how many times Harold Barrington was arrested? Thirty-two. His son had been arrested with him, according to our records, three times. Twice he spent his summer vacation in a juvenile detention center because both his parents were in jail and they preferred their son to spend his summer vacation in jail rather than with relatives—"

"What relatives?" interrupted Tatiana.

"Harold had a sister, Esther Barrington."

Alexander had only ever mentioned his father's sister once in passing. Gulotta's low voice was disturbing Tatiana, as if he were measuring his words so as not to spill the really awful news behind them.

"Can you tell me what all this means?" Tatiana said. "What you saying to me?"

"Let me finish. True, their son did not rescind his U.S. citizenship, but his parents rescinded, they surrendered their passports in 1933. Then in 1936 Alexander's mother came to the U.S. consulate asking for asylum for her son."

"I know. That trip cost her her life."

"Yes, indeed," said Gulotta. "But this is where our jurisdiction over Alexander ends. By the time he escaped on his way to prison, he was already a Soviet citizen."

"Yes."

"In 1936, the Soviet authorities came to us asking for our help in finding Alexander Barrington. They said he was a criminal and a fugitive, and we no longer had any right to grant him safe passage should he come to us, and in fact we were bound by international treaty to turn him over to the Soviet Union." Gulotta paused. "We were asked to immediately notify the Soviet authorities should Alexander Barrington come asking us for asylum, since he was a Soviet citizen and a political criminal who had escaped justice."

Tatiana stood up.

"He belongs to them," said Gulotta. "Not us. We can't help you."

"Thank you for your time," Tatiana said, her voice trembling, placing her hands on the handles of Anthony's carriage. "I sorry to bother you."

Gulotta stood up himself. "Our relations with the Soviet Union are stabilized because we're fighting on the same side. But the feeling of mistrust is mutual. What happens when the war is over?"

"I don't know," she replied. "What happens when war is over?"

"Wait," Gulotta said, coming around his desk and going to stand in front of his office door before he opened it for her.

"I go now," she barely said. "I must get train back."

"Wait," he repeated, putting his hand out. "For a second, sit."

"I don't want to sit anymore."

"Listen to me," Gulotta said, motioning her to sit. She was grateful to fall into the chair. "There is one more thing . . ." He sat in the chair next to her. Anthony grabbed hold of his leg. Gulotta smiled. "Have you remarried?"

"Of course I haven't," she said faintly.

Gulotta looked at the boy.

"That's his child," said Tatiana.

Gulotta didn't speak for a while. "Don't talk about this to anyone. About Alexander Barrington. Don't go to the Justice Department, don't go to the INS offices in New York or Boston. Don't go looking for his relatives."

"Why?"

"Not today, not tomorrow, not next year. Don't trust them. The road to hell is paved with good intentions. You don't want them making inquiries either on his behalf or out of some misplaced affection. If I contact the Soviets asking them for information on Alexander Barrington they will be less than accommodating. If I ask them the whereabouts of a man named Alexander Belov, who is really Alexander Barrington, if he is still alive, that might only lead the Soviet authorities to him."

"I understand that even better than you think I do," Tatiana said, looking down at her boy and away from Gulotta.

"You said you have residency here?"

She nodded.

"Get your citizenship as soon as possible. Your boy, he's an American citizen or—"

"He's American."

"That's good. Good." He cleared his throat. "There is one more thing . . ."

She said nothing.

"According to his files, last year, in March 1943, the Soviet authorities contacted the State Department about one of their citizens, a Tatiana Metanova, who was wanted for espionage, desertion, and treason, and was suspected of escaping to the West. They sent a telegraph wire asking if a Tatiana Metanova had either sought asylum in the United States or had tried to make inquiries about her husband—an Alexander Belov who is suspected of being Alexander Barrington. Tatiana Metanova apparently has not revoked her Soviet citizenship. Last year we said she had not contacted us. They asked us to get in touch with them if she did and requested she be denied asylum status."

For the longest time, Tatiana and Sam were utterly quiet. Finally Sam asked, "Has a Tatiana Metanova tried to make inquiries about an Alexander Barrington?"

And finally Tatiana answered. "No." It was just a breath.

Sam nodded. "I didn't think so. There will be nothing for me to put in the file."

"No," said Tatiana. She felt his hand on her back, easing her up, patting her slightly.

"If you give me your address, I can write if I hear anything. But you understand—"

"I understand everything," whispered Tatiana.

"Maybe this cursed war will end, maybe what's going on in the Soviet Union will end, too. If things get more relaxed, we can make some inquiries. After the war might be better."

"After which war?" asked Tatiana, without raising her eyes. "Maybe I write you myself. This way you don't have to keep my address on record. You can always find me at Ellis Island hospital. I don't actually have address yet. I don't live—" She broke off. With her teeth grit and her jaw set, she could not even extend her hand to Sam Gulotta. She wanted to, she just couldn't.

"I'd help you if I could. I'm not the enemy," he said quietly.

"No," she said, moving past him and out of his office. "But it turns out that I am."

⚬﹏⚬

Tatiana took two weeks off work, she said for a "needed vacation." She tried to convince Vikki to come with her, but Vikki was juggling two interns and a blind musician and couldn't come.

"I'm not going on some surprise train trip. Where do you think you're going?"

"Anthony wants to see Grand Canyon."

"Anthony is one! He wants to see his mother find herself an apartment and a new husband, not necessarily in that order."

"No. Just Grand Canyon."

"You told me we would look for an apartment."

"Come with us and maybe I look for apartment when I come back."

"You're such a liar."

Tatiana laughed. "Vikki, I am good here at Ellis."

"That's the whole problem. You're not *good here* at Ellis. You're all alone, you live in one room with your child, you share a communal bathroom. You're in America, for God's sake. Rent yourself an apartment. That's what we Americans do."

"*You* don't have an apartment."

"Oh, for the love of Jesus and Mary! I have a home."

"I do, too."

"You deliberately don't want a place of your own. Because that keeps you from getting involved with someone."

"I don't need to be kept from getting involved with someone."

"When are you going to start being young? What do you think, if he was alive, he'd be faithful to you? He would not be waiting for you, I'll tell you that. This very second, he would be knocking his brains out."

"Vikki, how do you go around thinking you know so much when you know nothing?"

"Because I know men. They're all the same. And don't start telling me yours is different. He is a soldier. They're worse than musicians."

"Musicians?"

"Never mind."

"I'm not having this talk. I'm not talking to you. I have patients. I have to go to Red Cross. Did I tell you I been hired on part-time basis for American Red Cross? They really need people. Maybe you should apply."

"Mark my words. Knocking his brains out. Just like you should be doing."

CHAPTER TWENTY-TWO

Majdanek, July 1944

THEY HAD STOPPED NEAR the woods in eastern Poland and were re-arming and taking a drink.

"Why do we have to keep talking about God and about the Germans and the Americans and the war and Comrade Stalin?" said Ouspensky.

"We don't talk about that," said Telikov. "You do. You're the only one who brings that shit up. Before you walked over, do you know what Commander Belov and I were discussing?"

"What?" barked Ouspensky.

"Whether the river perch or the river bass is easier to clean and which fish makes a better soup. I personally think the perch makes a great soup."

"That's because you've never had soup out of bass. Look, you're dropping your ammo as you're standing up," said Alexander. "What kind of a soldier are you?"

"I'm a soldier that needs to lie down with a woman, sir. Or stand up with a woman. Basically anything with a woman," replied Telikov, picking up his magazines.

"We got it, Telikov. The army does not supply women at the front."

"We've noticed that. But I also heard that the 84th battalion a few kilometers south has three women nurses who accompany them in the rear. Why do we have only medics?"

"You're a bunch of fucking convicts. Who will give you a female nurse? There are two hundred of you. That woman wouldn't be alive in an hour."

"I hardly think that matters, sir, to men like us."

"And that's why you're not getting a female nurse," said Alexander. Telikov glanced at him in surprise. "Are *you* the reason we don't have a woman nurse?"

Ouspensky said to Alexander, "I really don't think it's very fair of you, Captain, just because your own balls have been melted and frozen into igneous rock, that we should suffer. The rest of us are actually made of flesh and blood."

"Yes, and we're about to spill some of that blood, Lieutenant. Stop talking about my balls. Order your men to the firing line."

Alexander went forward with 200 men, and by the time they reached Majdanek, at the end of July 1944, they had eighty.

They trod into Majdanek, which had been liberated by the Soviets barely three days earlier. The Nazi camp lay on a plate-flat field of brown-green grass and its squat, long green barracks looked almost like camouflage. Alexander smelled the acrid-sweet smell of burning flesh in the air, but said nothing, though by the gradual quieting down in his tank and around his formations, he could tell his men smelled it, too.

"Why did they want us to come here?" asked Telikov, coming up to Alexander and staring with him at the city of Lublin through the barbed wire fence. Lublin was just over the field and down a slope.

"The high command wants us to see what we're dealing with as we force our way into Germany," said Alexander. "So we don't feel pity for the Germans."

Ouspensky asked if the residents of Lublin could smell what he smelled, and Alexander replied that they had probably been smelling it every day for months.

The camp was small and seemed almost serene—as if the humanity had left it, leaving behind only ghosts—

And ash—

And bones—

And blue remnants of Zyclon B gas on the concrete walls.

Femur bones, and clavicles . . .

And spy holes in steel doors.

A "bathhouse" on one side of the small camp.

And ovens with one long tall chimney stack on the other.

A road that connected them.

Barracks that divided them.

A commandant's house.

SS barracks.

And nothing else.

The men walked through slowly and silently, and then bent their heads, and finally, standing at the back of the camp, they took off their caps.

"Can't pretend this was a forced labor camp, can you?" Ouspensky said to Alexander.

"No, can't."

But something else, too—past the ovens with white ash and white pieces of human skeletons, there were mounds of white ashes. Not ant mounds but sand dunes, pyramids, two stories high of white ash, and on even ground nearby the white ash was spread out, and on it grew enormous cabbages. Alexander, and his lieutenant and his sergeants and his corporals and his privates, stared at the ash and the cabbages the size of mutant pumpkins, and then someone said that he had never seen cabbages so big before, and if they took one, they would have dinner for eighty men tonight. Alexander didn't let them touch it. In the long wooden warehouse full of shoes and boots and sandals, shoes of all sizes, boots lined and leather, he did let them take a pair of boots each, mindful of how hard it was to get requisitioned footwear in the Red Army, particularly in the penal battalions. The shoes were piled from floor to ceiling, jammed three meters high behind a wire netting.

"How many shoes you think there are here?" asked Ouspensky.

"What am I, a mathematician?" snapped Alexander. "Hundreds of thousands, I would guess."

They left the camp silently and didn't stop at the barbed wire fence to glance at the steeple churches of Catholic Lublin just a couple of kilometers away.

"Who do you think they did that to, Captain? Poles?"

"Hmm. Poles, yes. Mainly Jewish Poles, I think," Alexander replied. "The command won't say, though. They don't want the Soviet army to be less outraged."

"How long do you think it took them?" asked Ouspensky.

"Majdanek became operational eight months ago. Two hundred and forty days. Slightly less time than it takes one woman to make one life, they managed to snuff out a million and a half lives."

No one spoke until they were a kilometer away.

༄

Afterward, Ouspensky said, "A place like that just shows me the communists are right. There is no God."

"That didn't look like God's work to me, Ouspensky," said Alexander.

"How could God allow that?" Ouspensky exclaimed.

"The same way he allows volcano eruptions and gang rape. Violence is a terrible thing."

"There is no God," Ouspensky repeated stubbornly. "Majdanek, the communists, and science have shown us there is no God."

"I cannot speak for the communists. Majdanek showed us only man's inhumanity to man—this is what man sometimes does with the free will God gave him. If God made all men good, it wouldn't be called free will, would it? And finally it's not science's place to show us if there is a God behind the universe."

"It absolutely is. What else is science for?"

"Experiments."

"Yes?"

"Experiment with this—on such and such a day I slept so many hours and felt this way afterward. I ate x amount of food and was able to work for this long. In my forties my face began to line—science has told us this is the beginning of old age. How can the science that measures and combines and mixes and observes tell us what is behind the sleep?" Alexander laughed. "Ouspensky, science can measure how long we sleep, but can it tell us what we dreamed about? It will observe our reactions, it can tell if we twitched or laughed, or cried, but can it tell us what was inside our own head?"

"Why would it want to?"

"It can only report on the visible, on the ostensible, on the tangible. Science has no place inside my head, nor yours. How can it possibly tell you if there is a God? It cannot tell me what even you are thinking about and you are as transparent as glass."

"I am, am I? You'd be surprised, Captain. I'll tell you what I'm thinking about—"

"Where the nearest cathouse is?"

"How did you know?"

"Transparent as glass, Lieutenant."

They drove on in their tank.

Later: "Captain, what are you thinking?"

"I try not to, Lieutenant."

"What about when you can't help it?"

"I think about the Boston Red Sox," said Alexander. "And whether they're having a good season this year."

"The who?"

"Never mind."

"Oh, my dear God."

"There you go, calling on Him again. I thought He didn't exist?"

"I thought you tried not to think?"

Alexander laughed. "I'm going to prove the inability of science to disprove the existence of God to you, Ouspensky." He turned around and looked at the column of men marching doggedly behind the tank. "Now, look. Over there we have Corporal Valery Yermenko. This is what the army knows about him: he is eighteen years old, he has never lived away from his mother. He went straight from his family farm to Stalingrad. He fought in the city, surrendering to the Germans in December of 1942. When the Germans themselves surrendered a month later, he was "freed" and sent up the Volga to a forced labor camp. My question to you is, how did he get *here*? How is this young man walking with us through eastern Poland, in a penal battalion with the dregs the Siberian camps didn't want? That's my question: How did he get here?"

Ouspensky stared at Yermenko and then at Alexander. "Are you telling me that there is a God because some bastard named Yermenko managed to claw his way into your penal battalion?"

"Yes."

"And I understand this why?"

"You don't. But if you talk to him for two minutes, you will understand why God created the universe and the universe did not create itself."

"We have time for this?"

"You have some place else to go?"

Very close to Lublin, they made their slow way through a field that was heavily mined in staggered row formations. The chief combat engineer got almost all of the mines, except for the last one. They buried the engineer in the hole made by the mine. "All right," said Alexander. "Who wants to be the new chief engineer?"

No one spoke.

"One of you will either volunteer or I will volunteer one of you. Now which will it be?"

A small private in the back of the formation raised his hand. He was tiny, he could have been a woman, Alexander thought. A small woman. Private Estevich trembled as he stepped forward and said, "We won't be hitting another field for some time, sir?"

"We will be coming into a town that has been occupied by the Germans for four years and before they retreated, they mined it to welcome us. If you want to sleep tonight, you will have to prepare to un-prime our sleeping quarters, Private."

Estevich continued to tremble.

Inside the tank and in motion, Ouspensky said, "Will you tell me the end of your fascinating theory? I'm aflutter with anticipation."

"Well, aflutter further, Lieutenant. I will tell you tonight, if we make it into Lublin alive."

Estevich did well. He found five round mines in a small, largely intact house. The Germans left one place in town for the Soviet soldiers to rest in and then mined it to kill them. Eighty men made their beds in a broken dwelling, and when they were sitting in front of the fire outside in the yard, Alexander said, "Ouspensky, do you ever think of how many things you don't know?"

Ouspensky laughed.

"Think of how many things you stumble on and say, how should I know?"

"I never say that, sir," said Ouspensky. "I say, how the fuck should I know?"

"You don't even know how an insignificant corporal in the first brigade ended up under my command when by all rights he should have been somewhere else, and yet you can sit there and assure me with all confidence that you are certain there is no God."

Ouspensky thought first and then said, "I'm starting to *hate* this Yermenko."

"Let's call him over."

"Oh, no."

"Before I call him, I will remind you that for the last four hours you have been performing a scientific experiment on him. You have been observing him, you have been watching him carefully. The way he marches, the way he carries his rifle, the way he holds his head. Is he out of step? Does he show signs of tiring? Is he hungry? Does he miss his mother? Did he ever lie down with a woman?" Alexander smiled. "How many of these questions have you been able to answer?"

"Quite a few, sir," said Ouspensky indignantly. "Yes, he is hungry. Yes, he is tired. Yes, he wants to be someplace else. Yes, he misses his mother. Yes, he lay down with a woman. All he needed was half a month's salary back in Minsk."

"And you know all this how?"

"Because that describes me," replied Ouspensky.

"All right. So you know the answers to these simple questions because you know yourself."

"What?"

"You know the answers because you've looked inside yourself and you know that though you're marching and though you're holding your rifle high, and though your step is with your fellow soldier, you're tired, you're hungry, and you want to get laid."

"Yes."

"So, you're saying there is something behind what you see, and the reason you're saying there is something else is because you know there is something behind *you.* There is something inside you that makes you say one thing and do another, that makes you march yet feel melancholy, that makes you look for whores yet love your wife, that makes you shoot an innocent German yet not want to hurt the rat that's running among the mines."

"There's no such thing as an innocent German."

Alexander continued. "The thing that makes you lie and feel remorse, that makes you betray your wife and feel guilt, the thing that makes you steal from the villagers knowing all the while you're doing wrong, that thing is inside Yermenko, too, and that's the thing science can't measure. Let's go and talk to him, and I will show you how far from the truth you were."

Alexander sent Ouspensky to get Yermenko. He offered both men a cigarette and a glass of vodka and put more wood on the fire. Yermenko was wary at first, but then drank and warmed up. He was young and extremely diffident. He wouldn't look Ouspensky in the eye, kept shifting from place to place, and said, yes, sir, no, sir, to every question that was asked of him. He talked a little about his mother in Kharkov, about his sister who died of scarlet fever at the start of the war, about his farming life. When asked about the Germans, Yermenko shrugged and said he didn't read any newspapers and didn't listen to much news. He didn't know what was going on, he just did as he was told. He made a small joke at the expense of the Germans, he drank another glass of vodka, and shyly asked for one more cigarette before going to bed. Alexander excused him and he left.

Ouspensky raised his eyebrows. "All right—so he's a cipher. He is everyman, he is like Telikov, and like the engineer who just got killed—he is like me."

Alexander was rolling cigarettes.

"He doesn't want to know about the Germans, he just goes and shoots them when you tell him to. He is a good soldier, the kind you want in your battalion. Has some war experience, listens to orders, doesn't complain. What?"

"So you've observed him closely, you've watched him, and now you called him over and you talked to him. We socialized with him. We warmed him up, we chatted, we joked, we know a bit about this person, science has made its conclusions, right?"

"Right."

"Just the same way that science has observed the earth and the motion of the moon and the sun and the stars in the galaxy. The same way the telescope helped science discover the Milky Way and the nine planets, the same way the microscope helped Fleming discover penicillin and Lister discover carbolic acid. Right? We put Yermenko under the telescope when he marched, and under the microscope when he sat with us. We observed him the way science observes the universe—the *only* way science can observe the universe. Perhaps for a shorter time, but we have used the scientific principles that scientists use to tell us of the universe and how it was made, of atoms, of electrons, of cells. Perhaps we could find out what Yermenko's blood type is? Perhaps we could find out how tall he is? How many push-ups he can do? Would all that help us, you think, to understand what is behind the man who marches on the field with us?"

"Yes," said Ouspensky. "I think it would."

Alexander lit a cigarette and offered one to Nikolai. "Lieutenant Ouspensky, Valery Yermenko is only sixteen years old. He killed his own father at the age of twelve. Village justice they called it, for the father was beating his mother daily. Yermenko simply got tired of watching it. He beat him to death with a stick. Do you know how hard it is to beat to death a grown man, especially for a small boy? He escaped village justice by running away and joining the army. He lied about his age—said he was fourteen—and they took him. During his training, he constantly had run-ins with his training sergeant, finally accosting him in the woods as the man was coming from mess and breaking his neck for humiliating him earlier at target practice. In Stalingrad, he distinguished himself by killing over three hundred Germans with his hands and his army knife—the army was too afraid to issue him a rifle. The building he took over remained under Soviet control from the beginning of the siege until the end. The Soviets gave up Yermenko to the Germans because they didn't want anything to do with him. When the Germans surrendered, the Red Army got Yermenko back. They sent him to the Gulag where he sliced open the guard on duty, took the guard's uniform and rifle and walked out of the camp compound, walking a thousand kilometers through the Soviet plains before coming to Lake Ladoga. Do you know where he was headed? To Murmansk. He wanted to get on one of the Lend-lease ships. Turns out he read just enough papers to learn about American Lend-lease: what they're sending, what they're producing, and in what numbers the ships are coming into the port. He was apprehended at Volkhov and our General Meretskov, not knowing what to do with him, decided to give him to me to dispose of."

Ouspensky did not take a single drag of his cigarette. "Lieutenant," said Alexander, "don't waste my precious cigarettes. Smoke or give them to me."

Dropping the cigarette on the floor, Ouspensky, without taking his eyes off Alexander, said, "You're bullshitting me."

"Because that's me?"

"You're lying."

"Me again." Alexander smiled.

"So let me understand . . ."

"Behind Yermenko is *himself* which only he knows. Only Yermenko knows the workings of his own soul. Only you know why you walk slightly in front of me at all times even though I am your commander, and only I know why I fucking let you. That's my point. Behind the exterior of us there is Yermenko's soul, and yours and mine, and everyone else's. And if science looked in on us, it would never know. How much more there must be behind the vast and unknowable universe."

Ouspensky was pensive. "Why does that bastard Yermenko show so much loyalty to you, Captain?"

"Because Meretskov told me to shoot him and I didn't. He is now mine till death."

By the fire, Ouspensky asked, "So because of fucking Yermenko you are sure there is a God?"

"No. It's because I have seen Him with my own eyes," replied Alexander.

BOOK TWO
The Bridge to Holy Cross

Come my friends
'Tis not too late to seek a newer world,
Push off, and sitting well in order smite, the sounding furrows;
For my purpose holds, to sail beyond the sunset and the baths,
Of all the western stars until I die.

Alfred, Lord Tennyson

CHAPTER TWENTY-THREE

The Bridge to Holy Cross, July 1944

IN LUBLIN, ALEXANDER'S TROOPS rested and liked it so much they unilaterally decided to stay. Lublin, unlike the scorched and burned and plundered villages they had found in Byelorussia, remained nearly intact. Except for a few bombed and burned houses, Lublin was whitewashed and clean and hot with narrow streets and yellow stucco squares, which on Sundays had markets which sold—!things! Fruits, and ham, and cheese, and sour cream! And cabbage (Alexander's men stayed away from the cabbage). In Byelorussia they encountered maybe a handful of livestock; here, succulent, already basted and smoked pigs were being sold for zlotys. And fresh milk and cheese and butter implied the presence of enough cows to milk, not to eat. Eggs were sold, and chickens, too. "If this is what it means to be German-occupied, I'll take Hitler any day over Stalin," whispered Ouspensky. "In my village, my wife can't pull the fucking onions out of the ground without the *kolkhoz* coming to take them away. And onions are the only thing she grows."

"You should have told her to grow potatoes," said Alexander. "Look at the potatoes here." The vendors sold watches, and they sold dresses for women, and they sold knives. Alexander tried to buy three knives, but no one wanted Russian rubles. The Polish people hated the Germans, and they liked the Russians only marginally more. They would lie down with anyone to get the Germans out of their country, but they wished it weren't the Russians they were lying down with. After all, the Soviets had carved up Poland alongside Germany in 1939, and it looked as if they had no intention of giving their half back. So the people were skeptical and wary. The troops couldn't buy anything unless they had barter goods. No matter which way they turned, no one would accept their worthless Russian money. The Moscow treasury needed to stop printing meaningless paper. Alexander finally managed to sweet talk an old lady out of three knives and a pair of glasses for his near-blind Sergeant Verenkov for two hundred rubles.

ᕤᜦᜦᜦᕩ

After a dinner of ham and eggs and potatoes and onions, and much vodka, Ouspensky came to Alexander and whispered excitedly that they had found a "whore's mess tent" and were all going; would Alexander like to come, too?

Alexander said no.

"Oh, come on, sir. After what we saw at Majdanek we need something to reaffirm life. Come. Have a good bang."

"No. I'll be sleeping. We are forcing the bridgeheads at the Vistula in a few days. We're going to need our strength for that."

"Never heard of the Vistula."

"Fuck off."

"Let me understand—because of a river in some nebulous future, you're not going to get some cully-shangy today?"

"No. I'm going to sleep because that is what I need."

"With all due respect, Captain, as your drudge, I am with you every minute of every day, and I know what you need. You need Sir Berkeley as badly as the rest of us. Come with me. Those girls *want* to take our money."

Smiling, Alexander said, "Oh, because you've had so much luck unloading your rubles earlier. Ouspensky, you couldn't buy a damn watch. What makes you think you're going to buy a whole woman? She is going to spit at your rubles." Alexander was polishing his new knives in front of the tent.

"Come with us."

"No. You go ahead. Maybe when you come back you can tell me all about it."

"Captain, you are like my brother, but I will not let you live vicariously through me. Now come on. I heard there are five lovely Polish girls, and for thirty zlotys they will have each and every one of us."

Alexander laughed. "You don't have thirty zlotys!"

"But you do. Come on."

"No. Maybe tomorrow. Tonight I'm exhausted."

Nothing inside Alexander lifted when he was alone. When he was in the midst of battle, when he was commanding the tank, or waiting to attack, or killing other human beings, he could will his heart to forget.

He wet a towel in a bucket of water and lay down on his makeshift bed, covering his head and face with the sopping cotton. There, there. The cold water ran down his neck, his cheeks, his scalp. His eyes were closed. There, there.

"Shura, lie down, right here on the blanket."

Alexander obeys gladly. It is a warm, sunny, quiet afternoon. He has been chopping wood, and she has been reading. He wants to go for a swim.

"All that wood chopping, has it tired you out?"

"No, I'm all right."

"Are you a little tired?"

He doesn't know what answer she wants. "Uh—yes. I'm a little tired."

Smiling, Tatiana plops down on top of him and pins his arms above his head.

Her scent meanders into his insides. Alexander fights the impulse to kiss her collarbone. "OK, now what?" he says.

"Now you have to try to get away."

"How far do I have to get?" Alexander asks, flipping her on the blanket and rising to his feet.

She shakes her head. "I wasn't ready. Get back here." She is trying not to smile. Failing.

He obeys gladly.

She pins his arms—her fingers unable to circle the very wrists she is so judiciously attempting to pin—back under his head. Her scent weakens Alexander's senses. He is aroused by her spirited fearless playful struggle with him, by her jumping on his back, pulling him down on the ground, by her attempts to wrestle with him, by her wild antics in the water—her shy, erotic woman-child self is an endless aphrodisiac to him, like ambrosia.

"Are you ready yet?" he asks, gazing at her determined face as she thinks of the best way to keep him in place. She moves his wrists close together and under his head. "That's good," he says. "What else?"

"I'm thinking." Tatiana's legs squeeze his ribs. She takes a deep breath. "Ready?"

Before she can finish talking, Alexander flips her over. This time he does not stand up.

Sitting up, she asks plaintively, "What am I doing wrong? Why can't I hold you in place?"

He lays her down on the blanket. "Could it be because you are one and a half meters and forty-five kilos, and I'm a meter ninety and ninety kilos?" He places his large, dark, messy hand on her alabaster throat.

Moving away, she says stubbornly, "No. First of all, I'm a meter fifty-seven, so there. And secondly, I should be able to—physics demands that I can—put enough weight on you in the right place to immobilize you."

Alexander is trying hard to remain serious. Straddling her, he pins her wrists above her head. And smiles. "Am I allowed to kiss you during this game?"

"Absolutely not," Tatiana declares.

"Hmm," he says. He stares down at her face. He really wants to kiss her. Bending his head—

"Shura, that's not part of the game."

"I don't care," he says, kissing her. "I'm making up the rules as I go."

"Like you do at poker, right?"

"Don't start with the poker thing."

She tries not to laugh. "Are you ready?"

He is looking down at her. "I'm ready."

She tries to get away but she can't move. Her ribs are between his knees. Her legs flail behind him, actually rising high enough to hit him on the back. Her head is bobbing from side to side as she tries to lift her torso and disentangle her wrists. "Wait," she pants. "I think I got it."

"I tell you what," says Alexander. "I'll hold your wrists with just one hand; will that help?" With his right hand he squeezes her wrists together above her head.

"Ready?"

He laughs. "Yes, babe." He is trying to catch her eye, but she won't have any of it. Alexander knows once their eyes meet, that will be the end for this portion of the game. Tatiana knows the look in his eyes so well, as soon as she sees it, she moans a little, even while she is still fighting with him. Especially if she is still fighting with him.

Her legs are still flailing. She can't even free her wrists. With his roaming hand, Alexander caresses her thigh under her dress.

"That's not allowed," she pants, struggling against him.

"Not allowed?" His hand becomes more insistent.

"No. I do not allow that."

"All right, tadpole, come on," says Alexander, kissing her lips, her freckles, her eyes. "Show me what you got."

Tatiana turns her cheek to him. "I think I know what I'm doing wrong," she says. "Let's try it again."

His hand tightens around her wrists. "Go ahead."

Nearly inaudibly she moans. But Alexander hears.

"Well, you have to let go of me," whispers Tatiana.

"I thought you knew what you were doing wrong."

"I do. But you have to let go of me and lie down."

Reluctantly this time, Alexander obeys her.

Tatiana kneels between his legs. She doesn't hold his hands but pulls off his trousers and climbs back astride him, lifting her dress. "Now . . ." she murmurs, pinning his wrists above his head and moving her lips to his face. "Go ahead, soldier."

Alexander doesn't move. Tatiana moves. Up and down.

"Go ahead," she murmurs again. "You were saying? Show me what you got. Try to get away."

Alexander emits a low groan. Tania kisses him. "Oh, husband . . ." she calls melodiously, to the rhythm of her heart, to the rhythm of her motion. "You were saying . . ."

"Nothing." He closes his eyes. Tatiana yields herself to remind him that her submission—the source of all his strength—is his privilege and not his right. Wrapped in her, he takes it from her as though it is an elixir he needs to continue living.

Afterward she is still holding his wrists and he is still not moving, except for his heart, which is pumping 160 beats a minute of Tatiana through his body.

"I knew I wasn't doing it right before," Tatiana says, grinning and licking his cheek. "I knew there had to be a way to beat you."

"You should have just asked me. I would have told you what it was."

"Why would I want to ask you? I had to figure it out for myself."

"Good job, Tatiasha," murmurs Alexander. "You only just figured it out?"

⌇

In the middle of the night, Alexander—with the moist towel still on his face—was startled out of sleep by the cheerful drunken whisper of Ouspensky, who was shaking him awake, while taking his hand and placing into it something soft and warm. It took Alexander a moment to recognize the softness and warmness as a large human breast, a breast still attached to a human female, albeit a not entirely sober human female, who breathed fire on him, kneeled near his bed and said something in Polish that sounded like, "Wake up, cowboy, paradise is here."

"Lieutenant," said Alexander in Russian, "you're going on the rack tomorrow."

"You will pray to me as if I'm your god tomorrow. She is bought and paid for. Have a good one." Ouspensky lowered the flaps on the tent and disappeared.

Sitting up and turning on his kerosene lamp, Alexander was faced with a young, boozy, not unattractive Polish face. For a minute as he sat up, they watched each other, he with weariness, she with drunken friendliness. "I speak Russian," she said in Russian. "I'm going to get into trouble being here?"

"Yes," said Alexander. "You better go back."

"Oh, but your friend . . ."

"He is not my friend. He is my sworn enemy. He has brought you here to poison you. You need to go back quickly."

He helped her sit up. Her swinging breasts were exposed through her open dress. Alexander was naked except for his BVDs. He watched her appraise him. "Captain," she said, "you're not telling me you are poison? You don't look like poison." She reached out for him. "You don't feel like poison." She paused, whispering, "At ease, soldier."

Moving away from her slightly—only slightly—Alexander started to put on his trousers. She stopped him by rubbing him. He sighed, moving her hand away.

"You left a sweetheart behind? I can tell. You're missing her. I see many men like you."

"I bet you do."

"They always feel better after they're with me. So relieved. Come on. What's the worst that can happen? You will enjoy yourself?"

"Yes," said Alexander. "That's the worst that can happen."

She stuck out her hand holding a French letter. "Come on. Nothing to be afraid of."

"I'm not afraid," said Alexander.

"Oh, come on."

He buckled his belt. "Let's go. I'll walk you back."

"You have some chocolate?" she said, smiling. "I'll suck you off for some chocolate."

Alexander wavered, lingering on her bare breasts. "As it turns out, I do have some chocolate," he said, throbbing everywhere, including his heart. "You can have it all." He paused. "And you don't even have to suck me off."

The Polish girl's eyes cleared for a moment. "Really?"

"Really." He reached into his bag and handed her some small pieces of chocolate wrapped in foil.

Hungrily she shoved the bars into her mouth and swallowed them whole. Alexander raised his eyebrows. "Better the chocolate than me," he said.

The girl laughed. "Will you really walk me back?" she said. "Because the streets are not safe for a girl like me."

Alexander took his machine gun. "Let's go."

They walked through the subdued night-time streets of Lublin. Far away there was the distant sound of men laughing in a crowd, of breaking glass, of revelry. The girl took his arm. She was a tall girl, but the feel of soft female flesh pressing on him was a bittersweet waterfall to Alexander.

He felt a tightening in his abdomen, he felt his pulsing heart, his pulsing everything. He held her arm to him, and as they walked he closed his eyes for a second and imagined the relief and the comfort. He opened his eyes, shuddered slightly and sighed.

"You're headed over to the Vistula, aren't you? To Pulawy?" she asked.

He didn't answer.

"I know you are, you know how? Two of your Soviet divisions, one armored, one infantry, a thousand men in all, went that way. No one came back."

"They're not supposed to come back."

"You're not listening. They're not moving forward either. They're all in the river. Every one of your Soviet men."

Alexander looked at her thoughtfully.

"I don't care a whit about them, no more than I do about the Germans. But you treated me with a bit of respect. I'm going to tell you a better way," she said.

Alexander was listening.

"You're going too far north. You're headed straight into the German defense. There are hundreds of thousands of them. They're lying in wait for you across the Vistula. They kill you all and they will kill *you*. Remember, it was a walkover in Byelorussia because they didn't give a shit about Byelorussia."

Alexander wanted to beg to differ that it was a walkover in Byelorussia but kept quiet.

The Vistula is the last large river before the Oder on the border of Poland and Germany and the Oder flows practically through Berlin. Across the river and north to Warsaw, you will never get through, I don't care how many tanks and planes you have."

"I don't have any planes," said Alexander. "And only one tank."

"You need to move fifty kilometers south and cross the river at its narrowest point. There is a bridge there, though I'm sure it's been mined—"

"How do you know this?"

She smiled. "First of all, I used to live in Tarnow, not too far from there. And second, the fucking Fritzes when they went out of here a month ago talked German as if I didn't understand. They think we're all idiots. I'm sure the short white-and-blue bridge there has been mined. Don't take the bridge. But the river is shallow. You can build pontoons for the deepest point, but I bet all of you can swim. You'll even get your tank across. The forest is not well defended: it's too thick and mountainous. I'm not guaranteeing it's undefended. Just not well defended. It's mostly partisan groups over there—both German and Soviet. If you can get across, you'll get right into the woods and past those woods is almost Germany! At least you'll have a chance. But if you cross the Vistula at Pulawy or Dolny, you're all dead."

She stopped. "Well, here we are." She pointed to a small residential house. The lights were all on. She smiled. "That's how you know us sinners. Any time of night, the lights are always on."

He smiled back.

"Thank you," she said. "I'm glad I didn't have to do one more tonight. I'm exhausted." She touched his chest. "Though I wouldn't have minded one more with you."

Alexander adjusted her dress. "What's your name?"

She smiled. "Vera," she replied. "Means faith in Russian, right? And you?"

"I'm Alexander," he said. "The white-and-blue bridge down near Tarnow . . . does it have a name?"

Vera kissed him lightly on the lips. "*Most do Swietokryzst.* The bridge to Holy Cross."

⁂

The next morning Alexander sent five men north to Pulawy on a reconnaissance trip to the Vistula. The men did not come back. He sent another five men straight across to Dolny. The men did not come back.

It was the start of August and the reports coming from Warsaw were slow and grim. Despite much talk of pushing the Germans out of Warsaw, the Germans remained exactly as they were, reports of Soviet casualties were monumental and Poles, incited by the Soviets and spurred on by false promises of Soviet help had risen against the Germans by themselves and were now being massacred.

Alexander waited a few more days, but in the absence of good news, he took Ouspensky and they walked through the forest to the Vistula where they hid in the banks and watched the silent bulrushes on the other side. They were almost alone—if they looked straight ahead. Behind them were two NKGB troops, with slung rifles. No penal battalion officers were allowed to wander through Poland on their own even if it was ostensibly for a recon mission. The NKGB was the omnipresent police. They didn't fight the Germans, they just guarded the Gulag prisoners. There had not been a single day during the past year when they were not in Alexander's eyesight.

"I hate those bastards," muttered Ouspensky.

"I don't think about them." Alexander ground his teeth. He did not stop thinking about them.

"You should. They want harm to come to you."

"I don't take it personally." He took it personally.

They smoked. The morning was sunny and clear. The river reminded Alexander . . . He smoked, and lit up another and another—to poison his memory with nicotine. "Ouspensky, I need your advice."

"Honored, sir."

"I have been ordered to force the bridgehead at Dolny at sunrise tomorrow."

"Looks quiet," said Ouspensky.

"It looks it, doesn't it? But what if"—he inhaled—"what if I told you that you were going to die tomorrow?"

"Captain, you're describing to me my life for the last three years."

Alexander continued. "What if I told you we could go downriver where the German defenses aren't as heavy, and live? I don't know for how long, and I don't know if in the end it would make a bit of difference, but it certainly feels that the winds of destiny are at our heels this summer morning. Live or die, they whisper."

"Commander, may I just ask what in fuck's name you're talking about?"

"I'm talking about your path in life, Ouspensky. One way lies the rest of it. The other way the rest of it too—but shorter."

"What makes you think we'll do better downriver?"

Alexander shrugged. He didn't want to tell him about a soft-fleshed girl named Faith. "I know that Dolny is deceptively quiet."

"Commander, you have a commander too, don't you? I heard you on the horn this morning. General Konev was clearly giving you orders to take Dolny."

Nodding, Alexander said, "Yes. He is sending us to our death. The river is too deep and wide, the bridge is exposed. The Germans don't even mine the bridge, I bet. They just shoot us from Dolny across the Vistula."

Ouspensky backed off into the woods and said, "I don't think we have much choice, Captain. You are not General Konev. You have to go where he tells you. And even he has to go where Comrade Stalin tells him."

Alexander was thoughtful. He did not move from the bank. "Look at that bridge. Look at that river. It's carrying the bodies of thousands of Soviet men." Alexander paused. "Tomorrow it'll be carrying you and me."

"I don't see them," Ouspensky said casually, squinting. "And someone must make it through." That was less casual.

Alexander shook his head. "No. No one. All dead. Like us. Tomorrow." He smiled. "Look at the Vistula carefully, Lieutenant. Come sunrise, this will be your grave. Enjoy your last day on this earth. God has made it a particularly beautiful one."

Ouspensky chuckled. "Good thing then you had it off with that girl, isn't it?"

Alexander got up and as they were walking ten kilometers back to Lublin, said, "I am going to call General Konev about changing our mission. But I need your full support, Lieutenant."

"I'm with you till the day you die, sir, much to my infernal dismay."

༺ஐஒ༻

Alexander managed to convince Konev to let them travel fifty kilometers south down the Vistula. It wasn't as difficult as he had anticipated. Konev was well aware of what was happening to the Soviets at Dolny, and the main divisions of the Ukrainian front were not at the Vistula yet. He was not averse to trying a new position.

As Alexander's battalion set off for the woods, Ouspensky complained and whined the entire time he was breaking down Alexander's tent and getting their gear together. He complained up until the time he hopped into the open tank and told Telikov to step on it. He complained when he saw that Alexander was walking behind the tank and not getting on.

Alexander walked behind, through the narrow trampled path that led through the summer fields to the forest stretching for fifty hilly kilometers along the Vistula. He turned around. A squadron of NKGB troops armed to their miserable gills marched doggedly behind him.

They broke camp three times, and fished in the river, and carried carrots and potatoes with them from Lublin and stories of warm potatoes and warmer Polish girls, they sang songs and shaved until no hair was left on their bodies and behaved like Cub Scouts, not like convicted felons on the way to a road with no hope. Alexander sang louder than most and was more cheerful than all and walked faster than his men with the wind at his back.

Ouspensky, however, continued to grumble each and every kilometer. At one point during a late afternoon, he jumped down from the tank and walked next to Alexander for a bit.

"Only if I don't hear a breath of complaint from you."

"I am allowed to use my soldier's privilege," Ouspensky said grumpily.

"Yes, but why do you have to use it so much?" Alexander was thinking of the river and listening with only one ear to Ouspensky. "Walk faster, you one-lunged malingerer."

"Sir, the girl back in Lublin . . . Why didn't you avail yourself of her kindness?"

Alexander did not reply.

"You know, sir," said Ouspensky, "I had to pay for her regardless. The least you could have done was have her. Just as a courtesy to me, dammit."

"Next time I'll remember to be more considerate."

Ouspensky marched closer. "Captain, what is wrong with you? Didn't you see her? Did you not see her tit-for-tats? The rest of her was just as succulent."

"Oh?"

"Didn't you find her—"

"She wasn't my type."

"What is your type, sir? If you don't mind my asking. The canteen had all kinds—"

"I like the kind that haven't been to a canteen."

"Oh, dear God. It's war!"

"I have plenty to keep my mind occupied, Lieutenant."

"Do you want me to tell you about the Polish girl?" Ouspensky cleared his throat.

Smiling and looking straight ahead, Alexander said, "Tell me, Lieutenant. And you may not leave out any details. That's an order."

Ouspensky spoke for five minutes. When he was finished, Alexander was silent for a moment, taking in what he just heard, and then said, "That's the *best* you can do?"

"The story took longer than the actual knock!" Ouspensky exclaimed. "Who am I, Cicero?"

"You're not even a very good entertainer. Surely sex can't be that boring, or have I just forgotten?"

"Have you?"

"I don't think so."

"You tell me a story then."

Shaking his head, Alexander said, "The stories I can tell you, I've forgotten. The stories I remember, I can't tell you." Alexander felt Nikolai staring at him. "What?" He walked a little faster. "Go ahead, men!" he called to his formation. "Don't fucking die right in front of me. Faster! Hip hop! We've got another twenty kilometers before our destination. Don't dilly dally." He glanced at Ouspensky. "What?" Alexander barked at his lieutenant who was still staring at him.

"Captain, who did you leave behind?"

"It's not who *I* left behind," replied Alexander, marching faster, holding his machine gun tighter. "It's who left me behind."

෴

They got to the bridge by the third nightfall. Immediately the telephone stringer left to find an Army Group Ukraine division to run a wire from the high command to Alexander.

At pre-dawn, Alexander was up. He sat by the banks of the river, it was no more than 200 feet wide and looked onto the small innocuous bridge, an old, wooden, once-white bridge. "*Most do Swietokryzst*," Alexander whispered. It was very early Sunday morning and there was no one on it, but beyond the bridge in the distance, across the river, were the church spires of the town of Swietokryzst and beyond them were the dense oaks of the Holy Cross mountains.

Alexander was going to wait for a division of Army Group Ukraine to catch up with him, but he reconsidered. He was going to stop at nothing to cross the river first.

It was peaceful. It was hard to believe that in one day, the next morning, the sky, the earth, the water was going to be filled with the blood of his men. Maybe there are no Germans on the other side at all, he thought, and then we can cross and then somehow hide in the woods. The Americans entered Europe two months ago. Eventually they will be in Germany. All I have to do is live long enough to fall into American hands . . .

At one of these bridges, a painter would sit and on another Sunday would perhaps paint families rowing down the river in little boats, the women in white hats, the men with oars, the young children in white dresses. In his painting perhaps the woman is wearing a blue hat. Perhaps the child is about one. She holds the child in her arms, and smiles, and the man smiles back and rows a little faster, as the wake behind him increases, the goldenrod hue gleams, and the painter catches it all.

What Alexander wanted this morning was his childhood back. He felt as if he were eighty. When was the last time he ran with a smile to anything? When was the last time he ran to something without a gun in his hand? When was the last time he crossed the street in stride?

He didn't want to answer those questions, not before he crossed the bridge to Swietokryzst.

൭ᴍᴍᴏ

"OPEN FIRE! OPEN FIRE!"

The next day in the river they were dying under the oppressive popping din of enemy fire, and not slowly dying, either. His infantry ran in first, but they needed immediate help.

Their tank was stuck in the rocky bottom, immersed up to the treads in the water. Verenkov loaded a 100-millimeter shell into the cannon and fired. The explosion and resounding screams told Alexander that Verenkov did not miss. He reloaded with smaller ammunition, but didn't have enough time to open fire.

The tank was a large target. Alexander knew that it was about to be blown apart. He didn't want to lose his tank and his weapons, but he needed his men more. "Jump!" he shouted to his crew. "Live one coming!"

They all jumped—rather, they were thrown as the shell hit the tank nose and exploded on impact. With regret for his only piece of motorized artillery, Alexander began to wade through the water holding his machine gun above his head and shooting in short bursts at the small beachhead in front of him on the other side of the river. Ouspensky covered him from behind and to the side. Alexander heard Ouspensky yelling at him to MOVE BACK, to STEP BACK, to GET BEHIND, to HOLD, to DROP BACK, FIND COVER! FIND COVER! motioning at him, pulling him down, cursing, but all Alexander did was push Ouspensky off him, ignore him and continue forward. Telikov and Verenkov grabbed each other as they swam. Only Alexander was tall enough to wade through, water up to his neck. He was able to aim better than his men; swimming and shooting at the same time was inefficient at best.

All around him was machine-gun fire. He couldn't tell where it was coming from. Every round felt as though it were hitting his helmet.

His men were floating.

The Vistula was turning red. Alexander had to get to the other side. Once they were on dry land anything was possible. And *this* is better than Dolny, better than Pulawy? he thought. *Here* the German defenses are down?

In the water nothing seemed possible.

Ouspensky continued to shout, as always. This time it wasn't directed at Alexander. "Look at them all screaming like a bunch of pussies! Who are we fighting? Men or girls?"

Alexander spotted one of his own men clutching a corpse. It was Yermenko.

"Corporal!" Alexander yelled. "Where is your battle partner?"

Yermenko lifted the dead body. "Right here, sir!"

Alexander could see that Yermenko was struggling in the water. Quickly Alexander swam to him and yelled at him, but Yermenko was still struggling. He was using the body as a float. "What the fuck is wrong with you?" Alexander yelled. "Drop the soldier, and swim!"

"I can't swim, sir!"

"Oh, for fuck's sake!" Alexander got Ouspensky, Telikov and Verenkov to help Yermenko across. They were all ten meters from the shoreline when from the nearby bushes on the beach out jumped three Germans. Alexander didn't spend a second thinking. He fired; through the air they flew.

Then three more came. Then three more. He fired again and again. Four Germans jumped in the river and headed straight for Alexander, raising their weapons at him. Yermenko lunged in front of Alexander, pointed his weapon at the Germans and mowed them down. Ouspensky, Telikov, and Verenkov formed a wall in front of Alexander. Ouspensky yelled, "Back, Captain! Stand back!" He shot from above the shoulder and missed.

Alexander lifted his Shpagin above Ouspensky's head, shot from above the shoulder and did not miss. "If you miss, shoot again, Lieutenant!" he yelled.

But now five Germans were in the water, meters away, water up to their waists. Alexander kept shooting and trying to get closer to the beachhead. His men kept fighting off the Germans with the butts of their rifles and their bayonets, trying to get closer to shore, but they were having no luck. The wet band of them in the water were too exposed, and more and more Germans kept coming.

In battle, three out of Alexander's five senses were heightened. He saw danger like an owl in darkness, he smelled blood like a hyena, he heard noises like a wolf. He never got distracted, he never got confused, he never became uncertain, he saw and smelled and heard everything. He did not taste his own blood, he did not feel his own pain.

On his flank he saw a flash of light and had just enough time to lurch forward, the bullet missing him by half a meter. The German soldier was so livid at missing at point blank range, he stabbed Alexander with his bayonet. He was aiming for the neck, but Alexander's neck was too high for the German. The bayonet pierced him in the lower left shoulder, cutting into his arm. Alexander swung his weapon and nearly sliced off the German's head. The man went down, but now there were five of them on top of him, and he with his arm bleeding took out his knife and his bayonet and fought them until they went down and Ouspensky got their guns. Now that they had weapons in each hand, they became a wall of bullets moving to the shore and they weren't stopped.

There were no more Germans coming from the bushes, and there was no more firing, either. And suddenly all was quiet except for the panting of the still breathing, except for the death throes of the still dying, except for the bubbling of the river burying the dead.

Alexander's men crawled out onto the sand.

Alexander wanted a smoke, but his cigarettes were wet. He watched the NKGB troops cautiously swim across the river, holding their rifles and mortars above their heads.

"Fucking pussies," Ouspensky whispered to Alexander, who sat between him and Yermenko. Alexander didn't say anything to Ouspensky, but when the NKGB got to the beach, he stood up and without saluting said, "You should have taken the unmined bridge and walked across like the civilians you are."

The NKGB man—not a scrape on him—stared coldly at Alexander and said, "Address me properly."

"You should have taken the fucking bridge, comrade," said Alexander, bloodied from the helmet down, holding on to his machine gun.

"I am a *lieutenant* in the Red Army!" the man shouted. "Lieutenant Sennev. Weapons down, soldier."

"And I am a captain!" Alexander shouted back, lifting up the weapon with his good arm. "Captain Belov." One more word, and Alexander was going to see how many rounds his Shpagin still had in it.

The man stood down and motioned his men to leave the beach and follow him into the woods, cursing under his breath.

What was left of Alexander's men stayed on the beach. He wanted to assess the damage to his battalion (he was afraid it was more like a platoon now) but the medic, a Ukrainian by the name of Kremler, came to take a look at him. He washed out the arm gash with carbolic acid and poured sulfa powder right into the wound to disinfect it further. "It's deep," was the only thing Kremler said.

"You have thread for stitches?"

"I have a small spool. We have many injured men."

"Just give me three stitches. To hold it together, that's all."

Kremler sewed him, cleaned his banged-up head, and gave him a drink of vodka and a shot of morphine in the stomach. Afterward Ouspensky came and stood in front of him. "Captain, may I have a word?"

Alexander was sitting on the sand, having a smoke. The morphine was making him sleepy. He looked up. "First I'm going to have a word with you. How many men down?"

"All of them. We have thirty-two privates left, three corporals, two sergeants, one lieutenant—that would be me—and one captain—that would be you." Ouspensky said the last grimly.

"Yermenko?"

"Yes."

"Verenkov?"

"Neck wound, shell grazing on stomach, lost the fucking glasses you gave him, but yes."

"Telikov?"

"Broken foot, but yes."

"How in fuck's name did he break his foot?"

"He tripped." Ouspensky was not smiling.

"What's the matter? Are *you* all right?"

"I'm fine. My head has been bleeding out my brains for two hours."

"Did you start out with a significant amount, Lieutenant?"

Ouspensky crouched in front of Alexander. "Sir, I must tell you that I'm never one to second-guess my commanding officer, but I feel I'm not speaking out of turn if I say, what happened there—what you let happen there—was fucking lunacy."

"You're second-guessing me, Lieutenant."

"Sir—"

"Lieutenant!" Alexander stood up. His wound was oozing blood out of the bandage. "We had nowhere else to go." He paused. "And we crossed the river, didn't we?"

"Sir, that's not the point. Konev's 29th armored division is supposed to be a day behind us. We could have waited. Yet we went into the water, into direct fire, we did not wait, we did not recon, we did not try to knock them out of position first, we just fucking went! And more to the point—*you* just went. *You!* The only thing between all of us and instant death, you led us into the mouth of the Germans and lost nearly all of our men, and now you're sitting on the ground, half dead yourself, pretending you don't know why I'm raging!"

Alexander pressed his hand into the bandage and said, "You can rage all you want, Lieutenant, but don't do it in my presence. I wasn't going to sit and wait for Konev's men. He takes days to get here, there is no element of surprise, the Germans reinforce even more, and in the end, we get sent in first anyway. Except the Germans have more time to build up their defenses. We had to move out. Now we'll regroup, but we're in the woods. And we've cleared this path for Soviet reinforcements, Soviet armies. They'll thank us in their own ungrateful, grudging way." He smiled. "I guarantee you, we're the first Soviet men across the Vistula."

Ouspensky glared at him incredulously.

"We didn't do so badly. We didn't do great. We've lost men before, Lieutenant. Do you remember last April in Minsk? We lost thirty men de-mining one fucking field, not getting across a crucial river in Poland."

"Sir, you sent us into their rockets with nary a bullet!"

"I told you to hold your weapon above your head as you crossed."

"We have forty men left!"

"Are you counting the twenty NKGB?"

"Forty men and twenty pussies!"

"Yes, but we pushed the Germans away from the river bank. They've retreated into the woods. When we proceed into the woods, we will proceed with reinforcements."

Ouspensky shook his head. "We can't fight in the woods. I will not fight in the woods. It's completely different warfare in the woods. You can't see dick."

"No, you can't. I'm sorry I can't make war more palatable for you."

"We lost our tank. The only thing that protected *you.*"

"Me."

"Oh, Mother of Christ!" Ouspensky exploded. "You act as if you are fucking immortal, but you are not—"

"Do not," Alexander said loudly, "raise your voice to me, Ouspensky, do you understand? I don't give a shit what kind of liberties I allow you, I will not allow you this one. Do I make myself clear?"

"Yes, sir," Ouspensky said, quieter and stepping away. "You are still not fucking immortal, sir. And your men *certainly* aren't, but I don't give a shit about the men. It's you we can't replace. And I'm supposed to be here to protect you. How can you engage in hand-to-hand combat in the water when you are supposed to be in the rear? What do you think you are made of, Captain? Until just now when I saw you bleed red blood like the rest of us, I wasn't sure."

"It's not my blood," Alexander said.

"What?"

But Alexander shook his head.

"What's going to happen to us in the woods?"

"We are going to go into the mountains of Holy Cross. There's a good chance we will run out of ammunition because the Germans are better supplied. Konev will order us to fight until we die. That's what the penal battalion means. That's what being a Soviet officer means."

Ouspensky stared blankly at Alexander. "And coming here—this is your winds of fucking destiny blowing at your back?"

"Yes. Because there is just one thing, Lieutenant, that the Red Army overlooked."

"What's that, sir?"

"I," said Alexander, "have no intention of dying."

CHAPTER TWENTY-FOUR

Barrington, August 1944

"WHERE ARE WE GOING?" Vikki said. "And *why?* I don't want to take the train to Massachusetts. I don't want to go so far. What is it with you and these train trips? You just came back from Arizona, isn't that enough? It's raining, it's miserable, and I worked a double shift yesterday and I work another double on Monday. Can't I just stay home? Grammy is making her lasagna. I have to do my nails and iron my dress and my hair, and did you hear, women are shaving their legs and underarms now. It's all the rage. I was going to try. They told me that at Lady Be Beautiful, where by the way you promised me you were going to come with me. Why do we have to go anywhere? Couldn't I just stay home and have a bath?"

"No. We have to go," said Tatiana, pushing Anthony in the carriage, and pushing Vikki in the back.

"Why do I have to go with you?"

"Because I don't want to go alone. Because my English is not so good. Because you my friend."

Vikki sighed.

She sighed for five hours on the train, all the way to Boston. "Vikki, I counted. That was three sighs per mile. We went two hundred and forty miles. That's seven hundred sighs."

"That wasn't sighing," Vikki said petulantly. "That was breathing."

"Exasperated breathing, yes." She wished for her brother. Pasha would have gone with her and never uttered a word of misery, he would have just been stoic by her side. Her sister would have complained though, much like Vikki was doing. "I should've asked Edward," Tatiana muttered, covering up Anthony. It was raining in Boston, too.

"Why didn't you?"

"Can you *not* let me know every single thing you feeling at all times? I don't want to know that you grouchy about doing me favor. Just do it, and stop complaining."

Vikki stopped sighing.

The girls took a cab from Boston to Barrington since there were no local trains. The cabbie said, "That will be twenty dollars, going all that way."

Vikki gasped, then yelped as Tatiana squeezed her thigh. "That will be fine," Tatiana said to the cab driver.

"Twenty dollars? Are you crazy?" The girls settled into the back of the cab with Anthony on Tatiana's lap, and the taxi screeched off. "It's half a week's pay for me. How much do you get paid?"

"Less than that. How you think we going to get there?"

"I don't know. By bus?"

"Well, too far to walk to bus."

"But it's going to be twenty dollars more to get back."

"Yes."

"Can you tell me now what we're doing?"

"We going to visit one of Anthony's relatives." She knew she shouldn't do it, Sam had told her she shouldn't, but she could not help herself. For some reason she felt it was going to be all right. Besides, she might soon need a favor from one of Anthony's relatives.

"You have relatives in the United States?"

"I don't. He does. I need you with me for support. If I need help, I will pinch arm really hard, like this."

"Ouch!"

"Right. Until I do, you stand there, and smile, and say nothing."

An hour later they were at Barrington. Tatiana paid and the girls got out. Barrington was a white town with black shutters and green oaks lining the clean streets. It was homey and peppered with white spires peeking out over the trees. There were some open shops along Main Street, a hardware store, a coffee shop, an antiques gallery, and a few women on the streets. None of them were pushing carriages—no young babies in sight except for Tatiana's Anthony.

"Did you just spend more than two weeks' salary on his trip?" asked Vikki, taking out a brush for her tangled hair.

"Do you know how much money I spent to come to here from England? Five hundred dollars. Was that worth it?"

"Absolutely. But to come *here*?"

"Just push carriage for me."

"Wait, I'm busy." Vikki continued brushing.

Tatiana glared at her.

"Oh, all right."

"Let's go and ask where Maple Street is."

From the newspaper shop on the corner of Main, they learned that Maple was just a few blocks away. In the rain they walked there.

"Hey, something just occurred to me," Vikki said. "The town is named Barrington, and your last name is Barrington. Is that a coincidence?"

"That *just* occurred to you? Stop. We here." They stopped at a large white colonial clapboard house with black shutters, and overripe maples in the front yard. Up the brick walk they went, came up three steps, and stopped at the doorbell. They stood without ringing it.

"What are we doing?"

Tatiana couldn't get her courage up. "Maybe we should leave," she said.

"Are you joking? All this way, to leave?" Vikki rang the bell herself. Tatiana left Anthony's carriage at the foot of the steps and she held her son in her arms.

The door was opened by a stern-looking, properly dressed, perfectly coiffed, older woman. "Yes?" she said in a brusque voice. "You're collecting? Hold on, let me get my purse."

"We not collecting," Tatiana said quickly. "We come—I come to speak to Esther Barrington."

"I'm Esther Barrington," said Esther. "Who are *you*?"

"I—" Tatiana hesitated. She held out her boy. "This is Anthony Alexander Barrington," she said. "Alexander's son."

Esther dropped the keys she was holding in her hands. "Who *are* you?"

"I am Alexander's wife," said Tatiana.

"Where is he?"

"I don't know."

Esther's face turned red. "Well, I'm not at all surprised. To *think* you would have the nerve to come here, to my house! Who do you think you are?"

"Alexander's wife—"

"I don't care who you are! Don't you shove your son in my face, as if suddenly I'm supposed to care. I am very sorry for you—" Her stern voice belied Esther's wretched expression. "Very sorry, but you have nothing to do with my business."

Tatiana took a step back. "I'm sorry," she said. "You're right. I just wanted you to—"

"I know what you wanted! You're bringing me your bastard child. What? That's going to make it all better?"

"Make what better?" said Vikki.

Esther didn't reply to Vikki as she continued to raise her voice. "Do you know what your father-in-law said to me as he left my house for the last time fourteen years ago? He said, *My son is none of your business, cunt.* That's what he said to me! My flesh-and-blood nephew, my Alexander none of my business. I wanted to help them, I said I would keep the boy while he and his wife went to train-wreck their lives in the Soviet Union, but he spat on my offer. He didn't want any part of me, of our family. He never wrote to me, never telegraphed. I never heard from him." She paused, panting. "What's the bastard doing now, anyway?"

"He is dead," Tatiana said faintly.

Esther couldn't even mouth an "Oh." Her hands clutching the doorknob, she staggered back, and said, "Well, fine. Don't you, whoever you are, come to me now and tell me your stranger son is *my* damned business." With her trembling hand Esther slammed the door as loudly as she could and the girls were left standing on the porch.

"Hmm," said Vikki. "How did you expect that to go?"

Trying hard not to cry, Tatiana turned around and walked back down the steps. "Better than that, I think."

What had she expected? She didn't know the relations between Alexander's father and aunt before the Barringtons left the United States, but she was sure of one thing from Esther's reaction: Esther knew nothing—not about her brother, not about her sister-in-law and not about Alexander. And really, that was the only thing Tatiana had come to find out—whether Esther had any information that might help Tatiana. She didn't. Tatiana was done. The promise of distant family, of perhaps a familial bond for her son, was too much of an intellectual intangible for Tatiana at a time when she was single-mindedly set on just one thing— finding out the truth about what happened to Alexander.

She placed Anthony back in the carriage, and they walked down the path to the street. "Fourteen years," Vikki said. "You'd think she'd get over it. Some people have such long memories."

Slowly they made their way back to town. "Hey, what was that word?" Tatiana asked. "What did Alexander's father call her when he left?"

"Never mind. Ladies don't use that kind of language. Our Esther has a bit of the soldier in her. Someday I'll teach you the bawdy words in English."

Tatiana said, "I know bawdy words in English." Quietly. "Just not that one."

"How would you know anything? Dictionaries don't have them. Phrase-books don't have them." Vikki prodded her. "Not any phrase-books I've ever seen."

"I once," said Tatiana, "had very good teacher."

They were on Main Street when a car pulled up to the sidewalk and Esther jumped out, her makeup long gone, her eyes red, her gray coiffed hair disheveled. She went in front of Tatiana.

"I'm sorry," Esther said. "It was a shock to see you. And we had never heard a word from my brother since he left America. I didn't know what happened to them. No one in the State Department would tell us a thing."

Back at the house, the girls were fed to bursting with ham and bread and ham soup, and were given coffee, and Anthony was put upstairs into a bed, barricaded on all sides, and allowed to nap.

For someone who had harbored a grudge for over a decade, Esther cried like the wife of the hanged when Tatiana told her about her brother and his wife, and Alexander.

She insisted that the girls stay until Sunday, and the girls did. Esther was a decent woman. She herself had no children, was sixty-one, a year younger than Harold, and the only surviving Barrington. Her own husband had died five years earlier, and Esther now lived alone with Rosa, her housekeeper.

"Was this where Alexander lived?" Tatiana kept her eyes on Esther, afraid to look around, afraid she might see a vestige of a child Alexander.

Esther shook her head. "His house is about a mile away from here. I don't speak to the people who live in it now, they're right snobs, but if you want I could drive you past there so you can take a look."

"They had woods behind their house?"

"Not anymore," Esther replied. "All houses there now. The woods were nice. Alexander had a friend—"

"Teddy? Or Belinda?"

"Is there any part of his life you don't know?"

"Yes," said Tatiana. "The present part."

"Well, Teddy died in '42, in the Battle of Midway. And Belinda became a frontline nurse and is now in North Africa. Or Italy. Or wherever those troops are now. Poor Alexander. Poor Teddy. Poor Harold." Esther shook her head. "Stupid Harold. His whole family ruined, and that boy—that golden, unbelievable boy—do you have a picture?"

Tatiana shook her head. "He remained what he was, Esther. You haven't heard from him, then?"

"Of course not."

"Or anything about him?"

"Not a word. Why?"

Tatiana struggled up. "We really must be going."

On the train to New York, Vikki stared out the window.

"What's wrong, Vik?"

"Nothing. I was just thinking," said Vikki, "that when I first met you, except for that faded scar on your face, you seemed like the least complicated person I had ever met."

Staring at her boy, Tatiana put her hand on Vikki's leg. "I'm not complicated," she said. "I just need to find out what happened to my husband."

"You told me and Edward he was dead."

Tatiana stared out the window as the train whizzed through the wet summer Massachusetts countryside.

Have you been looking for me? she had once asked him, and he replied, All my life.

She said nothing further as she put her head back on the seat and, stroking Anthony's head, shut her eyes until they were in Grand Central Station.

CHAPTER TWENTY-FIVE

In the Mountains of Holy Cross, October 1944

DEEP IN THE DENSE thick forest of the mountains, a hundred kilometers and six weeks past the bridge to Holy Cross, Alexander and his men were under fire for three hours one cold autumn afternoon.

They lived in the woods and slept in the woods, setting up their canvas tents when the fighting stopped, or wrapping themselves in their trench coats on the ground when it didn't. They built fires, but food in the forest was more scarce than they would have liked. The rabbits scurried at the sound of a battalion of men. Neither the streams nor the fish were plentiful. But when there were streams, they at least managed to wash. The season for blueberries had passed, and they were all sick of mushrooms. Undercooked, the mushrooms gave Alexander's men terrible stomach upsets and he finally had to forbid their use. The telephone wire frequently broke on the uneven terrain, and the army supplies did not last between reinforcements. Alexander had to make his own soap out of lard and ashes. But his soldiers cared nothing for staying clean, for keeping off lice. They were aware of, but indifferent to, the symbiotic relationship between lice and typhus. The men wanted to eat the lard, and soap be damned. The gunpowder, the mud, the blood remained on their faces and bodies for weeks. Everyone had trench foot: they just could never get dry.

They were a battalion by themselves in the woods, making their way up the mountains to get to the other side, but the Germans took positions atop the mountains, as they had in Sinyavino and Pulkovo and they only needed a few men to ward off Alexander's many.

But at least before they had been making arduous progress. Suddenly they were stopped by the Germans at the foothills and they had not been able to penetrate the Nazi defense despite twice receiving reinforcements of men and ammunition. There had been no further reinforcements in eight days. In between bursts of fire from morning until night, German voices echoed through the woods. Not just above them, but to the left and right of them. Alexander began to suspect that the Germans had less of a defense *line* than an en*circle*ment. Alexander's troops had not moved a meter in the forest, and once again night was an hour away.

Alexander had to break the impasse or this forest was going to be his death. It had already been Verenkov's death. The poor bastard couldn't see the enemy, he fired blindly, but couldn't move out of the way of anything. Fortune had carried him alive to these woods and stopped here. Alexander and Ouspensky buried him in the hole ripped by the grenade that had taken him and left his helmet hanging on a stick rising out of the ground.

⌖

"Who the fuck is that?" Alexander suddenly asked when the gunfire ceased. "I swear to God, I can hear Russian. Am I hallucinating, Ouspensky? Listen."

"I hear the paper-ripping sound of the Maschinengewehr 43." That was the German sub-machine-gun.

"Yes, that, but listen. They're about to load another belt in, and you will hear someone barking commands in Russian. I swear to God it's Russian."

Ouspensky looked at Alexander with sympathy. "You miss Russia, Captain?"

"Oh, fuck," Alexander said. "I'm telling you it's Russian!"

"You think we're shooting at Russian men?"

"I don't know. Is that ridiculous? How would they have gotten here?"

"Hmm. Sir, have you heard of the Vlasovites?"

"The Vlasovites?"

"The Soviet POWs or partisans who have switched sides."

"Yes, I've heard of the Vlasovites," Alexander snapped. He did not want to be having this discussion with Ouspensky while he was trying to save his men. Ouspensky had absolutely no sense of urgency about anything. He was sitting behind a tree, reloading his Shpagin, setting up the shells in neat rows to load into Alexander's mortar, as peaceful as if he were at a Crimean resort.

Of course Alexander had heard about the Vlasovites. In the primordial morass that had become the partisan war on the Germans, the Vlasovites—led by the eponymous Russian general, Andrei Vlasov—were the Russian soldiers who, when taken prisoner by the Germans, switched to the German side and fought their Red Army brothers in arms— ostensibly fighting for a free Russia. Having organized his Anti-Stalinist

Russian Liberation Movement and having found no support from Hitler, Vlasov had long been under German house arrest, but many Russians continued to fight under his name in German-led brigades.

"It can't be the Vlasovites," Ouspensky said.

"General Vlasov is not here, but his men continue to fight on the German side. He had over a hundred thousand of them. And some of them are in those woods."

The fire died down for a minute and, as clear as skylight, they heard in Russian, *"Zarezhai! Zarezhai!"*

Alexander exchanged a look with Ouspensky, raised his eyebrows and said, "I hate it when I'm fucking right."

~~~

"Now what? We have no ammo."

"That's not true," Alexander said cheerfully. "I've got four magazines left and half of one drum. And reinforcements will be here soon." That was a lie. He suspected the telephone wire had been torn again, and now there was an added problem—the wire stringer was dead.

"There are at least thirty of them in the woods."

"I better not miss then, had I?"

"You're lying about the reinforcements. We already had our reinforcements. Konev brought you three hundred men with rifles and ammo two weeks ago. They're all dead."

"Stop your yapping, Lieutenant. Order your men to get ready to open fire."

Ten minutes later, Alexander had nothing left in his drum. The fire from his men subsided.

"How far is the German border?" Ouspensky asked.

"About a hundred thousand German troops away, Lieutenant." Ouspensky sighed. "Now what?"

"Take out your knife. Soon it will be hand to hand in the woods."

"You're fucking nuts." Ouspensky spoke quietly, so no one else could hear him.

"You have other suggestions?"

"If I had other suggestions, I wouldn't be a lieutenant. I'd be a captain and you'd be taking orders from me." Ouspensky paused. "Have you ever taken orders from anybody, sir?"

Alexander laughed lightly. "Lieutenant, in case you haven't noticed, I do have superior officers of my own."

"Well, where are they now? They need to order you to retreat."

"We cannot retreat. You know that. There are two dozen NKGB troops behind us to make sure of that. They'll shoot us."

Alexander was very quiet and very thoughtful.

The two men paused, sitting side by side on the mossy ground, their backs against a tree. Ouspensky said, "Did you say the NKGB will shoot us if we retreat?"

"Instantly." Alexander wasn't looking at Ouspensky.

"Did you say *shoot us*?"

Now Alexander looked at Ouspensky. "What are you suggesting, Lieutenant?" he said slowly.

"Nothing, sir. But you are implying, aren't you, that they have something to shoot at us with?"

Alexander was silent for a few minutes and then said, "Bring me Corporal Yermenko."

A few minutes later, Ouspensky returned with Yermenko, who was wiping blood off his arm.

"Corporal, how is your ammo holding up?"

"I've got three eight-round boxes, three grenades and a few mortar shells."

"Very good. Let me tell you the situation. We're low on ammo and there are at least a dozen Germans in the woods."

"I think, sir, more than a dozen. And they are armed."

"Corporal, how good a marksman are you? Will your two dozen rounds last you against a dozen men?"

"No, sir, they won't. I don't have a sniper rifle."

"Have you any ideas?"

"Are you asking me, sir?"

"I'm asking you, Corporal."

Yermenko paused, moving his mouth in a thoughtful manner, while he adjusted his helmet. He was standing at attention and his arm continued to bleed. Alexander motioned for Ouspensky to get the first aid kit. Yermenko was still thinking. Alexander motioned for him to crouch and took a look at the corporal's wound. It was a superficial grazing of the triceps, but it was bleeding steadily. Alexander applied pressure with a dressing, and while sitting next to Yermenko, said, "Tell me what you think, Corporal."

Lowering his voice, Yermenko said, "I think maybe we should ask the . . . back troops for some of their ammo, sir." He motioned behind him into the woods.

"I think you're right. But what if they refuse?"

"I think we should ask them in such a way as to make that impossible."

Alexander patted Yermenko on the back.

Lowering his voice further, Yermenko said, "I know they have dozens of semi-automatic rifles, at least three or four sub-machine guns, and they have not expended their rounds. They have grenades, they have mortar shells, and they have water and food."

Alexander and Ouspensky exchanged glances. "You're right, of course," Alexander said, wrapping the bandage over Yermenko's arm and tying the ends in a knot. "But I don't know if they're going to part with their ammo. Are you up to this assignment?"

"Yes, sir. I will need one man to distract them."

Alexander got up. "That will be me."

"Sir!" Ouspensky exclaimed. "No. You will send *me*."

"You can come with us. But whatever you do, don't tell them you have only one lung, Lieutenant." Alexander handed Yermenko the wooden club he had made. Small pieces of sharp shell fragments were wedged deep into the carved-out wooden head. At the other end, the handle was attached to a rope Alexander had made out of tree bark so it would be easy to swing. Yermenko took it, gave Ouspensky rounds for his Tokarev pistol, they loaded their weapons, Alexander loaded a fresh 35-round magazine into his Shpagin, and the three of them walked silently through the woods to the NKGB encampment. Alexander could see a dozen men sitting in a social circle around a welcoming fire, chatting, laughing.

"Ouspensky," he said, "stay here. I'm going to talk to them first. I'm going to ask for their help. You two wait for me here. When I turn around to walk back to you, if I sling my machine gun over my shoulder, it means we have peace. If I take a step with it in my arms, that means we don't. Understood?"

"Perfectly," said Yermenko, but Ouspensky, grim in the face, did not reply. Ouspensky took his job of protecting Alexander too seriously.

"Lieutenant! Understood?"

Sigh. "Yes, sir."

Alexander walked forward, leaving Ouspensky and Yermenko ten paces behind in the bushes, and came up to the circle in a small clearing. The men barely turned or raised their heads to look at him.

"Comrades," he said, coming up close to their circle, "we need your help. We have no ammo left, the replacement platoons aren't here, nor have I been able to reach anyone by field phone. I have twenty men left out of two battalions and I've got no support. We need your cartridges and your shells. We also need your first aid kits and some water for our wounded. And the use of your phone to call the command post."

The men stared at him in silence and then laughed. "You're fucking with us, right?"

"My orders were to break through the woods."

"You clearly haven't followed your orders, Captain," said Lieutenant Sennev, glaring at Alexander from a sitting position.

"Oh, I've followed my orders, Lieutenant," said Alexander. "And my men's blood is testament to my obedience. But now I need your weapons."

"Fuck off," said Sennev.

"I'm asking you to help your brothers in arms. We are still fighting for the same side, aren't we?"

"I said fuck off."

Alexander sighed. Slowly he turned his back on the circle of men, holding his Shpagin. Before he was turned around completely, he saw the shrapnel club hurled by Yermenko sail through the air and with a siren wail embed itself in Sennev's head. Yermenko must have been quite close to have heard it all, to have been so ready to throw the club. Alexander spun around, pointed his Shpagin and fired a shot at a time. He did not use the automatic fire. He didn't waste a bullet on Sennev, who didn't need one. Alexander fired five rounds, Yermenko fired six, and they were done. The NKGB men never had a chance to lift their weapons.

Ouspensky and Yermenko took all their arms and provisions, while Alexander piled the bodies one on top of another. When they were a sufficient distance away—twenty paces—Alexander threw his grenade into the pile of bodies and shielded his eyes. The grenade exploded. For a few moments the three men stood and watched the flames rise up.

"Perhaps they need a soldier's farewell from us," said Ouspensky, saluting them. "Farewell, and fuck you!"

Yermenko laughed.

As they walked back to their positions, Alexander slapped the corporal on the shoulder. "Well done," he said, offering Yermenko a cigarette.

"Thank you, sir," Yermenko said. He cleared his throat. "Request permission to go and find the enemy commander. I think if we take out their commander, their defense will fall."

"You think so?"

"Yes. They're very disjointed. In front, on the side, random fire, no purpose. They're not fighting like a trained army. They're fighting like a partisan force."

"We are in the woods, Corporal," said Alexander. "You're not expecting trenches, are you?"

"I'm expecting reason. I'm not seeing it. They are heavily armed and they're shooting at us as if they don't give a shit how long they'll hold out. They're defending the woods as if they have an endless supply behind them."

"And how will this change if you bring me the commander?"

"Without the commander, they will retreat."

"They'll retreat, but we'll still be in the woods."

"We can move laterally, south. We're bound to run into the South Ukrainian front."

"The South Ukrainian front will be overjoyed to see us. Corporal, my orders were to break through *these* woods."

"And we will. But sideways. We've been here two weeks, lost nearly everything, cannot replace our men and cannot move the Germans. Sir, please let me bring you the commander's head. You'll see, they'll retreat. The Germans don't do well without a commander. We'll be able to move sideways."

Ouspensky nudged Alexander. "Why don't you tell him they're Russian, Captain?" he whispered.

"You think that will make a difference to Yermenko?" Alexander whispered back.

Alexander got on the newly acquired field phone to contact Captain Gronin of the 28th non-penal battalion, four kilometers south of Alexander's position. He said nothing to Gronin about the downed NKGB but he did ask for reinforcements to come as soon as possible. It turned out that indeed the Germans had a bulge between Alexander and Gronin and to get reinforcements to Alexander, Gronin would have to move through German troops. Exhaustion in his voice, Gronin nonetheless managed to raise it high enough to shout, "Are you fucking joking with me, reinforcements? Who do you think you are? I'm sending you reinforcements when pigs fly! Fight with what you have until the rest of the army catches up with you." And he hung up with a slam.

Alexander replaced the receiver gently and looked up to see Ouspensky and Yermenko staring him in the face. "What did he say, Captain?" asked Ouspensky.

"He said reinforcements will be here in a few days. We have to hold out till then." Taking a sip of water from the flask, Alexander grunted—even the NKGB's water tasted better—and said, "All right, Yermenko. Go get me their commander. But take another man with you."

"Sir—"

"No. You *will* take another man with you. Someone silent and good. Someone loyal, someone you can trust."

"I'd like to take *him*, sir," Yermenko said, pointing at Ouspensky.

"What are you, a fucking madman? I'm a lieutenant—"

"Lieutenant!" That was Alexander. He lit a smoke, glanced from Ouspensky to Yermenko, grinned and said, "Corporal, you can't have the lieutenant. He is mine. Take someone else along." He paused. "Take someone better. Take Smirnoff."

"Thank you for your confidence, sir," said Ouspensky.

"You're welcome, Lieutenant."

⌒⌘⌒

In an hour, only Smirnoff returned. "Where is Corporal Yermenko?"

"He didn't make it," said Smirnoff.

Alexander was silent a moment before he said, "I didn't ask you that, Corporal. I asked where he was."

"I told you, he is dead, sir."

"And I asked you where he was. I will keep asking you until you tell me. Where is he?"

With a puzzled, slightly mortified, war-exhausted look, Smirnoff stared at Alexander. "I don't understand—"

"Where is the dead corporal, Corporal?"

"Back where he fell, sir. Tripped a mine."

Alexander straightened up. "You left your battle buddy, the man who covered your back, dead in enemy territory?"

"Yes, sir," Smirnoff stammered. "I needed to get out of there, to get back here."

"Corporal, you are not worth the uniform they put on you. You are not worth the gun they gave you to defend your mother country. To leave a fallen soldier in enemy territory . . ."

"He was dead, sir," Smirnoff said nervously.

"And soon you will be, too!" Alexander shouted. "Who will carry your body to the Soviet side? Your buddy is dead. It won't be him." Waving his hand at Smirnoff, he said, "Get out of my sight." Then,

"Before you go," he said to the corporal who had turned on his heels, "you will tell me if you've discovered anything we can use. Or did you just go into enemy territory to leave a soldier to die?"

"No, sir." Smirnoff didn't look at Alexander.

"No sir what?"

"Sir, I found out the commander is not German but Russian. Though I think there are a few Germans in their ranks. I heard German spoken. The commander is definitely Russian. He yells to the troops in German but speaks to his lieutenant in Russian. He's got about fifty troops left."

"Fifty!"

"Hmm. They look to him for their every move." Smirnoff paused. "I know because we got very close to him. That's when we found out the area around his tent is mined. But now I know where to go. I'll just find Yermenko's body, the mine there has already been tripped, and I figure I can throw a grenade into the commander's tent. He'll be blown to pieces and his men will surrender."

Alexander paused. "You sure he's Russian?"

"Positive."

Smirnoff left. A half-hour went by and he wasn't back. An hour went by and he wasn't back. After an hour and a half, with the woods black and impossible to see through, Alexander gave up on Smirnoff. The stupid cocky bastard had obviously alerted them with another casualty. Now he is lying there dead, waiting for me to come and retrieve him.

"I'm going in, Lieutenant," said Alexander. "If anything should happen to me, you're in command of our unit."

"Sir, you cannot go in."

"I'm going, and I'm not coming back until either me or their commander is dead. Fucking Smirnoff! Left poor Yermenko in the woods." Alexander cursed again. "At least now there are two of them for me to find. I'll know where to step. Wish I had a fucking tank. If I had a tank, I wouldn't be in this position."

"You had a tank. If you hadn't insisted on storming the river by yourself, you'd still have it."

"Shut up," said Alexander, taking his machine gun, tucking a pistol and five grenades into his shirt, and adjusting his helmet.

"I'm coming with you, sir," said Ouspensky, getting up.

"Yes, right," said Alexander. "They'll hear you wheezing in fucking Krakow. While I'm gone, stay here and grow yourself a lung. I'll be back in an hour."

"Be back, Captain."

In the dark, quiet as a Siberian tiger, Alexander made his way in the woods around the small flickering lights of the German camp. He had a small penlight that he held in his teeth and shined on the underbrush as he looked for a body, disturbed ground, anything. Alexander's pistol was cocked and the knife was in his hand.

He found Smirnoff, who had found a mine. A meter away he saw Yermenko. He made the sign of the cross on the men with his pistol.

After putting the penlight away, his eyes made out the commander's tent not five meters away in the clearing. He saw the mines lying flat on the ground. They hadn't even bothered to bury them in their haste. If only his men hadn't stepped on them in theirs.

He saw a flicker of a flashlight and a shadow in front of the tent. A man cleared his throat and said, "Captain? Are you awake, sir?"

Alexander heard a man's voice say something in German, then in Russian. In Russian, the captain asked the soldier to bring him something to drink and then not to step a meter away from the tent. "The mines have already killed two of them. But more will come, Borov. I'm well hidden, but we cannot take any chances."

That was helpful, Alexander thought, putting the knife between his teeth and getting out his grenade. He knew he had to be stealthy and very exact. He could not miss the tent.

The soldier came out of the tent and before he closed the flaps, he saluted the man. Alexander was about to pull the pin out of the grenade. The adjutant said, "I'll be right back, Captain Metanov—"

Alexander fell noiselessly to the ground. He dropped his grenade, and the adjutant went away.

Did he just say *Metanov*?

His tortured mind was playing tricks on him. With trembling hands, he picked up his grenade. But he couldn't throw it.

He was so close. He could have killed the commander and his assistant so easily. Now what?

If he had imagined the name, well, so much the worse for him, so much the fucking worse for the ceaselessly restless him. A little more forgetting, a little less lament and he wouldn't be within three strides of the German commander's tent imagining he had heard the name *Metanov*.

Alexander took one-two-three steps to the tent. He suspected the enemy captain wouldn't bury a mine within such proximity to his sleeping area and he was right. Reaching out, he touched the canvas with his fingers. Inside the tent a small flashlight shone. Alexander heard the rustling of paper. He couldn't even hear his own breath. It wasn't because he was quiet. It was because he wasn't breathing.

Silently he untied one of the ropes holding the tent to the stake. Crawling around, he untied another. Then another. Then the fourth. He took a deep breath, took out his sidearm—though couldn't cock it because it would make too much noise—gripped his knife, counted to three and jumped on top of the tent, pinning the commander inside the canvas. The man could not move. Alexander's body was on him and the barrel of his now-cocked Tokarev was pressed to the man's head. "Don't move," Alexander whispered in Russian. He felt for the man's hands, pinning them with his knees. With one hand, he reached under the loose straps of the tent and felt around the ground for the commander's gun. He found the gun and the knife, lying by what used to be the bed and the blanket. Feeling him stir slightly, Alexander said, "Can you understand me, or should I speak German?" He didn't trust the man to lie quietly. Alexander punched him hard, knocking him out. Then he pushed away the canvas and shined his penlight into the man's face. He was young, once dark-haired, completely shaven. He had a deep scar running down from his eye to his jaw; he had blood on his head; blood on his neck; he had only barely healed wounds; he was thin; he was pale in the white light of the flash; he was unconscious; he was either Russian or German. He was nothing, everything. Alexander gleaned no answers from this man's face.

Alexander pulled the commander out of the tent, flung him on his back and before the adjutant had a chance to return with water, walked with him down the slope through the forest back to his own camp.

Ouspensky nearly fell down and lost breath in his only lung when he saw Alexander carrying the enemy commander. He jumped up but before he could say a word, Alexander cut him off with a hand motion. "Stop talking. Get me some rope."

Alexander and Ouspensky tied the man to a tree in the back of the tent.

For the rest of the night, Alexander sat in front of the captured officer. At last he saw the man's eyes open and watch him angrily and questioningly. Moving closer, Alexander untied the bandana from his mouth.

"You bastard," were the man's first Russian words. "All you had to do was shoot me. No, you had me leave my men in the middle of battle."

Alexander still said nothing.

"What the fuck are you looking at?" the commander said loudly. "Are you figuring out how I'd like to die? Slowly, all right? And painfully. I don't give a shit."

Alexander opened his mouth. Before he spoke, he brought a flask of hot coffee to the man's mouth and let him have a few sips. "What is your name?" he said.

"Kolonchak," said the man.

"What is your real name?"

"That is my real name."

"What is your family name?"

"Andrei Kolonchak."

Alexander took his rifle into his hands. "Understand," he said, "if that's your real name, I'll have to kill you so your men make neither a hero nor a martyr out of you."

The man laughed. "What do you think? I'm afraid of death? Shoot away, comrade. I'm ready."

"Are the men you left behind ready for their death, too?"

"Certainly. We're all ready." The man sat straight up against the oak and stared unflinchingly at Alexander.

"Who are you? Tell me."

"Tell *you*? Who the fuck are *you*? What are you, my brother in arms? I won't tell you shit. You better kill me now because in a minute I'll yell my rallying cry and my men will charge. They'll die charging but you'll lose what pathetic troops you got left. You won't get a word out of me."

"You're in the back of my camp. You're a kilometer and a half away from your own troops. Scream all you want. Scream like a woman. No one will hear you. What is your name?"

"Andrei Kolonchak, I told you."

"Your last name is a combination of Alexander Kolchak, the leader of the White Army during the Russian Civil War and the woman partisan Kolontai?"

"That's correct."

"Why did your aide call you Captain Metanov then?"

The man blinked. For just one moment, he glanced away from Alexander, but that one moment was enough. Alexander caught that one glance away square in the chest. Recoiling back from the man, he couldn't look at him when he said, "Captain Pavel Metanov?"

There was silence from under the tree. There was silence from Alexander. Looking at his rifle, at his hands, at the moss, at his boots, at the stones, Alexander took one deep breath, one shallow breath, one aching breath and said, ". . . *Pasha* Metanov?"

When he looked up, the man was staring at him with the perplexed, stunned, emotional face of someone who had heard an English voice in China, who had traveled a thousand miles and saw one white face, one black face, one recognizable, familiar face. As if an imprint of childhood were snapped with a black-and-white camera and it caught the smiling face of a young boy and of a soldier near death sitting roped to a tree, all at once and more.

"I don't understand," the man said faintly. "Who *are* you?"

"I," said Alexander, and his voice broke; he couldn't continue. I . . . I . . . I scream to the deaf sky.

But it's not deaf. Look at what's in front of me.

Alexander stared at the man by the tree with a mixture of sadness, confusion, and disbelief. "I'm Alexander Belov," he finally managed to utter. "In 1942 I married a girl named Tatiana Metanova—" However much it hurt Alexander to say her name, it must have hurt the man at the tree even more to hear it. He flinched, coiled up, bent his shaking head. "No, stop. It can't be. Take your weapon. Shoot me."

Alexander put down his Shpagin and inched his way to the man. "Pasha, oh my God, what the fuck have you been thinking? What are you doing?"

"Forget me," said the man named Pasha Metanov. "You're married to Tania? She's all right then?"

"She's gone," said Alexander.

"She died?" He gasped.

"I don't think so." Alexander lowered his voice. "Gone from the Soviet Union."

"I don't understand. Gone where?"

"Pasha . . ."

"We got time. We got nothing but time. Tell me."

"She escaped through Finland." Alexander spoke in a whisper. "I don't know if she made it, if she's safe, if she's free. I know nothing. They arrested me, put me in charge of this penal battalion."

"What about . . . my"—Pasha's voice faltered—"family?"

Alexander shook his head.

"Did anyone make it?"

"No one," Alexander breathed out.

The warrior fought his words. "My mother?"

"Leningrad took them all."

Pasha was speechless for a few terrible moments, and then he cried. Alexander's head was lowered so far, the chin was on his chest.

An unconsoled Pasha said, "Why? You could've killed me, and I would have never known. I would have been all right. I thought they had evacuated, were safe. I thought they were in Molotov. I had comfort thinking of them alive. Why did you spare me? Can't you see I have no interest in being spared? Would I have joined the other side if I thought for a moment my life was worth saving? Who asked you to come along and save me?"

"No one," said Alexander. "I didn't ask you to come along either. I was ready to throw the grenade into your tent. You would've been dead, your troops annihilated by morning. Instead, I heard someone calling you by your rightful name. Why did I have to hear that? Ask yourself." He paused. "Can I release you?"

"Yes," said Pasha. "And I will tear out your heart with my bare hands."

"If only I fucking had one," said Alexander, getting up off the ground, and replacing the gag on Pasha's mouth with a heavy hand.

⁂

Morning broke and with it came anger. Alexander didn't understand as he watched Pasha sitting sullenly gagged and bound. He wished he had leisure to worry about it. At the moment it was raining, as if all other iniquities were not enough. They came to the mountains of Holy Cross to die, and now they were going to die wet.

Alexander offered Pasha some food. Pasha refused. A cigarette? Also a no.

"What about a bullet?"

Pasha wouldn't even look at Alexander.

The enemy was quiet this morning. Alexander wasn't surprised, and he knew Pasha wasn't either. The commander of their unit had gone.

"What the fuck is wrong with you?" Alexander asked, taking the gag out of Pasha's mouth.

"Why did you have to tell me about my family." There was no inflection.

"You asked me."

"You could have lied. You could have said they were all right."

"You would have wanted that?"

"Yes. A thousand times yes. A small comfort to a dying man in the rain, I would have wanted that."

Alexander wiped the rain off Pasha's face.

Then he regrouped his men, and they all took their positions along the trees. After a morning smoke, they opened feeble fire that was not returned. In the woods the sound of war was too close. A meter away, a kilometer away, the canopy of the leaves, the denseness of the underbrush, the slight damp echo made the fire sound oppressively close. Fields were better, mines were better, tanks were better. This was the worst.

He had only nineteen men left. Nineteen men and a hostage that both sides wanted dead.

They stopped firing and sat under the trees. Alexander sat mutely next to Pasha. He had tried to get Gronin on the phone again, but the telephone was cutting out and he could hardly hear. His men were nearly out of ammunition.

Ouspensky came and whispered that they needed to kill the commander to make headway in the woods. Alexander said they would wait.

And through it all, it rained.

Hours went by before Pasha finally moved his head, gesturing for Alexander, who took off the gag.

"Maybe now a cigarette," Pasha said.

Alexander handed Pasha a cigarette.

After taking a long satisfying drag, Pasha said, "How did you meet her anyway?"

"Fate brought us together," Alexander replied. "On the first day of war, I was patrolling the streets and she was eating ice cream."

"Just like her," Pasha said. "She nods and then does what she wants. Her instructions were very clear: don't dawdle; go and get food." He glanced at Alexander. "That day was the last day I saw her. Saw my family."

"I know." With a hurting heart, Alexander said, "What am I going to do with you, Pasha Metanov, the brother of my wife?"

Pasha shrugged. "That's your problem. Let me tell you about my men. I've got fifty of them in the woods. Five commissioned lieutenants. Five sergeants. What do you think they're going to do without me? They will never surrender. They will retreat just far enough to join up with the Wehrmacht motorized divisions protecting the western side of the mountains. You know how many troops are waiting there for you? Half a million. How far do you think your nineteen men are going to get? I know how the penal battalions work. No one will resupply you if they need the supplies themselves. What are you going to do?"

"My lieutenant thinks we should kill you."

"He is right. I'm the commander of the last vestige of General Vlasov's army. After I'm dead, there won't be any of us left."

"How do you know?" asked Alexander. "I hear the Vlasovites are running amok in Romania, raping the Romanian women."

"What does that have to do with me? I'm in Poland."

Alexander sat defeated with his hands on his legs. "What happened to you? Your family would have liked to know."

"Don't tell me anymore about my family," Pasha said, his voice catching.

"Your mother and father were torn up after you vanished."

"Mama was always so emotional," Pasha said and started to cry. "I thought it was kinder that way. Not to know. Suspect the worst. This is all slow death anyway."

Alexander didn't know if it was kinder. "Tania went to your camp in Dohotino looking for you."

"She's a fool," he said, his voice full of weeping affection.

Alexander moved a little closer. "The camp was abandoned, and then she moved on to Luga days before the Luga line fell to the Germans. She wanted to make her way to Novgorod to find you. She was told that's where the Dohotino camp members were sent."

"We were sent..." Pasha shook his head and laughed miserably. "God looks after Tania in mysterious ways. Always has. Had she gone to Novgorod, she would have died for sure, and I was never even close to Novgorod. The closest I got to Novgorod was passing Lake Ilmen in a train that the Germans blew up just south of the lake."

"Lake Ilmen?"

Neither man could look at the other. "She told you about that lake?"

"She's told me everything," said Alexander.

Pasha smiled. "We spent our childhood on that lake. She was the queen of Lake Ilmen. So, she came looking for me? She was always something, my sister. If anyone could have found me, it would have been her."

"Yes. But it turns out that *I* found you."

"Yes, in fucking Poland! I wasn't in Novgorod. The Nazis blew up our train and with dead bodies piled house-high, they set us on fire. Me and my friend Volodya were the only ones who survived. We scrambled our way out of the compost heap and tried to find our own troops but of course the entire countryside belonged to the Germans by then. Volodya had broken his leg in camp weeks before. We couldn't get very far. We were taken prisoner in hours. The Germans had no use for Volodya. They shot him dead." He shook his head. "I'm glad his mother didn't know. Did you know his mother? Nina Iglenko?"

"I knew his mother. She wheedled food from Tania for the two sons that remained with her."

"What happened to them?"

"Leningrad took them all." Alexander lowered his head another notch. In a moment, his head was going to be in the mud he was sitting in.

Alexander wanted to talk to Pasha about the Vlasovites but couldn't find the words. How to express that never before had a million soldiers turned away from their own army and joined the side of the hated enemy on their own soil against their own people. Spies yes, double spies, individual traitors, yes. But a million soldiers?

All Alexander could manage was, "Pasha, *what* were you thinking?"

"What was I thinking? About what? Have you not heard what happened in the Ukraine, how Stalin abandoned his own men to the Germans there?"

"I've heard it all," Alexander said tiredly. "I have been fighting for the Red Army since 1937. I've heard everything. I know about everything. Every decree, every law, every edict."

"Don't you know that our great commander made being taken prisoner a crime against the Motherland?"

"Of course I know. And the POW's family gets no bread."

"That's right. But know this: Stalin's own son was taken prisoner by the Nazis."

"Yes."

"And when Stalin learned of this, and saw the potential ironic conflict, do you know what he did?"

"The lore is that he disowned his son," said Alexander, drawing his helmet tighter over his ears.

"The lore is correct. I know because I heard from the German SS that he was sent to Sachsenhausen concentration camp near Berlin, and there he died in the execution pit."

"Yes."

"His own son! What hope is there for me?"

"None for any of us," said Alexander, "except this: Stalin doesn't know who we are. That might help us. Save us."

"He knows who *I* am."

Alexander feared Stalin might know who he was, too. Foreign espionage in his officer ranks. His eyes bore into Pasha's face. "All of this put together and heaped on top of all the dead Chinese in 1937 cannot equal fighting on the side of the enemy against your own people. I think the army calls it high treason. What do you think they will do to you when they catch you, Pasha?"

Pasha wanted to wave his hands with emotion; he struggled against the ropes and whirled his head from side to side. "The same thing they would do to me if I were returned to them a prisoner of war," he said at last. "And don't sit there and judge me. You don't know me. You don't know my life."

"Tell me." Alexander moved closer. They were huddled near the same tree, their backs to the silent line of battle.

"The Germans put me into a camp at Minsk for that first winter of 1941 to '42. There were sixty thousand in our camp, and they couldn't feed us, nor did they want to. They couldn't cover us, or clothe us, or heal us. And our own leaders made sure that extra help wouldn't be coming from the Red Cross. We certainly wouldn't be receiving any parcels of food from home, or letters perhaps, or blankets. Nothing. When Stalin was asked by Hitler about reciprocity for the German prisoners, Stalin replied that he didn't know what Hitler was talking about, because he was *sure* there were no Soviet prisoners, since no Soviet soldier would ever be so unpatriotic as to surrender to the fucking Germans, and then added that he certainly wasn't interested in unilateral rights of parcel just for the Germans. And so Hitler said, right, that's just fine with us. There were sixty thousand of us in that camp, I tell you, and at the end of that winter eleven thousand remained. Much more manageable, wouldn't you agree?"

Alexander mutely nodded.

"In the spring I escaped and made my way on rivers down to the Ukraine, where I was promptly seized by the Germans again, and this time put not in a POW camp, but in a work camp. I thought that was illegal, to make prisoners work, but apparently it's not illegal to do anything to Soviet soldiers or refugees. So the work camp was full of Ukrainian Jews, and then I noticed that they were disappearing en masse. I didn't think they were all escaping to join the partisan movement. I found out for sure when they made us non Jews dig out massive holes in the summer of 1942, and then cover up the thousands of bodies with dirt. I knew I was not safe for long. I didn't think the Germans had any special affinity for the Russian man. They hated Jews the most, but the Russians weren't too far behind, and Red Army men seemed to breed a special kind of hostility. They didn't just want to kill us, they wanted to destroy us, to break our bodies, first, then our spirits, then set us on fire. I had enough of it, and escaped that summer of 1942, and that's when I, plundering through the countryside, hoping to make my way to Greece, was picked up by a band of men fighting for Voronov who fought for Andrei Vlasov of the ROA, the Russian Liberation Army. I knew my fate. I joined."

"Oh, Pasha." Alexander stood up.

"You think my sister would prefer that I die at the hands of Hitler or at the hands of Comrade Stalin? I went with Vlasov—the man who promised me life. Stalin said I would die. Hitler said I would die. Hitler, who treats dogs better than the Soviet POWs."

"Hitler loves dogs. He prefers dogs to children."

"Hitler, Stalin, they offered me the same thing. Only General Vlasov stood up for my life. And I wanted to give it to him."

Slamming a magazine upward into his machine gun, Alexander said, "So where is this Vlasov when you need him? He thought he was helping the Nazis, except the Fascists and the Communists and the Americans all seem to have one thing in common. They all despise traitors." Alexander took out his army knife from his boot and bent over Pasha, who flinched. Looking at him with surprise, Alexander shrugged and cut the ropes that tied Pasha's hands. "Andrei Vlasov was captured by the Germans, spent time in their prison and was finally turned over to the Soviets. You've been fighting on the side of Vlasov who's been a nonentity in this war for years. His glory days are over."

Pasha stood up, groaned under his compressed and aching body being in one position for too long, and said, "My glory days are over, too."

They stared at each other. Compact Pasha reminded Alexander of Georgi Vasilievich Metanov, Tatiana's father. Pasha looked up and said, "We're a fine pair. I command what's left of Vlasov's men, a nearly extinct breed. My battalion is first on the line of defense because the Germans want us all to be annihilated by our own people. And you are being sent in to kill me, commanding a penal battalion full of convicts who can't fight, can't shoot, and have no arms." He smiled. "What are you going to tell my sister when you see her in heaven? That you killed her brother in the heat of battle?"

"Pasha Metanov," said Alexander, motioning him to come, "whatever I was put on this earth to do, I'm almost sure it was not to kill *you*.

Now come. We've got to put an end to this senselessness. You're going to tell your men to lay down their arms."

"Didn't you hear what I told you? My men will never surrender to the NKGB. Besides, do you have any idea what's ahead for you if you continue onward?"

"Yes. The Germans will get trounced. Maybe not by us on this fucking hill, but everywhere else. Have you heard about the second front? Have you heard about Patton? We're going to meet the Americans on the Oder river near Berlin. That's what's ahead. If Hitler had any sense he would surrender and spare Germany an unconditional humiliation for the second time this century and maybe save a few million lives in the process."

"Does Hitler seem like the kind of man who would unconditionally surrender? Or care about saving one life, or a million? If he's going down, he's going down dragging the whole world with him."

"He's certainly doing that," said Alexander, and was about to whistle for Ouspensky when Pasha put his hand on Alexander to stop him.

"Wait," Pasha said. "Let's think this through for a minute, shall we?"

They sat down on a log and lit their cigarettes. "Alexander," said Pasha, "you've really done it by not killing me."

"I have, haven't I?" Alexander smoked. "One way or another we need to figure it out immediately. Or you and I won't have any men left to command."

Pasha was quiet. "And then just you and me in the woods?" he asked.

Alexander glanced at him. What was he saying?

Leaning in, Pasha said, "I will have my men surrender if you will guarantee not to give them up to the NKGB."

"What do you propose I do with them?"

"Absorb us into your unit. We have arms, we have shells, we have grenades, mortars, carbines."

"I was going to take your weapons no matter what, Pasha. That's what the vanquished do—they surrender their weapons. But your men? Are they going to switch and fight for the other side now?"

"They will do what I tell them to do."

"How can they do it?"

"What do you suggest? Dispersing?"

"Dispersing? Disbanding? Do you know what that's called? Desertion."

Pasha was silent. "Alexander, there is no hope. There are five hundred thousand men over that hill."

"Yes, and thirteen million men are coming over that hill to kill them."

"Yes, but what about you and me?"

"I need your unit's arms."

"So you'll have my arms. You've got nineteen men. What on earth are you thinking?"

Alexander lowered his voice to a whisper. "Don't worry about what I'm thinking. Just . . ."

"Just what?"

"Pasha, I need to get inside Germany. I need to live long enough to do it."

"Why?"

Because the Americans are coming to Berlin. Because the Americans are going to liberate Germany, and they're going to liberate the POW camps, and eventually they're going to liberate me. But Alexander didn't say any of this.

"You've lost your mind," said Pasha.

"Yes."

Pasha stared at Alexander for a long time, in the crackling, wet, absorbing woods, standing miserably next to him, his cigarette burning bleakly to ash between his ravaged fingers. "Alexander, don't you know about the Germans? Don't you know anything?"

"I know everything, but I still have hope. Now more than ever." He glanced at Pasha. "Why do you think I found you?"

"So you could torture a dying man?"

"No, Pasha. I'll help you, too. Just—we've got to get out of here. You and I. You have medical kits?"

"Yes, plenty of bandages, plenty of sulfa, morphine, even some penicillin."

"Good, we'll need it all. What about food?"

"We've got canned everything. Dried milk even. Dried eggs. Sardines. Ham. Bread."

"Canned bread?" Alexander nearly smiled.

"What have *you* been living on?"

"The flesh of my men," replied Alexander. "Are most of your men Russian?"

"Most of them, yes. But I have ten Germans. What do you propose we do with them? Certainly they are not going to go on your side and fight their own army."

"Of course not. That's unimaginable, isn't it?"

Pasha turned away.

"We'll take them prisoner," said Alexander.

"I thought the penal battalions had a no-prisoner policy?"

"I make my own policy here in the woods," replied Alexander, "having been abandoned by my suppliers. Now, are you going to help us or not?"

Pasha took a last smoke, stubbed out his cigarette and wiped the wet off his face, a useless gesture, Alexander thought. "I will help you. But your lieutenant will not approve. He wants to kill me."

"You let me worry about him," said Alexander.

~

Ouspensky was not easy.

"Are you out of your mind?" he whispered hotly to Alexander, when Alexander outlined his plan for the absorption of Pasha's unit.

"You have better ideas?"

"I thought you said Gronin was coming with supplies?"

"I lied. Get me my troops, please."

"I say we kill the commander, and then lie in wait in the woods until we get arms and men."

"I'm not killing the commander, and I'm not waiting for anything. They are not coming."

"Captain, you are not acting according to the rules of engagement. We cannot take the Germans prisoner. We have to kill their commander."

"Lieutenant, get me my men and stop this foolishness."

"Captain—"

"Lieutenant! Now!"

Ouspensky, his face full of squinting suspicion, turned to Pasha, who stood by Alexander's other side, untied. Ouspensky and Pasha glared at each other for a few moments. "Captain, you've untied him?" Ouspensky said in a low voice.

"Why don't you worry about what you have to worry about, and let me worry about everything else. Go!"

Alexander, Ouspensky and Telikov had fourteen privates and two corporals under their command. With Pasha's battalion, they would have over sixty men, not including the German prisoners of war. He motioned Pasha to come.

Pasha said, "My men need to know it's me when I call to them."

"Fine," said Alexander. "I'll stand by you, you yell. They'll know."

Ouspensky stood in Alexander's way. "With all due respect, sir, you are not headed toward the firing line."

"I am, Lieutenant," Alexander said, moving Ouspensky out of the way with his machine gun.

"Captain," Ouspensky said, "sir, have you ever played chess? Do you know that in chess you will often sacrifice your Queen to take the opponent's Queen? His men will kill you and him both."

Alexander nodded. "All right, but *I'm* not the Queen, Ouspensky. They will have to do better than kill *me*."

"They kill you, they win the game. Let the bastard go by himself. He can stop the bullets with his teeth for all I care. But if something happens to you, we've got nobody else."

"You're wrong, Lieutenant. We've got *you*. Now look. We are under a direct order to plow through the woods." He lowered his voice. "And I've finally figured out why. It's because of them—the Vlasovites. Stalin wants his Soviet dregs—us—to kill his Soviet dregs—them." Pasha was standing nearby. Alexander didn't want him to hear. He led Ouspensky away. "We have only one directive—to go forward—and only one responsibility—to save our men. We're nearly all out. To save our men you'd save Metanov's life, wouldn't you?"

"No," Ouspensky said. "I'm going to shoot the motherfucker myself."

"Nikolai," Alexander said quietly, "if you touch him, you'll die. Just so you understand my position and won't accidentally fly into patriotic fervor, I want you to know your life is at stake. Anything happens to him, anything at all, I will blame you."

"Sir—"

"Do you understand?"

"No!"

"That man is the brother of my wife," said Alexander.

Something appeared on Ouspensky's face. Alexander couldn't quite place it. Some clarity, some understanding, some completion, almost as if Ouspensky had been waiting for something like this. Alexander couldn't tell, the expression in the eyes was too fleeting. Then Ouspensky said, "I did not know that."

"Why would you?"

Alexander and Pasha began their mission. It was mid-afternoon. Quiet in the woods except for the sound of drizzle on the evergreens. Disturbing, unexplained quiet. A burning branch broke and fell to the ground. It burned reluctantly, dampened by November. Pasha

Metanov stood ten meters away from Alexander and yelled, "This is Commander Kolonchak. Can you hear me? Bring me my Lieutenant Borov immediately."

There was no sound from the woods. "Hold your fire! And bring me Borov," he yelled.

A shot rang out. It narrowly missed Pasha. Alexander closed his eyes and thought, this is crazy. I'm not putting him in front of the firing squad before my own eyes. He called Pasha back, and sent for a corporal to shield Metanov next time he called out for his lieutenant. There was no more fire from the other side. Soon they heard a voice calling, "Commander Kolonchak?"

"Yes, Borov," said Pasha.

"What is the password?"

Pasha glanced at Alexander. "If they asked you, would *you* know?"

"No."

"Would you guess?"

"Don't play games. This is for the lives of your men."

"No, it's for the lives of yours."

"Give him the password, Pasha."

"The Queen of Lake Ilmen," yelled Pasha Metanov, waving a white handkerchief.

After a pained silence, Alexander said, "Well, I'm sure your sister would appreciate her name being summoned in the heat of battle."

Borov walked forward from behind the gray trees not thirty meters away—that's all that separated the two enemy battalions. In one hour this would have turned into hand-to-hand combat. Alexander had been in the woods too many times, up on hills, in the mud, in the marsh, shooting at phantoms, at shadows, at branches falling. He bowed his head. He was glad that at least for now the fighting would be over. He heard Pasha speaking to Borov, who was disbelieving and reluctant. "Permission not to surrender, sir."

"Permission denied," said Pasha. "You see a way out?"

"Die with honor," said Borov.

Alexander stepped forward. "Tell your men to lay down their arms and come forward."

"Captain!" Pasha cut in. "I'll handle this." He turned to Borov. "And the Germans are to be taken prisoner."

Borov laughed. "We're surrendering *them*? They're going to love this."

"They will do as they're forced to."

"What about the rest of us?"

"We're going to fight for the Red Army."

Borov stepped back with a look of disbelief on his face. "Captain, what's happening? This is impossible."

"What's happening, Borov, is that I've been taken prisoner. And so you have no choice. This is for my life."

Borov bowed his own head, as if he truly had no choice.

A little while later Pasha explained, "Borov will always be loyal to me. He is to me what Ouspensky is to you."

"Ouspensky is nothing to me," said Alexander.

"Ah, you're joking." Pasha paused. They were walking back to the Soviet camp, their men in front of them, the ten Germans with their hands tied. "Alexander, do you trust him?"

"Who?"

"Ouspensky."

"Inasmuch as I trust anyone."

"What does that mean?"

"What are you getting at?"

Pasha coughed. "Do you trust him with personal things?"

"I trust no one with personal things," Alexander said, looking straight ahead.

"That's good." Pasha paused. "I don't know if he can be trusted."

"Oh, he's proven his loyalty to me over the years. He can be trusted. Nonetheless, I don't."

"That's good," said Pasha.

ᏆᎷᏆᎢᎷᏟ

Alexander was right about many things. Soviet reinforcements did not come. And there were no Red Army Imperial uniforms for Pasha and his Russian soldiers. Though he had lost many more than forty-two men himself, he buried his dead in their wet and bloodied resplendent velvet garb. Now he had forty-two men in German uniforms with German haircuts. Alexander ordered them shaved, but they were still in German uniforms.

Pasha was right about many things. German reinforcements moved to the foot of the mountain looking for their Russian battalion, expecting to find Pasha's men and instead found Alexander's battalion and not a Vlasovite in sight. Though their shells and grenades were more plentiful than Alexander's, Alexander had the advantage, for the first time in his military career, of being at the top of the hill. The German artillery unit was repelled, with difficulty, then an infantry unit was repelled with ease, and his men moved down the mountain, having lost only five soldiers. Alexander said he would never fight again unless it was from a great height.

Pasha said maybe the first time the Germans had sent in a handful of troops to block Alexander, but next time they would send a thousand, and the time after that ten thousand.

⌒⍟⍟⍟⍟⍟⍟⍟⍟⍟⍟◦

Pasha was right about many things.

On the other side of the Holy Cross mountains was more forest and more fighting, and another day brought a heavier artillery, heavier machine-gun fire, more grenades, more shells, less rain, more fire.

Alexander's battalion was again reduced by five. The next day brought more Germans, and the battalion became three squads. No bandages, no sulfa helped. His men had no time to construct defenses, pillboxes, trenches. The trees covered them but the trees were felled by mortar fire, by grenades, by shells, and his men were, too. Nothing could sew back their severed limbs.

After four days, two squads remained. Twenty men. Alexander, Pasha, Ouspensky, Borov and sixteen foot soldiers.

One of Alexander's men was bitten by something in the woods. The next day he lay dead. Nineteen men. Back to where they were before Pasha. But they had eight bound prisoners to barter their lives with.

The German army was not advancing. It certainly wasn't retreating. Nor were they sitting still. Their singular purpose seemed to lie in finishing off Alexander's battalion.

Alexander managed to hold out for a fifth day. But then there were no more bombs, no more shells and the guns were nearly empty. Borov had been killed. Pasha cried when he buried him in the mud under wet leaves.

Then Sergeant Telikov. Ouspensky cried when they buried Telikov.

The bandages were gone. The food was gone. They collected rain water into leaves and poured it into their flasks. The morphine and the medic were gone. Alexander bandaged his own men.

"What now?" asked Pasha.

"I'm fresh out," said Alexander.

Retreat was the only option.

"We can't retreat," Alexander said to Ouspensky, who was ready to turn back.

"Yes, Lieutenant," said Pasha. "You know retreat is punishable by death."

"Fuck you," said Ouspensky. "I'd like to punish you by death."

Alexander and Pasha exchanged a look. "And you wonder why I chose the Germans over death," said Pasha.

"No," said Ouspensky. "You chose the Germans over your own people, you bastard."

"Look at the way our own people are treating their army!" Pasha exclaimed. "They've put you in here without any support, they've sent you to certain death, and to add insult to your injury, they made surrender a crime against the Motherland! Where have you ever heard of such a thing happening? In what army, in what place and time? You name me where." Pasha made a scornful sound. "And you ask why."

Alexander said, "Oh, Pasha, you take it all so personally. Who do you think cares for our death?"

He and Pasha mutely glanced at each other, and then Alexander stopped talking. He was sitting on a broken tree, pushed up against another, covered with his wet trench coat, carving a stake with his knife. From another tree Ouspensky called to Alexander to stop his useless tasks. Alexander replied that with the stake he was going to catch a fish, eat it himself and let Ouspensky starve for all he cared. Pasha mentioned mournfully that Borov always caught the fish for them, that he was his best friend and his right hand for three years. Ouspensky said, cry me a fucking river Vistula, and Alexander told them both to shut up. Night fell.

⚬⚏⚬

Alexander and Tatiana are playing war hide and seek. Alexander stands very quietly in the woods, listening for her. He can't hear a thing except for the bugs and ticks and flies and bees. Many insects, no Tatiana. He looks up above him, nothing. Slowly he moves forward. "Oh, Tania," he calls for her. "Where are you, tiny Tania? Where are you? You better have hidden yourself good from me, because I'm getting the feeling that I need to find you." He is hoping to make her laugh. He stops talking and listens. There is no sound. Sometimes if she is near he hears her cocking the pistol he gave her. But today not a sound.

"*Oh, Tania!*" *He walks through the woods, turning around every few seconds, watching his back. This game ends once she is behind him, his own gun in his kidney.* "*Tatia, I forgot to tell you something really important, are you listening?*"

He listens. Not a sound. He smiles.

Moss lands on his head. She is doing it again. Where did that come from? He immediately looks up. Not there. He looks around. Can't see her. During this game she puts on his camouflage undershirt and becomes nearly invisible. He is already laughing. "*Tatiasha, stop throwing moss at me, because when I find you—*" *He hears a noise and looks up. Water pours on him from above; not just water, but a whole bucket. He is doused. He swears. The bucket is in full view dangling from a branch, but she is nowhere to be seen. The rope connecting to the bucket descends and disappears behind a fallen log to Alexander's right.* "*All right, that's it. The gloves are off. Just you wait, Tania,*" *he says, taking off his wet shirt.* "*You are in so much trouble.*" *He moves towards the log, and suddenly he hears a little whoosh, and in the next instant he is covered with a white powder that gets into his hair and face. It is flour; now it is moist glue around his wet hair and head. Alexander can't believe it. How long had she been planning this, to lure him into the woods, to an exact position first for the water, then for the flour? Marveling at her, at what a formidable opponent she makes, Alexander says,* "*Oh, that's it, Tania, that's just it. If you think you were in trouble before, I can't even tell you what—*" *He moves towards the log, but hears a soft tread behind him, and without even turning around extends his hand and grabs her as she is at his back. He doesn't actually grab her, he grabs the gun. Tatiana squeals, lets go of the gun, which remains in his hands, and runs wildly through the woods. He chases her. The forest near this part of the river is sloppy—not the neat pine forest leading from Molotov to Lazarevo, or like the one around their clearing, but overgrown with the underbrush of the oaks and the poplars, the nettles and the moss. The low-hanging branches, the fallen trees slow Alexander down. Nothing slows her down. She jumps over them, passes underneath them, zigzags, and squeals. She even manages to pick up moss and a handful of leaves and throw them back at him.*

He has had enough. "*Watch your back!*" *he yells and flanks her on the side; ignoring the bushes in his way, Alexander jumps over three logs and comes out in front of her, holding the gun and panting. He is covered with water and flour. Tatiana shrieks and turns to run away, but before she can move, Alexander is on her, toppling her flat on the mossy ground.* "*Where do you think you're going?*" *he pants, holding her down as she tries to get away.* "*What do you think you're doing, you clever girl, too clever by half for your own good, where are you going to go now?"* He rubs his floured cheek against her clean face.

"Stop it," she pants. *"You're going to get me dirty."*

"I'm going to do more than get you dirty."

She struggles valiantly underneath him; her hands find his ribs as she tickles him without much success. He grabs her hands and pulls them over her head. *"You won't even believe what kind of trouble you're in, you flour-throwing Nazi. What were you thinking, how long were you planning this?"*

"Five seconds." She laughs. *"You're so gullible."* She is still fighting to get away.

He holds her hands above her head. Gripping her wrists with one hand, Alexander yanks up the camouflage T-shirt to her neck, exposing her stomach and ribs and breasts. *"Will you stop fighting with me?"* he says. *"Do you give up?"*

"Never!" she cries. *"It is better to die on your feet—"*

Alexander brings his stubbled face to her ribs and tickles her with his chin. Tatiana chortles. *"Stop it,"* she says. *"Stop torturing me. Put me in the kissing prison."*

"The kissing prison is too good for the likes of you. You're going to need a harsher punishment. Do you give up?" he asks again.

"Never!"

He tickles her ribs again with his mouth and his stubble. Alexander knows he has to be careful. Once he tickled her for so long, she fainted. Now she is laughing uncontrollably, her legs kicking up in the air. He puts his own leg over them, still holding her hands above her head, his tongue tickling her up and down her side. *"Do—you—give—up?"* he asks again, panting.

"Never!" she squeals, and Alexander raises himself slightly and grabs her nipple with his mouth. He does not cease until he hears her squealing change tone and pitch.

He stops for a moment. *"I'm going to ask you again. Do you give up?"*

She moans. *"No."* She pauses. *"You better kill me, soldier . . ."* Pause. *"And use all your weapons."*

Gripping her hands above her head, Alexander makes love to her in the moss, refusing to stop, refusing to be more gentle until she gives up. He continues through her first crashing wave, and then pants, *"What say you now, prisoner?"*

Tatiana, her voice barely above a murmur, replies, *"Please, sir, I want some more."*

After he stops laughing, he gives her more.

"*Do you give up?*"

She is nearly inaudible. "*Please, sir, I want some more . . .*"

He gives her more.

"*Let go of my hands, husband,*" *Tatiana whispers into his mouth.* "*I want to touch you.*"

"*Do you give up?*"

"*Yes, I give up. I give up.*"

He lets go. She touches him.

After he is done with her, her face and breasts and stomach are all covered in flour too. Flour and moss and Alexander.

"*Come on, get up,*" *he whispers.*

"*I can't,*" *she whispers back.* "*I can't move.*"

He carries her to the Kama, where they cool down and clean off in their shallow rocky canopied water hole with the fishes.

"*How many ways are there to kill you?*" *Alexander murmurs, lifting her up onto himself and kissing her.*

"*Just one,*" *replies Tatiana, her wet warm face rubbing against his wet neck.*

⁂

In the frozen forests of Poland past, Alexander, Pasha, Ouspensky, and their one remaining corporal, Demko, hid in the bushes, surrounded, out of ammunition, blackened, bloodied and wet.

Alexander and Pasha sat and waited for inspiration or death.

The Germans poured kerosene and set fire to the woods in front of them, and to the left of them, and to the right of them.

"Alexander—"

"Pasha, I know." Their backs were against the thick oaks. They were a few meters from each other. The fire was warm against Alexander's face.

"We're trapped."

"Yes."

"We've got no bullets left."

"Yes." Alexander was carving a piece of wood.

"This is it, isn't it? There is no way out."

"You don't think there is, but there is. We just haven't thought of it."

"By the time we think of it, we'll be dead," said Pasha.

"We'd better think faster, then." He watched Pasha. One way or another, he had to get Tatiana's brother out of these woods. One way or another he had to save him for her, though every once in a while during moments of blackness, Alexander did fear that Pasha was unsaveable.

"We can't surrender."

"No?"

"No. How do you think the Germans will treat us? We've just killed hundreds of their men. You think they'll be lenient?"

"It's war, they'll understand. And talk lower, Pasha." Alexander didn't want Ouspensky to hear, and Ouspensky always heard everything.

Pasha talked lower. "And you know perfectly well I can't turn back."

"I know."

They fell silent, while Alexander—to calm his idle hands—continued to carve out a spear from a wooden branch. Pasha cleaned his machine gun and suddenly snorted.

"What are you thinking, Pasha?"

"Nothing. I was thinking how ironic it is to end up here."

"Why ironic?"

"My father came here, long time ago. During peace. Came here on business. To Poland! We were so impressed. To around this part, actually. Brought us all back exotic gifts. I wore the tie he brought me till it frayed. Pasha thought there was nothing tastier than Polish chocolates, and Tania, her skinny arm broken, wore the dress my father gave her."

Alexander stopped carving. "What dress?"

"I don't know. A white dress. She was too skinny and young for it and her arm was in a cast, but she wore it anyway, proud as anything."

"Did"—Alexander's voice caught—"did the dress have flowers on it?"

"Yes. Red roses."

Alexander breathed out a groan. "Where did your father buy the dress?"

"I think in a market town called Swietokryzst. Yes, Tania used to call it her dress from Holy Cross. Wore it every Sunday."

Alexander closed his eyes and stilled his hands.

He heard Pasha's voice. "What do you think my sister would do?"

Alexander blinked, trying to get the image of Tatiana out of his tortured mind, sitting on the bench in that dress, eating ice cream, walking barefoot in that swinging dress through the Field of Mars, on the steps of the Molotov church, in his arms, his new wife, in that dress.

"Would *she* go back?" Pasha asked.

"No. She wouldn't go back." His heart squeezed in his chest. No matter how much she wanted to. No matter how much he wanted her to.

Picking up his machine gun, Alexander came up to Pasha, and before Ouspensky lumbered up off his stump and came too close to them, Alexander whispered, "Pasha! Your pregnant sister got out of fucking Russia all by herself. She had weapons but she would never use them. They were moot to her. Without killing anyone, without firing a shot, her belly full of baby, by herself she figured a way out of the swamps to Helsinki. If she got as far as Finland, I have to believe she got farther. I have to have faith. I found you. I can't believe that was for nothing. Now we have four good men, eight if you count the Germans. And they are our hostages. We have knives, we have bayonets, we have matches, we can make weapons, and, unlike Tania, we will use them. Let's not sit here and pretend we're finished. Let's *attempt* to be stronger men than Tatiana. It won't be easy, but we will have to try. All right?"

He stood still, his back against the oak, mud covering his face and hair. Alexander crossed himself and kissed his helmet. "We have to get through that burning forest to the other side, Pasha. Closer to the Germans. We have to, that's all."

"It's fucked up, but all right."

The remaining prisoners and Ouspensky took some harder convincing.

"What are you worried about?" said Alexander. "You have half our breathing capacity; in smoke and flames that's actually to your advantage."

"I won't be inhaling smoke, I'll be incinerating," Ouspensky replied.

Finally everyone was braced for the forge. Alexander told them to cover their heads.

Pasha said, his empty machine gun over his shoulder, "Are you ready?"

"I'm ready," he replied. "Be very careful, Pasha. Cover your mouth."

"I can't run and keep my mouth covered. I'll be all right. Remember, the fucking Fritzes burned my train down. I've been in a little fire before. Let's go. I'll breathe into my cap. Just promise me you won't leave me high and dry."

"I won't leave you high and dry," Alexander said, slinging his empty mortar onto his shoulder and covering his mouth with a wet bloody towel.

They ran into the fire.

Alexander breathed through the wet towel tied around his head as they ran through the burning woods. Ouspensky held his breath for as long as he could, breathing through his trench coat sodden with rain. But Pasha pummeled right through it. Brave, thought Alexander. Brave and foolish. Somehow they got through the flames. In this case, their wet clothes were to their advantage: they refused to catch fire. And the men's hair had all been shaved, it wasn't flailing in the flames. One of the prisoners wasn't lucky: a branch fell on him and he lost consciousness. One of the other Germans slung him on his back and continued forward.

With the fire behind them, Alexander took one look at Pasha and saw that he was more foolish than brave. Pasha was pale. He slowed down, then stopped. They were still amid the smoke.

Alexander stopped running. "What's the matter?" he said, taking the rag away from his mouth and immediately choking and coughing.

"I don't know," Pasha croaked, holding on to his throat.

"Open your mouth."

Pasha did, but it didn't help. He suddenly went down like a felled tree, and the sounds coming from him were those of a man who was choking on food or a bullet; they were the sounds of a man who could not breathe.

Alexander put his own wet towel against Pasha's nose and mouth. It wasn't helping, and he himself was gagging. The open flames had been better than the enemy smoke in the oppressive forest. Ouspensky was pulling on his arm. The rest of the German men were up ahead already, held together by Demko's—the last remaining foot soldier's—machine gun. They were dozens of meters ahead, but Alexander couldn't get through the bush and could not leave Pasha. Couldn't move forward, couldn't move back.

Something had to be done. Pasha was hacking, wheezing, gasping for the breath that wouldn't come. Alexander grabbed Pasha, threw him over his shoulders, took the rag from him to cover his own mouth and ran. Ouspensky ran with him.

How much time had Alexander lost carrying Pasha? Thirty seconds? One minute? It was hard to tell. Judging by the man's stifling inability to draw in a breath, it was too long. Soon it would be too late. He called for Ouspensky when the air was slightly clearer.

"Where's the medic?" Alexander panted.

"Medic's dead. Remember? We took his helmet."

Alexander could barely remember.

"Didn't he have an assistant?"

"Assistant died seven days ago."

Carefully Alexander moved Pasha off his back, and sat down holding him in his arms. Ouspensky glanced at them. "What's wrong with him?"

"I don't know. He wasn't hit, he didn't swallow anything." Just in case, Alexander elongated Pasha's neck to be in a straight line with the rest of his body, and stuck his fingers into Pasha's mouth, feeling around for any obstructions. There weren't any, but deeper near the esophagus, he felt around for the opening to the trachea and there wasn't one. The throat felt pulpy and thickened. Quickly Alexander kneeled over Pasha, held his nose shut and blew quick breaths into Pasha's throat. Nothing. He breathed long breaths into Pasha's throat. Still nothing. He felt for the opening in the mouth again. There wasn't any. Alexander became frightened. "What the hell is happening?" he muttered. "What's wrong with him?"

"I've seen it before," Ouspensky said. "Back at Sinyavino. Seen a number of men die from smoke inhalation. Their throat swells; *completely* closes up. By the time the swelling goes down, they're dead." He took a wet breath from his coast. "He's finished," said Ouspensky. "He can't breathe, there is nothing you can do for him."

Alexander could swear there was satisfaction in Ouspensky's voice. He didn't have the time to respond to it. He lay Pasha on the ground, flat on his back, and placed the rolled-up bloody towel under his neck, with his head slightly tilted backward to expose his throat. Rummaging through his rucksack, Alexander found his pen. Thank God it was broken. For some reason the ink didn't drip down to the nib. Thank God for Soviet manufacturing. Dismantling the pen, he put aside the hollow barrell and then took out his knife.

"What are you going to do, Captain?" said Ouspensky, pointing to the knife in Alexander's hand. "Are you going to cut his throat?"

"Yes," said Alexander. "Now shut up and stop talking to me."

Ouspensky kneeled down. "I was being facetious."

"Shine a light on his throat and hold it steady. That's your job. Also hold this plastic tube and this twine. When I tell you, give the tube to me. Understood?"

They got ready. Alexander took a deep breath. He knew he had no time. He looked at his fingers. They were steady.

Feeling down Pasha's throat, Alexander found his protruding Adam's apple, felt a little lower and found the skin stretching over the tracheal cavity. Alexander knew there was nothing but skin protecting the tracheal lumen right under Pasha's Adam's apple. If he was very careful, he could make a small incision and stick the tube into Pasha's throat to allow him to breathe. But just a small incision. He had never done it. His hands weren't meant for delicate work, not like Tania's. "Here goes," he whispered, held his breath, and lowered his knife to Pasha's throat. Ouspensky's hands were shaking, judging by the shaking of the flashlight. "Lieutenant, for fuck's sake, hold still."

Ouspensky tried. "Have you ever done this before, Captain?"

"No. Seen it done, though."

"With success?"

"Not much success," said Alexander. He'd seen two medics do it twice. Both soldiers didn't make it. One was cut too deep, and the fragile trachea was sheared in half by a knife that was too heavy. The other never opened his eyes again. Breathed, just never opened his eyes.

Very slowly, Alexander cut two centimeters of Pasha's skin. It was resistant to the knife. Then the skin bled, making it hard to see how far he was cutting. He needed a scalpel, but all he had was the army knife he shaved with and killed with. He cut a little deeper, a little deeper, and then put the knife between his teeth and opened up the skin with his fingers, exposing a bit of cartilage on both sides of the membrane. Holding the skin open, Alexander made a small cut in the membrane below the Adam's apple, and suddenly there was a sucking sound in Pasha's throat as air from the outside was vacuumed in. Alexander continued to hold it open with his fingers, letting the lungs fill with air and force the air out through the opening in the throat. It wasn't as efficient as using the upper airways such as the nose and mouth, but it would do.

"The pen, Lieutenant."

Ouspensky handed it over.

Alexander stuck the short plastic barrell halfway into the hole, taking care in his expediency not to ram it against the back of the trachea.

Alexander let himself draw a breath. "We did all right, Pasha," he said. "Ouspensky, the twine." He tied one end of the barrell to the rope, the other around Pasha's neck, so the pen would hold steady and not slip out.

"How long before the swelling goes down?" Alexander asked.

"How should I know?" replied Ouspensky. "All the men I've seen with their throats closed up died before the swelling went down. So I don't know."

Pasha was lying in Alexander's arms, erratically, sporadically, ecstatically breathing through the dirty plastic tube while Alexander watched his mud-covered struggling face, thinking that the whole war had been reduced to waiting for death while Pasha's life piped through the inkless barrell of a broken Soviet pen.

One minute Grinkov, Marazov, Verenkov without his glasses, Telikov, Yermenko, one minute Dasha, and one minute Alexander, too. One minute he was alive, and the next minute he was lying on the ice on Lake Ladoga bleeding out, his icy clothes entombing him. One minute, alive, the next face down, helmet down, in his white coat, lying on the ice, bleeding out.

But in less time than it took to draw a breath, Alexander had been loved. In one deep breath, in one agonized blink, he had been so beloved.

"Pasha, can you hear me?" asked Alexander. "Blink if you can hear me."

Pasha blinked.

Tightening his mouth, taking shallow breaths, Alexander remembered a poem, *The Fantasia of a Fallen Gentleman on a Cold Bitter Night*:

> Once in finesse of fiddles found I ecstasy
> And in a flash of gold heels on the hard pavement
> Now see I
> That warmth's the very stuff of poesy
> Oh, God, make small
> The old, star-eaten blanket of the sky,
> That I may fold it round me, and in comfort lie.

CHAPTER TWENTY-SIX

New York, October 1944

EDWARD LUDLOW CAME THROUGH the double doors of the hospital quarters in Ellis Island and pulled Tatiana by her hand out into the hall. "Tatiana, is it true what I saw?"

"I don't know. What you see?"

He was pale from anxiety.

"What?"

"Is it true? I saw the NYU Red Cross roster for the nurses about to be sent to Europe, and the name Jane Barrington was on it. Tell me it's a different Jane Barrington, just a coincidence."

Tatiana was quiet.

"No. Please. No."

"Edward—"

He took her hands. "Have you talked to anyone about this?"

"No, of course not."

"What are you thinking? The Americans are in Europe. Hitler is getting squeezed on both fronts. The war is coming to an end soon. There is no reason to go."

"The POW camps are in desperate need of medicine and food and packages and care."

"Tatiana, they have care. From other nurses."

"If they have care, how come army asking for Red Cross volunteers?"

"Yes, for *other* volunteers. Not for you."

When she did not reply, Edward pressed her. "God, Tatiana," he said in a shocked voice, "what are you planning to do with Anthony?"

"I wanted to leave him with his great-aunt in Massachusetts, but I think she won't be able to run after small boy." Tatiana saw the expression in Edward's eyes. She took her hands away. "Esther say I could leave him with her. She says her housekeeper Rosa could help look after the baby, but I do not think that's good idea."

"You don't *think*?"

Tatiana did not reply to the sarcasm in his voice but instead said, "I thought I would leave him with Isabella—"

"Isabella? A complete stranger!"

"Not complete stranger. She offered . . ."

"Tania, she doesn't know what I know. She doesn't even know what you know. But I know things even you don't know. Tell me the truth, are you going because you are planning to look for your husband?"

Tatiana did not reply.

"Oh, Tatiana," said Edward with a shake of his head. "Oh, Tatiana. You told me he was dead."

"Edward, what you worried about?"

He wiped his brow, stepping away from her slightly in his confusion and anxiety. "Tania," he said, his low voice trembling. "Heinrich Himmler has taken control of the German POW camps this fall. The first thing he did was to refuse any packages or letters to be passed on to the American POWs or to have the camps inspected by the IRC. Himmler assured us the Allied forces are getting fair treatment, all but the Soviets. Right now, the Red Cross does not have permission to examine the German POW camps. Which only speaks to their desperation. They know the war is so close to being lost, they don't even care anymore about the fate of their own prisoners. They cared last year, the year before, but not now. I'm sure the ban on the Red Cross will be lifted, but even so, how many prisoner camps do you think there are, two? Do you know how many? Hundreds! And dozens more Italian, French, English, American camps. How many prisoners do you think that is? Hundreds of thousands would be a conservative estimate."

"Himmler will change his mind. They did this before in 1943, and then quickly changed when they realize their prisoners are going to be treated bad, too."

"Yes, before, when they thought they were winning the war! Since the Normandy landings, they know their days are numbered. They don't care anymore about their stranded men. You know how I know? Because since 1943, they have not asked the Red Cross to inspect the American POW facilities here in the United States."

"Why should they? They know Americans treat German prisoners good."

"No, it's because they know the war is lost."

"Himmler will change his mind," Tatiana said stubbornly. "Red Cross will inspect those camps."

"Hundreds of thousands of prisoners in hundreds of camps. At a week per camp, that's two hundred weeks, not allowing time for travel between them. Four years. What are you even thinking?"

Tatiana did not reply. She had not thought that far ahead.

"Tatiana," Edward said. "Please don't go."

Edward seemed to be taking it personally. Tatiana didn't know what to say.

"Tatiana, what about your son?"

"Isabella will take care of him."

"Forever? Will she take care of him when his mother is found dead from disease or battle wounds?"

"Edward, I not go to Europe to die."

"No? You won't be able to help it. Germany is about to become the front. Poland is in Soviet hands. What if the Soviets have been looking for you? What if you go to Poland, and are discovered by the Soviet authorities? Jane Barrington, Tatiana Metanova, what do you think they will do with you? If you go to Germany, to Poland, to Yugoslavia, to Czechoslovakia, to Hungary, you are going there to die. One way or another, you are not coming back."

That's not true, she wanted to say. But she knew the Soviets were looking for her. She knew the risks. They were enormous. And Alexander? He was minuscule. Her plan was a bad one, she knew. Alexander had had Luga—a place—to go to. He had had Molotov, had her concrete evacuation, had a place, a name, had Lazarevo to go to. She had his death certificate. With his death certificate clutched and crumpled in her hands, she was going to travel to every POW camp open for inspection and look for him, and if he wasn't there, she would somehow make her way back to Leningrad and find Colonel Stepanov and ask him about Alexander, and if he didn't know, she would ask Generals Voroshilov and Mekhlis; she would go to Moscow and ask Stalin himself if she had to.

"Tania, please don't go," Edward repeated.

She blinked. "What is Orbeli?"

"Orbeli? You already asked me that. How should I know? I don't know. What does Orbeli have to do with anything?"

"He said, 'Remember Orbeli' to me last time I saw him. Maybe Orbeli is place somewhere in Europe where I supposed to meet him."

"Before you leave your child to go to the front, shouldn't you find out what Orbeli is?"

"I tried," she said. "I couldn't find out: no one knows."

"Oh, Tania. It's most likely nothing."

Edward's anxiety ate at Tatiana's insides. How to justify it? "My son will be fine," she said feebly.

"Without a father, without a mother?"

"Isabella is wonderful woman."

"Isabella is a stranger, a sixty-year-old stranger! Isabella is not his mother. When she is dead, what do you think will happen to Anthony?"

"Vikki take care of him."

Edward laughed joylessly. "Vikki can't take care of tying the bow on her blouse. Vikki can't come in on time, can't tell time. Vikki beats not to your son, not even to you, or her grandparents, but to herself. I pray Vikki never has children of her own. Vikki doesn't help you take care of Anthony now. What makes you think she will take care of him when her only emotional link with him—*you*—is gone? How long do you think she will keep that up?" Edward took a deep breath. "And do you know where they will send him when he is an orphan? The city home for boys. Maybe before you travel to Europe to kill yourself, you should take a look at one of those places to see where your fifteen-month-old son will end up."

Tatiana paled.

"You haven't thought this through," said Edward. "I know that. Because if you had, you wouldn't do it. I know that for a fact. Do you know how I know?"

"How?" she asked faintly.

"I know," Edward said, taking her hands, "because I've seen what you do for the people who come through the golden door. I know because you, Tatiana, always do the right thing."

She made no reply.

"He already lost a father," Edward said. "Don't let your son lose a mother, too. You're the only thing he has in this world that connects him to himself and to the past and to his destiny. Once he loses you, he will be an unmoored ship for the rest of his life. That's what you will do to him. That will be your legacy to him."

Tatiana was mute. She felt suddenly and acutely cold. Edward squeezed her hands. "Tania," he said. "Not for Vikki, not for me, not for the veterans upstairs, or for the immigrants at Ellis, but for your son—don't go."

༄

Tatiana didn't know what to do. But the seeds of doubt were formidable and growing. She called Sam Gulotta, who told her he had heard nothing about Alexander, and confirmed for her the dire situation in the German POW and concentration camps, and the fate of the Soviet prisoners incarcerated there. The more Tatiana thought about it, the crazier the plan sounded even to herself and the more guilt she felt about her child.

⚭

She asked everybody she could about Orbeli. She asked all the German soldiers and all the Italian soldiers, and the nurses, and the refugees, and then Tatiana went to the New York Public Library, but even there, amid the research books, the microfilm, the magazines, the periodicals, the atlases, the maps, the reference indices, she could not find a mention of an Orbeli.

The very fact of its obscurity made her think less of it, not more. The pointlessness of it diminished it in her eyes instead of magnifying it. It wasn't a forest or a village, or the name of a fortress, or the name of a general. More and more it seemed a meaningless remark, less to do with her or Alexander than with perhaps a small unrelated thing he had wished to convey to her, like a joke or an anecdote to be promptly forgotten when larger things overtook it. It wasn't a message, it was an aside, and then he was in the lake, and it should have been forgotten. It wasn't forgotten because what followed expanded it out of proportion, not because Orbeli deserved expanding.

But the medal, the medal? The *Hero of the Soviet Union* medal? How did that end up in her backpack?

But finally Tatiana had an explanation for that also. When Dr. Sayers first told her about Alexander, perhaps he had neglected to tell her that he had taken the medal off a dying man's neck instead of burying him in the lake with it, and then larger events had overtaken it, he had meant to tell her he put it into her backpack in a tiny secret compartment so she would find it someday but not right away, but he was dying and forgot.

⚭

She did not go back.

CHAPTER TWENTY-SEVEN

Poland, November 1944

ALEXANDER SLEPT, SITTING UP against the tree with Pasha's head on his lap. At dawn Pasha's throat swelling subsided. He put his finger over the opening in the plastic tube and took a few gasping breaths through his mouth. Alexander, encouraged, used some medical tape he carried to tape around the tube, to close up the opening as much as possible. He refused to take out the plastic pipe, worrying that if Pasha needed it again, he wouldn't be able to reproduce his work. Pasha placed his index finger over the opening in the tubing and croaked, "Tape it up, I can't speak with it open."

Alexander taped the end shut and watched for a few minutes as Pasha spluttered and struggled to take deep breaths.

"Alexander, listen," he finally whispered, weakly and faintly. "I have an idea. Carry me on your back out of this no-man's land to the defense line. I'm still wearing a German uniform, aren't I?"

"Yes."

"You'll save yourself by my German uniform. If you want to save him"—he pointed to Ouspensky and breathed hard—"have him carry one of the German wounded. Do we have any, or are they all dead?"

"I think we have a concussed German."

"Perfect." Breath. "Surrender to them carrying their own wounded. You will save your life."

"The other three can walk."

"Good. Remain in charge though, don't let the prisoners talk for you. When you get to the defense line, say *Schießbsen Sie nicht*. Don't shoot."

"Is that all I have to say?" said Alexander. "Why didn't we say that back in 1941? Or even 1939, for that matter?" He smiled. Pasha breathed.

"What are you two conspiring to do there?" said Ouspensky, overhearing. "You're not planning to surrender, are you?"

Alexander said nothing.

"Captain, you know we can't surrender."

"Can't retreat, either."

"We're not retreating. We're staying put. We'll wait for reinforcements to come."

Pasha and Alexander exchanged a look. "We are surrendering, Ouspensky. I have a wounded man. He needs to be treated immediately."

"Well, I'm not doing it. They'll kill us," said Ouspensky, "and then our own army will disown us."

"Who says we're ever going back to our army?" said Pasha, struggling up with Alexander's help.

"Oh, you're a fine one to talk. Certainly you, a dead man walking, have nothing to lose and nowhere to go, but the rest of us have families at home."

"I have no family," said Alexander. "But Ouspensky is right."

Ouspensky smiled with satisfaction at Pasha.

Alexander said, "Stay here, Nikolai. Wait for the Red Army to get to you."

The smile was wiped off Ouspensky's face. "Captain! You have a family. I thought you said you had a wife? And he"—pointing derisively to Pasha—"has a sister?"

Alexander and Pasha said nothing.

"Why don't you two care about her? She'll be sent to Bolshevik Island in Archangelsk because of your surrender." No one returned from Bolshevik Island.

Ignoring Ouspensky, Pasha glanced at Alexander. "Ready?" he said.

Alexander nodded, motioning for the four German prisoners. One was delirious. One had a superficial but very bloody and gloriously conspicuous head wound.

Ouspensky was barely able to get out a breath. He was wheezing like Pasha. "Is this what it's coming down to? You, Captain Belov, rode for fifteen hundred kilometers, you barreled through divisions and regiments, through minefields and death camps, through every river and every mountain, all so you could surrender to the Germans?" He was so incredulous he was hyperventilating.

"Yes," Alexander said, his own voice shaking. That is exactly why. "I'm done. Now, either you come with us or you stay here."

"I'm staying here," said Ouspensky.

Alexander saluted him.

"It's him," Ouspensky spat out. "Before him, you were an honorable man. You found him, and since he sold his soul to the devil and lived, you decided why not you, too."

Alexander was watching Ouspensky. "Why are you taking this so personally, Lieutenant? What does this have to do with *you*?"

"For some reason," said Pasha, "everything."

"Oh, fuck you! No one is talking to you. Why don't you breathe through your pen and shut the fuck up. You'd be blessedly rotting already if it weren't for him!"

"Ouspensky!" Alexander said. "You're out of line. Commander Metanov is a rank above you."

"I don't respect his rank. I don't recognize his Satan rank," snapped Ouspensky. "Go ahead, Captain, what are you waiting for? Go! Leave your live men behind."

Corporal Demko said timidly, "He's not leaving me. I'm going with him."

Ouspensky widened his eyes. "I'm the only one you're leaving behind?"

"Looks like it," said Pasha with a smile.

Ouspensky went for him. Alexander stepped between them just in time. Pasha, brave but foolish, could not have fought even a one-lunged Ouspensky. Breathing took all of Pasha's effort.

"What is it with you two?" Alexander said, pushing Pasha away. "Pasha . . ."

"I don't trust him, Alexander. I don't trust him at all."

"Oh, you're a fine one to talk," Ouspensky snapped.

"Since the moment I laid eyes on him," Pasha continued, "I've had a feeling about him." He panted and fell quiet.

Alexander took Pasha slightly aside. "He's all right," Alexander whispered. "He's been by my side this whole time. Like Borov was for you."

"Right by your side," Pasha echoed.

"Yes. Let's just take him and go before we make so much noise here the Germans will ready for another battle."

Pasha said nothing. Alexander bent Pasha's head back and adjusted the tape on his throat. "You've got to stop talking, we've got to get you to a medic and get this sewn up. So just shut up for the time being. Let me handle it."

He walked back to Ouspensky. "Nikolai, you may not respect his rank, but you have no choice but to respect mine. I cannot leave you in the woods by yourself. I might as well shoot you. I'm ordering you to lay down your arms and to surrender with the rest of us." He lowered his voice. "It's for your own good."

"Oh, just fucking fine," said Ouspensky. "I'll go. I'm doing it under protest, I tell you."

"You've been in this whole war under protest. Name me one thing you've done of your own volition."

Ouspensky said nothing.

"Pasha over there thinks you are not fit to live with pigs, Lieutenant."

"But you defended me, sir. You told him I was."

"Exactly. You have been my good friend, Nikolai. I cannot leave you behind. Now come."

The men laid down their weapons.

Walking behind the two able-bodied, limping Germans, Alexander carried Pasha on his back, Ouspensky carried the head-wounded German on his, and Demko the concussed. In this manner, single file, they moved through the woods, through the felled trees and the trench holes, through the pillboxes and the bushes. Unarmed, Alexander slowly walked to the German defense line that stretched for maybe half a kilometer. He knew he couldn't talk them out of shooting him no matter how much he said *Schießben Sie nicht.* Instead, he walked a kilometer to the flank.

He was stopped by a cry from the woods. "*Halt! Bleiben Sie stehen. Kommen Sie nicht naheres!*"

Alexander made out two sentries with machine guns. He stopped and did not go any farther just as instructed. "*Schießben Sie nicht, schießben Sie nicht,*" he shouted back.

Pasha whispered into his ear, "Tell them you've got wounded Germans with you. '*Wir haben verwundetes Deutsch mit uns.*' "

Alexander called out, "*Wir haben—*"

"*Verwundetes—*"

"*Verwundetes Deutsch mit uns.*"

There was silence from the German side, as if they were conferring.

Alexander raised his bloodied, once-white towel. "*Wir übergeben!*" We surrender.

"Very good," said Pasha. "So they taught you how to say it, just forbid you to do it."

"I learned in Poland," Alexander replied, waving his flag. "*Verwundetes Deutsch!*" he called out again. "*Wir übergeben!*"

The Germans took the four of them prisoner. They took Pasha and the other Germans to the medic's tent, sewed up Pasha's throat, gave him antibiotics. Then Alexander was interrogated, why had he taken German prisoners when it was against Soviet policy? They had also questioned the German soldiers, and from them learned that Pasha—taken care of like a German—was not German. They promptly relieved Pasha of his German uniform and rank, put him into prisoner clothes, and when he was better, transported him, Alexander, and Ouspensky to an Oflag internment camp in Catowice, Poland. Corporal Demko, being an enlisted man, was sent to a Stalag elsewhere.

Alexander knew that the Germans spared their lives only because he came to them bearing not weapons but wounded *German* men. The Germans thought the Soviets were worse than animals for letting their own soldiers perish of wounds on the battlefield. Alexander, Ouspensky and Demko were spared because they acted like human beings and not like Soviets.

⚮

Pasha had told Alexander the Germans had two kinds of POW camps, and he was right. This one was divided into two parts—one for the Allied prisoners, one for the Soviets. In the Allied camps, the prisoners were treated according to the rules of war. The text of the 1929 Geneva Convention on treatment of prisoners was proudly displayed in those camps. In the Soviet camps, separated from the Allies by barbed wire, the prisoners were treated according to the rules of Stalin. They weren't given medical attention, they weren't given food beyond bread and water. They were interrogated and beaten and tortured and finally left to die. The other Soviet prisoners were forced to dig graves for their fallen comrades.

Alexander didn't care how he was treated. He was near Germany, a few kilometers from the Oder river, and he was with Pasha. He waited patiently for the Red Cross nurses to come through the camps and was surprised and slightly disheartened when they did not. There were soldiers sick and dying even on the Allied side. Yet even for the French and the English there was no Red Cross. No one would give him a clear answer as to why, not even the major who interrogated him, not even the guards who manned his barracks. Pasha said something must have happened to make the Germans forbid the Red Cross access through their camps.

"Yes, they're losing the war," said Ouspensky. "That's bound to make anyone less agreeable to the rules."

"No one was talking to you," snapped Pasha.

"Oh, God, the both of you!" exclaimed Alexander.

"Lieutenant," said Pasha to Ouspensky, "why can't you leave us alone for just a moment? Why are you always at our side?"

"What do you have to hide, Metanov?" asked Ouspensky. "Why such need to be alone all of a sudden?"

Alexander walked away from them. They followed him. Pasha said, sighing with resignation at Ouspensky's presence, "I think we should try to escape. What's the point of staying here?"

Alexander snorted mildly. "There are no floodlights and no watchtowers. I don't think it can be called escaping, Commander," he said, pointing out a hole five meters wide in the barbed wire fence. "I think it's called leaving."

He himself did not want to run at first, hoping for the IRC to come through. But as weeks went by and the conditions in the camp deteriorated and the IRC was nowhere in sight, he concluded they had no choice. The barbed wire had been fixed. They used wire cutters, found in the engineer's tool shed, to cut through another hole and run. The three of them were picked up four hours later by two guards from the camp who came after them in a Volkswagen Kübel. Upon their return, the commandant of the camp, Oberstleutnant Kiplinger said, "You're crazy. Where did you think you were headed? There is nowhere to go, there is just more of this. I'll let you off this time, but don't do it again." He gave Alexander a cigarette. They both lit up.

"Where is the Red Cross, Commandant?"

"What do you care where the Red Cross is? Like they ever come for you. No packages for the Soviet men, Captain."

"I know that. Just wanted to know where they were, that's all."

"New decree. They're forbidden to inspect the camps."

Alexander kept as clean as he could, shaved scrupulously, and made himself useful by offering to work for the commandant. Kiplinger, against the rules of the Geneva Convention and in accordance with Alexander's wishes, gave him a saw, nails and a hammer and let him build more barrack housing for the prisoners. Ouspensky helped him, but it was too hard for him in the wet winter with only one lung.

Pasha volunteered to work in the kitchen, and that way managed to steal enough extra food for himself and Alexander, and reluctantly for Ouspensky also.

That was at the end of November 1944. December came and went, the camps filled up. Alexander couldn't build the new barracks fast enough in the freezing weather. The barracks in both the Allied and the Soviet camps normally held a thousand men. Now, stretched beyond limits, they held ten thousand.

"Lieutenant Ouspensky," Alexander said, "I find it ironic that they should have so many Soviet men here when the law against surrender is so clear. I just can't understand it. Can you explain that?"

"They're obviously renegades like you, Captain."

There was not enough food or water for everyone. Soldiers remained filthy and bred disease on their soiled bodies. The barbed wire came down, the camps became as one. The Germans were clearly unable to figure out what to do with 5,000 Soviet POWs. Aside from the Soviet contingent, there were Romanians, Bulgarians, Turks and Poles.

There were no Jews anywhere.

"Where are all the Jews?" one Frenchman asked, in broken English, and Alexander in Russian replied dryly that they were all in Majdanek, but the Frenchman and the Englishman didn't understand and stepped away from him. Ouspensky was nearby, and Alexander did not want to arouse suspicion by talking in English.

"Captain, how do you know there aren't any Jews in this camp?" asked Ouspensky as they walked back to their barracks.

"Don't you remember getting bathed and deloused when they first brought us here?" asked Alexander.

"Yes. They don't want to interrogate us filthy. They bathe and delouse us as a matter of course."

"Indeed they do, Lieutenant. They also, while you're naked, as a matter of course make sure you aren't Jewish. If you were, I guarantee you would not be here."

◌▨◌

In the meantime, there were rumors of grave American losses in Hürtgen Forest near the Ardennes in Belgium and of carnage and bestial fighting and no relief or capitulation in sight.

Each morning Alexander worked, repaired, built, supervised other prisoners, and each afternoon he repaired the barbed wire fence on the perimeter of the camp, or the windows in the broken compounds, or cleaned empty weapons, anything to keep his hands busy. For that he was fed a bit better. But it wasn't enough. Pasha reminded Alexander of his own experience in the prisoner camp at Minsk, where the Germans, unable to figure out what to do with all those Soviets, just let them all die.

"Well, they can't let all the Allied POWs die."

"Oh, they can't, can't they? What are we going to do, chase them straight to hell to hold them accountable? I say we try to escape again. You repair that stupid fucking fence all the time. It's constantly falling down."

"Yes, but now they have a sentry watching just me."

"Let's kill him and run."

"It's Catholic Christmas tomorrow. Can we not kill him on Christmas perhaps?"

"Since when are you so religious?" asked Pasha.

"Oh, the Captain and God go back a long way," said Ouspensky, and both he and Pasha laughed at Alexander's expense, which he thought was better than the enmity that existed between them all other hours of the day.

They were given extra coal to heat their barracks rooms for Christmas. They were also given a bit of vodka. There were twenty officers in their quarters. They drank and played cards, and chess, and then got drunk enough to sing rowdy Soviet songs, "Stenka Razin" and "Katyusha," and were all unconscious by morning.

The day after Christmas, the sentry was sick and they didn't have to kill him. He was sick and he fell asleep on the job. So they ran again, but it was winter and hard to get anywhere. The only trains were military trains. They caught one such train and were apprehended by a policeman at the very next stop, who thought their stolen uniforms were too ill-fitting. By the time they were returned to Catowice, the sentry was dead of pleurisy before he could be shot for dereliction. The three of them were called to Commandant Kiplinger again.

"Captain Belov, you see I run my camp very lax. I don't care what you do. You want work, I give you work. You want more food, if there is some, I give it to you. I let you run around the whole camp, I don't watch you as long as you stay within the boundaries. I think that's fair, you obviously don't think so, and under your command these two fools follow like sheep. Well, now you're done, you're leaving. I told you last time, you try it once more and you're finished here. Didn't you believe me? I don't want any problems with you. Don't you know they shoot us for losing prisoners under our command?"

"Where are we going?"

"To a place from which there is no escape," Kiplinger said with satisfaction. "Colditz Castle."

CHAPTER TWENTY-EIGHT

New York, January 1945

ON NEW YEAR'S DAY, Tatiana went across the bay with Anthony for a solitary walk, and then met up with Vikki to go skating in Central Park. They took a bus uptown and finally stopped at the corner of 59th Street and Sixth Avenue. Tatiana sent Anthony and Vikki into the park, saying she had to run a quick errand.

She went to a phone booth near the Plaza Hotel. She waited a few moments, fingering the dimes in her pocket. She took the dimes out and counted them, though she knew how many she had. Finally she dialed a number.

"Happy New Year, Sam," she said into the phone. "Is this bad time?"

"Happy New Year, Tatiana. This is fine, I was catching up on some urgent work at the office today."

She waited. She held her breath.

"I have nothing for you," he said.

"Nothing?"

"No."

"They did not contact you—"

"No."

"Not even about me?"

"No. They're probably busy with other things, like how best to carve up Europe."

She breathed out. "Silly of me to keep calling, making it uncomfortable for you."

"I don't mind. Really. Call again in a month."

"I will. You are really too kind to me. Thank you." Tatiana hung up and waited a few seconds, her head pressed into the cold metal frame of the phone.

Finally Tatiana agreed to find an apartment to share with Vikki. The girls moved in together in January of 1945. Tatiana had found a three-bedroom, two-bathroom, rent-controlled place on Church Street on the sixth floor. It was very close to Bowling Green and Battery Park. From her living room window she could see New York Harbor and Lady Liberty, and Ellis Island if she went out onto the fire escape.

The apartment cost the girls fifty dollars a month, and though Vikki said in the beginning that she was not used to working to pay the rent instead of buying new clothes, they were both quite happy in the new place. Tatiana because there was a place finally to put all the books she was buying, and because her son finally had his own room, and because she herself had her own room. Mostly that was just brave talk. Tatiana slept with her son, her blankets and pillows on the floor next to Anthony. She said when he stopped nursing, she would go to her own bedroom. At eighteen months, he stopped nursing. She remained on the floor.

⌘

Bread. Flour, milk, butter, salt, eggs, yeast. A complete food. Bread.

Vikki tried to figure out why every other night at eleven they had to make yeast dough by hand, and Tatiana finally said to her, "So that in morning, I don't have to leave my house to go get warm bread for my family." Vikki did not ask again, but every morning before she had Tania's fresh croissants or fresh rolls or fresh crusty loaf with some black coffee and a cigarette, she smacked her lips and said, *"Give us this day our daily bread."*

"Amen," said Tatiana.

"Hey Men!" repeated Anthony.

"Who taught you to make such delicious bread, Tania?"

"My sister. She taught me how to cook."

"She must have been a very good cook."

"She was good teacher." She taught me how to tie my shoes and how to swim and how to tell time.

"How did she die?"

"She . . . she didn't get enough of her daily bread, Vikki."

⌘

Can't do enough, she thought, staring at the ceiling. Too many minutes and seconds to fill the day. Look at me now. I got up at six, and got Anthony up for Isabella, thank God she comes here to take care of him. I was at Ellis from eight until four, and then at Red Cross until six to take blood for an hour and to fill their POW medical kits to be sent overseas. I picked up Anthony from Isabella's, took him to the park, bought food, cooked dinner, played with him, bathed him, put him to bed, and listened to the radio and listened to Vikki, and made bread dough for tomorrow. Now it's after one and Vikki and Anthony are asleep, but here I still am, staring up at the ceiling, because there is not enough for me to do.

I need to do until I'm too tired even for nightmares.

Until I'm too exhausted by my American life to see his face.

He holds her waist in his hands, his face wet, his hair wet, his teeth gleaming like the river. He counts one, two, three, and flings her as far as he can into the Kama, and then hurls himself on top of her. She dives under him, wriggles free and swims away. He chases her, threatening her with all kinds of bodily harm when he catches her, and she slows down a bit, so that he can.

⚭

With her heart resolutely turned to the east, Tatiana made bread and bought seven varieties of bacon with her ration cards, she bought pots and pans and kitchen utensils, towels and sheets, she so liked the stores, the fruit stands, the butchers, the supermarkets, the corner delis. With inexorable force, Tatiana's physical body moved forward while the spirit of Tatiana languished relentlessly in the past. He had found her, a Lazarevo orphan waiting for him, and made her whole.

But she couldn't find him. She barely even tried. What a poor effort it had been. Not: I'm not going to stop until I find you, Shura, but I couldn't find a babysitter, sorry, Shura. She began to hate herself, a first for her. Not even in the days when she played the moral roulette with Dasha and Alexander, did Tatiana feel such a gnawing self-loathing.

No matter how many times Vikki asked, Tatiana would not go dancing at a club called Ricardo's up in Greenwich Village on Astor Place on Saturday night. She would not buy a new dress, she would not buy new shoes.

"You must come with me to Elks Rendezvous in Harlem," Vikki said. "It's some place! Great dancing, lots of doctors."

"There is no fury like a woman trying to find herself a new lover," said Tatiana, quoting from a book she just read. "Have you read *The Unquiet Grave* by Cyril Connolly? I highly recommend it."

"Forget this reading business. Do you want to go see Bette Davis and Leslie Howard in *Of Human Bondage* at the Apollo?"

"Maybe other time."

"There is no other time! This Friday night, let's go to Lady Be Beautiful. I've been telling them about you, they're very eager to meet you. We'll get manicures, and then go out for dim sum on Mott Street, you have to try Chinese food, it's fantastic, and then we'll go to Elks Rendezvous."

"All the way to Harlem?"

"It's the best for a bit of jitterbug."

"Is *that* what you call it?"

"Are you being saucy?" Vikki studied her with a grin. "Will you come?"

"Maybe other time, okay?"

"Tania," Vikki said one evening as the girls curled up on the couch, "I've finally decided what's wrong with you. Besides you making bread and eating bacon all the time."

"What's wrong with me?"

"You're a moper. You need to learn how to curse like a sailor, you need to learn how to walk with bravado as if the entire world belonged to you, you need to come to Lady Be Beautiful and get a beauty treatment, but mostly you need a man."

"All right," said Tatiana. "Where do we find this man?"

"I'm not talking about *love*," Vikki said, as if explaining was what Tatiana needed.

"Of course not."

"No. I'm talking about a hair-raising good time. You're too uptight. You worry too much. You're always fretting, always working, being a mother. Ellis, Red Cross, Anthony, it's too much."

"I not always fretting," Tatiana defended herself.

"Tania, you're in America! I know it's war, but the war is not here. *You're* here. Didn't you always want to come to the United States?"

"Yes," Tatiana said. But I didn't want to come alone.

"Isn't it better here than your Soviet Union?"

They're in two rowboats and they're racing across Lake Ilmen, seeing who gets to the middle of the lake first—a kilometer of flat-out rowing. Tatiana, barely smiling, is methodical and unflappable. Pasha is crazed by his inability to beat his sister. And back on shore, their sister Dasha and their cousin Marina are jumping up and down rooting for Tania, and the grown-

ups behind them are waving left and right and rooting for Pasha. It's sum-mer and the air smells of fresh water.

But they're not there anymore. Not on Lake Ilmen, not in Luga, not in Leningrad, not in Lazarevo. Yet they never leave her.

And *he* doesn't leave her.

Tatiana blinked away her life as she drank her tea. "Tell me about your first love," she said.

"His name was Tommy. He was a lead singer in a band. God, he was cute. Blond and small and—"

"But you tall."

"I know. I smothered him as if he were my son. It was perfect. He was seventeen and so talented. I used to sneak down the fire escape to go watch him perform at Sid's at the Bowery. I was awed by him."

"What happened to you two?" Tatiana asked, looking into her cup.

"Oh, I found out what musician boys did after they finished playing their sets."

"I thought you went to watch him."

"I had to be back home. He would tell me he'd be by to see me *later*. And then I found out that between the end of set and *later*, he would have a number of girls in the back room of the bar. He would have them, and then come up the fire escape into my bedroom at five in the morning, and be with me."

"Oh, no."

"I cried for three weeks straight. And then I met Jude."

"Who's Jude?"

"The second boy."

Tatiana laughed.

Vikki placed her hand on Tatiana's back and caressed her hair softly. "Tania." Her voice was soothing. "There *is* a second love. And a third love. And if you're lucky, a fourth and a fifth, too."

"That feels nice," Tatiana said, holding her cup tighter and closing her eyes.

"I think you're only supposed to wear black for a year, mourn for a year. And I'll tell you—Jude was better than Tommy. I felt more for him. He was a better—" Vikki paused. "He was a better person. Better at everything."

Tatiana nodded.

"Tania, you've forgotten what a great man feels like."

"If only I forgotten."

Vikki pressed Tatiana to her. "Ah, Tania," she said. "We'll get you there. I promise. We'll get you forgetting yet."

Once upon a time, young girls met young boys when the moon was full and the nights were dark, when there was a fire and singing and joking, when there was wine and taffeta and dancing, when the music was loud and the laughing, too, when one pair of eyes stared at another, and the girl's chest swelled and the boy came up close, and suddenly she looked up, he looked down and . . .

Once there was first love.

Vikki had one. Edward had one. Isabella and Travis had one.

First love, first kiss, first everything.

Once when they were so young.

And then they got older.

Time passed with the cycles of the moon, and the music stopped, and the girl took off her dress, and the fire went out, and they stopped laughing. But eventually, as surely as the sunrise, another man stood in front of the girl in the taffeta dress and smiled, and she looked up at him, and he gazed down at her.

It wasn't first love.

It wasn't a first kiss.

But it was love nonetheless.

And the kiss was sweet.

And the heart still pounded.

And the girl went on. She went on because she wanted to live, and she wanted to be happy. She wanted to love again. She didn't want to sit by the window looking out onto the sea. She didn't want to remember. She wanted to forget the first man. All she wanted was to remember the first feeling.

She wanted to take that feeling and place it on another man, and smile again, because the heart was too full and too bright not to love again. Because the heart needed to feel and needed to soar.

And because life was long.

She went on and stopped grieving, and she smiled and put on another dress and stood close to another man. She sang again, and joked again, after all, she did not die, she was still on this earth and she was still the same person, the person who needed to laugh every once in a while, to laugh with the roses, even if she knew that she would never again in all those many days ahead love as she loved when her heart was seventeen.

To protect herself she walked through life favoring the bleeding half of her body. She was careful not to step too harshly, she was careful to shield it from other eyes, from other cries. Her greatest asset became her greatest liability. And what time allowed her to do was to become an expert at hiding her deformity from the world. What time allowed her to do was say, as she walked hunched uphill carrying the cross on her back, that everyone had one, and this was hers.

She was so lucky to have her baby boy, to not be alone, to have love, to have *life*. And yesterday when she was young, she had been given more than she deserved.

Someday, she would stand from the couch, step away from the window sill, leave the fire escape, put away the black backpack, take the rings off her neck. Someday when the music played, she would not feel him waltzing with her through the clearing under the crimson moon on their wedding night.

Oh, how we danced on the night we were wed . . .

Someday. But today with every breath of the past she colored her breath of the future, with every blink of her eye, Alexander bore himself deeper and deeper inside her until the whole of what they were together blinded her from seeing what else might be in the world for her.

All she thought about was what he had loved in her, what he had needed from her, what he had wanted from her.

Memory—that fiend, that cruel enemy of comfort.

There was no forgetting; worse, the bloodletting that went on every minute became more intense as time went on. It was as if his lips, his hands, his crown, his heart, the things that seemed almost normal, almost right in Lazarevo acquired a prescient, otherworldly sense; it was as if in their totality they took on a life they had not had before.

How did they fish, or sleep, or clean? How did she go to her sewing circle? She hated herself now, flagellated herself for doing anything else, how could she have tried to live a normal life in Lazarevo with him, knowing even then that time and they were as fleeting as snowflakes?

Knowing what was at stake, could he have lowered his head and walked by her, if he had known what he would lose for the hour of rapture, for the minute of bliss?

How he loved to touch her. And she would sit quietly, with her legs not too close together, so that anytime he wanted to, he could: and he did. *Anytime.* Yes, he said, it was what a soldier on furlough wanted.

Anytime wasn't often enough. He would touch her with his fingers as she sat quietly on the bench, and then he would touch her with his mouth as she sat less quietly on the bench, there was no other time for him but now, there was no later, there was only insanity now.

I will make you insane, her memory screamed at her near the winter window sill as Tatiana smelled the brine of eternity. On the outside you will walk and smile as if indeed you are a normal woman, but on the inside you will twist and burn on the stake, I will never free you, you will never be free.

CHAPTER TWENTY-NINE

Colditz, January 1945

PERHAPS THEY WERE RIGHT in what they said about Colditz. There was no escape. And there was no work, either. There was nothing for the men to do except sleep and play cards and go for two walks a day. They got up at seven for roll call, and turned off their lights every evening at ten. In between there were three meals and two walks.

Colditz was the sprawling fifteenth-century fortress castle in northern Saxony, in the triangle between three great German cities: Leipzig, Dresden, and Chemnitz. Colditz stood on a steep hill above the river Mulde. And it wasn't just a hill. Colditz was surrounded by moats on the south and vertical drops on the east and leg-buckling precipices on the north and west. Colditz was built out of the rocky hill. When the mountain ended, the castle began.

The castle was extremely well run by high-minded, well-organized Germans who took their jobs very seriously and would not be corrupted, as Alexander learned from the five Soviet officers already residing in their small, cold, single stone cell with four bunks.

Colditz had a sick ward and a chapel, it had a delousing shed, two canteens, a movie theater, even a dentist. And that was just for the prisoners. As if it were their permanent residence, the German guards lived and ate very well. The commandant of Colditz had a quarter of the castle all to himself.

The most notorious escapees in all the other POW camps in Germany were brought to Colditz, where the sentries with machine guns stood every fifteen meters, on level ground, on raised catwalks and in round towers, and watched them twenty-four hours a day. Floodlights covered the castle at night. There was only one way in and one way out, over a moat bridge that led to the German garrison and the commandant's quarters.

There must have been two sentries for every one of the 150 prisoners; it certainly felt like it. Alexander spent thirty-one January days watching the sentries as they went out for their walks in the large inner courtyard, cobbled with gray stones that reminded him slightly of Pavlov barracks in Leningrad. He wondered whatever happened to Colonel Stepanov.

For thirty-one days he watched the guards in the canteen, in the showers, in the courtyard. Twice a week for an hour—with good behavior only—the prisoners were allowed, in small clusters of twelve, to take walks on the outer terrace facing west. It was an enclosed stone space, and below it over a parapet was a grassy, completely enclosed garden, but the prisoners weren't permitted there. Alexander, always on his best behavior, went out to the terrace for his two walks a week and watched the men who were watching him. He even watched them changing guard out of the window of his room. His bunk was next to the window, on the third floor over the sick ward, facing west. He liked that he was facing west. Something hopeful about it. Below him was the long and narrow terrace, and below that the long and narrow garden.

Colditz certainly looked impenetrable.

But how did Tania do it? How did she make it to Finland, with Dimitri dead and Sayers fatally wounded? He wished he knew, but he knew one thing—somehow she ended up in Finland. So there must be a way out of this place, too. He just couldn't see it.

Pasha and Ouspensky were a lot less optimistic. They had no interest in watching the guards. Alexander wanted to talk to the British POWs in the courtyard, but he had no interest in explaining his flawless English to Pasha or Ouspensky. There were no Americans in sight, only British and French officers, one Polish officer and the five Soviets with whom they shared their cell.

The one Polish officer was General Bor-Komarovsky. Alexander and he got talking in the canteen. Komarovsky had taken over the Polish Underground Resistance to Hitler and to the Soviets in 1942. When he was caught he went straight to Colditz, to ensure his permanent incarceration. And though he was very willing to tell Alexander stories of previous escape attempts out of the castle, and even gave Alexander his old relief maps of the area, in Russian, Komarovsky told Alexander that he could forget about escaping from here. Even those who had gotten outside the fortress walls were all caught within days. "Which goes to show you," Komarovsky said, "that what I've always believed is especially true of a place like Colditz. Despite the most meticulous planning and organization, there is no successful way out of any difficult situation without the hand of God."

Tania got out of the Soviet Union, Alexander wanted to say. I rest my case.

At night on his top bunk, he thought of her arms. He thought of trying to find her . . . Where would she be? If she were still waiting for him, where would she be so he could find her? Helsinki? Stockholm? London? America? Where in America, Boston, New York? Somewhere warm, perhaps? San Francisco? The City of Angels? When she left Russia with Dr. Matthew Sayers, he was going to take her to New York. Though the doctor had died, perhaps Tatiana headed there as planned. He would start there.

He hated these blind alleys of his imagination, but he liked to picture what her face might look like when she saw him, what her body might look like as it trembled, what her tears might taste like, how she would walk to him, maybe run to him.

What about their child, how old was it now? One and a half. A boy, a girl? If a girl, maybe she was blonde like her mother. If a boy, maybe he was dark-haired like his once dark, now hairless father. My child, what is it like to hold a small child, to lift it up in the air?

He would get himself into a self-defeating frenzy thinking of her hands on him, and of his own on her.

When she had first left him, the aching for her in his body was unabated, through windy March and wet April, and dry May and warm June. June was the worst. The aching was so intense that sometimes he thought that he would not be able to continue another day, another minute of such want, of such need.

Then a year passed and another. And little by little the aching was numbed, but the want, the need—there was no escape from that.

Sometimes he thought of the girl in Poland, blowzy Faith, who offered him everything and to whom he gave a chocolate. Would he be as strong now if a Faith walked through these parts? He didn't think so.

In Colditz, there was no escape, not from the thoughts, not from the fear, not from the throbbing. Not from the realization that it had now been many months, many years, and how long could one faithful wife wait for her dead husband? Even his Tatiana, the brightest star in the sky. How long could she wait before she moved on?

Please, no more. No more thoughts. No more desire. No more love. Please. No more anything.

How long could she wait before she put her blonde hair down, and walked out of work, and saw another face that made her smile?

He turned his own face to the window. He had to get out of Colditz, at whatever the cost.

⌇⌇

"Comrades, look here," he said to Pasha and Ouspensky, when they were out on the terrace one freezing February afternoon. "I want you to see something." Without motioning he pointed to the two sentries one on each side of the rectangular terrace, seven meters wide by twenty meters long.

Then he walked them casually across the terrace to the stone parapet and casually looked over the ledge while lighting a cigarette. Pasha and Ouspensky also looked over the ledge. "What are we looking at?" said Pasha.

In the walking garden far below, same shape as the terrace but twice as wide, two sentries with machine guns stood at opposite sides, one in an elevated pagoda, one on a raised catwalk.

"Yes?" said Ouspensky. "Four guards. Day and night. And the garden is over a vertical drop. Let's go." He turned.

Alexander grabbed his arm. "Wait, and listen."

"Oh no," said Ouspensky.

Pasha leaned forward. "Let him go, Captain," he said. "We don't need him. Go to hell, Ouspensky, and good riddance."

Ouspensky stayed.

Alexander, without pointing, said, "There are two guards down in the garden during the day, and two up here on the terrace. But at night the two guards here are relieved until morning because there is not much point in looking right at the floodlights. The guards here are replaced by one additional sentry in the garden below for a total of three. The third sentry watches the barbed wire fence over the fifty-foot—" Alexander coughed—"sixteen-meter precipice that leads to the bottom of the hill and to freedom." He paused. "At midnight, two things happen. One is the changing of the guard. The other is the turning of the floodlights to light this terrace and the castle. I've been watching it all out of our window at night. The guards walk off their posts, and new ones come to take their place."

"We're familiar with what changing of the guard means, Captain," said Ouspensky. "What are you proposing?"

Alexander turned away from the precipice and toward the castle.

He continued to smoke leisurely. "I propose," he said, "that when the guard is changing and the floodlights aren't on, we jump out of our window carrying a long rope, run across this terrace, jump down right here into the garden below, run to the barbed wire, cut it, and then descend on ropes the sixteen meters down to the ground to make our escape."

Pasha and Ouspensky were quiet. Ouspensky said, "How much rope would we need?"

"Ninety meters in all."

"Oh, can we just pick that up at the canteen? Or should we ask housekeeping?"

"We will make it out of bed linen."

"That's a lot of bed linen."

"Pasha has been making friends with Anna from housekeeping." Alexander smiled. "You can get us extra sheets, can't you?"

"Wait, wait," said Pasha. "We have to jump out of our window, nine meters above concrete . . ."

"Yes."

Pasha tapped his foot twice on the ground. "Concrete, Alexander!"

"Hold on to the rope and run down the wall."

"And then hold on to the rope to scale another thirteen meters down into the garden, run fourteen meters across, cut the barbed wire, and descend on another rope sixteen meters to the ground?"

"Yes, but the second rope we can attach in the dark. Won't be any floodlights on the wall down there."

"Yes, but the sentries will have taken their places."

"We will have to be on the other side of the barbed wire and in the trees when they do."

"Ah!" exclaimed Pasha. "What about the long white rope that's hanging out of our window? You don't think the guards will notice that, with the floodlights illuminating it so discreetly?"

"One of our bunkmates will have to brace us and then pull up the rope. Constantine will do it."

"And he will do this why?"

"Because he has nothing better to do. Because you will give him all your cigarettes. Because you will introduce him to Anna in housekeeping." Alexander smiled. "And because if it works, he can escape himself the following night. The barbed wire will already be cut."

Ouspensky said, "Comrade Metanov, as usual, there is something you have overlooked to ask the captain. What about time? How long do we have before the new guard takes his place and the floodlights come on?"

"Sixty seconds."

Ouspensky opened his mouth and laughed. Pasha joined him. "Captain, you are always so amusing, wry, witty."

Alexander smoked and said nothing. Pasha did a double-take, his mouth still open, still wanting to smile. "You're not serious about this?"

"Absolutely am."

"Comrade, he will have us on," said Ouspensky to Pasha, "until Friday if necessary. He is a terrible prankster."

Alexander smoked. "What would you two rather do? Spend two years digging a tunnel? We don't have two years. I don't know if we have six months. The British here are convinced the war will be over by the summer."

"How do you know?" said Ouspensky.

"I can understand rudimentary English, Lieutenant," Alexander snapped. "Unlike you, I went to school."

"Captain, I enjoy your sense of humor, I really do. But why do we have to dig a tunnel? Why do we have to fling ourselves out of windows on sheets? Why don't we just wait the six months for the war to be over?"

"And then, Ouspensky?"

"Then, then," he stammered. "I don't know what then, but let me ask you, what now? You're throwing yourselves off a cliff, why? Where are you hoping to go?"

Pasha and Alexander both stared at Ouspensky and didn't reply.

"As I thought," said Ouspensky. "I'm not going."

"Lieutenant Ouspensky," said Pasha, "have you ever in your entire fucking miserable life said yes to anything? You know what's going to be on your grave? 'Nikolai Ouspensky. He said no.'"

"Both of you are such comedians," said Ouspensky, walking away. "You are just the height of hilarity. My stomach is hurting. Ha. Ha. Ha."

Alexander and Pasha turned back to the garden below them.

Pasha asked how they were going to get through the barbed wire.

"I've got the wire cutters with me from the Catowice Oflag," said Alexander, smiling. "Komarovsky gave me his military maps of Germany. We just need to get to the border with Switzerland."

"How many kilometers?"

"Many," Alexander admitted. "A couple of hundred." But fewer than from Leningrad to Helsinki, he wanted to add. Fewer than from

Helsinki to Stockholm. And certainly fewer than from Stockholm to the United States of America, which is what he and Tania had planned.

Pasha didn't say anything. "Failure cost is high."

"Oh, Pasha, what are *your* options? Even if you for a moment thought I might have some, which believe me I don't, where does staying in Colditz leave *you*?"

Shrugging, Pasha said, "I didn't say I wasn't with you, I didn't say I wasn't going. I just said . . ."

Alexander patted him on the back. "Yes, the risk is high. But the reward is also high."

Pasha looked up to the third-floor window of his cell, to the terrace they were standing on, down to the garden below. "How in the world do you expect us to do all this in sixty seconds?"

"We'll have to hurry."

⟲⟳

They planned for another two weeks until the middle of February. They got medical supplies and canned goods and a compass. They stole sheets out of the laundry room and at night cut them in the dark and braided them together and then hid them in their ripped-apart mattresses. While helping to make rope Ouspensky kept saying he wasn't going, but everybody in the cell knew he was. The hardest thing was to get some civilian clothes. Pasha finally managed to sweet-talk Anna into stealing them from the laundry at the German senior officers' quarters. Their weapons had long been taken away from them, but Alexander still had his rucksack, which had a titanium trench tool, wire cutters, his empty pen, and some money. Anna even stole them some German IDs the night before their escape.

"We don't speak German," said Ouspensky. "It won't do us much good."

"I speak a little," said Pasha, "and since we'll be wearing German clothes, it's only right we should have German IDs."

"And what did you promise this young naïve girl for risking her job and livelihood for you?" Ouspensky asked with a sneer.

"My heart." Pasha smiled. "My undying devotion. Isn't it what we always promise them? Right, Alexander?"

"Right, Pasha."

Finally the planned night in February came and the time was near. Everything was ready.

It was eleven in the evening and Ouspensky was snoring. He asked to be woken up ten minutes before departure. Alexander thought it was smart to rest, but he himself could not sleep since yesterday.

He and Pasha were sitting on the floor by the closed window, tugging on the rope that was securely—they hoped—attached to one of the bunkbeds cemented into the floor.

"Do you think Constantine is strong enough to hold the rope steady? He doesn't look that strong," Pasha whispered.

"He'll be fine." Alexander lit a cigarette.

So did Pasha. "Will we succeed, Alexander? Will we make it?"

"I don't know." Alexander paused. "I don't know what God has planned for us."

"There you go with your God again. Are you prepared for anything?"

Alexander paused before answering. "Anything," he said, "except failure."

"Alexander?"

"Yes?"

"Do you ever think about your child?"

"What do you think?"

Pasha was quiet.

"What do you want to know? If I think she still remembers me? Do I think she has forgotten me—found a new life? Assumed that I was dead, accepted that I was dead." Alexander shrugged. "I think about it all the time. I live inside my heart. But what can I do? I have to move toward her."

Pasha was quiet.

Alexander listened to his palpitating breathing.

"What if she is happy now?"

"I hope she is."

"I mean—" Pasha went on, but Alexander interrupted him.

"Stop."

"Tania is at her core a happy soul, a resilient person. She is loyal and she is true, she is unyielding and relentless, but she also feels a child's delight for the smallest things. You know how some people gravitate toward misery?"

"I know how some people do that, yes," said Alexander, inhaling the nicotine.

"Tania doesn't."

"I know."

"What if she is remarried and has made herself a fine life?"

"I'll be happy to find her happy."

"But then what?"

"Then nothing. We salute her. You stay. I go."

"You're not risking your life to just *go*, Alexander."

"No." I am a salmon, born in fresh water, living in salt water, swimming 3,200 kilometers upstream over rivers and seas back home to fresh water to spawn, and to die. I have no choice.

"What if she's forgotten you?"

"No."

"Maybe not forgotten, but what if she doesn't feel the same way anymore? She is in love with her new husband. She's got kids. She looks at you and is horrified."

"Pasha, you have a twisted Russian soul. Shut the fuck up."

"Alexander, when I was fifteen, I had a crush on this girl, we had a great time for a month, and the next year I went back to Luga thinking we would continue our romance, and you know what? She didn't even *remember* who I was. How pathetic was that?"

"Pretty pathetic." They both laughed. "You obviously were doing something wrong if she forgot you that quick."

"Shut up yourself."

Alexander had no doubt—whatever Tatiana's life was, she had not forgotten him. He still felt her crying in his dreams. Every once in a while he dreamed of her not in Lazarevo but in a new place, with a new face, speaking to him, begging him, imploring him—but even in a new place with a new face, Alexander could smell her pure breath, breathing her life into him.

"Alexander," Pasha barely whispered, "what if we never find her?"

"Pasha, you're going to make a chain smoker out of me," Alexander said, lighting up. "Look, I don't have all the answers. She knows that if I am able, I will never stop looking for her."

"What are we going to do with Ouspensky?" Pasha said. "Couldn't we leave him here? Just forget to wake him."

"I think he'll notice when he wakes up."

"So?"

"He'll send them after us."

"Ah, he would, wouldn't he? That's the thing about him. He's a bit . . . baleful, don't you think?"

"Don't think twice about it," said Alexander. "It's a Soviet thing."

"Even stronger in Ouspensky," Pasha muttered, but Alexander sprung up and shook Ouspensky. It was near midnight. It was time.

Alexander opened the window. It was a rainy and stormy night, and it was hard to see. He thought that might play to their advantage. The guards wouldn't willingly be looking up at the rain.

With the ends of the ropes tied around their waists, the slack rolled up in their hands, their belongings tied around their backs, the wire cutters in Alexander's boot, they stood and waited for the signal from Constantine. The guards on the terrace had already left for the night. Constantine would wave as soon as the guards were gone from the garden, and then Alexander would jump first, then Pasha, then Ouspensky.

Finally, a few minutes after midnight, Constantine waved and moved out of the way. Alexander flung himself out of the small window. The rope had four meters of slack. He bounced hard—too hard—against the wet stone wall, and then quickly released the roll of rope bit by bit as he ran down the wall to the ground. Pasha and Ouspensky were right behind him, but a little slower. He ran across the terrace and jumped over the parapet, releasing the rope bit by bit in a great hurry. The rope was too short, fuck, it yanked him up two meters above the grass, but it was all right, because he let go, fell into the sloshing, icy wet grass, rolled, jumped up and ran to the barbed wire, his cutters already out of his boot. Pasha was behind him, Ouspensky, breathing heavily, was behind Pasha. By the time they got to him, seconds later, the barbed wire was already cut. They squeezed through the hole and hid in the trees over the precipice. The floodlights came on. The guards took longer tonight to come out. It was windy and raining hard. Alexander glanced at the floodlit castle to see if the rope had been pulled up by Constantine. It could have been, it was hard to see through the rain. The guards were still not out and Alexander had extra time to attach one rope fifteen meters long to the branches of the three-hundred-year-old oak. This time he let Ouspensky and Pasha go first. The three of them slowly edged down the slippery wall, suspending themselves over the precipice. It was dark, and a good thing too because Ouspensky called out, "Captain, did I ever tell you I'm afraid of heights?"

"No, and now is not the fucking time."

"I was thinking now is a very good time."

"It's pitch black. There is no height. Just come on! Move a little faster."

Alexander was soaked to the skin. German trench coats were made of thick canvas, but weren't waterproof. What good were they?

They all released the rope and jumped to the ground a minute later. Alexander cut through the barbed wire fence surrounding Colditz at the bottom of the hill and they were out.

Now he wished the weather would quieten. Who wanted to run at night in this weather?

"Everybody good?" Alexander said. "We did great."

"I'm good," said Ouspensky, panting.

"I'm good, too," said Pasha. "I scraped myself on something when I landed. Scraped my leg."

Alexander got out a flashlight. Pasha's trousers were slightly ripped at the thigh, but he was barely bleeding. "Must have been the barbed wire. Just a scratch. Let's go."

൭ഝഄ

They were running, running all day and night, or maybe they slept in barns at night, but they dreamed of running, and when they opened their eyes, they were exhausted. Alexander ran slowly, Pasha ran slower, and Ouspensky barely moved. In the fields, in the rivers, in the woods. A day went by, then another, how far had they gotten from Colditz? Maybe thirty kilometers. Three grown men, five healthy lungs between them, and thirty kilometers. They weren't even past Chemnitz, just south-west. There were no trains, and they did their best to avoid paved roads. How were they going to get to Lake Constance on the border of Switzerland at this rate?

Pasha slowed down even more on the third day. He stopped chatting in between breaths, and stopped eating on the third night. Alexander noticed because when he said, Pasha, eat some fish, Pasha replied that he wasn't hungry. Ouspensky made a joke, something like, I'll eat everything, don't have to ask me twice, and Alexander gave him the fish without a second glance, but he stared at Pasha. He took a look at Pasha's thigh. It was raw and red and oozing yellow liquid. Alexander poured diluted iodine on it, sprinkled some sulfa powder on it and bandaged it. Pasha said he was feeling cold. Alexander touched him. He felt warm.

They made a lean-to with their sheets for all three of them, and they crawled in and kept barely warm, and in the middle of the night, Alexander woke up because he was sweating. He thought there was a fire in the lean-to, he jumped up with a start. But it wasn't a fire. It was just a burning Pasha.

What's wrong with you, Alexander whispered.

Don't feel so good, Pasha mouthed inaudibly.

Everything was silent and mute. Alexander used the last of their water, placing rags on Pasha's head. It helped a little. The water was gone, and the rags were hot from Pasha's forehead, and Pasha was burning. Alexander went out in the cold rain and got more water.

Don't feel so good, Pasha's mouth moved. By morning his mouth was cracked and bleeding. Alexander unbandaged his leg. It looked the same as yesterday. More green than yellow. He disinfected it, and poured sulfa powder on it, and then he diluted the sulfa in some rainwater and made Pasha drink it, and Pasha did, and then threw up and Alexander cursed and yelled, and Pasha mouthed, I been wet too long, Alexander. I think I was cold and wet too long.

It was just above freezing. The rain was turning to sleet. Alexander wrapped Pasha in his trench coat. Pasha was burning. Alexander took his trench coat off Pasha.

When it stopped raining, he built another fire and dried all of Pasha's clothes and gave him a smoke and a small drink of whisky out of their flask. Shaking, Pasha drank the whisky.

"What are we going to do?" asked Ouspensky.

"Why do you have to talk so much?" snapped Alexander.

They decided to walk on.

Pasha tried, he tried to put one foot in front of the other, he tried to move his arms across his body to help propel him forward, but his shaking knees kept buckling. I'm going to rest a bit, mouthed Pasha, and then he said, I'll be all right. He sat down on the ground. Alexander held him up, stood him up, raised him up, then lifted him and threw him on his back.

"Captain—"

"One more word, Ouspensky, and with my bare hands—"

"Understood."

They walked, Alexander carrying Pasha all the gray morning. Alexander lowered him, gave him a drink of rain, raised him, carried him all the gray afternoon. Lowered him, gave him a drink of whisky, stuffed a piece of bread into his mouth, raised him, carried him.

Somewhere on a dirt road in south-east Saxony, Pasha felt heavier and heavier. Alexander thought he was getting tired. It was the end of the day. They broke camp, sat by the fire. Alexander went ice fishing in the pond by the woods. Caught one perch, cooked it in water. He made Pasha drink the fish broth with some diluted sulfa powder, and then he and Ouspensky divided the fish and ate it, head and all.

Ouspensky slept. Alexander smoked. And sat holding the ice rag against Pasha's burning head. Then Pasha was cold, and Alexander covered him up with two trench coats, and took the coat from Ouspensky for Pasha.

No one spoke anymore, not even to mouth the words.

Next morning, Pasha, his eyes swollen with fever, shook his head, as if to say, leave me. And Alexander shook his, and lifted Pasha and carried him. There was no sun, it was February in central Germany. The slate sky was meters above their heads. Alexander knew they couldn't stop and ask for help—they spoke no German without Pasha. He also knew that the Saxony police had no doubt been notified about three escapees and was looking for precisely three men, masquerading as Germans yet not speaking a word of German.

They couldn't get too far with a sick Pasha. He had to get better. They found a small barn and waited out the cold morning covered by hay. Sitting, listening to Pasha's breaking-up breathing, watching Pasha's struggle and his inflamed face was too much for Alexander. He got up. "We have to go. We have to keep moving."

"Can I have a word with you?" Ouspensky said.

"Absolutely not," said Alexander.

"Outside the barn, for a moment."

"I said no."

Ouspensky glanced at Pasha, whose eyes were closed. He seemed unconscious.

"Captain, he is getting worse."

"All right, Dr. Ouspensky, thank you, that will be all."

"What are we going to do?"

"We're going to continue. We just need to find a Red Cross convoy."

"There weren't any Red Cross personnel in Colditz or Catowice. What makes you think there will be some here?"

"Maybe Red Cross. Maybe Americans."

"Have the Americans gotten this far?"

"Ouspensky, like you, I've been in prison these last four months. How the fuck should I know how far the Americans have gotten? I think probably yes, they're here somewhere. Didn't you hear war planes headed to Dresden?"

"Captain—"

"Not another word about this, Lieutenant. Let's go."

"Go where? He needs help."

"And we have to get him help. Help isn't going to come to us in a barn."

He picked up Pasha and flung him on his back. Pasha could not hold on.

Alexander barely saw the road in front of him. It took all his effort to continue walking. Every hour he stopped and gave Pasha a drink, and pressed a cold rag against Pasha's head, and wrapped him tighter in two coats, and walked on again, without his own coat.

Ouspensky walked by his side.

Alexander heard Ouspensky's voice. "Captain," he called. "Captain."

"What?" He did not look sideways, as if he could. He continued walking. Ouspensky came up in front, crossed Alexander's path, made him stop. "What, Lieutenant?"

Ouspensky placed his hand on Alexander. "Captain. I'm sorry. He is dead."

Alexander moved him aside with his hand. "Get out of my way."

"He is dead, Captain. Please, let's not do this any longer."

"Ouspensky!" He took a deep breath and lowered his voice. "He is not dead. He is unconscious. Now, we have only a few hours of daylight left. Let's not waste it by standing in the middle of the road."

"He is dead, Captain," whispered Ouspensky. "Look for yourself."

"No," said Alexander. "He cannot die. It's impossible. Leave me alone. Either walk with me, or walk the other way, but leave me alone."

And he continued to walk with Pasha limp on his back, for another half-hour, another hour, and then Alexander slowed down on the unpaved empty road, stopped by a lone bare tree, and lowered Pasha to the ground. Pasha was no longer hot, and he was no longer struggling for breath. He was white and cold and his eyes were open.

"No, Pasha," whispered Alexander. "No." He felt Pasha's head. He closed Pasha's eyes. For a few moments he stood over Pasha, and then he sank to the ground. Wrapping him tightly with the trench coat, Alexander took Pasha's body into his arms and, cradling him from the cold, closed his own eyes.

For the rest of the night Alexander sat on an empty road, his back against the tree, not moving, not opening his eyes, not speaking, holding Tatiana's brother in his arms.

If Ouspensky spoke to him, he did not hear. If he slept, he did not feel it, not the cold air, nor the hard ground, nor the rough bark of the tree against his back, against his head.

When morning broke, and gray close light rose over Saxony, Alexander opened his eyes. Ouspensky was sleeping on his side, wrapped in his trench coat next to them. Pasha's body was rigid, very cold.

Alexander got up from under Pasha, washed his own face with whisky, rinsed out his mouth with whisky, and then got his titanium trench tool and started to carve a hole in the ground. Ouspensky woke up, helped him. It took them three hours of scraping at the earth, to make a hole a meter deep. Not deep enough, but it would have to do. Alexander covered Pasha's face with the trench coat so the earth wouldn't fall on it. With two small branches and a piece of string, Alexander made a cross and laid it on top of Pasha's chest, and then they lifted him and lowered him into the hole, and Alexander, his teeth grit the entire time, filled the shallow grave with fresh dirt. On a wide thick branch, he carved out the name PASHA METANOV, and the date, Feb 25, 1945, and tying it to another longer branch made another cross and staked it into the ground.

Alexander and Ouspensky stood still. Alexander saluted the grave. "The Lord is my shepherd," he mouthed inaudibly to himself. "I shall not want. He maketh me lie down in green pastures. He leadeth me to high waters, to the valley of death . . ." Alexander broke off. Sinking down near his tree by the road, he lit a cigarette.

Ouspensky asked if they were going to get going.

"No," Alexander said. "I'm going to sit here a while."

Hours went by.

Ouspensky asked again.

"Lieutenant," said Alexander, in a voice that was so defeated he did not recognize it as his own, "I am not walking away from him."

"Captain!" Ouspensky exclaimed. "What about those winds of fate you said were blowing at you?"

"You must have misunderstood, Nikolai," said Alexander, not looking up. "I said they were blowing *by* me."

The next day the German police picked them up, loaded them onto an armored truck and took them back to Colditz.

Alexander was badly beaten by the German guards and taken to solitary, where he spent so long he lost track of time.

With Pasha's death came the death of faith.

Release me, Tatiana, release me, forgive me, forget me, let me forget you. I want to be free of you, free of your face, free of your freedom, free of your fire, free, free, free.

The flight across the ocean was over, and with it all the warmth of his imagination. A numbness encroached on him, freezing him from the heart out, the anesthetic of despair creeping its tentacles over his tendons and his arteries, over his nerves and his veins until he was stiff inside and bereft of hope and bereft of Tatiana. Finally.

But not quite.

CHAPTER THIRTY

New York, April 1945

IN APRIL THE AMERICANS and Russians swarmed over Germany, and in the first week of May, Germany unconditionally surrendered. The European war was over. In the Pacific theater, the Americans continued to suffer bloodletting even as they beat back the Japanese from every beach head, from every island.

June 23 quietly came and went. Tatiana turned twenty-one. How long did they say you would mourn before the years dulled your pain? How long before the hand of time, tick, tick, tick, relentless days and nights and months and years chipped away at the stone of sorrow inside your throat until it was no more than a pebble with smooth sides? Every time you think his name, the air can't get past it, every time you look at his son, the air can't get past it. Every time it's Christmas, your birthday, his birthday, March 13, you can't breathe for a day, another day, another year. They fly by, the years, and yet the grief remains lodged in your throat, through which everything else in your life has to pass. Everything else: happiness for yourself, affection for other people, joy at living, at comfort, at convenience, laughter at your child, food on your plate, drink at your table, every prayer, every clasping of the hands, past it, past it, past it.

∽

In the summer of 1945, Vikki agreed to go to Arizona by train with Tatiana and Anthony. Tatiana wanted to take a vacation to celebrate her becoming a U.S. citizen.

On the way, Tatiana told Vikki they needed to make a short stop in Washington DC.

She did not go inside the State Department building this time but sat patiently on the bench on C Street under the trees while Vikki smoked and Anthony played on the grass, and Vikki finally said, "This is your idea of a short stop? We took only two weeks off."

Tatiana watched the workers saunter out for lunch. She watched Sam Gulotta come out and walk past her bench. Tatiana did not acknowledge him. He walked another ten yards, slowed down, then stopped. Turning around, he stared at her for a few moments, and slowly came back.

Raising her eyes to him, Tatiana said, "Hello. I don't want to bother you." She introduced him to Vikki.

Gulotta smiled and sat down next to her. "You're not bothering me. It's nice to see you. I have nothing new to tell you."

"Nothing at all?"

"No. Europe is becoming an awful mess." He paused. "I know I told you that when things relaxed a bit, I could perhaps make inquiries . . . but I was wrong about things becoming easier. They've become worse than ever. Us, France, Britain, the Soviets, all in Germany, and worse—all in Berlin. One diplomatic faux pas and we're in another world war next week."

"I know." She stood up. "Well, thank you."

"Have you become an American citizen yet?"

"Yes, just."

Gulotta said, "Do you want to go have a bite to eat? It's lunch, we can get a sandwich."

"I'd like to, maybe another time. But I brought you something. I made them this morning." Tatiana took out a bag full of meat *pirozhki*. "Last time you said you liked them . . ."

"Very much, thank you." He took the bag from her. "I would have liked lunch, too."

Tatiana and Sam said goodbye.

Vikki pinched Tatiana very hard after Sam was out of sight. "Tania, you vixen! You strumpet! You libertine! All this time you've been up to this!"

"Vikki, up to nothing," Tatiana said calmly.

"Oh yes? Is he married?"

"He was, yes." Tatiana paused, wondering if she should tell Vikki about Sam. She decided to tell. "His wife died three years ago in plane crash carrying medical supplies to our troops in Okinawa. He is raising his two boys by himself."

"Tatiana!"

"Vikki, I don't have time to explain to you."

"You've got two weeks. But we have thirteen million troops abroad, and as soon as we win this war, they're all coming home through the Port of New York."

"Oh yes? Because United States has no other coastal city?"

"That's right. Now tell me why you have to go all the way to Washington to find a man when our beautiful New York is going to have thirteen million?"

"Not speaking to you about it."

ᏱᎷᏒᎯᎧ

After spending five days at the Grand Canyon, Tatiana drove a rented car south through Arizona, headed for Tucson. Vikki, being a city girl, did not know how to drive.

They stopped in Phoenix. "Just a dusty, one-horse village," Vikki called it. One scorching summer evening they were sitting on a blanket on the hood of their car, looking at the sunset. The Sonoran Desert, covered with white saguaros, stretches for hundreds of miles across southeastern Arizona. Home to 298 varieties of cactus, it is the largest desert in North America, spanning much of Arizona and New Mexico. In the near distance are the foothills of the Maricopa mountains. The indigo blue sky stands in stark contrast to the brick and cream hue of the earth. Except for the flickering of an occasional jackrabbit chasing a previously motionless Gila monster, the desert is silent.

They sat on the hood of the sedan, their backs to the windshield, northwest of the Superstition Mountains. Anthony crawled on the ground, at two years old interested in only two things: getting as mucky as possible and finding a snake, not necessarily in that order.

"Anthony," called Vikki, wiping the perspiration off her face. "Get off the ground. Do you know that snakes swallow their food whole?"

"All right, Vikki," said Tatiana. "Enough."

"Whole, Anthony," Vikki repeated.

"But I big boy. I want small snake." Anthony was verbal for a boy of two.

"You're not a big boy. You're a small boy."

"Vikki."

"What?"

Tatiana said nothing, just stared at Vikki.

"Why do you do that? You call out my name, as if that's enough for me to know exactly what you want. Vikki what?"

"You know what."

"No, I'm not going to stop. Aren't you at all concerned?"

"Not really," said Tatiana. "Anthony, you find snake, you let me know. We take snake back to New York and cook it."

"That'll be a nice change from bacon. For your next birthday," said Vikki, leaning back and taking a drink, "I'm going to buy you a book on mothering, a book on cooking, and also some 'a's and 'the's. You don't seem to have any."

"Some what?"

"Never mind. But seriously though, Tania, you eat Planter's peanuts, don't you?"

"What?"

"Planter's peanuts."

"No, I don't like peanuts."

"What does the ad for them read in Times Square? We passed it the other day."

"I don't know. I think it reads, *Planter's peanuts: a bag a day for more pep.*'"

"Exactly. Very good. Now, if you had your way with that line, it would read, *'bag day for more pep.'* Do you see the difference?"

"No." With a straight face.

"Oh, God."

Tatiana turned away and smiled. She got out a bottle of Coke from her bag and passed it to Vikki, saying, " *Drink Coca Cola. A pause that refreshes.'* "

"Very good!" Vikki said, her eyes, her teeth gleaming at Tatiana.

Anthony did not find a snake but did become exhausted by his search efforts. He climbed onto the car, onto Tatiana's lap, dusty, hands grimy, and nuzzled his head into her chest. She gave him a drink of water.

Sitting close against Vikki with Anthony cradled on her lap, Tatiana said, "Quite beautiful, no?"

"Your son?" Vikki leaned over and kissed him. "Yes. The desert's barren." She shrugged. "It's nice for a change of pace. I wouldn't want to live here, there's nothing but cacti."

"In spring all wildflowers bloom to life. It must be even better here in spring."

"New York is beautiful in the spring."

Tatiana didn't say anything at first. Then she said, "The desert is amazing—"

"Desert is okay. Have you ever seen a steppe?"

Tatiana paused before replying. "Yes," she said slowly. "It's not this. The steppe is cold and bleak. Here, yes, it's over ninety degrees now, but in December, near Christmas, it will be seventy. The sun will be high in sky. It won't be dark. In December, all I will wear for cover is long-sleeve shirt."

"What do they wear in this Arizona in the winter?" Dasha asks Alexander.

"A long-sleeve shirt."

"Now I know you're telling me fairy tales. Tell them to Tania. I'm too old for fairy tales."

"Tania, you believe me, don't you?"

"Yes, Alexander."

"Would you like to live in Arizona, the land of the small spring?"

"Yes, Alexander."

"So?" said Vikki. "It's broiling here right now. We're going to become scrambled eggs if we don't start driving."

Tatiana shuddered briefly, to shake off the memories. "I'm just saying. It's nothing like steppe. I like it here."

Shrugging, Vikki said, "But Tania, it's the middle of nowhere."

"I know. Fantastic, isn't it? No people anywhere."

"That's fantastic?"

"A little . . . yes."

"Well, I can't imagine anyone wanting to buy this land or live here."

Tatiana cleared her throat. "What about your friend?" she said.

"Which one?"

"Me."

"You want to live here?" Vikki paused and turned her head. "Or do you want to buy this land?" she said incredulously.

Quietly, Tatiana said, "Imagine I purchased some saguaro cactus and sagebrush land in Sonoran Desert."

"Not for a second."

Tatiana was silent.

"Did you buy this land?"

Tatiana nodded.

"This very land?"

She nodded.

"When?"

"Last year. When I come here with Anthony."

"I knew I should have come with you! Why? And with what?"

"I liked it." She looked at the expanse of earth stretching out to the mountains. "I never own anything in my life. I bought it with money I brought with me from Soviet Union." With Alexander's money.

"But God, why *this* land?" Vikki looked at her. "I bet it was cheap."

"It *was* cheap." It cost only four lives. Harold's. Jane's. Alexander's. And Tatiana's. Tatiana pressed Anthony closer to her chest.

"Hmm," Vikki said, studying Tatiana. "Are you going to be full of these kinds of surprises? Or is this it?"

"This is it." Tatiana smiled and didn't say anything after that but stared west into the valley, into the sunset, into the mighty saguaro cactus, into the desert, into four thousand eight hundred and fifty dollars that had bought ninety-seven acres of the United States of America.

CHAPTER THIRTY-ONE

Out of Colditz, April 1945

THE AMERICANS LIBERATED COLDITZ in April after three days of fighting, or so it was rumored, for though Alexander heard the gunfire, he saw only a handful of Americans out in the courtyard. He managed to approach a group of them, asking for a cigarette, and, while bending over the lighter flame, he said to one private in English that he was an American named Alexander Barrington and maybe if his story checked out, he could be helped?

And the U.S. soldier laughed and said, "Yeah, and I'm the King of England."

Alexander opened his mouth and Ouspensky came up to ask for a cigarette himself.

Alexander thought he would have another chance, but there was to be no other chance, because very early the next morning after the American liberation, Soviet officials, a general, two colonels, a deputy associate foreign minister or something, along with a hundred troops, came into Colditz to take the seven Soviet men "to join up with their brothers in the victorious march on defeated Germany."

They were put on a train. A whole train for only *seven* of them? thought Alexander, but it turned out the train was full of Soviet men. Not all of them were soldiers, some were workers, some were residents of Poland. Thousands of such men were on that train. One, a concrete mixer, said he was living with his family in Bavaria, a wife and three children, when he was apprehended. Others echoed that. "I had a family, too. A mother, two sisters, three nieces after my brother died." Where were the family members? Alexander wondered. "We left them, left them where they were," said the man.

"But why didn't you take your family with you?" inquired Ouspensky, who was shackled to Alexander.

The concrete man didn't reply.

The train continued slowly west through central Germany. Most of the road signs had been destroyed, it was impossible to tell where they were. They seemed to have traveled hundreds of kilometers. Alexander saw a small sign that said, Gottinger, 9. Where was Gottinger?

The train was stopped and they were all told to get off. After walking for two hours, they found themselves at what looked like an abandoned POW camp. The NKGB troops—by now Alexander realized they couldn't be Red Army men, since the Red Army men were all roped to each other—requisitioned the grounds and called it a transit camp.

"A transit camp to where?" ask Ouspensky. No one answered him.

Then they changed the camp's name to a screening and identification camp.

In this camp they lived for the last two weeks of April 1945, surrounded by barbed wire, watching perimeter lights being put up and watchtowers being hastily built. Then they heard that the war was over, that Hitler was dead.

The day after Germany's surrender, the fields beyond the electrified barbed wire were mined. Alexander and Ouspensky knew this because they watched at least a half-dozen Soviet men—including the concrete mixer—go to war with those mines and lose.

"What do they know that we don't know?" Ouspensky asked with suspicion, as they watched with a group of others as the bodies of the escapees were dumped into mass graves.

"Not just that," said Alexander, "but what do they know that makes them run across a mined field rather than remain in a fairly innocuous transit camp?"

"They don't want to go home," said another man.

"Yes, but why?" said Ouspensky.

Alexander lit a cigarette and said nothing.

He wondered why the camp was being run under military discipline, despite having so many civilians in it. There was reveille and taps, there was curfew and military inspection of the barracks and clear assignation of duties. It was all peculiar and puzzling.

ᨑᨒᨑᨑᨒ

A few days later, Ivan Skotonov, deputy associate foreign minister, sent straight from Moscow, came to speak to the men. They were not allowed to stand as a crowd; they were made to stand in rows. It was a windy May day; Skotonov, greasy-haired and in a suit, could barely be heard. Finally he took a loudspeaker. "Citizens! Comrades!" he said. "Proud sons of

Russia! You have helped to defeat an enemy such as our great nation has never known! Your country is proud of you! Your country loves you! Your country needs you again to rebuild, to reconstruct, to help make once again great the land that our Splendid Leader and Teacher Comrade Stalin saved for us. Your country calls for you. You will come back with us, and your country will greet you as heroes and shower you with applause!"

Alexander thought back to the concrete mixer from Bavaria who had left his wife and children behind and then run across a mined field to get back to them.

"What if we don't want to come back?" someone shouted.

"Yes, we had a life in Innsbruck, why should we have to leave it?"

"Because you are Soviet nationals," Skotonov shouted back amiably. "You don't belong in Innsbruck. You belong back home!"

"I'm from Poland," the man shouted back. "From Krakow. Why do *I* have to go back?"

"That part of Poland has been disputed for centuries, and the Soviet Union has decreed that it is part of our Motherland!"

That evening after the speech, twenty-four men attempted to escape. One even unprimed a clean swathe through the mined field before he was stopped by a bullet from the sentry's rifle. "He was wounded, not killed," Skotonov assured the skittish mob the following morning. But the man was not seen again.

There seemed to be three types of people in the camp: refugees from the German occupation of places like Poland, Romania, Czechoslovakia, and the Ukraine; forced labor workers who were taken in by the Germans for their own war machine; and Red Army soldiers like Alexander and Ouspensky.

These three groups were separated at the end of May, and quartered and fed separately. Little by little the refugees started filtering out of the camp, and then the forced labor workers.

"Always at night, have you noticed?" said Alexander. "We wake up, they're not here. I wish I could keep my eyes open at three in the morning, I have a feeling we'd see quite a bit going on."

In the yard while on his daily walk, he met a forced labor man who asked for a cigarette and said to him, "Have you heard? Five of the guys I been with the last four years have disappeared last night. Did you hear them? They were taken out and sentenced, right in the common area."

"Sentenced for what?" said Ouspensky.

"For treason against the Motherland. For working for the enemy."

"Maybe they should have explained that they were *forced* to work."

"They tried. But if they really didn't want to work for the Germans, why didn't they try to escape?"

"Maybe we could try to escape," said Ouspensky. "Huh, Captain?"

A Polish man came up behind them, laughed and said, "There is no escape. Escape to where?" Alexander and Ouspensky turned around. There was now a small crowd standing in the yard. The Polish man shook their hands and said, "Lech Markiewicz. Pleased to make your acquaintance. No escape, citizens. Do you know who delivered me into Soviet hands, all the way from Cherbourg, France?"

They waited.

"The English."

"And do you know who delivered my friend, Vasia over here, into Soviet hands, all the way from Brussels? The French."

Vasia nodded.

"And do you know who delivered Stepan into Soviet hands, all the way from Ravensburg, Bavaria, just ten kilometers from Lake Constance and Switzerland? The Americans. That's right. The Allies are helpfully returning us, millions of us, to the Soviets. In the transit camp I was in before this one, in Lübeck, north of Hamburg, there were refugees from Denmark and Norway. Not soldiers like you, and not forced labor workers like me, but refugees, made homeless by war, trying to find a place to hang their hat in Copenhagen. All returned to the Soviets. So don't talk to me about escape. Time for escape has long passed. There is nowhere to go anymore. All of Europe used to belong to Hitler. Half of Europe now belongs to the Soviet Union."

And he laughed and walked away, linking his arms with Vasia and Stepan.

But that night, Lech Markiewicz, an electrician by trade, shorted out the electrified fence and ran. He was not in camp the following morning. No one knew what became of him.

෴

The convoys came each night to take the men away, hundreds by hundreds, and during the day, the camp was maintained as a waystation to somewhere else. They were fed badly, they were allowed a bath once a week, they were regularly shaved and deloused. Yet, little by little new Russians kept coming in, old Russians kept shipping out.

One late July night, Alexander and Ouspensky were woken with all their quartermates, told to pack what was theirs, and taken out to the back of the camp. Three trucks were waiting for them. They were all paired up and tied to their partners. Alexander was chained to Ouspensky. They were driven some distance in the night, Alexander guessed to a train station, and he was right.

CHAPTER THIRTY-TWO

New York, August 1945

ON THE LOWER EAST Side, Tatiana, Vikki, and Anthony were strolling one summer Saturday, late morning, through the outdoor market under the El on Second Avenue. They were talking, like every person on the street, about the Japanese surrender a week ago following the atomic devastation of Nagasaki. Vikki thought the second bomb was unnecessary. Tatiana pointed out that the Japanese had not surrendered after Hiroshima. "We didn't give them enough time. Three days, what's that? We should have given them extra days for their imperial pride. Why else do you think they kept killing us these last three months even though they knew they would never win?"

"I don't know. Why did Germans? They knew their war was lost in 1943."

"That's because Hitler was a madman."

"And Hirohito, what was he?" Suddenly, Tatiana was stopped—no, besieged—by a family of what seemed like sixty. Actually it was six people, a husband, a wife, and their four teenaged children. First, they grabbed Tatiana's hands, then her arms, then enveloped her entire body.

"Tania? Tania? Are you there?" Vikki said.

Stroking Tatiana's hair, the woman murmured in Ukrainian. The man wiped his eyes and handed Anthony an ice cream and a lollipop, which Anthony took with a two-year-old smile and promptly dropped on the sidewalk.

"Who are these people?" Vikki asked.

"Mama knows a wot of people," said Anthony, tugging at Tatiana's skirt.

Straightening up, Vikki muttered, "That's certainly true. Just no men."

"Ice kweem, Mama. I want ice kweem."

The family talked to Tatiana in Ukrainian and she spoke Russian back to them. They kissed her hands and at last moved on. With Anthony, Tatiana and Vikki moved on, too.

"Tatiana!"

"What?"

"Are you going to explain to us the scene we just witnessed?"

"Anthony needs no explanation, do you, honey?"

"No, Mama. Need ice kweem."

After getting her son another ice cream and a lollipop, Tatiana glanced at Vikki and shrugged. "What? Slavic people very emotional."

"They weren't overreacting. They were genuflecting. I think they sprinkled gold dust at your feet. By their hand gestures alone, I could tell they were about to sacrifice their firstborn at your altar."

Tatiana laughed. "Listen, I tell you, it was nothing. Few months ago, they came in to Port of New York. The man had sent his wife and children at beginning of German occupation of Ukraine to Turkey. He was POW for two years, then escaped into Turkey and spent over year looking for them in Ankara. Finally found them in 1944. They arrived month ago in July in PNY without papers but in good health. But we getting too many refugees. The man, even without papers, could stay, because he do work, do something. Lay bricks, paint, whatever. But his wife can't sew, can't knit and can't speak English. She lived in Turkey for three years begging on streets for her children." Tatiana shook her head. "I wish they spoke bit of English. Everything would be much more easy. So what can I do? They were all going to be sent back." She leaned down, adjusting the baseball cap on Anthony's head and wiping the vanilla ice cream off his chin. "Imagine their reaction when I say husband can stay but rest have to go back. Go back where? they asked me. Go back to Ukraine? We escaped! We are going straight to camps, we are never coming out. Five women, do you know what would happen to us in camps? So what I can do, Vikki? I went and found mother job cleaning house for shop owner. The daughters become baby-sitters for shop owner's three young children. They stayed in Ellis until I got INS man to issue them temporary visas." Tatiana shrugged. "It's crazy over at Ellis, these days, crazy. They want to send everybody back. Just today, man was being sent back to Lithuania, and there was nothing wrong with him, he had little infection in his right ear! They put him in detention center, and tomorrow, he was going back just like that. Because his ear was red!" Tatiana was flushed in the face. "I found this poor thing, sitting in room bawling his eyes out. He said his wife had been in United States waiting for him for two years. They were tailors. So I checked his ear out—"

"Wait, wait, what INS man?" Vikki asked. "You don't mean the vulture, the viper, Vittorio, the marauder, Vassman?"

"Yes, him. He nice man."

Vikki laughed. "His own mother can't get a parking space in her son's garage. You got him to issue temporary visas? What did you have to do for him?"

"I made *pirozhki* for his ailing mother and *blinchiki* for him and told him he was making success of very difficult job."

"Did you go to bed with him?"

Tatiana sighed. "You impossible."

⁂

"Edward, have you heard what Tania is doing at Ellis?"

"Oh, I know all about it."

They were having lunch at the Ellis cafeteria, which was now full of nurses and doctors, since Ellis had become, once again, a refugee port. One of those nurses was not Brenda, who, to everybody's enormous surprise, quit in June 1945 when her husband came home from the Pacific. No one even knew that Brenda had a husband.

Vikki told Edward the Lower East Side story.

Edward nodded, looking fondly at Tatiana; in fact, looking at Tatiana in a way that made Tatiana look away and Vikki's eyes widen. "Vik," he said, "the entire Ellis Island knows about Tatiana. Why do you think they don't let her go on the refugee boats anymore? She lets in every single person on those boats. They know of her halfway across the ocean. Oh, to get into Tatiana's inspection line, to get her to touch them."

"The refugees I understand. But how does she get Vassman to issue them visas?"

"She hypnotizes him every morning. If that doesn't work, she slips something into his coffee."

"You're implying she sees him in the *morning?*"

"You two have to finish, all right?" said Tatiana. "You just have to stop."

Edward continued. "Just the other day, I had three women come looking for her on a Saturday afternoon. They took a ferry to Ellis to look for her."

"Much like your wife used to look for you?" Tatiana asked mildly.

"No, not quite," Edward returned. "My soon to be former wife was not coming to offer me her life services the way these people come to Ellis seeking you."

"I don't know what you talking about," Tatiana said. "They come to bring me apples."

"Apples, a shirt, four books." He smiled. "You weren't there. I told them I could give them your address—"

"Edward!" The girls shouted in unison.

He laughed. "Apples delivered right to your door, no?"

"No." Tatiana said.

⟨ೲ⟩

At the newspaper stand, the man who sold Tatiana and Vikki the *Tribune* looked at Tatiana and said, "You're Nurse Tatiana, aren't you?"

Instantly alert, Tatiana said, "Who wants to know?"

The kiosk man smiled. "They call you the Angel of Ellis. Take the paper. Don't pay me. Take it. I have a hundred customers because of you."

As they walked away, Vikki said, "I'm beginning to understand. Oh, my God. You're not doing it for *them*."

"Doing what?"

"You're doing it for *you*. You said to that man, *who wants to know*, as if you're waiting for the person who wants to know if you're Nurse Tatiana."

"Wrong again. How can you be so wrong in one day?"

"Who are you waiting for?"

"It remains from old days," Tatiana said. "Someone looking for you, it's bad sign."

"You're full of shit. Who are you waiting for?"

"No one."

"When do you find the time? You have a child. You have two jobs. And I live with you. When do you have time to lead a secret life?"

"What secret? I do nothing. Occasionally I ask our building super if they looking for another doorman. Is that so hard?"

"I don't know. I don't ask. Why should *you*?"

"Because it costs me nothing," Tatiana replied. "But now Diego from Romania is gainfully employed."

"What a gas you are," said Vikki, as she opened the door, putting her arm around Tatiana. "Is this your legacy to America?"

"It is not my legacy," said Tatiana, walking inside. "It is my thanks."

⟨〜〜〜⟩

Vikki was frequently not home in the evenings. She went out dancing, and to the pictures, she went to dinner, she met friends at bars. When she came home late at night, she often had had too much to drink and wanted to talk, and Tatiana, usually awake no matter what time Vikki came home, obliged her. One evening, though, Tatiana was already in bed sleeping. This did not deter Vikki, who threw off her dress and climbed in next to her. Vikki put her hands over her head and then sighed extravagantly.

"Yes?" said Tatiana.

"Oh, you're not asleep?"

"Not anymore."

Vikki took her hands away from her face. She looked tipsy. "Oh, Tania, Tania. I couldn't get a taxi. Walked all the way home from Astor Place in my high heels. I'm so sore."

Tatiana heard Vikki crying. Drinking at night tended to make all the Italian emotions come out in Vikki. Tatiana reached over and stroked Vikki's hair. "What's the matter, Gelsomina?"

"What am I looking for, Tania? What? I went out with a real idiot tonight, no, such a creep. Todd. From last week."

"I told you stay away from him."

"He was so nice at first."

"You mean last week?"

"Yes. But this week he is all demanding and creepy. Roughed me up outside Ricardo's. Grabbed me too hard. Thank God a car drove by. He wanted to come home with me and wouldn't take no for an answer."

"Why should he? You said yes to him first time you saw him."

"I just want to meet a nice man who loves me. What's wrong with that?"

Did Dasha go out every Friday and Saturday night after work and get involved with her boss, a married dentist, because she wanted to meet a nice man who loved her, too? And then she met a nice man, a tall Red Army officer in Sadko. ("Tania, wait till you meet him. You've never met anyone so handsome!")

"Nothing."

"I want that Harry back. Harry—he was such a sweetie."

He was a drunk. Tatiana didn't say anything.

"I want Jude back, or Mark, or even my former husband. Before the war ended it was better. Now they come back and they want us, they just don't know how to treat us. They want us to be like their war buddies."

"Do we know how to treat them?"

"I want my loving heart back," said Vikki, crying. "You know what I'm afraid of? That I will turn out like my mother. Rootless. I don't want to be like her. They say we all turn out like our mothers, you believe that?" Before Tatiana had a chance to answer, Vikki went on. "My mother left me, left New York, went abroad, traveled, loved, I guess, but ended up in a home somewhere in Montecito, imagine, I don't even know where Montecito is and my mother found a loony bin there."

"I'm sorry for her. And about her."

"You know what I think sometimes?" Vikki whispered with a small sob. "Sometimes I think I want my mother back. Isn't that ridiculous?"

"No," said Tatiana. "I want *my* mother back."

"Did you have a good mother?"

"I don't know. She was my mother, that's all."

"Did you have a good sister?"

"I had a very good sister," Tatiana whispered. "She carried me on her back when I was young and protected me from bad boys her whole life. I want them all back. My sister, my brother." She closed her eyes. *Pasha and Tania holding on to the same rope, swinging over the River Luga, one swing, two, three, letting go, and falling in, Pasha and Tania running flat out to the banks of the Luga, taking a running jump and diving in.*

"But don't you want love, too? I want love. A nice two-bedroom Levitt house in the suburbs of Long Island, a car, two kids. I want what my grandparents have. For forty-three years they've had each other."

"Vikki, you don't want that. You don't want kids. It's not for you. You have wandering heart."

Vikki squinted in the dark at Tatiana. Mascara was spread in black globs under Vikki's eyes. "I *could* have that."

Without taking her hand away from Vikki's hair, Tatiana shook her head.

"What do you know about anything? You never leave this apartment."

"Where do I have to go? I'm home."

"Do you?" asked Vikki, reaching out and touching Tatiana's hair. "Do *you* have a wandering heart?"

"I wish I did."

Vikki moved over and put her arms around Tatiana, who shut tight her eyes and lay nestled into Vikki, the way she once, a lifetime ago, used to sleep at the Fifth Soviet apartment, nestled into Dasha.

"Tania," said Vikki, "how could you have not given yourself to anyone all this time?"

Tatiana made no reply.

"Have you been with a man other than your husband?"

Tatiana moved away in the bed. To bear it in the night next to someone else was beyond her strength, beyond her limits. "No," she said in a low voice. "I fell in love when I was sixteen. I never loved anyone else. I never been with anyone else."

"Oh, Tania. My Grammy was right about you. She said that girl is still getting over her Travis."

Tatiana said nothing. Vikki inched over, putting her arms around her again.

"But you have his son. Isn't he a comfort to you?"

"When I don't think of his father, yes."

"But don't you want love again? Happiness? Marriage? God, Tatiana," Vikki breathed out. "You have . . . so much to give." She held Tatiana closer. "Edward's divorce has come through. Why don't you go to dinner with him? Why do you always keep him at lunch length?"

"Edward deserves better than me."

"Edward doesn't think so. I don't think so."

Tatiana laughed lightly, caressing Vikki's arms. "I'll get there," she whispered. "You said so yourself, I'll get there."

Hours in the dark, and they were not sleeping. Vikki sobered up a bit, drank some water. She was smoking and lying in bed under the covers.

"Please tell me you'll go to dinner with him. What can one dinner hurt?"

"What do you matter about all this?"

Vikki laughed. "I *care*," she emphasized, "because I know he wants to. And because I think you would be adorable together."

"Together? Forget everything. You said dinner."

"Yes. Dinner together."

"Together implies a number of dinners. Maybe even Levitt house."

"And that would be wrong, why?"

"I go to sleep now. You do what you like."

She couldn't tell Vikki about the ugly thoughts. She couldn't tell Vikki about the beautiful thoughts. She couldn't tell Vikki about the sky, or the sorrow.

How comforting it was to sleep next to another human being. Not to be alone. How comforting it was to feel a breathing body, and a trembling heart, to feel someone's dark hair on your shoulders, to feel, to feel.

⌒⌒⌒

All Vova has to say is, "Don't worry, Alexander. We'll take good care of Tania when you're gone."

At home she sits helplessly before him in the chair, looking flummoxed.

"Let me ask you," Alexander says, his voice dripping with sarcasm, and Tatiana says, "Shura, darling—"

"Let me ask you," he repeats, louder. "Don't interrupt me." He is pacing in front of her like a caged animal. "Just tell me, how long do you think you might wait before you let Vova take care of you? Oh, and maybe the guitar-wielding Vlasik, maybe you can ask him what else he wields. Ask him if he delivers the goods. Or would you like me to speak to him personally?"

She looks at him slightly aghast. She says nothing. She is not angry with him, how could she be when she knows he adores her, when she knows all he wants to do is to love her less.

"Answer me, dammit," he says, taking a menacing step toward her.

She sits in the chair, her hands clasped between her breasts. "I beg you—"

"Beg me all you want," he returns cruelly. "Would you like me to speak to Vlasik personally? Or are you going to use the words I taught you on him, perhaps when you're missing me?" His eyes are flaming. He grabs her by her arm and yanks her to her feet.

Tatiana pulls at his hand. "Let go of me." Backing away from him, she finds herself wedged between her sewing table and the brick wall of the peasant oven. Stepping forward, she tries to get past him into the open space of the cabin, but Alexander doesn't move out of her way and does not let her pass, shoving her lightly back into the corner with his body. "We're not done here," he says.

"Shura!"

"Don't raise your voice to me!"

"Shura! Stop it!" she says loudly and again attempts to get past him, but he does not let her out of the corner, this time pushing her back with his hands. "I said stop it! Stop. This is all for nothing."

"*To you it's nothing.*"

"*Are you out of your mind?*" She rams her body against him. "*Get out of my way.*"

"*Make me.*"

"*Shura!*" she screams. She tries very hard not to cry. She is shaking. "*Please, stop.*" From the effort not to cry, her lower lip begins to tremble. Above her, Alexander slams his head against the wall. And then he steps away.

"*What do you think, Alexander, that I will care less you're leaving if you do this? Keep going. Do you think this will make me glad to see the back of you? That anything in the world is going to make it easier for me once you're gone?*"

"*You seem to think so,*" Alexander replies, backing farther away from her.

Tatiana watches him, her eyes clearing for a moment. "*Wait a minute. This isn't about me. This isn't about me at all.*" She emits a stifled groan. "*It's you—you think that if you imagine me taking up with every village idiot, your feeling for me will fade? You think, if only Tania betrays me, it will be so much easier for me to die, to leave her, to abandon her.*"

"*Tania, shut up.*"

"*No!*" she shouts. "*That's what you want, isn't it? Imagine the worst, and then suddenly I'm not your wife, I'm just some slag with no heart, how perfect, and my husband is free. I'm a slag who has found another knocker to replace yours in minutes.*" She is so upset that she clenches her fists.

"*Tania, I told you, shut the hell up!*"

"*No!*" she yells, jumping on the hearth so she can be a little taller, feel a little braver. "*That's what you want, what you need, to imagine the impossible to rid yourself of me.*" Tears trickle down her face. "*Well, I don't give a damn how much you need it,*" she says furiously. "*I'm not giving it to you. I'm not giving that to you. You can have anything else, but I will not pretend to whore myself out just so you can feel better about leaving me.*"

"*You're going to stop, do you hear?*"

"*Or what?*" she says. "*Make me, Alexander. Because I'm not keeping quiet about this.*"

"*No, of course not!*" he shouts, helplessly kicking their kettle across the room.

"*That's right!*" she shouts back. "*You won't have this. You want a fight? I'll give you a fight for this.*"

He grits his teeth and comes for her. "*You don't know what a fight is,*" he says, yanking her off the hearth, ripping her dress from her chest to her *hips, pulling her down to the wood floor, holding her down, tearing off her underwear, prying her legs open, descending on her.*

Tatiana closes her eyes.

He is rough with her. She doesn't want to hold him at first, but it is impossible not to hold his anguished body. "Soldier . . ." she manages through her groans. "You can't take me, you can't leave me—"

"I can take you," he whispers.

Suddenly uttering a helpless groan, he pulls away and goes outside, leaving Tatiana on the floor, where she lies curled into a ball, coughing, panting.

He is on the bench, smoking. His hands are shaking. Tatiana, wrapped in a white sheet, stands in front of him. Her voice is shaking. "Tomorrow," she says, barely able to get the words out, "is our last day here in Lazarevo." She can't look at him and he can't look at her. "Please, let's not do this."

"All right, let's not."

She lets the sheet fall to the ground and comes close to his knees. "Careful," Alexander says quietly, glancing at his lit cigarette.

"It's too late for careful," replies Tatiana. "Our destruction is close. What do I care about your cigarette?"

For a long time in bed in the dark Alexander holds her to his warm chest, without talking, without moving, nearly without breathing, without finishing what he had started earlier.

Finally he speaks. "I cannot take you with me," he says. "You'll be in too much danger. I cannot risk—"

"Shh." Tatiana kisses his chest. "I know. Shura, I'm yours. You may not like it today, you may not want it tonight, you may wish for it all to be different now, but it remains, and I remain, as always, only yours. Nothing can change that. Not your wrath, your fists, your body, or your death."

He emits a grinding rasp.

"Darling, honey." She starts to cry. "We are orphans, Alexander, you and I. All we have is each other. I know that you lost everyone you ever loved, but you're not going to lose me. I swear to you on my wedding band, and on my maiden ring that you broke, on my heart you're breaking, and on your life, I swear to you, I will forever be your faithful wife."

"Tania," he whispers, "promise you won't forget me when I die."

"You won't die, soldier," she says. "You won't die. Live! Live on, breathe on, claw onto life, and do not let go. Promise you will live for me, and I promise you, when you're done, I will be waiting for you." She is sobbing. "Whenever you're done, Alexander, I will be here, waiting for you."

⟨∞⟩

Such brave words near their death in the moonless Lazarevo.

⟨∞⟩

Life showed itself in small things. In the dockhand sailor who stood near the gangplank of the ferry she boarded each morning, who smiled and said good morning, offered her a cup of coffee, a cigarette, and then sat with her on deck for the thirteen-minute ride. In Benjamin, the second baseman, who ran into her when he was trying to catch a foul ball, knocked her over, and then lay almost directly on top of her, not getting up for a few moments. Enough moments for Edward, the catcher, to come over and say, all right, break it up here, this is a softball game, not Ricardo's. In Vikki putting lipstick on Tatiana's face every morning before leaving for work, and kissing her on the cheek, and Tatiana wiping the lipstick off as she left the house.

In the one morning Tatiana not wiping the lipstick off.

And in the one Friday night not saying no to Ricardo's.

Life showed itself in the stockbroker in his suit in the coffee shop on Church and Wall Street sitting next to Tatiana and Vikki, laughing at their conversation.

In the father of a family Tatiana helped get into the country coming to see her at Ellis and asking her to marry his oldest son, who was a bricklayer and could support her well. The father brought the lad by so Tatiana could take a look for herself. He was a tall, strong, smiling boy of about eighteen, and he looked at Tatiana with the sweet expression of a long-term crush. Tatiana had coffee with him in the Ellis dining room, telling him she was flattered but couldn't marry him.

Life showed itself in the lunch she had with Edward twice a week.

In the construction workers and the Con Edison workers downtown and the smiling hot dog man who had sold her a Coke and a hot dog.

Tatiana spent all day on the ships, inspecting the new post-war refugees, shepherding them onto the ferry to Ellis, or else at Ellis examining them in the medical rooms. In the afternoons, she went to NYU hospital, walking through all the beds, looking at every male face. If *he* were going to come, he would come into one of those two places—Ellis or NYU. But the war had ended four months ago. So far only a million troops had been sent back home, a good 300,000 through New York.

How many times could Tatiana ask the wounded, where did you fight? Where were you stationed? In Europe? Did you meet any Soviet officers in the POW camps? Did any Soviet soldiers speak English to you? Tatiana met every boat that came in through the Port of New York, looking into the countless faces of the escapees from Europe. How many times could she hear from American soldiers about the horrors they saw in Nazi Germany? How many stories of what happened to Soviet prisoners in German camps? How many accounts of the numbers dead? Of the hundreds of thousands dead, of the millions dead? No plasma, no penicillin could have saved the Soviet men as they were starved by the Germans. How long could she hear the same thing over and over?

And then at night, she collected Anthony from Isabella's and she and Vikki had dinner there and chatted about books and movies and the latest fashion trend. And then they went home and put Anthony to bed. And then they would sit on the couch and read, or talk. And the next day it would begin again.

And then another week would begin.

And another.

And another.

Every month she went with Anthony to visit Esther and Rosa. They had no news.

Every month she called Sam Gulotta. He had no news.

New York's new construction was happening at a rate seven times the rest of the country's. The refugees to Ellis stopped being refugees and became immigrants once more. The veterans left NYU except for the long-term ward. Every week, she checked her post office box. But no one wrote to her. She waited for him against all reason, and danced on Saturday night, and went to the movies on Friday night, and cooked dinner and played softball in Central Park, and read books in English, and went out with Vikki and loved her boy, and through it all, she looked at every man's face that came her way, at every man's back, hoping for his face, for his back. If he could have come to her, he would have. He didn't.

If he could have found a way to escape, he would have. He didn't. If he were alive, she would have heard from him.

She hadn't.

"This is just the beginning of your life, Tatiana," he says to her. "After three hundred million years, you'll still be standing, too."

"Yes," she whispers. "But not with you."

CHAPTER THIRTY-THREE

The Motherland, 1945

THE TRAIN WAS STOPPED, once, twice, fifteen times along the way, the way to where? Alexander told Ouspensky they would know when it was their turn. But they didn't. They changed trains always in the middle of the night. Alexander felt as though he were hallucinating when he rattled his chains across the tracks, up the metal steps. He couldn't wait to lie down on the wooden shelf and close his eyes.

Alexander's train pushed east on the tracks. The train car shook the bodies of the chained men headed from war back to the Motherland, while Alexander and Nikolai ate thin gruel out of one bowl that spilled each time the train lurched.

Over the plains and the forests and over the Elbe, the train continued.

Alexander covered his face with the crook of his arm. The Kama was covered in ice. Through the night in front of him was her laughing, freckled face.

Through the mountains the train sped, past the pines and the moss and the stone treasure caves.

Days and days and nights and nights, a cycle of the moon, and still they were not done.

They had gruel for breakfast, for dinner.

It got cold inside the train car at night. The northern German plateau lay vast around them.

He slept.

He dreamed of her.

She wakes up screaming, and sits up in bed pushing away something in front of her. Alexander, murky from sleep, sits up slightly behind her. "Tania," he says and gets hold of one of her arms. With astonishing strength, she rips herself away from him in defined fear and fury and without even turning around, with the back of her clenched fist, punches him square in the face. He is unprepared and has no time to move. His nose opens up like a dam. He is less sleepy. Concerned for her, he grabs her by the arms, this time much tighter, and says in his loudest, deepest voice, "Tania!" All the while the blood streams from his nose down his mouth and chin and chest. It is the middle of the night, and the bright blue moon outside illuminates just enough of the cabin to see her bare silhouette panting in front of him, and to see black drops falling on the white sheet.

Tania comes to, breathes and starts to shake. He figures it is safe to let go of her arms.

"Oh, Shura," she says, "you wouldn't believe the dream I just had," and then turns to him and gasps. "Dear God, what happened to you?"

Alexander sits and holds the bridge of his nose.

Tatiana jumps over him, jumps from the bed, runs to get a towel, climbs back up and sits against the wall, pulling him to her. "Come here," she said, "come here, quick." She cradles his head against her knees, keeping him slightly elevated as she holds his nose with the towel.

"Dis is great," Alexander says, "but I can't breede." He gets up for a moment, spits out blood, and lies back down on her, lifting the towel slightly away from his mouth.

"I'm sorry, honey," Tania whispers. "I didn't mean to—but you won't believe the dream I had."

"I had better beed caught with adother womad," Alexander says.

"Worse," she replies. "You were alive, but motionless, lying in front of me, and you were being fed to me piece by piece. They—"

"Who's they?"

"Couldn't see their faces. They were pinning my arms back, and one was cutting flesh from your side and shoving it in my mouth."

He looks up at her. "You were eating me alive?" he asks.

She gulps.

Alexander raises his eyebrows.

"A chunk of your side"—she touches him below his right rib—"was missing."

"How do you know I was alive?"

"Only your eyes were moving, blinking, pleading with me to help you." She closes her eyes. "Oh, God . . ."

"So you were helping me by punching your captors?"

She nods, looking down at him with misty eyes. "What did I do?" she whispers.

"Break my nose, I think," he says casually.

Tania starts to cry.

"I'm joking," he says, reaching for her. "I'm joking, Tatia. It's just a nosebleed. It'll stop in a minute."

Alexander catches her remorseful expression. Remnants of the dream are lodged in her squared jaw, in the tense bones of her face.

"I'm all right," he says. *He turns his head and kisses her breast next to him and then presses his cheek against her as she holds him to her, squeezing the bridge of his nose with one hand and stroking his hair with the other.*

"You were alive," *she whispers,* "and pieces of you were being fed to me. Do you understand?"

"Extremely well," *Alexander says.* "I'm bleeding to prove it."

Tania kisses his head. Soon he stops bleeding. "I'll go and wash off. Tomorrow we'll deal with the sheets."

"Wait—don't go. I'll get something to clean you with. Hop down, can you get down? We have water in the cabin. Do you want me to help? Here, hold my arm."

"Tania," *says Alexander, holding her arm, hopping down and perching on the hearth,* "I have a nosebleed. I'm not dying."

"No, you're going to be quite bruised tomorrow." *She wets a small towel, sits on the hearth and gently cleans the blood off his face and neck and chest.* "I'm dangerous," *she murmurs.* "Look what I did to you."

"Hmm. I'll say this—I've never felt you that crazed before. You were in that state. I sometimes see men in war like that when their normal strength becomes the strength of ten people."

"I'm sorry. Come, you're all cleaned up. Don't have a bad dream about me, Shura, all right?"

"Where you're lying in front of me and I'm eating you?" *he asks, smiling.* "That would be a terrible dream."

"Not that one, or any other one, either. Climb up. Do you need my help?"

"I think I can manage."

She says she will be right back and leaves, returning a minute later with the towel washed in the Kama's cold night-time water. "Here, put this on to stop the swelling. Maybe you won't be too black and blue tomorrow."

He lies on his back with a wet cold towel covering his face. "I can't sleep like this," *he says in a muffled voice.*

"Who wants to sleep?" *he hears her say, as she kneels between his legs. He groans through the towel.* "What can I do to make it up to you?" *he hears her ask.*

"I can't think of anything . . ."

"No?"

She purrs, her gossamer fingers stroking him, her warm mouth breathing on him. He is in her mouth, and the cold wet towel is covering his face.

დოო

The train stopped, they disembarked and were arranged in columns outside the small, war-ruined station. Alexander got his boots on; he was sure they weren't his. They were too small for his feet. They stood groggily in the dark, illuminated hazily by one flickering floodlight. A lieutenant guard broke open a piece of paper out of the envelope and in a pretentious voice read aloud that the seventy men in front of him were accused of crimes against the state.

"Oh, no," whispered Ouspensky.

Alexander stood impassively. He wanted to be back on the wooden shelf. And nothing surprised him anymore. "Don't worry, Nikolai."

"Stop talking!" the soldier yelled. "Treason, colluding with the enemy, working against Russia in the enemy's prisoner camps, cooking for the enemy, building for the enemy, cleaning weapons for the enemy. The law is very clear against treason. You are all remanded under the provisions of Article 58, code 1B and will be incarcerated for no less than fifteen years in a series of Zone II corrective work camps ending with Kolyma. Your term begins when you will start to shovel coal into our steam train to refuel it. Coal is there by the side of the tracks. So are shovels. Your next stop will be a work camp in eastern Germany. Now, let's move it."

"Oh, no, not Kolyma," said Ouspensky. "There must be some mistake."

"I'm not finished!" yelled the guard. "Belov, Ouspensky, step forward!"

They shuffled forward a few steps, dragging the chains behind them. "You two, aside from allowing yourselves to fall into enemy hands which carries an automatic fifteen-year prison term, have also been charged with espionage and sabotage during times of war. Captain Belov, you are to be stripped of your rank and title, as you are, Lieutenant Ouspensky. Captain Belov, your term is extended to twenty-five years. Lieutenant Ouspensky, your term is extended to twenty-five years."

Alexander stood as if the words had not been spoken to him.

Ouspensky said, "Did you hear me? There must be some kind of mistake. I'm not going away for twenty-five years, speak to the general—"

"My orders for you are clear! See?" He waved a document in front of Ouspensky's nose.

Ouspensky shook his head. "No, you don't understand, there's definitely been a mistake. I have it on good authority . . ." He glanced at Alexander, who was looking at him with cold bemusement.

Ouspensky did not speak again while they were shoveling the coal into the furnace of the train and then into storage compartments, but when they were back in their berth, he was seething in a way Alexander could not understand.

"Will the day ever come when I will be free?"

"Yes, in twenty-five years."

"I mean free of you," said Ouspensky, trying to turn from Alexander. "When I won't be chained with you, bunked with you, assisting you."

"Hey, why are you so pessimistic? I heard the Kolyma camps are co-ed. Maybe you can pick yourself a little camp wife."

They sat down together on the shelves. Alexander lay down instantly and closed his eyes. Ouspensky grumbled that he was uncomfortable and had no room next to a man as large as Alexander. The train lurched forward and he fell off the shelf.

"What's wrong with you?" Alexander said, extending his hand to help him up. Ouspensky did not take it.

"I shouldn't have listened to you. I shouldn't have surrendered, I should have minded my own business, and I'd be a free man."

"Ouspensky, have you not been paying attention? Refugees, forced labor workers, people who lived in Poland, in Romania, all the way in Bavaria! From Italy, from France, from Denmark, from Norway. They're all being sent back, all under the same conditions. What makes you think you, of all of them, would be a free man?"

Ouspensky didn't reply. "Twenty-five years! You got twenty five-years, too, don't you even give a shit anymore?"

"Oh, Nikolai." Alexander sighed. "No. Not anymore. I'm twenty-six years old. They've been sentencing me to prison terms in Siberia since I was seventeen." Had he served out his first one in Vladivostok, he'd be nearly done by now.

"Exactly! You, you. Christ, it's all about you. My whole life since the cursed day bad fucking luck had me in a bed next to you in Morozovo has been all about you. Why should I get twenty-five fucking years just because some damn nurse put me in the adjacent bed?" He railed and rattled his chains. The other prisoners, trying to sleep, told him in no uncertain terms to "Shut the fuck up."

"That damn nurse," said Alexander quietly, "was my wife." He paused. "And so you see, dear Nikolai, how inexorably your fate is linked with mine."

For many minutes Ouspensky didn't speak.

"Did not know that," he said at last. "But of course. Nurse Metanova. That's where I heard her name before. I couldn't figure out why Pasha's last name sounded so familiar." He fell quiet. "Where is she now?"

"I don't know," said Alexander.

"Does she ever write you?"

"You know I get no letters. And I write no letters. I have one plastic pen that doesn't work."

"But I mean, there she was, in the hospital, and then suddenly she was gone. Did she go back to her family?"

"No, they're dead."

"Your family?"

"Dead, also."

"So where is she?" he exclaimed in a high-pitched voice.

"What is this, Ouspensky? An interrogation?"

Ouspensky fell silent.

"Nikolai?"

Ouspensky did not reply.

Alexander closed his eyes.

"They promised me," Ouspensky whispered. "They swore to me, *swore* that I would be all right."

"Who did?" Alexander didn't open his eyes.

Ouspensky did not reply.

Alexander opened his eyes. "Who did?" He sat up straight. Ouspensky backed away slightly but not far enough, chained as he was to Alexander.

"Nobody, nobody," he mumbled, and then, with a surreptitious glance at Alexander, he shrugged.

"Oh, it's as old as the sea," he said, trying to sound casual. "They came to me in 1943, soon after they arrested us, and told me I had two choices—I could be executed by firing squad for crimes committed under Article 58. That was my first choice. I thought about it and asked what my second choice was. They told me," he continued, in the deliberate and flat tone of a man who doesn't care much about anything, "that you were a dangerous criminal, but that you were needed for the war effort. However, they suspected you of heinous crimes against the state, but because ours was the kind of society that abided by laws of the constitution and wanted to preserve your rights—they would spare your life long enough for you to hang yourself."

That's why Ouspensky had never left his side. "And did they ask you to be my noose, Ouspensky?" asked Alexander, gripping his leg irons.

Ouspensky didn't reply.

"Oh, Nikolai," Alexander said in a dead voice.

"Wait—"

"Don't tell me anymore."

"Listen—"

"No!' Alexander shouted, throwing himself on Ouspensky. Grabbing him by the scruff of his neck, helpless and irate, Alexander smashed his head against the wall of the train. "Don't tell me anymore."

Red and panting, Ouspensky, who did nothing to free himself, whispered hoarsely, "Listen to me—"

Again Alexander smashed Nikolai's head against the wall.

Someone said, "Keep it down over there," but feebly. No one wanted to get involved. One less man was one more hunk of bread for someone else.

Ouspensky was choking. His nose was bleeding from the trauma to the back of his head. He did not fight back.

Alexander punched him in the face, and Ouspensky fell off the berth to the floor. Alexander kicked him with the boot that was too small for him. Alexander scared even himself. He was dangerously close to killing another human being in hot blood. It wasn't like the anger at Slonko that had been immediate and unstoppable. His fury at Ouspensky was tinged with fury at himself for letting his guard down, and tinged even more with the black hurt at being betrayed for so long by the person closest to him. This made Alexander weaker instead of stronger, and he pulled back and moved away, sinking onto the berth. He and Ouspensky remained shackled to one another.

For a few minutes, Ouspensky did not speak as he struggled to get his breath back. When he spoke his voice was quiet. "Back then I didn't want to die," he said. "They offered me a way out, they said if I brought them information on you—if you helped your wife to escape, or if you were an American like they suspected, that for that information they would set me free. I would be given back my life and reunited with my wife and children."

"They certainly offered you enough," said Alexander.

"I didn't want to die!" Ouspensky cried. "Surely you of all men can understand that! Every month I had to provide them with reports on everything you said and did. They were very interested in our God discussion. Once a month, I would be called to the NKGB command and questioned about you. Did anything raise my suspicions? Did you do anything to trip yourself up? Did you ever use phrases or words that were either unacceptable or foreign? For all that my wife got an extra monthly ration and an increase in her share of my military pay. And I got a few extra rubles to spend on—"

"You sold me out for a few pieces of silver, Nikolai? You sold me out to buy yourself a couple of whores?"

"You never did trust me."

"I did trust you," replied Alexander with clenched fists. "I just didn't tell you anything. But I had thought you were worthy of my trust. I defended you to my brother-in-law." And now Alexander understood. "Pasha suspected you from the start, and he kept trying to tell me." He had a sense about people the way Tatiana had a sense about people. Alexander groaned aloud. He hadn't listened, and now look. He would have told Ouspensky everything, but he hadn't wanted to endanger him with information that might have cost him his miserable life.

Ouspensky paused. "I told them everything I knew about you. I told them you talked to the Americans in Colditz in English. I told them you talked to the English in Catowice. I told them you wanted to surrender. I told them everything I knew. Why did I still get twenty-five years?"

"See if you can figure it out."

"I don't know why!"

"Because!" Alexander yelled. "You sold your mortal fucking soul for some phantom freedom. Are you really surprised that you now have neither? What do you think they care for their promises? You think they care for you because you gave them a bit of worthless information? They still haven't found my wife. And they never will. I'm surprised they gave you only twenty-five years." Alexander lowered his voice. "Their rewards are usually eternal."

"Oh, you're taking this all so personally! I'm going to fucking prison and you're—"

"Nikolai, I've been manacled to you for the last two months," Alexander said in a broken voice. "Manacled! For nearly three years you and I ate out of the same fucking helmet at the front, drank out of the same flask . . ."

"My allegiance was to the state," Ouspensky said. "I *wanted* it to be. I wanted them to protect me. They told me you were as good as dead with or without my help."

"Why tell me now? Why tell me anything?"

"Why not tell you now?" Ouspensky was down to a whisper.

"God, when am I *ever* going to learn! Don't speak to me again, Ouspensky," said Alexander. "Ever. If you speak to me, I will not answer you. If you persist, I have ways of forcing you to be silent."

"Then force me." Ouspensky's head was lowered.

Alexander kicked the chains at him and moved a full, stretched-out iron meter away. "Death is too good for you," he said and turned to the wall.

Where they were going it was hard to tell; it was summer outside, and warm, and it didn't rain, and the night air coming through the small opening smelled of trees. Alexander closed his eyes, and rubbed the bridge of his nose, viscerally recalling the wet towel on his face and Tatiana's mouth on him. The longer they traveled, the sharper the memory became until he would nearly groan out loud at the sensation of blood from his nose dripping down onto the white sheets and Tatiana cradling his head to her breasts, murmuring, *"You were being fed to me alive, Shura."*

CHAPTER THIRTY-FOUR

Jeb, November 1945

TATIANA AGREED TO GO to dinner with Edward. Vikki looked after Anthony. Tatiana dressed up a little, putting on a blue skirt and a beige merino wool sweater, but no matter how much Vikki asked her to, she did not let down her hair, leaving it pinned back in one very long braid, and she did not put on any makeup. Then she put on her coat and scarf, sat on the couch and waited with Anthony on her lap and a picture book in front of them.

"What are you worried about?" Vikki asked, milling around them, picking up the newspapers that had piled up. "You go to lunch with him all the time and talk. Only the title of the meal will change."

"And time of day."

"Yes, that, too."

Tatiana didn't say anymore, pretending to be preoccupied with Anthony's book.

Edward arrived dressed in a suit. Vikki commented on how handsome he looked. Tatiana agreed that Edward looked nice. Edward was fairly tall, thin, composed. He carried himself well—in a suit, in doctor's whites. He had serious, kind eyes. She felt comfortable and yet intensely uncomfortable around him.

Edward took her to Sardi's on 44th Street. Tatiana had a shrimp cocktail and a steak followed by some chocolate cake and coffee.

After an initial awkward silence, she spent the entire dinner asking Edward questions and listening to him. She asked him about medicine and surgery and the wounded and the dying and the sick, she asked him about the hospitals he had worked in and why he chose to be a doctor and whether it still meant something to him to be a doctor. She asked him about where in America he had traveled to and which place out of all he had seen he liked best. She looked him straight in the eye and laughed in all the right places.

And somewhere in the space between the taking way of the chocolate cake and the bringing of the check, Tatiana, while nodding, while listening, her head slightly tilted to one side, saw a color image of herself sitting across a table just like this from Edward, except the table was longer and they were much older, and around the table with them sat their grown children, all daughters.

She leaped up and asked the waiter the time. "Ten o'clock? My, look how late it is. I must get back to Anthony. I had really nice evening, thank you."

Looking a little shellshocked, Edward took her home in a taxi.

She sat all the way from 44th looking out the side window. Somewhere around 23rd Street, Edward said, "How do you do that? I can't believe what a bore I must have been, talking only about myself."

"Not at all," she said. "You were fascinating. As you know, I like to hear everything."

"Maybe next time, we can talk about you."

"I'm so boring," she said. "Nothing to talk about."

"Now that you've been here a couple of years, what do you like about America?"

"The people," she said without thinking.

Edward laughed. "But Tania, all the people you know are immigrants!"

She nodded. "True Americans. They are here in New York for all right reasons. New York is great city."

"What else do you like? What do you like the most?"

"Delicious bacon," she said. "I guess I like the comfort. Everything Americans do, produce, create is to make life little bit easier. I like that. Music is pleasant, clothes are comfortable. Blankets don't itch. Milk is right around corner. So is bread. Shoes fit. Chairs are soft. It's good here." She looked out the window as they passed through 14th Street. "So much to take for granted," she added quietly.

The cab pulled up in front of her building. "Well . . ." she said.

"Tania," he said in an emotional voice, reaching for her.

She leaned over to Edward, pecked him on the cheek, said, "Thank you so much for lovely evening," and got hastily out of the car.

"I'll see you on Monday," he called out, but she was already running inside the doors, opened instantly and reverentially by Diego from Romania.

Tania Tania.

I hear him shouting for me.

I turn and there he is, still alive and calling my name.

Tania Tania.

I turn, I must turn and there he is, wearing his fatigues, rifle slung on his shoulder, running towards me, out of breath.

Still so young.

Why do I hear him so clearly?

Why is his voice an echo in my head?

In my chest.

In my arms and fingers, in my barely beating heart, in the vapor of my cold breath?

Why is he loud, why is he deafening?

At night all is quiet.

But during the day, amid the crowds . . .

I walk, always slowly, I sit, always motionlessly, and I hear him calling my name.

Tania, Tania . . .

Why do I hear it?

Didn't he tell me to listen for the stellar wind at night?

It will be me, he whispered, calling you back.

To Lazarevo.

Then why is he SHOUTING now?

Here I am, Shura! Stop calling for me. I'm not going anywhere.

Tania Tania . . .

⁊

One cold and sunny Saturday afternoon, a bundled-up Tatiana, Vikki, and Anthony were walking as usual through the outdoor market on Second Avenue. Vikki was idly chatting, Tatiana was idly listening and holding Anthony by the shoulders. He wanted to push his own carriage today—into the ankles of the pedestrians. Vikki carried all their shopping, never missing an opportunity to complain about how unfair it was.

"And explain to me why you refuse to go out with Edward again?"

"I don't refuse," Tatiana said gently. "I told him I need little time, little more adjustment. We still have lunch."

"Lunch shmunch. It's not dinner, is it? He knows a brush-off when he sees one."

"No brush-off. Just . . . slow-off."

Vikki was already onto something else. "Tania, I know you want bacon for dinner today, bacon and bread, but I was thinking maybe you could make something other than bread and meat. What about spaghetti and meatballs?"

"What is spaghetti made of?"

"How do I know? It grows in Portugal, like olives, and my grand-mother buys it in special shops."

"No. Spaghetti made of flour."

"So?"

"Meatballs made of meat."

"So?"

Tatiana didn't answer. Half a block ahead of her, she saw a tall male shape. She held Anthony's hand tighter as she stared through the crowds, trying to see. Second Avenue was busy and she tilted her head, then moved three steps to the right, and then tried to speed up.

"So?"

"Come on, little faster. Excuse me," she said to the people in front of them. "Excuse me, please."

"Hey, what's the hurry? Tania! You didn't answer my question."

"Question?"

"So? That was my question. So?"

"Spaghetti and meatballs are also bread and meat. Excuse me," Ta-tiana said again to the people in front of her, pulling Anthony faster than his short legs could carry him. "Come on, son, let's not dawdle." But she wasn't looking at Anthony, or at Vikki, or at the people she was pushing out of her way with the carriage. No one liked to have their an-kles rammed by an aggressive Russian woman, even in a Russian neighborhood—especially in a Russian neighborhood. Tatiana heard some very unkind words in her native tongue. "Hurry, Vikki, hurry."

She picked up Anthony, thrust the carriage into Vikki's already full hands and said, "I've got to—" Then, breaking off, she started to run. She couldn't restrain herself. She ran out into the street and alongside the curb, trying to catch two men about a block ahead of her. Short of shouting at their backs, she didn't know what to do; panting, her heart pounding, she caught up with them at the light and before speaking— because she couldn't speak—she placed her free hand, the one that wasn't holding Anthony, on the man's arm, and tried to say, *Alexander?* But no words would come out.

The man was very tall and very broad. She kept her hand on him long enough for him to turn around, and see her staring. He smiled. Turning red, Tatiana took away her hand and averted her gaze, but it was too late.

"Yes, sweetheart?" he said. "What can I do you for?"

She backed away. Temporarily forgetting her English, she started yammering in Russian. Then went back to a broken language even she didn't recognize. "I sorry, I think you was someplace, someone else . . ."

"For you, I'll be anyone you want me to be. Who do you want me to be, sweetheart?"

Vikki had caught up by now, with the carriage and shopping bags, flushed and put upon. "Tania! What do you think you're—" She broke off when she saw the two men, and smiled.

The tall man introduced himself as Jeb and his friend as Vincent.

Jeb was dark-haired, but his face was all wrong. It was Jeb's face. It wasn't Tatiana's husband's. Nonetheless, on a Saturday afternoon, in standing close to him, in looking up into his friendly smiling eyes, Tatiana felt a twinge of want. A breath of desire.

A few minutes later, as they were walking away, Vikki said, "Tania, why is it feast or famine with you? You completely ignore all men for years, then you knock down old ladies to chase one down the street. What is wrong with you?"

The next day Jeb called.

"Are you crazy?" Vikki said. "You gave him our number? You don't know where he's been."

"I know where he been," said Tatiana. "Japan. He was sailor."

"I don't understand. You don't know him at all. I've been trying to get you to go out with Edward for two years—"

"Vikki, I don't want Edward to be my rebound. He too good for that."

"Edward doesn't think so. You want Jeb to be your rebound?"

"I don't know."

"Well, I don't like him for you," Vikki stated flatly. "I didn't like the way he was looking at you. I can't believe of all the men out there, you had to pick the *one* I don't like."

"He will grow on you."

But he didn't grow on Vikki. Tatiana was too ashamed of being attracted to Jeb to go out alone with him, but she did invite him for dinner.

"What are you going to make him? Eggs and bacon? Bacon, lettuce and tomato on bread? Or stuffed cabbage—with bacon?"

"Stuffed cabbage sounds good. Stuffed cabbage and bread."

Jeb came and had dinner with them. Vikki would not disappear into her room for a moment, and Anthony was underfoot all evening. Finally, Jeb left.

"I didn't like the way he looked at you the first time he saw you and I like him even less now," Vikki declared. "Don't you find him condescending?"

"What?"

"He cut you off every time you spoke, didn't you notice? Always with a smile, the fraud. And don't tell me you didn't notice how he ignored your boy?"

"How could he ignore him? Thanks to you, Anthony was under table entire night!"

"Don't you think Anthony is worth a better man than Jeb?"

"I do," said Tatiana. "But better man is not here. What am I supposed to do?"

"Edward is a better man than Jeb," Vikki said.

"So why don't you go for Edward then? He is available."

"Don't think I haven't tried!" rejoined Vikki. "He is not interested in *me*."

Vikki was right about Jeb. He *was* possessive and he was condescending. But Tatiana couldn't help it—she wanted the agony of his big arms around her.

Tatiana thought of Alexander; she imagined Alexander whole and in the imagining created the kind of hell for herself that only the true masochist can create, the *thinking* male praying mantis who creeps to the female fully knowing that as soon as she is finished with him, she is going to snap off his head and devour him. And still he creeps, with his eyes closed, with his heart shut tight, creeps to the gates of life and death, and thanks God for being alive.

〇〜〜〇

A couple of weeks before Christmas, when Tatiana came to pick up Anthony from Isabella's, Isabella sat her down and, giving her a hot cup of tea, said, "What's wrong, Tania?"

"Nothing."

Isabella studied her.

Tatiana looked at her hands. "I wish having faith was easier."

"Faith in what?"

"Faith in this life. In me. Faith in doing what I am supposed to." I don't want to forget him, she wanted to say.

"Darling, of course you're doing what you're supposed to," Isabella said. "Go on the way all women do when their husbands have died."

"But what if he is not dead?" Tatiana whispered. "I need some proof to have faith."

Isabella replied, "But, darling, then it wouldn't be called faith, would it, if you had proof?"

Tatiana didn't say anything.

"You grit your teeth and go on," Isabella said, "just as you have been doing."

"Dear Isabella," said Tatiana, "as you know, I'm queen of grit teeth. But every day that moves me farther from him, I hate that day."

"But that's when you need faith the most—when it's darkest around you." Isabella watched Tatiana thoughtfully. "Honey, it must be better now than it was? You were so sad when you first came to New York. It's better now?"

"It is, Isabella," Tatiana replied. On the outside her life was right. But inside was his damn medal. And his damn Orbeli.

"Would you feel better if you had more proof than his death certificate?"

Tatiana made no reply. What *could* she say?

"Pray he is dead, darling. Pray he is at peace, that he is not tormented anymore. He is not hurting. He is free. He is your guardian angel, looking over you."

"Isabella," said Tatiana. "Don't tell me he is dead, because if I believe that, it's harder for me to go on living—knowing that with one bullet, I could be with him."

"Who'd take you," asked Isabella, "if you died and left your son an orphan?"

"Why not?" said Tatiana. "He died and left his son an orphan."

"So if it's easier, believe he is still alive."

"If he's still alive, then how can I go on with my life?" Tatiana emitted a cry of such physical pain that Isabella paled and moved her chair *away* from her.

"Oh, Tania," Isabella whispered. "How can I help you?"

Tatiana stood up. "You can't help me." She called for Anthony, taking her bag from the floor. "Must be pleasant to see things so clearly. Well, why not? You are still with Travis. Your faith is easy—you have living proof right here."

"And you do, too—here he is," said Isabella, pointing at Anthony who came bounding out of the den, leaped into his mother's arms and said, "Mama, I want ice krrreeeem for dinner."

"All right, son," said Tatiana.

And he did.

⚬⚬⚬

"Mama, how come Timothy has a daddy, and Ricky has a daddy, and Sean has a daddy, too?"

"Honey, what's your question?" They were walking to school near Battery Park. It was Anthony's second week in playgroup. Tatiana was intent on introducing Anthony to more children his own age. She thought he was around grown-ups too much. Around Isabella too much. His brow was creased in an adult manner; Tatiana didn't like it. He spoke too fluently, he was too pensive, too solemn for a boy of two and half. She thought playgroup would do him good.

And now this.

"Why I don't have a daddy?"

"Baby, you have daddy. He is just not here. Just like Mickey's daddy, and Bobby's daddy, and Phil's, too. Their daddies aren't here, and their mommies take care of them. You're lucky. You have your mommy, and Vikki and Isabella—"

"Mama, when is Daddy going to come back? Ricky's daddy came back. He walks him to school in the morning."

Tatiana stared into the middle distance.

"Ricky wished for his dad for Christmas. Maybe I can wish for my dad for Christmas."

"Maybe," whispered Tatiana.

Anthony didn't let his mother kiss him at the doors of the school or walk him inside. Squaring his shoulders and creasing his solemn brow, he went through the doors himself, carrying his small lunch bag.

⚬⚬⚬

The four stages of grief. First there was shock. And then there was denial. That lasted until this morning. Today, onward to the next stage. Anger. When will acceptance come?

She was so angry at him. He knew perfectly well she didn't want this life without him. Did he think that she'd be better off in America amid post-war small appliances and radios and the promise of a television than she would have been in the Gulag?

Well, wait. What about Anthony? The boy is not a specter. He is a real boy, he would have been born regardless. What would have happened to him?

She looked into the water on the harbor. How long would it take me to jump and swim, swim like the last fish in the ocean to where it's winter and the water is cold? I would swim slower and slower and slower, and then I would stop, and maybe on the other side of life he would be waiting for me with his hand outstretched, saying what took you so long to come to me, Tatia? I've been waiting and waiting.

She stepped away from the railing of the boat. No. On the other side, he is looking at me, shaking his head, saying, Tania, look at Anthony, he is the perfect son. How lucky you are to lay your hands on him. How I wish I could. Wherever I am—know that's what I'm thinking. How I wish I could touch my boy.

Anthony needed his mother. Anthony could not be an orphan, not here in America, not there in the Soviet Union. His mother couldn't abandon him, too. That sweet boy, with his sticky hands, with his chocolate mouth and his black hair. Tatiana coiled when she looked at, when she touched his black hair.

"Shura, let me wash your hair for you," she says, sitting on the ground, looking out onto the clearing.

"Tania, it's clean. We just washed this morning."

"Come on, please. Let's go swim. Let me wash it for you."

"All right. Only if I can wash—"

"You can do whatever you like. Just come."

She coiled every time she looked at her son.

༺∼∽༻

That night she went out on the fire escape, without a coat or a hat, and sat mutely breathing in the cold ocean air. It smelled so good.

"Alexander," Tatiana whispered. "Are you there? Can you hear me? Can you see me?" Up on the fire escape, she lifted her arms to the sky. "How am I doing? Better, right?" She nodded to herself. Better.

New York, every day pulsing as if indeed it was the heartbeat of the world. No dim-out at night anymore, every building illuminated like endless fireworks. There was not a street that was not teeming with people, a street where the manholes were not open, where steam wasn't coming out of the underground, an avenue where the men didn't sit on top of telephone poles and electrical poles, laying new pipe, hanging new wire, breaking down the El. The constant clang of construction, every day from seven in the morning, along with the sirens and the buses, and the honking horns and the yellow cabs. The stores were filled with merchandise, the coffee shops with donuts, the diners with bacon, stores with books and records and Polaroid cameras, music poured every night from the bars and the cafés, oh, and lovers, too, under trees, on benches, lovers in uniform and in suits and in doctors' coats and nurses' shoes. And in Central Park where they went every weekend, each blade of grass had a family on it. The lake had a hundred boats in the daytime.

But then there was night.

In the ocean, her arm outstretched to God, was Lady Liberty and on the fire escape was Tatiana, sitting in the three-in-the-morning air, listening across the ocean for the breathing of one man.

The fire embers are flickering out. He is finally done. Not only is he done, but asleep, too. He hasn't moved off her. He had exhausted himself and, spent, nuzzled for a few moments and fell soundly asleep. She doesn't even try to move him. He is heavy, what bliss. He is on top of her, so close. She can smell him and kiss his wet hair, and his stubbly cheek. She caresses his arms. It's sinful for her to love his muscled arms so much. "Shura," she whispers. "Can you hear me, soldier?"

She doesn't sleep, for a long time cradling him to her, listening to him breathe, hearing the wood turn to ashes and the sound of the crackling rain outside and willowy wind, while inside it is warm, dim, cozy. She listens to his happy breathing. When he sleeps he is still happy. He is not bothered by bad dreams, by sadness. He is not tormented when he sleeps. He is breathing. So peaceful. So fulfilled. So alive.

⌒౼⌒

Why did her present life suddenly start to feel so desperate? On the surface, there was so much. But under the surface she felt herself settling in—as if, as if—

She could close her eyes and imagine life . . .

Without him.

Imagine forgetting him.

The war was over.

Russia was over.

Leningrad was over.

And Tatiana and Alexander were over, too.

Now she had words to dull her senses. English words, a new name, and covering it all like a warm blanket, a new life in amazing, immoderate, pulsating *America*. A sparkling new identity in a gilded immense new country. God had made it as easy as possible to forget him. To you, I give this, God said. I give you freedom and sun, and warmth, and comfort. I give you summers in Sheep Meadow and Coney Island, and I give you Vikki, your friend for life, and I give you Anthony, your son for life, and I give you Edward, in case you want love again. I give you youth and I give you beauty, in case you want someone other than Edward to love you. I give you New York. I give you seasons, and Christmas! And baseball and dancing and paved roads and refrigerators, and a car, and land in Arizona. I give it all to you. All I ask, is that you forget him and take it.

Her head bowed, Tatiana took it.

A week would fly by, filled with work and the people in whose eyes she could see what she meant to them, and filled with Edward, in whose eyes Tatiana could see what she meant to him, and with blessed, impossible Vikki. Tatiana endlessly saw in Vikki's eyes what she meant to Vikki. They went to the pictures and took in Broadway shows, and advanced nursing classes at NYU. Tatiana got dressed up in high heels and pretty dresses and went to Ricardo's, and it was there that she would realize she had lived another week, almost as if she were *meant* to, as if Alexander were indeed becoming . . . remote.

There was a settling of the stellar dust. Soon the first love would fall into the recesses of memory, like childhood, it would all fall through the cracks in the cement of life, and weeds would grow over it.

But every morning, Tatiana took the ferry to Ellis, and as the boat broke the water of the harbor, she saw Alexander's eyes, showing her what she had meant to him. Every day of forgetting, of wanting life, was another day of his eyes telling her what she had meant to him.

America, New York, Arizona, the end of war, feverish reconstruction, a baby boom, dancing, her high-heeled shoes, her painted lips—what *she* had meant . . .

To *him*.

What would she have, had she meant *less* to him? Why, nothing. She would have the Soviet Union, that's what. Fifth Soviet, two rectangular rooms, and a domestic passport, and maybe a *dacha* in the summers for her child. She would be fifth in line forever, pulling the quilted hat down over her ears in the blizzard.

Every day of forgetting was a day of increased remorse. How could you forget me so quick, she thought Alexander was saying to her, when I have paid for you with my life?

Quick?

She was getting tiresome even to herself. Quick.

Quicksand into the earth.

Quicksilver into the water.

Quick quick quick, forget him so you can lie down with Jeb. Forget, Tania, so you can lie down with your third and fourth and fifth, Alexander is dead; hi ho, hi ho.

The months, the months, the months, the months.

Alexander, Alexander, Alexander, Alexander.

Tania, Tania . . .

That's you, I know, that's the pitiless horseman calling me back, calling me back to. . . .

Lazarevo . . .

We lived it in our rapture and abandon as if we knew even then it had to last us our whole life.

Do you see our rumpled bed, our kerosene lamp? Do you see the kettle of water I boiled for you and do you see the counter top you had built for me, for the potatoes we never got, and for our cabbage pie? Do you see the cigarettes I rolled for you and the clothes I washed for you and do you see my hands on you, and my lips, and my ear pressing against your chest to listen to your beating heart, tell me, do you see all this before you and around you and inside you, too?

God keep you if you are alive, you unrelenting Alexander.

But if you are an angel watching over me, don't come here, don't follow me into the Superstition Mountains, don't come here where it's black around me and cold. I live in the desert, watching the winds and the wildflowers in the spring.

Don't go here.

Come with me instead to the place I fly to, follow me over the oceans and the seas and the rivers between us, take my hand and let me lead you down through the pine cones, through the pine needles to wet our feet with the River Kama, as the sun peeks over the barren edges of the Urals, promising us one more day, and one less day every sunrise times twenty-nine, one more day, one less day, and gone again. Come with me into the river, flow with me as you and I swim across to the other shore against the rushing current. You swim slightly afraid I'm going to be carried away downstream into the Caspian Sea. I call *swim faster, faster,* and you smile and swim faster, your eyes on me. You're always just ahead, your shining face to me. Come with me there for one more morning, one more fire, one more cigarette, one more swim, one more smile, one more, one more, one more, *alskär* into the eternity we call Lazarevo, my Alexander.

CHAPTER THIRTY-FIVE

Oranienburg, Germany, 1945

ALEXANDER DIDN'T KNOW WHAT month it was when the train finally stopped for good and they were told to get out. He had long been removed from Ouspensky and chained to a small, blond, pleasant lieutenant Maxim Misnoy, who spoke little and slept much. Ouspensky, with a broken jaw, now traveled in a different car.

During their time on the train, Maxim Misnoy told Alexander a little about his life. He had volunteered for the front when the Germans invaded Russia in 1941. By 1942, Misnoy had yet to be issued a revolver for his empty holster. He had been taken prisoner by the Germans four times and escaped three times. He was liberated from Büchenwald by the Americans, but, being a loyal Red Army soldier, traveled to the Elbe to join the Russians in the Battle of Berlin. For his heroism, he had been given the *Order of the Red Star*. In Berlin afterward he was apprehended and sentenced to fifteen years for treason. He was too pleasant to be angry about it.

After alighting from the train, they were made to march in double file for two kilometers through a road in the woods to a path in the tall trees that led to a white ornate gatehouse. They passed a large yellow house before the gates. On top of the gatehouse was a clock, and flanking the clock were two machine-gun sentries.

"Büchenwald?" Alexander asked Misnoy.

"No."

"Auschwitz?"

"No, no."

The iron lettering on the gate read *"Arbeit Macht Frei."*

"What do you think that means?" asked a man from behind them in line.

"Abandon hope all ye who enter here," replied Alexander.

"No," said Misnoy. "It means, 'Work will set you free.'"

"Like I was saying."

Misnoy laughed. "This must be a Class One camp. For political prisoners. Probably Sachsenhausen. In Büchenwald, the engraving didn't say that. It was for more serious, more permanent offenders."

"Like you?"

"Like me." He smiled pleasantly. "Büchenwald read, '*Jedem das Seine*. To Each His Own.'"

"The Germans are so fucking inspiring," said Alexander.

It was Sachsenhausen, they were told by the new camp commandant, a repulsive fat man by the name of Brestov, who could not speak without spitting. Sachsenhausen was built at the same time as Büchenwald, and was a full-time forced labor camp and a part-time extermination camp, mainly for the homosexuals who worked at the brick factory just outside the gates, for the few Jews who had found their way here, and certainly for the Soviets—nearly all the Soviet officers who entered the gates were buried within them. It was now called Special Camp Number 7 by the Soviets, implying of course that there were at least six more just like it.

As they were led through the camp, Alexander noticed that most of the prisoners walking from barracks to canteen or laundry, or working in the industry yard, did not have the hangdog Russian look. They had the tall, unbent Aryan look.

He turned out to be right. The majority in the camp were Germans. The Soviets were taken to a special place, slightly beyond the main camp walls. Sachsenhausen was built in the shape of an isosceles triangle, but the Nazis had discovered during the war that there was no room to house the Allied POWs in the forty barracks within camp walls. So twenty additional brick barracks were built, jutting out on the right side of the camp at the farthest corner from the gatehouse. The Nazis called it Class II and that's where the Allies were kept.

Now, Special Camp Number 7 was split into two zones—Zone I in the main camp as "preventive detention" for the German civilians and soldiers picked up during the Soviet advance on Germany, and Zone II, in the additional housing, for the German officers released by Western Allies but recaptured and tried by Soviet military tribunals for crimes against the Soviet Union. The Soviets were also kept in Zone II.

Though in the same general area as the German officers, the Soviets had six or seven barracks all to themselves, they ate at separate times and had separate roll call, but Alexander wondered how long it would be before the camp, stretched to its limits, would start intermingling its prisoners, treating them all as enemies of the Soviet Union.

The first thing Alexander and his group of men were ordered to do when they got to the camp was build a perimeter fence around a square area just to the side of their barracks. This was to be a cemetery for those who died in Special Camp Number 7. Alexander thought it was quite prescient of the NKGB to be so forward-thinking as to be building a cemetery before there were any casualties. He wondered where the Germans had buried prisoners who had died—Stalin's son, for one.

On a walk through the camp, Alexander's group was shown a small enclave built out from the main wall into the industry yard. The enclave contained a concrete execution pit and next to it a crematorium. The Soviet guard told them that that was where the German pigs disposed of the Soviet prisoners of war, shooting them in the neck through a hole in the wall as they stood near a wooden yardstick that measured their height. "No Allied soldier has seen this pit, I can assure you," the guard told them.

Alexander, shaking his bewildered, scornful head, said, "And why do you think *that* was?"

For that he received a knock with the rifle and a day in the camp jail.

Alexander started out working in the industry yard, a large fenced-in area where the Soviets took their exercise and chopped wood that was brought in from the forests around Oranienburg. Soon he volunteered to go and log himself. Every morning he was taken out with a convoy at seven fifteen, just after roll call, and did not return until five forty-five. He never stopped working, but for that he was fed a bit better, and he was out in the open air, left with his own thoughts. He liked it until it started getting cold at the end of September. By October he was hating it. He wished half-heartedly he were in one of the warm rooms soldering or hammering, making cups or locks. He didn't really want to be stuck inside a factory-floor room, but he wouldn't have minded being warm. He was outside, his boots were falling apart and leaking, held together with jute, and the gloves they had given him had holes in the fingers—an unfortunate flaw for gloves. But at least he was moving his body, metabolizing warmth. The ten men guarding the twenty prisoners were certainly dressed for the weather, but they stood for the entire ten hours, moving from foot to frozen foot. A small satisfaction, Alexander thought.

As it got colder, the cemetery started filling up. Alexander was made to dig graves. The Germans were doing poorly in Soviet-run camps. They had lived through six years of vicious war, but stuck in Special Camp Number 7, they withered and died. More and more were brought in. Clearly there was not enough room. The barracks started getting more and more crowded. The bunkbeds made in the industry yards were placed closer and closer together.

Special Camp Number 7, formerly known as Sachsenhausen, was not run by the military administration of Berlin. It fell under the USSR Government Administration of the Camps, or GULAG.

And there was something about being imprisoned in the Soviet-run Gulag that abjectly pervaded Alexander and the other five thousand Soviet men, gave them a bleak sense of terminal malaise. Many of the men had been in POW camps, they were not unfamiliar with restraints of movement and limits to activity. But even during the worst of the winters in German POW camps, the situation did not feel permanent, did not feel obliterating. They were soldiers then. And there was always hope—of victory, of escape, of liberation. But now there was victory, and liberation meant surrender to the Soviets, and there was no escape from Sachsenhausen into Soviet-occupied Germany. This prison, these days, this sentence felt like the end of hope, the end of faith, the end of everything.

☙

Little by little, the torrent, the torment of memory ebbed.

At war he had imagined her whole—her laughter, her jokes, her cooking. In Catowice and Colditz, he imagined her whole—oh, but didn't want to.

Here in Sachsenhausen he wanted to imagine her whole, and couldn't.

Here she had become tainted with the Gulag.

His hands are on her. She is shuddering, her body in spasms breaking up into his hands. Alexander takes hold of her legs as he moves against her, and through it all, she moans and shudders helplessly, every once in a while breathing, "Oh, Shura," and Alexander is breaking into pieces from his excitement and his terror. The excitement is inside her. The terror is in his hands as he grips her quivering body tighter and pulls out for a moment, hearing her nearly scream in frustration, but he is not having any of it. She is his right now, he will do with her as he needs to. He knows what he needs—to hold her closer than his own heart, to feel her dissolve in his hands, and all around him. The more helpless she is and the more he feels her need, the more he feels like a man. But sometimes what he needs as he holds her tighter is for Lazarevo not to vanish with the moon. He can't give her that—what she wants most. What he wants most. He gives her what he can.

"*You like it, babe?" he whispers.*

"*Oh, Shura," she whispers back. She can't even open her eyes. Her arms go around his neck.*

"*You're not done yet," he says. "God, you're trembling."*

"*Shura, I can't—I can't—I can't—oh, that's it—*"

"*Yes, honey, yes. That's it."*

He closes his eyes, and hears her cry out.

And cry out. And cry out.

He is not stopping.

And cry out.

Now I'm a man, now when I've made my holy maiden shiver in my hands, I've become a man.

And cry out.

"*God, I love you, Tania," he whispers into her hair, his eyes still closed.*

And wants to cry himself.

Her body limp underneath him, she lies, gently stroking his back.

"*Done?" he asks.*

"*Done* for," *she replies.*

Alexander hasn't even begun.

That's the only thing Alexander imagined now. There was no clearing, no moon, no river. There was no bed, no blankets, no grass, no fire. No tickling, no games, no foreplay, no afterplay. There was no end and no beginning. There was only Tania underneath him, and Alexander on top of her, holding her close and tight. Her arms were always around his neck, her legs were always wrapped around him. And she was never silent.

Because she had become tainted with the Gulag, where there were no men.

We are not men. We do not live like men, and we do not behave like men. We do not hunt for our food—all except me when the guards aren't looking—we do not protect the women who love us, we do not build shelter for our children, nor do we use the tools God gave us. We use nothing—not our brains to live by, not our strength to live by, not our cocks to live by.

War defined you. You always knew who you were during war. You were a major. A captain. A second lieutenant, a first lieutenant. You were a warrior. You carried weapons, you drove a tank, you led men into battle, you obeyed orders. You had categories and roles and passages. You didn't always sleep and you weren't always dry and many times you were hungry, and every once in a while you got shot or shelled or snipered. But even that was expected.

Here we give nothing of ourselves to anyone. We haven't just become less as human beings, we have become less as men—we lost the very thing that made us what we were. We don't even fight like we did at war. We were all animals then, but at least we were male animals. We *drove* forward. We *thrust* into enemy lines. We *penetrated* their defense. We *broke* their ring. We fought as *men*.

And now we're being reconstructed before we are sent back to society as eunuchs. Emasculated, we are sent back to our faithless wives, into cities in which we cannot live, into life with which we cannot cope. We have no manhood to offer, not each other, not our women, and not our children.

All we have is our past, which we detest and dissect and wring our hands over. The past in which we were men. And behaved like men. And worked like men. And fought like men.

And loved like men.

If only—

Only nine thousand days like this to go.

Until—

We're given back to the world we saved from Hitler.

⚭

And soon even her breasts were gone from him, and her face, and her voice calling for him. All was gone.

What remained was his male impact upon her female moaning.

⚭

And soon even that was gone.

⚭

His hands flung up over his right shoulder, he paused in introspection of the wood and crashed down. And with every swing of the axe, Alexander cut apart his life.

Did he think so little of it—to have so quickly given it up? How many times had fate twisted him to Finland? When he was young, hadn't he refused the path given to him, offering excuses to the gods instead?

He had always been in the middle of something else.

Stepanov's son—there was nothing else he could do that day.

But during the blockade, when he pushed the Finns north to Karelia? He had an automatic weapon against five NKVD men with single-shot rifles. He could have been free.

He swung his axe, dumbstruck by himself.

Alexander could have gone, and forgotten her, and she him. She would have forgotten him and lived through the war, remained in Leningrad, and married. She would have had one child. She never would have known the difference. But Alexander *had* known the difference. And now they both knew the difference. Now they both were split apart—except she is wearing high heels and red lipstick somewhere, and all the soldiers returning from war are fawning over her and she says, oh I had a husband, and I made some vows but now he is dead, and come dance with me, come, look at my heels and my glorious hair, come dance away the war with me, I live and he is dead, I was sad, and then the war was over and I breathed again and now I'm dancing.

He swung his axe.

I inhale the frozen earth, I inhale ice that fills my lungs, and I breathe out fire.

I didn't go because I was an arrogant bastard. I thought I could always run. I thought I was fucking immortal. Death would never get me. I was stronger and smarter than death. Stronger and smarter than the Soviet Union. I jumped thirty meters into the Volga, I made my way through half the country with nothing on my back, Kresty didn't get me, Vladivostok didn't get me, typhus didn't get me.

Tatiana got me.

I will be fifty-one when they let me out of here.

He felt so old, having been young with her.

Alexander had been in the woods too long. And the deathly, eerie silence of the forest was icily frightening. He looked around. Suddenly he heard a noise. What was that? It sounded almost familiar. He held his breath.

There it was. In the middle distance, the sound of soft laughter.

Again the soft trilling sound, so familiar his bones ached. *Tatiana,* he whispered.

She comes to him, and she is pale. She is wearing a polka dot bathing suit, and her hair is long. She comes up to him and sits down on the stump so he can't cut his wood. He lights a cigarette and watches her mutely. He doesn't know what to say to her.

"Alexander," *she speaks first.* "You're alive. And you've grown so old. What happened to you?"

"How do I look?" *he asks.*

"You look like you're nearly fifty."

"I am fifty."

She smiles. "You're fifty, but I am seventeen." *She laughs melodiously.* "How unfair life is. La-la-la."

"Lazarevo, Tania, do you remember it? Our summer of '42?"

"What summer of '42? I died in '41. I'm forever seventeen. Remember Dasha? Dasha! Come! Look who I found."

"Tania, what do you mean, you died? You didn't die. Look at you. Wait, don't call Dasha."

"Dasha, come! Of course I died. How do you think my sister and I could have survived that Leningrad? We didn't. We couldn't. One morning I couldn't carry the water up anymore. Couldn't get the rations anymore. We lay down together in our bed, and we were fine. We couldn't move. I covered us with a blanket. The fire went out. The bread ended. We didn't get up again."

"Wait, wait."

Tania smiles at him, white teeth all, freckles all, braids, breasts, all.

"Tania . . . what about me? Why didn't I help you?"

"Help me with what?"

"With bread, with rations? Why didn't I get you out of Leningrad?"

"What do you mean? We never saw you again after September. Where did you go? You said you were going to marry Dasha, and then you disappeared. She thought you had run out on her."

"On her?" *Alexander says, aghast.* "What about you?"

"What about me?" *she asks brightly.*

"What about our talk at St. Isaac's? What about Luga?"

"What St. Isaac's? What Luga? Dasha, where are you? You won't believe who I ran into!"

"Tania," *he says.* "Why are you acting as if you don't know me? Why are you pretending? You're breaking my heart. Please stop. Please say something to comfort me."

She stops bouncing, bounding, skipping, flinging her braids around, stops cold, looks at him and says, "Alex, what are you—"

"What did you just call me?"

"Alex—"

"You've never called me that."

"What do you mean? We called you that all the time."

Alexander is desperately trying to wake up. He can't dream this anymore. He will go mad. Except he is awake. The axe is in front of him. She is skipping on one leg. *"Luga, Tania? What about Luga?"*

"Luga is where our dacha was. We thought we'd go back there after the war, but we never made it."

"How do you know me?" he asks. *"How do you know who I am?"*

"What do you mean?" Peals of her soft laughter ripple the water in the river. *"You're my sister's guy."*

"How did you and I meet?"

"She introduced us. She'd been talking about you for weeks. Finally you came for dinner."

"When?"

"I don't know. July sometime."

"What about June? June 22? You met me in June, didn't you? The war started and you and I met at the bus stop, remember?"

"June 22? Of course we didn't."

"Did you have ice cream on the bench?"

"Yes . . ."

"Didn't a soldier—me—see you from across the street?"

"There was no soldier," she says adamantly. *"The street was empty. I had my ice cream and the bus came to take me to Nevsky Prospekt. I went to Yelisey, got some caviar. Didn't last us long. Didn't help us through the winter."*

"But where was I?" he cries.

"I don't know," she chirps, jumping up and down. *"I never saw anyone."*

Ashen, he stares into her face. Not a flicker of affection moves across it. *"Why didn't I help your sister during the blockade?"* he barely gets out.

Lowering her voice in an excited whisper, she says, *"I don't know if this is true about you, Alexander, but Dimitri told us that you escaped! Escaped and ran to America—all by yourself. Can that be true? Did you leave us all behind and run?"* She laughs. *"That's so delicious. America! Wow. Dasha, come here."* She turns to Alexander. *"Dasha and I talked and talked about it through the winter months. Even as we lay in bed our last morning, we said, can you believe, Alexander must be warm now and full. Was there heat in America during the war? White bread?"*

Alexander has long ceased to stand. He has dropped to his knees on the snow. *"Tania . . ."* he says desperately, looking up at her. *"Tatia . . ."*

"What did you call me?"

"Tatiasha, my wife, Tania, mother of my only child, don't you remember our Lazarevo?"

"Where?" she says frowning. "Alexander, you're acting so odd. What are you talking about? I'm not your wife. I was not anybody's wife." She laughs briefly and shrugs. "Child? You perfectly well know I never even had a boyfriend." Her eyes twinkle. "I had to live through my angel sister. Dasha, come here, look who I found. Tell me more about this Alexander of yours. What was he like?" She skips away without a backward glance. And soon her laughter fades away.

Alexander dropped his axe, got up and started walking.

∽∽∽

They caught him in the woods and brought him back, and after two weeks in the camp jail, Alexander picked the lock on the leg chains with a pin he carried in his boots. They rechained him and took away the boots. He picked the lock on the leg chains with a small straight piece of straw he found on the cement floor of the isolation cell. They beat him and strung him up by his legs upside down for twenty-four hours. The effort of pulling his body up dislocated both his ankles.

After that he was left on the straw in the jail, his arms chained above his head, and three times a day someone came in and shoved bread down his throat.

One day, Alexander turned his head away and refused the bread. He took the water.

The next day, he refused the bread again.

They stopped bringing it.

One night he opened his eyes; he was cold and thirsty. He was filthy and his body hurt. He could not move it. He tried to sweep up some straw to cover himself with. It was no use. He turned his head to the left and stared at the dark wall. He turned his head to the right and blinked.

Harold Barrington was sitting on his haunches against the wall. He was wearing slacks and a white shirt, his hair was brushed. He looked young, younger than Alexander. He was quiet for a long time. Alexander didn't blink; he was afraid his father would be gone if he did.

"Dad?" he whispered.

"Alexander, what's happening to you?"

"I don't know. It's all over for me."

"Our adopted country has turned its back on you."

"Yes."

"Have you married?"

"I married."

"Where is your wife?"

"I don't know." Alexander paused. "I haven't seen my wife in many years."

"Is she waiting for you?"

"I think she is long past that. She is living her own life."

"Are you? Are you living your own life?"

"Yes," Alexander said. "I'm living my own life, too. I'm living the life I made for myself."

Harold was silent in the dark. "No, son," he said. "You're living the life I made for you."

Alexander was so afraid to blink.

"I had thought you would go far, Alexander. Your mother and I both thought so."

"I know, Dad. I was all right there for a little while."

"I imagined a different life for you."

"Me, too."

Harold stood over Alexander. "Where is my son?" he whispered. "Where is my boy? I want my son back. I want to carry him to sleep in my arms, just like I did when he was born."

"Here I am," said Alexander.

His voice cracking, Harold said, "Ask for some bread, Alexander. Please. Don't be so proud."

Alexander did not respond.

Harold leaned over him and whispered: "If you can force your heart and nerve and sinew, to serve your turn long after they are gone, and so hold on when there is nothing in you, except the will which says to them, 'Hold on!' "

Now Alexander blinked. And Harold was gone.

CHAPTER THIRTY-SIX

New York, December 1945

TATIANA WAS PUTTING ANTHONY to bed when he suddenly said, "Mama, can Jeb be my daddy?"

"Probably not, honey."

"Can Edward?"

"Yes, maybe him. You like him?"

"I like him. He is nice."

"Yes, honey, Edward is a good man."

"Mama, tell me a story."

She kneeled by the side of Anthony's bed, and clasped her hands together as if in prayer. "Want to hear about how Pooh Bear and Piglet found an endless pot of honey and Pooh Bear got so big he had to be put on a diet—"

"No, don't want that one. Tell me a cary one."

"I don't know scary ones."

"Cary one," he said, in a declaration that invited no argument.

Tatiana thought about it. "All right, I'll tell you about Danaë, the woman in the chest."

"The woman in the chest?"

"Yes. A painting of her, by great painter named Rembrandt, used to be in big museum of city I was born, Leningrad. But when war started, paintings were all shipped out from museum, and I don't know if Danaë and all others are safe."

"Tell me about woman in chest, Mama."

Tatiana took a deep breath. "Once upon a time, there was cowardly man named Acrisius. He had a daughter named Danaë."

"Was she young?"

"Yes."

"Was she a bootiful princess?" Anthony giggled.

"Yes." Tatiana paused. "But Acrisius had the oracle—"

"What is oracle?"

"Person who tell you future. He had oracle warn him that his daughter's son was going to kill him. So he got very scared—"

"He didn't want to die?"

"That's right. So he locked Danaë away in bronze chamber so no one could get to her and give her a baby."

Anthony smiled. "Someone got to her?"

"That's right. Zeus." Tatiana's hands were clasped. She was on her knees. "Zeus found way into Danaë's bronze chamber by making himself into golden rain, and Danaë was loved by a god . . . and he gave her a baby, a son. Do you know what they called him? They called him Perseus."

"Perseus," Anthony repeated.

Tatiana nodded. "When Acrisius found out that his daughter had son, he became so scared that he didn't know what to do. He did not dare kill boy, but he couldn't let him live, either. So he had mother and child put into chest and set adrift in stormy sea."

Anthony was listening raptly.

"They were set adrift with no food and all alone. Danaë was scared, but Perseus wasn't scared." Tatiana smiled. "Perseus knew in his baby heart that his father wouldn't let anything happen to him. Nor to Danaë." She paused. "And his father didn't. Zeus asked god of sea—Poseidon—to still the waters and calm the waves to let them pass safely in their frail ark to wash ashore on island in Greece."

Anthony smiled. "I knew they be safe." He breathed in deeply. "Did they live happily ever after?"

". . . Yes."

"What happened to Perseus?"

"Someday, when you are older, I will tell you what Perseus's future held."

"You will be my . . . *oracle?*"

"Yes."

"But he didn't die?"

"Oh, no. He grew up nicely. All people on island could guess right away that Perseus was of royal birth—the son not just of a king, but of a god. He grew up strong, played all games, always beat his playmates, but his mind was set only on brave deeds by which he might prove himself to be hero among men."

Anthony stared at his mother. "Did Perseus become a hero?"

"Yes, son," answered Tatiana. "Perseus became spectacular hero. When you are little older, I will tell you what he did to Gorgon Medusa and to sea monster. But now I want you to have sweet dreams. I want you to dream of Luna Park and cotton candy and playing hide and seek under the boardwalk. All right?"

"Mama, wait—was the oracle right? Did Perseus kill . . . that man?"

"Yes, son. Perseus did kill Acrisius. Accidentally. Without meaning to."

"So he was right to send them away."

"Suppose so. Didn't matter much, though, did it?"

"No. That wasn't very cary, Mama. Maybe sea monster next time?"

"Maybe. I love you." She closed the bedroom door behind her.

❧

Vikki had gone out for the evening, to another Christmas party at the hospital. She had invited Tatiana, but Tatiana had gone to several holiday parties in the last few weeks and was all partied out. She was at the kitchen table with a cup of tea and the *New York Times* spread out in front of her, and the radio on with the latest from Nuremberg, when the doorbell rang.

It was Jeb. He was wearing his naval whites, and he looked tall and wide, and . . .

"What you doing here?" she asked, surprised. She was not expecting him.

"Why, I've come to see you," Jeb said, pushing past her and inside.

She closed the door behind him. "It's late."

"Late for what?"

Tatiana went to the kitchen. "You want cup of tea?"

"How about a beer? You have a beer?"

"No, no beer. Just tea."

She made him a cup of tea and settled tensely on the couch next to him. Jeb took a sip and put the cup down. "House is quiet," he said. "That *Vikki* not here?"

"She stepped out for minute," said Tatiana.

"At eleven at night?"

"She be back any minute."

"Hmm." Jeb eyed her. "You know, you and I never have a chance to be alone." He rubbed her thigh.

Tatiana did not move away from him.

"Yes. Why won't you come over to my place?"

"Don't you share apartment with Vincent?"

"What does *that* have to do with anything?"

"You not alone, either."

"Yes, but Vikki is *always* around," he said tendentiously. "And Anthony, too."

Tatiana squinted. "Anthony has nowhere to go," she said slowly.

"Hmm. He's sleeping now?"

"Restlessly, yes,"

"Hmm." He pushed her down on the couch. His mouth was on her neck.

"Wait," said Tatiana, turning her head this way and that. "I can't breathe." She was pushing him away, but he wasn't going anywhere.

"Hey," he said, "you smell *great* . . . and we're alone."

"Get off, please."

"Oh, Tania, sweetheart, you don't know who you're dealing with."

"And you don't know who you're dealing with," she said, forcibly moving his face off her, and slipping onto the floor from under him. Panting, she said, "Jeb, I'm sorry, I'm tired. I have to get up very early. Can you go?"

"Go?" he said in an irritated voice. "I'm not going anywhere. Not going anywhere, till I—" He broke off. "What do you think I came here for?"

"Jeb, I don't know. I'm not going to guess. Fight with me, I reckon. I'm not in mood to fight."

"I won't fight with you, Tatiana," he said, getting up off the couch and coming toward her. "That's not what I'm in the mood for."

"Well, I'm not in mood to fight or anything," she said, souring on him and his naval uniform and his height and his hair, souring on him, gleaning a displeasure at herself, and remorse, and suddenly a clearing of her senses. Could she have been *so* transparent?

"Tania, I feel you've been stringing me along," Jeb declared, stepping away and sitting down on the sofa.

"Not at all. We are getting to know each other, that's all."

"Yes, we've gotten to know each other plenty. Plenty! Frankly, I want to get to know you a little better."

Tatiana stared coldly at Jeb, sitting with his legs spread open, his arms spread open on the back of the couch. "I have child in bedroom. What are you thinking, raising your voice, acting this way?" She started to walk to the door.

Jumping up, he grabbed her by the arm. "I'm not leaving."

"You *are*, Jeb," she said. "If you want to see me again, you will leave now."

"Is that a threat?" he said, yanking at her sweater. "What are you going to do?" He laughed. "Kick me out? Stop me?"

"Yes, and yes," she said.

He grabbed her, bringing her to him. "I see the way you look at me," he whispered. "You think I don't see, but I see. I know you want it too, Tania."

"Stop it," she said, struggling to wrest herself away from him. A pang of sadness shot through her. Sadness for herself.

He laughed and held her tighter. Tatiana took his arm and pinched him very hard on the wrist. "Get control of yourself."

"Ouch!" he said loudly. "You want it rough? Is that what you want?" He forced her back onto the couch.

"Don't you understand?" she said, panting. "I don't want it at all. I've made terrible mistake."

"Too late for mistakes, dearie. I'm done walking around you on eggshells."

She was trapped beneath him, and she was so fed up, and so sick and tired of herself, she didn't know what to do. I have been loved by Alexander, she thought. This will not be my life. Pretending to kiss Jeb, Tatiana bit down hard, breaking the skin of his lip with her teeth. He yelled, and she pushed him off her and jumped to her feet. He jumped up too, and before she could move or duck or turn away, Jeb swung and struck her. She tottered, dropped to the couch, wavered, saw white light, but struggled to keep conscious because she heard a low noise near the bedroom door. Anthony stood in his pajamas, melting into the wall, looking at Jeb and trembling. "Don't—" he said in a small voice. "Don't you hurt my mama."

Tatiana crawled to him.

Jeb cursed, wiping the blood off his mouth.

Tatiana pushed Anthony inside the bedroom and whispered, "Stay here, and don't come out no matter what, do you hear me?" Quickly she went to the closet, and reached down into the corner on the floor to get to the black backpack.

Anthony didn't respond, his lip curling down in a shudder.

"Do you hear me? Not for *anything*."

He nodded.

Tatiana closed the door behind her.

Tatiana looked at Jeb as if she had never seen him before. How could she have been so swayed by what Alexander had been? She had thought she could replace just a part of him, that it would be all right if she replaced the one part she so desperately missed of Alexander, the one part she craved and wanted for herself, that she would feel better, that she would be comforted. And now look at what she had done.

Breathing hard, Tatiana pointed her German P-38 pistol at an amused and panting Jeb, and said, "Get out of my apartment."

He glared at the gun with surprise and then laughed. "Where on earth did you get *that* little playtoy?"

"My husband and father of my child gave it to me to protect me from cannibals," she said. "My husband was major in Red Army and he knew how to use this, and he taught me. Now get out."

She was holding the gun with both hands and her feet were apart.

"Is that even loaded?" he asked with contempt.

Tatiana paused, cocked the hammer, moved the muzzle slightly to the left of Jeb's face, took a deep breath, and fired. Jeb staggered backward and fell to the floor. The bullet blew a hole in the plaster and got lodged in the outside brick of the building. It had made a very loud noise, but Anthony did not come out of the bedroom. There was some half-hearted banging from downstairs, warning her to keep it down.

Tatiana came up to Jeb and hit him hard on the face with the barrel of the gun. "Yes. It's loaded," she said. "Now get the hell out."

"Are you fucking crazy?" he yelled, his hands up in front of him.

She stepped away and pointed the weapon at him. "Out."

"You'll be sorry for this! Very sorry. I want you to know I am *not* coming back," Jeb said to Tatiana, scrambling to his feet.

"I'm hoping somehow I'll manage. Get out."

After he had gone, Tatiana bolted and chained the door. She washed her face and hands, and then went in to see her son, who was huddled in the corner of the room. Bringing him back to bed, Tatiana covered him up, sat with him a moment but couldn't speak. She patted his blanket and left the room.

She went out onto the fire escape and sat in the cold night. Six flights below was the whine of an ambulance rushing down Church Street.

That's it for me, Tatiana thought. That's it. I feel it. I can't continue.

I am going to lie down on his sled and close my eyes and he will pull me along the snow to my Fifth Soviet building, except when we get there, I will not feel his hand on my cheek.

She looked at the gun in her lap, with seven bullets still in the clip, and she thought, it would take just one split second. Not even that. It would take one one-thousandth of a second, and it would all be over. So easy.

She closed her eyes. What comfort. Not to have to wake up again. Not to have to wake up and think of him on the ice.

What comfort not to suffocate.

Not to love.

Not to hurt, to want, to grieve. As if grief is not only my prerogative but my comeuppance. I caress the grief as I once caressed him; as long as it's here, he is here; as long as I'm pretending to live, I can be near him. I've paused over it, one, two, three years nearly, going on the fourth cartwheel of despair, I'm bereaved, let me alone, and let me gaze at my grief with passion and ardor.

We thought I was strong. We thought I could live through it all.

But we were wrong.

I just can't seem to live through you.

Though I want to. I want to so much.

What a relief it would be not to have to live for both of us. What joy. She stared at the gun in her raised hands.

In her darkest hour, Tatiana heard her son's voice say, "Mama?"

He was standing in his cotton pajamas near the open window, his lower lip quivering, watching her hold the pistol.

"Anthony," she said. "Go back to your room."

"No. I want you to put me to bed."

"Go back to your bed. I'll be right there."

"No. Come with me now." He was crying.

She put the gun down on the metal floor of the fire escape and climbed inside.

"Vikki will be here soon," she whispered, laying him back down and covering him up.

"No," said Anthony. "I don't want Vikki. I want you. Lie down next to me."

"Anthony—"

"Mama, lie down next to me."

In her clothes, Tatiana lay on Anthony's bed, and put her arm around him. "Stay here," he said. "Fall asleep with me, Mama."

They lay quietly. Minutes passed. "Son, everything is going to be all right from now on," she said. "I promise you. One of your father's promises. Not your mother's. Everything is going to be all right."

Quietly Anthony said, "Was my daddy really a major in the Red Army?"

"Yes."

Pause. "He wouldn't have missed."

"Shh, Anthony."

Tatiana thought about tomorrow.

Continuing through fear, living through fear. And worse. Living through death. Loving through *him*. Courage, Tatiana. Courage, babe. Get up, get up for me, and go on. Go on, go take care of our son, and I will take care of you.

Her guardian angel Alexander, her sweetest angel Alexander, floating above her veiled in sorrow, whispering to her: *Tania, do you remember what you said to your sister as she was dying on the ice, on the Road of Life, as she was collapsing into the snow unable to walk, you said to her, come on, Dasha, get up. Alexander is trying to save your life. Show him your life means something. Get up and walk to the truck, Dasha.*

Well, I'm saying it to you now. Show me your life means something. Get up and walk to the truck, Tania.

Tatiana lay next to Anthony until he was asleep. It was very late, and Vikki was still not home. Finally she got up off the bed, and went to put the pistol away into her backpack. She did not look at anything else there, but she did take the wedding rings from around her neck, kissed them once quickly and placed them in the pack too, to rest with his cap, and his *Bronze Horseman* book and the picture of him receiving his medal for rescuing Yuri Stepanov. To rest with his medal for rescuing Dr. Matthew Sayers from the ice—his *Hero of the Soviet Union* medal. Rings, medals, pictures, book, money, cap. Their two wedding photos.

All of it inside, and Alexander, too.

And Tatiana, too.

CHAPTER THIRTY-SEVEN

New York, January 1946

NEW YEAR'S DAY. TATIANA, as usual, went ice skating in Central Park with Vikki and Anthony.

After they were done and walking to 59th Street to take a bus home, Vikki was staring at Tatiana.

"What you looking at?"

Vikki didn't reply.

"What?"

"We've passed three phone booths."

"So?"

"Aren't you going to ask me to mind Anthony for just a few minutes and run off to make your phone call?"

Tatiana stared down Fifth Avenue.

"No," she said. "But do you think Edward might be interested in going out with me again?"

Vikki beamed. "I think he's going to fly to the moon!"

⌒⌒⌒

She and Edward were having lunch at NYU hospital, soup and tuna sandwiches. Tatiana really liked tuna with mayo, lettuce and tomato. She had never had tuna before she came to America. Or lettuce.

"Hey," she said brightly, reaching across the table and taking his hand. "*Mildred Pierce* is hailed as the next masterpiece. Want to go and see it?"

"Sure. When?"

"How about Friday evening? Come over after work. I'll make you dinner, and then we'll go."

Edward paused. "You want me to come over *in the evening?*" he asked slowly.

"Please."

Edward looked at her hand on his, then at her. "Something is terribly wrong. What is it? Have you found out you only have five days to live?"

"No," she said. "I found out I have seventy years to live."

⌇

The next day, she was in the examination room at Ellis, filling out papers on one of the Polish refugees, when another nurse walked in and whispered, "There is someone outside to see you."

Tatiana didn't look up from the application for residency. "Who?"

"Never saw him before. Says he's from the State Department."

Tatiana looked up immediately.

Outside in the corridor, Sam Gulotta stood, dressed in a suit, waiting for her.

"Hello, Tatiana," he said. "How are you? Did you have a happy New Year?"

"I'm good, yes, and you?" she replied, and then couldn't say anything else, but reached out slowly, hoping Sam wouldn't notice, to get hold of the wall behind her.

"I've been waiting for you to call."

Very carefully, she shrugged. She didn't want him to notice she was shaking. "I didn't want to bother you anymore. You have been so patient with me over the years . . ."

Sam looked up and down the hall. "Is there somewhere we can go and talk?"

They went outside and sat on the benches by the swings where Anthony used to play.

"I was hoping you'd call me," Sam said.

"What's happened?" she said. "Are they still looking for me?"

He shook his head. Tatiana's white fingers bored into the sides of the bench. She was grateful for the cold that allowed her teeth an excuse to chatter.

"What?" she whispered. "You have information for me? He is dead?"

"I have something, yes. I have an inquiry on his file. As always, it went to the wrong department—Global Affairs, who forwarded it to Population, Refugees and Migration Bureau. They said it wasn't their jurisdiction, and sent it to the Department of Justice to EOIR, Executive Office for Immigration Review." Sam shook his head. "Someone should explain to them the polar difference between immigration and emigration—"

"Sam," was all Tatiana said.

"Oh, yes. I just wanted to explain the bureaucracy of our government. Everything moves in geological time. Let me tell you what the inquiry is: it's very short. An Allied American soldier, PFC Paul Markey of the 273rd Infantry Division contacted the State Department—*last summer*, no less—asking if they had any information about an American named Alexander Barrington."

Tatiana swayed and sank into the bench.

For a very long time she remained mute.

"Tania?"

"Yes?" In a voice that wasn't hers. "Sam, who is Private Markey?"

"Private First Class Paul Markey of Des Moines, Iowa. Twenty-one years old, three years in the armed forces. I called his home last week. Spoke to his mother." Sam lowered his head. "He was returned from Europe and discharged from duty last summer, I guess that's when he made the inquiry. I'm afraid there is bad news about him. In October he took his own life."

Tatiana sucked in her breath. Blinked. "Sam, no, I'm sorry for him, but . . . I mean, *who* is Paul Markey? Where was he?"

"I know little about him except his inquiry, which he made verbally by phone."

"Who did he speak to at PRM?"

"A woman by the name of Linda Clark."

"Should we go talk to her?"

"I already have. She is the one who got me the notes of that conversation."

Tatiana held her breath.

"Paul Markey told her that when his regiment liberated Colditz Castle—a fortress used as an Oflag during the war—when the Americans liberated Colditz on April 16, 1945, among the hundreds of Allied officers, there were a few Soviet officers, half a dozen, maybe. One of them approached Markey in surprisingly good clean English, asking for his help. He said he was an American named Alexander Barrington, and asked if Markey could check out his story and help him."

Tatiana started to cry. Her shoulders shook and the tears ran between her fingers with which she covered her face. Sam's hand was on her back, patting her gently.

A few minutes went by. Tatiana calmed down. "I knew he lied to me. I just knew," she whispered. "I could feel it in my bones, I had no proof, but I knew."

"What about the death certificate?"

"Fake, all fake." She sucked in a pained groan. "Just to make me leave Soviet Union."

"How did he end up in Colditz all the way from Leningrad?"

"Like I already tell you. He was put in penal battalion. When Soviet army pushed Germans out of Soviet Union, he went with his battalion. Obviously he ended up in POW camp, this Colditz."

"Do you want me to tell you the rest of what Markey told Clark?"

"Yes," she said with a short sob. "What happened to the liberated men?"

"Everybody but the Soviets went home. Markey told Clark that the morning after liberation, on April 17, a Soviet convoy came into Colditz and took the handful of Soviet officers away, including that man."

"Took them where?"

"Markey did not know. He told Linda Clark that he returned to the United States in the summer and made the call out of curiosity. In October, Consular Affairs called his home in Iowa to tell him that indeed Alexander Barrington had been born in the United States but had been residing in the Soviet Union since 1930. Three days after that Markey took his own life, his mother told me."

Tatiana was quiet, trying to compose her voice. "What kind of liberation is that?" she finally said. "Americans come in to liberate Colditz. Why didn't the Soviets also get liberated? Why was he there even a day later?"

Sam said nothing.

Tatiana looked up and wiped her face. "Sam?"

"What?"

"I thought I was asking rhetorical question, but by your heavy silence I suspect question has answer."

He was silent.

"Sam!"

"Why do you do that? Sam what?" He sighed. "Look, this is just what I hear, I can't confirm or deny this, but the buzz in the State Department, connected to a much larger buzz from the Defense Department, was that the liberating Americans were ordered to keep any Soviet officers or refugees in place until the Red Army came to pick them up."

"Why?"

"I don't know why."

"Where did this order come from?"

"From up the ranks."

"How high up the ranks?"

Sam didn't answer for many ticking seconds. "All the way," he finally said.

⁊⁊⁊

That night, Tatiana came home and said, "Vikki, we have to take little trip."

Vikki fell back on the sofa. "No, God, no. Please. Every time you say the word little, it means somewhere unbelievably far. Where to, this time?"

"Iowa. Poor Edward. I'm afraid I will have to cancel our plans."

"Iowa? No! I refuse. Go by yourself. I'm not going. Anthony is not going. We refuse. Do you hear me?"

⁊⁊⁊

Looking out the train window, Vikki was saying to Anthony, "Look, it's quite pretty here, so many fields. What do you think they grow on these fields, Anthony?"

"Wheat," he said. "Corn."

Vikki glanced at Tatiana, who sat pretending to be immersed in a book. "Anthony, and you know this how?"

"That's what Mama calls them. Wheat fields. Corn fields."

"Oh."

Tatiana smiled.

Des Moines was a city rising up out of those fields. It was brutally cold in Iowa in January. Vikki said she had not expected it. "Why did I think it was warm here? They keep talking about the dust bowl droughts. How can you have a drought in frigid temperatures?"

"They don't have droughts in wintertime, Vikki," said Tatiana, buttoning her coat. "Come on, we'll take *a* taxi."

"You and your taxis. Is this person expecting us?"

"I wrote her."

"Did she write you back?"

"Not really."

"Not really? Is there a middle ground with something like that? Did she or did she not write you?"

"I know she was going to, but we are coming to see her so soon, she didn't get chance to."

"I see. So we're barging in uninvited on a farm widow who has just lost her son?"

The small Markey farmhouse was on the outskirts of Des Moines. Their silo nearby was obscured by snow drifts and trees, giving the impression that it had not been used for some time. The door to the house was opened by a frail, pale woman who nonetheless smiled and said, "Tatiana? Come in. I been expecting you. I'm Mary Markey. This your son? Anthony, come with me." Stretched out her hand. "I just made corn muffins, you can help me serve them. Do you like corn muffins?"

Vikki and Tatiana followed them into the kitchen with Vikki whispering, "How do you do that?"

"Do what?"

"Show up in strangers' homes and have them invite you in as if they've known you all their lives?"

The kitchen was neat and plain and old. They sat behind the wooden kitchen table and drank coffee and had corn muffins. Then Vikki took Anthony out in the snow. Mary cupped her mug of coffee and said, "Tatiana, I want to help you. Since you wrote, I been trying to remember what my boy said to me. You understand, I didn't see him in three years, and when he came back he was all closed up. Closed up to me, to his old friends, to the world. The girl he used to see in high school married someone else. Who'd wait that long when you're so young? So Paul would sit around here, or he'd go in the truck down to the local bar. He talked a little about opening the farm again, but with his dad gone that seemed so unlikely." She paused. Tatiana waited. "And he seemed so detached. And then he just gone and killed hisself, too many guns around here, so I been kind of reeling from it and much of what he said to me flew my mind."

"I understand. I'm sorry. Anything you can recall would be helpful."

"I know Paul got that phone call a few days before he died. He didn't tell me nothing, just sat here at this table for the rest of the afternoon. Refused dinner. Went out for a drink, came back, and late at night was sitting here again, or out in the back on the porch. I asked, believe me, I asked several times what the matter was. Finally he said, 'Mom, we liberated that castle and there was a man there who said he was an American, and I didn't believe him. I said . . . something smart in return. And I didn't see him after that . . . and the next day, the Red Army came to get their POWs. Except that this man's perfect English stuck in my memory. So when I came back stateside, I called Washington, just to put my mind at ease.' He sort of made a choking sound then. He said, 'The phone call I got this afternoon? Someone from the State Department. That man *was* an American once upon a time. He was an American, trapped there somehow.' And I tried to say something comforting like, well, he was just sent back to his own country. Just like you was sent back to your own country. And Paul waved me off and said, 'Mom, you don't understand. Our orders—my orders—were to keep all the Soviet officers under surveillance until their army came to reclaim them.'

" 'So?' I said.

" 'Why does an army need to reclaim them? Why don't they just go back in mobs and crowds, of their own accord, like we did, like the English did? Our armies didn't come to reclaim *us*. But the point is, that man wasn't a Soviet.' I didn't understand, you know? I told him that there was nothing he could have done, and he said, 'I don't feel better because I'm helpless, Mother.' And he wring his hands so, and I said, 'Son, but what does the Soviet Union have to do with you? *You're* not sending those people back.' And he put his head down on the table and said, 'Maybe I could have done something for just that one.' "

Tatiana got up and came round Mary's side of the table. She put her arms around the woman. "And he did, Mary. He did."

Mary nodded.

"I'm very sorry."

"I'll be all right. My other daughter lives nearby. I been alone since my husband died in '38. I'll be all right." She looked up. "Do you think that man was your husband?"

"Without a doubt," replied Tatiana.

☙

On the train back, Tatiana was engrossed in the way the snow lay on the fields outside her window. Anthony was asleep. So was Vikki, Tatiana thought, but then Vikki opened one eye, then the other, and said, "So what now?"

Tatiana didn't answer.

"So what now?" Vikki repeated.

"I don't have all answers, Vik," replied Tatiana. "I don't know what now."

But suddenly the world made a bit of sense again. Alexander was not in the lake.

Somewhere in the world Alexander was still living. In the largest country in the world, sprawled over one sixth of the earth's land mass, one half tundra and permafrost, one quarter steppe, one eighth coniferous forest, part desert, part arable land, with the largest lake in the world, the largest sea in the world, the largest protected border in the world, the largest socialist experiment in the world, was Alexander.

All her small paths of faith had led her to an alive Alexander.

And now what?

⚭

Upon her return Tatiana immediately called Sam, but he could not find out what had happened to the Soviet prisoners from Colditz. The Soviet military wasn't speaking, relations were icy, and though Sam had contacted two other privates who were with Markey at Colditz, they had not heard an English voice from the Soviet prisoners and Markey had not spoken to them about it.

"Contact Soviet Department of Defense and ask what happened to Soviet officers at Colditz."

"What should I say? Have you got that Alexander Barrington stowed away somewhere?"

"You're just joking. You know you can't mention him by name."

"Oh, that's right. I'm not allowed to actually make any inquiries on his behalf."

"Sam, call our Defense Department."

"Anyone in particular at the Defense Department? Maybe Lieutenant Tom Richter?"

"Yes, if he has answers. Ask him what happened to the Soviets at Colditz. If he doesn't know, ask what happened to Soviet officers in Germany."

"Tania, you know what happened to them!"

"I want to know where they were taken," she said. "And there is no need to shout."

"Even if I did find out, what are you supposed to do with that information?"

"Why you always worry about my part? Just do your part."

She didn't reschedule her plans with Edward.

A few days later, she called Sam again. He told her that a major general in Patton's army said that last year the Soviets were rounding up all of what they called their nationals and keeping them in transit camps until they could transport them back to the Soviet Union.

"How many is everyone?"

"The major general did not say. He did not hazard a guess."

"Can you?"

"Even less than him."

"Where are these transit camps?"

"All over Germany."

Tatiana was thoughtful.

"Tania, for certain he is in the Soviet Union by now. Liberation of Colditz was nearly ten months ago. But regardless of where he is, the Soviets aren't giving *their* men back to us no matter how nicely we ask. They won't give *our* men back to us! We have soldiers MIA on the Soviet side. They aren't giving us any information at all."

"Alexander is MIA," Tatiana said.

"No, he isn't! The Soviets know precisely where he is!" And quieter, Sam said, "Tania, haven't you heard the death statistics for the Soviet POWs? They're staggering."

"Yes," she said. "I'm still holding death certificate you placed so much faith in. You told me he was most certainly in lake."

"This is worse."

"How is this worse? We just have to find where he is."

"He is in the Soviet Union!"

"Then find him in Soviet Union, Sam. He is American citizen. You have responsibility to him."

"Oh, Tatiana! How many times do I have to tell you? He lost his citizenship in 1936."

"No, he did not. Sam, I have to go. I have patients. I will talk to you tomorrow."

"Of course you will."

CHAPTER THIRTY-EIGHT

The Nuremberg Trials, February 1946

"COME ON, LET'S GO out," Vikki said petulantly. "What are you listening to that for? Let's go to a movie, or a coffee bar, or for a walk." She pounded the kitchen table. "I'm so tired of it. We've been listening to it for months. We're never getting a television, I just want you to know that."

Tatiana had her ear to the radio as she was listening to the audio transcript of the Nuremberg trials.

"I'm not listening just for sake of something to do," said Tatiana, turning up the radio. "I'm listening because it's riveting."

"Do you see me riveted? The war is over, they're all guilty, they're all to be hanged, when is enough enough? It's been going on for months. The generals have all been convicted. These are just the lackeys. I can't take much more."

"Can you go for walk?" Tatiana said without turning her head. "Go now, and stay out for two hours."

"You'll be sorry if I leave for good."

"Yes. But not if you leave for two hours."

Vikki, with a harrumph, sat in the chair next to her. "No, no. I want to hear."

"They're talking about my Leningrad," said Tatiana. "Listen."

In the criminal plans of the Fascist conspirators, the devastation of the capitals of the Soviet Union occupied a particular place. Among these plans the destruction of Moscow and Leningrad received special attention.

Intoxicated by their first military successes, the Hitlerites elaborated insane plans for the destruction of the greatest cultural and industrial centres dear to the Soviet people. For this purpose they prepared special Sonderkommandos. They even advertised their "decision" in advance.

It is necessary to note that such expressions as "raze to the ground" or "wipe from the face of the earth" were used quite frequently by the Hitlerite conspirators. These were not only threats but criminal acts as well.

I shall now present two documents which reveal the intentions of the Hitlerite conspirators.

The first document is a secret directive of the Naval Staff dated 22 September, 1941. It is entitled "The Future of the city of Petersburg." In this directive it is stated: "The Fuehrer has decided to wipe the city of Petersburg from the face of the earth"; that it is planned to blockade the city securely, to subject it to artillery bombardment of all calibres and by means of constant bombing from the air to raze the city to the ground. It is also decreed in the order that should there be a request for capitulation, such a request should be turned down by the Germans.

The second document is also a secret directive of the Supreme Command of the Armed Forces dated 7 October, 1941, and signed by the defendant Jodl. I read into the record a few excerpts from this letter:

". . . The Fuehrer again came to the conclusion that a capitulation of Leningrad or later of Moscow is not to be accepted even if it is offered by the enemy . . ."

And further, the next to last paragraph of this page:

". . . Therefore, no German soldier is to enter these cities. By the fury of our fire we must force all who try to leave the city through our lines to turn back. We cannot take the responsibility of endangering our soldiers' lives in order to save in their entirety all Russian cities, nor that of feeding the population of these cities at the expense of the German Homeland."

The Hitlerite conspirators began to put their criminal ideas regarding the destruction of Leningrad into effect with unprecedented ferocity.

I read:

"As a result of the barbarous activities of the German Fascist invaders in Leningrad and its suburbs, 8,961 household and adjoining buildings—sheds, baths, etc.—with a total volume of 5,192,427 cubic metres were completely destroyed, and 5,869 buildings with a total volume of

14,308,288 cubic metres were partially destroyed. Completely destroyed were 20,627 dwellings, with a total volume of 25,492,780 cubic metres, and 8,788 buildings, with a total volume of 10,081,035 cubic metres were partially demolished. Completely destroyed were 295 buildings of cultural importance, with a total volume of 844,162 cubic metres, and 1,629 buildings with a total volume of 4,798,644 cubic metres were partially ruined. Six buildings dedicated to religious sects were completely, and 66 such buildings partially, destroyed. The Hitlerites destroyed, ruined and damaged various kinds of buildings valued at over 718,000,000 rubles, as well as industrial equipment and agricultural machinery and implements worth over 1,043,000,000 rubles."

This document establishes that the Hitlerites bombed and shelled, methodically and according to plan, day and night, streets, dwelling-houses, theatres, museums, hospitals, kindergartens, military hospitals, schools, institutes and streetcars, and ruined the most valuable monuments of culture and art. Many thousands of bombs and shells hammered the historical buildings of Leningrad, and its quays, gardens and parks. For the bombardment of Leningrad, there was in the batteries a special stock of munitions supplied over and above the average, to an unlimited amount . . . All the gun crews knew that the bombardment of Leningrad was aimed at ruining the town and annihilating its civilian population.

Vikki said to Tatiana, "Did you know any of this when you were there?" "I didn't know any of it," Tatiana replied. "I lived through all of it."

GENERAL RAGINSKY: Mr. President, in order to exhaust fully the presentation of evidence in regard to the subject-matter of my report, I ask your permission to examine witness Josif Abgarovitch Orbeli—

Tatiana dropped the cup of tea she was drinking, and it fell on the tile floor and broke, and Tatiana fell on the floor, too, on her knees, and began to pick up the pieces, every moment or so emitting cries of such distress that Vikki, who was nearby, jumped up, backed away and said in a stunned voice, "What's *wrong* with you?"

Tatiana waved her off with one hand, her other hand holding a ce-

ramic shard which covered her mouth as she continued to listen to the
bare echo that was the radio broadcast as it ceaselessly continued. A
crash on the road, but the radio still plays music, still transmits sounds
no matter how incongruous it is that the ear can somehow hear, that the
brain can somehow listen—

—Orbeli will testify in regard to the destruction of the
monuments of culture and art in Leningrad.
Q. What is your name?
A. Josif Abgarovitch Orbeli.
Q. Witness, will you tell us, please, what position you occu-
pied?
A. I was Director of the State Hermitage Museum—

Tatiana groaned in pain.
"What?" Vikki said with alarm. "What?"
"Shh"—

Q. Were you in Leningrad at the time of the German
blockade?
A. Yes, I was.
Q. Do you know about the destruction of monuments of
culture and art in Leningrad?
A. Yes.
Q. Can you tell us in your own words facts that are known
to you?
A. I was an eye-witness of the measures undertaken by the
enemy for the destruction of the Hermitage Museum. During many long months these buildings were under system-
atic air bombardment and artillery shelling. Two aerial
bombs and about thirty artillery shells hit the Hermitage.
The shells caused considerable damage to the building, and
the aerial bombs destroyed the drainage system and water
conduit system of the Hermitage.
Artillery shells caused considerable damage to the Hermitage and to the surrounding areas.
Q. In what part of Leningrad were these buildings—in the
south, the north, the south-west or south-east section?
A. The Winter Palace and the Hermitage are right in the
centre of Leningrad on the banks of the Neva.

Q. Can you tell me whether near the Hermitage and Winter Palace there are any industries, particularly armament industries?

A. So far as I know, in the vicinity of the Hermitage, there are no military enterprises. If the question meant the building of the General Staff, that is located on the other side of the Palace Square, and it suffered much less from shelling than the Winter Palace. The General Staff building, which is on the other side of the Palace Square, was, so far as I know, hit only by two shells.

Q. Do you know whether there were artillery batteries, perhaps, near the buildings which you mentioned?

A. On the whole square around the Winter Palace and the Hermitage there was not a single artillery battery, because from the very beginning steps were taken to prevent any unnecessary vibration near the buildings where such precious museum pieces were.

Q. Did the factories, the armament factories, continue production during the siege?

A. I do not understand the question. What factories are you talking about—the factories of Leningrad in general?

Q. The Leningrad armament factories: did they continue production during the siege?

A. On the grounds of the Hermitage, the Winter Palace, and in the immediate neighborhood, there were no military concerns. They never were there and during the blockade no factories were built there. But I know that in Leningrad munitions were being made, and were successfully used.

Q. Witness, the Winter Palace is on the Neva river. How far from the Winter Palace is the nearest bridge across the Neva river?

A. The nearest bridge, the Palace Bridge, is about fifty meters from the Palace, at a distance of the breadth of the quay, but, as I have already said, only one shell hit the bridge during the shellings; that is why I am sure that the Winter Palace was deliberately shelled. I cannot admit that while shelling the bridge, only one shell hit the bridge and thirty hit the nearby building.

Q. Witness, those are conclusions that you are drawing. Have you any knowledge whatsoever of artillery from

which you can judge whether the target was the Palace or
the bridge beside it?

A. I never was an artillery man, but I suppose that if German
artillery was aiming only at the bridge then it could not possibly hit the bridge only once and hit the Palace, which is
across the way, with thirty shells. Within these limits I am an
artillery man. (Commotion in the court.)

Q. One last question. Were you in Leningrad during the entire period of the siege?

A. I was in Leningrad from the first day of the war until 31
March, 1942. Then I returned to Leningrad when the German troops were driven out of the suburbs of Leningrad.

GENERAL RAGINSKY: We have no further questions.

THE PRESIDENT: The witness can retire. (The witness
leaves.)

Tatiana looked up at Vikki from the floor and then struggled up to the
table where she put her head down and closed her eyes. Vikki's hands
were on her back.

"I'm all right," she mouthed inaudibly. "I need one minute."

Alexander, to the last.

Orbeli standing in the street, saying goodbye to his crates.

Tatiana had been very moved by his face. She never forgot it.

*It was these crates he was looking at with such heartbreak, as if they
were his vanishing first love.*

"Who is that man?" Tatiana asks.

"He is the curator of the Hermitage Museum."

"Why is he looking at the crates that way?"

*"They are his life's sole passion. He doesn't know if he is ever going to
see them again."*

*Tatiana stares at the man. "He's got to have more faith, don't you
think?"*

*"I agree, Tania. He's got to have a little more faith. After the war is
over, he will see his crates again."*

*"The way he is looking at them, after the war is over he will have to
bring them back single-handedly," she replies.*

Tatiasha—remember Orbeli.

Orbeli was in Alexander's eyes as Tatiana sprinted away from him
in Morozovo hospital, flickered away with nary a thought, barely a look
back, ta-da, darling, and be well, oh, and tell me about that Orbeli an-

other time, Shura, tell me about him next time you see me, and one last time she turned around, laughing, and saw Josif Abgarovitch Orbeli in his eyes. She could never put her finger on his expression. Now she knew.

Every day I stand at the edge of your bed, and I salute you. *I'll see you, Major. Sleep well*. And you say, *I'll see you, Tania*.

I walk away. You call back to me, and I turn around, my trusting eyes on you.

You say to me, in your bravest voice, deep and calm, your stoic voice, you say to me, *Tatiasha—remember Orbeli*.

I frown for a second, but not even a tick goes through me because I'm so busy and you're so calm and Dr. Sayers calls me. And I say, Shura, darling, I have to run, tell me tomorrow, and now I know—you can't speak anymore, you've used it all up. You are mute and you nod, and I blithely mosey through the beds, and at the drab doors I turn around carelessly, one last time, and here I stop.

And there I am going to be.

Orbeli.

৩৩৩৩

In the February night, in the aqua silence, Tatiana sat on the cold fire escape, wrapped in Alexander's cashmere blanket, and smelled the ocean air beyond her, as Manhattan flickered beneath her.

You will find a way to live without me. You will find a way to live for both of us, Alexander had said to her, once.

She knew now, knew for certain what she had long feared, long suspected: Alexander had handed her his life and said, this is for you. I cannot save myself, I can only save you, and you have to go and live your life the way you and only you were meant to live it. You have to be strong, and you have to be happy, and you have to love our child, and eventually, you have to love. Eventually, you have to learn to love again, and to smile again, and to put me away, you have to learn to hold another man's hand, and kiss another man's lips. You have to marry again. You have to have more children. You have to live your life—for me, for you. You have to live it as we would have lived it. All in one word: Orbeli.

Things were clearer in war: right, wrong, so easily defined, so easily defiled. Peril, absolution, privation. *Emotion, anguish, passion*.

I see *him* clearly, even in peace.

Oh—but how much life I have to mask him.

How many traditions, celebrations. Christmas, Thanksgiving, Easter, Labor, Columbus, Independence, and birthdays birthdays birthdays, every one, even mine, the cursed mine, the twisted mine, the suffering mine, the gold mine. Celebrations, food, sunshine, warmth. From dawn to dusk I fill my life with life.

With all the things he wanted for me.

My foundation is buried underneath the building, tall with windows and high with rafters; the foundation covered by trees and shrubs, pansies in the winter, tulips in the spring and my heart is covered too, healed, concealed. Sometimes I run my hand over my chest and in the running of the hand over my heart, the nerves send a small sharp shudder through my body to my brain, a shudder slightly longer than a breath, a long breath. In, out, hold. Breathe out:

Alexander.

Forgive me for leaving you to the dogs of war, for being so quickly willing to believe in your death. I was slow to love, but quick to abandon you.

Where is he? Where is the splendid horseman, my gold ring and my chain, my black bag and my brightest day?

And here Tatiana was, sitting by the bay, wanting her life to begin, to end, but she was not ended, and she was not begun.

The truth was, she was nowhere.

This stage, how long did it last? And would there ever come a time when she wasn't in a stage anymore? When she was just in life?

Before finding Alexander's *Hero of the Soviet Union* medal? No.

After finding Alexander's *Hero of the Soviet Union* medal? No.

After Paul Markey, no.

And never again after Orbeli.

The soul was at war.

She wanted one word from him? Here it was.

I am trying to send you to a place where you will be safe. Don't despair, he was saying, and have faith.

But what to do now? Something had to be done, must be done, but what?

Whatever she did, wherever she went, it meant leaving behind her son. Was that not folly? Was it not lunacy? Was it not madness?

It was all those things.

To go and leave her son behind? What would Alexander say if he were to find out she had left his son to go traipsing through the world looking for him among its horror stores?

Tatiana sat motionless and smelled the air, smelled the water, smelled the sky, tried to find Perseus in the sky and couldn't, tried to find the full moon in the sky and couldn't. It was late and the moon was under cloud cover.

Her baby boy needed his mother.

Did he need his mother more than Alexander needed his wife?

And was that the choice?

Was the choice between the father and the son?

Was she abandoning one for the other?

She had to entertain the possibility she would not be back. Was that the life she was prepared to give her child?

All she had to do was stay where she was, go on as she was.

But there was no Tatiana here. Tatiana remained with Alexander. Her arms were around him in Lake Ladoga, where she lay down with him every night. Her arms were holding him bleeding out into the Lake Ladoga ice. She could have let go of him then, could have given him to God; God was certainly calling for him.

But she didn't.

And because she didn't, she was here in America, sitting on the ledge of the rest of her life. It certainly felt that way, that seminal moment where she knew that whatever her decision, her life would take either one course or it would take another.

One way the path was plain and vivid.

And the other was black and fraught with doubt.

To stay was to accept the good.

To go was to embrace the unknowable.

To stay was to make his sacrifice not be in vain.

To go was to go into death.

Could she accept life without him?

Could she imagine life without him? Maybe not now, but could she imagine herself in ten years' time, in twenty years' time, in fifty years' time? Could she imagine herself being seventy and without him, married to Edward, having Edward's children, sitting with Edward at the long table?

That Bronze Horseman would pursue her into her grave. She felt it. Into her eternity, clambering behind her in the night and in the day, in every hour of sorrow, in every minute of weakness, in darkness, in light, through all of America he would be rattling at her heels, the way he had been relentlessly rattling at her through the past eleven hundred days, through the past eleven hundred nights, right into her maddening dust. How much longer for Tatiana's life?

How much longer for the Bronze Horseman?

Orbeli—was that not proof that wherever he was, in his own blackest night, Alexander was calling for her?

And if she believed that he was alive and did not try to find him, she would be turning her back on him.

What did that say for her?

Maybe she could close that dark window that led to night and not listen for him anymore. Perhaps she could even convince herself that Alexander would forgive her for her turned back, for her indifferent heart.

Ask yourself these three questions, Tatiana, and you will know who you are.

What do you hope for?

What do you believe in?

But most important, what do you love?

She climbed back inside, closed the window and went to lie in bed next to her son.

ᏬᎲᎪᎾ

"Vikki, I have to talk to you," Tatiana said the next morning as they were standing in the kitchen eating croissants and drinking coffee before they rushed off to work.

"Can it wait till tonight? We're late already. Anthony needs to be in playgroup."

Tatiana took Vikki's hand. Vikki's mouth was covered with croissant crumbs. She looked very endearing and skinny and dark-haired standing at the counter, her mouth full, looking down at Tatiana with exasperated affection. Tatiana hugged her. "I love you so much," she said. "Now, sit down. I have to talk to you."

Vikki sat down.

"Vik, you know that I work at Ellis, and I volunteer for Red Cross, and I walk through the veterans' hospitals, and I look through every refugee boat that comes into New York. You know I call Sam Gulotta in Washington every month, and that I got in touch with Esther that first time, all for only one reason?"

"What izh that weason?" Vikki said, chewing.

"To find out what happened to Alexander."

"Oh."

"But I haven't been able to find out anything."

Vikki patted Tatiana's hand.

"It's time for me to do more."

Vikki smiled. "More than Iowa?"

"Now I need your help."

"Oh, no." Vikki rolled her eyes. "Where are we going now?"

"I would like nothing more than for you to come with me," said Tatiana. "But I need you for even bigger things."

"What things? And where are *you* going?"

"I'm going to find Alexander."

A small piece of croissant fell out of Vikki's mouth. "Go find Alexander where?" she said disbelievingly.

"I will start in Germany. Then I go to Poland, then Soviet Union."

"You're going to go *where*?"

"Listen . . ."

Vikki threw her arms down in front of her, flat on the table. Several times she banged her forehead on the tabletop, and flailed her head from side to side.

"Vikki, stop."

"Okay, this one is the best one yet. I don't think you're going to top this one. Massachusetts was good, Iowa was better, Arizona was best, but this one, this one is out of the park."

"I wait until you finished."

"What are you talking about?" Vikki said, finally swallowing her food and banging the table with her fist. "I know you're just joking. No one goes to Germany."

"International Red Cross goes. I'm going."

"The Red Cross doesn't go!"

"It does. And I'm going with it."

"You can't go! Anthony and I can't come with you if you go with the Red Cross to occupied territories!"

"I know. I don't want Anthony and you to come with me. I want him to stay here where he is safe . . ."

Vikki's mouth fell open. This time it was empty.

"I want him to stay here with *you*." She took Vikki's hands. "With you," she repeated. "Because you love my boy, and he loves you, because you will take care of him, as if he were your own, take care of him for me and his father."

"Tania," Vikki whispered hoarsely. "You're crazy, you can't go."

Tatiana squeezed Vikki's hands. "Vik, listen to me. When I thought he was dead, I was dead. I have been resurrected by Paul Markey and by

Josif Orbeli. My husband needs me. He is calling for me, trust me when I tell you he needs my help. Paul Markey saw him *alive* in April last year all way in Saxony, Germany, when he was supposed to be dead in Lake Ladoga, Leningrad, thousand kilometers away. Edward talked me out of going in 1944 because he said I had nothing. And he was right. This time I have something. And I'm going. I just need you to look after my son. Your Grammy and Grampa will help you." Tatiana paused. "No matter what happens."

Helplessly, Vikki shook her head.

"I can't live out my ice cream life here and leave him to rot away his Soviet life there. You do understand how impossible that is, don't you?"

Vikki continued to shake her head.

"He needs me, Vikki. What kind of wife would I be if I did not help him? I help complete strangers at Ellis. What kind of wife does not help her own husband?"

"A sane wife?" whispered Vikki.

"A not very good wife," said Tatiana.

⁂

That same day she took the train to Washington.

Sam Gulotta motioned three people out of his office and shut the door.

"Sam, how are you? I need your help," she said.

"Tatiana, I'm tired of hearing that. Look, you think I don't understand? You think I don't know? Why do you think I've been helping you all these years? You think if there were some way I could bring my Carol back, I wouldn't do it? I would, I would sacrifice everything to have her back. And so I've bent over backwards for you. I did everything I could for you. But I can't help you anymore."

"Yes, you can," she said calmly. "I need you to get me passport for Alexander."

"How can I get him a passport?" Sam yelled. "On the basis of what?"

"He is American citizen and to come back he needs passport."

"Come back from where? How many times do I have to tell you . . ."

"Not one more time. Your own State Department says he has not lost his citizenship."

"They say nothing of the kind."

"Oh yes, they do. Doesn't the federal code for dual nationals read, and I quote"—she took out a piece of paper and brought it to her nose—"'The law requires that the U.S. national must apply for the foreign citizenship *voluntarily*.'" She put special emphasis on *voluntarily* and then, just in case Sam didn't get it, she repeated it. "Voluntarily."

Then she sat with a satisfied expression on her face.

"Why are you looking at me like the cat that ate the canary?"

"I say for third time—voluntarily."

"I heard you the first time."

"I quote more." Paper to nose again. "'He must apply for foreign citizenship by free choice and with the intention of giving up U.S. citizenship.'"

Sam rubbed his eyes. "The code *might* say that. What is your point?"

"Military conscription in Soviet Union for boys sixteen years of age is *compulsory*!" Just in case he didn't get it, Tatiana repeated it. "Compulsory."

"Oh, for God's sake, what is this, kindergarten? I got it the first time you said it to me."

"Voluntary. Compulsory. Do you see, two words have polar, opposite meanings?"

"I see, thank you for defining English words to me, Tania."

"That's what I'm saying. He did not give up his citizenship by free choice, he did not surrender it voluntary . . . ly. He was *forced* to join Red Army at sixteen."

"You told me he enrolled in an officers' program at eighteen. That sounds voluntary to me."

"Yes, but sixteen comes before eighteen. At sixteen he was already forced to conscript and made to believe he had no right to America." She paused. "And he does. And I need you to help him."

Sam stared blinklessly at Tatiana. At last he said, "Do you know something about his whereabouts I don't know?"

"I know nothing. I wish you could help me with that. But I know that one way or another he is going to need passport."

"Passport? Tania! The Soviets have him. Do you understand? Why can't you accept that he is more lost now than ever, without a doubt in the clutches of the Soviet machine that threw millions of their boys at the Germans?"

Tatiana said nothing. Her lower lip quivered slightly.

"And I can't issue a passport without a photo. Without a regulation black-and-white, face only, nothing-covering-the-head photo. I suppose you have one of those?"

"I don't have one of those."

"Then I can't help you."

She stood up. "He is American citizen and he is behind Iron Curtain. He needs *you*."

Sam stood up, too. "The Soviets are refusing to give us information on our MIAs. How do you suppose they will give us information on a man they've been hunting for the last ten years?"

"One way," she said, "or another. I go now. I will wire you when I need you."

"Of course you will."

BOOK THREE
Alexander

She is coming, my life, my fate;
The red rose cries, "She's near, she's near;"
And the white rose weeps, "She's late;"
The larkspur listens, "I hear, I hear;"
And the lily whispers, "I wait."

Alfred, Lord Tennyson

CHAPTER THIRTY-NINE

Eastern Germany, March 1946

TATIANA WENT TO GERMANY on faith.

She was partnered with a short nurse named Penny—shorter than Tatiana!—and a doctor just out of residency named Martin Flanagan. Penny was a bubbly, heavy, funny gal. Martin was medium height, medium weight, medium paunch under his dress shirts, and excruciatingly serious. Martin was losing what thin hair he was born with, which Tatiana thought might have contributed to his humorlessness. Still, she thought Martin was all right until the day before they were leaving when he told her she was putting too much gauze in the medical kits.

"Is there such thing as too many medical supplies?" she said.

"Yes. Our instructions say one gauze, one adhesive tape, and you're putting in two of each."

"So?"

"That's not what we're supposed to do, Nurse Barrington."

Slowly she pulled out the second gauze, but as soon as he turned his back, she threw another three in the cardboard box. Penny saw and suppressed a giggle. "Don't get under his skin. He is very meticulous about how things are supposed to be done."

"He obviously doesn't have enough to worry about," said Tatiana. What would Martin think when she colored her hair and put on makeup? What would he think when she called him Martin? She found out the next morning when she said, "Ready to sail, Martin?"

He coughed and said, "Dr. Flanagan will be fine, Nurse Barrington."

The hair and makeup he did not comment on. Tatiana had colored her hair black that morning, after she said goodbye to Anthony. She didn't want him to see his mother looking like a different person, and so she took him to playgroup as usual and hugged him as usual and said in as calm a voice as possible, "Anthony, now you remember what we been talking about, right? Mama has to go on business trip for Red Cross, but I'm going to be back as soon as I can, and we'll go somewhere fun for our vacation, all right?"

"Yes, Mama."

"Where did you say you wanted to go?"

"Florida."

"That sounds great. We go there."

He didn't say anything, just kept his hand on her neck.

"You're going to be all right with Vikki. You know how much she loves to take care of you. She make you eat donuts and ice cream every day."

"Yes, Mama."

She watched him walk through the classroom doors, his backpack on his back, and then went after him. "Anthony, Anthony!"

He turned around.

"Just one more hug for your mommy, honey."

Vikki took the day off to help with the hair color and to see her off. Tatiana wanted to dye her hair and put on makeup because she didn't want to be accidentally recognized. It took them three hours to dye Tatiana's very long hair. "Remember, this is the toughest part. After this, you just do touch-ups at the crown, every five, six weeks. You think you'll be back by then, maybe?"

"I don't know." She didn't think so. "You better give me enough color for several touch-ups."

"How many?"

"I don't know. Give me enough for a dozen."

Vikki put mascara on Tatiana, some liquid black eyeliner, some cake makeup to cover up her freckles, and some rouge. "I can't believe this is what you go through every day," said Tatiana.

"I can't believe this is what it takes to get you to wear makeup. A suicide mission to the war zone."

"Not suicide. And how am I going to apply it without you? Easy, easy on the lipstick!" Lipstick made her mouth too full and conspicuous—not the effect Tatiana was going for. She glanced at herself in the mirror. She wasn't recognizable even to herself. "Well, what do you think?"

Vikki leaned over and kissed the corner of Tatiana's mouth. "You're completely incognita."

But Martin—Dr. Flanagan—said nothing when they met at the docks that morning, though he did clear his throat and look the other way. Penny was stunned, however. "You have the most beautiful blonde hair, and you went and colored it black?" she said incredulously, her own hair a short thin brown.

In a solemn tone, Tatiana said, "I don't think people take me seriously. I color my hair black, I put on a little makeup, maybe they take me seriously."

"Dr. Flanagan," said Penny, "do you take Tatiana seriously?"

"Very seriously," replied Martin.

It was all the girls could do to keep from laughing.

Vikki, who went with Tatiana to the docks, would not let go of her for some minutes. "Please come back," she whispered.

Tatiana did not respond.

Martin and Penny stared. "Italians are so emotional," Tatiana said, walking up the plank with them and turning around to wave to Vikki.

Tatiana traveled in white slacks and a white tunic and a white kerchief with a red cross on it. She had gone to an army supply store and bought the best and largest canvas backpack, with many zippered pockets and an attached waterproof trench blanket/coat/tent. She packed another uniform for herself, sundries (toothbrushes for two), undergarments, and two olive drab civilian outfits—one for herself and one for a tall man. She packed the third cashmere blanket she had bought during her first Christmas in New York. She packed the P-38 gun Alexander had given her during the siege of Leningrad. She overstocked her nurse's bag with gauze and tape, and syringes filled with penicillin, and Squibb morphine syrettes. Into another compartment in the backpack, she put a Colt Model 1911 pistol and an outrageously expensive ($200) Colt Commando, apparently the best revolver, which fired not bullets but practically bombs. She also bought a hundred eight-cartridge magazines for the pistol, a hundred .357 rounds for the revolver, three 9-millimeter clips for the P-38 and two army knives. She bought the weapons at the "world famous" Frank Lava's. "If you want the best," said Frank himself, "you have to get the Commando. There is simply no heavier-duty, more accurate, more ferocious revolver in the world."

Frank raised his bushy eyebrows only once—when she asked for the box of a hundred magazines. "That's eight hundred rounds you got there."

"Yes, plus revolver rounds. Not enough? Should I get more?"

"Well, it depends," he said. "What's your objective?"

"Hmm," said Tatiana. "Better give me another fifty for . . . *the* Commando." She was doing so well with her definite articles.

She brought cigarettes.

She couldn't lift the backpack when she was done, plain could not lift it off the ground. She ended up borrowing a smaller canvas back-pack from Vikki and putting the weapons into it. She carried the personal items on her back and the weapons bag in her hands. It was very heavy, and she wondered if perhaps she hadn't gone a bit overboard.

From her black backpack she took out their two wedding rings, still threaded through the rope she had worn at Morozovo hospital, and slipped the rope around her neck.

When she resigned from the Department of Public Health and Edward found out, he didn't want to talk to her. She went to say goodbye to him at Ellis, and he stared at her grimly and said, "I don't want to speak to you."

"I know," she said. "I'm sorry for that. But Edward, what else can I do?"

"Not go."

She shook her head. "He is alive—"

"Was alive. Nearly a year ago."

"What am I supposed to do? Leave him there?"

"This is crazy. You're leaving your son, aren't you?"

"Edward," Tatiana said, taking hold of his hand and looking at him with understanding eyes. "I'm so sorry. We almost . . . But I'm not single. I'm not a widow. I'm married, and my husband may be alive somewhere. I have to try to find him."

⚬₥₥₥₯

They sailed on the Cunard White Star liner, and it took them twelve days to reach Hamburg, Germany. The cargo vessel was filled with the prisoner medical kits from the United States, 100,000 of them, plus food kits and comfort parcels. The longshoremen spent half a day loading them onto large trucks to be transported to the Red Cross hospital in Hamburg and then distributed among the many Red Cross jeeps.

The white jeeps themselves were meant to be self-sufficient, to supply and feed teams of three Red Cross personnel—two nurses and a doctor, or three nurses—for a period of four weeks. The doctor was there to tend to the sick and wounded if need be, and there was certainly a need for tending: the refugees in the Displaced Persons camps they visited suffered from every malady known to man: fungus infections, eye infections, eczemas, tick bites, head lice, crab lice, cuts, burns, abrasion, open sores, hunger, diarrhea, dehydration.

In one such white jeep, Tatiana, Penny and Martin traveled to refugee camps scattered all over northern Germany, Belgium, the Netherlands. They may have had enough food to feed themselves, but the DPs didn't, and there were not nearly enough food parcels to distribute. Several times a day, Martin had to stop driving so they could help someone limping or walking, or lying by the side of the road. The whole of western Europe was reeling with the homeless and camps for them were springing up all over the countryside.

But one thing that was not springing up all over the countryside was Soviet refugees. Those were nowhere to be seen. And although there were plenty of soldiers, French, Italian, Moroccan, Czech, English, there were no Soviet soldiers.

Through seventeen camps and thousands and thousands of faces, Tatiana did not even come close to finding a Soviet man who had fought near Leningrad, much less to finding anyone who had ever heard of an Alexander Belov.

Thousands of faces, of pairs of hands reaching up, of foreheads she touched, desperate people infected and unwashed.

He was not here, she knew it, she felt it. He was not here. She walked each discouraging day from one camp to another, without Penny or Martin. The next camp was close—seven miles—and she did not want company, nor their chatter, she wanted to march herself into a life where she could feel for him and find him. Her heart sinking, fading in her chest, she could not feel for where he was.

She withdrew from Penny and Martin, wishing instead upon a New York sunset, wishing instead upon the face of her son, now three months going on forever without his mother. Wishing idly for warm bread, for good coffee, for the happiness of sitting on a couch covered up by a cashmere blanket reading a book with Vikki a nudge away, with Anthony a room away. Her blonde roots grew out faster than she could find a private bathroom with a mirror for her touch-ups. She took to wearing her nurse's kerchief at all times.

Three months. Since March, she had been driving the truck, handing out parcels, bandaging wounds, administering first aid, driving through destitute Europe, and every day bending to the ground in prayer as she bandaged another refugee. As she buried another refugee. Please let him be here. Another barracks, another infirmary, another military base. Be here, be here.

And yet . . . and yet . . .

The hope had not died completely.

The faith had not died completely.

Every night she went to sleep and every morning she woke up with renewed strength and looked for him.

She found another P-38 on a Ukrainian man who had died practically in her arms. She took his ruck which contained eight grenades and five eight-round clips. She crawled into the jeep and hid her new-found loot along with her weapons bag inside the hidden compartment underneath the floor, a thin, narrow hutch that held crutches and folding stretchers, or litters, and now held an arsenal of fire.

But when Tatiana finally realized that Alexander could not be where there was no trace of him, she quickly lost interest in this part of Europe and suggested they go elsewhere.

"What, you don't think the DPs need our help, Nurse Barrington?" said Martin. They were in Antwerp, Belgium.

"No, they do, they do. But there are so many others who need our help. Let's go to U.S. military base here and talk to base commander, Charles Moss." They had received from the International Red Cross the names and the maps of all U.S. installations and known DP camps in Europe.

"Where do you think they need us most, Colonel Moss?" she asked the commander of the base.

"I'd say Berlin, but I wouldn't recommend going there."

"Why not?"

"We're *not* going to Berlin," confirmed Martin.

"The Soviets have rounded up the German soldiers and imprisoned them," said Moss. "I hear the conditions there make the DP camps here seem like resorts on the Riviera. The Soviets have not allowed the Red Cross to distribute parcels in the camps, which is too bad. They could use the aid."

"Where are these Germans held?" Tatiana wanted to know.

"Ah, in a fitting irony, they're being held in the very concentration camps they themselves built."

"Why wouldn't you recommend going there?"

"Because Berlin is a ticking war bomb. There are three million people in the city that cannot be fed."

Tatiana knew something about that.

Moss continued. "The city needs three and a half million kilos of food—a day—and Berlin produces two per cent of that."

Tatiana knew even more about *that*.

"You figure it out. The sewers are out, the drinking pumps are out, there are no hospitals beds and almost no doctors. Dysentery, typhus, not our little eye infections. They need water, medical attention, grain, meat, fat, sugar, potatoes."

"Even in western zones?" asked Tatiana.

"A little better there. But you have to go to the Soviet zone to get to the concentration camps in eastern Germany. I wouldn't recommend it."

"Are the Soviets amenable?" she asked Moss.

"Yes," he replied. "Like the Huns."

After they left Antwerp, Tatiana said, "Dr. Flanagan, what you think? Should we head for Berlin?" The Soviets were in Berlin.

He shook his head. "Absolutely not. That wasn't on our agenda. Our mission is clear: the Low Countries and northern Germany."

"Yes, but Berlin needs us most. You heard the colonel. There is plenty for these parts."

"Not plenty. Not nearly enough," said Martin.

"Yes, but in eastern Germany, there isn't *any*."

Penny stepped in. "Tania is right, Martin. Let's go to Berlin."

Martin sniffed.

"Hey, how come you allow her to call you Martin?" asked Tatiana.

"I don't allow her," he said. "She just does it."

"Martin and I have traveled together through Europe since 1943," said Penny. "He was just an intern then. If he's going to make me call him Dr. Flanagan, I'm going to make him call me Miss Davenport."

Tatiana laughed. "But Penny, Davenport isn't your last name. It's Woester."

"I always liked Davenport."

All three of them were sitting in the front, squished together in the cabin of the jeep. Tatiana was squeezed between the stiff Martin, who was driving, and the soft Penny.

"Come on, let's see these work camps, Dr. Flanagan," said Tatiana. "Don't you feel needed? Berlin doesn't have enough doctors. You're a doctor. Go where you are needed."

"Doctor are needed everywhere," said Martin. "Why should we go into the quicksand that is Berlin? We're going to be sunk there."

But they went, first stopping off at Hamburg to replenish the supplies. Martin balked at filling the jeep with too many kits and food parcels, pointing out that regulations clearly stated that the trucks were not to be filled more than four feet high, but both Tatiana and Penny insisted, and their jeep was packed from floor to ceiling. Tatiana couldn't get to her stash under the floor. She figured if and when she needed it, the jeep would be less fully packed.

Tatiana could have firebombed the city of Berlin herself, so well armed and well stocked was she. She even brought a case of twenty liter-and-a-half bottles of vodka from Hamburg, buying it with her own money.

"Why do we need that? We don't need vodka!"

"You will see, Martin, without it, we will get nowhere."

"I don't want to allow that in my jeep."

"Believe me, you won't regret it."

"Well, I think drinking is a filthy habit. As a doctor I don't want to condone that sort of behavior."

"You're so right. Please don't condone." Tatiana slammed the doors of the jeep as if the matter had been closed.

Penny stifled a laugh.

"Nurse Woester, you are not helping. Nurse Barrington, did you not hear me? I don't think we should bring that alcohol."

"Dr. Flanagan, have you ever been in Soviet territory before?"

"Well, no."

"I didn't think so. Which is why you should trust me on this one. Just this one, all right? We will need the vodka."

Martin turned to Penny. "What do you think?"

"Tatiana here is the chief nursing practitioner at Ellis Island for New York's Department of Public Heath," said Penny. "If she says we should bring vodka, we should bring vodka."

Tatiana didn't want to correct her, she didn't want to say *was* the chief nursing practitioner.

In the DP camps as they traveled hundreds of kilometers through Allied-occupied western Germany, Tatiana found something else besides money, jewelry, pens and paper: the many hands of the desperately lonely-for-home soldiers. Nearly each one, as she bent over him, touched her and whispered something, in French, or Italian, or German, or in familiar warming English, about what a nice girl she was and what a dark girl and what a pretty girl, and was she lonely too, was she married, was she willing, was she, was she, was she, and to every one of them, Tatiana—who did not stop touching their heads to bring them comfort—would quietly say, "I'm here to look for my husband, I'm here to find my husband, I'm not one for you, I'm not the one."

Penny, however, was not attached and was not looking for her husband. What was *she* looking for? Tatiana was glad Vikki had not come to this cauldron of reckless male want. Vikki would have thought the gods were finally answering her prayers. Penny, less attractive than Vikki—and maybe therein lay the problem—could not stop herself from feeling flattered and from succumbing to their pleas, and every week or so, needed to take injections of penicillin to ward off sicknesses the thoughts of which made Tatiana a little bit sick herself.

There were some wards and some camps, in Bremen for instance, where things were so heated that the Red Cross nurses were not allowed to go into the wards by themselves, either without an armed convoy or without a male Red Cross representative. Trouble was, the convoy sometimes was paid to look the other way, and the Red Cross male reps were unreliable. In all honesty, who could Martin have stopped?

Tatiana took to carrying the P-38 on her at all times, tucked into her belt at her back. Often she did not feel safe.

⊙≈∞≈⊙

To get to Berlin, they had to pass through a number of Soviet checkpoints. Every five miles or so, they were stopped by another military post on the road. Tatiana thought of them not as checkpoints but as ambushes. Every time they looked at her American passport, her heart thumped extra loud in her chest. What if one of them was alerted to the name Jane Barrington?

As they pulled away after one checkpoint, Martin said, "Why do you call yourself Tania if your name is Jane Barrington?" He paused. "Rather, why did you name yourself Jane Barrington if your name is Tania?"

"Martin! Don't be such a clod," exclaimed Penny. "Don't you know anything? Tania escaped from the Soviet Union. She wanted to give herself an American name. Right, Tania?"

"Something like that."

"So why would you be going back into Soviet-occupied territory if you escaped from the Soviet Union?"

"Oh, that *is* a good question, Martin," said Penny. "Why, Tania?"

"I go where I'm needed most," said Tatiana slowly. "Not where it's most convenient."

Every other checkpoint, the Soviet soldiers asked to inspect the jeep. Since the truck of the jeep was packed to the gills, all the soldiers did was open the doors and close them again. They did not know about the hidden compartment so they never requested to look in there, nor did they look through the personal belongings. Martin would have had a conniption if he saw how much morphine Tatiana was carrying in her nurse's bag.

"Where is this Berlin already?" said Tatiana.

Penny replied, "You're in it."

Tatiana looked around at the long rows of houses. "This is not Berlin."

"Yes, it is. What were you expecting?"

"Big buildings. The Reichstag. The Brandenburg game."

"What do you think firebombing means?" Martin said loftily. "There is no more Reichstag. There are no more big buildings." They drove on to the center of town.

Tatiana pointed. "I see the Brandenburg gate is still standing."

Martin fell quiet.

Berlin.

Post-war Berlin.

Tatiana didn't know what she was expecting, but having lived through a bombed Leningrad, she had braced herself for the worst, and was still surprised by the destruction she found. Berlin wasn't a city, it was a ruin of biblical devastation. Most buildings in inner Berlin were lying in rubble, and the residents lived in the shadow of those ruins, as their children played amid the broken concrete, as they hung their washing out to dry from one mangled steel post to another. They built tents around the places where they used to live, and made fires in pits in the ground, and ate what they could and lived how they could. That was the American sector.

The Tiergarten Park that had made Berlin famous was now the stomping ground for thousands of displaced Berliners, the River Spree was polluted with cement ash, glass, sulfur, sodium nitrate—the debris of firebombing that left nearly three quarters of the central city razed to the pavement.

Penny was right. Berlin was not cramped like New York into a cigarette pack of an island, was not even like Leningrad, a neat ink blot stopped by the gulf. Berlin sprawled in all directions, broken buildings jutting out for miles.

No wonder the sectors were so hard to contain, Tatiana thought. There isn't one way in and one way out, there are hundreds of ways in. Tatiana wondered how the Soviets were keeping all the Germans from escaping into the American, French and English sectors.

Martin explained. "I told you, because all the Germans are in jail."

"All the Germans?"

"The rest are dead."

They met with the American military governor in Berlin, an ageing brigadier general by the name of Mark Bishop originally from Washington Heights in Manhattan, who fed them, was very interested in news from back home, and let Tatiana telegraph a wire to Vikki and Anthony ("AM WELL AND SAFE. MISS YOU. LOVE YOU.") and one to Sam Gulotta ("IN BERLIN. ANY NEWS? ANY HELP?") and put them up in a hostel for the night. The building was badly damaged but inhabitable. The inside walls had partly collapsed and the windows were all blown out. But many medical and military personnel used the building to sleep in, and so did Tatiana, Penny, and Martin. Tatiana and Penny shared a room. It was June, it was breezy and cool and there was the constant noise of awake men coming from the outside. Tatiana slept lightly with her hand heavily on the pistol.

Alexander of the broken hearted! Alexander of the innocent, the eloquent, the invincible, the invisible, the inordinate, Alexander of the warrior, the combatant, the commander, Alexander of the water and the fire and the sky, Alexander of my soul—good Lord, deliver me to you, to my soldier man of the tanks and the trenches, of the smoke and the sorrow, to Alexander of all my bliss and my longing, to you wherever you may be—I am searching for you. Please O God be on this earth, Alexander of my heart.

༺∞༻

The next morning, there was a telegram from Sam waiting for her at Bishop's administrative offices. "YOU ARE MAD. JOHN RAVENSTOCK CONSULATE. HE WILL HELP."

Vikki also telegraphed: "COME HOME. WE HAVE NO BREAD."

Mark Bishop himself, eager to get the Red Cross inside the Soviet zone of occupation, took the three of them through the Brandenburg gate to meet with the lieutenant-general of the Berlin garrison who was also the military commander of Berlin.

"He doesn't speak English. Do any of you speak Russian, or do I have to get an interpreter?" asked Bishop.

Martin volunteered Tatiana. "She speaks Russian."

She would have to talk to him about volunteering her for things.

"Tania, you don't mind translating, do you?" said Penny.

"Not at all. I do my best," Tatiana replied, and then took Penny aside. "Penny," she whispered, "don't call me Tania, all right? We're in Soviet territory. Don't call me by my Russian name. Call me Nurse Barrington."

"I didn't even think, I'm sorry," Penny said and smiled. "All that lovin' must be going to my brain."

"Did you take your penicillin shot today? Yesterday you forgot."

"I took it. I'm nearly all better. Thank God for penicillin, huh?"

Tatiana smiled wanly, cringed slightly.

The buildings on the boulevard Unter den Linden in the district of Mitte that had been commandeered to quarter the Soviet army were as decrepit as the hostel Tatiana had slept in. Tatiana was stunned most of all not by the destruction, but by the absolute and foreboding lack of reconstruction, a year after the war. New York, which was not even bombed, was building feverishly as if it were gearing up for the next century. Yet the eastern section of Berlin was stagnant and ruined and sad.

"Commander Bishop, why is it so quiet here? Why isn't Berlin rebuilding?"

"We are rebuilding. Slowly."

"Not that I can see."

"Nurse Barrington, the tragedy that is Berlin I cannot explain in the five minutes before we meet the Soviet garrison commander. The Soviets don't want to pay for the rebuilding. They want the Germans to pay for the rebuilding."

"All right," said Tatiana, "Berlin is a German city. They should."

"Ah. But first the Soviets want to rebuild the Soviet Union. It's only right."

"It is."

"So there is no money for eastern Berlin. Or brains. They're sending all the engineers and all the money to the Soviet Union."

"Why don't the western Allies help?"

"If only it were that simple. The very last thing the Soviets want is our help in their occupied zone. They hate us being in Berlin. They wish we weren't here. They're going to try to force us out, you'll see. They accept nothing from us. You'll see how impossible it will be to convince the garrison commander to enter the concentration camps even for humanitarian reasons."

"They just don't want us to see how badly they're treating German men," said Tatiana.

"Maybe. But they want us out. I'm not looking forward to this meeting."

The stairs inside the building were marble. It was broken and chipped marble, but it was marble nonetheless. The lieutenant general was waiting for the four of them in his quarters.

They went in. He turned around and smiled. Tatiana gasped out loud.

It was Mikhail Stepanov.

⌒⌒⌒

Penny and Martin turned around to look at her. She stepped behind Martin to collect herself. Would he recognize her with her black hair and no freckles and all that makeup? After making the introductions, the governor said, "Nurse Barrington, will you come forward and translate for us, please."

There was nowhere to go. Tatiana stepped forward. She did not smile and Stepanov did not smile at her. He stood completely still and his eyes barely blinked. The only movement his body made in acknowledgement of her was his hand gripping the edge of his desk.

"Hello, General Stepanov," she said in Russian.

"Hello, Nurse Barrington," he said.

Her lips were shaking as she translated for the military governor. The Red Cross was offering to help disperse much needed medical help to the thousands of Germans held by the Soviets in eastern Germany. Could they have permission to administer the aid?

"I think they will need quite a lot of aid," said Stepanov. He still stood straight, but he looked older. He looked tired. There was a worn-out expression in his eyes that said he had seen too much and was finished with nearly all of it. "The camps are not run very well, I'm afraid. The Germans were taken prisoner as part of the reparations effort to help rebuild Soviet Russia, but we're finding that many of them have simply lost their will to work."

"Let us help them," said Tatiana.

Stepanov invited them to sit down. They sat. Tatiana fell into her chair. Thank God she didn't have to stand anymore. "There is a real problem, unfortunately," Stepanov said, "and I don't know if your little parcels are going to do the trick here. There is a growing hatred toward the German prisoners in Berlin and the surrounding areas, a lack of the military discipline essential for running the camps properly, no training for our prison guards, no experience. This all provokes an endless cycle of crime—escape, resistance to the guards and violence. The political costs are quite harsh. Many German workers, who would otherwise work for us and help us, are refusing. In their rebellion, the workers are fleeing to the western zones. It's a problem that we're going to need to address, and soon, and I fear that the Red Cross might simply inflame an already unstable situation."

When Tatiana translated Stepanov's words, Martin said, "The lieutenant general is absolutely right. We have no business here. We don't know what we're playing with."

But Tatiana did not translate that into Russian. Instead she said, "The International Red Cross is a neutral body. We do not take sides."

"You would if you saw these camps." Stepanov shook his head. "I have been trying to get something done about the inequitable distribution of food, the unsanitary conditions, the arbitrary and unfair enforcement of rules. Four months ago I ordered the squalid conditions of the camps to be corrected, to no avail. The army contingent responsible for the Russian camps refuses to punish abuses in its own ranks, leading only to more hostilities."

"The Russian camps?" said Tatiana. "You mean the German camps?"

Stepanov blinked. "Russians in there, too, Nurse Barrington," he said, staring at her. "Or at least there were four months ago."

Tatiana began to tremble.

"What army contingent is responsible for the camps? Maybe I— we—should go talk to them."

"You'd have to go to Moscow and speak to a Lavrenti Beria," said Stepanov. He smiled grimly. "Though I wouldn't recommend it— rumors say that *having coffee* with Beria can be a life-ending experience."

Tatiana clasped her hands between her legs. She did not trust her body to remain impassive. So the NKVD governed the concentration camps in Germany!

"What did he say, Ta—Nurse Barrington?" Penny asked. "You're forgetting to translate."

Martin said, "Our minds are already made up. This is a waste of our resources."

Tatiana turned to him. "We have plenty of resources, Dr. Flanagan. We have the whole United States of America as our resource. The commander is saying that camps desperately need our help. What, are we going to back out now when we discover to our dismay that they need help even more than we thought they did when we came here?"

"Nurse Barrington makes a good point, Dr. Flanagan," said Penny, keeping a serious face.

"The point is to help those who have a way of saving themselves," Martin declared.

"You know what? Let's help first, then we let them sort out if they can help themselves." She turned back to Stepanov. Quietly she said, "Sir, how did you get here?"

"What are you asking him?" said Bishop.

"They transferred me after the fall of Berlin," Stepanov replied. "I was doing too good a job in Leningrad. That'll teach me. They thought I could do the same here. But this isn't Leningrad. Leningrad doesn't have any of these problems. Different problems, with food and housing and clothing and fuel, yes, but Berlin has all that plus a clash of countries, of people, of economies, of justice, of reparations, of punishment. The morass I'm afraid is sinking me." He fell quiet. "I don't think I'm going to last much longer here."

Tatiana took his hand. The military governor, Martin, and Penny all gaped at her.

"He who brought your son back," she breathed out. "Where is he?"

Stepanov shook his head, his eyes on the hand that held his.

"Where?"

He raised his eyes. "Sachsenhausen. Special Camp Number 7."

Tatiana squeezed him, and released him. "Thank you, Lieutenant General."

"What did the general say about Sachsenhausen?" Martin said. "You're forgetting to translate. Maybe we should get an interpreter."

"He was telling me where I'm needed most," Tatiana said, with an effort getting up out of her chair and standing on her unsteady legs. Her mouth was dry. "We would appreciate directions to the camps, sir. Maybe a relief map of the area, just in case? Will you please telegraph them to let them know we're coming? We will telegraph Hamburg for more Red Cross convoys to come to Berlin. We will get enough kits and food into your camps, we promise. It won't correct all the ills, but it will be something, it will be better."

They all shook hands. Stepanov nodded to Tatiana. "Go soon," he said. "The Russian prisoners are doing very poorly. They've been getting transferred to the Kolyma camps over the last several months. You may already be too late for them."

As they were leaving, Tatiana turned around one last time to glance at Stepanov, who was once again standing stiffly beside his desk. He raised his hand. "You're not safe," he said. "You're on the class enemies number one list. I'm not safe. And he is not safe most of all."

❦

"What did he say?" asked Martin as they left.

"Nothing."

"Oh, it's ridiculous! Governor." He turned to Bishop. "Nurse Barrington is obviously keeping important information from us."

"Dr. Flanagan," said Bishop, "you obviously don't speak another language. Whenever you translate, you translate only the salient points."

"I have certainly done that," said Tatiana. When they got outside, she had to sit down on a hunk of mortar that was lying near what used to be an esthetically pleasing fountain.

Bishop came over and perched next to her. "He said the word *vrag* to you as we were leaving. I know that means enemy. What was he saying?"

Tatiana had to take a number of breaths before she could find her composed voice. Quietly she said, "He told us the Soviet army regards us—the Americans—as the enemy. Nothing we can do about that. I didn't want to say that out loud. The doctor"—she nodded in Martin's direction—"is weak-stomached as it is."

The governor smiled. "Understood." He patted her arm, looking at her with approval. "Not like you?" They walked back to Penny and Martin.

"Governor," said Martin, "do you think we should go to Sachsenhausen?"

"I don't see how it can be avoided, Doctor. That's what you came here for. Your nurse here got him to agree to let us into the camps. How did you do it, Nurse Barrington? That's a huge breakthrough for the Red Cross efforts. I will telegraph Hamburg immediately, ask them to send another forty thousand kits."

"Wait, Tania," said Penny, "I want you to explain how you took hold of a Soviet general's hand, got him to let us into the work camps, and not have him call the secret police on you?"

"I am a nurse," said Tatiana. "I touch them all."

"You shouldn't be getting so friendly with the Soviets," said Martin censoriously. "Remember we're neutral."

"Neutral does not imply indifferent, Martin," said Tatiana. "Neutral does not mean unhelpful, uncomforting. Neutral means we do not take sides."

"Not in your professional life," said the governor. "But Nurse Barrington, the Soviets are barbarous. Do you know that they closed off

Berlin for eight days after the German surrender? Closed it off to our armies. For eight days! No one could get in. What do you think they were doing here?"

"I don't want to guess," she said.

"Raping young women like you. Killing men like Dr. Flanagan. Pillaging every house still standing. Burning Berlin."

"Yes. Have you seen what the Germans did to Russia?"

"Ah," said Martin. "I thought we did not take sides, Nurse Barrington?"

"Or the enemy's hands," said Penny.

"He was not the enemy," Tatiana said, and turned away from the others so they wouldn't see her cry.

CHAPTER FORTY

Sachsenhausen, June 1946

MARTIN WANTED TO START the next day. Tatiana said no. They were going immediately. They were getting into their jeep and driving. Immediately.

Martin had a hundred reasons why they should wait until tomorrow. Stepanov's telegraph wire would not have reached the camps yet. They could wait for more Red Cross jeeps and go as a true convoy, the way the Red Cross entered Buchenwald after the war ended. They could have more support. They could go via the hospitals in Berlin itself to see if they needed help. They could have some lunch. The military governor invited them to lunch and was going to introduce them to the generals of the U.S. Marines stationed in Berlin. Tatiana was listening while making them sandwiches and taking all their belongings into the jeep. Then she took Martin's keys, unlocked the doors, pointed to the wheel and said, "Tell me everything, but tell me on the way. Should I drive, or do you want to?"

"Nurse! Have you not been listening to a word I was saying?"

"I've been listening very carefully. You said you were hungry. I have sandwiches for you. You said you wanted to meet a general. You will meet the commandant of the largest concentration camp in Germany in just over an hour if we hurry and don't get lost." Sachsenhausen was about twenty-five miles north of Berlin.

"We need to call Red Cross in Hamburg."

"Governor Bishop is doing that for us. It's all taken care of. We just need to go. Right now."

They got into the truck.

"Where do you think we should start?" said Martin in sulky capitulation. "Apparently Sachsenhausen has one hundred subcamps. Maybe we should start with a few of those. Show me the map. They're small, we could get through them quickly."

"Depending on what you find there," said Tatiana. "But no, we should head for Sachsenhausen." She did not show Martin the map.

"Hmm, no, I don't think so," said Martin. "On my information sheet it says the population of Sachsenhausen is twelve thousand prison-ers. We don't have enough kits."

"We'll get more."

"What's the point? Why don't we just wait until we get more?"

"How long would you wait to give life support, Dr. Flanagan?" said Tatiana. "Not too long, right?"

"They've waited for us all these months, they can wait another cou-ple of days, no?"

"I don't think they can, no."

⁓

Evgeny Brestov, the commandant of the camp was surprised, "shocked, actually," to find the three of them at his doorstep. "You're here to in-spect my *what*?" he said to Tatiana in Russian. He had not asked to see her credentials. Her uniform seemed to be enough for him. He was an overweight, underwashed, sloppily dressed man who quite obviously drank unconscionably.

"We're here to tend to the sick. Hasn't the military commander of Berlin been in touch with you?" Tatiana was the only one able to speak to him.

"Where did you learn Russian?" he asked her.

"At an American university," Tatiana replied. "I don't think I'm very good."

"Oh, no, no, your Russian is excellent."

Brestov walked with them down the road to his administrative of-fices where a telegraph wire from Stepanov marked "Urgent" was wait-ing for him.

"Well, if it's urgent, it's urgent," said Brestov. "Why hasn't anyone brought me this!" he bellowed. And then, "Why such urgency now, I don't understand. Everything is good. We are keeping up with the new regulations. If you ask me there are too many of them. Regulations. They ask us to do the impossible, then they complain when we don't do it to their liking."

"Of course. It must be very difficult."

He nodded vigorously. "So difficult. The guards have no experi-ence. How are they going to manage a trained killing force like the Ger-mans? You know they put up that sign on the gate to the camp, 'Work Makes You Free' or something. You'd think the Fritzes would do a little bit of it."

"Maybe they know it won't make them free," said Tatiana.

"It might. We're discussing terms with the Germans. It certainly won't if they continue to be so recalcitrant."

"So who does the work?"

Brestov fell quiet. "Oh, you know . . ." he said, and changed the subject. "I'm going to introduce you to my superintendent, Lieutenant Ivan Karolich. He oversees the daily routine of the camp."

"Where can we safely keep our truck?"

"Safely? Nowhere. Park it in front of my house. Lock it up."

Tatiana looked down the wooded path and saw that the commandant's house was several hundred yards from the camp's gatehouse. "Could we park it inside the camp? Otherwise, too hard for us to carry thousands of kits. You have what, twelve thousand in there?"

"Give or take."

"Which is it, give or take?"

"Give."

"How many?"

"Four thousand."

"Sixteen thousand men!" Then with less inflection Tatiana said, "I thought the camp was built to house only twelve thousand. Did you construct new barracks?"

"No, we stuffed them all in the sixty barracks we have. We can't build new barracks for them. All the lumber we log in Germany goes back to the Soviet Union to rebuild our cities."

"I see. So can we park inside the gate?"

"Well, all right. What do you have in your truck, anyway?"

"Medical supplies for the sick. Canned ham. Dried milk. Two bushels of apples. Wool blankets."

"The sick will get better. And they're eating too much as it is. It's summer, we don't need blankets. Have you got anything to drink there?" He coughed. "Besides dried milk, that is?"

"Why, yes, Commandant!" Tatiana said, glancing at Martin, and taking Brestov's arm as she led him to the back of the jeep. "I've got just the thing you need." She took out a bottle of vodka. Brestov relieved her of it swiftly.

A sheepish Martin drove the jeep through the gatehouse and parked it on the right-hand side. "The camp looks like an army base," he said quietly to Tatiana. "It's so well designed."

"Hmm," she said. "I bet when the Germans ran it, it was cleaner, better kept. Now look at it."

And true, the walls of the buildings were chipping, the grass was sloppy and uncut, wooden planks from broken window frames lay haphazardly on the grass. The iron was rusting. It had an unpainted, dogged, Soviet look.

"Did you know," Brestov said, "and translate for your friends here, that this camp used to be a model camp? This is where SS guards were trained."

"Yes," said Tatiana. "The Germans really knew how to build camps."

"A lot of fucking good it did them, excuse my language," said Brestov. "Now they're all rotting in their model camps."

Tatiana pulled herself up to stare gravely at the commandant, who coughed in embarrassment. "Where is your superintendent?"

Brestov introduced Lieutenant Karolich, and left the four of them to get oriented. Karolich was a tall, neat man who enjoyed his food. Though he was fairly young, he had the jowly look of someone who'd been eating lard too long. His hands were meticulously clean, Tatiana noticed, as she gave him her hand to shake. How someone with such sanitized hands managed a disease-ridden camp full of unwashed men, Tatiana had no idea. She asked for a walk-through of the camp grounds.

The camp was large and though poorly maintained, the original pie-shaped design of being widest at the front and narrowest at the back made it easy to shoot at prisoners from the gatehouse all the way to the back apex four hundred yards away. The barracks, laid out in three concentric smaller and smaller semi-circles in front of the gatehouse, housed most of the German civilians and soldiers.

The hangings used to take place prominently in the middle of the first semi-circle, perhaps after morning roll call. "Where are your officers housed?" asked Tatiana as they came up to the infirmary.

"Oh, they . . ." Karolich trailed off. "They're in the former Allied barracks."

"Where is that?"

"Just beyond the perimeter, at the back of the camp."

"Well, Lieutenant Karolich, are the German officers so well taken care of that they don't need our help?"

"No, I don't think that's true."

"So? Let's see them."

Karolich coughed. "I think there might be some Russians there, too."

"All right."

"Well, it's a problem to let you into those barracks."

"Why? We will help them, too. Lieutenant, perhaps you misunderstand me. We are here to feed your prisoners. We are here to administer alms. The doctor is here to heal your sick and ailing. So why don't we start? Why don't you escort Dr. Flanagan and Nurse Davenport to the infirmary and leave them to do their work, and then you and I will walk through the barracks to help your men. Let's start at the officers' camp, shall we?"

Dumbfounded, Karolich stared at her. "The commandant told me you would like to have—um—some lunch." He stumbled on his words. "I'm having the kitchen prepare something special. Perhaps have a rest in the afternoon? The commandant has made nice rooms available to you and your staff."

"Thank you so much. We will eat and rest when the work is done, Lieutenant. Let's begin."

"What can you do without the doctor?"

"Why, nearly everything. Unless you need brain surgery performed, but I don't know if even our doctor can help there."

"No, no."

Tatiana was too tense to smile. She continued. "Everything pertaining to the sick and wounded, I can do. I can stitch, and wash and bandage, I can administer blood and morphine, treat any kind of infectious disease, prepare medications, make diagnoses, treat lice, reduce fever, shave heads to prevent further problems." She patted her nurse's bag. "Most everything I need is in here. When I run out, my jeep is full of additional supplies."

Karolich muttered something unintelligible, mumbled that the camps didn't need blood, or morphine, they were just internment camps.

"Nobody has died in your camps?"

"People die, Nurse," Karolich said haughtily. "Of course they die. But you can't do much for those, can you?"

Blinking, Tatiana didn't reply, flying fleetingly back to all the people in her life she had tried to save and could not.

"Tania," Martin whispered, "the commandant had mentioned lunch, no?"

"Oh, yes," she said, taking her nurse's bag. "But I told them we just ate." She leveled Martin with a look. "Dr. Flanagan, we did just eat, didn't we?"

He stammered.

"I thought so. You and Penny head right to the infirmary barracks. I will start with the officers' barracks and see what I can do there."

Since Tatiana was the only bridge between the cultures and the nations and the languages, she was the only one in charge. Martin and Penny went to the infirmary.

She and Karolich came back to the jeep and opened the back doors. Tatiana stared at the medical kits, at the food parcels, at the apples, trying to get her bearings. She turned away from Karolich for just a few moments because she was afraid. She didn't want him to see her fear. Without looking at him, she said, to stall for time, to give herself another moment, "Do you have an adjutant? I think we need an extra person. Also maybe a handtruck." She paused. "To carry the medical kits and the apples."

"I'll carry them," Karolich said.

Now she turned to him. She was calmer, more in control. "Then who will carry the machine gun, Lieutenant?" They stood silent in front of each other for a few moments, until Tatiana was sure he had absorbed the meaning of what she was getting across to him.

Karolich flushed uncomfortably. "The men are all right, Nurse. They won't bother you."

"Lieutenant Karolich, I don't for a moment doubt that in another life many of them were decent men, but I've also had four months of reality and three years of nursing the German POWs on the American front. I have few illusions. And I think it's bad form for a nurse to brandish her own protection, don't you?"

"You are completely right." He wasn't looking at her anymore. Asking her to wait, he retrieved his assistant, a sergeant. They precariously loaded a bushel of apples and thirty kits onto a wobbling handtruck and set off for the officers' barracks.

The sergeant waited outside with the kits. Tatiana, lugging a burlap bag full of apples in one hand, walked through the first two barracks, holding on to Karolich's arm with the other. She didn't want to, but she suddenly realized that if she saw Alexander on one of those nasty, filthy, too-close-together bunks, she might not be able to hide what was inside her.

She glanced through the bunks, two men per bunk, handed them an apple and moved on. Sometimes, if they were sleeping, she touched them, sometimes she pulled back their blankets. She listened to their calls, their banter, to the sound of their voices. She ran out of apples very quickly. She didn't open her nurse's bag once.

"What do you think?" Karolich said, when they stepped outside.

"What do I think? Terrible," she said, deeply breathing in the fresh air. "But at least the men were alive."

"You didn't stop to examine any of them."

"Lieutenant," she said, "I will give you my full report when we have gone through all the barracks. I need to write down the few I have to come back to, the few that require immediate medical attention from Dr. Flanagan. But I have a method for doing this. I can tell by the odor who is sick with what, who needs what, who is alive and who is dying. I can tell by the temperature of their skin and by the color of their face. I can also tell by their voices. If they, like those men were, are calling out, shouting things in German at me, reaching out for me, then I know things aren't too bad. When they don't move, or worse when they follow me with their eyes but don't make a sound, that's when I start to worry. Those two barracks had live men in it. Have your sergeant give out the small medical kits to each and every one of them. Next."

They went through the next two. Not as good here. She covered two of the men lying in their beds and told Karolich they needed to be taken out and buried. Five men had raging fevers. Seventeen had open sores. She had to stop and dress their wounds. Soon she ran out of bandages and had to return to the truck to get more. She stopped by the infirmary on her way back and got Penny and Dr. Flanagan to come with her. "The situation is worse than I thought," she said to them.

"Not as bad as in here. The men here are dying of dysentery," said Martin.

"Yes, and it's breeding in the barracks," said Tatiana. "Come look."

"Any signs of typhus?"

"Not so far, though a number of the men have fever, but I've only been through four barracks."

"Four! How many are there altogether?"

"Sixty."

"Oh, Nurse Barrington."

"Doctor, let's walk quickly. They pack those barracks with one hundred and thirty-four bunks each. Two hundred and sixty-eight men. What do you expect?"

"We're not going to be able to get through this."

"That's the spirit," said Tatiana.

The men from one of the barracks were in the yard. The men from another were in the showers.

After going through barrack number eleven, Martin wiped his face and said, "Tell Carol-itch, or whatever his name is, tell him that every healthy man in that one is going to die if the diphtheria cases don't immediately get sent to the infirmary."

In barrack thirteen, Tatiana was bandaging the upper arm of a German man when he suddenly heaved himself off his bunk and fell on top of her. At first she thought it was an accident, but he immediately started grinding against her, keeping her pinned to the floor. Karolich tried pulling him off, but the man wouldn't budge, and none of the other prisoners would help. Karolich had to knock him very hard on the head with the barrel of his Shpagin, and he only stopped after he lost consciousness.

Karolich helped Tatiana up. "I'm sorry. We'll take care of him."

Dusting herself off and panting, she picked up her nurse's bag and said, "Don't worry. Let's go." She did not finish bandaging her attacker.

It was eight o'clock at night when they got through barrack fifteen. Karolich said they had to stop. Martin and Penny said they had to stop. Tatiana wanted to continue. She had heard Russian spoken only in the last two barracks. She went extra carefully through those, pulling back all the covers, handing out the medical kits and apples, talking to some of them. There was no Alexander.

And then Karolich and Martin and Penny all shook their heads and said they had to stop, they couldn't do it anymore, they would start fresh the next day. She couldn't continue without them. She couldn't walk through those barracks alone. Reluctantly, she returned to the commandant's house. They washed up, scrubbed down. Penny took another dose of penicillin. They met Brestov and Karolich for dinner.

"So what does your doctor think, Nurse?" Brestov asked. "How are we doing?"

"Poorly," said Tatiana without even bothering to translate. Martin and Penny were scarfing down their food. "You have a real health situation with those men you've got there. I'll tell you your biggest problem. They're unclean. They're scabby and furfuraceous. Are your showers working? Is your laundry working?"

"Of course," Brestov said indignantly.

"They're not working around the clock, though, and they should be. If you kept your men clean and dry, you would prevent half of what's going on in there. Disinfectant in the toilets wouldn't hurt, either."

"Listen, they're getting up, they're walking, they can't be that sick. They get a little exercise in the yard, they eat three times a day."

"What are you feeding them?"

"This isn't a resort, Nurse Barrington. They eat prison food."

Tatiana looked at the steak on Brestov's plate.

"What, gruel in the morning, broth for lunch, potatoes for dinner?" she asked.

"Also bread," he said. "And sometimes they get chicken soup."

"Not clean enough, not fed enough, bunks too close together, those barracks are incubators for disease, and lest you think it has nothing to do with you, *your* men have to guard them, and your men are getting sick, too. Remember, diphtheria is contagious, typhoid from eating spoiled food is contagious, typhus is contagious—"

"Wait, wait, we don't have typhus!"

"Not yet," Tatiana said calmly. "But your prisoners have lice, they have ticks, their hair is unshaven and too long. And when they get typhus, your men will still have to guard them."

For a moment, Brestov said nothing as the piece of steak hung suspended from his fork, and then he spoke: "Well, at least they're not being eaten alive by syphilis." He threw his head back and laughed. "We've taken care of *that* little problem."

Tatiana got up from the table. "You're mistaken there, Commandant. We found sixty-four men with syphilis, seventeen of them in advanced tertiary stages."

"That's impossible!" he cried.

"Nonetheless, they're ill with it. And by the way, your nationals, the Soviet prisoners, seem to be in worse shape than the Germans, if *that's* possible. Well, thank you very much for a pleasant evening. I will see you all tomorrow."

"We don't want the men *too* healthy," said Brestov after her, taking a large gulp from his vodka glass, "do we now, Nurse Barrington? Good health makes men less . . . cooperative."

Tatiana continued walking.

The next morning she was up at five. No one else was, though. She had to sit on her hands—literally—until six o'clock.

They got ready—slowly; they ate—slower, and finally resumed inspection of the remaining five officers' barracks.

"Are you all right?" Karolich asked her with a polite smile. His uniform collars were starched, his hair clipped and brushed neatly back. He was incongruous. "Yesterday shake you up?"

"A little. I'm fine," she said.

"He's been sent to the brig because of what happened."

"Who? Oh, him. Don't worry."

"Does it happen often?"

"Not that often."

He nodded. "Your Russian really is very good."

"Well, thank you. I think you're just being kind."

They gave out the kits and apples, treated what they could, and got the infectious cases out of the common barracks. Tatiana took a walk through the infirmary beds. He was not there, either.

"I'm surprised at the condition of the Soviet men," Martin said when they went outside to take a break. It was raining, and they stood under an awning for just a breath of reprieve.

"Why?" said Tatiana.

"I don't know. I would have thought they'd be treated better than the Germans."

"Why would you think that? The Soviet men are not in danger of being scrutinized by international eyes. It's all about appearances. Those Soviet officers are about to be shipped back to the Soviet Union work camps. What do you think awaits them there?" She shuddered. "At least here, there's a summer."

It was in barrack nineteen, as Tatiana was perched on one bunk, cleaning out an old burn wound with boric acid that she heard a voice behind her and a familiar laugh. She turned her head, looked across the row and found herself eye to eye with Lieutenant Ouspensky from the Morozovo hospital. Instantly she looked elsewhere, then turned back to her patient, but her heart was beating wildly. She waited for him to call out to her, "Why, Nurse *Metanova*, what brings *you* here?"

But he didn't. Instead, when she was finished and stood up to leave, he said, speaking Russian to her. "Oh, nurse, nurse, looky here."

Slowly she looked. He was smiling widely. "I have a number of things very wrong with me that I know only you can fix—being a nurse and all. Can you come hither and help me?"

The makeup, the hair worked. He didn't recognize her. Collecting her things and snapping shut her bag, Tatiana stood up and said, "You look perfectly healthy to me."

"You haven't felt my head. You haven't felt my heart. You haven't felt my stomach. You haven't felt my . . ."

"I'm an old professional. I can see you are fine from a distance."

He laughed joyously, and then, a smile still big on his face, said, "What is it about you that looks so familiar to me? You speak such good Russian. What's your name again?"

She had Penny give him a small medical kit and a food parcel while she herself left in a hurry. How long before Ouspensky put her face together with his memory?

Slower and slower she walked through the last barrack. She dawdled and paused at every bed, even talked to some of the men, slower, slower. If Ouspensky was here, wouldn't it mean that Alexander was here, too? But barrack twenty proved just as fruitless. Two hundred and sixty-eight men, none of them Alexander. Twenty barracks, five thousand men, none of them Alexander. There was the rest of the camp to get through, but Tatiana had few illusions. Alexander would be where the Soviets were. He wouldn't be with the German civilians. Besides, Karolich told her as much. All the Soviets were together. The camp didn't like to mingle the German and Russian prisoners. In the past, violent conflicts erupted over nothing.

When they stepped outside, she left the others for a minute and walked over to the short barbed-wire fence that separated the housing units from the cemetery. It was June, and wet. It had been lightly drizzling since dawn. She stood, in her soiled white pants, her soiled white tunic, her black hair falling out of her hat, her arms around herself, and motionlessly gazed at the small freshly dug elevated hills without markers, without crosses.

Karolich came up to her. "Are you all right?" he asked.

With a pained sigh she turned to him. "Lieutenant, the men who died in the barracks yesterday, where are they buried?"

"They're not buried yet."

"Where did you take them?"

"For now they're in the corpse cellar, in the autopsy barracks."

She didn't know how she got the next words out. "Could we see the corpse cellar, please?"

Karolich laughed. "Sure. You don't think the dead are getting fair treatment?"

Martin and Penny returned to the infirmary and Tatiana went with Karolich. The autopsy room was a small, white-tiled bunker with high tiled berths for the bodies.

"Where's the cellar?"

"We slide them to the cellar this way." Karolich pointed.

At the back of the room Tatiana saw a long metal chute that led down twenty feet into darkness.

She stood silently over the chute.

"How do you"—her voice was untrustworthy—"how do you bring the bodies up from there?"

"We often don't. It's connected to the kilns in the crematorium." Karolich grinned. "Those Germans thought of *everything*."

Tatiana stood and stared down into the darkness. Then she turned and walked outside.

"I just need a couple of minutes, Lieutenant, all right? I'm going to go over there and sit on the bench." She attempted a smile. "It will be a little easier for you when some of the Soviets get shipped out, no? You'll have more room."

"Yes." He waved dismissively. "They bring more in. It never stops. But the bench is wet."

She sank down. He waited a bit. "Do you want me to, um, leave you alone?"

"Would you mind? For just a few minutes."

Tatiana's lower stomach was burning. That's what it felt like, a slow charring away of her insides. There was such a thing, wasn't there, as feeling better, eventually and forever? She couldn't feel this old into eternity, could she?

In eternity, wouldn't she be young, wearing her white dress with red roses, her golden hair streaming down past her shoulders?

She would be walking in the Summer Garden late at night, strolling down the path with the ghostly sculptures standing to attention before her, and she would break into a run, as her hair flowed, and a smile was on her face.

In eternity she would be running all the time.

Tatiana thought of Leningrad, of her white-night, glorious flowing river Neva, and over it Leningrad's bridges and in front of it the statue of the Bronze Horseman, and St. Isaac's Cathedral rising up, beckoning her with its arcade, with its balustrades, with its wrought-iron railing above the dome, where they had stood once before, a lifetime ago, and looked out onto the blackest night, waiting for war to swallow them.

And it did.

She sat in disbelief.

Something was finishing inside her, she felt it.

Had it been raining all this time and she didn't even notice?

Tatiana lay down on the bench in the rain.

"Nurse Barrington?"

She opened her eyes. Karolich helped her up. "If you're not feeling well, I'll be glad to take you back to the house. You can have a rest. We can do the camp prison and the rest of the barracks another time. There is no hurry."

Tatiana stood up. "No," she said. "Let's do the camp prison now. Are there many in there?"

"It's in three wings, two of them we closed, but the operational one is half full." He spat. "They break the rules all the time. Disobey, don't come to roll call, or even worse, constantly try to escape. You'd think they'd learn."

There was only one way into the prison wing and one way out, and it was guarded by a man in a chair with his machine gun propped up against the wall. He was playing cards with himself.

"How has it been today, Corporal Perdov?"

"Quiet today," the corporal said, standing up briefly in salute. He smiled at Tatiana. She did not smile back.

The prison was a long corridor, floor covered with sawdust and cells on each side. They went through the first five cells.

"How many prisoners are you keeping this way?" Tatiana asked.

"About thirty," Karolich replied.

In the sixth cell, the man had fainted and Tatiana put smelling salts under his nose to revive him. Karolich had left to open cell number seven. Cell number six revived. Tatiana gave him a drink of water and walked out into the corridor.

From inside cell number seven, she heard Karolich say in a mocking voice, "How is my favorite prisoner doing this morning?"

"Fuck you," came the reply.

Her knees buckled.

Tatiana stepped from the corridor into the doorway. The cell was long and narrow with a step down divider, and on the straw beneath the tiny window that shed no light on the floor, twenty feet in front of her, lay Alexander.

The moments of silence fell through the cell. They fell onto her face and her shoulders. Her breath taken away, her burning stopped, her heart stopped too, she stood and looked at the bearded, thin man in manacles, in dark slacks and a blood-drenched white shirt. She dropped her nurse's bag, and her hand went over her mouth stifling a racking sob.

"Oh, I know. This is our very worst, Nurse," said Karolich. "We're not proud of this one, but there is just nothing we can do with him."

❧

When the door opened and light streamed in, Alexander had been sleeping. Rather, he thought he had been sleeping. His eyes were closed, and he had been dreaming. He had not eaten in two days: he hated his food left on the floor for him as if he were a dog. He was planning on eating soon.

Alexander was furious with himself. The last escape had been so close to being successful. The orderly, bringing some medical supplies into the infirmary, was dressed in civilian clothes, and as usual was coming freely in and out of the camp, waving to the sentries, who would wave back and without a second glance open the gate for him. What could be easier? Alexander had been in the infirmary for the previous three weeks with broken ribs. He knocked out the orderly, took his clothes, shoved him in a closet, and walked up to the gatehouse, waving to the guards. And one of them came down and opened the gate for him. Never even looked at Alexander.

He waved a thanks, a goodbye and started walking.

Why did Karolich have to come out of the green casino just on the left, why at that very moment? He looked through the gate, saw Alexander's back and screamed for the sentries.

Now, three days later, bloodied and worn out, he had been dreaming of swimming and of the sun and of cool water on his body. He dreamed of being clean, of not being thirsty. He dreamed of summer. It was so dark in the cell. He dreamed of finding a corner of order in the infinite chaos that his world had shown him. He dreamed of . . .

. . . And through the small bars he heard voices and then the door lock turn and the door open. Squinting, Alexander saw Karolich walk in. That Karolich! How he enjoyed flaunting Alexander's failure to Alexander. They had their usual exchange, and then a shadow of a small nurse appeared in the doorway. For a moment, just a single moment, coming out of a dream as he was, the small shape of the nurse looked almost like . . . but it was hard to see, and, besides, hadn't he been hallucinating her enough? He couldn't get far enough from his delusions of her.

But then she gasped, and he heard her voice, and while the hair was different, the voice belonged only to her, and he heard it so clearly. He tried to see her face, he peered, he tried to sit up, to move away from the wall, but he could do nothing. She took one step forward. God, it looked like Tatiana! He shook his head, he thought he was delirious again, the visions of her in the woods in her polka dot bathing suit with her love-less eyes chasing him through every night, through every day. He raised his arms as far as his chains would permit, raised them in supplication: vision, comfort me this time, don't afflict me again.

Alexander shook his head and blinked, and blinked again. *I'm imagining her*, he thought. I've imagined her for so long, what she looks like, what she sounds like. She is an apparition, like my father, my mother; I will blink and she too will be gone—as always. He blinked and blinked again. Blinked away the long shadow of life without her, and she was standing in front of him, and her eyes shined and her lips were bright.

And then he heard Karolich say something to her, and it was then that Alexander knew that the bastard Karolich could not be imagining her, too.

They stared speechlessly at each other and in their eyes were min-utes and hours, months and years, continental drifts and ocean divides. In their eyes was pain and there was vast regret.

The scythe of grief fell evenly upon their stricken faces.

⌇

She tripped on the step and nearly fell. Dropping to her knees by his side, she did what she did not think she would do again in this lifetime.

Tatiana touched Alexander.

He had dried blood on his hair and face, and he was shackled. He looked at her and did not speak.

"Nurse Barrington, we don't treat them all this way, but he has proven himself to be incorrigible and beyond rehabilitating."

"Lieutenant Karolich," she croaked. "Lieutenant," she repeated, but lower, her body trembling so badly that she thought Karolich would not only notice but become alarmed. But he noticed nothing. It was dim in the cell; the only light came from the corridor. "I think I left my nurse's bag in cell number six. Could you get it for me, please?"

As soon as his back was turned, Tatiana whispered, "Shura," in a barely audible voice.

Alexander groaned.

Tatiana touched his trembling arm, moved closer, and just as Karolich was coming back, she placed both hands on Alexander's face.

"How is he?" Karolich said. "Here is your bag. You've got quite a few tubes of toothpaste in there. Why do you carry toothpaste in your nurse's bag?"

"It's not toothpaste," she said, with extreme effort taking her hands away. "It's morphine." Could she continue to speak normally, sitting so close to Alexander, unable to lay her hands on him? No, not unable. "What's happened to him?" she asked as she put her hands on Alexander's chest. His heart was pummeling into her palms. Sitting beside him, tears trickling down her face, she said, "He's got a head wound that has not been treated. We will need to get some water and soap, and a razor. I will clean him and bandage him. Let me give him a drink first. Can you hand me my flask, please?"

Motionlessly, Alexander continued to lie against the wall, his eyes on Tatiana, who could barely look at him as she brought the flask to his lips. He tilted his head back and drank. Her fingers were shaking and she dropped the flask.

The lieutenant noticed. "Are you all right?" he asked. "Is this too much for you, seeing them like this? You don't seem cut out for this kind of work. You seem kind of . . . fragile."

Without responding, Tatiana said, "Lieutenant, would you please get me a large bucket of preferably warm water for the head wound, some soap, some strong shampoo, and one of my medical kits from the truck?"

"Yes, but come outside. You can't stay here by yourself with the prisoner. You know what happened to you yesterday. It's not safe."

"He's in shackles. I'll be fine. Go ahead. But hurry. We have many more to do." Her hand was on Alexander.

As soon as Karolich was around the corner, Tatiana pressed her forehead to Alexander's head. "God, it can't be," she whispered in Russian. "It can't be you."

She felt his body shudder.

Tatiana was bent over him. Alexander's eyes were closed.

They remained that way, not moving and not speaking.

A groan left her. She couldn't find a single word, a single word when she had thought books, when she had screamed and wept and railed against the unjust fate, when she had grieved and in her sorrow been so angry, when she had grieved and in her sorrow been so lost. Now she pressed her face into his bloodied black head and couldn't find a word. Groans, yes. Wretched cries, yes. Not much silence, but no actual words.

On her knees by his side, through her barely moving lips, Tatiana whispered, "Oh, Shura . . ." She put her shaking hands to her face and cried.

"Tania, come on, now."

Doubled over, she took deep breaths, covering her face, hiding it from him in his blood-stained shirt in an effort to get calm.

"How have you been, Tania?" Alexander asked in a rupturing voice.

"Good, good." She clasped his chained hands.

"What about—" He broke off. "What about . . . the baby?"

"Yes. We have a son."

"A *son*." Alexander breathed out. "What did you name him?"

"Anthony Alexander. Anthony."

His eyes filled up and he turned his head away.

Tatiana stared at him, her mouth opening and closing. "Is it really *you*?" she whispered. "Tell me, before I break down, tell me it's *you*."

"*Before?*" he said.

He was more gaunt than she had ever seen him, even during the worst of the Leningrad blockade. "Alexander . . ." she whispered. *Blink. The cheek was unshaven. Foam on his cheeks. And she held the mirror between her breasts. Blink.* She ran her fingers over his beard, his lips. He kissed her fingers. "Tatiana . . ." he whispered. "Tania . . ."

"What happened to you? You were arrested, weren't you?"

"Yes."

"Let me guess. You knew you were going to be arrested—" She stopped. "Somehow, I don't know how, you knew you were going to be arrested and you faked your own death to get me out of Russia. Sayers helped you."

"Sayers helped me. I didn't fake my own death. I thought it was imminent. I didn't want you to stay behind and watch me die. I knew you wouldn't leave any other way."

They spoke quickly, afraid any minute Karolich was going to return.

"Stepanov helped you?"

"Yes."

"He's in Berlin."

"I know. He came to see me a few months back."

"How did you get Sayers . . . ? I don't care." She couldn't sit away from him, or move away. She couldn't even breathe away. "You think that's what I wanted? To leave you behind?"

Shaking his head, he said, "I knew you didn't."

"I would've never left."

"I knew that." He paused. "Too well."

She stopped touching him. "You and your impossible ego," she said. "Leningrad, Morozovo, Lazarevo. You always thought you knew what was best."

"Ah," he said. "So there was a Lazarevo?"

"What?" she said, momentarily puzzled. "I told you I would have waited for you, and I would have."

"Like you told me you would not leave Lazarevo? You would have lived there without me," said Alexander. "I've been sentenced to twenty-five years' hard labor."

She flinched.

"Tania, why aren't you looking at me?" he asked haltingly. "Why are you looking down at your lap?"

"Because I'm afraid," she whispered. "I'm so afraid."

"Me, too," Alexander said. "Please lift your eyes. I need your eyes on me."

She lifted her eyes. Tears were rolling down her cheeks.

They fell mute. She was bending under the weight of her heart.

"Thank you," she whispered, "for keeping yourself alive, soldier."

"You're welcome," he whispered back.

⚭

There was the sound of the outside door opening and closing. Moving away, Tatiana quickly wiped her face. Her mascara was running. Alexander closed his eyes.

Karolich walked into the cell with a pail and gauze.

"Lieutenant, let's begin, but I need you to unlock him. His wrists and ankles are raw from the iron. I need to clean them and bandage them or they will get infected if they haven't already."

Karolich took out his key and brought his machine gun into his hands. "You don't know this one, Nurse Barrington. I wouldn't have much sympathy for him, if I were you."

"I have sympathy for all the afflicted," she replied.

"This is all his own doing."

Tatiana could see that Karolich's genial manner changed when he was around Alexander. He was cold and rough as he unlocked the shackles and dropped them noiselessly to the straw. "Why do you use irons here?" she asked. "Why don't you use leather restraints? They do what you need but are easier for the prisoner."

Karolich laughed. "Nurse, you obviously have not been paying attention. *We* don't use the irons, the Germans used the irons. This is what they've left behind for us. Besides, this one would gnaw through the leather in three hours."

She sighed. "We should at least change the straw when we're done."

Karolich shrugged, then sat back against the wall, on clean straw, his legs stretched out comfortably, and took the machine gun into his hands. "One wrong move, Belov, and you know what's going to happen?"

Alexander said nothing.

Tatiana kneeled by Alexander. "Come on," she said. "Let me clean you, all right?"

"All right."

"Tip your head back. It will be easier for me to clean your hair."

He tipped his head back.

"What happened to him, Lieutenant?" asked Tatiana, as one of her hands went around Alexander's neck, supporting his head, his face nearly in her nurse's uniform, nearly at her breasts, as she with a towel wiped the dried and bloodied mats out of his hair. It was as long as his beard. "I will shave and trim him, but you know you need to keep your men's hair short, you can't let it grow this long and not keep it clean. Not just him, all your men."

"Why are you looking at him like that?" Karolich asked suddenly.

"Like what?" she whispered.

"I don't even know."

"I'm tired. I think you're right. This has been too much for me."

"So leave him. Let's go to the house. We'll have a decent lunch." He smiled. "Yesterday you didn't have any wine. The wine is very good."

"No. I will finish here." She snipped away the hair and gently cleaned Alexander's wound. He had been cut in the skull above the ear and had bled down onto his neck and shirt. The blood had dried where it fell. How long had he been here? His face looked swollen with blood-ied bruises under his eyes, below his jawline. Was he beaten? In the dark, she could make out the black of the blood and the white of his shirt, and the black of his hair, and the black of his eyes. He was long unshaven, long unwashed. Long untouched. He lay in her arms, his eyes closed, barely breathing. Only his heart thundered through his veins. He lay in her arms so still, so comforted, so hers, so relieved, so afraid, she felt it all in him, and felt it all in her, and was so desperate to bend to him, to say something to him, that through the effort she was expending to remain composed, she bit her lip so hard it bled, right onto Alexander's face.

"Nurse, you're bleeding on the prisoner."

Alexander blinked, and mutely raised his eyes to Tatiana.

"It's nothing." Tatiana licked the blood off her mouth as she dipped her rag in cool water. "Tell me what happened to him."

Karolich chuckled. "He's been with us nearly a year. He was well behaved at first, worked hard, logged, was quiet, a model prisoner, a tireless worker and was amply rewarded. We wished we had more prisoners like him. Unfortunately, since November he has been trying to escape every time we let him out of here and back into the barracks. He thinks he's in a hotel. Comes and goes as he pleases. You'd think he would learn after seventeen failures, but you'd be wrong."

"Fuck you," said Alexander.

"Tsk, tsk. The man has no manners in front of a lady. Well, it doesn't matter." Karolich lowered his voice. "He's not staying here."

"No?" Tatiana was cleaning Alexander's wrists. As she did so, she slipped two pins from her hair into his palm and squeezed it shut.

Karolich shook his head. "No. He and a thousand others are leaving for Kolyma tomorrow." He laughed lightly and poked Alexander in the ribs with the muzzle of the machine gun. "Try to escape from there."

"Please don't provoke the prisoner," said Tatiana, beginning to shave his beard. "Why isn't he wearing prison clothes?"

"He stole these from an orderly in the infirmary. When we caught him, we threw him in here as he was. He obviously likes it here. He always wants to return."

"Why is he bleeding, so bruised? Was he beaten?"

"Nurse, did you hear me? Seventeen times! Beaten? He's lucky he's alive. What if the man yesterday did what he did to you seventeen times? How many times would you take it before you said, enough already and beat him to death?"

Tatiana glanced down at Alexander. His eyes blackened.

"Nurse, you're getting his filth all over your nice white uniform," said Karolich with distaste. "Lay him down on the straw. He doesn't care if he's shaved. He is not used to this kind of treatment. Nor should he be getting it."

She did release Alexander. His wrists were clean and dressed, his hair was cut and washed, his scalp wound cleaned and bandaged. She even had him swill his mouth out with baking soda and peroxide. Now she needed to look at the rest of him, to make sure nothing was broken.

"Does this man have a rank?"

"Not anymore," said Karolich.

"What *was* his rank?"

"He was a major, once. Demoted to captain."

"Captain, how are your ribs? Do you think they're broken?" asked Tatiana.

"I'm not a doctor," said Alexander. "I don't know. Perhaps."

Unbuttoning his shirt, she slowly ran her hands from his throat down to his ribs, whispering, "What hurts, what hurts?"

He did not answer. He said nothing, nor did he open his eyes.

His body was unclean and black and blue. She thought his ribs were broken, but when she touched them he did not flinch. That could just be Alexander—he didn't flinch when she cleaned his head, either—but decided to leave the matter.

She moved down to his leg irons, detached them, and washed his feet in soapy water. His ankles felt pulpy. The skin on them felt eaten away and raw. It was hard to see in the dark.

Karolich continued to sit. He even lit a smoke, sat coolly and enjoyed it.

"Would you like a smoke, Nurse Barrington? These cigarettes are very good."

"Thank you, Lieutenant, but I don't smoke. Perhaps your prisoner would like one?"

Karolich laughed and shoved Alexander's hip with his boot. "Prisoners in camp jail do not get cigarette privileges, do they, Belov?" He took a deep drag and blew the smoke into Alexander's face.

Tatiana got up. "Lieutenant, stop provoking the prisoner in front of me. We're finished here. Let's go."

Alexander emitted a despondent sound.

Tatiana collected her things. Karolich locked Alexander's wrists and ankles to the manacles once again.

"How long has it been since this prisoner was fed?" she asked.

"We feed him," Karolich replied gruffly. "More than he deserves."

"How does he eat? Do you take the irons off him?"

"The irons never come off him. We put the food in front of him, and he crawls to it and bends his face and eats it off the ground."

"He didn't eat his food. Do you see the state of him? Is this his old plate? He didn't eat it, but the rats did. You have rats here, Lieutenant, because you leave the food on the ground for days, and they know where to come for their supper. You do know that rats carry the plague, don't you? The International Red Cross is here to ensure that exactly these kinds of abuses do not happen. Now, let's get the old straw out and sweep some clean straw under him."

After they had done so, Karolich picked up the plate off the ground. "He'll be brought fresh food later," he said brusquely.

She glanced at Alexander, who lay with his eyes closed, his hands clenched in shackles at his stomach. She wanted to tell him she would be back, but she didn't want Karolich to hear her quivering voice.

"Don't go," he said, without opening his eyes.

"We'll come back later to see how you are," Tatiana said weakly, and was grateful that his hands were manacled because she knew he would not have let her go had he been able to move them.

‍

Tatiana was blinded for a moment by the gray daylight. She stopped cold to get her bearings, and when Karolich asked if she wanted to get some lunch, she said, no, thank you, because she had to count how many supplies they still had left. She told him to go on ahead, that she would soon follow.

The camp prison was located just to the right of the gatehouse and just to the right of her parked Red Cross jeep. The two guards stood sentry above it on the roof. One of them waved to her. She opened the jeep and looked inside. The truck was a quarter full of supplies, there was another bushel of apples and some food parcels left. She knew she had only minutes to think. She stood quietly, and then loaded up the handtruck with sixty medical kits and walked by herself to the nearest barracks. The fact that she could think of entering a barracks by herself, a woman amid 266 men, only spoke of her desperation, but she was not a fool. Her nurse's bag hung on the handtruck handle and her P-38 was tucked into the front of her pants where everyone could see it.

She handed out one medical kit per bed, told them as she passed them that she would be back with the doctor, quickly ran back to get more kits, and more, and more, rushing, rushing. When she got back to the commandant's house everyone else was finishing lunch. After downing a glass of water, she went to change her clothes, retouched her makeup and then took Penny and Martin aside and said, "Listen, I think we should return to Berlin to get more kits. We have none left, and we're running out of bandages and penicillin. We'll go back tonight and return here tomorrow."

"We just got here and you want to leave already? She is so fickle, Martin, isn't she?" Penny said with a twinkle.

"Fickle is the least of what she is," Martin said. "I told you we shouldn't have come to a place like this without proper support."

Tatiana patted him on the shoulder. "You were so right, Dr. Flanagan," she said. "But we did get through five thousand people between yesterday and today, and that's quite an achievement."

They agreed to leave at eight in the evening, though Martin expressed reservations about driving on unfamiliar roads at night. While Penny and Martin went with Karolich through the German civilian barracks that Tatiana had just been through, she said that she was going to finish inspecting the rest of the jailed men. When Karolich said he would come with her, Tatiana said, "Nurse Davenport and Dr. Flanagan need you more. The jailed men are the safest, you know that. After all, they can't touch me, and I'll have Corporal Perdov with me."

Reluctantly, Karolich left with Martin and Penny, and Tatiana ran to the commandant's kitchen and got them to prepare a hot lunch of sausage, potatoes, squash, bread with butter, and oranges. "I haven't eaten and I'm starved," she said gamely. There was a carafe of water, and a large glass of vodka that she poured herself.

As she walked through the jail door, this time she smiled at Corporal Perdov, and he smiled back. "Corporal, I'm here to feed cell number seven. I've discussed it with Lieutenant Karolich. The prisoner hasn't eaten in three days."

"I can't unchain him."

"It won't be necessary. I'll feed him."

"Hey," Perdov said, looking at her tray. "Is that a glass of something *extra* special?"

"Why, yes!" She smiled. "But I don't think our prisoner should have that, do you?"

"Absolutely not!"

"Exactly. Why don't you have the whole thing."

Perdov took the vodka and downed it in two gulps. Tatiana watched him amiably. "Very good," she said. "I might come back later with his dinner, and maybe I can bring the prisoner another glass." She winked at Perdov.

"Oh, yes," he said, "but don't be so stingy next time." And burped.

"I'll see what I can do. Now, can you open cell seven for me?"

Alexander was sleeping in a sitting position.

"I think you're wasting your time," Perdov said. "This one doesn't deserve a nurse's attention. Don't take too long, all right?"

Leaving the door open, he walked back to his chair and Tatiana descended the step and came to Alexander. Setting the tray on the ground, she kneeled by him and whispered, "Shura . . ."

He opened his eyes. She threw her arms around him and pressed herself to him, his bandaged head cradled near her neck. She held him as tightly as she could, every once in a while whispering, "Shura . . . Shura . . ."

"Tighter, Tania, hold me tighter."

She held him tighter. "How are the locks?"

Alexander showed her they were open. His wrists lay in them freely. "What happened to your hair?"

"I colored it. Keep your hands in the manacles. Perdov can come in at any time."

"Are you always on a name basis with the gatekeeper? Why did you color it?"

"Didn't want to be recognized. Just as well. Nikolai Ouspensky is here."

"Be very very careful with Nikolai," he warned. "Like Dimitri, he is the enemy. Come closer."

She did.

"What happened to your freckles?" he whispered.

"Makeup over them."

They kissed. They kissed as if they were young once again in the Luga woods, and it was the first summer of their life, or standing on the ledge of St. Isaac's under the moon and the stars, they kissed as if they were in Lazarevo, raw for each other, they kissed as if she had just told him she was getting him out of Russia, bending over him in the Morozovo hospital ward. They kissed as if they had not seen each other for many years. They kissed as if they had been together for many years.

They kissed away Orbeli and Dimitri, they kissed away war and communism, America and Russia. They kissed away *everything*, leaving behind only what remained—pale fragments of Tania and Shura.

His hands moved out of the manacles. She pulled away instantly and shook her head. "No, no, I'm serious. He can come in at any time and then we're sunk."

With great reluctance he slipped his hands back in the open iron rings. "Makeup can't hide the scar on your cheek. Where did you get it? Finland?"

"I'll tell you all about it later if we have time. Now I'm going to feed you, and you are going to eat your food and listen to me."

"I'm not hungry. How on this God's earth did you find me?"

"You will eat your food because you need to be strong," she said, bringing the spoonful of sausage and potatoes to his mouth. "And you left a short trail of yourself in this world."

Contrary to his words, he ate ravenously. She didn't speak while she watched his great hunger.

"Shura . . . we have seconds, are you listening?"

"Why is this suddenly so familiar?" he said. "Tell me another one of your plans, Tatiasha. How is our boy?"

"Our boy is great. He's a great, smart, beautiful boy."

"Where are you living?"

"New York. We have no time. Are you listening?"

He was chewing the bread and could only nod. "What was the name of the man who assaulted you?"

"I'm not telling you."

"You are telling me. What was his name?"

"No."

"Tania! What was his name?"

"Grammer Kerault. He is Austrian."

"I know him." Alexander's eyes were cold. "He's always in here. Dying of stomach cancer, doesn't care what he does." Then they warmed as he turned his gaze on her. "How are you going to get me out of here?" he whispered.

She bent over him. They kissed desperately. "Honey," she whispered. "Honey, I know you're afraid."

"I don't want food, I don't want drink, or even a smoke. Just . . . just sit by me for two seconds, Tania. Press yourself to me for two seconds to let me know I am real."

She pressed herself to him.

"Where are our wedding rings?"

She pulled the rope out from her tunic. "Until we can wear them again," she whispered—and suddenly heaved herself away.

Perdov stepped into the doorway. "Are you all right, Nurse? You've been here a while. Do you need me to help you?"

"No, that won't be necessary, Corporal, thank you," Tatiana said, tucking the rings back into her tunic and giving Alexander the last bit of potato. "I'm almost finished. I'll be just another minute."

"Give a holler if you need me." He smiled and disappeared.

"Are you here with a convoy?" Alexander asked.

"There are three of us in one Red Cross jeep. Me, another nurse, and a doctor. We have to get you on that jeep."

"Tomorrow Stalin is coming for me to take me back to the Soviet Union."

"Stalin, my love, is late," said Tatiana. "I'm here for you today. We are leaving at eight p.m. sharp. I'm coming for you promptly at seven. I'm coming with Karolich, so please be ready. I'm bringing you dinner, and you will eat it in front of him, slowly. We need twenty minutes for the secobarbital to work on Perdov."

Alexander was silent. "You better give him a large amount of seco-barbital."

"An unconscionable amount."

Alexander stopped chewing his food as he stared at her. "What are you thinking? That you'll just put me in your little truck and drive me to Berlin?"

"Something like that," she whispered.

He stared at her for a longish moment and then shook his head. "You're underestimating the Soviets. How far to Berlin?"

"About twenty-two miles—I mean, thirty-five kilometers."

Alexander allowed himself a small smile. "You don't have to convert for me, Tania."

And she allowed herself a small smile back.

"Any checkpoints?"

"Yes, five."

"What about your two colleagues?"

"What about them? In one hour, we're all in the American sector and safe. There is no problem."

Alexander stared at her incredulously and grimly. "Well, let me tell you, your Red Cross truck will be stopped after twenty minutes. You'll be lucky to get out of Oranienburg before they'll come for me, and for you, and for the rest of your gallant crew." He shook his head. "I'm not doing it."

"What are you talking about?" she gasped. "How will they know? They won't know for at least a few hours. And by that time, we'll be in Berlin."

Alexander shook his head. "Tania, you have no idea."

"Then we'll get off earlier, if you want," she said. "We'll get off . . . wherever you want."

"They'll find me before we leave. The guards will inspect the truck."

"They won't. You're going to walk out as Karolich, and drive out of the gate with me, and then you will hide in the crutch and litter compartment in the back. They don't know there is a compartment in the back."

"Where are the crutches and litters?"

"Back in Hamburg. We'll get off, and Martin and Penny will drive on to Berlin, knowing nothing."

Perdov stood outside the door, swaying. He held on to the door. "Nurse? That's enough now."

"I'm coming." She stood up. Someone called for him, and Perdov staggered down the corridor.

They had a myriad details to go over, but there was no time. From her nurse's bag she retrieved the Colt 1911 and two extra clips. "Much *much* more in the truck," she said, hiding the gun underneath him in the straw. "When we're on our way for a bit, I'll knock twice, and you make a distraction for me to stop the truck."

He said nothing. "And then?"

"Then? There is a hatch on the roof. We climb out onto the roof and jump."

"While the truck is moving?"

"Yes." She paused. "Or we can just do it my way and drive the truck into Berlin."

He said nothing at first. "Not as good as your last plan, Tania," he said. "And that one failed."

"That's the spirit. I'll see you at seven. Be ready," she said, and saluted him. "O Captain, my Captain."

Tatiana pretended to eat dinner with Brestov and Karolich, to listen to banter between Penny and Martin, even to smile. How? She didn't know. To save him.

She didn't want to keep looking at her watch, but couldn't keep herself from staring at Martin's wrist until she realized she was making him twitch with her unexplained scrutiny. She excused herself and said she would go and pack. Penny excused herself and said since she was already packed she would go and check on barrack nineteen. Tatiana knew there was a man there Penny wanted to say goodbye to. It was 6:00 p.m. For fifteen minutes Tatiana agonized in her room, looking over the map of the area between Oranienburg and Berlin. She could not still her unquiet heart.

At 6:20 she carried her pack to the jeep and returned to the commandant's kitchen to get another plate of food for Alexander. At 6:45 she filled a glass with vodka and secobarbital and, with her nurse's bag on her shoulder, picked up the food tray and went to find Karolich.

⚭

At 6:55, Penny walked through the beds in barrack nineteen, moving past the bunk of Nikolai Ouspensky.

"Hey, nurse, where is the rest of your crew?" he called out in Russian. "Where is that other, hmm, little nurse?"

"It's a good thing I don't understand a word of what you're saying," Penny retorted in English with a smile, without stopping.

With a smile himself Ouspensky fell back on his bed. Penny brought back the image of the other nurse, the small, black-haired one. He had forgotten all about it, but something had niggled him about her. What was it about her that was so faintly familiar, and why for such a faint familiarity was that niggling so sharp?

⚭

"Lieutenant, could you come with me?" Tatiana smiled. "It's getting late. I want to bring the plate of food for the prisoner in cell number seven, and I don't want to go alone. And this way you and I could drive the jeep back to the commandant's house to retrieve Miss Davenport and Dr. Flanagan."

Karolich walked gladly through the forested path with her. He seemed flattered.

"You are a very good nurse," he said. "You shouldn't care so much about the prisoners, though. Take it from me. It makes it too hard to do your job."

"Don't I know it, Lieutenant," she said, walking a little faster.

"You can call me Ivan if you wish." He coughed.

"Let's stick with lieutenant for now," she said, walking faster still.

It was 7:00 when they walked into the jail corridor. All was quiet. Perdov stood up in a salute. Tatiana winked at him, glancing at the vodka glass. Perdov winked back. Karolich passed first, then Tatiana, who nodded and moved the tray over to Perdov who grabbed the full glass, downed it, and put it back on the tray. Karolich was opening cell seven. "Are you coming, Nurse?"

"Coming, Lieutenant."

Alexander was lying on his side.

Karolich sank down onto the straw with a yawn. He was facing Alexander's back and his machine gun was on his lap angled at Alexander.

"Feed him quickly, Nurse. I want to be done with my day. That's the thing about this work. Begins early, ends late, feels like it's never done."

"I know what you mean." Putting the tray on the ground, Tatiana pretended to examine Alexander. "He doesn't look so good, does he?" she said. "I think he's getting a terrible infection."

Indifferently, Karolich shook his head. "He'd look worse dead, don't you agree?" He lit a cigarette.

"Captain, would you like something for the pain?"

"Yes, thank you," said Alexander.

"Before or after you eat?"

"After."

He turned onto his back and she fed him. He ate quickly, and then groaned, rolling back on his side. "My head hurts. Maybe something for the pain now?"

"I'm going to give you a little morphine to help you."

Alexander continued to lie on his side. He opened his eyes and glanced at Tatiana without blinking. His hands were in front of him, his back was to Karolich, and in his hands, he held the Model 1911.

"So, how long have you been working for the Red Army, Lieutenant?" Tatiana asked Karolich, opening her nurse's bag and taking out three syrettes—small, toothpaste-type tubes each filled with a half-grain of morphine solution.

"Twelve years," he said. "How long have you been a nurse?"

"Just a few," she replied, fumbling with the needle and safety seal. Her hands were useless. Usually she could do this in her sleep. "I worked with German POWs in New York." She needed to get all three syrettes ready, and she couldn't even break the safety seal on one.

"Oh, yeah? Any escapees?"

"Not really. Oh, yes. One. Knocked out one of the doctors and took a ferry across the water."

"What happened to him? Ever catch him?"

"Yes," she said, walking between Alexander and Karolich and kneeling down. The three syrettes were in her right hand. "He was caught six months later living in New Jersey." She laughed. Her laugh sounded fake. "He wanted to escape to New Jersey."

"What is this New Jersey? And why are you using so many tubes on him? One is not enough?"

"He is too big a man," she said. "He needs an extra dose."

"Last thing we need around here is a morphine addict. Although, do you think it will make him pliant?"

At that moment, there was a loud thump from the corridor as if something heavy had fallen. Karolich turned his head toward the cell door and immediately reached for his machine gun.

"Now!" said Alexander.

Tatiana, without another breath, pushed the machine gun off Karolich's lap with her left hand and plunged the three syringes into his thigh with her right, puncturing his pants and his skin, squeezing the morphine through all the needles. He opened his mouth in a gasp, and struck out, hitting Tatiana with his forearm square across the jaw, and with his other arm grabbing for his falling machine gun. But Alexander was already up behind Tatiana, pushing her aside. He kicked the machine gun against the wall and struck Karolich violently on the head with the butt of the Colt. Karolich's head opened up like a dropped watermelon. It had all taken maybe four seconds.

"I'll show you fucking pliant," said Alexander, kicking a convulsing Karolich with his bare foot.

"Take his clothes, Shura, quick, before he bleeds all over them."

Karolich was bleeding copiously.

Alexander ripped the lieutenant's uniform off Karolich's body and quickly undressed. Tatiana, a little wobbly from the blow, peered out of the doorway. Perdov had fallen off the chair and was unconscious on the floor.

Alexander threw his bloodied white shirt and brown slacks on Karolich and shackled the man's wrists and ankles. Then he put on the lieutenant's boots, his cap, took his Shpagin, and in Karolich's uniform appeared in the corridor. "He is just the right size," he said to Tatiana. "A little shorter and bigger, the fat fucking bastard."

Walking over to Perdov, he lifted him and sat him back in the chair. Perdov kept falling. Finally they got him to sit straight, his head bent all the way forward.

"That did not take twenty minutes," Alexander said.

"I know. I decided to give him a little, hmm, larger dose."

"Good. How much morphine did you give Karolich?" Alexander asked.

"One and a half grains, but I think it's going to be his open skull that will keep him quiet."

Alexander hoisted the machine gun over his shoulder. The cocked Colt was in his hand. "Where is the truck?"

"Fifty yards in front of you, as you walk out the door. When we get to the truck, look up at the sentry on the gatehouse and salute them. That's what he always does when we pass. He opens the gate himself with his master key. He's left-handed, though. You might . . ."

Alexander switched the jangling key from his right hand to his left. "Okay. Better for me. I shoot with my right. Are you ready? Does he walk in front of you or behind you?"

"Next to me. And he doesn't open any doors for me. He just salutes them and gets in the truck."

"Who drives?"

"I do."

Before she opened the door, he put the hand that held the pistol on her. "Listen," he said very quietly. "Get in the truck as fast as you can and start the engine. If something goes wrong, I will shoot the guards but I need you to be ready to drive."

She nodded.

"And Tania . . ."

"Yes?"

"I know you like to do as you please, but there can only be one person in charge—me. If we're both in charge, we both die. Understood?"

"Understood. You're in charge."

He pulled open the door. They were outside. It was dark and cool. Alexander walked quickly in long strides across the illuminated courtyard; Tatiana could barely keep up. As the sentries looked down and watched him, Alexander walked over to the gate, the one that said, "Work Makes You Free," unlocked it, pushed it open and walked back to the truck. Tatiana was already inside with the ignition on. In fact, the truck lurched before Alexander had a chance to get in.

He looked up at the sentries, smiled, and saluted them. They saluted him back.

He got in, and Tatiana drove him out of Sachsenhausen, down the leafy forested road to the commandant's house. In the dark of the trees, halfway between the gatehouse and the commandant's house, she stopped the jeep. They got out, ran to the back doors. Tatiana opened them, climbed in and raised the hatch to the long compartment. Suddenly seeing Alexander next to her, she wondered if he would fit. She had forgotten how tall he was.

He himself seemed to wonder that, because he looked at the narrow space, looked at her and said, "It's a good thing I haven't eaten in six months."

"Yes," she breathed out, taking out the bags with the weapons. "Get in, quick. When we're on the road a little while, I'll give a knock and you do something."

"Tania, I don't forget. You don't have to repeat it. Are those your two packs?"

She nodded. "Plus my backpack over there."

"Weapons? Ammunition? Knife, rope?"

"Yes, yes."

"A flashlight?"

"Below in the compartment."

He grabbed it.

"In."

He squeezed in sideways, and she slammed the hatch shut. "Can you hear me?"

"Yes," came his muffled voice. He opened the hatch from inside. "But knock loudly so I can hear above the noise of the jeep. What time is it?"

"Seven forty."

"Get them in as soon as possible and start driving."

"Right now."

Before she climbed into the jeep, Tatiana ran to the side of the path and threw up.

"I don't know what the hurry is," said Penny plaintively. "I'm tired, I had some wine, why can't we just go to sleep and drive back tomorrow?"

"Because we have to be back here tomorrow," said Tatiana, pushing her to the jeep. "Dr. Flanagan, are you coming?"

"Yes, I'm coming, I'm coming. I just want to make sure I haven't forgotten anything."

"We'll be back tomorrow, even if you did."

"That's true. Should we say goodbye to the commandant?"

"I don't think that's necessary," said Tatiana as casually as she could. She wanted to scream. "I already made our goodbyes to him. Besides, we'll see him tomorrow."

They walked outside, dropped their bags in the back.

"Where are *your* bags, Tania?" Penny asked.

She pointed to them.

"You have so many bags," Martin said. "More and more, it seems like."

"You're never sure what you're going to need on a trip like this. Would you like me to drive? My head is clear. I've had no wine."

"Yes, why don't you?" said Martin, sliding in past the wheel. "But do you know the way in the dark?"

"I mapped out our route earlier to make it easier for us. We go down to Oranienburg and make a left."

"I guess." Martin closed his eyes. "Let's go."

Tatiana drove away from the commandant's house and made her way slowly in the darkness, and then faster and faster. It impressed on her that she wanted to be as far away as soon as possible from Special Camp Number 7.

⚭

At 7:55, Nikolai Ouspensky opened his eyes and screamed. He jumped out of bed and ran waving like a madman to the guard by the door of the barracks.

"I must see the commandant!" he yelled. "I must see him now! It's a matter of great urgency, believe me, great urgency!"

"Easy now," the guard said calmly, pushing him away. "What's so urgent all of a sudden?"

"One of their prisoners is about to escape! Tell Commandant Brestov that Captain Alexander Belov is about to escape!"

"What are you talking about? Belov? The one who is shackled in isolation until the trains come?"

"I'm telling you, one of the Red Cross nurses is not an American. She is his Russian wife, and she is about to help him escape!"

❦

Tatiana drove for a minute, two, three. Time and distance suddenly stood still. She could not drive fast enough, nor get enough time to pass before they needed to make their move. She couldn't remember if there was a checkpoint at Oranienburg, and didn't know if she should chance it. Could Special Camp communicate with the checkpoint? Was there a phone? What if someone came into the cell block? What if Karolich came to and started screaming? What if Perdov fell off his chair and became revived by the fall? What if, what if, what if.

"Tania, we're talking to you, did you hear us?" Martin said.

"No, sorry, what?"

They reached Oranienburg and made a left onto a paved road. As soon as the dim lights of the small town were behind them, Tatiana rapped her knuckles twice on the cabin. Penny and Martin were talking and didn't notice.

❦

Ouspensky was brought before Brestov at 8:15.

"What is this all about?" Brestov said, inebriated and smiling. "Who did you say is escaping?"

"Alexander Belov, sir. The Red Cross nurse is his wife."

"What Red Cross nurse?"

"The black-haired one."

"I thought they both had . . . dark hair."

Ouspensky through his teeth said, "The small one."

"They were both small."

"The thin one! She was a Russian nurse by the name of Tatiana Metanova, and she escaped from the Soviet Union some years back."

"And you're saying she came back for him?"

"Yes."

"How did she know he was here?"

"I don't know that, but sir . . ."

Brestov laughed and shrugged. "Where is Karolich?" he said to the guard at the door of his quarters. "Ask him to join us, will you?"

"I haven't seen him, sir."

"Well, find him."

"Why don't you talk to the nurse?" said Ouspensky. "She's his wife, why don't you talk to her?"

"I'll have to do that tomorrow, prisoner."

"Tomorrow will be too late!" Ouspensky nearly screeched.

"Well, tonight is not possible. They've left."

He gasped. "Left where?"

"Back to Berlin. Ran out of supplies. They'll be back tomorrow. We'll talk to her then."

Ouspensky took one step back. "Sir, she won't be coming back tomorrow."

"Of course she will."

"Yes. But though I am not a betting man, I will bet that Alexander Belov is no longer in your custody."

"I don't know what you're talking about," Brestov said, rubbing his head. "Belov is in the camp brig. We'll wait for Karolich and then look into it."

"Call the next checkpoint on the road," said Ouspensky. "Have them at least stop the truck until you know Belov is still here."

"I'm not doing anything until my lieutenant gets here." When Brestov tried to get up, he sloppily knocked a number of papers off his table. "Besides, I liked that nurse. I don't think she is capable of what you say."

"Just check on your prisoner," said Ouspensky. "But if I am right, perhaps the commandant could do me a small service and speak to Moscow on my behalf? I'm supposed to be getting shipped out tomorrow. Perhaps a commutation of some sort?" He smiled thinly and beseechingly.

"Let's stop counting the eggs until they've hatched, shall we?"

They waited for Karolich.

⚬⚬⚬

There was the sound of doors banging hard against the sides of the truck and then a loud thump as if something fell or was run over.

"Geez, what was that?" exclaimed Penny. "Tania, oh my, did you run over a dog?"

They stopped the jeep and all got out onto the empty road and hurried to the back. The doors of the jeep were swinging open. They stared at them mutely.

"What in heaven's name happened here?" Penny asked.

"I think I must have forgotten to lock them all the way," replied Tatiana. She looked deeper inside the truck. Her backpack was gone.

"Yes, but what did you run over?"

"Nothing."

"Then what was that noise?"

She turned around. A bulky form was lying some twenty meters back. She ran to it.

It was her backpack.

"Your backpack fell out?"

"We must have hit a nasty bump in the road. Look, everything is all right."

"Well, let's get back in," said Martin. "No use standing idly on a dark highway."

"No, you're right," said Tatiana, and then she rushed over to the side of the road and retched, pretending to throw up. They gave her a flask of water to clean her mouth, and stood solicitously by her side. She said, "I'm sorry, I guess I'm not feeling as well as I thought. Martin, would you mind driving the rest of the way? I think I'll lie down in the back."

"Of course, of course."

They helped her in. Before Martin closed the doors, Tatiana looked at them fondly. "Thank you both. For everything."

"Not to worry," said Penny.

Martin, being most careful, locked the doors from the outside. Before he was in the driver's seat, Tatiana opened the hatch to the litter compartment. Alexander was looking at her. The truck pulled away from the roadside.

Martin was driving cautiously—at some thirty kilometers per hour. She knew he wasn't comfortable driving on foreign roads in the dark.

Tatiana heard the muffled talking in the cabin through the small pane of glass. Alexander got out of the compartment and pulled out Karolich's sub-machine gun.

"You should have left the backpack on the road," he whispered, nearly inaudibly. "Now we'll have to throw it and it will be harder to find."

"We'll find it."

"We should leave it."

"All our things are in it. We also have to take this." She pointed to the smaller canvas bag and the ruck.

"No. We will have to make do with one backpack."

"This one has pistols, grenades, a revolver, and rounds for all your weapons."

"Ah."

He stood on his tiptoes, reaching for the latch that kept closed the hatch in the roof.

"Let me get out first," he whispered, "you'll hand me our things, I'll throw them down, and then I'll pull you up."

Once he threw down the backpack, her nurse's bag, the weapons, and pulled her up onto the roof of a moving vehicle from which they were going to jump down a black slope, Tatiana nearly reconsidered. The slope looked like a bottomless pit, but in less than seventy minutes of comfortable driving they could be in the French sector.

The wind was ripping through her hair and she could hardly hear him, but she heard him well enough. "We *have* to jump, Tania. Push off as hard as you can, land in the grass. I go first."

Alexander didn't even take a breath or count or look back. He just sprang off from a crouching position and jumped, the bag of ammo on his back. He was down the slope and she couldn't see him.

Holding her breath and tensing her body, she crouched and jumped. She fell awkwardly and hard. But she fell onto the grassy slope, into bushes, and rolled down underbrush, not concrete. Because it had rained, the ground was soft and muddy. Clambering up to the side of the road, she saw that the truck had not stopped. It continued moving down the highway. Something hurt. She didn't have time to think what it was or where. She began to run back, every once in a while stopping and whispering, "Alexander? Alexander?"

◦⟁⟁∾

It was 8:30. Karolich was nowhere to be found. The guard who reported this was unconcerned, and so was Brestov. He asked that Ouspensky be taken back to his barracks. "We'll check this out tomorrow morning, Comrade Ouspensky."

"Couldn't you just check Belov's cell, Commandant? Just to make sure. It will take two minutes. We can check the jail as you're walking me back to barracks."

Brestov shrugged. "Go ahead, Corporal, walk by the jail, if you want."

Ouspensky and the guard walked back to the gatehouse.

"Have *they* seen Karolich?" asked Ouspensky, motioning to the sentries.

"Yes, they said they saw him and a Red Cross nurse get into the jeep and head for the commandant's house about forty-five minutes ago."

"But he's not at the commandant's house."

"That doesn't mean anything."

The guard pushed open the door of the jail and walked inside the cell block corridor. Perdov was sprawled out on the floor, unconscious. He reeked of vodka. "Oh, just great," muttered the guard. "Some fucking sentry you are, Perdov." He grabbed the master key from him and unlocked cell number seven.

Ouspensky and the guard stood in the doorway. The man on the straw was chained and was wearing a bloodied white shirt and dark slacks. His head was tilted back. He wasn't moving.

"Well?" said the guard. "Satisfied?"

Ouspensky walked down to the prisoner and looked into his face. Then he turned around. "I'm satisfied," he said. "Come look for yourself."

The guard stepped down. Dumbly he stared into the open eyes of Ivan Karolich.

⌘

"Tania!" She heard his voice.

"Where are you?"

"Down here, come."

She ran down the slope to him. He was waiting for her by the trees. He had already found the weapons and her backpacks. In his hands he was holding the nurse's bag. She wanted to come closer, but he was holding too many bags.

"Will you be all right carrying the smaller bag with the ammo and your nurse's bag?" he asked. "I'll take the rest of the ammo, the weapons and the large backpack. What did you put in here, rocks?"

"Food. Wait. I have clothes for you. Once you change into them, it'll be lighter."

"I'll wash first, then change." Alexander led the way, carrying the flashlight.

"What river is this?" he asked.

"Havel."

"How far south does it run?"

"To Berlin, but it runs along the highway nearly the whole way."

"Ah, too bad." He undressed. "I'll be happy to get out of the uniform of that motherfucking bastard. And just a lieutenant, too. Do you have any soap? Did you get hurt?"

"No," she said, her head slightly leaden. She handed him the soap.

He walked naked into the water. Sitting down on the embankment she shined the light on him.

"Turn it off," he said. "You can see light for miles in the dark."

She wanted to look at him. But she turned it off and listened to him instead, splashing, lathering, diving under.

She was facing his dark form in the river. He was facing her and the incline to the road. Suddenly he stopped moving. All she heard was his breath.

"Tatiana," he said.

She didn't have to be told anything. When she turned around and looked up, she already knew what she would be seeing. Bright lights, moving down the highway, engine noise getting closer, the sound of men shouting, and dogs barking.

"How could they have found out so quickly?" she whispered.

Quickly she handed him his clothes. He got dressed. He kept Karolich's boots, because otherwise he would have been barefoot. ("I can't think of everything," she said.)

"We have to lose our scent. The Alsatians will find us. The Soviets are really enjoying the fruits of Hitler's superior military machine."

"But they passed us."

"Yes. Where do you think they're going?" he asked.

"To the truck."

"Are we in that truck?"

Ah. "But where can we go?" she asked. "We're stuck between the river and the road. They'll smell us here for sure."

"Yes, the dogs will find us. It's a windy night."

"Let's cross the river and head west."

"Where's the nearest river crossing?"

"Forget about a crossing" she replied. "There may be one five miles down. Let's just cross here. We'll swim across and then move west, away from Berlin, before we turn south and return back east into the British sector."

"Where's the American sector?"

"All the way south. But all four zones in the city have open borders, so the sooner we leave Soviet-occupied territory the better."

"You think?" he said. "The river is not that deep, maybe eight feet."

She was already undressed down to her vest and underwear. "That's fine. We'll swim to the other side. Let's go."

"We can't swim," he said. "If our weapons and ammo get wet, they'll be no good to us until they dry." They stood for a moment, their eyes on each other. "Get on top of my back," Alexander said, quickly taking off the clothes he had just put on. "I'll swim across and you hold all our things on your back."

Tatiana climbed onto Alexander. The feel of his naked back against her vest produced such a peculiar aching inside, such a sense of familiarity and loss—and not temporal but permanent loss—that she couldn't help it, she groaned, and he misunderstood and said, "Hey," and she, to keep from breaking down, bit down on the strap of the backpack.

With the packs and the machine gun on her back, and her on his back, Alexander waded into the river and began to swim. The river was less than half the size of the Kama. Did he notice? She couldn't say for sure, but she knew one thing for sure—he was having trouble. She could almost feel him sinking. He kept upright, but he wasn't able to speak. All she heard was his bubbling breath, in from the air, out into the water. When they reached the other side, he lay for a minute on the ground, panting. She sat down next to him, pulling off the backpacks. "You did great," she said. "Is it hard for you?"

"Not hard, just . . ." He jumped up. "Six months in a cell will do that to you."

"Well, let's rest. Lie back down." She touched his leg, looking up at him.

"Do you have a towel? Hurry."

She had one small towel. "Tania," he said, drying off quickly. "You're not thinking this through. What do you think that posse is going to do five miles down the road when they stop the Red Cross truck and when your friends open the back and find you not there? Do you think everybody will just go on as before? Your friends, being unprepared and not knowing they have anything to hide, will say, 'Oh, but we just saw her right down the road.' And they will lead the guards to the spot from where we just swam. They'll get an armored vehicle across to here in forty seconds. Ten men, two dogs, ten machine guns, ten pistols. Now—can we go, please? Let's put as much distance between us and them as possible. Do you have a compass, a map?"

"Do you think they'll get into trouble with the Soviet authorities?"

He stood silent for a moment. "I don't think so," he said at last. "They don't like to bring their darkness out into the open. They'll interrogate them for sure. But they're not going to trifle with U.S. nationals. Let's go."

They dried off as best they could, threw on their clothes, and ran to the woods.

👁

Meandering they walked through the night-time woods for what seemed to Tatiana tens of miles. He was ahead with the knife, clearing the way. She was doggedly behind him. Sometimes they ran if the woods were clear. Most of the time it took a grunting effort to get through the thick underbrush. He would shine the flashlight for three seconds to illuminate the way just ahead of them. He often stopped and listened for sound, and then continued forward. She wished they could stop moving. Her legs weren't carrying her. He slowed down and said, "Are you tired?"

"A little. Can we stop?"

He stopped to look at the relief map. "I like where we are, we're much more west than I think they would expect, and not nearly as far south. We've moved laterally very well."

"Yet we're no closer to Berlin."

"No, not much closer. But we're farther away from them, and that's better for now." He closed the map. "You don't have a tent?"

"I have a waterproof trench. We could make a lean-to." She paused. "I'd rather find a barn, maybe? The ground is so wet."

"Fine, let's find a barn. It will be warmer and dryer. There will be farms just the other side of the woods."

"So we have to walk some more?"

Alexander pulled her up and, for a moment, held her close to him. "Yes," he said. "We still have a way to go."

Onward and slowly, they moved through the woods.

"Alexander, it's *midnight*. How many miles west do you think we've gone in total?"

"Three. In another mile there will be fields."

She didn't want to tell him she was scared to be in the constantly creaking woods. He probably didn't remember the story she had once told him about herself, about being lost in the woods when she was

younger. He had been wounded and near death, and probably didn't remember her telling him that being lost in the woods was the most terri-
fying experience of her life up to then.

They came out onto a field. The night was clear; Tatiana could just
make out the shape of a silo at the other end.

"Let's walk across," she said.

Alexander made her walk around. He didn't trust fields anymore,
he told her.

The barn was a hundred yards away from the farmhouse. Popping
open the latch, Alexander motioned her inside. A horse whinnied in
surprise. Inside was warm and smelled of hay and manure and old
cow's milk. They were familiar smells to Tatiana, as familiar as Luga.
Again a pronounced aching hit her. All the things America had nearly
made her forget, she was remembering now with him.

Alexander pulled up a ladder next to a hay loft above the cows and
prodded her upward.

In the loft, sitting in a heap on the hay, Tatiana found a flask of water, drank some, gave him some. He drank, and then said, "Got anything else in there?"

Smiling, she rummaged and pulled out a pack of Marlboros.

"Ah, American cigarettes," he said, lighting up. He smoked three
cigarettes without saying a word while she sat collapsed on the hay and
watched him. Her eyes were closing.

When she opened them, she found Alexander sitting mutely and
staring at her with an expression of profound emotion. She crawled on
her hands and knees to him and buried herself inside his fierce arms,
and somewhere near her head, she heard his whisper, *Shh, shh.*

They could not speak. To be in Alexander's arms, to smell him, to
hear his breathing, his voice again . . .

Shh, shh, he was still whispering and holding her, pulling off her
hat, her hairnet, her hairpins, letting her black hair fall down.

His hands were in it. His eyes were closed. Perhaps he was imagining her hair was not black but blonde again.

The way Alexander was touching her now, she could tell that he
was blind and had not yet learned to see—he was holding her in that
impossible choke that had to do not quite with love or passion, but somehow with both and with neither. The embrace wasn't an alloy, it was a
conflagration of anguish and bitter relief and fear.

Tatiana could tell Alexander would like to have spoken more, but he couldn't, and so he sat on the hay with his legs open, while she kneeled in front of him, folded into his arms, and every once in a while from his shuddering body would come a *Shh, shh* . . .

Not for her. Not for Tatiana. For himself.

Continuing to hold her, Alexander lowered her onto the straw. His trembling limbs surrounded her. Tatiana was barely breathing, her own body convulsing. To rage, to quell—

They didn't know what to do—to undress? To stay clothed? She couldn't move, nor want to. His lips were on her neck, her clavicles, he was clawing at her, ripping open her tunic, baring her breasts to his desperate gasping mouth. She wanted to whisper his name, to moan maybe. Tears kept trickling down her temples.

He removed from himself and her only what was necessary. He didn't so much enter her as break her open. Her mouth remained in a mute screaming O, her hands clutched him, not close enough, and through the whisper of grief, through the cry of desire, Tatiana felt that Alexander, in his complete abandon, was making love to her as if he were being pulled from the cross to which he was still attached by nails.

His gripping her, his ferocious, unremitting movement was so intense that Tatiana felt consciousness yield to—

Oh my God, Shura, please . . . she mouthed inaudibly.

But it could not be any other way.

Violent release came for Alexander at the expense of Tatiana's momentary lapse of reason, as she cried out, her pleas carrying through the barn, to the basin, to the river, to the sky.

He remained on top of her without moving, without pulling away. His body was shaking. He couldn't be any closer. She held him closer still . . . And then . . .

Shh, shh.

That wasn't Alexander.

That was Tatiana.

They both fell asleep.

Still they hadn't spoken.

ᘒᙏᘐ

She woke up to find him inside her again.

And night, though lengthened by gods, wasn't long enough.

She spread the trench coat on the hay. He took the clothes off her.

In the unmuted darkness, Tatiana cried and cried out, stretched out on the rack of his famine.

Time and again she was imprisoned and released—barely, just for breath; time and again she burned for Alexander, in the *hands* of Alexander, and cried out again, *Oh, Shura* . . . endlessly, endlessly.

During brief respite, he continued to lie with his limbs over her, and again she was crying.

He whispered, "Tatia, what's a man to think when every time he makes love to his wife, she cries?"

"That he is his wife's only family," said Tatiana, crying. "That he is her whole life."

"As she is his," he said. "You don't see him crying." Tatiana could not see his face—it was buried in her breasts.

There was no night.

There was only twilight; the sky turned blue then lavender, then pink again within minutes that weren't long enough.

The night was not long enough.

Not long enough for the floor in Mathew Sayers's office, for Lisiy Nos, for the swamps of Finland, not long enough for Stockholm.

Not long enough for the punishment cell in Morozovo, for the ten grains of morphine in Slonko, for the drive across Europe with Nikolai Ouspensky.

Not long enough for the river Vistula.

And nothing was long enough for the forests and mountains of Holy Cross.

ᎾᏇᎧᎧᎧᎧᎧ

"Don't tell me another word." Tatiana's voice was defeated. "I don't have the strength to hear it."

"I don't have the strength to tell it."

After Tatiana heard about Pasha, she could not talk or look at Alexander, as she lay supine, her legs drawn up to her chest, while he lay behind her whispering, "I'm sorry, Tania. I'm sorry."

Just a gasp from a bereft Tatiana.

"I was dying in 1944 before I found him," said Alexander. "You can't imagine what stormed inside me as I pushed my penal battalion across every fucking river in Poland."

"Alexander, what I would have given for a penal battalion."

He kissed the soft flesh between her shoulder blades.

She rolled into a tighter coil, seeking to return to the place she had once shared with her brother.

Alexander didn't even bother uncoiling her to return to the place he shared with her.

⚊⚊⚊

Alexander was not so much sleeping as unconscious, while Tatiana was propped up on her elbow, tracing the scars on his body. She didn't want to wake him but she couldn't stop touching him. He had marks on his body that defied her understanding. How could a body bear all this yet live, thinner than before, less whole than before, raggedly tearing apart at the seams, yet live?

Her hand cupped him softly, then ran down to his shins, and up again to his arms, where it stayed, caressing him, while Tatiana stared at his sleeping face.

There is one moment, a moment in eternity. Before we find out the truth about one another. That simple moment is the one that propels us through life—what we felt like at the very edge of our future, standing over the abyss, before we knew for sure we loved. Before we knew for sure we loved forever. Before the dying Dasha, the dying Mama, the dying Leningrad. Before Luga. Before the divinity of Lazarevo, when the miracles you heaped upon me with your love and your body alloyed us for life. Before all that, you and I walked through the Summer Garden, and once in a while my bare arm touched your arm, and once in a while you spoke and that gave me an excuse to look up into your face, into your laughing eyes, to catch a glimpse of your mouth and I, who had never been touched, tried to imagine what it might be like to have your mouth touch me. Falling in love with you in the Summer Garden in the white nights of Leningrad is the moment that propels me through life.

⚊⚊⚊

He woke up, saw her. "What are you doing?" he whispered.

"Watching over you," she whispered back.

And he closed his eyes and reached for her, taking her almost without waking, and then slept.

⚊⚊⚊

The next morning at dawn, the farmer came in to milk the cows. They lay silently in the loft and listened to him, and after he left, Tatiana dressed, went down the ladder and squeezed some milk for her and Alexander into a cup she carried to dispense medicine. He came with her, holding both pistols in his hands.

They drank to bursting.

"My God, you're thinner than I've ever seen you," she said. "Have some more milk. Have all of it."

He drank. "You're curvier than I've ever seen you." He bent to her on the little stool. "Your breasts are bigger."

"Motherhood, I guess," she muttered, kissing him.

"Let's go up," he said, his hand on her.

They went up. But before they had a chance to undress, they heard the sound of an engine outside. It was seven in the morning. Alexander looked out the small, four-pane loft window. A military truck was outside and four Red Army officers were talking to the farmer in the clearing.

He glanced back at Tatiana.

"Who's there?" she whispered.

"Tania, sit back against the wall but not too far. Hold the P-38 and the ammo."

"Who's there?"

"They've come for us."

She emitted a cry, creeping to the window. "Oh, my God, there are four of them, what are we going to do, we're trapped up here!"

"Shh. Maybe they'll leave." Alexander readied the machine gun, all three pistols and the Commando. She watched them out of the corner of the window. The farmer was opening his hands, shrugging his shoulders. The soldiers were coming up too close to him, pointing to the house, the fields, and finally the barn. The farmer moved out of their way, motioning with his hand in the direction of the barn.

"The revolver, is it double action, or single action?"

"What?"

"Never mind."

"Double action, I think. I'm almost sure," she said, trying to remember. "Does it recock by itself you mean? Yes."

Alexander lay flat with two bales in front of him, the machine gun and pistols by his right side, the Commando in his hands pointed at the ladder. Tatiana, her shaking hands full of clips, sat against the barn wall behind him.

He turned around. "Not a single sound, Tania. Stop shaking."

Mutely she nodded. Tried to stop shaking.

The barn door opened and the farmer came in with one of the officers. Tatiana's heart was beating so loudly that she could barely hear. The officer spoke very poor German intermingled with Russian. The farmer must have told him that no one had been through these parts, because the officer yelled in Russian, "You're sure of this, you're sure?"

They went on in circles like this for a few seconds, and suddenly the officer stopped speaking and looked around. "Do you smoke?" he asked in Russian.

"Nein, nein," said the farmer. *"Ich rauche nei in der Scheune wegen Brandgefahr."*

"Well, fire or no fire, somebody has been smoking in your fucking barn!"

Tatiana put her hand over her mouth to stop herself from crying out.

The officer ran out of the barn. She looked out the window. He said something to the rest of the men. One of them turned off the engine and they all retrieved their machine guns.

"Shura," Tatiana whispered.

"Shh. Don't speak. Don't even breathe."

The farmer was still standing in the middle of his barn when the four Soviets walked in with their weapons.

"Get the fuck out of here," one of them said to the farmer. He ran.

"Who's here?" they called.

Tatiana held her breath.

"There's no one here," said one of them.

"We know you're here, Belov," said another. "Just come out and nobody will get hurt."

Alexander said nothing.

"You have a wife you should think about. You want her to live, don't you?"

Tatiana heard the quiet creaking of the ladder.

Alexander lay so still you could have walked by him and not known he was there. There was another creak.

One of the officers below said, "If you come out peacefully, your wife will get amnesty."

Another said, "We are all heavily armed. You cannot escape. Let's do this reasonably."

Alexander barely even leaned over. He just tipped the Commando downward and fired a .357 bullet into the head of the man on the ladder. The man flew backward in a spasm, the other men crouched, raising their guns, but they couldn't raise them fast enough, nor hide. Alexander aimed fired, aimed fired, aimed fired. The men didn't have a chance to take cover, much less open fire.

He jumped up and turned to Tatiana. "Let's go," he said. "Can't stay here another second. If the farmer has a telephone, he's on it right now."

"Maybe he doesn't have a telephone," Tatiana muttered.

"Can't count on that, can we? Hurry."

She quickly collected their things while Alexander reloaded the revolver.

"Nice weapon, Tania," he said. "Some recoil on it, though. What's the muzzle velocity, do you know?"

"The man who sold it to me told me it was four hundred and fifty meters per second."

Alexander whistled. "Immense power. Almost like my Shpagin. Are you ready?"

They glanced out the window to make sure no one was coming, and then descended the ladder, stepped over the dead men at the door—though not before Alexander reached into their pockets and relieved them of their Soviet cigarettes—and were out. From their truck, Alexander took one light machine gun and one ammunition belt. Tatiana asked how he was going to carry another machine gun, this one with a bipod, plus a sub-machine-gun, three sidearms, and all the ammo.

"Don't worry about my end," he said, throwing the metal ammunition belt around his neck. "Just worry about yours."

"We could take their truck," Tatiana suggested.

"Yes, good idea, we'll drive it to the next checkpoint."

They ran through the fields, away from the farm, into the forest.

They walked until noon.

"Can we stop?" Tatiana pleaded. They were about to cross a stream. "You must be tired. We'll wash up, maybe have a bite to eat. Where are we, anyway?"

"Nowhere," he said, reluctantly stopping. "Barely four miles from the farm and the Soviet army."

"Four miles south?" she said with hope. "That would mean that we're only about—"

"West. We're not heading south."

She stared at him. "What do you mean, we're not heading south? Berlin is south."

"Hmm. That's where they think we'll be going."

"But eventually we have to go south, no?"

"Eventually, yes."

She didn't want to say anymore. They washed their faces and brushed their teeth. "Just don't give me any of that morphine toothpaste," Alexander said.

She unpacked a few things to eat. She had Spam—with a smile. And he actually smiled back, and said, "I like it. But how do you plan to open it?"

"Ah, because it comes from America," she said, "it has a little can opener built into the cap."

She had some dried bread, dried apple chips. They ate, drinking water out of the stream.

"Okay, let's go," he said, springing up.

"Shura," she said, glancing up at him. "I'd like to go in the water. Wash. All right? It won't take long."

He sighed.

After he had smoked two or three cigarettes, he undressed and went into the water after her.

∽⟶

They were sitting on a log next to the stream in the canopied and secluded woods. They were both astride the log, she in front of him, with her back to him. He was wearing his skivvies. She was wearing a white tank top and underwear. They weren't speaking.

Presently Alexander leaned down to her and, kissing her neck under her ear, whispered, "I want to see those freckles." Tatiana purred in a soft chime, and turned her head to him. They looked at each other a moment, and then they kissed. The brush fell from his hands as they went around her neck, touching the wedding bands.

He bent her head all the way back, as his hand moved down to her breasts, to her stomach, to between her thighs. She undressed and straddled him on the log, standing against him. He cupped her breasts, and pulled her to sit on top of him, bending to her nipples.

Her soft moans echoed through the woods.

Alexander carried her to their open trench blanket. She lay on the blanket in front of him, and he kneeled in front of her and put his fingers on her, but only for a short while, too short a while. She was too fevered. He climbed on top of her, and she began to cry out and cry—

Suddenly Tatiana stopped moving. Stopped making a single sound except the panting which she could not control. Clutching Alexander to herself, she whispered, "Shura, oh my God, there is a man watching us."

He stopped moving, too. "Where?" he said into her ear, not turning his head.

"Over to my—"

"Clock, Tania. Tell me where he is on the clock. I'm in the middle."

"He's at four thirty."

Alexander lay very still, as still as he had lain up in the barn that morning. Tatiana emitted a puppy whimper.

"Shh," he said without a breath. The P-38 lay on the trench blanket by his left hand. He lifted himself slightly off Tatiana and in one fluid motion, cocked the lever, turned his left hand and fired three times. There was a cry from the woods and the sound of a body crashing into the bushes.

They both jumped up. Alexander threw on his shorts, Tatiana her underwear. He went to look, armed with his Commando and his Colt. She followed close behind, her hands on her breasts.

A man in a Soviet uniform lay spurting blood. Two of the shots hit him, one in the shoulder, one in the neck. Alexander took away the man's loaded pistol and went back to the clearing. Tatiana kneeled down in front of the man and pressed her hand against his neck wound.

From behind she heard Alexander's incredulous low voice. "Tatiana, what are you doing?"

"Nothing," she said, loosening the man's collar. "He can't breathe."

With a guttural growl, Alexander grabbed her, pulled her out of the way, pointed the Colt and shot the man twice, point-blank in the head. She screamed, fell down, and in her terror tried blindly to get away from Alexander who yanked her up off the ground, still holding the Colt in his hand. She shut her eyes, struggling so hard she was on the verge of becoming hysterical.

"Tatiana! What the fuck are you doing?"

"Let go of me!"

"He can't breathe? I fucking hope not! Certainly not anymore. Are you trying to save him or us? This is not a fucking joke, your life and mine! You can't be bending down, making his last moments better when we're seconds away from death!"

"Stop it, stop it, let go!"

"Oh, for fuck's sake!" Alexander threw down his weapons and squared off against her, who stood in front of him, her trembling hands palms out at her chest. "What do you want? Why did you come here? Was your goal to leave our son without his mother? Don't you understand it's either you and me, or it's them? There is no middle ground. It's fucking war, don't you understand that?"

"Please—just—"

"No, I don't think you do!" He grabbed her, squeezed her. "He was watching us, watching *you*, probably from the very beginning, he saw everything, heard everything, and you know what he was waiting for? For me to finish so he could kill me and then have you all to himself. And then he would have killed you. We don't know who he is, he may be an army man, he may be a deserter, but one thing I know, his intentions were not to partake in our lunch!"

"Oh my God, what's happened to you?"

He shoved her away. "What, are *you* of all people judging me?" He spat on the ground. "I'm a soldier, not a fucking saint."

"I'm not judging you. Shura, please ..." she whispered, opening her hands to him.

"Us or them, Tatiana."

"You, Alexander, *you*." She swayed. He took hold of her with one arm to steady her, but did not press her to him, did not comfort her.

"Don't you understand anything? Go clean his blood off and get dressed. We have to move out."

They left the clearing within ten minutes, and back in olive drab, they walked through the woods not speaking except to stop, have a drink, move on. Alexander smoked as he walked. He would stop to listen for the ambient noise of the countryside and then cautiously proceeded forward.

They avoided villages and paved roads, but the farms were also problematic. It was summer, planting season, crop season, harvest season. The combine harvesters, the simple threshers, the tractors, the field-hands were out everywhere. They had to walk around the perimeter of busy fields just to avoid the workers.

They walked through the meadows and woods for six hours, *finally* heading in a southerly direction. Tatiana wanted desperately to stop. But he wasn't slowing his stride and so she wouldn't slow hers.

They came to a potato field and she, very hungry, walked out in front of him. He immediately grabbed her and pulled her back. "Don't walk in front of me, You don't know anything about this field."

"Oh, and you do."

"Yes, because I've seen thousands like it."

"I've seen a field before, Alexander."

"A mined field?"

This gave her pause. "It's a potato field. It's not mined."

"And you know this how? Did you look at it through your binoculars? Did you examine the ground? Did you crawl through it, your bayonet in front of you feeling for the mines? Or are you just thinking that when you were a little girl growing up in the Luga fields, they weren't mined?"

"Stop it, okay?" she said quietly.

He took out the binoculars. He examined the earth. He said he thought it looked safe, but he wasn't taking any chances. He pored over a relief map for a few minutes, and said, "Let's go to the left. On the right there's a highway. Too dangerous. But the woods on the other side are thick and cover about ten miles."

He let her dig out five or six potatoes from the edge of the field.

The sun was setting by the time they got to the woods. When they stopped at a stream for a drink, Tatiana said, "Maybe we could catch a fish? If you build a fire, I can cook these potatoes and a fish. We'll eat. Break camp, you know." She wanted to smile at him but he looked so grim that she reconsidered.

"Fire? You've completely lost your mind, haven't you? They smelled my cigarette in a barn. What do you think their dogs are trained to sniff out, if not the scent of cooking fish?"

"Oh, Alexander. They're not looking for us anymore. They're not here."

"No, they're there." He waved in a nebulous direction. "By the time they're here, it'll be too late."

"So we're not going to eat?"

"We'll eat the potatoes raw."

"Great," muttered Tatiana.

They ate the potatoes raw. They had their second to last can of Spam. Tatiana would have brought more, but who would have thought they weren't going to be able to build a fire, to cook a fish, a potato? They washed again, he smoked again and said, "Ready?"

"Ready for what?"

"We have to go."

"Oh, please no more, no more! It's eight in the evening. We need to rest, we'll walk tomorrow during the day." She wanted to add that she was afraid to walk at night, but didn't want him to see her weakness, so she said nothing, waiting for him to do the right thing.

He was silent.

She was silent.

"Let's go until ten," he said with a sigh. "Then we'll stop."

She stayed very close behind him. But she hated that there was no one behind *her*. She kept feeling that there was someone there, and would whirl around every time Alexander stopped to listen to the woods. Once, something fell, a rock rolled, or a branch hit something, and Tatiana cried out and grabbed for Alexander.

He put his hand on her. "What, Tatiasha?" he said softly.

"Nothing, nothing."

Patting her, he said, "Let's stop."

She had to bite her lip to keep from begging him to find a barn, a shed, a ditch near a house, a mined field even, anything as long as they didn't have to spend the night in the woods.

He built them a small lean-to with some sturdy branches and the trench blanket. He said he would be right along, but after fifteen minutes of not being right along, she climbed out and found him sitting against a nearby tree, smoking.

"Shura," she whispered. "What are you doing?"

"Nothing. Go to sleep. We have a long day tomorrow."

"Come in the lean-to."

"It's too small, I'm fine here."

"It's not too small. We'll sleep side by side, come." She pulled on his arm. He pulled it away.

Kneeling by him, she studied him and then her hands went on his face. "Shura . . ."

"Look," he said, "you've got to stop fighting with me. I'm on your side. You have to let me do what I know we need to do. I can't have it out with you every time we're in danger."

"I know," she said. "I'm sorry. But you know I can't help it. It's my nature."

"You *have* to help it. I know it's hard, and I know you're overwhelmed, but you have to win that battle inside yourself. One way or another, you have to make it right inside you. Or don't you care if the Huns win?" His arms went around her.

She pressed her face into his throat. "I care if the Huns win. I will try, all right?" she whispered.

"You will *do*," he said, holding her. "You will do as I say, and you will not heal those who mean to kill us, that's what you will do." He took her face into his hands. "Tania, last time in Morozovo, I let you go, but not this time. This time we live together or we die together."

"Yes, Alexander," she breathed out.

"I've put away everything in my nature except what I need to do to get us out of here, and you will put away everything in yours."

"Yes, Alexander. Come in and sleep."

He shook his head.

"Please," she whispered. "I'm scared at night in the woods."

He came inside and fit in behind her. She covered them up with her cashmere blanket. "I bought this for you," she said. "My first Christmas in New York."

"It's light and warm," he said. "Good blanket. *Oh, God, make small the old, star-eaten blanket of the sky, that I may fold it round me, and in comfort lie.*"

They lay fitted into each other, like two metal bowls.

"Tania," he said, "tell me, I won't be upset. I wanted you to be happy. Have you been with someone else?"

"I have not," she said, pausing slightly, remorsefully, remembering how close she had come with Jeb, how close she had come with Edward. "Who is blessed like you, endowed like you with gifts from the gods?" Tatiana felt Alexander's body tense. She wanted to ask him, but couldn't.

"I haven't." He paused. "Though I would have liked to once, twice, to stave off death."

She closed her eyes. "Yes, me too," she said. "You want to finish the earlier . . . staving off?"

"No," he said.

When she opened her eyes again, it was still dark and he was not behind her. He was sitting outside the lean-to by the trees, with a machine gun in his hands.

"What are you doing?" she asked.

"Watching over you," he replied.

Tatiana brought the blanket out and covered him with it, and then lay down on the ground with her head in his lap. She closed her eyes and restlessly slept.

When she awoke, her head was covered by the blanket. She moved it off her and found him staring at her in the near darkness and smoking. His body was as stiff as a springboard.

"What's wrong?" she whispered.

"I didn't want to drop ashes on your hair."

"No, I mean . . . what's *wrong?*"

Alexander looked away. "I don't think we're going to make it, Tatiana," he whispered.

She watched him for a moment and then closed her eyes, settling deeper into his lap. "Live as if you have faith," she said, "and faith shall be given to you."

He said nothing.

She took the rings off her neck. She fitted the small one onto her ring finger and took his hand—though it took some doing to get him to release the gun—and slipped the larger band onto his finger. He squeezed her hand, and then picked up the M1911 again.

"Do you want to sleep? *I'll* sit."

"No," he said. "I can't sleep."

She caressed his arm. "What can I do?" She nudged him. "*Anything* I can do?"

"No."

"No?" With surprise.

"No," he repeated flatly. "Too much around us. I'm not losing the edge, not even for a moment. Look what nearly happened."

Tatiana slept. He shook her awake sometime when the trees turned blue with dawn. Silently they brushed their teeth, picked up their things. She went a few meters away into the woods and when she returned, his back was to her.

"Are you hungry?" Tatiana asked, and before she was finished inflecting, Alexander whirled around, two cocked pistols pointing at her. A second went by before he lowered his arms and without a word turned back to what he was doing.

She went to see what he was doing. He was going through every inch of her backpack.

"What are you looking for?"

"You have any more cigarettes?"

"Of course. I brought six packs."

He paused. "Besides them."

She paused. "You smoked *six* packs of cigarettes last night?"

He resumed looking through the backpack.

"What about the pack you took from the Soviets?"

"What about it?" said Alexander.

Tatiana came to him, took the backpack out of his hands. She tried to take the weapons out of his belt but he wouldn't let her. She hugged him with the pistols and the ammunition belt between them. "Shura," she whispered. "Darling, husband, it'll be—"

"Let's go," he said, moving away. "Let's get going."

They got going. This time they headed south. Gradually he stopped letting her get even a meter away. There was no swimming in streams, no fire, and they were out of Spam and crackers. They picked some blueberries while walking. They found another field of potatoes.

At the end of the day, she asked if they could build a fire. After all, they hadn't heard anything suspicious all day. He told her no. She was surprised they had gone only ten miles, they seemed to be moving so slowly. Tatiana wondered if he was for some reason afraid to get to Berlin. But why? "I think we're very close. We seem close. Don't you think?"

"No. We're—yes, we're only about six miles away."

"We can do that by tomorrow."

"No. I think we should wait in the woods for a while," he said.

"Wait in the woods? But you insist on walking, you don't want to stop."

"Let's stop."

"When we stop, we can't build a fire, can't cook, can't eat, can't swim, or sleep, or . . . anything. What are we waiting in the woods for?"

"They'll be looking for us now. Don't you hear it?"

"Hear what?"

"Them. Around the edges, in the distance, agonizing back and forth, don't you hear it?"

Tatiana didn't. "Even so," she allowed, "North Berlin is spread out. They're not going to be looking for us everywhere."

"They are. We should stay here."

She put her hands on him. "Come on, Alexander," she said. "Let's go, let's push on, push on until we're done."

He moved away and said, "Fine, if that's what you want. Let's go."

The woods became sparse in the last stretch before Berlin. There was a sloping countryside, a flat countryside, some trees partitioning the fields. They were moving slowly, and once they sat in the bushes for two hours because, on the horizon, Alexander glimpsed a truck gliding by.

There were no streams and nowhere to hide. He was getting more and more tense, holding his sub-machine-gun in front of him as he walked. Tatiana didn't know how to help him. They were out of cigarettes.

At nine in the evening, as he was letting her rest her feet, she said, "You don't think the countryside is quiet?"

"No," he said. "The countryside is anything but quiet. On the periphery of the fields, in the echo of distance, I hear trucks constantly, I hear voices, I hear dogs barking."

"I don't hear them," she said.

"Why would you?"

"Why would *you*?"

"Because that's what I do. Come on, are you ready?"

"No. Can you show me on the map where we are?"

Sighing, he brought out the relief map. She followed his finger. "Shura, but that's great! A few kilometers ahead of us is a hill, with not too big an elevation—six hundred meters is not too big? Six hundred meters up, six hundred meters down. When we get down on the other side, we'll stop, and Berlin is just a few kilometers away. We'll be in the American sector by noon tomorrow."

Alexander watched her. Without saying a word, he put the map away and began walking.

The moon was out in the clear sky and it was possible to walk at night without shining a flashlight. When they got to the top of the hill, Tatiana thought she could almost see Berlin in the distance. "Come on," she said. "We can run the last six hundred meters to the bottom."

He sank into the ground. "It's obvious to me you were not paying attention to the war around Leningrad. Have you learned nothing from Pulkovo, from Sinyavino? We're not moving from the top of the hill. It's the only advantage we have, height. Perhaps a small element of surprise. At the bottom of the hill, we might as well wait for them with our hands up."

She remembered the Germans at Pulkovo and Sinyavino. She just felt too exposed here on the bare hilltop, with only a tree and a few bushes. But Alexander said they weren't going. Therefore they weren't going.

He didn't build a lean-to, telling her to take nothing out of the backpack except the blanket if she needed it, so they could be ready to run at any moment.

"Run? Shura, look how quiet everything is, how peaceful."

Alexander wasn't listening. He walked away and began doing something on the ground. Tatiana could just make out his silhouette. "What are you doing?" she asked, coming closer.

"Digging. Can't you see?"

She watched him for a moment. "What are you digging?" she asked quietly. "A grave?"

Without glancing up, he said, "No, a trench."

Tatiana didn't understand him. She feared the lack of cigarettes and his acute anxiety were turning into a temporary (temporary, right?) madness. She wanted to tell him he was being paranoid, but she didn't think that would be helpful, so she bent down and helped him dig with a knife and her bare hands until the pit was long enough for him to lie down in and be covered.

He was finished around two in the morning.

They sat under the linden tree, Alexander against the trunk, Tatiana in his lap. He refused to lie down or to put down his machine gun, but once she felt it fall on top of her only to scare her and make him jump up, knocking her to the ground.

After they sat back down, she tried to sleep, but it was impossible to relax into sleep with his body so tense around her.

She heard him say, "You shouldn't have come back for me. You had a good life. You were taking care of our son. You were working, you had friends, the promise of new things, New York. We were over. You should have let it be."

What are you talking about? she wanted to cry out. He didn't mean what he was saying, no matter how grim he sounded. "Well, why then did you give me Orbeli in my nightmare if you wanted me to let it be?" she asked. "Why did you give me a glimpse of your wasted life?"

"I didn't give you Orbeli for a nightmare," he said. "I gave you Orbeli to have faith."

"No!" She jumped up and away from him.

"Keep your voice down," he said, without jumping up.

She lowered her voice, remaining standing. "You gave me Orbeli to damn me!" Here came the deluge.

"Ah, yes, because *that's* what I was thinking during those last moments." He twisted his boot into the ground.

"You gave me Orbeli to torture me!" Tatiana cried.

"I said keep your voice down!"

"If you really wanted me to think you were dead, you would have said nothing. If you really wanted me to think you were dead, you would not have asked Sayers to put your damned medal into my bag. You knew, *knew*, that if I had any hint, a single word that you were alive, I would not be able to live my life. Orbeli was that word."

"You wanted a word, you got a fucking word. Can't have it both ways, Tatiana."

"We were supposed to be all about truth, and you ended our life on the biggest lie imaginable. You put me on the rack every day. Your life, your death were my meathooks. I couldn't twist my way out. And you knew it!"

They stopped for a moment. Tatiana tried to compose her trembling body. "That horseman has chased me every day, every night of my life and you're telling me I shouldn't have come back for you?" Leaning down, she grabbed him and shook him. He didn't protest, didn't defend himself, but after a moment pushed her slightly away.

"Take off my clothes," he said. "Come to me, lie with me uncovered, lie naked with me and tear the raw flesh off my bones with your teeth, just like in your dream. As you have been doing, eat me alive piece by piece, Tatiana."

"Oh my God, Alexander." Helplessly she sank to the ground.

And so they sat, under the linden tree in June, his back to one side, hers to another. Covering her face, she lay down on the earth. He sat with all the guns around him.

Hours passed. She heard his voice. "Tatiana," he said very quietly, and he didn't have to say anymore, because she heard them herself. They were coming. And this time, the sound of their engines and their shouting and their dogs wasn't off on the distant horizon, this time, the insistent barking of the dogs was just a hillside away.

She was about to jump up when his hand held her down. He didn't say a word, just held her down. "What are you doing," she whispered. "Why are you sitting? Let's run! We'll be down the hill in sixty seconds."

"And they will be at the top of the hill in sixty seconds. How many times do I have to tell you?"

"Get up! We'll run—"

"Where? There are rolling hills and fields all around us. You think you can outrun German shepherds?"

He was still holding her to the earth. She stopped hyperventilating. "Will those dogs sniff us out?"

"No matter where we are, yes."

Tatiana looked down the hill. She couldn't see them, but she heard their frantic noise, and the sound of men holding them, ordering them to be quiet, in Russian. But she knew the dogs were only barking because they were so close to their prey.

"Go into the trench, Shura," she said. "I'm going to climb this tree to hide."

"Better tie yourself to it. They'll throw a smoke bomb, you won't be able to hold on."

"Go. And give me the binoculars. I'll tell you how many of them there are." He let go of her and they jumped up. "You might as well give me my P-38." She paused. "We have to kill the dogs. Without the dogs, they won't know where we are."

And here Alexander smiled. "You don't think two dogs lying dead at their feet will give them an inkling?"

She didn't smile back. "Give me the grenades, too. Maybe I can throw them."

"I'll throw them. I don't want you popping the pin too early. When you fire the pistol, watch for the recoil. It's not bad with a P-38, but still it'll give you a jolt back. And even if you have one round left in the clip, if you have a moment, reload. Better to have eight bullets than one."

She nodded.

"Don't let anyone get too close to the tree, the farther they are away, the easier it is for them to miss." He gave her the gun, the rope, all the 9-millimeter clips in a canvas bag, and nudged her forward. "Go," he said, "but don't come down for anything."

"Don't be silly," she said. "I'm coming down if I'm needed down. If you need me down then that's where I'll be."

"No," he said. "You will come down when I tell you to come down. I cannot be worrying about where you are and what you're doing."

"Shura . . ."

He loomed over her. "You will come down when I tell you to come down, do you understand?"

"Yes," she said in a small voice. She tucked the weapon into her slacks and raised her arms. The first branch of the tree was too high for her to reach. He lifted her up, she grabbed on and climbed. He ran

to the trench and lined up all of his pistols and magazines, threaded
the ammo belt into the light machine gun he set up on a bipod, wrapping the rest of the belt around himself and finally settling down behind the bipod. The Shpagin was by his side. The belt had 150 rounds
in it.

Tatiana climbed as high as she could go. It was hard to see: the linden tree, known for its shade, was leafy in the summer. She broke off
some of the softer branches and perched herself astride a thick branch
close to the trunk. From her height she could make out the sloping
countryside even in the first haze of dawn. The shapes of the men were
small and far down below. They were scattered, meters from each other,
not a formation but a blot.

"How many?" Alexander called out.

She looked through her binoculars. "Maybe twenty." Her heart was
pulverizing her breastbone. At least twenty, she wanted to add, but
didn't. The dogs she couldn't see. What she could see, however, was the
men holding the dogs, because they were moving faster than the others
and more jerkily, as if the dogs were yanking them forward.

"How far now?"

She couldn't tell how far. They were down below, still small.
Alexander would be able to tell how far, she thought, but he can't do
both, spot them and kill them. The Commando had a sight and was extremely accurate, maybe he could spot the dogs with it?

"Shura, can you see the dogs?"

She waited to hear from him. She saw him picking up the Commando, aiming it; there was a sound of two shots being fired and then
the barking stopped.

"Yes," he replied.

Tatiana looked through her binoculars. The commotion below was
considerable. The band started dispersing. "They're moving out!"

But Alexander did not have to be told. He jumped up and opened
machine-gun fire. For many seconds that's all Tatiana heard, the bursts
of popping. When he stopped there was a whistling sound, and a
grenade exploded a hundred meters below them. The next one exploded fifty meters below them. The next one twenty-five.

"Where, Tania?" he yelled out, machine gun rest still propped against
his shoulder.

She kept looking through her binoculars. Her eyes were playing
tricks on her. The men now seemed to be crawling in their dark uniforms,

crawling along the ground, moving closer. Were they crawling or writhing?

A few got up. "There are two at one o'clock, three at eleven," she called out. Alexander opened fire again. But then he stopped suddenly and threw the machine gun off him. What happened? When Tatiana saw him picking up the Shpagin, she knew he must have run out of ammunition. But the Shpagin had only half a drum in it—maybe thirty-five rounds. They were gone in seconds. He picked up the Colt pistols, fired eight times, paused for two seconds, fired eight times, paused for two seconds. The rhythm of war, Tatiana thought, wanting to close her eyes. The three men at eleven o'clock suddenly became five at two o'clock, and four more at one. Alexander, crouching down, never stopped firing except for the two seconds it took him to reload.

There was rapid fire from below. It was haphazard fire, but it was coming their way. She looked again. The men firing were giving off a flame charge every time their machine guns went off. It made them much easier to spot. Alexander spotted them. It occurred to Tatiana that his pistols were giving off a flame charge that made him also easier to see, and she yelled for him to get down. He was back on his stomach in the trench.

One man was coming up the hill, only about a hundred meters below them, right in front of Tatiana's tree.

She saw him throw something, and it whistled through the air, landed very close to Alexander and exploded. The bushes and the grass in front of him burst into flames. Alexander popped the pins out of two grenades and threw them, but he threw them blindly, he couldn't see where the men were.

Tatiana could. She cocked her P-38, aimed it at the shape in front of her, and before she had a moment to reconsider, fired. The recoil was violent, it threw her shoulder back, but the deafening sound was worse, because now she could not hear. The bushes and the grass in front of Alexander's trench were burning.

Alexander? she thought she whispered, but could hear no sound coming out of her mouth. She looked through the binoculars. It was getting lighter, and the shapes on the ground were still. She fired again and again. There were no more mortar shells, but suddenly there was sporadic machine-gun fire from below, all aimed at Alexander's small trench. Tatiana found them, lying behind the bushes, halfway up the hill. Because she couldn't speak to Alexander, and could not hear his response to her, she aimed her weapon again, not sure if the bullets would carry two hundred meters, but fired anyway. She wished she could hear sounds from below, but she couldn't. She reloaded six times.

Alexander continued to fire. The bushes may have gone up in flames from the explosives out of his own weapons. Tatiana couldn't be sure of anything anymore. She pointed her gun down the hill, closed her eyes and fired and reloaded and fired until all the bullets were gone.

Then all was quiet. Maybe all wasn't quiet.

She opened her eyes.

"Watch your back!" she screamed, and Alexander rolled out of the trench just as a soldier, coming up behind him, shot into the pit. Alexander kicked the rifle out of the man's hands, kicked him again in the legs, pulled him down and they grappled with one another on the ground. The man grabbed a knife out of his boot. Tatiana, losing all sense of self, nearly fell out of the tree. She ripped off the rope around her, scrambled down and ran across the clearing to the two fighting men. Stop, stop, she shouted, raising her pistol, cocking it, knowing it didn't have any bullets left. Stop, but she couldn't hear herself so how could they hear her? The man was forcing his knife toward Alexander, who was barely stopping him.

Tatiana ran up close and, raising her empty-chambered pistol, brought it down hard on the soldier's neck. He jumped from the blow but did not release Alexander—his fingers remained around the knife handle, Alexander's remained around the man's wrist, just stopping him from sinking that knife into his abdomen. Crying out, Tatiana hit the man again, but she couldn't hit him hard enough. Alexander grabbed the man around the neck, twisted him fast and hard, and he went slack. Throwing the man off him, he sprang to his feet, all bloodied and wired. He said something, she didn't hear. He motioned her back. Tatiana dropped her gun and backed away. Picking up her pistol, Alexander aimed at the soldier and pulled the trigger, but there was no sound.

The gun is empty, Tatiana wanted to say, but Alexander knew that. He picked up the Commando which still had bullets in the cylinder, aimed at the soldier, but didn't fire. The man's neck was broken. Dropping the gun, he came to her then and held her to him for a few moments to calm her down.

They were both panting hard. Alexander was covered with black ash and bleeding from his arm, his head, the top of his chest, his shoulder.

He said something and she said, what?

He bent to her ear. "Well done, Tania. But I thought I was clear: don't move until I tell you to move."

She looked up at him to see if he was joking. She couldn't tell.

Squeezing her, he said, "We have to go. We have only revolver rounds left."

Did you get them all? she mouthed.

"Stop shouting. I'm sure I didn't, and in any case, they'll be sending a hundred men next, with bigger bombs. Let's run."

"Wait, you're injured—"

He put his hand over her mouth. "Stop shouting," Alexander said to her. "You'll get your hearing back in a little while, just keep quiet and follow me."

Tatiana pointed at his bleeding chest. Shrugging, he crouched down. She ripped away the sleeve of his shirt. It was a shell grazing; she pulled the pieces of shrapnel out of his shoulder; one was deeply stuck in his deltoid and pectoral. Shura, look, she thought she said.

He leaned to her. "Just grab it with your fingers and pull it out."

She yanked it out, nearly fainting at the pain she knew he must have felt. He winced but did not move. She washed out the wound with an antiseptic and bandaged it.

"What about your face?"

His scalp wound had reopened.

"Stop speaking. It's fine. Later. Let's just go." Her face was stained with his blood from when he had pressed her to him. She didn't wipe it off.

Leaving the empty machine gun, Alexander picked up his pistols, the sub-machine-gun, and the backpack; Tatiana grabbed her nurse's bag and they ran as fast as they could down the hill.

ᘉᕮᕲᘉ

Around the perimeters of the fields along tree walls and stone walls they ran and walked and crawled for the next two to three hours until the dwellings became progressively more residential and less farm-like, and finally there were streets and finally there was a white sign posted on the side of a three-story bombed-out building that said, "YOU ARE ENTERING THE BRITISH SECTOR OF THE CITY OF BERLIN."

Tatiana could hear now. She grabbed his good arm, smiled and said, "Almost there."

There was no reply from Alexander.

And in a few hundred feet she knew why. Berlin was not abandoned, and there were trucks and jeeps on the road, and though many of them belonged to the Royal armed forces, quite a few of them didn't. They saw a truck up ahead barreling forward, honking, with the hammer and sickle on the crest, and Alexander yanked her into a doorway and said, "How far to the American sector?"

"I don't know. I have a street map of Berlin."

It turned out to be five kilometers. It took them all day. They would run from building to building and then stop in broken-down entranceways, hallways, doorways, and wait.

By the time they got to the American sector it was four in the afternoon.

They found the U.S. embassy on Clayallee at four thirty.

And they could not cross the street to it, because the hammer-and-sickle jeeps were parked four in a row across the entrance.

This time it was Tatiana who pulled him inside the doorway, under the stairs.

"They're not necessarily here for us," she said, trying to sound optimistic. "I think it's standard procedure."

"I'm sure it is. You don't think they've been notified to be on the lookout for a man about my size and a woman, yours?"

"No, I don't think so," she said in a doubting voice.

"All right then, let's go." He began to get up.

She stopped him.

"Tatiana, what are you thinking?"

She thought about it. "I'm an American citizen. I have a right to ask to go into the embassy."

"Yes, but you'll be stopped before you get a chance to exercise that right."

"Well, we have to do something."

He was quiet. She kept thinking, looking him over. He wasn't so tense as before. The fight seemed to have left his body. Reaching out, she touched his face. "Hey," she said. "Rear up. We're not done fighting, soldier." She pulled on him. "Let's go."

"Where to now?"

"To the military governor's house. It's not too far from here, I think."

When they got to the U.S. command headquarters, Tatiana hid inside a building across the boulevard, changed from olive drab into her grimy nurse's uniform, and motioned Alexander to follow her to the armed, gated entrance. It was five in the evening. There were no Soviet vehicles nearby.

"I'll wait here, you go in by yourself and then come out for me," he said.

She took hold of his hand. "Alexander," she said, "I'm not leaving you behind. Let's go. Just put your weapons away."

"I'm not crossing the street without my weapon."

"It's empty! And you're coming up to the military governor's house. Who is going to let you in brandishing weapons? Put them away."

They had to leave the machine gun—it was too big. With the other weapons in the backpack, they walked up to the gate and Tatiana, standing shoulder to shoulder with Alexander, asked the sentry if she could see Governor Mark Bishop. "Tell him Nurse Jane Barrington is calling for him," she said.

Alexander was looking at her. "Not Tatiana Barrington?"

"Jane was the name on the original Red Cross documents," she replied. "Besides, Tatiana sounds so Russian."

They stared at each other. "It *is* so Russian," he said quietly.

Mark Bishop came to the gate. He took one look at Tatiana, one look at Alexander and said, "Come through." Before they got inside he said, "Nurse Barrington, what a ruckus you've been causing."

"Governor, this is my husband, Alexander Barrington," Tatiana said in English.

"Yes," was all Bishop said, before falling completely silent. "Is he injured?"

"Yes."

"Are you?"

"No. Governor, could one of your men please give us a ride to the embassy? We need to see the consul, John Ravenstock. He is waiting for us."

"He is, is he?"

"Yes."

"Is he waiting for your husband, too?"

"Yes. My husband is American citizen."

"Where are his papers?"

Tatiana leveled a look at Bishop. "Governor," she said. "*Please.* Let's have *the* consulate take care of everything. No use getting you involved, too. I would really appreciate *a*"—special emphasis on the indefinite article—"ride."

Bishop summoned two of his on-duty privates. "Would you like a jeep, Nurse Barrington, or . . ."

"A covered truck would be best, Governor."

"But of course."

She asked Bishop if Dr. Flanagan and Nurse Davenport had reached the American sector.

"Not without a fight, but we did get them back two days ago, yes."

"I'm very sorry. I'm glad they're back and safe."

"Don't apologize to me, Nurse Barrington. Apologize to them."

Two privates drove Tatiana and Alexander to the embassy. They sat in the back on the floor, close together, not speaking. Tatiana tried to wipe the dried blood off his temple. He pulled his head away.

When the doors opened, they were on American soil.

"Everything will be all right, Shura," she whispered before they got out. "You'll see."

But when the summoned John Ravenstock, wearing black tie, came out of the embassy doors into the paved courtyard where they were standing, he was neither smiling nor friendly. Either he was always a serious man wearing a tuxedo or else he did not want to make a single gesture that could be interpreted as warm.

"Mr. Ravenstock, Sam Gulotta in Washington told us to come see you," said Tatiana.

"Oh, believe me, I've been hearing quite a lot from everybody these past three days, including Sam, yes." He sighed deeply. "Nurse Barrington, come with me. Have your husband wait here. Does he need a doctor?"

"Later," she said, taking hold of Alexander's hand. "Right now he needs to come in with us. We will speak privately if you wish and he will wait outside, but he has to come in. Or we speak now in front of him."

Ravenstock shook his head. "You know," he said, "it's six in the evening. My working day finishes at four. I have a reception to go to tonight. My wife is waiting."

"My husband is waiting," Tatiana said quietly.

"Yes, yes. Your husband, your husband. But the working day is over! Come in, but I'm telling you, I can't deal with this properly at the moment. I'm going to be egregiously late."

They walked through the embassy doors and up the wide stairs to the second floor, to Ravenstock's wood-paneled office. He called a guard to come and stay by Alexander in the waiting room and led Tatiana inside.

Tatiana turned to glance at Alexander, not wanting to leave him, but they were inside the American embassy, and it was better than leaving him in Soviet-occupied Berlin in an abandoned building. Alexander was already taking out his light and asking the guard for cigarettes.

"Please don't sit down, we don't have that kind of time," said Ravenstock, closing the door. He was a heavy, gray-haired man in his fifties; he had a long sloping gray mustache and gray eyebrows that grew over his eyes.

Tatiana remained standing.

"Do you have any idea what kind of trouble you have caused?" said Ravenstock hotly. "You don't, do you? Nurse Barrington, you are in Berlin by privilege! To abuse your Red Cross uniform and to so incite our former allies is pure folly. But I don't have time to get into it right now."

"Sir, the consulate office in United States will authorize the issuing of a passport to my husband—"

"Passport! Yes, Sam Gulotta has been in touch with me about this. Forget about a passport. We have a very big problem on our hands, a very tough situation, you do realize that, or no?"

"I realize—"

"No, I don't think you do. The Commander of the Berlin garrison, the Soviet military administration in Germany, heck, the National Security Department in Moscow, have been completely overwrought about this matter!"

"The Commander of the Berlin garrison?" Tatiana said with surprise. "General Stepanov has been overwrought?"

"No, not him, he was replaced two days ago, by a Moscow man, a veteran general, Rymakov or something."

Tatiana paled.

"And they are all in unison, crying for your blood!" He paused. "For you both. Your husband apparently broke every military and civil law on their books. He is a Soviet citizen, they say, a *major* in their army. First they accused him of treason, of espionage, of desertion, of anti-Soviet agitation, and when we said that we did not have him in our custody, they accused him of being an American spy! We asked if he was both, a traitor to them and a spy for us? We asked them to pick. They refused and upped the ante on you, too. You've been on their class enemies list since 1943, did you know that? You didn't just escape apparently, you deserted your Red Army post as a military nurse, and you killed five of their border troops, including a decorated lieutenant, in order to get out of Russia. They told me your brother is a . . ." Ravenstock scratched his head. "I can't remember the word they used. Apparently a traitor of the worst kind."

"My brother is dead," said Tatiana, holding on to the back of a chair.

"Bottom line is, Nurse Barrington, they want you both extradited into their hands here in Berlin. So when you ask about a passport, you have no idea what you're talking about. Now I really have to run, look, it's six fifteen!"

Tatiana sat down in the chair in front of Ravenstock's desk.

"I asked you not to sit!"

"Mr. Ravenstock," she said calmly. "We have a small son in United States. I am U.S. citizen now. My husband is a U.S. citizen, he came to Russia with his parents when he was a small boy, he could not help that he had to register for compulsory draft, he could not help that his parents were shot and killed by the NKVD. Do you want me to read you the regulations on citizenship?"

"No, thank you. I know them by heart."

"He is an American citizen. He wants to come back home."

"I understand that's what he *wants*, but do you understand that he has been convicted by the Soviet authorities under the laws of their country for desertion and treason? And just to make matters more complicated, not only has he escaped, which is a crime in itself, escaping just punishment, or so they tell me—and you colluded to help him, which is also a crime—but you and he cut a swathe through sixty of their men! They are *screaming* for your blood!" He glanced at his watch, ripping off his bow tie in frustration. "Oh, no. Oh, no. I can't tell you how late you are making me."

"Sir," said Tatiana. "We desperately need your help."

"Of course you do. But you should have thought of what you were doing before you embarked on this lunatic mission."

"I came back to Europe to find my husband. He never meant to be Soviet. Not like me. I was Soviet-born, and Soviet-raised." She swallowed. "But it doesn't matter. I don't matter in this, the only one who matters is my husband. If you talk to him you will find out he served on the side of the Allies honorably, you will see he was a great soldier who deserves to go back home. The U.S. Army would be proud to commission a man like my husband." Tatiana's voice did not tremble. "I was Soviet citizen. I did not kill those men on the Finnish border, but I did escape, they are right about that. You have every right, to turn me over to the Soviet authorities. I will willingly go, as long as I know my husband returns home where he belongs."

She realized even as she was saying it how absurd it was, how ridiculous! As if Alexander would allow any scenario in which Tatiana would be handed over to the Soviets while he moseyed off safely home. She lowered her head, but couldn't let Ravenstock know of her bluff. She raised her eyes.

Ravenstock sat on the edge of his desk and watched her. His body stopped fidgeting for a short spell until it remembered again it needed to be someplace else. He started fumbling with his torn-off tie. "Look, we are not in the business of judging our allies." He fell quiet. "But the Soviets are proving themselves to be a determined and vicious force in the occupation of Europe. It's true they do not want to make any concessions to the Allies. But you both did break a number of their laws. This is not in dispute."

Tatiana remained mute, her intense gaze on Ravenstock.

The consul tapped nervously at his watch. "Nurse Barrington, I would *love* to sit here with you and discuss the merits and demerits of the Soviet Union, but you are making me *impossibly* late. I have to, I simply must resolve this matter, but I have to resolve it tomorrow."

"Please telegraph Sam Gulotta," she said. "He will give you all information on Alexander Barrington you need."

Ravenstock lifted a heavy file off his desk. "A copy of that information is already in my hands. Tomorrow morning at eight sharp we will speak to your husband."

"Who is we?" she breathed out.

"Myself, the ambassador, the military governor, and the three inspector generals of the armed forces here in Berlin. After he is questioned by our military, we will decide what to do. Be aware, though, that the army is very strict on military matters, be they pertaining to soldiers of our own army or someone else's. Desertion, treason, these are grave charges. There is nothing graver."

"What about me? Are you going to question *me*?"

Ravenstock rubbed the bridge of his nose. "I don't think that will be necessary, Nurse Barrington. I've spoken to you plenty. Now, will you please stand up from my chair and go tend to your husband?"

They opened the door to his office. Alexander was sitting in the reception area, smoking.

Ravenstock came up to Alexander. "You will be questioned tomorrow, um—what is your rank now, anyway?" he said in English.

"Captain," Alexander replied in English.

Ravenstock shook his head. "You say captain, they told us major, your wife says they took away your rank. I understand nothing. Tomorrow at eight, Captain Belov." He looked him over. "You may eat in the embassy canteen, or . . ."

"Brought up to the room will be fine," said Alexander.

"A military man indeed." Ravenstock mulled Alexander's shredded, muddied, bloodied clothes. "Do you have anything else to wear?"

"No."

"Tomorrow at seven, I will have housekeeping bring you a spare captain's uniform from headquarters. Please be ready to be escorted to the conference room at seven fifty-five."

"I'll be ready."

"You're sure you don't need someone to take a look at your injuries?"

"Thank you, I have someone."

Ravenstock nodded. "See you tomorrow. Guard, please take them to the sixth-floor residences. Have housekeeping make up a room for them and bring them some dinner. You two must be starving."

○◦◦◦◦○

Their room was large, with wood floors, area rugs, three large windows and high ceilings. The ornate crown molding ran around the perimeter of the walls. There were comfortable chairs and a table and even a private bathroom. Alexander dropped all their things on the floor and sat in an upholstered chair. Tatiana walked around the room for a few minutes, looking at the pictures, at the crown molding, at the area rugs, at anything but Alexander.

"So how apoplectic are the Soviets?" he asked from behind her.

"Oh, you know," she said, not turning around.

"I can imagine."

"They replaced Stepanov with someone else," Tatiana said, turning to him.

Alexander's hands twitched. "He told me when he came to see me in February that he was surprised he had lasted as long as he had. Things are getting particularly nasty for the generals in the post-war Soviet army. Too many campaigns gone wrong, too many men lost, too much blame to lay." He lowered his head.

"How did he know you were there?"

"He saw my name in the Special Camp rolls."

"They wouldn't let *me* look through the rolls."

"You are not the military commander of the Soviet garrison in Berlin."

Tatiana collapsed onto the window ledge and put her face into her hands. "What's happening?" she said. "I thought the hard part was behind us. I thought this was going to be the easy part."

"You thought this was going to be the easy part!" Alexander exclaimed. "What about our life has ever been easy? Did you think you would step onto American soil and they would welcome us with a reception?"

"No, but I thought after I explained it to Ravenstock—"

"Perhaps Ravenstock is not familiar with *all* your powers of persuasion, Tatiana," said Alexander. "He is a consul, a diplomat. He follows orders and he has to do what's best for the relations between the two countries."

"Sam told me to ask for his help. He wouldn't have—"

"Sam, Sam, and who is this Sam, and why do you think the NKGB will listen to him?"

She wrung her hands. "I knew it," she said. "We should have never come here! We should have run north where they wouldn't be expecting us. We should've taken a cargo boat to Sweden. Sweden would've given us asylum."

"That's the first I'm hearing of *this* plan, Tania."

"We didn't have time to think. Berlin, Berlin! Why would I ever have taken you to Berlin if I thought for a second we wouldn't find help here?"

There was a knock on the door. They looked at each other. Alexander got up to answer it, but Tatiana pointed to the bathroom and said, no, go there, don't come out, just in case.

It was housekeeping, with dinner and fresh towels.

"Do you have any cigarettes?" Tatiana asked, her voice cracking on every word. "I'll pay you if you have a pack—or two maybe?" The girl returned with three packs.

"Alexander? Are you all right?" It had been so quiet in the bathroom and Tatiana had been waiting for the girl to come back and didn't go get him, and it suddenly occurred to her that he could have hurt himself in there, and she ran to the door and pushed it open with such force, screaming, "ALEXANDER!" that she nearly knocked him off his feet.

"What's the matter with you?" he said. "Why are you screaming?"

"I don't—I . . . you were very quiet, I didn't—"

He took the cigarettes from her hands.

"Look, they brought you food," she said, quieter, showing him the food trays. "They brought steak." She tried to smile. "When was the last time you had steak, Shura?"

"What's steak?" he said, and tried to smile, too.

They sat down at the table and moved the food around on their plates. Tatiana drank water. Alexander drank water and smoked.

"It's good, right?"

"It's good."

They moved it around some more, not looking at each other, not speaking. It got dark. Tatiana went to turn on the light.

"No, don't," he said.

The only light in the room was the short fuse of his cigarette, one after another.

Nothing was said, but there was no silence. Tatiana was screaming inside and she knew Alexander was smoking to mute his own screaming. To drown out hers.

Finally he said, "You learned English well."

And she said, "I once had a very good teacher," and started to cry.

"Shh," he said, looking not at her but past her to the open window. "Russian is somehow easier for us, more familiar."

"Yes, it hurts more to speak it," she said.

"Feels so comforting to speak it with you."

They stared at each other across the table.

"Oh, God," she said, "what are we going to do?"

"Nothing to do," he replied.

"Why do they need to speak to you? What's the point?"

"As always, whenever it's a military matter, it has to be dealt with in a military way. The Soviets took away my rank when they sentenced me, but they know they will get nowhere with the U.S. military if they say the man seeking safe passage is a civilian. The governor would not even think about it then, the matter would pass straight to Ravenstock. But the Soviets invoke treason, desertion, all highly provocative military words, especially to the Americans, and they know it. I haven't been a major for three years, yet they call me major, a commissioned high-ranking officer to incite them further. These words beg a correct military response. Which is why they will question me tomorrow."

"What do you think? How will it go?"

Alexander didn't reply, which to Tatiana was worse than a bad answer because it left her to imagine the unimaginable.

"No," she said. "No. I can't—I won't—I will not—" She raised her head and squared her shoulders. "They will give me over, too, then. You are not going alone."

"Don't be ridiculous."

"I'm—"

"Don't—be—ridiculous!" Alexander stood up but didn't come near her. "I don't . . . I refuse to have even a theoretical discussion about it."

"Not theoretical, Shura," said Tatiana. "They want me, too. I spoke to Ravenstock, remember? Stepanov himself told me. Class enemy list. They want us both handed over."

"Oh, for fuck's sake!" he exclaimed. "You've really done it, haven't you?" Suddenly he went to the window and looked outside, as if calculating the distance to the ground from the sixth floor. "Tania, unlike me, you actually carry an American passport."

"Just a technicality, Alexander."

"Yes, a vital technicality. Also you're a civilian."

"I was a Red Army nurse, on a grant to the Red Cross."

"They won't hand you over."

"They will."

"No. I will speak to them tomorrow."

"No! Speak to them? Haven't you spoken enough? To Matthew Sayers, to Stepanov, you looked me in the eye and lied to my face, isn't it enough?" She shook her head. "You won't be speaking to anyone."

"I will."

She burst into tears. "What happened to we live together or we die together?"

"I lied."

"You lied!" She trembled. "Well, I should have known. Know this, they're *not* taking you back. If you're going to Kolyma, I'm going, too."

"You have no idea what you're saying."

"You chose me," Tatiana said in a breaking voice, "then in Leningrad, because I was straight and true."

"And you chose *me*," Alexander said, "because you knew I fiercely protected what was mine; as fiercely as Orbeli."

"Oh, God, I'm not leaving without you. If you go back to the Soviet Union, I go, too."

"Tania!" Alexander was not sitting anymore. He was standing in front of her, his despondent eyes glistening. "What are you talking about? You're making me want to tear my hair out, and yours, too. You're talking as if you've forgotten!"

"I haven't forgotten—"

"The interrogators will torture you until you tell them the truth about me or until you sign the confession they put in front of you. You sign and they shoot me dead on the spot and send you to Kolyma for ten years, for subverting the principles of the Soviet state by marrying a known spy and saboteur."

Tatiana put her hands up. "All right, Shura," she said. "All right." She saw he was losing control.

He grabbed her by the arms, pulled her up to stand in front of him. "And then do you know what will happen to you in the camps? Lest you think it's going to be just another adventure. You'll be stripped naked and bathed by men and then paraded naked down a narrow corridor between a dozen trustees who are always on the look-out for pretty girls—and they will notice a girl like you—and they will offer you a cushy position in the prison canteen or the laundry in exchange for your regular services, and you, being the good woman you are, will refuse, and they will beat you in the hall, and rape you, and then send you out logging, as they have done with all the women since 1943."

Tatiana, afraid for Alexander and his inflamed heart, said, "Please—"

"You'll be hauling pine onto flatbeds and by the time you are done, you won't be able to function as a woman, having lifted what no woman should lift, and then no one will want you, not even the trustee who takes anyone except women loggers because everyone knows they are damaged goods."

Pale, Tatiana tried to disengage herself from him.

"At the end of your sentence in 1956 you'll be released back into society, with all the things that once made you what you are gone." He paused, not letting go of her. "All the things, Tania. Gone."

All she could manage was a broken "Please. . . ."

"All without our son," said Alexander, "without the boy who might grow up to change the world, and without me. There you will be— without your front teeth, childless and widowed, broken down and barren, sodomized, dehumanized—going back to your Fifth Soviet apartment. Is that what you prefer?" he asked. "I haven't seen your life in America, but tell me, will *that* be your choice?"

Grim but determined, Tatiana said quietly, "You survived. I will, too."

"That *was* you surviving!" Alexander yelled. "You didn't die in that scenario, did you? You want death? That's different." He let go of her and stepped away. "Death, all right. You will die from the cold, from the hunger. Leningrad didn't kill you; Kolyma will for sure. Ninety per cent of all the *men* who are sent there die. You will die after performing an abortion on yourself, from infection, from peritonitis, from pellagra, from TB, which will kill you for certain, or you'll be beaten to death after your streetcar gang rape." He paused. "Or before."

She put her hands over her ears. "God, Shura, stop," she whispered.

He shuddered. She shuddered, too.

Alexander drew her to him, into his chest, into his arms. Though every breath out of him sounded as though exhaled from a throat lined with glass spikes, she felt better pressed against him.

"Tania, I survived because God made me a strong man. No one was going to get near me. I could shoot, I could fight, and I was not afraid of killing anybody who approached me. What about you? What would you have done?" His hand went on top of her head, and then he lifted her face to him. Pulling her arms away, he pushed Tatiana backward, and she fell on the bed. Sitting next to her, he said, "You can't protect yourself against *me*—and I love you as much as it is possible for a man to love a woman." He shook his head. "Tatiasha, that world was not meant for a woman like you—which is why God didn't send you into it."

She placed her hand on his face. "But why would He send *you* into it?" she asked with quiet bitterness. "You—the king among men."

He didn't want to speak anymore.

She wanted to and couldn't.

He went to have a shower, and she curled into a ball in the chair by the window near the bed.

When he came out, just a towel around his waist, he said, "Will you come and look at my gash? I think it's getting infected."

He was right. He knew about such things. He sat very still while she gave him a shot of penicillin and cleaned the rip on his chest and shoulder with carbolic acid. "I'm going to stitch it," she said, taking out her surgical thread, suddenly remembering that she had used surgical thread to sew the Red Cross emblem onto a Finnish truck that took her out of the Soviet Union. She swayed from her weakness. She couldn't save Matthew Sayers.

"Don't stitch it, it's been too long already," Alexander said.

"No, it needs it. It will prevent infection, it'll heal better." How did she continue to speak?

She took out a syringe to anesthetize the area and he took her hand and said, "What's this?" He shook his head. "Stitch away, Tania. Just give me a cigarette first."

He needed eight stitches. After she was done, she placed her lips on the wound. "Sore?" she whispered.

"Didn't feel a thing," he said, taking another drag of the cigarette.

She bandaged his shoulder, his arm down to his elbow, bandaged his hand that was raw from gunpowder burns. She didn't want him to see her face so close, but she cried as she took care of him and she could tell by his breathing how hard it was for him to listen to her, to be so close to her without touching her. She knew he could not bring himself to touch her the closer they were to the very end.

"Would you like some morphine?"

"No," he said. "Then I'm unconscious all night."

She stumbled away a step.

"Shower was good," he said. "White towels. Hot water. So good, so unexpected."

"Yes," she said. "There are many comforts in America."

They turned away from each other. He left the bathroom, she went into the shower. When she came out wrapped in towels, he was already asleep, on his back, naked over the quilt. She covered him and then sat in the chair by the bed and watched him, her hand inside her nurse's bag, touching the morphine syrettes.

Tatiana could not, would not allow him to be taken back to Russia. God would have him before the Soviet Union ever had him again.

Taking her nurse's bag with her, she climbed under the covers, to his naked body, and spooned him from behind. She held him in her arms and cried into his shorn head. The Soviet Union had left only skin and bones on him.

And then he spoke. "Anthony," he said, "is he a nice boy?"

"Yes," she replied. "The nicest."

"And he looks like you?"

"No, husband, he looks like you."

"That's too bad," said Alexander, and turned to Tatiana.

They lay naked face to face.

Their regrets, their breath, their two souls twisted between them, bleeding and shouting grief into the unquiet night.

"With or without me, you have lived and will always live by only one standard," he said.

"I tried harder for you. Wanted to do even better for you. I imagined what *you* might have wanted for the both of us, and I tried to live it."

"No. *I* tried harder for you," said Alexander. "I wanted to do better for you. I held you before my eyes, hoping whatever I did, however I managed, you would be pleased. That you would nod at me and say, you did all right, Alexander. You did all right."

A pause.

A hoot of an owl.

Maybe a bat flapping by.

Dogs barking.

"You did all right, Alexander."

He wrapped his arms around her and pressed his lips to her fore-head. "Tatiana, my wife, we never had a future. We'll live tonight for five minutes from now," he whispered. "That's how we always lived, you and I, and we will live like that again, one more night, in a white warm bed."

"Be my comfort, come away with me," said Tatiana, weeping. "Rise up and come away, my beloved."

His hand caressed her back. "You know what saved me through my years in the battalion and in prison?" he said. "*You*. I thought, if you could get out of Russia, through Finland, through the war, pregnant, with a dying doctor, with *nothing* but yourself, I could survive *this*. If you could get through Leningrad, as you every single morning got up and slid down the ice on the stairs to get your family water and their daily bread, I thought, I could get through this. If you survived *that* I could survive *this*."

"You don't even know how badly I did the first years. You wouldn't believe it if I told you."

"You had my son. I had nothing else but you, and how you walked with me through Leningrad, across the Neva and Lake Ladoga and held my open back together and clotted my wounds, and washed my burns, and healed me, and saved me. I was hungry and you fed me. I had nothing but Lazarevo." Alexander's voice broke. "And your immortal blood. Tatiana, you were my only life force. You have no idea how hard I tried to get to you again. I gave myself up to the enemy, to the Germans for you. I got shot at for you and beaten for you and betrayed for you and convicted for you. All I wanted was to see you again. That you came back for me, it's *everything*, Tatia. Don't you understand? The rest is nothing to me. Germany, Kolyma, Dimitri, Nikolai Ouspensky, the So-viet Union, all of it, nothing. Forget them all, let them all go. You hear?"

"I hear," Tatiana said. We walk alone through this world, but if we're lucky, we have a moment of belonging to something, to someone, that sustains us through a lifetime of loneliness.

For an evening minute I touched him again and grew red wings and was young again in the Summer Garden, and had hope and eternal life.

CHAPTER FORTY-ONE

Berlin, July 1946

THE NEXT MORNING THEY woke at six. At seven, housekeeping brought breakfast and a U.S. commissioned uniform for Alexander. They laundered Tatiana's nursing uniform.

Alexander had coffee and toast and six cigarettes. Tatiana had coffee and toast but couldn't keep it down.

At seven fifty-five, two armed guards escorted Alexander and Tatiana to the third floor. They sat down silently in the antechamber in wooden chairs.

At eight, the doors opened and John Ravenstock came out. "Good morning, you two. Much better in clean clothes, no?"

Alexander stood up.

Ravenstock glanced at Tatiana. "Nurse Barrington, you might want to wait in your room. We're likely to be a good few hours."

"I will wait right here," said Tatiana.

"Suit yourself," Ravenstock said.

Alexander walked behind the consul. Before he disappeared inside he turned around. Tatiana was standing. She saluted him. He saluted her.

⁙

Six men sat at a long conference table, while Alexander remained standing.

John Ravenstock introduced Military Governor Mark Bishop ("We've met"), Phillip Fabrizzio, the U.S. ambassador, and the generals for the three branches of the U.S. armed forces stationed in Berlin—Army, Air Force, Marines.

"So?" Bishop said. "What have you got to say for yourself, Captain Belov?"

"Excuse me, Governor?"

"Do you speak English?"

"Yes, of course."

"Because of you we have an international situation brewing here in Berlin. The Soviets are demanding, *insisting*, that the minute you come through our doors we surrender an Alexander Belov to the proper Soviet authorities. Your wife, however, is telling us that you are an American citizen. Indeed Ambassador Fabrizzio has read your file and things seem to be a bit murky with the nationality of a man named Alexander Barrington. And look, I don't know what you did or didn't do for the Soviets before they threw you in Sachsenhausen. But one thing I *do* know—in the last four days you killed a battalion of their men and they are demanding justice for them."

"I find it ironic that the Soviet military command here in Berlin, or anywhere for that matter, should suddenly care about their men, when I myself buried at least two thousand of their men in Sachsenhausen during time of peace."

"Yes, well, Sachsenhausen is a camp for convicted criminals."

"No, sir, soldiers like me. Soldiers like you. Lieutenants, captains, majors, one colonel. Oh, and that's not including the seven hundred German men—high-ranking officers and civilians—who have been either buried or cremated there."

"Do you deny killing their men, Captain?"

"No, sir. They were coming to kill me and my wife. I had no choice."

"You did escape, however?"

"Yes."

"The Commandant of the Special Camp claims you are an inveterate escapee."

"Yes, I was not happy with the living conditions. I was voting with my feet."

The generals exchanged looks. "You were convicted of treason, is that correct?"

"It is correct that that is what I was convicted of, yes."

"Do you deny charges of treason?"

"Whole-heartedly."

"They say you had deserted the Red Army when they were coming to resupply you and after meandering through the woods, you willingly surrendered yourself to the enemy and fought alongside them against your own people."

"I did give myself up to the enemy. I had not had any reinforcements in two weeks, I was out of bullets and out of men on a defense line of forty thousand Germans. I never fought against my own people. I was in Catowice and then Colditz. But surrendering *was* against the law for Soviet soldiers, so I am guilty as charged."

The generals were silent. "You are lucky to still be alive, Captain," said General Pearson of the Marines. "We heard that out of six million Soviet prisoners of war, the Germans let five million die."

"I am sure that figure is not inflated, General. Perhaps if Stalin had signed the Geneva Agreement, more would be alive. The English and the Americans POW weren't all killed, were they?"

There was no answer from the generals.

"So what is your rank now?"

"I have no rank. My rank was taken away from me when I was sentenced for treason."

"Why are the Soviets calling you Major Belov, then?" Bishop asked.

Half-smiling, Alexander shrugged. "I don't know."

"Captain Belov, why don't you start at the beginning, from the moment your parents left America and came to the Soviet Union, and tell us what has happened to you? That will help us greatly. We have too much conflicting information here. The NKGB has been looking for an Alexander Barrington for ten years. But they also maintain you are Alexander Belov. We don't even know if that is one and the same man. Why don't you tell us who you are, Captain."

"Be glad to, sir. Request permission to sit."

"Granted," said Bishop. "Guard, bring this man some cigarettes, and some water."

✿

Alexander had been in for six hours. Tatiana thought he could have been taken away through a secret passage, but she kept hearing dim voices through the thick wood doors.

She paced, she sat—she crouched, she rocked. Her life and his floating before her eyes in the anteroom of the United States Embassy in Berlin.

They were learning to swim, and each minute did not get easier, each day did not bring new relief. Each day brought just another minute of the things they could not leave behind. Jane Barrington sitting on the train coming back to Leningrad from Moscow, holding on to her son, knowing she had failed him, crying for Alexander, wanting another drink, and Harold, in his prison cell, crying for Alexander, and

Yuri Stepanov on his stomach in the mud in Finland, crying for Alexander, and Dasha in the truck, on the Ladoga ice, crying for Alexander, and Tatiana on her knees in the Finland marsh, screaming for Alexander, and Anthony, alone with his nightmares, crying for his father.

But there he is! With the cap in his hands, crossing the street for his white dress with red roses, there he is, every day coming to Kirov, stone upon stone, corpse upon corpse, there he is, in the Field of Mars under the lilacs with his rifle and she is barefoot next to him, and he is whirling her around on the steps of their wedding church, waltzing with her under the red moon of their wedding night, coming out of the Kama, coming at her broken and destroyed, bare, smiling, smoking, drowning Alexander. He is not gone yet. He is not vanished. Perhaps what remains of him can still be saved.

And there he is once again, standing on the river Vistula, looking out onto the rest of what's left of his life. One path leads to death; the other to salvation. He doesn't know which road to take, but in his eyes is the girl on the bench, and across the river is the Bridge to Holy Cross.

∽∞∾

When Alexander was finished, the generals sat still, the ambassador sat still, the consul sat still.

"Whew, Captain Belov," said Bishop, "that's some life you got there. How old are you?"

"Twenty-seven."

Bishop whistled.

General Pearson of the United States Marines said, "You're telling us that your wife, without knowing where you were, came to Germany bearing weapons, found the camp you were in, found your cell, found you, and orchestrated your escape out of the maximum security Special Camp Number 7?"

"Yes, sir." Alexander paused. "Perhaps we can keep the reference to my wife out of this tribunal's report?"

John Ravenstock was quiet. The generals were quiet. "And what would you call yourself, Captain, if your American citizenship were reinstated?"

"Anthony Alexander Barrington," he said.

The men stared at Alexander. He stood up and saluted them.

∽∞∾

The door opened and the seven of them came out of the conference room. Alexander walked out last. He saw Tatiana struggle up from her chair, but she couldn't stand without holding on to it, and she looked so alone and forsaken, he was afraid that she would break down in front of half a dozen strangers. Yet he wanted to say something to her, something to comfort her, and so slightly nodding his head, he said, "We are going home."

She inhaled, and her hand covered her mouth.

And then because she was Tatiana and because she couldn't help herself, and because he wouldn't have it any other way, she ran to him and was in his arms, generals or no generals. She flung her arms around him, she embraced him, her wet face was in his neck.

His head was bent to her, and her feet were off the ground.

ᏯᎷᎯ

Though much is taken, much abides; and though we are not now that strength which in old days moved earth and heaven, that which we are, we are—

Unyielding.

Barrington, Leningrad, Luga, Ladoga, Lazarevo, Ellis Island, the mountains of Holy Cross, their lost families, their lost mothers and fathers, their brothers in arms and brothers are etched on their souls and their fine faces and like the mercurial moon, like Jupiter over Maui, like the Perseus galaxy with its blue, imploding stars they remain, as the stellar wind whispers over the rivers all run red, over the oceans and the seas, murmuring through the moonsilver skies . . .

Tatiana . . .

Alexander . . .

But the bronze horseman is still.

ACKNOWLEDGMENTS

Grateful and overdue thanks:

To Larry Brantley, the voice of the Army, for the hours spent detailing for me things I could never have known.

To Tracy Brantley, his wife and my true friend, who in a very amigo-like fashion, gave me early on what I needed most by weeping in all the right places and loving Tania and Shura for all the right reasons.

To Irene Simons, my first mother-in-law, for giving me the name under which I write my books.

To Elaine Ryan, my second mother-in-law, for giving me her perfect second son.

To Radik Tikhomirov, my father's friend for sixty years, for photocopying diaries of blockade survivors at the St. Petersburg library and sending me hundreds of pages in original Russian.

To Robert Gottlieb, a fellow Russophile, for performing miracles, and to Kim Whalen for a decade of hard work.

To Nick Sayers, my former publisher, my editor, my friend.

To Pavla Salacova who works so hard making my life easier she makes me believe she has twenty hands.

To my second and last husband Kevin—you are the bomb.

And to my father, who, a long time ago, hoped and believed and loved, and brought his family to the promised land for a free life.